THE SHADOW SW

MW00658586

THE 19TH BLADESMAN

S.J. HARTLAND

Dark Blade Publishing

Dark Blade Publishing
52 Walker St, Townsville

VAL ARQUES

YEAR TWO IN THE REIGN OF CATHMOR

Archers tugged bowstrings back to their ears. Warriors drew swords in a clatter of iron as they ringed armed riders protecting the woman who had vowed to take this land by storm.

Every bowman, every bladesman looked to their lord on the castle walk, willing his hand to fall.

So tempting to drop his arm. So easy to snatch up his sword and unleash the rage carefully shackled within. Slaughter her guards, take her captive—and call it duty.

But a heartbeat before seizing the blade at his hip, Vraymorg reined in his yearning. Unseemly for a lord, self-indulgent even, to desire bloodshed. Embrace it. But anger filled the hollow place within, and he feared who he was without it.

“Well, where is he?” A rider at the woman’s side shouted up at the guard walk. Wind whipped auburn hair across a surly, young face Vraymorg at once disliked.

“Where is this fiendish bladesman whose deeds maudlin poets spin into legend, this terrible lord of the abyss? Cowering in the shadows? Show yourself, Vraymorg.”

Vraymorg. Yes, they called him that.

But it was just a name to hide his secrets.

They called him lord, too. Lord of these mountains where wind brawled with frosted grass and a bleak sky curved to a rusted horizon. Lord of this gaunt, grey, iron-gated castle.

Its lord? An ugly laugh soured his throat. No. Its prisoner—though the nauseating poets and the singers wandering from hall to hall with their crystal voices did not know it.

A captive of wretched duty, of shame who belonged in this dismal, repellent fortress.

An eternity of pain drenched its ancient keep. Its hulking walls blistered the edge of a rolling gorge like ugly, naked spines. The fangs of its portcullis, crafted from the teeth of the dead, grated into an eerie silence.

Hideous. Forbidding.

Yet for all the spells woven with blood and bone into its stone, she dared ride through this castle's gates, head disdainfully high, wind streaming a cloak of black dog hair.

She dared bring armed men to this outpost of Telorian rule, their murmurs, chafing metal, and jingling harnesses a discordant riot in the ward.

Rozenn, Queen of Cahir. Young, pretty.

His enemy.

"Wherever you're hiding—my lord—tell your archers to lower their bows." The surly man slapped a glove against his horse's flank. He paused. Smirked. "We have your pup."

Air swooped in Vraymorg's gut. He sought Kaell's blond head among the riders. The boy sat unbowed upon a horse roped to another's.

"How?" He turned to his captain. "How? We couldn't find him. How did they?"

Arn Tranter's scowl guttered an angry scar on his jaw. "Seems these foul Cahireans scooped the boy up somewhere beyond the gorge."

"The gods take them. I can only hope they don't know who

Kaell is. But take no chances until they surrender him."

"I assure you, my lord." Arn clasped fingers about a belted knife, his face stiff with outrage. "They will surrender him." With a curt nod, he hurried down the stairs to the ward.

Vraymorg braced the parapet, the worn stone beneath his calloused hands barely warm from a bleached autumn sun.

Rozenn's fire-banners slapped air as cold as liquid silver. Its scents of dried mud, dying wildflowers, and distant smoke stank of emptiness, of the wild, steep hills and lonely hollows of this remote wasteland—unsettling to a man born on the sea cliffs of the Isles.

He swept his eyes across cleared land to wind-scarred rocks. No streaked movement. No sun glittering on helms.

Rozenn was too clever to bring an army against him.

Yet should she threaten Kaell, he'd fall to his knees and surrender this castle, his body, his cursed blood—whatever she demanded in return for the boy.

"I'm losing patience, Vraymorg," the rider said. "If you want your pup, show yourself."

At another insolent challenge, fury pricked his skin. His men looked to him. Wind buffeted dying grass. A crow's caw faded away into an expectant hush.

For a span of wing beats, Vraymorg did nothing but brush his fingers over his worn sword hilt. Anger harnessed for Kaell's sake, he called from the walk, "Show me the boy."

Leisurely, the man dismounted. Sunlight gleamed on jewelled steel sheathed in his belt beneath a flowing cloak of finely woven wool. From the garments, the sword, his arrogance—wellborn.

He pulled Kaell off his horse and shoved him forward. "Show yourself." The man's grin twisted with malice. "Orphan brat."

The boy stiffened. Glared. Vraymorg half expected bared fangs and a snarl.

"The bastard calls himself Kaell of Vraymorg," the man said. "He's a little knight, apparently. Or a lord. The lord of mud from the look of him."

His companions hooted laughter and nudged each other. Rozenn said nothing, only looked towards the broken tower, into the murk that hid him.

Wind plucked at a hood covering hair of baked gold. That hair and her banners betrayed who she was, but not why she risked a perilous journey through the gorge. What she wanted.

What she knew…

Nothing. She couldn't. Not his name. Not his past.

Vraymorg shook off his unease. Still he didn't move, reluctant to leave the walk. But pitiless duty intruded. As it always did.

Men parted as he trod down the stairs to the ward, his blade's slap against his thigh the music of slumbering death. Their gazes fell hard, their tongues silent.

The Cahireans, though, murmured behind their hands. "That's him… Gods, such stories. They can't be true." Then even their whispers faded. A hush plunged in the courtyard, taut and eager.

Kaell followed his every step with low-lidded green eyes. A small sword tucked into his belt around a dirty, ripped, woollen tunic. But for the silver bracelet circling his upper arm and kersey cloak, he looked as wild as a wolf's-head's whelp.

"You reckless, young fool." Vraymorg's relief poured out in fury. "My men searched the gorge for days with no sign of you. Thank the gods you're safe."

"Thank the gods, *we* found him," the surly man said. "Before ghouls did."

Kaell spun, jeering. "Stay safe in your bed if you fear ghouls, old man. I want them to come. So I can kill them."

"Arrogant whelp." The man chuckled indulgently. "He has more spirit than the rest of you milk-blood Telorians." He faced his queen. "We should keep him, Your Majesty."

Rozenn made a poor attempt to hide a smile. "And do what with him?"

"Keep me?" Kaell snorted. "Am I a pet? You can't keep me. My lord." He shot Vraymorg a glance stiff with all the affront and elaborate hauteur a nine-year-old boy could muster.

"He teases you, whoever he is."

The man carelessly bowed. "Tarvan Blackstone. You'll have heard of me."

"Nothing good." Vraymorg lifted a glare to Rozenn. "And you—the queen who vowed to take this land by storm. That was your word. Storm. You say this and dare approach this castle? Tell me why I shouldn't arrest you and surrender you to my king?"

A silence deepened, thick with menace, ready to accompany him in a bladesman's dance of blood. How he longed for its familiar, dread steps. That relief of gnawing rage.

One or two Cahirean warriors aware of his reputation edged back. Though the boldest among Rozenn's women offered appreciative, lingering looks he hardly heeded.

Their queen dismounted. She pushed back her hood. The blue gaze that slowly passed over him ghosted with strangeness, a dusting of the otherworld.

Strange rumours swirled about Rozenn of Cahir. Dangerous rumours. She was, as those fool poets might say, of a mystical bloodline.

"Then you didn't hear?" Her voice was cool, like shards of moonlight.

"Hear what?"

"All is forgiven. We are, in fact, journeying to Dal-Kanu. Your king invited me to celebrate peace between our lands. I seek nothing more than hospitality, Vraymorg."

"Then it appears I must offer you that—Your Grace."

At his discourtesy, Rozenn smiled. In a tone equally insincere, she said, "I thank you for your warm reception. In return, I bring a gift. And give you back this child found wandering."

Indignant, Kaell said, "I don't wander. I hunt."

"Hunt," Vraymorg echoed in disbelief. He grasped Kaell's shoulders. "Hunt? What if ghouls or Varee slavers found you?"

The boy mimicked his lord's usual stance with a thrust of hands to hips. Such a small gesture, yet Vraymorg tasted brackish sadness. The boy looked up to him. But he could never be what Kaell wanted. What he deserved.

"I can take care of myself." Kaell's prideful tone also echoed his.

"With no boots and a useless blade? Did your wits desert you?"

Beneath his lord's stare, Kaell's boldness wilted. He scuffed toes across dirt. "I—I'm sorry. I didn't mean to disappoint you."

And there it was. The undercurrent of need beneath the words. Almost unbearable.

Vraymorg beckoned to a slender, ruddy-faced man. "Ewen, take Kaell to his room. Have the physician see to his cuts and scrapes."

As Kaell trailed after the servant, he traced the boy's steps, a faceless fear weighing his shoulders. The gods willed he keep this child safe. Prepare him for the malign struggle ahead. But how to protect Kaell from himself?

At a swift intake of breath behind, he turned. Rozenn's hand stilled on a fold of her gown, her brows arched, her stare on his exposed wrists.

Vraymorg dragged an etched bronze bracelet over his scars. He looked at his wind-whipped banners, their insignia that of a king he despised but would follow to the tower tomb. All the while self-loathing roiled, its bitterness in his mouth.

"I'm obliged to you for returning Kaell, Your Grace," he said, his tone elaborately polite. "The gods only know why he ran off."

Rozenn tore her eyes from the bracelet, a disarming smile burying a flicker of speculation, even triumph. "Surely it's obvious, Vraymorg." She paused as if to let the stillness settle about her words. "The boy ran off to do as his gods bid him—kill ghouls."

Men muttered uneasily. Arn's grope at his blade rattled steel against a belt clip, the sound brittle. Angry.

"For what else"—she clearly relished their discomfort—"can Khir's bonded warrior do?"

Vraymorg flinched as if struck. Whispers faltered. Tense looks flicked from him to Rozenn. A caw as a bird flapped from a tower lifted hairs along his arms.

"I don't know what you mean, Your Grace."

With ringed fingers, Rozenn tapped an impatient rhythm on a low-slung girdle. "Do you take me for a fool, Vraymorg? Khir's signs mark his flesh. The battle god claims this boy. You train him to slay ghouls. How desperate you must have been when he ran off, my lord."

Desperate? Maybe so. But now he owed her something for Kaell's return?

"You spoke of hospitality." Annoyance clipped his words. "The ancient lords did not build this fortress to accommodate a queen. We shall, however, try to make you comfortable. Once you've rested, it will be my pleasure to entertain you in the feasting hall."

"The pleasure will be mine."

Vraymorg frowned. Her provocative smile held meaning he could not unravel.

"First, let me give you this." Rozenn drew out a book, its leather cracked with age.

"A book?"

"No. It is a warning."

He glanced up sharply. Fading light shadowed her face. Hard to read. But a sibilant murmur prickled his spine. The wind? Its whisper coiled all day, sentient, a portent of danger that soaked down into him like rain.

"I don't understand." A lie. He knew too well the malevolence within this book.

"It contains writings about the boy. Kaell is, after all, the Nineteenth Bonded Warrior."

Reluctantly, panic scraping his gut, Vraymorg took the book in his fingertips. How did she get hold of this? "Even if that were true, it hardly concerns you—Your Grace."

Only the knifing wind sat between them. That, and centuries of secrets.

Rozenn leaned close. "You know," she said. "You know the truth."

He did not reply. His heart drummed against ribs.

"We must talk." Rozenn grasped his arm. "Alone."

"We'll talk, yes." Vraymorg snatched at duty to mask his alarm. "First, my steward will find you suitable rooms. See to your men."

Shrugging off her touch, he strode away. He would not look at the book. He would not. But it drew his glance. And his shudder.

A BRANCH TAPPED STONE like gnarled talons scouring iron. The wind brushed his skin, damp and cool.

Beyond Vraymorg's window, the moonless night fell away into a basin of soft sounds and shadows, broken only by braziers flaring on the wall walk where sentries muttered and stamped their feet.

How vast the wilderness beyond the rutted great gorge seemed with its abandoned cities of red stone, its knotted forests, and sleek, turgid rivers where only Varee slavers flourished and ghouls hunted human prey.

Against such lawless chaos, the decay of civilisation far from the reach of kings and queens, this Telorian castle was surely as impotent as a buckle shield against Seithin steel.

Loneliness boiled up. He was just as impotent. An Isles man displaced. Alone. Damned.

At first Vraymorg mistook the knock at his door for a shutter whipped by a gust. Until it came again. Insistent.

With a weary sigh, he looked up from tedious accounts. Perhaps Ewen might stomp in with complaints about their Cahirean guests camped in the ward, or Arn with a report from the watch. Even Kaell, his eyes clouded, seeking comfort from tormenting dreams.

"Yes?"

The door creaked. Seeing who stood there, he blinked, tried not to gape. Cold foreboding hammered down his backbone, but his heart sprang.

Rozenn said not a word, only walked inside. Her satin cloak whispered over floorboards like fingertips on skin. Her bare feet sank into a threadbare rug.

She possessed a sleepwalker's ethereal fragility. Her unbound hair tangled and beautiful, lids languidly lowering over her glistening, long-lashed eyes.

"Your… Grace?" Vraymorg stammered. "I… can I help you?"

She looked at him. Just looked.

Wind gnashed stonework. An owl hooted. Wings beat air. A bell tolled sweetly in the distant well house. A candle guttered with a last fizzle against cool air.

"I know who you are." Her voice was breathy. "Who you really are, Val Arques. I know what you've done, why you hide here. I know who hunts you and what they will take from you if they can. But for all your menace, you're too young to be the keeper of such secrets."

With deliberate care, Vraymorg pushed back his chair and rose to light a new candle. He did not bother to deny her words. But they tore a bitter laugh from him. "You expected a grizzled, grey-haired man, stooped beneath the burden?"

Candlelight glowed on golden hair. Her rose and vanilla perfume wisped as she moved very close.

"You are younger and more beautiful than I expected, true. But you move with the grace and confidence of a man certain of his formidable skill. Like an Isles bladesman trained in the mysteries and mysticism of the Serravan."

"There is no Serravan. Not for centuries."

"And yet, only a Serravan bladesman could hold these mountains against ghouls. Or hold on to himself beneath this shroud of duty."

Her gaze dropped to his wrists. "Hold on to himself," she repeated, her smile ironic.

"What do you want, Rozenn of Cahir? Why are you here?"

A shrug. "I brought you a gift."

"You brought me a curse. That book is evil."

Rozenn released a breath. "I am right. You *do* know about the boy."

Vraymorg flung his glance from her. By candlelight, the few objects in his drab room looked jarringly unfamiliar. A cloak flung carelessly over his chair, his discarded weapons belt and long-bladed sword, a knife with a jewel-clustered hilt.

Few possessions and he valued none of them.

"I know."

"And what will you do?"

"Nothing."

She swung on him with words. "Are you so arrogant? Give me Kaell, and I'll do what you're afraid to."

"You'd spill his blood? A child's?"

"And bring Khir's curse upon my head? Even I, a Cahirean, respect the old gods of Telor. I won't spill a drop. Though, if the omens prove true, I'll bloodlessly execute Kaell when he is older. I am not cruel. It'll be quick."

"How old is old enough to die?" Vraymorg forced his fist through air to beat back her meaning. "Do your vicious gods set an age?"

"The priests and priestesses did. Yes."

They glowered across a chasm of mistrust. The room filled with a yowling wind, a rattle of shutters, the fire's crackle. Yet something else ripened, too strange, ripped from his longing, his emptiness.

Her glare softened to a sad smile. "How alone you must feel here, Val Arques. An Isles bladesman in these desolate mountains."

He made no reply. Not just her beauty, but a yearning to feel, to escape his loneliness just for one night, quickened his heart to chaos.

She took a step closer, even closer, touching fingertips to his lips. “Such a sensuous mouth for a killer, my lord.”

Vraymorg did not draw away. The atmosphere needled with that intimacy of warriors locked in a fight to the death, akin to passion. Enlivening but dangerous.

Rozenn’s cloak slid from her shoulders to puddle on stone. Candlelight gleamed on bare skin, shadowed soft, sweet curves.

“Is that what you want of me, Rozenn of Cahir?” he whispered, his hand moving to the nape of her neck. Her hair was as soft as a child’s.

Beneath his palm she trembled as she fell against him. He closed his arms about her. Desire blazed hot and fast in his groin, a carnal ribbon of fire through every muscle.

With ragged breaths, Rozenn stripped off his garments.

He pressed his lips to hers with a savagery born of loneliness, his caresses roaming hungrily from tangled hair to breast to hip.

When they tumbled onto the bed, wind fanged his naked back. Vraymorg thought he heard a warning in its moan. Though it might only be Rozenn’s cry as she arched beneath him.

A GRINDING WOKE HIM. The creaking portcullis. The room was cold; the blankets were tangled about his ankles, the indented bed empty but still warm from where Rozenn slept.

Vraymorg sat up fast. He rose and padded to the windows. Moonlight gleamed on faces beneath hoods, on sword hilts as riders threaded through the gatehouse.

The Cahireans. Leaving before dawn.

Vraymorg turned for his cloak. His breath cut.

A thin, silver blade, its hilt ivory, protruded from his pillow. A forbidden Seithin temple knife that pinned parchment to spilled feathers.

Heart clamouring in his chest, he ripped the knife out, snatched up the paper, and took it into the moonlight. He read:

Generous, indeed, Val Arques. Tonight you gave me the throne of Telor. You, my lord, have brought on the very storm you fear.

KAELL

YEAR 12 IN THE REIGN OF CATHMOR

The man on the ground squirmed beneath Kaell's blade. Sunlight drummed his dropped helm. "Bastard," he said. "Bastard."

Kaell grinned. Probably. "You yield to this bastard, then?"

His opponent scraped words through gnashed teeth. "Curse you. Yes. I yield."

Kaell's grin widened. That made six. All heralded warriors vanquished at the point of his sword, its clank, its whir a sweet, sweet melody for this dance of death upon a field streaked with blood and purple wildflowers.

But for the needle-thin keep of Knight's Spike circled by forest-crusted hills, it might be any tournament ground, anywhere in Telor. The silk and canvas of pavilions and banners snapped in the breeze. The cacophonic roil of clashing metal and squeaking leather cut air hazy with summer's honeyed warmth and smoke from a distant forest fire.

A milling crowd, vividly clad in a rainbow of dyed linens and straw hats, shouted and jeered as bladesmen hewed, hacked, sweated, bled for their amusement.

Kaell whipped his sword from his opponent's throat. As he

stepped back, spectators cheered. A muted roar.

They desired a tangle of steel and flesh. Black fountains of blood. Sheared limbs. Screams. They wanted the victor to rip off his helm, brazenly kiss a young woman in the crowd and thrust his sword skyward with all the theatrics of a bawdy farce.

Not a quick, controlled victory from an unnamed warrior, iron hiding his face and hair.

Too bad. He didn't fight to please them.

Nor did he fight to please the grim-faced Downs lord, Nate Caelmarsh, watching in comfort from his cushioned seat upon a platform.

Kaell fought to please one man. A man who wasn't here to see his victories. Though again and again his gaze sifted the jostling mob, half dreading, half hoping that man might come.

"A bet," cried one of Caelmarsh's companions. The speaker wore a plain-dyed but embroidered doublet, stained with wine. He clasped his goblet with a nobleman's soft hands.

"Two pieces of silver says the next challenger puts this too-tidy swordsman in the dirt."

"Done," said a young woman with tumbling brown curls and curved, red lips. She tossed Kaell a bold smile. "Win for me, stranger."

He bowed, his glance shifting uneasily to Caelmarsh, master of these soft, green lands sweeping north to the Mountains, south to the Isles, fat with wheat and citrus orchards and scented of rich, resinous earth.

But the Downs lord only gulped wine, unaware the young man he had vowed to kill stood a mere few lengths from him.

Kaell choked a careless laugh. He'd die young. Bloody. But whatever his fate, it wasn't to rot in some dank prison because time failed to soften an ageing lord's grudge.

"Stop that man."

A warrior with age-blackened iron covering his face and hair shouldered past a protesting marshal onto the field. A herald scampered after him, plucking at the newcomer's scarlet tunic. "Stop. You're not on the lists."

The warrior spun. Threw a fist. The herald hit the ground hard.

Outrage erupted. Agitated marshals shouted for soldiers. Sensing the unexpected, spectators rushed to the fence. A low murmur rippled, built to shouts.

Ignoring the tumult, the stranger strode right at Kaell as if intent on fighting only him.

Kaell gripped his hilt. His scalp prickled with that thrill of challenge, of danger that banished all else. Smothered the lump of fear in his gut.

Not fear of death. Fear at what he could do. At how easily he could lose control and hurt this man. Fear he wanted to.

Still the stranger came at him. He ignored the groaning herald, the stirred-up crowd. With no warning, no word, his sword flashed as he thrust at Kaell's thigh.

Out of position, Kaell shuddered back. His leaping blade barely scraped the blow aside.

The stranger laughed. As though gripped by battle trance, he blinked sleepily through his helm's slits.

Kaell bit down on a surge of anger. He dipped a shoulder and shoved.

The man lazily yawed a step. "Is that all you've got?" His wilted blade invited an attack.

Willingly, Kaell jabbed a probe. Swordplay was a conversation. A lunge or beat was a question, a parry an answer. Even a false reply uncovered patterns in an opponent's slashes.

The warrior responded with a limp, disinterested stroke.

Knowing this game, Kaell swung hard, forcing the man to dodge.

The stranger unleashed a maelstrom of shrieking hacks and cuts. Kaell leapt back. Then he counterattacked with battering, flurried steel. Slash, stab, hew.

Swords collided, scraped, leapt, cut, the combatants at once swept up in a torrent of slashing swordplay. Boots churned dirt and flattened blood-splattered blossoms. Breath hissed from tightening chests.

Thrust, retreat, thrust again. Steel whistled through steaming air, singing blades seeking flesh but finding only metal in a lethal tempest that surely pleased the most demanding gods.

The crowd roared at every blow, at every dizzying step. Cheering as blades pealed in a whirlpool of blue-sparked steel.

Kaell hacked, hammered at shoulders, smashed low, determined to wound, not kill. For all his speed and skill, a metallic assault dogged him, a deceptive hunt of whirring death.

Soon sweat drenched his armpits and matted hair beneath his helm. Thought condensed to staccato notes. *Wear him down. Keep control. Do not kill. A bonded warrior must kill only ghouls, not men.*

Nor would he yield. He was too proud. So his sword streaked like lightning, seeking openings to wound.

The stranger answered every stroke then rained blows with a catlike balance and an unnatural calm. Unable to pierce Kaell's defence, he changed tactics to retreat with a lowered blade. Kaell shadowed his steps but refused to rush an attack.

As if recognising the bait dangled uselessly, his opponent smote deep and fast.

Kaell's training screamed parry, but he recklessly leapt into the thunderous strike, hilt grinding from tip to pommel. Swords caught, the two pressed blade to blade, body to body, their eyes locked in a private, perverse bonding.

The stranger's breath steamed his cheek. The helm's slits rimmed eyes like dark crystal. "They said you were fearless—Kaell."

Kaell jolted with alarm. His face hidden, no one here knew his name. Who was this man?

Sunlight sparked on metal. The stranger fisted a knife in his other hand. He stabbed. Kaell jerked back. But the knife followed.

It ripped through cloth and skin, its bite sharp. Blood pooled below his hip.

No time to recognise pain. The man already cleaved at his legs. Kaell smashed his sword down. The shudder of blades nearly wrenched his from his hand.

Unbalanced, he flung an arm at his opponent's chest. The stranger stumbled. Enraged, he bellowed and swung high.

Kaell spun to one knee. Steel swished a hair's breadth from his scalp. He sprang up with a yell and punched the man in the jaw.

The warrior crumpled. His dislodged helm clunked to the ground.

Ponderously he rose, kicked the helm away, and stood tall and unbowed, with a finely chiselled face, arrogantly stretched neck—

And an inhuman shade of blond hair. Freed from the helm it tumbled about broad shoulders, darkly golden, long, and glinting.

Shock anchored Kaell. He could only stare at that hair, a creep at the back of his neck.

All sound drained away. Marshals circled. One pointed a wavering finger at the blond warrior. In a voice thick with horror, he cried, "Ghoul. He's a ghoul."

Swords scraped from scabbards. Guards ran onto the field. The crowd's whispers rose to gasps, then shrieks of terror. Most shrank back. The braver, or drunker, pressed forward.

The ghoul's gaze held on Kaell. "Khir's warrior. Well, well. You're a long way from home, little flower."

Kaell snapped from his trance. Waving the guards back, he curled gloved fingers tighter about his hilt.

"So are you. This is the Downs. Doesn't your kind prefer to cower in the Mountains?"

"My kind." The ghoul only laughed. "What do you know of my kind, orphan brat?"

A clumsy taunt. Kaell grinned chillingly. No need now to check his strokes, to limit his sword arm. Before him stood a monster, and his god and his lord bid him to slay monsters.

"Here to kill me, ghoul?"

"Sadly, my master forbids it. Though he says nothing about making you bleed while I deliver his message."

"I have a message for you too."

Roaring, Kaell leapt in. His sword sliced, stormed, thrashed. A song burst up. No longer restrained, his body, his will, gladly surrendered to training and instinct. To darkness.

The ghoul edged back, then back again, grunting in surprise as he struggled to keep out streaming thrusts.

Kaell sprang again, his blade humming as it devoured distance.

A cold joy bolted within. Hard to kill a ghoul warrior, but his god had gifted him with unnatural strength and speed. This would end as it always did when he fought ghouls. In blood—but not his.

The ghoul blocked and swept steel. Again, their swords locked. The two strained against each other, rasped breath expelled in air sharp with the odour of sweat, damp hair, and skin.

"This is amusing," the ghoul said. "Why I've even worked up a sweat. But you cannot beat me. I am Lastenarron, a Lord of the Night."

"Lord of the Night or not," Kaell said. "You'll still die the same."

"You're sweet, but you know nothing, child. Soon you'll journey to the Waste Mountains. My master says if you come to him, he promises the answers you seek. The truth about who you are."

"What?" Kaell shivered. "Who is this master?"

As slippery as a fish, Lastenarron freed his blade, ducked beneath Kaell's whirring sword and ran. The young warrior spun to follow.

A marshal shouted, "After the ghoul. Don't let him get away."

Guards wearing Downs badges took up the chase. Lastenarron reached the fence and vaulted into the crowd, light striking his drawn sword, discordant shouts and screams scattered in his wake.

Kaell forced a path after him. Lost his target. Hearing shrieks, he ran towards them.

The crowd splintered around him, desperately charging in the other direction. A dazed woman clutched a bawling girl to her breast as he ran by. A man pointed, "That way."

The ghoul dashed past billowing pavilions, a guard on his heels. Panicked figures dispersed like a flock of squawking birds.

The guard shouted a challenge. Lastenarron pivoted. Thrust. His pursuer parried.

Their violent clash of blades spun the guard's sword high.

Unarmed, he tried to back up, but the ghoul grabbed him.

Kaell broke into a sprint, shouting, "No!"

"There you are, Kaell." Lastenarron squeezed an arm about the guard's throat. "I want you to know you can't save him. You can't save anyone. The true god of this land will soon be free. He's coming."

The guard writhed, his face contorted in terror. Lastenarron did not look at him. He held his eyes on Kaell as he sank his teeth into soft flesh. Blood spouted from the man's neck. A woman wailed, the sound quickly drowned by horrified cries.

Lastenarron flung his prey down, lunged at a nearby man, and with one wrench, tore his head from his neck.

As blood and bone from the man's crushed vertebrae sprayed, the ghoul roared in glee and dropped the convulsing torso. He shouldered into a thinning mob, bunting bodies aside with his fists.

Seething with outrage, Kaell tore after him, ready to leap and cleave with steel.

A staff shot out. Kaell hit it, coiled, dropped, and lay breathless, his sword at his side. A dark-haired man reached down a hand with an apologetic grimace. "Sorry. I didn't see you."

Wind nibbled at his sky-blue linen shirt, red bandana, and green cowl. A low-slung belt about leather pants sheathed a jewelled knife. Silver coiled his arms and ears.

Kaell growled. Ignoring the offered hand, he jumped up, snatched his sword, and whirled this way and that. No sign of the ghoul.

He rushed back to find others gathered around the decapitated body. Nearby, a grey-haired, beak-nosed man bent over the fallen guard. “Is he—?”

The man looked up from his knees and shook his head.

Kaell heaved an angry, helpless sigh. It fell to him to stop Lastenarron. To save these men. Curse the silvered peacock who got in his way.

An uncomfortable thought struck him. The peacock spoke with a Mountains lilt and dressed like the gaudily colourful Varee—slavers and thieves from the wastelands beyond the great gorge. Did he deliberately interfere? Why?

A hand brushed his sleeve. Kaell turned.

“The ghoul got away?” A marshal led a knot of ill-assorted warriors hastily called from their pavilions.

“Yes.”

“Or maybe you let him escape. Given how well you fight, maybe you’re a ghoul too. That one also hid his face. Is that why you’ve hidden yours too? Take off that helm. Let us see who—or what—is beneath.”

“No one.” Kaell took a step back.

“Stop that man.” A new voice rang out.

Kaell wheeled. Trailed by armed retainers, the Lord of the Downs stomped towards him.

He looked older, his lank hair receded, shoulders stooped towards his mound of a belly, at odds with his gaunt limbs.

The vicious, ruby-lipped mouth was the same though. Still made for sly insults and quick judgements. Just as it had been all those years ago when this man travelled to Vraymorg on the king’s orders to judge him.

Nate Caelmarsh jabbed a gnarled finger at Kaell. “Show your face. Or we’ll gut you.”

HE WOULD NOT REMOVE the helm. He would not reveal his dark-blond hair that drew glances so hostile they fell like a slap.

I'm not Seithin, Kaell wanted to shout when strangers whispered behind their hands and traced signs against evil at the sight of him. *How can I be? The Seithin are dead. Hunted down.*

The crowd thickened. Necks craned, men and women jostled for the best view, attracted by the marshal's threats, their lord's booming voice and the scent of bloody entertainment.

A drunken voice slurred, "Kill the ghoul." Others pressed forward, fists clenched, shouting, "ghoul, ghoul, ghoul."

Caelmarsh poked a finger again. "His face. I must see his face."

Soldiers blocked Kaell. He tried to edge around. "Here, what is this?" They shadowed him.

The marshal leaned, his breath unpleasantly warm. As if worried he was wellborn, he used his knife to lift a stray strand of Kaell's sweat-darkened hair.

"You're Mountains-born from the way you speak, stranger. With the same colour hair as that ghoul. And you fight too well—like a ghoul. How many men did you put in the dirt? Five? Six?"

"I'm no ghoul," Kaell muttered. Angrily he poked straying fair hair beneath his helm.

"Gut the ghoul," a woman said. Other drunken voices picked up the cry amid a smattering of fearful mutterings and hisses. Spectators strained to get closer.

The marshal bellowed for silence. He faced Kaell. "Remove the helm. Or I'll ask my lord for permission to rip your head off with it."

The mob's stares stabbed with macabre excitement. Desiring blood. How long before they attacked him? How long could Kaell bluff before an impatient Caelmarsh ordered his arrest?

He tore off his helm and flung it at his feet. Unlaced and shrugged out of his leather doublet.

Was this what they wanted? What would they see? A celebrated warrior? Or someone not quite human?

Kaell lifted his head, daring them to judge him as he stood arms bared from shoulder to wrist, clad only in a thin tunic, pants, and boots.

He could be any warrior aged twenty. Muscles knotted his back and arms, his thighs moulded by years drilling with the blade.

Once Kaell complained that though he was tall, his lord still towered over him, only for Vraymorg to smile and assure him his build offered better balance in swordplay.

He looked exactly as a Telorian bladesman should. Except—

Except for his dark-blond hair falling to his shoulders, its shade uncommon since the fall of Seithin. Except for the tattoos disfiguring his arms, their dark whorls swirling across his shoulders onto his neck.

Onlookers gaped, gasped. They nudged each other, poking fingers at his hair then Khir's sigils on his skin. A soldier recoiled.

The marshal stammered, "Apologies, I'm sure. We didn't know the battle god's bonded warrior fought here today." He backed away.

"Wait," Caelmarsh said. "Hold him. I permit you to lay hands on him."

Soldiers grabbed Kaell's arms. Indignant, he struggled, but their grips only tightened.

The Lord of the Downs stepped through his guards, lips moving in soundless fury. He grasped Kaell's chin with a bony hand. "You," he said. "You dare come here."

Unblinking, Kaell met Caelmarsh's glare. A silence fell about them and lengthened… and still lengthened. Beneath it crept barbed memory neither would look at.

Caelmarsh clawed a cracked wheeze from deep in his throat. "No," he said. "Not here. Not while others watch."

He let Kaell go with a shove, turned, and shouldered past the startled marshal. His soldiers followed.

KAELL'S BREATH HAMMERED OUT. Stupid to think he could come to Knight's Spike without trouble. Bitterly he scooped up his helm and doublet and pushed into the crowd. Their murmurs picked up then fell away as he parted them.

At twenty he was old enough, surely, to laugh off the whispers, the stalking glances, but they prickled like coarse sackcloth against his skin.

It didn't matter that the gods chose him, that he'd die young to keep these people safe in their soft lands far from the Mountains. They still feared him. Resented him as a son of privilege, arrogant and spoilt—just as his lord had warned him long ago.

Kaell, just fifteen, had laughed it off. "Why should I care what others think? I know who I am."

Vraymorg's dark eyes flashed with amusement. He reached to ruffle Kaell's hair, only to whip his hand back as if afraid to show affection.

"I don't care," Kaell repeated stubbornly.

But he did. Not about the judging stares. He cared that Vraymorg didn't muss his hair the way he patted the heads of young grooms or girls playing hopscotch in the castle ward.

A hard man, Vraymorg. The king's man in the Mountains.

The closest to a father Kaell had ever known.

Sometimes he lay in his bed at the fortress of Vraymorg, moonlight carving patterns on the ceiling, wondering about his mother, his real father. Perhaps he was Venivan, given his blond hair. Or Tarlean-ah, from beyond the Ice Sea.

The one time he dared ask his lord, Vraymorg's curt, "I don't know," his stiff shoulders, the edge to his voice meant: we don't talk about this.

Forcing the past away, Kaell dragged his doublet down over his head and walked on.

Men exchanging coins glowered as they looked up. No doubt they bet against him, not knowing who he was. More fool them.

A stringy man with dirt-smeared, hollowed cheeks bounded after him.

"So the unheralded swordsman is unmasked," he said. "Khir's bonded warrior. We are privileged, I'm sure. You want some advice, bonded warrior? You fight too cleanly. Spill a little blood, and the crowd will warm to you."

Kaell ignored him. He needed to be far from Caelmarsh before the Downs lord thought better of letting him leave.

The man dogged him. "Aw, don't go off sore. I'll wager you can win the tournament."

He blew his nose on a dirty sleeve. Sniffed. "Not that it's much of a tournament. No Isles warriors here. With their harsh training, you always bet on Isles bladesmen at tournaments, don't you? Once I saw Aric Caelan fight. Years ago, but I'll never forget it."

Kaell pushed past. The words, though, kindled a fierce longing.

You always bet on Isles bladesmen.

The Isles produced the best swordsmen. Always had. Could he call himself a bladesman without matching steel and wits against the best?

Yet no Isles man had risked entering a tournament for two years. Their lord warred against the King of Telor. Hatton's warriors, especially his son Aric, were called upon to defend its walled towns, not defend their reputations in games.

His gaze drifted to the field as heralds announced new combatants. Men swaggered out to fight, legs brushing wildflowers that bowed and waved in the soft breeze. Kaell envied the flowers their nakedness. Sweat trickled uncomfortably down his neck.

Idly he slapped a fly and turned to search the crowd again for one man.

His lord was not here.

Deep within, Kaell knew Vraymorg would not come. Not this time. But nothing rational took away his longing, his constant, mortifying need for proof his lord cared about him. He badly wanted this man to follow—even if drawn only by anger.

His throat lumped at an echo in his mind of their argument two days ago. His unprovoked, sharp words. The way Vraymorg's face tightened just before his lord hit him.

Kaell touched his bruised cheek. The blow fell too fast to avoid. It didn't hurt. But it humiliated. And he did what he always did when ashamed.

He ran. Hid his face beneath a helm, disobeyed Vraymorg to enter a tournament to prove he controlled both his formidable skill and his temper.

If only his lord watched him fight, how he faced the ghoul, unafraid—

What? He might be proud?

A stale taste rolled about his mouth. Vraymorg ruled the Mountains, with more to concern him than—what? What was he to this man?

"You're a burden," a sly-tongued brute had told Kaell at sixteen. "A possession. No better than a slave." Kaell had run from his vile words. The man laughed and shot an arrow into him.

Vraymorg carried him wounded to the keep, his face etched with misery. Emboldened by his lord's concern, comforted by the strength of his arms, Kaell fought tears of pain to whisper, "Am I? Am I a burden?"

He might have asked: *Am I loved? Who am I?* He didn't. He wasn't ready for those answers. Not really.

His lord's eyes were wet. Yes, he remembered that. But sinking into a poppy-juice sleep, he couldn't recall Vraymorg's reply. Only knew he didn't hear "You're loved. Like a son."

A HAND FELL upon his arm. With a hopeful gasp, Kaell snapped from the past back to the tournament field and its blur of cheers, scraping metal, and colours. Did his lord come after all? Did he care enough to follow him?

His shoulders fell. "Arn."

The man before him stood taller than most, heavy with muscle with huge calloused hands and thick legs. Braided, greying hair clumped at his sun-darkened neck like a cropped tail. A worn leather scabbard drooped at his hip. Its plain sword, the hilt unadorned by niello or gems, was like the man—straightforward, practical, no-nonsense.

"Who did you expect? Vraymorg?"

Kaell scuffed a boot across ground. "No."

Arn dropped his hand. He sighed heavily. "He won't come, boy. Not this time."

"Why should I care?"

"You're hurt." Arn said. "Bleeding."

Kaell clamped a palm over the seeping wound. "It's nothing."

"I heard talk of a ghoul—"

"He came for me, Arn." A torrent of words spilled. "Here. In the Downs. Can you believe that? We fought. The ghoul ran off. Killed a guard and another man. I couldn't save them—"

Kaell stopped, dismayed. He had failed his gods. Failed his lord.

Arn's dark-eyed look rested knowingly. "I wonder how the ghoul found you. It took me two days to track you down."

"I wasn't hiding. I was just—"

"What? Fighting tournaments for a handful of gold?"

Kaell rolled his sword's pommel beneath his palm, its knurl cool and smooth as though worn by hundreds of hands before his. He scraped the blade from its scabbard, jammed it back. In and out. In and out. The sound jarred. A fingernail down his spine.

"Why not?" He laughed without humour. "I could use that gold to go anywhere in Telor. Perhaps fight Venivan raiders and pirates as a bladesman in service to the Lord of the Isles."

"The Lord of the Isles who rebels against the king." Arn shook his head. "The Lord of the Mountains—your lord—is loyal to that king. Are you ready to turn traitor?"

Kaell shrugged. "The Lord of the Falls, then. Or even the Icelands."

"The Icelands." Arn scoffed in disbelief. "You? Serve the

haughty Damadars? No, this is nonsense. A warrior bonded to Khir doesn't fight for Ice lords. Nor should he waste his skills fighting tournaments. The truth, lad. Why are you here?"

Arn's eyes held understanding, compassion. Kaell wanted to recoil from both.

"Why, Kaell?"

Again he groped for his sword, jagging it up and down. His need blurted out in a desperate flurry. "We argued. My lord struck me. I thought he might be sorry, might come after me." Kaell broke off with a self-mocking laugh. "I don't know what I thought."

Arn squeezed his shoulder. "What do you want from him?"

Kaell shrugged, unable to voice his longing.

"It's always my lord this, my lord that with you." Arn gently teased. "You're no longer a child wandering the gorge with a wooden sword pretending to hunt ghouls. You're a warrior chosen by the gods. You need not bend your knee to any man, even Vraymorg."

"It's not that simple." Unbidden, those sly words echoed in his mind again: *No better than a slave, a burden.* He shoved them aside.

"What did you and Vraymorg fight about?"

"Why do you have to know everything? You're not my father."

Arn's face clouded with hurt. Quietly he said, "No, but I am your friend."

Kaell rubbed the pommel, regretting his sharp words. Arn never tried to take Vraymorg's place. As his captain and friend, he had every right to ask why Kaell ran.

Why did he? What did he hope to prove? Was it as childish as hoping his lord would chase after him to show he cared? Was that the painful, pathetic truth?

If he couldn't admit the truth to himself, then he'd never be truthful with others.

Vraymorg taught him that. Vraymorg. Vraymorg. His lord shaped him. Everything he knew, what he was, even what he owned was all because of Vraymorg.

No better than a slave.

"I wanted to test myself at this tournament." He gulped a breath. "To show I'm a warrior like any other. Nothing less, but nothing more. Nothing unnatural—inhuman."

"Unnatural. Inhuman. Don't do that to yourself."

"My Lord forbade me to come, insisting I must prepare to ride to Dal-Kanu, that the king bids us kill ghouls in the Waste Mountains. That I can't waste my skills at tournaments. I told him I'll do as I liked, that just because he's too cowardly to defy the king—"

"You called him a coward? Vraymorg? What madness possessed you?"

Kaell grimaced. "It just came out."

Did it? Or did he deliberately provoke his lord? Wanting a reaction so badly that even a slap was better than nothing.

"It just came out," he repeated stubbornly. "Of all men to call a coward. I know how he fights. Fearlessly."

"Recklessly, you mean. As if he doesn't care if he lives or dies." Arn shook his head. "Tell me about the ghoul. I heard a Downs guardsman died."

"The ghoul killed two men to taunt me. It was deliberate, cold." Horror scraped the back of Kaell's neck. "He said his lord waits for me in the Waste Mountains."

Arn tensed. "What lord?"

"No clue. But the ghoul knew the king intends to send us to the Waste Mountains. How?"

"Ghouls are clever. They heard a rumour and hoped to unsettle you. Don't let them get to you, Kaell. Wherever the king sends us, it will be like any other hunt."

When he didn't answer, his captain squinted harder.

"Ah," Arn said softly. "The dream."

Kaell broke away. The doublet suffocated him. He forced his focus on a black cloud of birds, torpid in flight, on the sounds of the stirred crowd and thundering swords.

Arn slid an arm about his shoulder. "It's back? The dream about that ruin? The door?"

The door. Kaell passed an unsteady hand over his eyes.

The familiar dream had struck near dawn. A deep sleep chained him to it.

It had started with a girl's kiss. A wondrous, sweet kiss. But Kaell could never hold on to her, finding himself alone in a desolate castle, the wind gnawing through empty towers. The air had smelt of dew and frosted grass. Of a forgotten past.

He had wandered into a tallow-scented passage of ancient, blackened stone. Torches in sconces barely breached welling shadows. Curling smoke hurt his eyes. He swiped it away.

And there it was. The door. It was iron hinged and brass handled. Its imposing length depicted carved warriors wearing exotic, flowing robes and turreted castles rising from sand.

Numb with terror he couldn't explain, he tried to run, but a voice always called his name. Such a voice. As rich as gold, as dangerous as a blade's edge.

"The dream starts in the Waste Mountains." The words thickened in his throat. Kaell couldn't say the rest. *In the dream, I die. Behind the door.*

Arn's hands fell helplessly to his side. "I've never seen you afraid," he said. "Not you."

"I'm not—" Another lie? What was wrong with him? Did the dream unsettle him that much? His lord taught him to face the truth, to examine his motivations and thoughts.

"Kaell." Arn's tone softened. "You know your duty. Not only to the gods, but to the Lord of Vraymorg. To the men who ride with us. You never balked at that duty before."

"Duty." Kaell scoffed. "Duty." It was his duty to die. Behind that door. Unless he ran.

"Everything will be all right, Kaell. We've crossed the great gorge more than once."

"Not into the Waste Mountains. Where that ghoul's master waits for me."

"Khir gifts you with visions. Even if that ruin from your dream is close to whatever stinking ghoul den the king wants us to clear out, nothing can harm you, or any of us. Khir would warn you of danger."

"So you say."

"Kaell."

He looked up. Arn's expression was bleak. "Vraymorg sent me to bring you back."

Steel clanged. A man howled. A sigh stirred through the crowd. Kaell glanced towards the sounds, wondering at the contest unfolding. A favourite warrior beaten?

Laughter rang as boys shook a tree to loosen apples. Leaves scattered about a still figure clad in a cowled cloak. The figure stared right at him.

Coldness brushed his neck. He blinked. When he looked again, no one was there.

"Did you hear me? Vraymorg ordered I bring you back. To do your duty."

Duty. Always duty. Those scraps of his lord's regard, his interest, so desperately fought for, all because the gods compelled this man to train him. Prepare him.

"He sent you rather than come himself." Bitterness tore up his voice. "It should hardly surprise me how little I mean to him. But as you just reminded me—I answer to no one. Tell him, I'll return when I'm ready."

KAELL STRODE a rough coil of path below dark-trunked trees, helm in one hand, his swinging sword tapping his hip.

His thoughts churned. His lord did not care enough to seek him out. Why should he? The stares, the mutters from the tournament crowd said it all. He wasn't like them. He was different, a freak even, and his lord knew it.

Lost in thought, he tripped over a stone and fell forward with a jarring thump. Kaell cursed as he rose, brushed dirt from his pants, and bent to retrieve his helm.

His arms tingled. He spun.

Bilberry bushes swept slopes tangled with gnarled roots and drooping, budding branches. Sunlight shattered upon leaves. The air scented of jasmine, grass, and dried mud shimmered with heat. From the nearby tournament at Knight's Spike, steel clanked.

Warmth dusted his skin like a golden mist. Wind gently fluttered his cloak.

Yet a misplaced sound, whisper thin, swirled. A fluttering of warning not so much in his ears as down his backbone. Someone watched from the trees.

The ground rumbled. Horses thundered along the path.

Kaell ripped his sword from his belt as armed riders surrounded him.

The horsemen slowed. Unhurried, they moved in. Kaell whipped about. More men wearing Downs' uniforms closed at his back. He tilted his chin and spat a defiant: "What do you want?"

A rider broke free of the others, his captain's badge a curled salamander and lavender sprig. Dark-brown hair matted his ruddy cheeks beneath dented capped steel.

"Our lord desires the pleasure of your company," he said.

"Oh, pleasure is it? The pleasure of my company in a foul cell?" Determined to hide his alarm, Kaell swept the man an insolent bow. "Tell Caelmarsh I'd rather ghouls skewer me."

The captain grinned viciously. "I'm bid only to bring you to him. Skewering you must discuss with Caelmarsh. I'm sure my lord will oblige."

Warily Kaell circled within a noose of horseflesh and steel.

"You may thank Caelmarsh for his kind invitation, but I am too busy."

"Too busy to answer to a great lord of Telor?"

"Too busy." Kaell patted his mouth. "And a little tired. Another day perhaps?"

"My lord did say you're an arrogant brat who doesn't know his place." The captain gestured. His companions dismounted, slid swords free and advanced, unsmiling. Nervous.

"Really?" Kaell sighed. "Another dance? I had my fill for today."

Despite his bold words, fear stirred. The soldiers numbered eight. The odds were against him. Especially as he must only wound and not kill.

"Then put up your sword," the captain said complacently.

"The first thing a bladesman learns is never, ever lose hold of your weapon. The second—that attack offers better odds than defence."

With a roar, Kaell leapt at the knot of soldiers. His slash opened a long cut in an arm. The wounded man yelled in pain, his sword spilling to the dirt as Kaell twisted and swung. The stroke put a second man on his knees. He clutched his hip and howled.

Kaell thrust at a third. The soldier reeled. His thigh gushed blood.

Two Downs guards confronted him. Kaell backed up, watchful. They advanced together as though intent on combining their attacks.

In position, he let them come. They struck in unison. Kaell veered from their blows, sunlight blazing off his sword as he parried. He fought with grim resolution, taking no pleasure in any contest against men. But they must not overwhelm him.

Again the pair attacked as one. Kaell knocked their blades aside and jabbed low. One collapsed, moaning. The other circled.

With one fluid movement, Kaell whipped his knife from his belt and hurled. It snagged the man's shoulder. The soldier yelped and dropped.

The captain kicked his horse forward to ride him down. Sword levelled, Kaell retreated a step then another.

Beneath his heel the earth crumbled into emptiness. For a heartbeat he clawed air, toppling on the edge of a gaping hole.

Then he tumbled, flailing at nothing until he smacked hard ground, his breath knocked from his lungs, his limbs sprawled on a bed of stone.

Kaell moaned. The stones tore clothes and flesh alike, his inflamed back a mass of bloody cuts. Blood trickled from his gashed temple.

A tattered cloth ripped by his weight fluttered above like a ragged curtain, its camouflage of dirt and grass layering grime over his face and garments.

Flinty rock and clouding dust settled into a tense silence, broken only by wind stealing through branches. Kaell could not take in what happened. He fell. Into some hole?

The captain peered down, laughing with surprised glee. "I'll leave a man or two to make sure you stay put while I fetch Caelmarsh. Maybe he'll just bury you alive."

"He wouldn't dare," Kaell said. He wished he believed it.

"My lord will risk not only the king's displeasure but the wrath of the gods to make you suffer. He intends—"

A bowstring twanged. An arrow clattered on earth.

A man called, "The next pierces your throat."

The captain whipped about. "Show yourself, coward."

More arrows strummed heat-simmering air. "To your horses," the captain cried. "Ride."

A ruckus broke out above. Scuffling boots, men's groans, then grating leather, jangling harnesses, and the captain's angry gibe: "You'll be sorry. We'll return with more men."

The drum of hoofs exploded then faded. Kaell's breath shuddered out into a bewildering quiet. But from a creep at the nape of his neck, he knew he wasn't alone.

Footsteps crunched. A man's low, deep voice rumbled, "And they shall. Caelmarsh fostered me as a boy at Knight's Spike. He is a vile man but a determined one."

A woman answered, "And a patient one."

"What's his grudge against the boy?"

"Rumour is something to do with Caelmarsh's daughter. I don't know the story."

Kaell twitched with unease. Whoever stood above knew rather too much about him.

Dizzy, his battered body protesting at movement, he pushed to his elbows. Hoping the drop broke no bones.

"We'd best finish this quickly, Your Grace." The man hesitated. "If you still intend—"

The woman sighed. "It seems the abhorrent deed falls to me after all. Get him out. If he's conscious after the fall, I don't want—I do not want to see his eyes. Cover them."

A shadow fell on the hole. Kaell glanced up at a figure silhouetted against bright sunshine. Wind slapped at a woman's long gown. A tendril of memory sparked. The tournament. Someone beneath that apple tree. Watching.

Men appeared at the pit's edge. Their indistinctive clothes and swords revealed nothing about who they were.

Kaell passed a hand over his damp brow. "What happened?"

"You fell into a hole." A man joined the woman, a hood shading his face.

Dazed, bruised, Kaell squinted into sunlight. "Someone dug a hole and covered it up?"

"Are you hurt?"

"I hit my head." He staggered up. "Someone filled this cursed hole with sharp stones."

The man reached down. "We'll get you out. Pass your sword up."

Kaell looked at his spilled weapon then at the man. Doubt curdled into a harsh laugh. He scooped up the blade and drove it into his belt. "I'm not in a trusting mood. For all I know you dug this cursed pit. No, I'll find my own way out."

The man muttered to someone unseen. An archer took

position at the edge, bowstring drawn back.

"Be reasonable," the man said calmly. "Keep the sword if you must, but we'll haul you out one way or the other."

Kaell glared at the bowman. With an angry hiss, he swept his palms over dirt and rock for a foothold. It hurt his pride to be so helpless. Trapped.

Seething, he peered up. "What do you want with me?"

The man dropped a dark cloth into the hole. "We want a word. It's a better option than Caelmarsh will give you. Cover your eyes, and get ready to grab the rope."

Kaell caught the cloth. "Have I any choice?"

"It's a poor one, I'll grant you that. We could leave you here for Caelmarsh to take captive. Or our archers cripple you, and I climb in to get you. Now, the blindfold."

"Why a blindfold?"

"A precaution. You're wasting time arguing. Just do it."

Kaell cursed and swung a fist at crumbling earth. He paced in a tight circle, muttering. Helpless anger jagged through him.

"You choose an arrow in the leg, then? Come, be sensible." Coiled rope dropped.

Nowhere to go. No footholds. Futile to stomp about in this pit. With a heavy sigh, he tied the cloth about his eyes, groped for the rope and clambered up. Men hurled him over the top, set him on his feet but held his arms.

"You said you wanted a word. Well, I'm listening. So let me go."

Someone pulled Kaell's sword from his belt. He glared blindly. "I want that back. I also demand to know why you're holding me."

When they did not release him, he broke into a frenzied thrashing, shouting, "Let me go."

"What's he saying? It's like he speaks Venivan or something."

"They all sound like that in the Mountains. Can't understand them half the time."

Kaell kicked towards the voices.

"Here you, keep still."

At a numbing slap to his face, Kaell fell against his captors. They roped his wrists together and dumped him on his knees. He swayed and moaned, every breath painful. Fresh blood dripped from his temple.

"There's no need to be so rough." The woman drew so close he caught a snatch of her perfume. Roses and vanilla.

"I am sorry," she said.

"Sorry?"

"Who you are is not your fault. I shall make this quick. Painless if I can."

Kaell had no time to think what that meant when someone pushed his chest. His bruised, torn back hit the ground. Guards pounced, their knees pinning his hips.

He writhed, bucked, and twisted, shouting in outrage. They held him until at last, exhausted by pain, Kaell stilled—all but his heart's ragged rhythm against caging ribs.

"What do you mean quick?" His voice thinned in horror. "Do you mean to kill me? Why?"

"Hush."

"No." Kaell rocked his head weakly. "Let me die as a warrior. If not in battle, at least in combat. Give me a sword."

"Hush."

Cloth rustled in grass as if someone knelt. Dread banded his throat.

"Don't struggle." She touched fingertips to his cheek. "It will be over fast."

Beneath the blindfold, Kaell's blinkered eyes snagged on her ring of silver and emerald. Alarm narrowed his thoughts to that ring. Only that ring.

Cloth clamped hard over his nose and mouth. He jerked in shock, then fought pressing hands, desperate for air. His lungs choked. A scream was buried within him, unheard. Panic flamed. Thoughts splintered. Too weak to fight. Blackness rushing. Dying. He was dying.

"Mother, no." A boy's high-pitched voice.

"I told you to wait in the trees."

"You're hurting him. Please don't hurt him."

The cloth and hands lifted. Kaell rasped a breath.

"There. I stopped hurting him. Though it is cruel to pause, to give false hope."

"You can't kill him. Mother, you can't. My tutors say the gods punish those who spill a bonded warrior's blood."

"I'll not spill his blood. Not a drop. That's why we dug the pit. To capture him, execute him bloodlessly."

Kaell shuddered. They even knew of the curse.

"Don't hurt him. I don't want you to."

"Nor is it my wish. But my fire visions show me a terrible truth. I warned his lord, but he did nothing. Nothing. Clearly Vraymorg values this young man's life above the lives of thousands. This foul act falls to me."

Kaell uneasily shifted his hips. Did she expect his lord to kill him?

He struggled to his knees. No one stopped him. Panted breath beat in his skull. Hot air wisped his arms, leaving gooseflesh in its wake. A breeze carrying a whisper of pine and mud stirred branches. Pungent sweat trickled uncomfortably down his neck.

"We make our own choices," the boy said. "You taught me that."

"None of us cheats fate," she said. "Whatever path you choose, fate twists to find you."

Duty chased like fate. Kaell could not flee from it either, no matter the nonsense he told Arn.

He chanced getting to his feet. This time his captors pushed him back to his knees and held his shoulders. The rancid stink of their unwashed bodies, the damp touch of hands soaked into him.

"You know who my father is," the boy said. "You chose him so I may become king. But I will not be a king with a bonded warrior's death on my conscience, Mother."

"It shall be on mine."

"Please. I'm not asking because I'm weak, Mother. But isn't there another way?"

A breathless, empty stillness battered. Into its void, she whispered, the words indistinct like a storm-scattered murmur. Did she softly say, "Is my son right? Show me. Speak."

Wind tunnelled furiously through trees. Branches creaked, snapped, and fell in whirl-pooled leaves. Inhuman cries boiled beneath the gusts. Nervous men muttered.

Kaell trembled. He lived close enough to the otherworld to recognise magic.

"Is there another way?" Her plea rose to a shout. "Tell me!"

The wind swirled, a fury of sounds like spirits shrieking all at once. Kaell dug his knees into the ground, cold fear dampening his skin.

The woman moaned. "I understand. It is your will he dies somewhere else. Very well. I'll spare him. But the next time you put him in my power, I will do what I must."

The wind died. Sunlight once more beat on Kaell's scalp. He groaned, his strength leached by pain and blood loss, unsure he could fight them even if they freed his hands.

"We have wine?"

"Yes, Your Grace."

"Do not call me that. Get wine into him—until he passes out." A pause. "I want him very, very drunk, so he recalls less."

It could work. Poison him with alcohol, and he might doubt what he saw and heard. Kaell stored memories. Her scent. A jewelled ring. Betraying words—*Your Grace.*

"You are young to show your mettle, my son," the woman said to the unseen boy. "You are not fire, like me. You are steel like your father—cold, bright, sharp."

Her laugh bubbled. Sweet, almost innocent. "I am satisfied with that."

His captors forced wine down his throat. Spluttering, Kaell

tried to turn his head, clamp his lips shut, but again and again they pummelled his belly until he gasped and swallowed. When they dumped him on grass, he curled, wretched.

He was a bonded warrior. Blessed by the gods. Strong.

But he didn't feel like that now.

After a time, footsteps closed on him. Warm breath misted his cheek. "None of us eludes fate, Kaell," the woman said. At least he thought she did. Maybe he dreamt it. The wine and sleep weighing his eyelids fragmented reason.

She stroked his face, her touch tender. "Every path twists back to what must happen. There can be no escape for you, I think. Still, I offer what warning I can."

Cloth wisped his arm as she leaned against him. "He'll call you to him." Her voice was soft but iron edged. "Archanin. You must never go into the Waste Mountains. If you do, he'll take you."

Kaell fell away into a wine-sodden dream of blood and misery and death.

SOMEONE SHOOK HIM. He surfaced with a groan, his skull aflame, throat rough as unhewn stone. Dusk deepened about him, its soft web shrouding the first moon. Beneath a spreading tree, bilberry bushes cushioned his back, his dew-wet clothes stinking of wine.

Arn's face screwed tight with disgust. "Wine breath. Wine hair, too." The man threw Kaell a long look. "And you're bleeding. So now you're drinking and fighting. With what? Bilberry bushes? Shadows?"

Yes, shadows. The woman's voice drifted like a dream's fading fragment. *He'll call you to him. Never go into those mountains.*

"I fell in a hole—" Kaell broke off with a sigh. Too hard to explain when his head thumped and words grated his throat.

Arn pulled him up. "Talk quietly. Caelmarsh's men are

searching for you. I heard your name and followed them. Little did I know I had only to follow the odour of stale wine."

"You came after me."

"I always do, Kaell. But I clearly missed the fun. A hole, you say?" Arn clapped a palm to his brow, groaning.

"Cyrah protect us, I just had a terrible thought. You'll torment us with a song or worse, one of your awful poems, about your adventure in the hole." He grinned. "With luck, you won't think of anything rhyming with the word witless."

Kaell started to laugh then moaned. "Oh, my head."

"Don't expect sympathy. You stink like an Isles tavern. Caelmarsh's men can hunt you with their noses."

"The woman forced wine on me."

"Found a woman in the hole? Was that before or after the fighting?"

"You're as funny as a log, Arn."

His dulled wits scrambled memories. Vanilla and rose. Her sigh of regret. Words about duty that struck deep, like a forgotten truth.

He whirled, hearing his name. Darkness welled beneath the trees. The wind rattled dead leaves and gnarled boughs. The forest surely sat empty. Yet a shiver ran through him. *Khir.*

Kaell stared, lost in a trance. It held him a long while, until he grew aware of Arn gripping his arm, an owl's distant hoot, cicadas humming, the scent of wet grass and leaves.

"I hate it when you do that," Arn said.

"When do we ride for the Waste Mountains?"

Arn brightened. "I thought you wanted to wear fur undergarments and fight for a Damadar Ice lord."

Kaell shrugged that off grimly. He belonged to Khir. If he peered deeply into his dreams, his god waited in the murk, demanding his surrendered will, his blood. He could not serve an Ice lord any more than he could the ghoul god, Archanin.

What did the woman say? You cannot flee fate. Something like that.

And Khir moulded his fate. He must go where the gods willed. Even beyond the great gorge into the Waste Mountains. Towards the door of his nightmares.

HEATH

The inn stank of stale wine and cold sweat. Of intrigue. Heath raked its gloom, spying his sister Judith alone at a corner table.

He ducked his head beneath a low-hung beamed roof, his cloak swishing leather boots as he dodged crowded benches to reach her. Discordant voices, laughter, the odours of tallow and roasted meat roiled in a chaotic blend so very typical of this dreadful city.

A girl in a low-cut, tight gown brushed past. Heath stared with undisguised interest at her sand-pale hair. She favoured him with a bold, nearly toothless smile.

A seaman at a nearby table glared. "Go find a goat, stranger. She's taken." He pulled the unprotesting girl onto his lap. Dice spilled as the table rocked. Another sailor sprang up, pointed an accusing finger at Heath, and jabbered.

Heath at once groped for his sword. *Though—think it through.* Killing drunken fools attracted attention. Reluctantly he weaved past two soldiers huddled over a table, their voices low and careful, their glances creeping over their shoulders as though they plotted treason.

An idle thought. His mind turned on schemes more dangerous than betraying kings.

He slid onto a bench opposite his sister, leaning to kiss her cheek. Judith's perfume tantalised with a fragment of blossoms. It reminded him of lazy, steaming summers, of billowing clouds above fields of cornflowers.

"That girl has yellow hair." He jerked his head. "Where'd she get that, do you think?"

"What do you care? This is Tide's End. Every stinking, sweating soldier, priest, sailor, and lordling washes up here. Maybe her mother bedded some blond Venivan. Or the girl's the whelp of a heathen from beyond the Ice Sea. They all have yellow hair there."

Heath laughed. "And how would you know, Judith, my precious?"

"I keep my ears open."

"And your mouth shut—when needs must," he teased. "A skill I'm yet to master."

"You've mastered talking nonsense," Judith said. "Made it an art form, in fact."

A greasy-haired man with sweat stains on his tunic thumped a carafe onto the table. Heath dropped coins into his outstretched hand and poured wine. He sipped.

"I tried the ale," Judith said. "Undrinkable. I ordered you wine."

He made a face. "The wine is fit only for pigs."

She laughed. "My poor Heath. If you can't get drunk, what will you do?"

"The gods only know. How do the not-so-respectable citizens of Tide's End live like this? Cursed heat, flies, wine a dog might spew up. What a wretched place."

"A wretched place?" Judith arched well-formed brows. "The jewel of the Isles? This famed city of stone, light, and air?"

"Give me the emptiness of the Icelands any day."

Tide's End, in comparison, crowded like an oppressive mire, crawling with jostling life.

The city sprawled about an ancient castle rising from cliffs into clouds, a haze of alleys, jutting harbours, and wharves lapped by a too-bright sapphire sea. Sleek, exotic ships with furled sails congested sea lanes or rocked beside long-fingered boardwalks.

Heath had prowled the sweeping harbour that morning, unnoticed in the wash of perfumed bodies thinly clad in silk and linen.

He listened to thuds and clunks as men unloaded goods off vessels from Wardour and distant Veniva, to creaking timbers, lapping waves, the cries of traders, and strident voices cursing or laughing or complaining about the heat.

Tide's End's scents—brine, citrus, and sharp sweat—tore at him with longing, a yearning for the lonely icescape of cutting winds and monotonous cold he and Judith called home.

"Surely we can soon return to the Icelands." Judith grabbed his hand. "No need to look further. Aric Caelan will please our gods."

"I must make sure."

"I'm sick of this, Heath. Sick, sick, sick. Can't we go home? It's been—" She broke off to stare at the door, murmuring, "No, don't look," when he turned.

"Is it Pairas, or whatever his stupid name is? What's he doing?"

"Laughing with some sweating fool. No doubt comparing jewellery or admiring each other's garments. Isles men." She gave a mocking roll of her eyes.

Heath tried the wine again. Still foul. "So what now?"

"We know his weakness." Judith tucked a strand of long hair behind her ear. "I'll bring him here and drop a little something into his drink."

"What a dull plan. More fun if I beat the information from him."

She patted his hand as she might a child's. "What's that old expression? Too much pleasure spoils a man. And I must protect you from yourself, dear brother."

"Must you? I'd rather be spoiled."

Scowling, Judith shot to her feet. "That cow."

"What?"

"Your yellow-haired lass is all over him. And now another. Well, I suppose he *is* deliciously masculine."

"An Isles man? They're all too pretty for my taste. Can't tell one from the other."

"*You* can't tell. Only because you're always drunk." She shed her cape and smoothed a gown hugging every curve.

Heath risked a glance as Judith glided away, hips swaying, torches dancing auburn light through her tumbling, dark hair. Men gaped. One, more brazen than his companions, called out. Her retort drew barks of laughter.

She reached a young man with burnished, black hair, a bladesman's curved shoulders, and press of muscle against a tight tunic. Whispered in his ear. The man laughed and shook his head. Women clinging to him glared.

Judith turned with a swirling gown and a flick of glossy hair.

The man discarded his admirers to follow like a puppy. Too easy. Heath yawned.

"Heath. I won our bet. This young man is Pairas. Not who you thought."

"If he's cost me money, the least he can do is drink with us."

Judith touched Pairas's arm. "Please join us."

Heath caught a thread of her perfume, too sweet for this wretched den and its licentious Isles patrons.

Pairas willingly sat. His helpless, doglike look reminded Heath of another old Icelands saying from the notorious long-dead lord and poet they called the Ice Rider.

Oh, what foolishness we men embrace, and all because of a pretty face.

"Pairas, this is my brother Heath."

"Brother?" The Isles captain brightened.

"So you're not Aric Caelan?" Heath gestured to the tavern keeper for more wine.

Pairas tore admiring eyes from Judith. "I'm honoured to serve Aric. Call him friend, even. But I'm nothing like him."

"Really?" And everyone said Isles men all looked alike.

The surly tavern keeper brought wine. Heath surrendered more coins as Judith eased an ampoule from her pocket.

"An acquaintance pointed you out as Aric. My mistake."

"Your acquaintance saw us together, perhaps? Where was this?"

An undercurrent of suspicion. Heath approved. "At a tournament, I think."

Pairas made no reply. His stare dwelled on a brooch on Heath's tunic. A tight frown burrowed his brow beneath soft, damp curls. "That's a curious pattern."

With a disarming smile, Heath drew his cloak tight.

"An old family thing. Wine? It tastes like piss, I'm afraid. Judith can buy the next carafe since she won our bet." He wagged a playful finger at his sister. "She always guesses right. Whether it's who wins the melee or if the king has a new mistress."

Or which pretty, sweating, ignorant Isles fool he might carve up next.

"A tournament, you said?"

Ah, still suspicious. Hardly surprising. The king wanted Aric Caelan dead.

Heath poured wine to deflect the question.

Pairas raised his cup to Judith. "Lady, to your beauty."

Judith threw him a bold, low-lidded look, her scarlet lips parted.

Pairas's breath stalled. His dazed look mimicked other men's around Judith.

Heath sighed. He expected a trickier hunt, given the young captain's wits cut as sharp as his blade. Or so men said. And men in Tide's End had a lot to say about Pairas—for a handful of coins.

"A good swordsman… not as good as Aric Caelan, mind you," they had told him. "But then who is?"

"True, so true," Heath had replied, nodding, "but about Pairas?"

"Oh, Pairas. Young for an Isles captain. Wellborn. The only son of an impoverished lord drinking himself to death on a crumbling rock in the middle of the sea."

Very sad. Heath hid another yawn as his sister clashed cups with Pairas. She slipped a hand beneath the table. A time-proved way to scramble a man's wits, sharp or not.

Pairas put down his cup. He drew Judith's hand onto the table and covered it with his own. "Can we just talk? I possess only your name. That isn't close to enough. I must know what's behind that beautiful face. I must know everything."

Judith sat back. She hid a blink of surprise. A small silence settled about her and Pairas.

Across the tavern, laughter broke up voices raised in discord. A man shouted for ale. But neither of Heath's companions spoke.

At length, Judith turned to him. "Heath, I thought you must meet a trader."

He forced a doubtful look. "And leave you alone in this dreadful place? It's too much to ask this young man to watch out for you, Judith, when we only just met him."

Solemnly, Pairas said, "It would be my honour to serve you and your sister."

"If you're sure." Pairas talked a lot about honour. An honour to serve Aric. An honour to service—ah, serve—Judith. "Then I am in your debt. I'll retire to change."

He rose, nodded, and made his way to the stairs. The seamen glared. Heath chuckled. Long memories in the Isles. They held a grudge for at least half an hour.

Upstairs, he left his door unlocked, lit a candle, and dropped onto the bed. Not long now. Judith's potion stunned as readily as her beauty.

Softly he whistled a stupid tune he heard all over Tide's End about a knight called Goffren who betrayed the king. It followed them everywhere. The Falls, the Mountains, the Plains.

The minstrel in the city of kings, Dal-Kanu, was a swarthy, balding man with plump cheeks. At Tide's End a pale-faced boy too thin to have breath in him belted out the words.

In a Downs tavern, a sallow-cheeked woman with braided hair amused drunken patrons with cheekily added lewd gestures.

Fat, thin. Old. All sang the same tune, it seemed. What tune might the young captain sing?

WIND WHOOSHED as the door thumped back. Heath leapt up to catch a slumped Pairas.

"Quickly." Judith pushed past. "Help me with him. He drained his wine in one swig. Silly boy. I could barely rouse him."

"You had no trouble rousing him before."

She glared at his crude humour. Heath muttered, "I am truly unappreciated," and dragged Pairas to the room's only chair. The man's head drooped.

"How much did you give him? I can't question him if he's senseless."

"Not my fault he gulped his wine." Judith knelt to search a chest. "However, I have another potion that will somewhat restore his wits."

Heath tapped fingers on the wall. She grew careless. He had known for a while but did not have the will to correct her. Not when he grew careless too. Sick to his gut of all this.

When they had first left the Icelands, Judith's artistic seductions required only a mere promise to hook and land their prey. Now—

"He gulped the wine so he could bed you quicker. Of late, you're reckless, clumsy even. I saw your hand. What did you do? Fondle him in public?"

"You have a wicked mind."

True enough.

"I touched his thigh. He"—her fingers stilled on the trunk, brow furrowed at the memory—"removed my hand."

"The chase, Judith. That keeps a man keen. On the Downs you let that swordsman with the grey eyes work to win you. This one? You could teach that yellow-haired wench a trick or two about plying her trade. If it's too easy, a man like Pairas will suspect you want more than his body."

"Shut your mouth." Judith surged up, clutching a vial. "How dare you judge me. I serve our family and our gods."

Heath gestured at Pairas. "He's out of it, Judith. I won't learn anything about Aric."

"I don't care. We learnt all we need. But you must make sure. Always making sure."

"Lower your voice." He pressed an ear to the door. "A poor choice will anger the gods."

"I'm beginning to think one swordsman is just like another."

"You don't mean that."

Hands on hips, Judith glowered. "No bladesman is Aric's match. Instead of this nonsense, it's time, surely, to come up with a clever plan, my *clever* brother, to abduct him."

"I have lots of clever plans in my clever head. I just need to know where Aric might be so we can snatch him. With luck, this man will tell me."

In answer she knelt and held the uncorked vial beneath Pairas's nose. He coughed.

Judith rose, arms folded. "Well, he's yours to torment. So make certain."

Heath slapped their captive's cheek. "Captain, you can sleep after we talk. You want to answer my questions. You must answer my questions. Can you do that?"

Pairas grunted. His dark eyes were hazy, his body and mind languid and soft.

Despite the dreamlike state, their sister Myranthe's potion compelled answers. She loved her draughts, her spells. Magic gave Myranthe control. Even of her scheming siblings.

"What was that?"

"Yes."

"Good. I want you to think back to a tournament in the Falls. Aric Caelan was there."

"Aric fell in the melee." Pairas smiled faintly. "Drank too much the night before."

"He lost? To whom?"

"Aric doesn't lose. He recovered, held off the Stone Knight, Sherrin Cross, I think—" His voice trailed off.

"Aric is the best swordsman you've seen?"

"We know this," Judith muttered.

Pairas hesitated. "The best."

"You sound uncertain."

"No. Aric never loses. It's just—"

"What?" Heath hammered.

"A Downs tournament years ago. There was this woman—"

"Yes, yes, forget the woman. What about this tournament?"

The Isles captain's voice blurred. "He was perhaps sixteen. His lord raged when he learned he entered the lists. I thought he might strike the boy."

"Strike who?"

"Kaell. Vraymorg dragged him away, shouting, 'A bonded warrior does not waste his talents at tournaments. He serves the gods.' Not a man to cross, the Mountains lord."

"Vraymorg." Judith frowned. "We keep hearing strange things about him."

Heath leaned in. "You watched Khir's bonded warrior fight. In a tournament?"

"Some Cahireans ambushed Kaell. Vraymorg killed—"

"Forget Vraymorg. Tell me about Kaell."

"Kaell?"

Heath heaved an impatient sigh. "Is this Kaell a better bladesman than Aric Caelan?"

"This is pointless." Judith threw up her arms. "We can't touch Kaell. You know that. He belongs to Khir."

Ignoring her, he gripped Pairas's wrist. "Just tell me. Then you can sleep."

"Tell you?"

"About Aric. And Kaell. Who is the better swordsman?"

"It's not that simple."

"Then how is it?" He no longer had a taste for this. Time he and Judith returned home.

Pairas's eyelids drooped. "That boy. He stunned everyone. His speed. His control."

"So he is better than Aric?" A flat despair emptied him. The old gods protected Kaell.

"Kaell is brilliant, his technique perfect. But he fights coldly, without passion."

That was a weakness? Not in the Icelands. Not in a fire arena.

"And Aric Caelan?"

Pairas smiled fondly. "Aric fights with both head and heart. Not that he'll fight much after he bends his knee to Cathmor."

Judith gasped. Heath's breath died. He knew nothing of this.

"Why should Aric Caelan, prince of the Isles, bend his knee to King Cathmor?"

"No." Pairas shook his head furiously. "It's still secret. I can't."

"You want to tell me."

The man's head sagged as if the compulsion in the command crushed his will.

"A treaty. An end to war between the false king Cathmor and Aric's father, King Hatton. Signed secretly. Aric is escorting his sister Azenor to Dal-Kanu to marry the false king."

Heath threw Judith a bewildered look. His sister shrugged a "don't ask me."

"And Aric? Will he stay in Dal-Kanu? Or return to Tide's End once Azenor weds?"

"Cathmor won't let him leave. I told Aric that. I told him not to go, reminded him the king had a price on his head, that he'd find an excuse to arrest him. He wouldn't listen."

Judith whispered, "Heath, what do we do?"

"About him?" He drew his knife. "I'll finish him, dump the body at sea."

"No!" She grabbed his arm. "There's no need. Leave him to sleep it off."

"Judith, this man is not some drunken Downs knight or an unwashed Mountains warrior with a dog's wits. He's an Isles captain. He saw my brooch, may even know what it means."

"No," she howled, fingernails in his flesh. "Please. I can't stand any more. I haven't slept properly since you cut that soldier's throat in Dal-Gorma. Please. Not this one."

Heath dragged his hands down his face, too weary to argue. Let the fool enjoy a few dazed hours of life. Time enough to kill him later. "Tie him up."

"Let's leave him here, Heath. He doesn't know who we are."

"Bind him. Let me think."

Judith dropped her hands to her side. "Heath, what do we do? If there's peace, we lose all. The prophecy says a true Caelan king must rule before fate draws the seer back to the Icelands. If Hatton bends his knee, he can't be king."

Heath snatched up his cloak. A restlessness twitched. "I must go out."

"Now?"

He nodded towards Pairas. "Watch him. I'll deal with him when I return."

THE GIRL STRAIGHTENED HER SKIRTS. She flashed Heath that toothless grin and brushed strands of blonde hair from her cheek. "My, you're a strong one."

Heath pushed off the rough wall. Flooded tides left a line of salt and grime on stone.

He wrinkled his nose against the vinegarish stench of the

narrow, mud-stained alley.

As he yanked up his pants, the girl held out her hand.

"I've a weakness for men with dark-brown hair. Reminds me of my first lover. But a girl's still got ex—" She struggled briefly with the word, then proudly pronounced, "Expenses."

"You've got more than that." Heath looped a lock of hair around a finger. Such a strange colour. With a laugh, he dug into his purse to find coins. She took them, again flashing gums.

"Why do you have yellow hair?"

"What's it to you? A quick poke doesn't mean you can ask questions."

He shrugged. "Curiosity. I've not seen a lass with pale hair in Telor before. You hear stories sometimes, nonsense I thought, that a few of the Seithin survived."

She slapped his hand away. "Don't you go saying that. Don't you dare. You'll get me arrested and killed and all. I'm not Seithin. That's stupid." She gulped in an outraged breath. "My father's Venivan. A ship's captain, my mother says."

"Oh, a captain."

"Yes, a captain." She tilted her chin. "Lazy cow can't remember his name, but he was Venivan, with yellow hair. So don't you go causing trouble, saying I'm Seithin."

Heath backed her up to the wall. "Cause trouble? But you've a weakness for men like me."

"I've a weakness for men with coins in their pockets."

Heath groped her breast, lazily aroused again. Ah well, he had a few more coins. From the moons, the night was not so old.

A bell tolled, its peal rippling silver in the clear, crisp darkness.

"What's that?"

"Nothing. Get off me."

"A bell in the middle of the night means something. Tell me."

The girl squirmed beneath his weight. Heath let her go and stepped back in one graceful movement. He held up a gold coin. "What's happening?"

"Some poor fool's about to die. You really don't know? Where have you been? The ends of the earth?"

Something like that. "What poor fool?"

"Cultist probably. There, I told you." The girl snatched the coin, backed up a step, then scuttled from the alley.

Heath followed. To his surprise, the black night awakened with nervous laughter and whispers as a stream of people hurried along the road beside the sea wall towards the docks. Some bristled with excitement. Others peered over shoulders with frightened expressions.

He pushed into the crowd, catching snatches of conversation as it carried him forward.

"Did they uncover another one?"

"What do you think? Why else summon everyone?"

The mob surged towards torches blazing upon jutting breakwaters in the stone-walled harbour then grumbled to a halt.

Squeezed shoulder-to-hip with men and women held back by a line of guardsmen, Heath could only stare as figures in sinister, purple robes appeared on a breakwater. Moonlight gleamed on white-painted faces.

Between the breakwater and the quayside where the expectant crowd waited, the tide lapped stone, a silver-streaked inky pool.

Hooded figures dragged a half-naked man onto the breakwater. Young, scrawny, with matted, black hair, he slumped in their grasp. Broken. Too exhausted to be afraid.

The bells stopped. In the taut silence, heavy with menace, cold slivered down Heath's spine as though something unseen and ancient breathed on his neck as it swept past.

A figure stepped forward. Torch flames cast a woman's silhouette upon the wall. As she addressed the crowd, Heath struggled to catch the words. Something about judgement. Gods.

A priestess then. He shrank back. Some called his gods cruel, but these Isles deities surely could frost even an Icelands winter.

The priestess lifted her voice. "An offence to our king, to our gods."

"What offence? What did the wretch do?" he asked a man near him. The stranger shushed him with a disapproving frown.

"Accept this traitor, accept his life as our offering, oh gods who protect us and grant us life," the priestess said. "May the Three always turn their faces towards us."

She nodded. Hooded figures threw the young man down. A muttering ran through the jostling crowd as he sprawled on his hands and knees, dirty hair spilled across his face.

At a grinding sound, the mob hushed. Metal clinked and rattled. Heath used his height and swordsman's bulk to force his way to the front of the human tangle as a stone slab rose from the water, its rusted chains creaking against the breakwater.

The prisoner scrambled back, clawing helplessly at the wall of robed captors, his mouth open in a noiseless scream. They grabbed his arms and pulled him towards the stone. The throng pressed close, straining to see.

Two robed priests leapt onto the wet stone. Their companions thrust the captive at them. They knocked him to his knees then onto his back. He arched and kicked, but they pinned him with their bodies until iron fastened his wrists and ankles.

The priests returned to the breakwater, their sacrifice uselessly struggling in fetters. The priestess lifted long-sleeved arms, her chant lost in an excited babble and the roar of water.

The stone rumbled into the sea.

With morbid anticipation, even an exhilarated fascination, Heath wondered at the young man's likely terror as he disappeared beneath the water.

He should feel something else. Shouldn't he? Compassion. Disquiet. Horror, perhaps.

A hush fell. The crowd stilled like a stalking beast. Waiting.

A woman near Heath swiped a tear from her cheek, saw him staring, took a startled breath, and disappeared into the mob. This time, unexpectedly, pity stabbed. Did she know the sacrificed man? A brother? A lover? Husband?

He tried to follow her with his eyes, but the crowd sighed as a grinding split the quiet. With a mighty splash, the stone broke above waves. The manacles lay open, the young man gone.

Not as dramatic as the deaths Heath delivered his gods in the fire halls. But curious.

"Praise the gods." The priestess's voice lifted. "They accept the sacrifice."

A ripple tore through onlookers. Relief. Excitement. Everyone spoke and laughed at once. A stranger slapped his back. "Cultists. It's too quick a death."

More talk of cultists. What were they? Why did they deserve this? "It's a trick," Heath said. "A mechanism releases the chains, so the body disappears. The tide does the rest."

The man sneered. "You don't know what you say, stranger. But best not say it too loud."

Heath peered into swirling, murky waters. Even if the tide carried the body off, it must float. No, he no longer liked this at all. Nor anything about these vicious Isles gods.

With heavy footsteps, he returned to the inn, wondering at his coldness. Was this what he had become after years fighting to survive in the arena? A man unable to feel even shame at his lack of sympathy, his hardness.

When he stepped into the room, he froze in surprise.

Like the sacrifice upon the stone, Pairas lay on floorboards, ringed by burning candles.

Judith stood over him, holding a cup. Blood smeared her brow.

"You can't kill him now," she said.

Heath tore the cup from her. Blood spilled on his wrists, dripped to the floor. He considered Pairas. Smears patterned his naked chest, but no wound marked him.

Judith thrust out a gashed arm. "It's my blood."

"What is this? What have you done?"

"A protection spell. Myranthe told me how. She knows what you're like."

Heath snorted a sigh. A restlessness crept back into his bones, a weariness of spirit.

"A protection spell," he repeated dully. "Against me?"

Judith held up a knife. "I used your knife for the spell. Myranthe said to take an object that's worn close to your body. It means *you* can't kill him now."

Heath snatched at his missing blade, then let his hands fall to his side. "Judith, please understand. He must die. We can't leave ends untied."

"Whatever you do to him, my spell means it rebounds against me."

He stared at her beloved face, enlivened by determination. How dare she take the side of some fool warrior from a gods-forsaken rock in the middle of nowhere against him. *Him.*

"Why him? Tell me that, Judith? You've never cared before."

"He reminds me of someone," she said, her eyes hazing with memory.

"Where does this leave us, Judith? How can I trust you after this?"

Her expression softened. She took his hands. "You can always trust me, Heath. How can you ask that? After everything that's happened. It's only this one thing."

Heath snatched his hands away. Only this one thing. He dug fingers into his aching temples. "I don't have time for this. If Aric Caelan is in Dal-Kanu, then you and I must follow."

"And we will. But first let this man go. It can do no harm."

He sighed. "Very well, nag. I'll leave him outside the city gates. Alive. I swear it."

Judith threw her arms around him. "Thank you."

He smiled at her. But alarm cut through him like sharpened steel. Heath Damadar, a lord of the ice, fire dancer and spy, knew he—they—just made their first mistake.

ARIC

Aric Caelan split the line of riders and carriages advancing slowly towards the river crossing, his gloved hand instinctive on the reins, his thoughts snagged on one thing.

His outriders. Where were his outriders? He had sent them into the forests beyond the forge and into the glare of noon. Now the light pearled towards dusk.

"Skull top. Talk to me." His sister Azenor leaned from the saddle to torment a man with a bald, shiny head. "My swaggering brother says he's too busy."

With an indulgent chuckle, Aric fell in beside Azenor and the Isles captain.

"I'm bored, Cass," Azenor said. "Tell me a story about Isles kings of old, sorceresses, warriors, and magic. The bloodier the better."

"The woman's a witch," Cass said. "She can't see me but always knows I'm there."

"She smells you." Just like he smelt something amiss, could taste it, metallic as blood on his tongue. Where were his scouts?

"These mud berries?" His captain scooped pear-shaped, purple fruit into his mouth and chewed aloud. "Try some, my prince. Put hairs on your chest."

"Hairs on my chest? You still think I'm a boy, you old fool?" Aric thrust a gloved hand over his nose. "You've been eating them since this morning and your breath reeks, Cass. The stench will fling me from the saddle."

"You're one to complain, Aric," Azenor said. "You doused yourself in Venivan perfume. It can't be for the king, so maybe you intend to charm the women of Dal-Kanu."

Her tone whipped with mischief—as it often did. Yet Aric sensed veiled unease beneath.

Because she must wed? Surely not. Azenor Caelan was every bit an Isles woman, fearless, hot-tempered. Quick to laugh, quick to love, quick to scorn.

He remembered a singer at his father's castle in Tide's End on a summer's eve, the heavy air drenched with brine and sweat. The man weaved flattering words about Azenor while warriors dazed by wine and rich food in their bellies slumped at tables complaining about the heat.

Daring be our sweet lass of the Isles,

And lovely be her face and smiles.

The fool singer left out the verse about her "daring, lovely tongue," though, and "its daring, lovely sting." Especially on a long journey to the city of kings when our sweet lass of the Isles sought to pass the time with teasing jabs.

Cass sniffed. "Venivan scent. Every fashionable Isles man wears it these days. Load of nonsense if you ask me. Women like the smell of sweat on a man, not perfume."

Aric swiped at his moist brow. "I'm bound to charm every woman in Dal-Kanu, then."

"Lord Charming, King of the Land of Sweat," Azenor said. "Women at Tide's End have another name for you. Shall I tell you?"

"Only if you want your hair mussed."

Cass laughed. "My wife told me that name. It's oddly flattering."

Aric summoned a mock glare of disapproval. "One more word, Cass, and you stay with Azenor in Dal-Kanu. The city stinks of rotting cabbage, I'm told. At least until you and your berries get there."

"Not that we'll ever reach Dal-Kanu." Azenor swatted a black curl. "How much farther?"

"What? In a hurry to wed?"

His sister lowered lids over eyes as untamed and dark as a mountain cat's. Black pearls, the singer said. *Black lances more like.*

She thrust out a palm. "I want berries, Cass."

"To pelt at Aric?" He shook his head. "I'm too old for this. I won't miss you and your brother bickering when you're wed, lass. I'm keen for a bit of peace."

"I don't bicker. He's just a big-headed, swaggering, sweet-scented lackwit."

"Now that wounds me," Aric said. "The sweet bit, I mean. The rest is fair."

A bird took to the air with beating wings and a screeched protest. Aric stole a look ahead. A shrill wind rattled branches of reedy, silver-barked trees along the river.

The road led through rustling grassland towards darkling shadows. Yellow wildflowers dipped and waved, their sickly sweet scent mingling with pungent earth, sweat, and horseflesh.

An ambush seemed unlikely this deep in the false king's lands. Still—a crow circled clumped trees. The light stripped away fast. The stillness crept thick and ugly.

He leaned to Cass. "Those outriders?"

"Not returned. But no telling how far ahead they tracked."

"Maybe something got them," Azenor said with morbid delight. "Pairas told me outlaws roam these roads. Packs of them. Like wolves."

There it was again. That undercurrent. Not fear exactly. More nervous expectation.

"They won't attack so many armed men. Besides." He punched her arm. "Your sharp tongue will wound wolf's heads better than any edged blade."

"Ha, ha. A perfumed jester. What a prize."

"Prize what, little one? Prize fool?" Aric said. That's what his elder brother Gendrick called him. Though he usually added the word "reckless."

Aric turned to Cass. "Pass the word. We wait at the ford."

"Yes, best be careful." His captain spurred his horse forward.

Azenor pouted prettily. "More delays. You fuss like an old woman, Aric. So we won't reach Dal-Kanu tonight?"

"Impatient to be queen, little one? So you can order me about?"

"It's beyond me why your head doesn't burst with conceit. It's not about you, dullard. *You're* not exiled to Dal-Kanu."

"Marrying a king, albeit a false one, is hardly exile."

"You sweet-scented liar. Pairas told me what you said: that I should elope with some penniless, unwashed Mountains goat rather than wed this scheming brute, Cathmor."

Pairas again. A name she should fast forget. "Azenor, don't talk of Pairas to the false king." The less Cathmor knew about that—he sought the safest word—relationship, the better.

His sister's knuckles whitened about the reins.

"I lost my sight, Aric, not my wits. Nor am I a child."

No, hardly a child. A strong-willed young woman with a wicked sense of irreverence. He almost pitied his cousin. Almost. The false king was a power-greedy deceiver.

"Still, best curb that tongue before we reach Dal-Kanu. What's acceptable in the Isles is treason in Dal-Kanu. A wrong word and you and I both end up in the king's head house."

"Or our heads will." Azenor laughed. "Or rather, just yours. Mine must remain attached to my body, or the king will find it hard to wed and bed me."

Gods take her. Now she grew amused. Aric released a long breath. The king filled his infamous tower with rotting heads in the war. Isles warriors captured, tortured, and executed. He pushed the thought aside.

"At least my head will smell sweet as it rots. Don't worry,

Cathmor won't dare arrest me now."

"But he hates you, Aric."

"It's as well then, what with my duties in Tide's End, I won't be in Dal-Kanu much, attracting the king's ire once you're wed."

"Yes, just as well." Her eyes were too bright.

Aric grasped her hand. "Azenor. It won't be so bad—"

She yanked her hand away. "I am not a child with a head full of romance, Aric. I'll do my duty and marry Cathmor. You'll do your duty and make me."

He would indeed do his duty. And even pretend to like it.

A crow screeched. Its caw sank into his gut with unease. Aric tilted his head, following the scavenger's languid circling. Did something lie dead in the trees?

They had passed a ragged skeleton in a crow cage near Dal-Breen that morning, a starved outlaw left as a warning to those who defied the false king's sheriffs. Azenor had complained about the stench. He'd told her it was a dead horse.

"Duty, though, is hot and dull." Azenor yawned. "I'm fed up with riding."

He seized his chance to bait her, just as he always did. "You should travel in the carriage with your women. You're a mere girl and hardly up to riding so far."

She swung her head his way, black eyes blazing like sunlight striking his sword. Lances, he thought again. "I can outlast you in the saddle, you blustering blaggard. You're not the only one with Caelan blood."

"Blustering blaggard. I like it. It's better than big-headed lackwit. No sting in that."

"Blustering lackwitted, big-headed, scented jester. Go away."

"Scented jester? How your cruel words cut me."

"What? Still there?" Azenor flicked a hand.

"Very well, Your Soon-To-Be-Majesty. I'm off. But you'll miss me—and my sweet scent."

Aric signalled to a man to watch her and urged his horse on.

Something lay in those trees. A dead fox? Or a dead man?

We're not in the Isles any more. Not among friends. An old expression but true.

He took a breath to shout to Cass riding ahead. Words choked in his throat. *What was that?* An awareness, nameless and indistinct, tingled at his neck.

Pulling hard on the reins, he listened. The wind drummed like hoofbeats, carrying the river's muddy scents and gurgling murmur. Isles banners flapped. Fading sunlight retreated behind gathering clouds. Dusk fell quickly, menacingly.

Lost within every other sound, a mere wrinkle in air, he heard a bowstring thrum.

"Ambush!" Aric flattened against his horse's neck. A bolt rippled his sleeve then thudded into earth. Horsemen scattered. A churned stone grazed his arm as he whipped out his sword.

"Archers. Behind you!" Cass yelled. A rider shrieked and toppled. A man plunged to the ground, a shaft in his neck, his startled horse bolting. Aric twisted, desperately searching tangled steel and flesh for Azenor. "To me!" he shouted.

Indignant crows exploded from grass in a black cloud. In their wake, figures leapt up, swords gripped in gauntleted hands. Wild with fury and outrage, Aric rode at them. Isles warriors charged after him, bellowing defiance.

Iron clashed in a thunderous clangour as the strangers fell upon his men like ravenous beasts. Aric thrust at one, his sword spilling guts. Gore and blood splattered his tunic. He kicked the body away.

Another attacker, pale-skinned with burning eyes, hammered with steel. Aric slashed his throat. By Saarn, who or what came at them?

Cass cut through attackers to him. "I sent men to protect Azenor's women. My prince, find Azenor and get—" Two figures fell upon him with streaking metal.

No! Aric hacked. A head flew. Splattered blood blinded him. He swiped his eyes.

The air steamed with cries. Shapes ran wild. Arrows twanged and zipped and clunked. A man screeched. Blades clanged.

Hands groped at his ankle. Aric swung, his sword cleaving flesh and bone. A shield smashed into his chest. For a heartbeat he had a sense of falling, falling. Then a boot struck his jaw. Darkness closed in.

"ARIC. ARIC, PLEASE BE ALIVE."

The words floated as formless as a dream. Flickering light scratched his weighted eyelids. His skull flamed. Cord bit into his wrists and ankles.

Memory rushed him. Cass riding ahead. Whirring arrows. Ambush. By Saarn, by Sauveroken—Azenor. Aric forced open blood-crusted eyes.

Wrists bound, his sister crouched against a crumbling wall, moonlight blinking on her frightened face. Starlight sprayed through fire-ravaged roof beams. Shadows scrabbled along ivy-tangled stone walls, inked with age. A ruin. Where? Who held them?

"Aric. Tell me you're not hurt. Please."

Dizziness hazed his vision as he moved his head. He managed, "I'm alive, Azenor."

She dragged in a sharp breath. "Thank The Three."

"Did they—did they harm you?"

"Someone pulled me from my horse. I heard screams. I feared they killed you."

"Do you know where we are? Or who holds us?"

"No."

"And the others? Cass? Any of them?"

"I didn't hear—I don't know. Aric, I have to tell you something."

At her tone, unease whipped his back. "What?"

Azenor didn't answer. She sank her teeth into her bottom lip.

A bite of wind riffled though hair to Aric's skull. The touch of creeping fingertips. Moonbeams threaded through gaps in broken stone.

Awkwardly he rose to an elbow. "Azenor?"

She dropped her head. "I didn't know, Aric. Oh gods, he didn't tell me anyone would die."

"What?"

"I knew about the ambush, but not like this—" She stopped. Her voice shrilled in panic. "They're coming."

Booted steps closed. A blurred figure yanked Aric up and slammed him against the wall.

He blinked to clear his sight. At first glance he might think he stared upon a man. Except something predatory marred the face close to his; the eyes were veiled with coldness beneath arched brows, the lips sensually red but pressed in a cruel, thin line.

Others prowled behind. Beautiful creatures with gold in their hair and night in their gazes, their tall, slender bodies muscular and elegant. Swords and jewelled knives decorated belts; silver circled wrists and long necks.

Belly sick, struggling to stay upright, Aric snatched at anger for strength, "How dare you attack us. You'll answer for it. Who are you, and what do you want with us?"

His captor grasped his throat with long, white fingers.

"Shut your mouth and listen, princeling." He stumbled over the Telorian words. "We have a task for you. Fail—and your sister dies."

Azenor gasped. Aric shot her a terrified look. Saarn, all the gods of the Isles, protect them. Protect her. "What task?"

"You will strike down Khir's bonded warrior with a poisoned blade."

Aric didn't understand. "Bonded warrior," he repeated stupidly. "Do you mean that boy from Vraymorg?" Why? Who would want a bonded warrior dead except… except…

Horrified, he whispered, “You’re ghouls.”

The ghoul shoved his face into Aric’s, his breath cool. “We are the ancient enemy, our name forbidden. Once we ruled every land with magic and strength. We serve a lord with real power, not like your petty kings.”

“Whatever you want, it can’t have anything to do with us.”

“Is that what you think, princeling? That you’re safe in the Isles, behind the high walls of Tide’s End? Nowhere is safe. Our lord is coming. But first, he needs you to poison Khir’s warrior. You’ll do it, too, or she,” he slid Azenor a glance, “dies painfully.”

Anger flamed through him. “No!” Aric shoved the ghoul back.

His captor staggered a step, grabbed Aric, and hurled him into the wall. “Be still.”

Aric tried to swing his arms. His wobbling legs yielded. The ghoul dragged him up. As he pummelled Aric’s belly, Azenor screamed his name.

Doubled over, he fought for breath. The ghoul fisted Aric’s hair to pull his head back.

“Listen, young fool. I will be brief as I find your language unpleasant. Do as we bid, and she lives. Fail, and she dies.”

Aric gagged on bile. The ghoul let him go. He sucked in air.

“Surely this warrior is in the Mountains killing monsters like you. May his gods help him.”

The ghoul punched his face. Aric grunted in pain. His lip split where a ring tore soft flesh.

“He is in the Place of Kings,” the ghoul said. “Dal-Kanu. Your king summoned him.”

Aric squeezed his eyes closed, wanting to shut out this ruin, the ghoul, his terrible words.

“How will I know him?” He knew precious little about Khir’s warriors. Ghouls infected the Mountains, the Downs, but ancient magic kept them from the Isles.

“By Khir’s sigils on his skin. By his hair, pale as daylight.” A monotone. As if the ghoul recited what others told him. “You will know him by his sword. Its ancient Seithin steel, blue in moonlight. The jewels in the pommel, red as blood, black as night."

"How will I kill him?" Could even he slay such a warrior?

The ghoul held up an ampoule. "This contains Night's Kiss. One smear on your blade—"

"I know what Night's Kiss is." Aric stopped him, his tone frigid with disgust. "I am no assassin. I will not hide in the night to strike a brave warrior in the back."

The ghoul shrugged. "Then poison him in the great hall at Dal-Kanu, before King Cathmor himself. Invite a crowd to your performance. But if Khir's warrior is not dying three days from now, the king will have no Isles bride."

Azenor's sobs raked the stillness, each a spear in Aric's flesh. If only he had words of comfort. Instead, his thoughts emptied into an abyss.

Did they really leave the Isles only two days ago, the rushing waves breaking on Tide's End's salt-crusted walls? Now ghouls held him and Azenor, their escort dead.

Guilt flushed through him. He thought only of Azenor.

"My men—" His voice shattered. "My sister's women."

"The women fled during the fighting. Your warriors, though"—the ghoul licked his fingers—"a feast of Isles blood. Rare. We usually feed on those Mountains-born."

Aric drove his knuckles hard into his thigh. He would avenge his men, repay blood for blood. "Why us? We have little to do with your kind in the Isles."

The ghoul peeled his lips back from white teeth. A grin or a grimace?

"You are the king's cousin, able to walk freely in Dal-Kanu. Further, you are a Serravan-trained bladesman, perhaps the only man who can poison Khir's warrior."

How skilled a swordsman might this bonded warrior be? No, he couldn't just slaughter a stranger. Aric shoved his back into stone, desperate to crawl through it to escape.

"Your answer?"

"Please. Do what you want with me. Kill me. I offer my blood. Just set Azenor free."

For a moment the ghoul's gaze hung on his face. Then he nodded at a companion. "Bring in the first. Our princeling needs a nudge."

Ghouls dragged Cass into the ruin and discarded him on his knees.

Aric jerked beneath his captor's hold. "No. No. Don't touch him."

Face bruised, his shirt sodden with blood, Cass managed a grim smile. "My prince—"

A whirring whipped up air.

Aric had no time to shout, no time to register alarm before a ghoul swung a chain. With simple, terrible ease, its spiked ball pulped his captain's head.

Cass crumpled. His blood and shards of bone splattered Aric's face. Robbed of thought, of breath, he could only stare at his friend's caved-in features.

The ghoul swung again. The ball smashed into the dead man's ribs with an awful, gut-wrenching crunch. Aric could not look away as the ball whirred again. Cass's body exploded, the torso and face mashed to red dough.

Released, Aric collapsed to his knees. He beat his roped hands against the ground. Shock offered no protection, no numbing of his mind against the sheer horror of what he'd just seen: the image of his captain's crushed form trapped in his memory.

"You sick, sick monsters. You'll pay for that. I swear it."

"A waste of blood." The ghoul nudged Cass's body with a boot. "Bring in the next."

"No," Aric said. "Please."

"You can stop this," the ghoul said impassively. "Just poison one man, and those few of your companions who still live die fast, and we spare your sister. But let Khir's warrior leave Dal-Kanu unharmed, and Archanin tortures our captives and slaughters her. Your answer?"

Archanin? Who or what was that?

In blank terror, Aric stared at his captor. The contrast between the ghoul's beauty and his ugly, callous disregard for life disgusted him.

With golden hair, his body as strong and straight as any Isles warrior's, this foul beast could be Venivan, from across the sea. The lines of his face were hawkish, the nose straight, his mouth full-lipped. How could something so beautiful be so unnaturally cruel?

He snatched a look at Azenor's frightened face. His will buckled.

"I have no choice."

"You will strike down Khir's bonded warrior? You'll poison him?"

"I will kill him."

This time the ghoul did smile. Just before he hit him.

ARIC WOKE OUTSIDE THE RUIN, his head throbbing. He sprawled, untethered, sword and baldric on the ground, his horse grazing nearby.

Flies buzzed about Cass's pulped flesh. Aric tore his eyes away fast.

Dazed, he stumbled from the ruin onto a windswept, treeless hill. Sunlight, too bright, mocked his despair.

At a stream below the hill he undressed and bathed, every movement pure habit, his tormented mind shut down. He banished Azenor from his thoughts. Nor could he think of Cass or the warriors who rode with him. Not yet.

Returning to the ruin, he searched his saddlebags for food. His fingers brushed smooth, cool glass. As he drew it out, his heart slammed against ribs.

The ampoule of Night's Kiss.

Aric sank to his knees. He clawed his wet hair.

Did he deserve this? Because he ignored what ghouls did in the Mountains, on the Downs. Let others fight and die in a malefic struggle. Not caring, just so long as the Isles was safe.

Help me, he implored his gods. Saarn, the voice in the wind, Sauveroken, the shadow beneath rolling waves. And Sartaen. Sartaen, the unseen.

For a long while, he huddled, rocking back and forth. At last, the ground too hard to bury Cass, he covered the man's body with rocks. Aric mounted and rode towards Dal-Kanu, his heart cold, his hand steady on the reins, his will resolute.

HEATH

Crows circled as Heath stepped onto the castle balcony, their caws a raucous accompaniment to clanking, ringing swords in the training field below. A warm breeze struck his face with the offal odours of the rambling, ancient city of Dal-Kanu.

"Mud and cabbage," his brother Velleran had once told him with his usual sneer. "That's what the fabled City of Kings stinks of."

That and the stench of rotting flesh carried by a wind sobbing through the gate tower and its bloody spikes. Eight spikes but just one spiked head. The king's sword Goffren, now more infamous than in life.

Heath hummed a few lines.

A knight who poorly serves His Grace,

Shall find the spike becomes his place.

He chuckled. Three figures watching men trade blows in the ward turned to stare.

"Damadar." Cathmor passed cool eyes over him. The king's uncle Cael-Carren grunted. Rozenn of Cahir threw him a tantalisingly bold smile.

He offered her a bow, then dipped his head to Cathmor. "Your

Majesty. I passed the grand constable's messenger just now. Surely there's no trouble so close to your wedding day?"

Cael-Carren answered for his king. "Ghouls attacked a Downs village. Nate Caelmarsh demands the king sends Khir's bonded warrior at once."

Demands? Heath edged up an eyebrow. The king surely disliked that word.

Cathmor knuckled the wall, muscular shoulders tense. Wind danced through dark-brown hair, the match in colour for eyes that should have been warm but instead froze men in their tracks.

Few signs of his Isles mother moulded that stern face. Though he looked every bit a king, elegantly confident with a liquid quickness to his steps and gestures.

"How dare he demand." Cathmor's voice tolled like a bell. "I should demand Caelmarsh and Aric Caelan joust for the title of most arrogant lord. The loser keeps his head."

At a shriek of metal and barked laughter from the training field, Cael-Carren clutched at his sparse beard. *As thin as a king's promises,* Heath thought.

"But on the Downs, Your Grace," Cael-Carren said. "No wonder Caelmarsh is afraid."

"It's too close to Dal-Kanu, I'll grant you that."

"Ghouls also attacked a village in the Isles. These things grow bolder."

They fell into an argument. Disinterested, Heath leaned his elbows on the balustrade. Warriors clad in the grey and black of the Mountains lord Vraymorg hewed and hacked with steel below. Occasional laughter broke up oddly accented words.

"A Damadar out of his icy lair." Rozenn rested ringed hands on the balustrade's stone.

She, too, might be made of stone with that exquisitely boned face, that sensuous, full-lipped mouth. Brushed hair fell so perfectly over one shoulder he wanted to touch it to see if it felt as silken as it looked.

"What brings you to Dal-Kanu, Heath Damadar?"

"Why the same thing as you, Your Grace. The king's wedding."

"Liar." Her wondrously blue eyes glistened with amusement. They masked secrets, and something beguiling, something mystical. "You're plotting, no doubt."

He returned her brazen smile, enjoying her teasing. Or flirting? They had met only once before, in passing, though few men forgot the Queen of Cahir. She must be about thirty now, a year or two older than Cathmor, and still impossibly striking.

"No doubt. I am a Damadar, so I am always up to mischief."

Rozenn clapped her hands. "Excellent. Weddings are tiresome, and Dal-Kanu is most unpleasant in this last week of summer. The stench is unbearable."

"I'm surprised you came, Your Grace," Heath said truthfully.

Rozenn shrugged. "Cathmor still doesn't trust me. I'm here not only to witness him wed some dreadful Isles girl but to bring my son, Alecc, to be fostered."

"I see," Heath said stiffly. "My brother Velleran took it as an insult when you refused his offer to take Alecc as his squire. I had hoped to instruct the boy in swordplay. He'd learn more from me than the king's sword masters."

Rozenn playfully slapped his shoulder. "Do not pretend to hurt feelings, Ice lord. No doubt you are a master bladesman, but I could hardly turn down the king." She paused, considering him with open interest. "I hear you dance with fire."

"I do, Your Grace. A fight to the death in the fire halls is an ancient Icelands tradition."

"And you are undefeated."

Heath laughed, his good humour restored. "Otherwise I would not stand before you."

"Aren't you afraid? The life of a fire dancer is notoriously short."

Heath shrugged. "No. I don't fear either the fire or death. I never lose."

"To never lose. To never fear death. Yet fear, death, and loss are beneath all we do and feel. That is life, no less. Without fear, a man might be dead inside."

At her unexpected words, Heath's breath caught. When it released, it seemed nothing more than a whisper stirred by wind. He passed his tongue over cracked lips, mouth stale.

Dead inside. How easily she, a stranger, uncovered that emptiness within. A remarkably shrewd insight, too, for a woman barely older than his twenty-seven years.

Except—were the words even for him? There was something distant about her gaze as if she no longer addressed him, that she was thinking of someone else.

"You see into men's hearts, I think." His uneasy laugh ground like rusted spears. "Boredom is my secret torment, Rozenn of Cahir. Long ago the exhilaration of victory tarnished to dull duty. I kill to please the gods, not myself."

How he longed to once more know delicious fear prickling his spine, that thrill of danger, wondering if he could lose and die.

He needed to face a bladesman who might just be better, swifter, smarter.

Where? Who? Was there even such a man?

"Even so." Rozenn's gaze fell on combatants trading strokes below. "I might choose boredom over that boy's torment. Kaell knows every bonded warrior dies young."

Heath sought a blond head among the Mountains men, guessing this must be Kaell.

Sword sheathed, the boy leaned close to an older man with plaited, grey-streaked brown hair who delivered a string of words with expansive gestures. Kaell threw his head back, laughing. His companion slapped his shoulder.

Without understanding why, he shivered. Rozenn's words? Or clouds momentarily shadowing land, driven by a wind brawling with pennants and flags?

Rozenn turned to Cathmor. "Kaell is still injured?"

"Bruised and battered after that Downs tournament," the king said. "Apparently the audacious brat hid his face and fought unheralded. Now he hurt his ankle falling down the stairs to the crypt. His men say someone pushed him."

"They like to make up stories in the Mountains." Cael-Carren sniffed in contempt. "Nothing else to do. That, or hump goats."

They liked to make up stories in the Icelands too. Heath wasn't sure about humping goats, though it might catch on.

"What did he want in the crypt? Up to no good if you ask me," Cael-Carren said. "The boy must have recovered. He fought that scarred warrior at dawn. Our captains took a keen interest."

"Any captain will surely wish to watch a bonded warrior fight," Rozenn said with poisonous sweetness. "But recovered? Kaell's footwork was off. His balance. A swordsman worth the weight of his blade could see he battled a strained ankle."

Cael-Carren bristled. "What do women know of fighting?" He whirled to plead to the king. "If Kaell can stand, he can fight. You must send him to Caelmarsh."

"Must? No king *must* anything." Cathmor tugged irritably at his fringe. "Caelmarsh *must* wait. I promised some villagers Kaell's help against a nest of murderous ghouls. What could I do? They fell to their knees to beg. So I asked the Lord of Vraymorg to give me the boy."

"Intolerable," his uncle said. "The king does not ask. Especially of Vraymorg."

"I don't know Vraymorg," Heath said with idle interest. "What manner of man is he?"

They fell silent. Telling.

He shrugged and turned away, hands pressed on warmed stone. Below Kaell corrected a man's stroke. Wind billowed his cloak. Sun struck his dark blond hair. He looked content. Again, nameless unease needled Heath's neck.

"Vraymorg is a contradiction." Cathmor's voice held a strained edge. "He reeks of power but never seeks it. A bladesman with a courtier's grace and wit but a tongue and temper as abrasive as straw."

"Bloodless," Cael-Carren said. "He murdered Caelmarsh's captain. Pushed Paulin from the ramparts of that Mountains fortress, all because Paulin put an arrow in that boy, Kaell. But not even Caelmarsh will accuse him. He's afraid of Vraymorg."

Afraid? A thrill menaced Heath's backbone. Vraymorg sounded ruthless, a man who could prove a worthy opponent in the fire halls.

That old ache burned. It started in his gut and rose into his breast. A tremor of anticipation. He had to learn more about the Lord of the Mountains.

"He unnerves me." Cathmor pressed his lips grimly.

Cael-Carren bobbed his head. "He unnerves us all. Best to keep Vraymorg in the Mountains as castellan of that dreadful fortress where the dead walk."

"He is very beautiful." Rozenn's laugh rippled.

Heath grinned. "A woman's perspective on a man is always useful." As with beautiful women, handsome men, in Heath's experience, behaved differently to plain men.

"You could just demand Vraymorg surrender Kaell to you for good," Cael-Carren said. "You are the king. Such a powerful weapon shouldn't be in another's hands."

"I don't need Vraymorg as my enemy." Cathmor gripped his sword belt. "If I openly cross one of Telor's great lords, the others will mistrust me. No, patience will get me what I want."

"And subtlety," said Heath. "That always works for me." *But not so well as murder, treachery, blackmail, and occasional mayhem.*

The wind gusted. Crows circled the tower. The king sniffed. "Let's retreat to my rooms. Goffren is beginning to stink."

Rozenn's fair hair blew about her cheeks. "I like the wind."

"You like watching young men sweat." Cathmor laughed as he moved towards the doors. "I'm coming to know you, my dear."

Heath lingered. “Which young man do you watch sweat?” A little forward, yet she had set the informal, almost confiding tone.

“I’m watching Kaell.”

“Why?”

“Because he’s dangerous.”

“He hardly seems old enough to be dangerous. Though”—he considered the young bladesman—“he looks cocky.”

Rozenn folded her arms over a swirling gown. Her hair streamed like golden ribbons. “He’s cocky because he’s not known defeat. One day he will. Every warrior does.”

Do they? Wind howled about Heath’s ears as though mocking him. Swords snarled and sang. Wings beat like whipped flames in the Iceland fire halls where he never lost.

Heath sighed. “If only you are right.”

ARIC

The seneschal at the king's door wrung his hands.

"I won't disturb His Grace. Not for anyone."

Aric half edged his sword out. "He'll see me."

The man gaped, stammered, "I'll—ask," as he quickly disappeared inside. Rumbling voices, a burst of savage laughter threaded through the open door, then the servant's pleading tone.

Aric slammed his blade back and nudged the door wider. The king and his uncle Cael-Carren stood near doors open to a balcony. The breeze carried the clang and clink of swords.

"Demands?" Cathmor said.

"I mean, I mean, he awaits your pleasure, Your Grace."

"None of my cousins gives me the least bit of pleasure. Get rid of whoever it is. I'm busy. My wedding is in two days."

The seneschal cleared his throat.

"Oh, very well. Which cousin? One has already bored me today. Why not another?"

"Aric, Prince of the Isles. Son of King Hatton."

A silence fell. The two men exchanged a look.

"Prince, indeed," Cael-Carren said. "I'll give him prince."

"My dear uncle, I admire ambition. Let Aric call himself what he likes. When I rule the Isles, this dog shall learn his place."

"You should put the dog in chains. In case he barks."

"Or put him down in case he bites." A drawn-out sigh. "But what's that old Telorian expression? Too many pleasures at once ruin a man's character."

"Then at least keep him close."

"Oh, I plan to keep him uncomfortably close. Once I'm wed and the Isles mine, I'll appoint Aric a chamber knight. He can hardly refuse the honour. I may put him in charge of my chamber pot. Ha, Prince of Piss Pots."

Aric bristled with prideful anger, his fingers seeking comforting steel. He shoved his fury down. He could not afford to let the king rile him. Not now.

"Well"—Cathmor waved a hand—"show in the Isles 'prince.'"

Aric retreated as the servant bustled back.

"His Majesty will see you now."

Rudely he shouldered past, his sword strapped to his back. Guards rushed to challenge him.

Cathmor pushed off the wall near the balcony doors. He sniffed. "Cousin, pretty as always but you dare come armed into your king's presence?"

With set lips, the belittling jibe stoking his anger, Aric unbuckled his strap and set it aside. *Get through this. Lie to Cathmor. Kill Khir's bonded warrior. Save Azenor.*

"I expected my bride, Aric," Cathmor said. "Don't tell me you misplaced her. The last man who misplaced something of mine ended up in my head house. Well, part of him did."

Aric fought down another flush of temper. Curse Cathmor's condescending tone. It got his back up as the king no doubt knew.

"She is at Dal-Decma, Your Grace. Azenor insisted on riding instead of travelling in the carriage with her women. The sun gave her a headache. She has taken to her bed until tomorrow."

"But the priests wed us in two days." Cathmor sighed. "She is often ill?"

"No, Your Grace. It's excitement about the wedding. Azenor is as healthy as a horse."

"She can look like a horse for all I care. Dal-Decma did you say? That's only half a day's ride. I'll send guardsmen to escort her safely here."

"No need," Aric said quickly. "*All* my men are with her."

"All?" Cathmor frowned. "You came alone?"

"To explain our delay, Your Grace."

"I always knew you were a reckless fool, cousin. Our wolf's heads don't frighten you? Or ghouls? But then, silly me—you are a bladesman."

"I am Serravan-trained, Your Grace. Undefeated with the sword from the age of fifteen."

"And they say I have a big head. I can't wait to hear more about how excellent you are." Cathmor yawned. "You'll dine with me, of course."

Aric bowed his neck, cheeks heated with indignation. Again Cathmor deliberately sought to provoke him. To what end?

"Oh." The king flapped a hand. "Heath Damadar must join us, given who he is. Or what he is. He and his sister Judith yesterday unexpectedly graced Dal-Kanu with their presence. At least, *she* has grace. *He* has presence, I suppose."

"He thinks he's witty," Cael-Carren said. "Full of themselves, these Ice lords."

"Damadar." A boyhood memory stirred of fishing with Heath at Tide's End while their elders hammered out a marriage contract. "Why is he here?"

"He says he represents his family at my wedding," Cathmor said.

Aric dismissed Heath. A distraction. He must focus on one task—murder. It was his job to protect his sister. He had already failed his men. He could not fail her.

"So cousin. Until tonight what amusement can we offer?"

"A mirror so he might admire his reflection," Cael-Carren said.

A guard at the door coughed to hide laughter.

"Shall I send a woman to bathe you?" Cathmor's sweetly innocent tone hid contempt. "I can't promise she'll be as pretty as you, but we will do our best."

The guards openly sniggered that time.

"Or perhaps you might like to see the castle library? I'm told you're fond of anything with dust and ink on it."

More mockery. More snide remarks about his appearance. Aric curled a fist.

Citizens in Dal-Kanu considered an Isles man's longer hair, silver bracelets, and earrings unmanly. The king's insults, though, exposed Cathmor's resentment.

Aric defeated him in battle. Made him look small. In return, the king sought to diminish him. Provoke him to lash out. An excuse to hurl the man he hated into a dark, dank cell.

Or did another twisted game play out? Aric had no time to learn its rules. He must get to Kaell and kill him.

Cathmor wagged a finger at his uncle. "You angered my cousin. How naughty of you."

Aric's patience exploded. "What game is this? Is this how you treat a guest, Cathmor?"

"You're not a guest," the king said. "You're about to become my new brother. That makes you a fair target."

Thudding blood in Aric's skull drowned sound. He snatched at calm. None of this mattered. Only Azenor mattered. "If Your Grace does not object," he said stiffly. "I need to swing a sword about after the long ride. Perhaps your men train in the ward?"

Cathmor jeered with lifted brows. "How frightfully dull. You have no interests apart from weapons and war?" He patted his mouth again, his manner and words deceptive. Aric knew the real menace beneath.

"Oh go and get sweaty if you must. Though I warn you, cousin. I summoned Khir's bonded warrior to Dal-Kanu. He and a mob of those dreadful Mountain warriors took over the training field this afternoon before they ride north."

Aric's crazed laugh even shocked him. "I hope he might honour me with swordplay."

Cathmor frowned as though the laugh jarred. "I'm told he enjoys a challenge. I'm also told Kaell is skilled with a blade. Gods forbid he might even mess up your hair."

Aric offered a formal bow. Retrieving his sword, he stalked past carefully impassive guards. No one waited outside the door. He paused, thinking about Cathmor's words. *Kaell enjoys a challenge.* A thin plan formed.

"I don't like him," Cael-Carren's voice carried into the passage. "He wears more jewellery than your mistress. And his hair is like a woman's."

"Very pretty hair. And a pretty head. Put it on a spike, and we could all admire it. The minstrels might even write another song. I tire of the one about Goffren."

Aric was about to move away when a woman said, "A man of Caelan blood is far too dangerous to keep here, Cathmor. He reeks of his disgusting gods."

"Aric reeks of sweat. And what stained his shirt? I should insist he bathe."

"You joke at everything," she said. "But you take the gods of the Isles lightly at your peril. Do not forget, they were Roaran's gods as well."

Cathmor's laugh tattered with unease. "Such a pleasant conversation until this talk of dead Telorian kings, Rozenn. Roaran this, Roaran that. Blah, blah, blah. The next fool to mention Roaran Caelan joins Goffren in the head house. At least his head will."

Aric turned. Cathmor and his insults, his nasty games, must wait.

He had to atone for failing his men. Save his sister.

He had to find a stranger and murder him.

HEATH

Heath braced against the wind blistering across the lake to his balcony as though he must fight it. That defined him—the fight. A fire dancer endlessly battled flames, chance, and fate, struggled against another man's hungry blade and will.

Do your worst, he taunted the fire before every contest. *Kill me if you can.*

Though it snapped with greedy fingers, he knew it could not. Nor could the too-confident fools who tried to dance with him as the inferno spat beneath their feet.

Heath remembered every man he killed. How their insolent smiles faded as they realised they would lose and die. How they stared in terror as the flames embraced them. Each time, triumphant, he raised his sword to shouts of adulation and felt his gods' pleasure.

They loved him. He knew it. Just as he knew exactly what he was, where he belonged.

So why, why, did Rozenn's words stir up doubt?

Dead inside.

He shook his head fiercely. Why question his purpose? He was not only a lord of the Ice but a fire dancer gifted by the gods with a keen eye, quick feet, a steady hand, and sharp wits.

Yes, the flames must have him in the end. When age weakened his limbs and clouded his sharp mind. The fiery pit took all fire dancers, eventually. But not yet.

Beneath his hands, the balcony's age-worn stone, bleached by sunlight, felt smooth but cool. A thread of pine stirred, very pure after the stench of the king's head house. Carelessly he slapped at a mosquito.

Still Rozenn's words niggled, his desire, his compulsion uncomfortably naked.

Once winning and surviving had thrilled like a dazzling glimpse of destiny. The danger raging through him. Knowing he stood a heartbeat, a thrust, a slip from death, enlivened like nothing else. Not power. Not sex.

Now he fought mechanically, driven by duty and pride. Now staring into the abyss of leaping flames, of spitting ash, there was only an emptiness, a yearning for that old delirium, for that exhilaration he used to feel that shouted: this is life, fight for it.

He might still turn to the flames and softly taunt, *do you worst. Take me. I dare you.* Knowing they would not. Knowing, deep down, no one could beat him.

It was madness surely, to desire that belly-clenching rush. To desire risk. Madness… or stupidity.

Judith would call it that. If ever he were to confess this longing, she'd slap his mouth. Call him a prancing poppy or some nonsense. And he'd grin like a stupid, prancing—whatever he was.

What was he? A serious question that. Even for a man who analysed his intent, his every act. No reason to ask it now—but for Rozenn's words.

All right, then. What was he? Obedient son? Devoted brother? Smooth-tongued spy? Cold-blooded enforcer? The old Icelands word for a Damadar son trained to serve with steel the older brother born to become lord.

Enforcer. Heath heard it whispered in awe behind his back.

That's Heath Damadar. An enforcer—with a cruel wit and a prideful swagger.

Only Myranthe used the word to belittle. Dismiss. "Enforcer," his elder sister said in that velvet voice, her dark, hooded eyes a void. "You are nothing less, but also nothing more."

Oh wicked, wicked Myranthe. She who heard otherworldly voices. She who stunned with a curse, summoned the dead with a song, fell into a trance to watch—

Heath shivered. He peered over the palace walls across the rambling, mud-stenched city of Dal-Kanu to its famed lake. The dipping sun, never warm in autumn, sparkled on its blue waters, the coldness tearing into him.

When a bird screeched in a distant tower, he turned fast. Was that Myranthe's terrible gaze on his back? Yes, he feared her. More than he feared the fire.

"You have that look." Judith appeared at his shoulder.

Heath wheeled. "What look?"

"That half-witted look when you're restless and dreaming up mischief."

He threw her an amused glance. "You think the best of me. This half-witted look is the effect of too much wine. What have you uncovered?"

His sister smirked.

From that smirk, he knew he must tease the information out. He would. Gladly.

Without games life ground to boredom. Every Damadar child learned that during long winters in cut-off ice caverns with nothing to do but torment each other. Alliances formed, broke, reformed. Schemes hatched amid tears, shouting, bruised pride, or bruised flesh.

"That smirk, sister dear, makes you look like a horny, deprived squire about to tumble into bed with a buxom wench."

"Crude." Judith squinted through sunlight. "And typical. You think of nothing but women and swordplay."

"And wine. Though that leads to thoughts of women and swordplay."

Bluntly, Judith said, "He's here."

"You ruined the game, Judith." He sighed. "Who's here?"

"Lackwit. Who do you think?"

Heath's heart brawled in his chest. "Aric? I was just with the king. No Aric."

"Well now he's here."

Wind whipped dark-brown hair about her face. Heath snatched at a strand. "Where's Aric now?"

Judith stabbed a finger at the air beyond the balcony.

"The training fields? How single-minded. Though Aric might prove a worthy opponent in a fire dance. Tournament champion and all that, Isles commander—"

"And in Dal-Kanu all alone. Isn't that sad? Left his men at Dal-whatever with his sister."

"The skinny one with freckles? Always pouting and hanging about like a rusting sword, whining about Aric not paying her enough attention."

"Azenor Caelan? She scrubs up well, now. Apparently."

Heath smoothed Judith's hair between his fingers. "But still Cathmor will have eyes only for you. It's unfair isn't it, how blessed our family is? Myranthe with wickedness. Velleran with ambition. Griffin earnestness. Me with my wits. You with beauty."

"I may have a beautiful head," Judith sweetly mocked. "But yours is entirely wit-free."

"You said I thought about women and swordplay. Now I'm empty-headed?"

She didn't reply. Her gaze fell on the ward. Through clouds of dust stirred by trampling feet, Kaell leaned against a stone wall, arms crossed, sun glinting on bright hair.

"Good gods, another one," Heath said. "What is it about him?"

"What are you on about now?"

"I just watched the lovely Queen of Cahir drool all over that young warrior. She called Kaell dangerous."

"Dangerous? Surely not. Interesting, though. Myranthe would love to play with him. Marked by his Mountains gods. She'd say he reeked of enchantment."

Heath grunted. "That's the stink of unwashed Mountains flesh. Forget him. We can't touch the Vraymorg child. You know that."

"He has secrets."

"We men merely pretend to have secrets, Judith. So women think we're intriguing. They want to unravel us, scratch away to what's beneath—"

"Where all they find is an empty head and a belly full of wine. No, listen. Kaell left his room after dark last night, taking care no one followed him."

"Except Judith Damadar, scourge of secret keepers. And he went?"

"To the temple first—"

"How the gods draw the wicked." Heath smothered a yawn. "It must be horrible to be a god. I'd want to be a deaf god."

"Looking furtive, he snatched up a torch and crept down to the crypt. Our young warrior laid a moonflower on a particular coffin. Then stood there a long while, saying nothing."

"A flower. How revoltingly sweet. Whose coffin?"

Judith sniffed. "I don't think I'll tell you. You're too annoying."

"Oh please, Judith." Heath wrung his hands and attempted an innocent look. "I let your pretty Isles captain live. I'm a good brother, really. Hardly annoying at all, or at least annoying only half the time. The rest of the time, I'm—"

"Tiresome."

"Charming?" He wiggled his eyebrows. "Dashing, loveable, sweet—"

"Like I said, annoying." Judith tried to hide a smile. "All right, charming, dashing Heath. Why should an unwashed warrior of distant Vraymorg sneak into the crypt to visit the tomb of Cathmor's first queen? The one who threw herself from a bridge and drowned."

"Caelmarsh's daughter, Annatise? That makes no sense. How could a Mountains warrior with no second name know a highborn lass like that?"

"A mystery," Judith said. Then at his suspicious look, she spread her arms. "No, really, I don't know. Though let me offer you a further puzzle, charming Heath. Someone followed Kaell. I heard her at the top of the stairs. It sounded like she pushed him."

"Did you see who?"

"No. But I smelt perfume before Kaell cried out."

"It's very curious. But hardly our concern." He threw her a look. "Why do you care?"

"I like to know things. Information is useful."

Heath smiled, thinking again of their childhood games when he and Judith teamed up to outwit Myranthe and the Icelands heir, Velleran. Judith always complained she possessed fewer weapons than her siblings, only whatever secrets she unearthed.

"Talking of curiosities that are our concern," Judith said. "What brews in that charmingly wine-sodden head? I am delighted you at last positioned us where Aric is, but how do you plan to snatch him? You *do* intend to snatch him, don't you?"

"Why, what do you think I should do with him? Dance with him? Give him the name of my new boot maker?"

Judith slapped his shoulder. "I know what I should do with you. It involves my hands and your neck. About Aric." She paused. Looked at him. "You were boyhood friends, but you won't go soft on me will you, brother? You will be all Heath-like, all cold and merciless?"

"I shall be heartless, ruthless, unpleasant, and entirely Heath-like. The only time I've been un-Heath-like was for you, Judith dear. Heath-like Heath would never let Pairas live."

Judith dug teeth into her lip, her expression shuttered. "I told you. He reminds me of someone. It was the right thing to do, Heath. I can't believe you're so soaked in violence you forgot that."

"I'm soaked in alcohol, actually. Now about Aric—"

"He'll no doubt join us at dinner with the king, being well-bred and Cathmor's cousin."

Heath flicked a ladybug off her cloak. "Don't worry Judith. I shall be polite, witty, charming, all non-Heath-like attributes, to show I'm also well-bred."

"You shall have to be on your best behaviour."

"But I'm at my best when I'm, well, bad. Or drunk."

"You're always at your best then. The plan?"

Heath rubbed a bristled chin. "You could seduce Aric. I'm told women think he's easy to look at, that he washes once a day, is vaguely amusing, terribly arrogant, and all that."

She pouted. "How dreadful. He sounds like you, except for the amusing bit. Can I seduce that Vraymorg warrior too?"

"They don't wash in the Mountains, you know." Heath tilted his head to consider her. "It's the pale hair isn't it?" He thrust a hand to his breast. "Oh Kaell, what pretty hair you have. Oh, Kaell, what big, strong arms you have."

"Oh Heath, what a big bag of wind you are. When we return to the Icelands—"

"With Aric."

"I'll beg Myranthe to find a spell to make you mute."

"That's very cruel, Judith. Just when we agreed I was charming and sweet."

"Not even asleep."

"How I suffer. And here I was about to impress you in my windy, wine-soaked way by explaining how we'll snatch a young Isles lordling from one of the most heavily guarded castles in Telor. And from right under the king's nose."

ARIC

Aric was already dead. He knew it.

He *would* cut down this warrior of Khir's. Slaughter him. Coldly. Precisely. Because he could. Because that's what he always did.

But then came the festering wound. The stain of murder. A killing blow within.

With quick steps he crossed the ward towards the training field. The execution ground.

The sword at his hip, always so familiar, no longer felt part of him. Nor did his body. It had become a shell, hollow of his warrior's spirit, nothing but a butcher's tool.

A rancid laugh burst up in his throat at the irony of it all.

Many men wished him ill. His brother Gendrick who stewed with envy. The king. But Cathmor's malicious plots, even Gendrick's jealousy, could not destroy him.

No, he'd do that himself. The moment he killed this bonded warrior. Reputation, honour, his life gone. But he had no choice. He must save Azenor.

Snatching a steadying breath, Aric passed men drilling with unblunted weapons, shields wrapped about sagging arms.

The odours of sweat and leather, the dust, reminded him of

Tide's End where grim-faced weapons masters had yelled about balance as he learnt the centuries-old dance of steel.

Who trained these warriors? The Lord of the Mountains? Vraymorg rarely competed in tournaments, though Pairas declared the man fought with calculated savagery.

Aric paused to watch a smooth-skinned youth trade blows with a thick-necked brute, their skulls capped by helms. The boy flashed a smile through broken teeth, but his eyes were dark and hard. Solid enough blade work. Feet as lumbering as a siege engine though.

He peered across the yard, absorbing every sight and sound. Men grunting, sweating, cursing, their boots scuffing dirt and flattening grass. Ringing, shuddering steel. Laughter. The squawks of black birds circling a spired tower an irregular chorus for the ragged melody of his heart.

Then his heart slammed still for a beat.

You will know him by the colour of his hair. As light as daylight.

The ghoul did not lie about that, at least. Among so many dark Telorian heads, the man he must kill stood out like a beacon. Kaell, the king had called him. Aric wished he never heard the name. Easier to murder an unnamed stranger.

His thoughts flew again to the song he heard on that hot Isles night:

A thousand times I'll kill the man I do not know.

But weep a thousand tears for the friend who falls to any blow.

Kaell.

With horrified fascination, Aric watched the young man move among his companions, nodding or frowning at swordplay. Men grinned or greeted him with words that drew a laugh. One or two threw Kaell a shadowed look, flinching as he passed.

"You." Kaell strode at Aric. "What do you want? Who are you?"

Aric unravelled the singsong words.

"Do you have a name?" Kaell halted before Aric, a smile curving an expressive mouth.

"Aric. The king sent me to train with you."

How the lies thickened. He might prove a courtier one day. No, thankfully he'd not live that long. This foul deed done, Cathmor would gleefully behead him.

"If that's the king's wish. Let me find you a sparring partner."

"I'll fight only you. Kaell."

"I rarely fight inexperienced bladesmen—friend." Kaell's tone held a friendly insolence, but his eyes hardened to clouded emeralds, the colour of the sea off Tide's End where ships floundered on hidden reefs.

"You make dangerous assumptions." Aric fought to steady his voice. His heart bolted free like a shutter banged by wind, hammering not with fear, but anger. He could not do this. Kaell was younger than him. A boy.

"And you throw out dangerous challenges. If you know my name then you know what I am."

"A boy too afraid to fight me."

Now amusement, not annoyance, danced in those striking eyes. "A cheap taunt." Kaell turned his back.

Other warriors lowered weapons to listen. *Use it. Embarrass him.* "Then here's another, even cheaper. I heard you had no honour and would never accept a challenge."

Kaell spun back. "Who said this?"

An older man, thick rather than tall, with a long braid of greying black hair and a pale scar disfiguring his jaw, stepped between them. "Just words, Kaell. Words." He glared at Aric. "Who sent you? Caelmarsh?"

"Caelmarsh?" What history did Caelmarsh have with this young Mountains warrior? "That snake? Do I look like a Downs man?"

That drew nervous laughter. Men crowded closer. The scarred warrior rounded on them. "You, Smiler. Leaning on your sword, your mouth flapping like a fish, won't keep you alive against ghouls. And you two—"

Aric slipped his hand to his dagger as he edged towards Kaell.

The older man blocked him. "Keep your distance, stranger. Or I'll gut you myself."

"You can try. I'll readily fight you after I've fought him. Unless you're craven too."

"Why you—" The man drew his sword.

Kaell patted his arm. "Just words, Arn." He grinned at Aric. "If you weren't such a conceited blowhard I might like you, whoever you are."

Aric made a self-mocking bow. The birds on the tower squawked approval as though he did it nicely. "The conceited blowhard assumed everyone knew me. My name is Aric Caelan."

Startled murmurs rippled among the Mountains men. Arn reluctantly bent his knees.

"Aric Caelan." Kaell whistled. "Such stories about you. You challenged the Black Lord of Long Rock to single combat when his ships turned pirate."

"A dead man the instant he agreed to fight," Aric said truthfully.

"And you defeated nine challengers in a row at Princes' Stone when the king offered a fat purse to any knight who put you in the dirt."

"The king should love me. I saved him all that gold."

"Why even before you turned seventeen, your father named you commander of the Isles."

Ten years ago. Aric could hardly remember what he was like then. He dangled a snare. "My ancestor, Roaran Caelan, first commanded the Isles at fifteen. He, too, trained as a Serravan bladesman. You see little of the Serravan style in the Mountains. But Isles weapons masters still teach their methods."

Those striking green eyes were too alive. Aric knew men who laughed as they turned a blade against your heart, their gazes flat and empty. Yet ghouls feared this young man enough to abduct an Isles prince, threaten his sister, and slaughter his men.

Fight me, he willed. *Let Azenor live.* The birds shrieked as if knowing a feast neared.

"You tempt me, Aric Caelan." Kaell eagerly tapped his sword sheath with fingers bare of rings. "I long to know more of Serravan techniques."

"Pick up your sword, then. Test my technique."

Arn rose, jaw clenched. "You're injured, Kaell. And we ride north soon."

"Who's he? Your nursemaid?" Aric returned Arn's glare.

Kaell laughed. "Arn, you always tell me I'll learn nothing more from you or Olier and must seek worthy opponents. Here's a worthy opponent. Only a few moments, I swear."

Aric only needed a moment to kill. "As long as your nursemaid agrees. If you're injured—a blunted sword, perhaps?"

Kaell glanced at steel strapped to Aric's back. "You don't carry a blunted sword."

"Nor do you." The young man wore a peculiar-looking blade. "What *is* that?"

Kaell ripped the sword out and cut the air. Seithin steel. The match of Aric's blade. "Every bonded warrior carries this blade. It's called Fortitude."

"Fortitude? You'll need more than that to beat me."

"I have more than that." He faced Aric with a smile. "You haven't encountered a bonded warrior before, have you?"

Aric shrugged. "One warrior's the same as another. They all fall readily to my blade."

"Shall we see?" Kaell stripped off his cloak and grabbed a helm.

So it was done. Just like that pirate lord, Kaell was dead the instant he agreed to fight.

Guilt and regret knotted in Aric's breast. A tight, hard clench.

The temptation to fling down his sword, drop to his knees, and confess it all gnawed at him. What if he didn't have to face this alone? If he asked Kaell to help save his sister?

No. This was his fault. His duty to keep Azenor safe. He could not risk her life on some chance a stranger would help him. No way out. He must shed blood.

Shed, shed, shed, the birds squawked. Aric tossed them a mirthless grin. *Maybe mine? Is that what you sing? Be patient. You'll feast on my spiked head soon enough.*

Drawing his sword, he took an offered helm and let coldness tame his mind as trained. It didn't matter how young this warrior was. How worthy. To save his sister, it fell to him to murder Kaell.

"A fine weapon," Kaell said.

Fine? Cursed—now. "It's called The Cup."

Kaell whistled. "That's an infamous blade."

"An infamous blade with a meaningless name." *After this, best call it Treachery.*

Arn again grasped Kaell's arm. "Think about this, boy. This lordling is champion of the Isles. Telor's best tournament fighter. You can't risk that ankle. Not before we ride out."

"Don't fuss so. I'll be careful." Kaell paused, considered, then turned a smile on Aric. "Since you're from the Isles, I must ask. Have you come upon a girl—?"

"Isles men come upon lots of girls," a man quipped, drawing leering laughter.

Kaell shook his head. "Ignore the would-be jesters, Aric Caelan. Our Mountains' humour is crude. What I mean is, I seek a young woman with a scar on her breast, just near the heart."

Aric's breath stalled. "Do you call that funny?"

"What?" Kaell's smile withered. "No."

"He asks everyone that," the thick-necked man said. "Some girl he dreams about."

"Do you want to babble about women? Or fight?" Aric snapped the visor shut. He exhaled slowly. *A coincidence. It must be.*

"Listen, boy." Arn fisted his hands at his side. "Your injured ankle aside, this isn't right. If he's really Aric Caelan, why is he here? Ask yourself that."

"In Dal-Kanu?" Aric sniffed. "Why, for the fetid air." More laughter.

“When else can I test myself against the Isles champion?” Kaell closed his helm. “You know, Arn, you do fuss like an old woman.”

“He’s right, nursemaid. Nag, nag, nag.” *Go away.* But which ankle? An injury he could use. Kill him. Wound him. Either way Kaell died, and he saved Azenor.

Dead, dead, the birds mocked. Aric shook his head at them. *Soon. You can have me soon.*

AS THE TWO TOOK STANCE, Aric considered tactics. No shields. The ground cracked and hard. Let Kaell set the rhythm. Assess his speed. His bladework.

He deliberately hung back. Kaell obliged with a probing lunge, shallow and easily parried. Then a quick thrust on a different line.

Aric lazily blocked. His opponent sought to uncover his patterns with false attacks.

Sure enough, Kaell feinted low to draw that same defence, then jabbed high. Aric slipped away without using the blade. Show him nothing.

Kaell slashed at his shoulder. Aric threw up a false defence. Circling, he tapped Kaell’s blade. No reaction. But his swift lunge drew a late, deliberate parry. His opponent, too, revealing only enough to deceive.

When he again misleadingly left an opening, Kaell stepped in to hammer Aric’s blade with ringing, thundering steel.

Somewhere in the chaos of biting, screeching metal, grunts, and glittering sun on blades, a deep feint sought Aric’s lateral block. But his circular parry caught his opponent’s sword.

Kaell skipped back from a quick riposte, his grin good-natured. Enjoying their contest. But this game he could not win. Because Aric meant to kill him and Kaell didn’t know it.

Wanting it done, he took up the attack. Unleashed a flurry of blows, of thrusts, cuts, jabs. But steel only jarred on steel; Kaell’s parries and counterattacks were as controlled as his.

A hush gripped enthralled spectators, broken only by occasional gasps. Every Mountains warrior and a few king's men circled as the screech of clangoring blades drowned the wind, as their feet stirred up dust and the air charged with danger.

When their swords caught, Aric glimpsed a warm light in Kaell's eyes. Not battle fever but pleasure, a simple joy in the challenge, the cut and thrust and manipulation of swordplay.

For all that, Kaell's blows fell hard. Cut, hack, hew, at his head, his chest, his belly. Aric flashed parry after parry, his mind sifting a rhythm in the furious strokes, found something but did not trust it.

Soon both men were panting. Sweat glistened on their arms and necks. Kaell did not let up. No surprises there. He was strong. Fast. Cocky.

Injured. *Use it.*

Aric rained metal, driving Kaell towards the ringed spectators, one step, another, but always back. The young bladesman effortlessly held off his thrusts, but each time he defended, he put less weight on his left foot. Or winced. Quickly hidden.

"Kaell, are you without sense?" Arn yelled. "Enough."

Catching his opponent's single distracted blink, Aric crashed steel down to cleave flesh and bone. At the last heartbeat Kaell deflected the blow. Just. Startled, he glared.

Too ferocious—boy? He had only just started.

Aric hacked so hard his stroke shuddered through his tight shoulders. Sparks flew as Kaell took the brutal blow high up, locking their swords and bodies close.

"By all your gods." His pulse leapt in his throat. "Just what counts as practice in the Isles?"

Aric only laughed, a shockingly vicious sound. Kaell shouldered him back, shifted his grip, and waited. There was a flatness to his eyes now, a wariness in his stance.

Willingly Aric rushed in. His sword shrieked as it struck. Kaell spun away. His riposte clunked so hard on Aric's helm his ears rang. Careless. Those wretched crows nearly got a meal. But Kaell still didn't want to kill him. Which was why he would die.

Kaell lunged, the thrust a fraction short. Aric stepped into the attack, swinging. A rapid parry flew, then quick-fire blows back and forth. Their rasped breath fogged air. Metal shredded blue sparks. Men pressed nearer, shouting.

Aric wanted to shout too. *Yield. Die. I've hardly slept since I left the Isles.* But he saved his breath to partner Kaell in a furious dance.

"How's that ankle?" he said as their swords again ground together. "About to give?"

He kicked.

Kaell collapsed to one knee.

Finish it.

"You made your point." Kaell reeled to his feet. "My balance, this cursed ankle—"

Aric slashed. A death stroke set to shatter bone. With breathtaking speed, Kaell smacked it aside, his face stiff with anger.

Yes, at last you see it, Aric thought. *You finally realise I mean to kill you.*

All deception over, he hailed lethal blows. Kaell ripped up steel to defend, metal clattering in showering blue.

Sensing something had changed, tension boiled through the onlookers. They stilled, their yells and curses dying away. A few shook their heads.

Stab. Hew. Jab. Sword scraped against sword. Aric upped his speed to cut the distance. He swung an arm. Beneath the unexpected whack, Kaell stumbled. Buckled on that weak ankle.

Aric struck. His blade tore into flesh. A red stain burst on his opponent's sleeve. As Kaell gasped, an angry mutter spread. The Mountains warrior flung his blade into his left hand.

Aric circled like the crows. *End this.* With a quick thrust in the heart. Not the cruel, slow death of Night's Kiss. He jabbed.

Kaell blocked hard. But Aric's blade dipped beneath.

The young man crashed steel across fast, partly deflecting the blade. It missed his heart, missed his belly. Sliced his thigh. Kaell cried out. His face contorted in pain. He dropped.

No quick release then. No cawing applause from the crows. But it was done. This bonded warrior was dead. He just didn't realise it yet.

Nauseous, appalled at what he'd just done, Aric let his sword wilt. Night's Kiss. A painful, lingering end. A hideous act, this. But Azenor—saved.

Silence. Then shock erupted to outrage. Men shook fists, heckled, but none dared yet touch him. The youth with chipped teeth shoved his face into Aric's. "You wounded him. A warrior who serves Khir. What's wrong with you?"

Sprawled in dirt, blood oozing through fingers clamped against his thigh, Kaell panted. He glared up. "Is this how you train in the Isles? Anyone would think you want to kill me."

"I *have* killed you," Aric said. "It hardly matters, but I'm sorry for it."

Arn grabbed Aric's sword. He sniffed the tip. "What have you done? Curse you."

Kaell tried to rise but failed. "Arn, something's wrong with me."

"The blade's tainted. Smells strange."

The young man stared at Aric. "You poisoned me?"

Now that was a philosophical question for men much smarter than Aric. *I poisoned us both,* he might say. *But only you with the sword.*

Crows circled. Soon they would feed on his flesh. He hoped they choked on it.

Again, Kaell struggled to get up. Fell back. He thumped a fist into the ground.

"Stay still," Arn said. "I'll fetch a healer."

He spoke quickly to a young warrior who took to his heels, then called two men to him. "Olier, Smiler." Arn shoved Aric at them. "Arrest him. If he resists, knock him out."

"But Arn, what if he's really the king's cousin?" the chip-toothed youth protested.

"Get him out of my sight before I kill him. He poisoned Kaell. If he's the king's cousin, then the king will have to deal with him."

HEATH

"No!" Cathmor sprang up, snatched a goblet from a table and smashed it against the wall. Wine splattered like blood.

Heath recoiled, bewildered. What had just happened? Had Aric lost his mind?

Cael-Carren grabbed the king's elbow. "Careful. Think before you act rashly."

"Rash?" Cathmor threw off his grip. "Aric Caelan struck down a bonded warrior under my protection. If Kaell dies, do you understand what it means?"

Cael-Carren poured wine with a shaking hand. "It means war."

War? Heath shot the man a look. The old fool cut to that conclusion quickly.

"You're right." Cathmor tugged at his fringe. "If Kaell dies, then I must execute Aric. It is the law. No leniency to a man who strikes a bonded warrior."

"Aric's father will use it as an excuse to attack," Cael-Carren said glumly. "The Isles will rise again."

That didn't sound right. Cathmor longed to attack the Isles again, to recover face after losing the last war. No, he'd tell his lords Hatton would resume hostilities to convince them to strike first.

"Why would Aric Caelan want this boy dead?" Heath said.

Cael-Carren stared into his wine cup. "Why does Aric Caelan do anything? You've missed the point, Damadar. If this boy dies, ghouls will overrun the Mountains and Downs, perhaps even breach the Falls."

"And when Aric's head comes off, the Isles will seek to overrun us." Cathmor squeezed a fist. "We must strike first."

Heath knuckled his chin. "But this Kaell might survive?"

"The physician says the boy sickens by the minute. It seems Aric laced his sword with poison, but the physician doesn't know what sort."

"Then Aric must tell us," said Heath.

ARIC

They gripped his shoulders as tightly as a miser clutched a bag of coins. No need. Hands bound, a split lip bleeding onto his tunic, Aric staggered, head down, no fight in him.

The two Mountains men threw him to the floor, then backed up. Cathmor yanked Aric to his knees by his hair.

"What have you done? Khir will punish you for this."

Aric flinched. Not his god. But his would surely judge him as he judged himself. Sick disgust rolled in his gut. This cowardly deed—murder no less—tainted everything he was. He deserved death.

"Yes, be afraid." Cathmor twisted his hair until he winced. "You deliberately struck a bonded warrior. Spilled his blood. Khir's curse rests upon you. But why? Why?"

"Someone paid him." Arn kicked Aric. "Caelmarsh. He bears Kaell a grudge."

Cathmor rounded on him. "What's this you're saying? I should cut you down for such treasonous words about my high constable."

"Forgive me, Your Grace." The scar on the man's jaw coloured as blood rushed to his face. "I spoke hastily. Out of fear for Kaell."

The king drove his boot into Aric's knee. "Well? You always had a lot to say before. Does nothing justify your actions? A blood dispute between you and Kaell? Did he wrong you?"

Aric squinted into flickering light. Glares as tangible as a whip fell on him. He could not regret poisoning Kaell to save Azenor. Nor did he expect or deserve mercy.

"I am guilty of the act, though it was not my choice."

"It was your sword." Arn's voice impaled with contempt.

Cathmor cut the Mountains man off with a gesture.

"Why no choice, cousin? Give me a reason to spare you."

"Ghouls hold Azenor." Aric licked his bleeding lips. "They ambushed us. Slaughtered all—" Gods help him. Cass.

Grief splintered his voice, his will. He shoved down gut-churning memories. "Slaughtered my men. Threatened to kill Azenor unless I murdered this boy."

A horrified silence fell. It was there in the swiftly drawn-in breaths, the fixed stares, the shuffling feet.

"Your Grace—" Cael-Carren began but could not continue.

"Where?" Cathmor's grim voice rolled like nearing thunder. "You rode with my bride to protect her. You, the Isles commander. Yet you live and she is—" He, too, could not finish.

"Ghouls attacked us at the ford." Aric stared at the swirls of the patterned mosaic floor. Nothing felt real. Not the ambush, not what he just did. It was as though he was watching another man, a ruthless man broken down to the beast within. A man already dead.

"The women got away, thank The Three. To where, I don't know. Ghouls took Azenor and me prisoner. Said someone called Archanin would kill Azenor—"

"Archanin?" Arn said sharply. "He took the lady?"

"This Archanin is a fairy tale," Cael-Carren said. "A story to frighten children. And you women from the Mountains, it seems."

"You let her be taken." Every part of Cathmor could be carved from stone. Taut. Still. Except his eyes. They glittered, dark and terrible with smouldered rage.

"Your task was to bring her safely to Dal-Kanu. To your king. You failed me."

"No. I saved my sister. Now this bonded warrior will die."

Cathmor struck Aric's cheek, his ring ripping skin.

"You believe the word of ghouls?" the king said. "Are you Isles demon worshippers guileless? These things care nothing for you or Azenor. They fear one man. He lies dying."

"Azenor is kin. The boy is nothing to me."

Cathmor jabbed a finger. "Kaell. He's called Kaell. He serves the gods, you heathen fool."

"Your gods," Aric said. "Not mine."

The king hit him again. This time the blow knocked Aric flat, cheek to stone. Dizzy, he could not rise. Blood from his torn cheek slowly puddled.

"Your Grace." Cael-Carren grasped his nephew's arm. "He might have the poison on him. If we at least knew what it was—"

Cathmor flicked a hand. "Strip him. Search him."

Cael-Carren waved at guards. "Take him away."

"Do it here. We're among friends. Kin." The king snorted vicious laughter.

"Do as His Majesty says."

No, no, no. What humiliation was this? The hall was full. Every servant who could slip away from their duties, every guard, every one of the Mountains warriors, jostled to watch.

Aric writhed as guards grabbed him. They struck him until he stopped thrashing. With rough hands they ripped off his garments, their touch moving impersonally over his body.

"Careful," Cathmor said. "Don't mess his hair."

Aric managed a sneer. "Find a bard to teach you new lines. Your obsession with my hair bores me."

A guardsman dumped him hard on the tiles and backed away. "Nothing, Your Grace."

"Find his horse. Search his saddlebag," Cael-Carren said. "Then deliver him to the king's interrogators. He must tell us."

More humiliation and pain. For what? Because he was ashamed to name the poison he'd used? No, he feared if he told them they might cure Kaell—and Azenor died. But there was no cure. “Night’s Kiss.” Aric slumped over his raised knees, a barrier against intrusive eyes. “It was Night’s Kiss.”

“You snake.” Arn rocked back. “You piece of filth.”

Others turned aside as though unable to look at him. Beneath the weight of their disgust, Aric hunched. No less than he deserved.

“So Kaell must die. Painfully.” Cathmor spoke softly so only Aric heard. “The law demands you die as well. No doubt your father will use this as a reason to attack, call it vengeance. By summer war will rip this land apart. Do you know what you’ve done?”

Aric lifted his chin, defiant. He knew exactly what he’d done. Saved his sister. He had to believe that. But war? No. His father would accept Aric wronged Cathmor. He had no desire to plunge Telor into war again, a war the Isles could not win—this time.

No, Cathmor *hoped* his father would march on Dal-Kanu for a flimsy reason like vengeance. Then every other Telorian lord would rally to the false king. Perhaps even the haughty Damadars with their formidable ice warriors.

“My cousin’s words condemn him.” Cathmor raised his voice. “Put him somewhere safe. See no harm comes to him. Not until my questioners are ready for him.”

Aric hugged his knees, fighting down panic. Torture, then. No quick death.

The king’s gaze passed over him again. It held a myriad of emotions: fury, sneering triumph, but disappointment too. Perhaps beheading was too swift an end for a man he hated.

Cathmor leaned close. In a low voice, the words for his captive alone, he said, “I don’t care what song you sing for my interrogator, Aric. Just so long as you take a long, agonising time to sing it.”

HEATH

Heath reeled from the scene in the hall. An echo of Cathmor's voice taunted as he strode through the castle. "My cousin's words condemn him."

Condemn. No. Aric could not die. At least, not yet. And not here.

Early moonlight frosted stone as he took the tower steps two at a time. The wind barbed his skin, its cool autumn breath layered with that distant scent of pine, woodsmoke, and rancid fat from the kitchens.

A door near the top stood open to an octagonal room. Curtains banished moonlight, trapping the stench of sickness and despair within circular, stone walls.

Kaell writhed on a bed. Still conscious. A Mountains man held him down as a physician salted his wounds in a useless bid to counter the poison.

Heath winced. A painful, lingering, and certain death. The fire, at least, was quick.

Light footsteps tapped. Torchlight blinked on hair like streaming gold as Rozenn emerged from the stairwell.

"Your Grace." He bowed.

She threw Heath a remote smile as she brushed past to the doorway.

"Do you know him? Kaell?"

Rozenn stopped. Turned. "I met him—once. How strange he should die like this. His gods are cruel. Far crueller than I could ever be."

HEATH LEFT Rozenn at the room's threshold, staring within.

As he reached their chambers, Judith sprang to her feet. "Is it true? Aric poisoned Kaell?"

"I can't take it in. Aric Caelan is no assassin. But he admitted his crime."

Judith dragged hands down her face. "I can hear Kaell's screams. Heath, it sounds so dreadful. Night's Kiss, they said."

"It's not a quick death."

"And Aric? Where is he? Did he flee Dal-Kanu?"

"He's in the tender care of Cathmor's interrogators. Until the king executes him. No, don't look at me like that, Judith. It's the law. A bonded warrior serves Khir. To kill such a man offends both king and gods."

His sister moaned. He shared her bewilderment, her frustration. All their endeavours to find the right bladesman and the man they chose had done this.

Every muscle clenched, he paced. Judith followed his steps with reproachful eyes.

It's not my fault, he wanted to shout. *Did I put a sword in Aric's hand? Did I offer him a sachet of poison? Did I tell him to throw his life away?*

"It's all been for nothing," she said. "If Aric dies, we must find another bladesman. Gods, we'll never get home. How will we get home?"

Heath buried his face in his hands.

"Tell me again, clever brother," Judith said. "Tell me how we'll snatch this lordling from beneath Cathmor's nose?"

Heath, for once, had no words.

KAELL

Beneath layers of racking torment, Kaell moaned. Sweat soaked his hair, streamed down his arms onto the cot. Every bit of his skin glistened, hot and damp, his body aflame.

The king's physician leaned over him. "Kaell. The king is here to see you."

A shadow fell over the bed just as a spasm of agony shook him. Kaell flung his head back and forth on the pillow, sobbing. He nearly shredded the sheet with his fingers.

"Can't you do something, Brenin?" Cathmor grimaced in distaste. "It's been three days."

Brenin helplessly tugged his grey beard. "Night's Kiss, Your Grace. He's survived longer than most but—"

Kaell groaned. The assassin, whoever he really was, wanted him to suffer.

A fist rapped the door. Through tears of pain, Kaell flicked a fevered glance to a guardsman who dipped his head to the king.

"Well? What is it?"

"Your Grace, an Isles representative is here with a small escort of soldiers."

"Curse them," Cathmor said. "That's all I need. Angry accusations from the Lord of the Isles. We found the women hiding in some ruin. My soldiers searched everywhere for Azenor. But Hatton will think I do too little."

The guardsman shuffled. "It is not a messenger from Lord Hatton, Your Grace. It is—she demanded I bring her straight here."

"She?"

"I'm called Ethne, Your Majesty." A young woman pushed into the room. Untamed, dark hair fell onto bare shoulders, her unblemished skin bronzed by the sun. A simple, ivory robe curtained sandalled feet. "I am a healer. Sent to help."

Brenin protested.

"Leave," Cathmor said.

The physician reddened but bowed and departed. The king beckoned the girl inside.

Kaell coughed blood onto the sheets, bracing as pain struck like venom burning in his veins, allowing no escape. He bucked, gasped, trembled.

The girl looked his way. "Let me help him."

"No one can help. It's Night's Kiss."

"Even so. I know something of this poison."

The king's brow furrowed. "Then you are no simple healer."

She said nothing. Kaell shut his eyes, fists clenched against his belly. A tension swirled in the room. He hardly cared. He wanted to die.

"Yes, Your Majesty," she said at last. "I am a healer, but I also serve The Three of the Isles. Not as a priestess. As something else."

"A sorceress."

Kaell snapped a startled look at her. Could a sorceress help him?

"If I let a sorceress touch this boy, the Lord of Vraymorg will raise a storm."

Vraymorg. At his lord's name, Kaell ached with yearning. As a child, whenever he was ill, Vraymorg was there with soft words or hands that smoothed hair from his brow. His lord would not care who healed him, only that he survived.

"Please." Kaell thumped the mattress as a wave of agony rolled through him. "Kill me."

The young woman edged closer. She brushed her palm over his moist hair. "Let me ease his suffering, Your Grace. My Lord only wishes to correct his son's foul deed."

"Even if it means his daughter dies?"

"Hatton believes Azenor is already dead. He does not trust ghouls."

A silence. Kaell could no longer hold a thought. A torrent of pain pulsed through every muscle, every vein, throwing him to the edge of blackness.

As he slipped away, he heard Cathmor say, "Do it."

THE DREAM AMBUSHED him near dawn: an assault of burning oil, wet stone, and dust, robed figures with crimson lips and clawing hands. Snatching at him.

Yelling in terror, he flailed his arms, scraped his fingernails on walls for a grip. But no matter how hard he fought or screamed, they dragged him along a torchlit passage.

To the door.

Kaell woke shouting, his palms moist. He clawed at nothing as he did in the dream. The ornate door, the city rising from red sand etched on its bronze, shimmered at the edge of his vision.

"Something's coming," he whispered.

A crack of light stole across the floor as a door opened.

"What's this noise?" Brenin stomped over to the bed. "I heard yelling."

Kaell swiped at sweat trickling into his eye. "A nightmare."

The physician touched his brow. "You're hot." Tut-tutting, he fussed with satchels. "Drink." He held a cup to Kaell's lips.

Kaell shook his head. “No more poppy juice.”

“You need rest.” Brenin swept a professional gaze along Kaell’s battered body. “No one survives Night’s Kiss. You should be dead. If not for the witch. What did she do to you?”

“I don’t remember her.”

“What did the poison feel like? A throbbing or more like fire?”

“I don’t remember.” Every choked scream, every wretched pulse of agony still tormented his mind. But his pain was his, not for a morbid stranger to paw.

“How did the pain spread? Did you feel as though it radiated from your wounds?”

“It’s all a blur.”

“Come, come. Even sentries in the towers heard your screams.”

“Did I scream?”

The man curled a lip in disbelief.

Reluctantly Kaell relented. “My flesh burned. My blood, too, like rivers of fire inside.”

Brenin nodded as though satisfied. He held the cup out again. “More.”

Kaell raised an eyebrow. “Dreamless sleep?” What he wouldn’t do for that.

“I cannot speak to a bonded warrior’s dreams. But sleep, assuredly.”

Kaell sipped, let his head drop onto the pillows, and sank into blackness.

When he woke, the nightmare’s remnants clung to him in his sweated fear, in the imprint of moist, impatient hands on his skin.

Not real. Only a dream. Stirred up by his fever and that ghoul’s taunts about his master waiting for him in the Waste Mountains.

A shudder iced his shoulder blades. What if this ghoul lord came for him? Weak, injured, he could not protect himself. Not if he couldn’t fight.

Panic swooped in his gut. Kaell tried to stand. Pain lanced his ankle. Gasping, he slumped and thrashed the mattress with his fist.

"Curse it." He beat the bed again, shouting to the walls, "I have to fight. I have to. And I can't with this useless leg!"

"What, by Khir, do you think you're doing?"

Arn leaned against the door, arms folded. He had *that* look on his face. Part anger, part irritation. All disappointment.

"Arn." Only at the sight of him, could Kaell name that churning within.

Loneliness. An unsettling feeling. Unfamiliar to a young man raised at a Mountains fortress where lessons and swordplay crowded his days.

A vivid image snapped into his mind of his first weapons master. How sweat stained the man's padded doublet. How he cursed in his native Venivan when Kaell used the wrong edge of the blade to defend. Grunted when he correctly parried.

Other tutors taught him languages, military history, and tactics. Kaell recalled one in particular, a grizzle-haired, stoop-shouldered man who squinted when he held books close to his face to read. By birth Wardorian, he officiously corrected every single syllable his student incorrectly pronounced. Mind-numbingly tedious.

Kaell tried to excel at everything. He didn't want to disappoint his lord, wanted Vraymorg to be proud of him.

Proud. The word caught in his throat. Oh gods, what would his lord think when he heard a stranger beat him? Poisoned him.

"Miss my poems, Arn?" He grinned, forcing down his disquiet. "Though, I didn't think that wearisome physician would let anyone in."

"The wearisome *guards* won't let anyone in," Arn said, his face stern.

"However many you killed to breach this room, thank Khir you're here. Get me out of here. I have to train."

A vein throbbed in Arn's throat. "You're not going anywhere. Get back into the bed."

But the dream, the door… In this strange room, far from his lord, weak from an assassin's blade, Kaell's utter powerlessness struck him.

"No, no, Arn, you don't understand. You don't know."

Kaell clenched his fists, unclenched them. Clenched them again. Dread tightened his chest. The door, the ghoul. This master waiting for him.

"I need a sword." He sliced air with his hand; the practised move dampened his alarm.

"No swords," Arn said. "Not even poetry. Rest."

Rest? No time for that. If he couldn't fight, he'd die. Die. Behind that door.

"I can't lie here. I need to get strong again. Be at my best." Better than that. The grin of the warrior who wounded him blazed in his mind. No longer mocking but sinister. "I have to be ready."

"For what?"

"For—" Kaell blinked hard. Why didn't Arn understand? If he couldn't defend himself against one man, how could he defeat ghouls or whatever waited beyond the door?

Breath stalled in his garrotted ribs. The need to lash out, yell, run, overwhelmed him. Anything to push back this terror. Kaell slammed his fist into the wall. Pain jagged his wrist.

Arn grabbed his shoulders. "What's wrong with you? Break your hand, and you won't hold a sword for a long while."

Kaell groaned. "He bested me, Arn. Me." There, he said the words. A bonded warrior couldn't lose in swordplay against one man.

Arn let him go. "Not bested. Outwitted."

Kaell tore up a laugh. Outwitted meant a hacked arm and a thigh wound still weeping pus.

He'd taken blows before, too many, but as Khir's warrior he healed fast. Except this time.

"And what of the next man who outwits me? The next thrust I'm too slow to hold out?"

"Listen, boy." Arn slumped onto a stool near the bed. "You didn't realise he was out to kill. None of us did. Curse that twisted salt head. Those Serravan-trained, prancing, bejewelled men of the

Isles know all the tricks. And Aric Caelan is the best of—"

"Wait." Kaell clutched at the bed frame. "It couldn't really be Aric Caelan? What quarrel has he with me? No, it was an assassin using that name. Sent by Caelmarsh."

"Caelmarsh is cunning. He won't attack you openly, only hunt you when you're alone. Like on the Downs. No, the assassin was Aric Caelan. The king's cousin. Identified by Cathmor and all the court."

Kaell dug fingers into his temples. "I don't understand. Why should an Isles lord, a stranger, try to kill me? Why didn't anyone tell me this?"

"Like who? The king?" Arn shook his head. "The Isles snake said ghouls seized his sister in an ambush—in daylight mind you—and unless he killed you, the Blood Lord killed her. The foul deed done, he didn't run, just let us arrest him."

The Blood Lord. Dread throbbed in Kaell's skull. Bewildered, he sank down on the bed. He wanted to shut out Arn's words, shut out the world.

"You don't believe him? About the ambush?"

"They're all liars in the Isles, Kaell. What with their bloodthirsty gods and their tongues as smooth as their perfumed skin. The king's questioners will rip the truth from this prince."

"What?"

Arn's ragged scar twisted his face as he grinned. Men who didn't know him backed off when Arn Tranter smiled. Kaell never had. As a boy, he'd followed Arn about like a puppy, firing questions the older warrior patiently answered.

The scar meant this man had fought battles—real battles against ghouls or outlaws—that he knew things.

"The king arrested Aric. What did you think would happen? That Cathmor would kiss his cheek and forgive him? You're a servant of Khir, boy."

"But he's the Lord of the Isles' son."

"So the great lords of Telor will recognise his head rotting on a spike. What do you care? He tricked you into fighting to kill you."

Kaell flushed. Arn had warned him. But he'd thought only of the contest, the chance to test his skill. "His fear for his sister surely drove him to this. To come at me openly, knowing his own death must follow. The girl. Is there word of her? Is she safe?"

"Azenor. The king's soldiers searched this past week while you shirked your duty." Arn's grin flashed but quickly faded. "She's dead. Especially if the ghoul story is true."

"Why shouldn't it be true?"

Arn's frown fell on the table beside the bed. "Did you bring your book?" His voice roughened. "That thing you scribble rhymes in all the time?"

Kaell brushed his palm over a leather-bound book. "This isn't mine. My 'thing' as you call it is in my room at Vraymorg. Anyway, I'm in no mood for rhymes right now."

"So what's this?"

"The physician found it by my bed. He mumbled something about 'her' leaving it. And how you can't trust Cahireans. Then called the book sorcerous nonsense. Sadly, there are no wicked, sorcerous pictures. Only stories about the seer king from the Isles. Roaran Caelan."

Kaell leaned forward, eager. "His friend, a Cahirean king, murdered Roaran here, Arn. In the great hall of this castle." The stains might be visible. Blood always left its mark.

Arn stood there saying nothing. A slow shudder ran through him.

He muttered, "I know the story."

THROUGH AN OPEN WINDOW, a rising moon pearled the gloaming. A breeze rippled curtains.

For all the coming night's gentleness, its beauty, it felt oddly remote. The world shifted, became an even more complex place where Isles princes faced impossible choices. Kill a warrior he'd never met, or let ghouls kill his sister.

Pity gnawed at Kaell. Could he do as Aric did? Murder a stranger to save someone he loved? Except Aric did not save her.

Kaell tore his hands down his cheeks. Groaned. He lived, and she died. How could he carry this guilt? No, it was too much to even think upon. If only his lord were here. To talk things through, to comfort with reason, to share this burden.

Whenever Kaell took a wound or suffered a winter cough, Vraymorg was there. Sometimes with words like "hush, it's all right" or just sitting in silence by his bed. Kaell always sighed and fell into a deep sleep. Safe.

But what if his lord walked in now with only disappointment in his eyes?

How he wanted to hide from that. As a child, seeing that look, he always dropped his head, shuffled his feet, swore to himself to do better, be better. Earn his praise. His affection.

THE DOOR CRASHED INWARD. A man stood huge and unbowed on the threshold.

Kaell's breath choked, then unwound in a muttered, "My Lord." He pulled his torn body up against the pillows, his dazzled gaze on Vraymorg.

He came. He came! Dizzying relief blazed through him. His lord's sheer presence and strength meant it would be all right.

But even within that comforting thought, the old yearning ached.

If only this man smiled and ruffled his hair, told him it didn't matter that Aric had fooled him. That he thought no less of him. That he cared.

Kaell nearly laughed aloud at his own foolishness. It was never like that. Not quite. For now, it was enough his lord had even come.

Vraymorg kicked the door shut on a protesting guard. Torchlight sparked on bracelets coiled up his muscular arms, its flame etching his furious face.

"How could this happen?" He slapped a glove against his palm. "Did this snake strike you when you turned away?"

Every muscle in Kaell's back stiffened. Why would he expect anything but anger? He'd failed, let Aric draw him into swordplay with clever words.

Sweet words. A poisoned blade. It sounded like a minstrel's song. Or even a poem he might write.

"If by snake you mean Aric Caelan, he didn't strike me in the back."

"Olier says you fell down the crypt stairs. Hurt that ankle Paulin put a bolt into years ago. Injured, you still took on Aric Caelan. A prince of the Isles—" Vraymorg's breath snapped out. "And then to let that woman, to let evil, touch you."

Evil? "She saved me."

"A sorceress. A servant of the Isles gods." Vraymorg struck his palm with the glove again. And again. And again.

"That's unfair. How could I stop—" Kaell broke off, his mouth dry. His lord had taught him obedience and respect, lessons he learned only too well.

At the lurking bitterness in that thought, shame wilted his shoulders. This man had trained him to obey, yes. But did he forget the rest? His lord taught him to survive, to hold his head high without fear. To laugh. To trust.

To love? No, that was too difficult to sift.

"My lord, so what if she used magic? Spell makers, wood witches, are all common in the Mountains. And the rituals, the training of bonded ones, are steeped in sorcery."

"What do you know?" The unflinching slap of leather struck like iron on an anvil. "You're a weapon of the Mountains gods, sharpened and used. That's all you were born for."

Hurtful, diminishing words. But his lord's gaunt cheeks, the shadows of sleeplessness beneath his tormented eyes, did not match them.

Kaell looked away fast, his heart straining at his rib cage. Cool air plucked at his sleeve. The camphoric fragrance of sage, of rosemary drifted from gardens below the window.

His lord's dishevelled clothes, his unshaven jaw meant one thing. Vraymorg had ridden from the Mountains without stopping. To get to him.

He cared. His lord cared. Enough to ride straight to him. Not wasting time to sleep nor seek the king. Beneath his anger, his lord feared for him.

Secretly pleased, Kaell managed, "My wounds will heal, my lord. I'm much recovered."

"At what price? That witch serves demons. What did she offer them to save you?"

"Would you prefer I died?"

"How could you ask that?" His lord thrust his gloves into his belt. "But you don't understand. Her magic comes from gods that aren't yours."

Could these Isles gods be so terrible? Yet—Kaell swallowed, deeply reluctant to tell his lord the truth. Not because he feared this man's wrath. No, he feared his expression clouding in disappointment.

"The dreams—"

"What?"

"My visions, they're gone. I dream, nightmares of that stupid door again, but not like before. It's more a memory now, the door. I don't see what's coming."

Silence. His lord filled it with his presence, imposing and terribly still, but for his fierce eyes flaring like newly lit onyx lanterns. His voice came out low, the words carefully placed as though he shackled inconvenient emotion. "The witch left you defenceless."

"My lord, why would she do that? It may be the poison. My

strength returns. Perhaps the visions will as well."

"Where did you get that?"

Kaell glanced up. Vraymorg's stare dwelt on the book.

"I—it was here."

"Did you take it from my room?"

"No," Kaell whispered, uneasy. "The physician thinks the healer left it."

Vraymorg smoothed its leather with his palm. "It's not the same." He briefly closed his eyes. "I know you'd never take anything, Kaell. Did you read this?"

First Arn and now his lord asking about this book, an undercurrent in their tones.

"Only the stories about King Roaran. The rest looked dull."

His lord brooded in that way of his, body held stiffly, his eyes dark, wide, and distant.

With his raven hair, the close-cut stubble shadowing his jaw, this man resembled Aric. That made no sense. An Isles prince and a Mountains lord.

"Describe what the witch did."

"She prepared a potion for me to drink. Said things." Kaell shrugged.

"Words? Like a chant?"

"My lord, I blacked out. But she saved my life."

Vraymorg looked past him into the murk along the walls.

"As soon as you can ride," he said. "You'll return to the Mountains. I'll summon the priests of Khir. They'll undo her mischief."

"I can't do that." Kaell's boldness shocked him. "I promised the king we'd destroy a nest of ghouls near the Waste Mountains."

"You're bound to the rulers of Vraymorg, boy, not of Dal-Kanu." His lord's tone did not yield so much as a handbreadth. "The king will return you until you are again ready to serve the gods."

He stormed out, leaving Kaell crushing the sheet with iron fingers.

VAL ARQUES

Men called it the Silent Keep. It wasn't. It creaked with whispers.

Vraymorg heard them all, every unearthly voice echoing through the Castle of the Lake's stone passages, every footstep that fell in emptiness.

Dead Telorian kings prowled, watchful. Their breath hunted like a wound along his backbone, their shadows unfolding in his wake.

Spirits paced his childhood home at Tide's End, too, with sorrowful songs as familiar as waves shattering on rocks below moonlit Isles cliffs.

He grew up hearing clashing blades, a relentless hammering from the forge, the tide thundering over reefs and wind groaning with ghostly voices through arrow slits in towers.

Every sound strangely comforting. Unlike the velvet hush of his prison, that bleak, iron-gated Mountains keep called Vraymorg.

He remembered with a shiver nights he stood at his window staring across the great gorge into a blackness that might hold—anything. And his neck prickled as if fingers brushed his skin.

Slowly he lifted his eyes to Cathmor. Seated in a high-backed chair in the hall, shoulders hunched, torchlight licking at a blunt, grim countenance, the king looked upon nothing.

Perhaps he, too, sensed judging spirits roaming dark corridors, shadows that flitted and darted. Or perhaps Cathmor merely pondered how to get rid of him.

Beyond the windows, sodden thunderheads blotted dusk, a fugue of black and grey. The air was as acrid as his frayed temper. He wanted nothing more than to sink down, back to the stone wall, and drop his head into hands.

Not yet. Not until Cathmor agreed to return Kaell. Not until he took Kaell safely back to the Mountains, far from treacherous Isles princes with poisoned blades.

"I won't leave without him, Your Grace."

Cathmor lurched from his chair. Loosely leashed menace enlarged a man already a head taller than Vraymorg. Soft, brown hair and slumberous eyes belied a face as hard as iron and a sarcastic, belittling tongue.

"And again, I say: You can't have him."

"Your Grace, Kaell must return with me."

"You argue with your king, Vraymorg? Is your loyalty suspect? Shall I throw you into a cell next to Aric? Let me say it one last time: I need Khir's warrior here."

Vraymorg forced repugnant words through gritted teeth. "I am loyal to Your Majesty." The Mountains might be his prison, but at least there he answered to no one. "Kaell is useless to you. An Isles sorceress cast incantations over him."

"I permitted her to tend him."

"You had no right. Better he should die."

Cathmor knuckled a fist against his hipbone. "A time in irons might soften your arrogance, Vraymorg. You do not even bow to your king."

Deliberately slowly, Vraymorg dropped to one knee. Cathmor might indeed arrest him. He could hardly help Kaell if he rotted in a cell.

The king rubbed his chin, pleased. "Well, well. So you can bend that stiff neck."

Vraymorg said nothing. Vanity blinded even clever men. And Cathmor possessed wit enough to be at least formidable—if not for that vanity. If not for his belief in his kingly rights and his need to dominate and slap others down with steel or words.

The king drove a hand through air. "I don't understand you, Vraymorg. I permitted the sorceress to tend to Kaell to save his life. You should be grateful."

"Only blood magic can cure Night's Kiss," Vraymorg said. "That means a life for a life."

"Whatever do you mean?"

"Was there—a death?"

"When the witch tended Kaell?" Cathmor shrugged. "A gardener's apprentice."

Vraymorg snatched a breath. "How?"

"Someone stabbed him."

"A young man? Healthy?"

Cathmor scoffed. "Not a supernatural death, Vraymorg. I'm told the boy accused a guard of cheating at dice."

Lightning scarred darkness beyond the window. Thunder pealed, a ripping ribbon of sound. An awakened wind carried the sharp scent of rain and stirred dust.

The witch *had* used blood magic. Vraymorg knew it. Sorcery demanded payment.

"I can't leave Kaell here," he said. "Injured. He's vulnerable."

"The boy is among friends." The king's look for once held neither menace nor impatience, only an odd, unsought sympathy. "No one here wishes him harm."

An intimacy awakened. Deeply uncomfortable. Vraymorg did not expect pity from this man. No, he did not *want* pity from him.

Cathmor crossed to a table spread with maps and parchments.

"Once Kaell can fight, he'll lead his men north. The villagers of Thom begged me for help. Two pitiful things made their way to Dal-Kanu to plead for warriors to save them."

"So your messenger said. Gods help them."

"Eleven villagers taken at night from some forsaken place here." Cathmor poked a finger at a map. "Slaughtered. The villagers set guards, but ghouls took them as well."

Vraymorg frowned. "I've not heard of ghouls near Thom before. Why now?"

"Caelmarsh brought me a strange story of a ghoul killing two men at a tournament on the Downs. Who knows what these beasts intend."

"But for their appetites, they're hardly beasts. Intelligent. Dangerous. A curse upon this land. In the time of Queen Devarsi, they killed so many the streams ran red with blood."

"Until the gods blessed us with the first bonded warrior. An old story." Cathmor yawned.

"Do I bore Your Majesty?"

"You're far too prickly to bore me. But you irritate me. Now, are we agreed?" A warning edge to his voice. "Kaell remains here until he rides north. I assure you, he has the best care."

Vraymorg freed a held breath. "You may have Kaell. But he returns to the Mountains once he destroys this nest of vipers."

"May have?" Cathmor swept the map from the table. "You don't give. I take. My father complained about your father's impudence. Arrogance, it seems, is in the blood."

An old complaint. Vraymorg shrugged it off. Cathmor resented him. Perhaps because the king recognised he couldn't easily bend or break him. To break or bend, a man must have something to lose. His position? His life? He didn't care about either.

But about Kaell…

"As for Aric Caelan—"

"No."

"No?"

"No. I will not give you my cousin, Vraymorg. Nor will I let you roam in the deepest, darkest places of this castle so you can play with him."

"This man." Vraymorg's clenched jaw ached. "Struck down

Kaell coldly, deliberately. Night's Kiss is a vicious death."

"I assure you Aric Caelan is in torment, with no thought beyond how to stop his agony. My interrogator knows many bloody joys."

"Your prisons are neither dark nor damp enough. There are holes in the Mountains where no one will ever hear from him again."

"That would never do." Cathmor mocked with a roll of his eyes. "When Aric dies—I think his execution will be quite an event, don't you?—everyone must hear him scream."

"I want him. He wronged me more than you."

"Really? You wish to play that tiresome game? Then let me remind you of this, Vraymorg. Aric's incompetence denied me my queen. If his father thinks he can send some sorceress to heal Kaell and all is forgiven, he's wrong. I will execute Aric."

To provoke Hatton into declaring war? Or to pretend to fear he might and attack first?

"As for Kaell," Cathmor said. "Aric attacked a warrior under my protection. So it seems, I win."

"Then I'll ride with Kaell to Thom. It's too close to the Waste Mountains. It could be dangerous. He'll need my help."

Cathmor snorted. "Your king needs your help. I must be ready to march on the Isles by the first week of spring. I need arrows. Rope. It will be a long, busy winter for you. You'll return at once to the Mountains."

"Your Grace, at least let me speak again with Kaell."

"Enough. Now you do bore me."

"Your Grace—"

"Enough, I said. You test me, Vraymorg. Another word and you'll get your wish and spend time with Aric. In my cells."

KAELL

Kaell climbed up to the balcony above his room. Stone cut his palms, bloodied his shins. He hardly felt it. A nervous edginess kept pain and exhaustion at bay. For now.

As he slipped into Cathmor's empty bedchamber, a key jangled.

The king walked inside. With a weary sigh, he shut the door at his back.

"Your Grace."

Cathmor whipped a knife from his belt as he spun. "By Cyrah. How did you get here?"

"Your Grace, I must talk to you."

"So you crept into my rooms? Are you witless? I should call the guards to arrest you."

"Forgive me." Kaell fell to one knee.

A silence plunged. Slowly it filled with Cathmor's breaths, with the tread of guards outside, a whisper of lambent flames in sconces.

"Well, well." Cathmor waved him up, a satisfied gleam darkening his eyes. "What is so important you break into your king's rooms in the middle of the night?"

"I must talk to you, Your Grace," Kaell said. "But the guards won't let me leave my room."

"You're guarded for your protection. Saying that." Cathmor

frowned. "How did you slip by my men?"

"The window. I climbed up."

"You embarrassed my guards. I'll discipline them. What if you were an assassin?"

"Your Grace, please." Kaell threw up his hands. "Don't punish anyone because of me."

Cathmor unbuckled his sword belt.

"This night proves illuminating, but it is becoming very long. Tell me what you came to say. I already put up with a tirade of nonsense from your lord, so why not you as well?"

Kaell swayed, fist clenched to focus on staying upright. "I came to beg you to spare Aric."

"You want mercy?" The king barked a startled laugh. "For the man who tried to kill you?"

"Yes," Kaell said.

Another laugh, bitter as limes. "A soft heart is a flaw for a killer, boy. Is that why my cousin bested you?"

Kaell stilled. Did Aric beat him because he was weak? Flawed? "Your Grace." His mouth tasted like ash. "Please be merciful and spare him."

"I think not." Cathmor's voice sharpened with contempt. "Aric is a ghouls' assassin."

"He is no assassin, Your Majesty. Aric did not strike secretly. He fought me openly before my men. And he failed. He didn't kill me."

"That doesn't excuse him."

"Your Grace, banish him. He only hurt me because he loves his sister."

"His sister—my betrothed—who Aric failed to protect." Cathmor said. "He deserves no mercy." He hurled up a hand to stop Kaell's protest. "No, I've spoken. And since you're well enough to climb through windows, you'll come with me."

The king beckoned with a curled finger. Kaell could only follow.

CATHMOR STRODE INTO THE PASSAGE. A flat-nosed, hard-eyed swordsman with flaked dandruff on his collar peeled away from the wall and trod after him. The new king's "sword," Janak, by repute was everything his disgraced predecessor wasn't. Single-minded. Humourless. Mean.

In the empty inner ward, biting pine overshadowed the death scent from the head house. Shadows huddled beside buttressed stone. Sentries shuffled on the wall walk.

The storm gone, the night fell softly as those mid-autumn nights often did, its nip through Kaell's tunic pleasurable as he followed the king up stairs and across a bridge to a tower.

As they passed inside, guards stiffened to attention then turned keys at each of three iron gates on the spiralling, rough-hewn staircase until they descended to a dimly lit passage.

Janak snatched up a torch and strode past cell after cell. The silence was hollow as though nothing lived beyond. Damp coldness needled Kaell's skin. Shivering, he drew his thin cloak tight across his breast. A desperate, hopeless place, apart from the world above.

The king clasped a hand over his mouth and nose. "Worse than a cesspool," he muttered.

A blank-faced guard fumbled at a lock to a metal door. A long, narrow tunnel led into gloom reeking of mould and decay. A man moaned. The torch-licked darkness swallowed the grim sound.

"Few leave here," Cathmor said. "A fortunate few, forgiven or bought free. But not Aric. He will be neither forgiven nor ransomed."

A jailer staggered up from behind a table, his dirty, sallow face creasing with surprise. "Your Grace." The man fell clumsily to his knees. His grubby clothes stank of ale.

"I wish to see my cousin. Take me."

The man stumbled to his feet. "This way, Your Grace." He

grasped another burning torch to lead them along a stale-aired passage, then through a grilled door into a dank, close room.

Despite an ember-red fire, its smoke disappearing into a hole in the roof, stone slabs chilled Kaell's bare feet. Water dribbled down cracked, stained walls, green and slippery with moss. Rusty iron chains dangled from roof beams. A rat squealed.

On dirty straw, his wrists and ankles fettered, Aric curled, naked. A red-soaked bandage was wrapped around his torso. Face grimy, thick hair matted and filthy, he looked nothing like the arrogant, handsome man who'd struck Kaell down.

Kaell shivered again, surprised by another niggle of compassion. Interrogators had held and tortured Aric for five days.

Cathmor wheeled on the jailer. "Why is he bleeding? I ordered his wounds treated. I don't wish him to die too soon, you fool."

"Your interrogator used the hook today, Your Grace." The jailer grinned nastily. "They always bleed, and they always scream when she uses the hook." He shrugged. "For all the stories about this man, he screamed no less than any other."

The king swept aside clanking chains to reach for a book on a wobbly, stained table.

"Question." He read aloud. "You and your father plot against His Majesty. You wanted Khir's warrior out of the way so you could kill Cathmor."

"Answer: No, how many times must I deny it? No, no, no. Please, no. Prisoner faints."

Cathmor flicked pages. Kaell knew enough of what happened in the dark cells below the Mountains fortress to guess the book detailed not only Aric's denials but what instruments the interrogator used and the prisoner's reaction to each.

"Who—" Kaell licked lips tasting of the prison's foul odours. "Who is your—"

Cathmor did not look up. "A Cahirean called Bellicent Blackstone, sister to Queen Rozenn's captain. She learned her bloody trade in the dungeons of Quisnaf."

An iron grate swung with a vicious creak. A woman with smooth black hair and round eyes squinted from the doorway. Kaell at once thought of a kitchen cat. Fat, sleek, sly.

She offered the king a slick bow. "Your Grace. Is there some difficulty?" A predatory gaze settled on Kaell. "You wish me to—examine this young man?"

Examine? Kaell blenched.

"Not tonight. He's here to learn, Bellicent," Cathmor said. "I came to see my cousin."

Bellicent swept another bow. "Excellent timing, Your Grace. Your cousin proved stubborn today. I intend to soften him up with the whip tonight, to poison his dreams."

Cathmor flicked up a brow. "The transcripts—"

"A day old, I'm afraid. The wicked boy lost his tongue." Bellicent rubbed her hands with pleasure. "Not literally. Unless you wish it?" She glanced hopefully at the king. "No? Then I shall use the whip—if it might amuse Your Grace."

"I cannot promise to be amused. But continue."

Kaell shuddered. He knew the bite of leather upon his shoulders.

"Do you know what they say, Kaell?" Cathmor leaned to whisper like a conspirator. "Blackstone, black heart. Her appetites are extreme, but she's thorough and inventive."

The interrogator snapped her fingers at the jailer. "Get him up."

The jailer splashed water over the prisoner. Aric twitched, his lips moving noiselessly as the man hoisted him up and swung his manacled wrists onto a hook. His eyes held barely a flicker of awareness.

Kaell fell back. His palm grazed rough stone. He had no taste for torture. No desire to see another man in pain. Why had Cathmor insisted on bringing him here?

The jailer cranked chains until Aric's toes brushed the stone floor. At the unnatural position, muscles strained in his shoulders and back.

Cathmor drifted his hand over the captive's shoulder. "Striking, isn't he? If my queen looked like her brother, she must have pleased the eye."

Kaell wrenched his head aside, uncomfortable at not only the confidence but the caress.

"I'll never know. Aric's failure to protect his sister robbed me of my Caelan bride. Robbed me of the Isles. Do you understand why he must suffer, Kaell? Do you understand the extent of his crimes? Not just against you, but against his king."

Kaell said nothing. He longed to be anywhere but here, about to witness the king's interrogator torture a man.

With as much care as a bladesman might select a sword, Bellicent chose a whip. She fingered its knotted leather, smiling faintly as she circled Aric.

Aric's head lolled. A pulse fluttered in his throat as Bellicent grasped his buttocks to pull his groin against her. At the intrusive touch, Kaell flinched with distaste.

The interrogator traced a bead of sweat down the prisoner's breast onto his belly. "Such a sweet lordling. And he screams so prettily for me."

She sighed with pleasure, stepped back, and lifted the whip. It whistled through air. Tore into flesh. Aric jerked. He made no sound. The lash cracked again. Blood streamed from welts in the captive's back to the floor. Kaell locked his eyes on its slow drip.

"He's strong." Bellicent stroked Aric's cheek. "Deliciously strong."

Disgusted, Kaell ground his fists together. "Your Grace. Is this necessary?"

"You'll watch this, Kaell. Just as two days from now you'll watch him die."

"No!" The protest ripped from him.

Cathmor considered him with displeasure. "No?" His fist struck out.

Beneath the blow, Kaell reeled. A snarling Janak moved in,

sword extended. The king waved him off. Breaths tight, he yanked Kaell up. "You will watch every stroke and be glad of his suffering. And you'll never question your king again."

Jaw aching, Kaell drew as still as a statue. He did not look at Cathmor. He forced his eyes to Bellicent as she slid her hands possessively all over Aric's naked body.

"He knows how to retreat from the pain." The interrogator's voice cracked with a sick desire. "Your Grace, I can break him. If you should only reconsider—"

"No."

"I've learned what he fears—"

"My orders stand. I don't want him crippled. Nor do I want you to drive him mad. That makes for a dull execution. Tonight I do, however, wish to hear him scream. Make him."

The woman flashed a radiant smile. "With pleasure, Your Grace. I know just the thing."

Bile shot up Kaell's throat. If only he could flee this foul cell with its stench of blood and misery. But he could only watch as Bellicent trod to the fire, humming as she drew on a glove to pull a glowing tong from the flames.

Bellicent thrust. The tong sizzled into skin.

Pain snapped Aric from whatever languor held him. He screamed. The drawn-out sound jarred down Kaell's spine.

He hazed his vision so he didn't see Bellicent's jabs. But he could not hide from Aric's terrible, gut-wrenching shrieks that surely carried through every one of these passages.

TIME BLURRED. There was only Aric's screams, the odour of burnt flesh. Bellicent's sickening smiles. Cathmor's intent, pitiless fascination.

"Cut him down," the king said at last. "Tend to his wounds."

Kaell blinked in surprise. A faint hope kindled. Perhaps the king might show mercy.

But Cathmor smothered that at once. "Move him to a tower cell to await execution."

No. Not that. Kaell jammed a fist in his mouth, biting back another protest. Helpless anger whirled within him. Whatever Aric Caelan did to him, this was punishment enough. The man did not need to die.

Cathmor turned. Shaken, Kaell trod after him, Janak a few steps ahead. As guards unlocked the door to the ward, the king said, "I hope you need never see that wretched place again, Kaell."

"I hope so, too, Your Grace."

"Of course, that depends on your lord."

"My Lord?"

"Yes, your lord. He came close tonight to finding himself in a cell next to Aric. I should hate for you to see him like that. A prisoner in such squalor." Cathmor wet his lips. "Although, I should enjoy seeing him in chains, I think. Such an arrogant creature."

Kaell braced a trembling hand against a wall. "I don't understand."

"No." Cathmor considered him. "I don't suppose you do. Let's just say upon your return from Thom you might like to consider who you bend your knee to."

The guard flung back the final grate. A covered bridge crossed to the mighty Kanu Tower. Its elegant length cut out the clear, star-bright sky, a silhouette etched by pallid moonbeams.

Cathmor paused to stare up. "As a boy I looked in awe upon this tower. I wondered which god made it. It disappeared into clouds. Now I live in those clouds, in the king's chamber."

He sighed and walked on. "And the tower seems small. Like the rest of the world."

Kaell hardly listened as he followed Cathmor into the tower, up twisting steps lit by blazing torches. After the bleak prison, even this indifferent glow seemed too brilliant. A mockery of pain.

What did the king mean? Bend his knee to him, or Cathmor imprisoned his lord? Surely he misunderstood. His Grace could not intend that. Yet his words contained menace.

Cathmor stopped. He flicked a hand at Kaell. "Janak, return my wayward guest to his room. Make certain he doesn't roam again."

The king brought his hard eyes to rest on Kaell's face.

"I'll leave you with your thoughts, Kaell. But before you pity my cousin, think about this. That man wronged you. If he hadn't wronged me as well, I might let you strike off his head."

VAL ARQUES

The blow felt good. Too good.

Vraymorg clenched his fists against roiling anger. It was always with him, this anger. Buried beneath a veneer of control. Long ago he'd learned to push it deep down through sheer will, so it leaked out as recklessness in battle, in his impatient, curt manner.

But now he wanted to surrender to it.

Arn did not rise. Sprawled in dirt in the castle ward as though shot from a trebuchet, he rubbed his jaw, watching Vraymorg warily. "I deserved that, my lord. But forgive me if I don't get up just so you can hit me again."

"I should have you whipped. I bid you to watch out for him."

"I failed you, my lord—and Kaell."

"Get up, fool."

Arn slowly got to his feet, shoulders hunched against another blow.

Vraymorg expelled cool air to check his rage. Darkness spilled about him but below streaked clouds beyond the castle towers, a flux of dawn's rose creased the horizon.

"How could this... *prince*"—Vraymorg spat the word in disgust—"wound him? The moment you learnt this man's name, you should have stepped in. Stopped Kaell at once."

“My lord, the king’s cousin dared Kaell to fight him. He couldn’t back down.”

“So for the sake of pride he nearly loses his life? I blame you. Kaell is eighteen, still with a boy’s hot-headed rashness.”

“He’s twenty. Nearly twenty-one.” Arn’s tone implied his lord should know as much. “Kaell—all of us—were curious to see how this man Aric fought.”

Curious? A fresh burst of anger heated his blood. Everyone knew how an Isles prince trained by Serravan-influenced weapons masters fought. With both wit and skill.

Still—Vraymorg had taught Kaell to defeat clever, expert bladesmen.

“You’re saying Aric Caelan is the better swordsman?”

“My lord, that’s not quite how it is.”

“Then how is it? Explain how a warrior dedicated to Khir, the God of Battles, only lives because some Isles sorceress cast spells over him.”

Arn folded his arms. “My lord, Kaell fought as he trains, precisely, fairly—until he realised this man wanted to kill him. Before that, he held back his arm.”

“And Aric?”

“The Isles man”—Arn’s voice held awe—“did not check his strokes. Aric Caelan is a splendid bladesman, at the peak of his abilities, but no better than the boy.”

“No better doesn’t leave a man dying. You’re wrong. Aric outthought Kaell, and that makes him the superior swordsman.”

HE STALKED TO THE STABLES. Arn’s words pursued him. *No better than the boy.* Yet no man, not even Aric Caelan, should match Kaell with steel. Not when he had trained him.

“My lord.” His servant Ewen tightened stirrups on their horses. “Where’s Kaell?”

"The king won't surrender him."

"Surrender? Is he a prisoner?" Ewen bristled. "Why? Does this Isles prince blame Kaell? Does he claim Kaell provoked him? Then he's a liar and a coward."

Vraymorg whipped up a hand before Ewen took it into his greying head to storm the castle, kill all the king's guards, and rescue Kaell. "Cathmor wants Kaell to hunt down those ghouls menacing villagers on the Downs."

"How many ghouls? As I hear it Kaell can hardly walk, let alone fight."

"Kaell's fine." He wondered why he lied to himself. "Arn will keep him out of trouble."

Ewen sniffed in disgust. "A poor job he's made of that. First Caelmarsh almost grabs Kaell on the Downs, no thanks to Arn. Then some woman tries to smother him. Now this."

Vraymorg nibbled his lip. His fault. Kaell only ran off to that stupid Downs tournament because he lost his temper and struck him. "If it's any comfort, Kaell had strength enough to answer me back just now."

"That sounds like him. I'm fond of the lad, the gods only know how much. He has an easy way about him, a warmth. But he doesn't always hold his tongue."

"Next he'll spin words at us again. Poems and such."

"Khir protect us." Ewen grinned. "Before he left the Mountains, Kaell came up with a poem about the cook. Rhymed cook with chook or sook or some other nonsense. She chased him from the kitchen with a spoon."

"A fierce woman, that one. The boy would be sore if she caught him."

Ewen ran his palm over a horse's flanks. "This thing with the king summoning Kaell to Dal-Kanu and now keeping him here. It worries me."

"Cathmor's plotting something, yes."

"He takes his rights as king seriously. Wants Kaell to answer to him, not you."

The king resented his power. Resented him. Vraymorg shrugged. “Kaell will always obey me.”

“The boy loves you, Val. Even though you don’t want to hear it. That’s why he argues with you, wanting attention all the time.”

Loves you. The temptation to turn the words over, sift them, tugged like a storm wind through sails. No. Shield his heart, or it would shatter. How many times could it shatter before he could no longer find himself among its pieces?

“At least tell me the king will surrender the Isles coward to us. There are men ready to show this Aric Caelan a few tricks, if you take my meaning, my lord.”

“No lordling pup to torment.”

Ewen thrust out his bottom lip. He grabbed the bridles to lead their horses outside.

Vraymorg tried to imagine him torturing Aric with hot pokers. No, Ewen would scold the prisoner until he sobbed and begged for quiet.

“Do we ride for home, my lord? Empty-handed, though we may be?”

“We’ll be at the foot of the mountains by dusk tomorrow. Home within a week if the gods feel charitable and the rivers aren’t high.”

He peered up at the castle’s towers masked against the lightening sky. Unease coldly snaked his arms. His past stalked this place, his memories ghosting like fog.

In this ward, he once danced with a bladesman with the ichor of gods in his veins. In a cell deep within the earth, a long-dead king had left him shackled and forgotten.

“My lord.” Ewen tore him back to the present. “Something you should know. Word is Heath Damadar is here with one of his sisters. Judith, I think. Wedding guests, apparently.”

“Heath. Not the eldest son, Velleran?”

“No, Heath. Though I don’t believe the wedding guest bit for one moment.”

"What are they up to, I wonder?"

"Can't be good. Ever come across a Damadar not intent on malice?"

He tried never to come across a Damadar at all. Fickle allies, the Ice lords. Dangerous enemies. Their purpose shrouded, but always to do with ambition and magic.

Vraymorg swung into the saddle. In streaked light, movement blurred. A young man watched him from the doorway to the blacksmith's forge, his raven hair lit by fires within. A hammer bent iron.

"Ah, trouble," Ewen said. "Saw him staring when we rode in."

The stranger walked resolutely towards them. "My lord. May I speak with you?"

"If you must. But be quick as we've a long ride. Who are you?"

The man halted a sword's length away. The aroma of ash clung to his guardsman's uniform. "From the wary look in your eyes, I think you might know."

"Insolence," Ewen spluttered. "How dare he address you so familiarly?"

Vraymorg held up his hand. Ewen had once leapt off a horse to slap a sharp-tongued squire about the ears. He'd spare this young man's ears.

"You're bold, whoever you are. What do they call you?"

"Philip. And as you are leaving, I must take my chance and be bolder still."

He paused. Looked Vraymorg right in the face. "You knew my mother."

"Knew my mother, *my lord,*" Ewen said. "Address your betters correctly."

Philip's stare did not move away. "You knew my mother—my lord."

Knew? What was he implying? "I think you mistake me for another."

"My uncle." The guardsman glanced at the forge. "Tells me

you're Vraymorg. That is the name my mother gave me when I asked…" He shifted his weight.

Vraymorg threw back a laugh to disguise his disquiet. That black hair. Those cheekbones.

"I know what you're hinting, Philip. By The Three, how old do you think I am?"

"I cannot explain your age. I only know you're the man she told me she… knew." His voice quavered. Too dark to see the blush Vraymorg guessed crept up his neck.

"Your mother—?"

"Izzy, my lord. She died last winter. A fever."

"My lord," Ewen said. "We have a long ride."

"As you say." He swept Philip another look. Unmistakable, the signs of his blood.

"Was there something you wanted, Philip?"

The man's gaze still did not falter. "With my mother gone, I have few ties in Dal-Kanu. Word is you always need trained warriors at Vraymorg. What with ghouls and the Varee."

"You need trained warriors—my lord." Ewen shook his head. "Young man, I hope your bladework is not as sloppy as your manners."

"My lord." Philip said with a faint smile. "I assure you my bladework is sharp enough."

"There's a Mountains captain called Arn Tranter," Vraymorg said. "Do you know him?"

"No, but I'll find him."

"Tell him we spoke. Two of my men return to the Mountains tomorrow. You can travel with them. If your bladework is as you say, I'm sure there's a place for you."

The soldier nodded. "I'm sure there is, too—my lord."

OUTSIDE THE GATES, Ewen whistled. "You bedded his mother, then? Of course you did. You never learn, do you?"

Gentle, lovely Izzy. She spent two afternoons in his bed, may The Three forgive his weakness. His impiety, though infrequent and always when he was lonely, haunted him.

"And you swore by 'The Three'. Careless. Do you want gossip about why a Mountains lord bends his knee to the Isles gods?"

Vraymorg smiled grimly. "Once an Isles man." *A weary Isles man.*

"That boy, Philip, looks like an Isles man too. It's unwise to bring him to the Mountains."

"What else can I do? I'm surprised no one mentioned the likeness to Cathmor."

"He'd just think your father didn't keep it in his pants. Let's hope this Izzy told no one else about your encounter."

Encounter. A cold word for the comfort he'd found.

Vraymorg listened to the steady thud of hooves, remembering warm sunlight streaming through an open window, the scent of a young woman's skin. He was miserable and lonely. Izzy, pretty and kind.

And her son? What was her son—oh gods, his son—like? Should he regret missing Philip's childhood? Dare he intrude on his life now? How would he answer his son's questions? For there would be questions.

Vraymorg dragged his tongue over dry lips, a twisting in his belly.

His son. What should he feel? No, no, no. A dizzying fear beat up. He pulled hard on the reins, slid from the horse, and staggered towards the trees.

"Val." Ewen came after him. "By Khir, Val, what is it?"

Vraymorg tugged a leaf from a branch. He twisted it in his fist.

"I can't do this," he muttered. "I can't. I'll never be what Kaell deserves, let alone this young man. I don't know how to be a father. At least, not a good one."

"I have two daughters, Val. You do it because they need you to."

Vraymorg violently shook his head. "What was I thinking inviting Philip to the Mountains? There can't be another young man to love and then mourn. Not again. I can't hurt like that anymore. I have to keep control."

Ewen touched his shoulder. "I understand. I do. You've raised so many young warriors only to see them fall in this malign fight to save Telor. But it's not all about loss. There's joy, too, Val. There's love."

Love. Vraymorg touched a corded scar on his wrist. Except he was cursed, broken in ways even he couldn't understand. How could Philip, how could Kaell want his love?

He had no right to pretend to be a father. How could anyone bear it? To look upon a son or daughter with that awful, writhing anguish. Silently swearing to keep them safe, immured from every hurt and danger.

Except no father could keep a child safe. No, not at all.

"Even beneath the joy, beneath those times when you laugh together, there's always fear," he whispered. "Because you know maybe not that day, maybe not the next, but one day you'll mourn that child. I can't do this. Love. Mourn. Not with Kaell, not with Philip."

"There are worse things than sorrow, Val."

Are there? He might have said.

They trod back to the horses. Vraymorg's skin was damp.

"It's safer if Philip is away from Dal-Kanu," Ewen said, always practical. "Less talk about you. Dangerous if the king thinks too much about who you are or are not."

A curious choice of words. Who he was or was not.

He knew who he wasn't. He wasn't Vraymorg. That was a mask worn by a cursed Isles warrior once known as Val Arques Caelan. A man who'd sobbed as he cut his wrists in a sunlit room.

Who he was? Even after 540 years he did not know the answer to that.

KAELL

His lord always put on a particular garment before he rode out to fight. It was black and padded like a quilt. Vraymorg wore it over a linen shirt but beneath leather armour. Iron and steel were expensive, mostly reserved for blades. It hurt Kaell's heart when his lord later gave him the only chain mail in the castle.

As a child, Kaell would sit upon his lord's bed and watch him dress for battle, a fluttering in his belly. He knew this ritual—shirt, gambeson, leather—would one day be his.

There was something in these quiet moments that Kaell didn't have a name for—then. He'd watch in awe, wondering if he'd ever be as powerful as this splendid man. Longing for the day when he grew old enough to take on the Varee or ghouls at Vraymorg's side.

He remembered the first time he watched his lord leave for battle, that odd feeling in his little, five-year-old body, that fear Vraymorg would not come back. Kaell stood in the ward with the servants, feeling very small and alone as his lord strode towards his horse and the group of mounted warriors.

"No." He wrapped his arms about his lord's leg.

"Oh, you don't want me to go, do you?" Vraymorg, often so stern, so aloof, looked amused.

"I won't let you."

"We'll see about that."

Vraymorg swung his leg in an enormous stride that lifted Kaell off the ground. It was so unexpected; he laughed.

His lord took another big step, then another. Kaell held on tightly. He was laughing in delight now, his fear gone. His lord was laughing too. Until at last he hoisted Kaell up, so high, and dropped him onto his horse's saddle.

"You can see me out the gate," he said.

Kaell could so clearly hear Vraymorg's voice from the past. It was a happy memory, a glimpse of what it could be like. Of that tenderness he longed for.

But there were other memories too. Especially here in this bedchamber where flickering candlelight drew the walls in close. Just as it did in that gloomy tower room where Vraymorg had always imprisoned him to punish disobedience.

Kaell was fourteen. Taller. Stronger. Rebellious. His lord had no patience with his adolescent tantrums. He remembered how he hugged his knees and rocked, impatient for that tap of Vraymorg's boots on the stairs. Listening for his heavy sigh as he paused at the door.

"Do you know why you're here, boy?"

Kaell scrambled to his feet. A bonded warrior did not cower. His lord taught him that.

"Because I kept the weapons master waiting."

His lord lifted a new candle in a tarnished iron holder to his face. "Yes. So where were you? If you lie, make me believe it."

"With the cook." He wanted out of that hateful room, away from its cold and its whispers. "I wrote a poem for her. Let me tell you how it goes."

"A lie. A poor one."

"In the stables. With Alyssa."

"The cook's niece? Doing what?"

"Nothing, my lord." Kaell looked at the ground. "Talking."

"Talking," his lord repeated softly.

Kaell's face burned. He had kissed Alyssa in the stables two days ago only for the girl to pull away. "You're like a brother, Kaell," she said, not unkindly. "And I love Will. My William."

"Alyssa is comely." His lord seemed younger as he smiled, his gaze hazy with unspoken memory. "But duty first, Kaell. Do you understand? Very well. You may go."

Head down, Kaell scuttled towards the door, letting out held a breath in a sigh.

"Wait."

Kaell stopped.

"Come here."

His feet dragged as he wandered back. "My lord?"

Vraymorg backhanded him. Humiliated, Kaell held his cheek. The blow was intended to shock, not hurt, but he hated what it represented. It meant he disappointed his lord.

"Another lie. Your shoulders fell as you walked away. Relief I believed you."

"No, I—"

"Kaell, do you think I want to punish you? It's only that I know what you must face. Listen. Never let your guard down until you're alone. Gods forbid your enemies ever capture you, then lies may be all that keep you alive. Do you understand?"

"Yes, my lord."

"So where were you?"

"Fighting with the blacksmith's sons, my lord."

Vraymorg gave him a measuring look, long and hard. "The truth, at last."

I never fooled him, Kaell thought, banishing the past where it belonged. *But somehow, I must fool the king and his guards.*

With a heavy sigh he stretched his throbbing leg. The physician had left poppy syrup by the bed to help him sleep, to drift through veiled nightmares Kaell knew too well.

"They're a gift." Vraymorg had reassured him one night when

he had crept shaking from his bed and found his lord drinking alone in the great hall. "Use them. Learn from them."

His lord's grim face had softened to a smile. He'd beckoned Kaell to join him by the fire, slung an arm about his shoulders, and held him until nearly dawn. Telling him stories about distant Quisnaf and Veniva and the rumoured lands beyond the Ice Sea.

FOOTSTEPS CLUNKED TO THE DOOR. Familiar voices argued with guards. Kaell grinned. About time. Anyone might think he had nothing better to do than just lie here.

"Let them in." He raised his voice. "You heard me."

The door inched open. A guard said, "No one enters without the king's permission."

"These are my captains. We must make plans for our campaign in the north."

"If the king hears, it's on your head." The man stepped aside to let two men through.

At the sight of Kaell, Olier gaped.

Arn flushed angrily. "What's this? Some fool manacled you to the bed."

Kaell shook his wrist so its chain rustled its merry tune. "My fault."

"But—"

He flashed a warning look.

Olier shut the door then crossed to the bed. "Why? I'd understand a gag to stop your out-of-tune singing hurting everyone's ears. But this?"

"So I don't wander. The king thinks I'll slit his throat while he sleeps."

His captains exchanged glances.

"Heard something about your night visit," Olier said. "The king's guardsman Merynn got duty on the castle walk. Just as it grows cold. Another enemy you made there, boy."

"And he doesn't even know me."

"Oh indeed, he'd love you if he knew you," Olier said. "All these soft lake dwellers would love you if sang to them or shared your silly poems."

"Flatlanders don't understand us." Back to them, Arn rested his palms on the windowsill.

"That town we're to help—" Kaell said.

"Thom," Olier said. "Some forsaken Downs hole."

"Is Thom near your home, Arn?" Kaell was curious about his friend's past.

Arn turned. "Not very. Though I've heard of it. Those villages along the Ridges are remote. The villagers more Cahirean than Telorian. They don't like outsiders."

"Charming," Olier said. "We're always sent to some dirt patch with unwelcoming, inbred villagers with two heads. Why can't the king send us to Tide's End? Women there love strangers. Real men for once, instead of those pretty Isles boys with their painted faces."

"No ghouls in the Isles." At this familiar banter, some of Kaell's tension seeped away.

"Got your message from that physician." Arn threw an irritated glance at Olier. The two captains bickered like siblings. "But we're not here to talk about our ghoul hunt, are we?"

"I'm sure you have the arrangements in hand."

"As always. Though you're hardly fit to ride."

"You won't have to tie me to my horse if that's what you're worried about."

"No need." Olier flapped a hand at the bed. "We've got chains now."

Arn grunted his disapproval at this nonsense. "Better spit it out, Kaell."

"Aric Caelan. The king plans to execute him."

Olier shrugged. "I don't care. Why should you?"

"Olier is right—for once." Arn's hard stare dwelled on Kaell. "I, for one, will gladly watch Aric's head roll."

Beneath his friend's scrutiny, the way it exposed his thoughts, Kaell looked away. "Aric doesn't deserve to die. Wouldn't you act as he did?"

Arn drew his brows together. "I'd ride fast for Dal-Kanu and seek the king's help to hunt down the ghouls who took the girl."

"And condemn her to a horrible death?"

"Just like this Isles snake condemned you to a horrible death?"

"But I'm not dead. So why execute Aric?"

"No, there's more to this. What's fermenting in that irritatingly restless mind of yours?"

Kaell dropped back on pillows with a sigh. "The king marched me down to the dungeons to watch his interrogator, some Cahirean called Blackstone, torture Aric."

They stared, shocked.

"Vile creature, Blackstone," Olier muttered.

"But that's still not it," Arn said quietly. "Is it, boy?"

Kaell dug teeth into his lip, uncertain how to explain the turmoil inside. "It's Azenor," he blurted. "She's dead. She must be. Because I'm alive."

"No, Kaell, no." Arn bunted the words away with his palm. "It's not your fault."

Kaell shut his eyes. With a twisted laugh, he said, "The ghoul, Lastenarron. He said I couldn't save anyone. So far, he's right. I have to try, at least, to save Aric."

"Who says you have to save everyone?" Arn said. "Where did that come from? No, you can't take the guilt of that girl's death on your shoulders. Her brother is a warrior. He rode into that ambush. This is his burden, not yours."

"She's dead. And I'm not," Kaell said. "Maybe it's stupid; maybe it won't make sense to anyone else. But if I help Aric—" He broke off with a helpless shrug.

Maybe this awful guilt might lift.

They exchanged looks. The night-time sounds of the castle

closed in. Footfall. An autumn wind whistling through stone passages. An owl's hoot.

"The king should exile Aric," Olier said at last. "Execute him, and the Isles will consider it a deliberate, hostile act. Lord Hatton will declare war."

Kaell snapped open his eyes. "Which is what Cathmor wants."

Arn glanced at the door. "Be careful."

"Cathmor wants the Isles." Kaell lowered his voice. "But he can't just attack Lord Hatton. Not every Telorian lord will support him. Not unless the Isles strikes first."

Arn crossed his arms. "Who cares about these flatlanders and their disputes? Our task is to kill ghouls. Besides, what would you have us do? Kill the king? Warn Lord Hatton? What?"

Kaell could not hold back a grin. "No."

"Spit it out, boy."

"Free Aric."

Olier gaped. "You're not jesting. That's why they chained you up—you lost your wits."

"I've had time to think how to do it, but I need your help."

"So now we come to it." Arn pressed his mouth into a harsh line. "No one chases trouble like you, Kaell. You swagger about the Downs tempting Caelmarsh to abduct you and string you up. Now you recklessly intend to snatch a man from the king's prisons."

"It's not reckless."

"Is that right? Free Aric, and Cathmor will know it's us. Then it won't just be Aric's head that rolls, yours will too. Then ours. After Blackstone spends a little time with us all."

"The king can't arrest us without evidence."

"You're not really that naïve are you, boy?"

Kaell shifted on the bed. "Cathmor will suspect me, yes. Especially as I asked him to free Aric. We'll have to prove it wasn't us."

"We didn't agree to help you yet."

"But you will. Olier, go to the watch tomorrow and seek

permission to leave Dal-Kanu. Tell them a blacksmith in Dal-Fast repaired a sword for you. It's brought you luck in battle, and you're eager to have it back. Take Smiler."

"Why him? Chatter, chatter. Mindless rubbish."

"He looks like you."

"No need to insult me, Kaell."

"Wait with horses in the woods. When we get Aric to you, take him to his uncle in Dal-Decma. Smiler rides for Dal-Fast. He pays the blacksmith for the sword and visits the taverns, loudly telling everyone he's the Vraymorg captain, Olier."

"So when the king sends men to check where I was—"

"The descriptions of Smiler will sound like you."

"Can we trust Smiler?" Arn said. "He serves under you, Olier. You know him best."

"He adores Kaell," Olier muttered miserably. "I could rip his every limb off, tell him it'll make Kaell happy, and he'll help me rip. Smiler will keep his mouth shut."

Kaell looked at Arn. "The king moved Aric to the Watcher's Tower. I need you with me."

"I'll play cards. Drink, pick a fight. It's the same every night. At the first punch, I'll stay down and slip away after they dump me on my bed to sleep it off."

"Risky."

"And you, Kaell? I trust you can remove that shackle. Can't count the times Vraymorg made you practise picking locks."

"Just leave me a knife or something, Arn."

"Putting manacles aside is one thing. Putting aside the king's suspicions another."

Kaell tapped his nose. "Quickness of hand, friend."

AINGEAR

The clearing closed in: the fire's stench of charred flesh, the hot rain, the silent ring of trees. Throat clenched, dizzy, Aingear swayed.

"Priestess?" A man poking a stick at ashes lifted his head.

She thrust a scented cloth to her nose. "I'm all right, Pairas. Is it true? Ghouls? Here?"

The man shrugged muscular shoulders. Even in this small movement he possessed feline grace. "They're dead, at least. Burned. The villagers did well to stop them."

"How did they breach the Isles? Roaran Caelan's magic protects us."

Pairas scuffed his boot to shake off ash. "Pitch forks and sticks against ghouls." He imitated a sword stroke in the air. "If only I'd been here—"

As he thrashed air, Aingear shook her head. Typical of a warrior to believe steel solved everything. In her youth, she'd known too many Isles men like him. Brave, strong, reckless.

Dead.

"You must stay here. The gods permit only their servants to enter this valley."

"Priestess, I can't let you go alone. I've heard tales of this place. It's dangerous."

"Dangerous for you if you follow. Wait."

She left him with the horses and walked into the forest. Its tangle of roots and boughs, its green canopy swallowed her at once, the breeze carrying scents of mud and the creamy nutmeg of dark-brown earth.

Like so much of the Isles, it was a lush wilderness of wildflowers, fat bushes dense with tiny, white blossoms, and trunks too thick to hug. Butterflies danced in secret sunlit groves where flame trees shed scarlet flowers.

In a narrow valley, the birdsong faded. The breeze stilled. A silent, eerie world sprawled before her, an ancient, hidden place caged by crouching mountains thickly pelted in forest.

Through dark-trunked trees, a burial tomb loomed. It was like others scattered across the Isles. Abandoned monoliths containing decaying shrouds and crumbling stone coffins.

At the sight of the slashed bushes at the tower's entrance, Aingear shuddered in dismay. Who dared cross this threshold? Who even knew of this place?

She rocked on her toes in the doorway, reluctant to enter this forbidding tomb.

Coward. A high priestess did not hesitate because of what she might find. With a quick, sharp breath, Aingear walked inside. A wall torch flared at her touch, casting pale light on ledges along the walls, empty of shrouds, and rough-cut stairs.

Her footsteps dragged as she climbed to the top chamber. A curtain of magic, invisible to others, shimmered. Aingear stepped forward, her neck prickling in anticipation.

For a moment nothing happened. Then with a wail, an avalanche of wind struck. It needled her skin, her scalp, whipped her gown up to her thighs as it swept her. Briefly it held her. Too briefly, its power fast fading.

Something was wrong. Roaran's magic was far stronger than that.

She stumbled to the bench. Brushed her palm over the shroud, a morbid, precious offering that had kept the Isles safe for eight centuries.

How had the seer king chosen this sacrifice? When Roaran Caelan cast this spell so long ago, did this man offer his life and body willingly, to lie for centuries as a voiceless sentinel?

And what of Roaran? Did he sacrifice a friend? Did he weep as he took up the knife?

Desperately she tore at the rotting cloth. She gasped, reeled, hands raised.

The corpse—defiled. The protective sigils tattooed on leathery skin burnt off. Fearfully she lifted her eyes to the walls. Every sigil, every one, defaced, the sacrifice useless.

Only ghouls would do this—destroy Roaran's magic.

Aingear's knees hit the floor, her will and strength drained. She wished she could beat her fists on the grimy stone floor, weep. But in her gut, in her breast, sat only flat, empty despair.

At last she rose from her knees, doused the torch, and staggered from the tower. Her sandals slipped often. More than once she fell. More than once she did not want to rise.

As she pushed through bushes, Pairas came forward in relief. Aingear let him help her onto her horse.

"Priestess." He frowned. "You look ill. What did you find?"

Aingear shivered. He had a right to know. If she did not restore Roaran's spells, ghouls would spill his blood—and that of too many young Isles men like him.

"Ghouls breached the tower." The reins nearly slipped through her trembling fingers. "Perhaps the ones the villagers killed. They defiled the offering."

"I don't understand. This place is hidden. How could they know? Sorcery?"

"Sorcery—or worse." For centuries, this tower had remained secret. Did someone tell?

Rain pattered, as hot as Aingear's skin. If only she could throw off her cape and wail at the sky.

"But the spells to protect the Isles can be recast. That girl, Ethne. I heard you say she's powerful."

"No one has magic to match Roaran Caelan's. And the seer king is long dead."

Pairas guided his horse cautiously along the overgrown path, one hand on the reins, the other close to his sword's hilt. Alert. Careful. Not quite the feckless captain she had judged him before this journey.

By reputation, he was intemperate with women, with ale. Though Aric trusted this man. He always said Pairas's dissolute ways shielded against a childhood hurt.

She sensed Pairas wished to confide something. More than once since they left Tide's End, he had blurted, "Priestess," only to shake his head.

"Is there something you wish to tell me?"

Pairas tensed, shoulders up. "I think I must tell someone about them. But not now."

Them? "I will listen if you confide in me."

They rode on. Beneath a cap of storm clouds, twilight's fugue of orange and peach frayed the darkness. Wild thyme spilling between grass released its scents.

"How did you know to come here?" Pairas said. "Even before the villagers sent word about the ghouls, you insisted upon going to that tower."

"A dream. The Three visit me often in my dreams."

Pairas slitted his eyes, knuckles white as he squeezed the reins.

Warriors trusted steel, not gods. But only the gods could save them now.

"I wish you dreamt of Aric," he said.

"I wish it as well." If only to reassure the king that his son lived. But she could not force a message from The Three. And on Aric's Caelan's fate, they remained silent.

As silent and elusive as Roaran's magic.

KAELL

"Such a mess." Brenin clicked his tongue to his teeth. "I heard bonded warriors heal fast, but the Isles traitor's sword chipped bone. Now you're stronger, I could dig around."

Kaell shook his head. "We leave in two days. I can't carry a wound."

"A pity. At least it heals cleanly." He shoved a cup at Kaell.

"More sleeping draughts? The king worries I'll roam in the night?"

"The king is concerned you rest and recover."

Kaell sighed and put the cup to his lips.

The physician gathered his lotions, cloths, and torturous instruments. "I'll return at midnight to make sure you're not in pain."

Kaell hid the full cup beneath the bed. The first moon streaked light through shutters. Not the best night to steal away lordly captives. But Aric died tomorrow. He had to act tonight.

CLOSE TO MIDNIGHT, cool air gusted as his door opened. Footsteps slapped over rugs. The physician bent to listen to his breaths. His steps retreated. The door clicked. A guard coughed.

Kaell slipped the knife under his pillow into his fingers and jiggled his hand free with the tip. Once dressed, he eased the window shutters open.

“Arn?”

“Here.” His captain peered down from the tower roof. A rope dropped. Kaell caught it.

“Lazy sod,” Arn said once he hauled Kaell up. “You just let me pull you. All this lying about made you slothful and heavy.”

“Weapons?”

Arn passed Kaell a double-edged blade.

He swished it back and forth. “The weight’s wrong. Not like Fortitude.”

“Oh, good idea.” Arn slung a sack over his shoulder and headed into the circular stairwell. “Let’s take Fortitude. And when the guardsmen describe their attacker’s distinctive Seithin blade to the king, he’ll never guess it was you.”

“What’s in the sack?”

“Rope. Cloth. Apparently you don’t want to kill anyone. Such a sook.”

“Did you get word to the Isles herald?”

“Delivered. The man told the king he rode for the Isles, but he’ll wait at Dal-Decma with Aric’s uncle.” Arn paused on the steps. “One thing, boy. Say little.”

Kaell grinned. With an exaggerated Mountains accent, he softly sang, “Sweet his voice, like love’s embrace, sweet his voice, but not his face.”

Arn shook his head. “Poets, singers. If I had my way, they’d execute them all.”

“Poets, singers, please our lords. But me, I’d put them to the sword.”

“You proved my point, Kaell.” Arn edged open the door. “That’s the Watcher’s Tower across the ward. Lots of guards. Distracted guards.”

“Distracted?”

His captain teased with twitched brows.

They stole along the tower base, darting beneath the walk as sentries tramped above their heads. Men of the watch hurried through the ward, grim-faced and shivering beneath cloaks.

A ruined palisade loomed ahead, waxen in moonlight, its rotted timbers once part of the wooden fort Caelan the Gormel Slayer replaced with this stone castle, the foundation of his new kingdom.

It was a place of shadows and guttering torchlight, eerily lovely. Vine entangled weathered stone. Weeds intruded through cracked slabs. Buttressed walls crumbled, and a carved gargoyle lay shattered amidst white alyssum and nut grass.

Opposite Caelan's first keep, the Watcher's Tower rose from a worn-down mound, its red, hewed blocks smooth and windowless until five storeys up.

Two guardsmen flanked the only door. The second moon blasted through streaked clouds. Sentries crossed on the wall walk, the dull beat of their steps aging the night too fast.

Crouched beside the first keep, Kaell tapped his foot against a loose cornerstone. What if the physician returned? The risk, already high, rose with every wasted minute.

Arn nudged him. The guards bent their heads close. One slipped inside.

Hood up, Kaell brazenly strode right up to the doors. The remaining guard levelled a blade. "Who's that? Stop."

He walked on.

The guard advanced. "Name yourself."

"Cael-Carren."

"Do you take me for a fool? Drop the hood. Show your face."

Arn stalked up from behind. He cracked his sword hilt against the guard's head. The man folded. Kaell snatched up the guard's spilled blade and helped Arn carry him into the tower.

"Extra sentry duty for this one, too," Arn said. "Soon the king will assign all his guards to the walls. But as Olier says, they'd love you if they knew you."

"Love me and my sweet voice."

Footsteps clattered on steps. The second guard returned. Kaell cut him off at the bottom of the stairwell, poked steel at his neck. "Still and silent."

The guard groped for his blade. Kaell punched him. "My apologies," he said as he caught the slumped figure.

"You're as soft and silly as a flatlander," Arn said once they had hidden the man with his companion. "If you insist on snatching Isles lords from prisons, someone will get hurt."

"And break my oath?" Kaell crept up the stairs. Torches lapped stone with a yellow glow. Crisp air nipped at their ankles. "Besides. This man did me no harm."

"No, the only one who harmed you is Aric. And we're risking our lives to free him."

"I thought you might understand," Kaell muttered. "If the king kills Aric because of me, that's another death on my conscience. How do I live with that, Arn?"

"Aric deserves to die. He poisoned you, Kaell. Not just with any poison. Night's Kiss."

"This is an old song. I thought you hated songs—"

Glass smashed above.

Arn threw up a warning hand. In a smoky, torchlit room off the stairwell, men rolled dice at a table. An empty wine flagon rocked on a stained, slabbed floor near broken glass. A guardsman snored in a corner, his shirt loose at the waist.

Kaell jerked his head at a second stairwell. Softly, they edged away.

"What was that?" A man slammed his cup down. "I heard something."

"A rat."

"You heard his lordship crying out for more," a third man said.

"You got it wrong. Men cry for mercy when the Pearl is in their bed."

They all laughed.

Kaell nudged Arn. "The Pearl?"

His captain smirked.

In an antechamber at the top, an oil lamp cast an eerie flicker about circular stone. Sword belts and blades lay upon a crude table, its scuffed legs uneven. Four men huddled near a wooden door, whistling and sniggering as they took turns to peer through the keyhole.

Hoods shadowing their faces, a cloth covering all but their eyes, Kaell circled from the right, Arn from the left. Both levelled their swords.

"Still and silent."

Guards spun. One sprang at Kaell. He slashed an arm. "That was stupid. Be still. Or die."

Arn shook his head at him, whispered, "Don't talk, fool."

"Who are you?" The wounded man clutched his bloody arm.

"On the floor."

Glaring, mouths thin with hate, the four men dropped to their knees.

"Flat. On your faces."

"You've made a big mistake," the injured man said. "We're king's guardsmen."

"You're poor guardsmen. Not worthy of serving any king." Kaell could not hold back a muffled retort. "No. Move and you're dead." He poked another man with steel.

Arn took cloth and rope from his sack to bind and gag the first man. He moved to the second, knee pressed to his backbone as he grabbed his wrists.

"You're the dead men," this one said. "The king will have your heads." Arn dug his knee harder into the guard's spine. "Shut your mouth, and you'll live to see our heads roll."

Kaell snatched bunched keys from the table and turned the lock to an inner chamber.

At the door's groan, a woman gasped. Candlelight glistened on moist, bare skin, on tangled sheets as two figures on a bed blinked in surprise.

Kaell's cheeks flamed. "Ah, my apologies."

The woman stared boldly. She was softly curved with heavy breasts and loosened brown hair that tumbled down her back in a thick, silky array.

Aric Caelan, completely naked, lifted his arm to shade his eyes. "Who are you?"

"A friend. Here to return you to the Isles."

"Did my father send you?"

"Dress quickly. We must go."

Kaell retreated, his face still flushed.

Arn grinned.

"You knew about this." Kaell drew his captain away from the bound guards.

"It's all over the barracks. Cathmor believes a man about to die should enjoy the pleasures of being a man before he does so."

"Who is she?"

"Word is for a man as highborn as Aric the king sent his mistress, a lovely lass called the Pearl of the Plains. In truth, the guards say her name is Jayne, and she's a sailor's daughter from the Bay of Wrecks. Well, is she beautiful? I didn't get the eyeful you did."

Kaell heaved an impatient sigh. "Yes, she's lovely. What do we do about her?"

"I suppose she heard your voice? Good gods, Kaell. I told you to say nothing. And there you were, blabbing away to the guards."

"The cloth muffled my voice."

Arn grimaced. "At least tell me the girl didn't see your face? Just lock her in."

Kaell strode back to rap on the doorframe. "We have little time."

Aric limped out, struggling to tie a woollen cloak about his broad shoulders. Cursing, he gave up and pressed his back to the wall, eyes shut, face gaunt with pain. Bruises on his cheeks shone as blue-black as his hair. Blood pooled on his crumpled tunic.

After what Kaell had just seen, Aric must take some blame for his reopened wounds. But he still could not banish the memory of that dismal prison, of Blackstone's groping hands, the whip tearing into flesh. Aric must be in pain.

"Can you walk?"

"I'll manage." Aric pushed off the wall. "Who are you?"

"Talk later." Kaell kept his face hidden. "What about the woman?"

"She asked me to hit her, so Cathmor doesn't punish her for not raising the alarm." His glance fell on the bound men. He muttered, "You've been busy," and staggered to the stairs.

Soldiers still rolled dice as they crept by. "Hear that? Something banging upstairs."

A snigger. "That's one word for it."

"No, no. Listen. A thumping. Like heels on floorboards."

Kaell helped Aric below. They circled the ward, keeping to the murk along the wall. The second moon swept high and full, spraying too much light.

A shadow bloated. Kaell turned fast, his neck prickling. No one. But he was almost certain someone trailed him. Who? Enemy or friend? And why?

A guard burst from the Watcher's Tower, shouting, "He's loose. The prisoner's loose."

Sentries clattered down stairs a sword's breadth from them. Kaell waited until they passed, then led the others to the Kanu Tower. But for the flicker of torches, a hush clung to its winding, empty stairwell, at odds with the alarm erupting in the ward.

The light revealed Aric's wan face, how his lips pinched at every laboured step. When they reached the roof, his breaths wheezed. A dark, wet patch soaked his tunic.

Arn caught Kaell's eye, mouthing "dead man" as he retrieved the rope.

"Please." Aric clutched the balustrade. The stain on his tunic spread by the minute. "Tell me who you are."

"Save your strength. You're bleeding badly."

"From places you don't want to know about." That mocking, amused glint stirred in his dark eyes. "Who are you? I must know."

Kaell glanced below. The ward enlivened with rushing men and bobbing torches. A long-cloaked figure barked orders. Men grouped, moved off. Soon they would wonder about him.

Turning to Aric, he dropped the hood and grinned.

The Isles prince whooped in surprise. "By The Three. You!" Then a shadow muddied his handsome face. "But I wished you dead. And that death was the most painful—"

"There's no time, Aric. See those trees? My captain has horses. He'll take you to your uncle at Dal-Decma."

"But—"

"No questions. Go. Just don't bleed out on the journey."

Aric looked down. "It's a long drop. My arm is useless."

"Then you must trust Arn's strength."

Aric offered both men a wavering smile as Arn roped his waist. "I can't think how to repay you. If ever I can do something—"

"There is something," Kaell said.

"Anything."

"The ghouls who ambushed you. It really was daylight?"

"Nearly dusk. Cloudy. They hid near the ford before Dal-Decma." Aric lifted his eyes to Kaell. "I keep thinking about that day. About what the ghouls said."

He paused. Dug fingers into a merlon. "This will sound stupid now, especially after what I did, but I think I got it wrong. They never used the word kill, you see."

"What?"

"The ghouls said to poison you. More than once they said poison but never kill. My wits were all over the place. I assumed they meant kill. But what if they didn't? What if they meant exactly what they said? Just poison."

Kaell shook his head, perplexed. "That makes no sense. They would want me dead."

"I hope there's nothing sinister in it." Aric swung his legs over the parapet.

Kaell touched his shoulder. "Will you tell me if you ever meet a dark-haired girl with a mark like a healed wound on her breast?"

A shadow flitted behind Aric's blink. He dropped his gaze. "I'll watch out."

That same look. What did it mean?

He and Arn lowered Aric to the ground. The Isles warrior untied the rope, raised his hand in a salute and stumbled into the trees.

"Now for you," Arn said. "Back to your room before the king feels your feverish brow."

"And back to the barracks for you. Do you want me to hit you so your story rings true?" Kaell playfully shook a fist.

"Your punches are like mosquito bites, boy. The only damage you ever do is to my ears when you sing. Now over the side. Don't forget to act like you're asleep."

"No deception needed." Kaell grasped the rope. "I'll drink the good physician's draught I pretended to before. When they come, not even the gods will wake me."

HEATH

When the last of his captains reported, Cathmor swept the candle from the table and lurched to his feet to prowl the chamber like an enraged beast. "No sign of him after Dal-Decma."

Heath stamped on the burning wick. "Aric will be in the Isles within days. Unless you're ready to raise an army and storm Tide's End, there's nothing you can do."

The king whirled. "Nothing I can do? I can execute Kaell in Aric's place. And anyone who helped him. What's his captain's name? The man with the scar."

"No idea." Heath lifted his shoulders. "How can you be certain Kaell did this?"

"He begged me to free Aric."

"Your physician swears Kaell drank a sleeping draught. We couldn't wake him."

Cathmor flung his hands up. "A trick. Or he ordered others to do it. The guards said their attackers spoke like Mountains brutes so it must be Kaell's men. Or—" The king poked a finger. "Unless it was you. Ice lords like to meddle. Where were you?"

"Drinking with you, Your Grace. Judith, too."

"That was earlier."

Heath barked an amused laugh. "Why should I wish to steal about draughty towers to free Isles princes? It all sounds very tiresome."

"I have no idea what runs through that twisted mind of yours, Damadar." Cathmor stared moodily at the fire. "No, you're right. It was Kaell. I know it."

"He was sunk in poppy dreams, a guard at his door."

"He climbed from the window. That's how he got into my chambers. I should have punished him then. A moment of weakness."

Heath poured more wine. "Another, Your Grace?"

Cathmor waved the cup away. "I have reason enough to arrest Kaell. Blackstone will force a confession from him."

"You would be within your rights, yes," Heath said. "But what of the villagers of Thom? Let the bonded warrior rid you of these ghouls first."

"And then what? Give him a bouquet and a kiss upon his return?"

"In Kaell's absence, seek evidence of his guilt. Or invent it. Arrest him the moment he rides through the gates. Threaten to execute him unless he bends his knee. I'm sure Blackstone will convince him if he's stubborn. Until then, be patient, Your Grace."

"Be patient? You tell me to be patient?" Cathmor returned hotly. "I'm the wretched king who patiently waited my entire life to win the Isles."

He paced. "My father couldn't take the Isles. He said if he couldn't I never would. I'll show him he was wrong about me. I'm every bit as strong a king as him."

The king stopped. He slid Heath a glance as if realising he'd said too much.

So that was what drove this man to conquest? Resentment against his dead father.

"You'll have the Isles," Heath said carefully. "Especially if I persuade my father to send fighting men to help you take Tide's

End. You'll have Aric Caelan in shackles, at your mercy. You can even have Kaell. In fetters or on his knees. Whatever pleases you."

Cathmor gritted his teeth. "Very well. If I must wait only a few weeks to see this insolent warrior from Vraymorg on his knees, then I'll be patient."

AINGEAR

The castle loomed severe and gaunt on the cliff, a ragged silhouette against a murky sky.

A low, fat moon silvered rocks below as grey-flecked waves foamed. Brine-scented mist rolled across the pebbled shore. Stillness brooded. The night belonged to gods and magic… and priestesses.

Yet a shape flitted on the breakwater. Aingear waved the lantern, annoyed at the intrusion. "Who's there?"

"Do I disturb you, priestess?"

"Pairas, is that you?"

"It is, priestess." Pairas jumped to the sand, his cloak billowing like wings. He wore a tunic and doublet, feet bare, his dark head uncovered, only a knife strung in his belt.

"May I accompany you to the Isle of the Gods? I must speak with you."

Aingear sighed. "If it's important."

Moonlight fell on Aingear's boatman Jordan as he stepped from the darkness, shaking an oar like an axe. "Who's this?"

"It's only Prince Aric's captain," Aingear said. "Is the boat ready?"

Jordan lowered the oar and gently took Aingear's arm to guide her to the boat. Their boots scuttled pebbles into blue-black waves nibbling the shore. Pairas trailed behind, silent.

Once upon the waves, passengers in the bow, Jordan fell to the oars. Pairas sat lost in thought, his face turned from the spray, hunched in his cloak.

A brooch wrought in silver—a present from Aric?—gleamed at his breast. Careless to let it tarnish in the salt. But not her business.

Aingear tilted her head to the bleak sky. Waves gurgled. The sea smelt fresh and new, the same perfume of that forest that hid the burial tower. She shivered at the memory of the defiled corpse. Roaran Caelan's centuries-old magic, destroyed.

Nothing now stopped ghouls with their sick appetite for blood breaching the Isles.

"Priestess." Pairas nervously broke the silence. "May I speak plainly?"

Her heart skipped. Face carved and curved by shadow, Pairas might be her dead lover. But Isles men all looked alike—at least lake dwellers of Dal-Kanu mockingly thought so.

"You may. Do not worry about Jordan. He knows all my secrets."

He nibbled his lip, hesitating. The boat slid on velvet water, ribboned by moonlight piercing the mist. Oars creaked. The Isle of the Gods hulked ahead like a dark, misshapen lump blistered on the horizon.

Pairas slumped on the bench. "I don't know how to start. I think I made a bad mistake."

"A mistake in a dress like the last one?"

"I deserve that."

He was no worse than his lord. But blame stuck more readily to lesser-born men.

"If you intend to tell me you seduced one of my priestesses, I can hardly admonish you after your lord's example."

Pairas sat straighter. "You know about Ethne? It's not serious."

Ethne thought she had snared a princely prize. But Aric upon occasion took lovers. Sometimes an enticing young woman, sometimes a charming man. The Isles celebrated beauty in both men and women and embraced sexuality with a hedonistic enthusiasm.

Aingear had no doubt Aric was fond of each of his paramours. But he loved only one man. Aiden Saltman. Always had. If Aric ever wed, it would be for nothing other than duty.

"No, priestess. I didn't seduce one of your women." Pairas's laugh self-mocked. "No, this is strange, hardly real."

"But there is a woman somewhere in this confession?"

Pairas snatched a breath. "A woman approached me in the Craven Beast tavern, whispered if I told her my name I'd win her a bet. Why wasn't I suspicious? I mean, she was beautiful."

"Now you tease me. Beautiful women surely seek you out."

At his silence, his hunched shoulders, Aingear frowned in surprise. This uncertainty—or regret—was new. Where was the irritably cocky Isles captain?

"She looked, she moved—even her scent was a noblewoman's." He trailed fingers through his wind-ruffled hair. "What did a woman like that want in such a den?"

"A taste of common life?" Aingear jested, unable to find threat lurking in his story.

"And her brother—" He fluttered his hands indecisively. "His lordly manner was that of a man always obeyed. Then there's her samite cloak, his jewelled knife. A peculiar brooch on his tunic he tried to hide. It was a sword and an oddly shaped rock."

Aingear clutched the boat's side. Stillness thickened as fog crept after the boat. Water lapped. Oars dipped, stroked. A gull soared by and disappeared towards the moon.

"Could it be"—she whispered at last—"a shard of ice?"

Another silence descended, taut with unease.

Pairas groaned. "I did not think of that. Curse it. It could be a shard of ice. It could."

Only an Ice lord or lady dared wear such an emblem. Aingear's throat constricted. “What did they want of you?” she croaked.

“Priestess, they drugged me. For information.”

“Go on.”

“The man made some clumsy excuse to leave me with his sister. I wanted him gone. She was lovely. I thought… the way she touched me, I thought…”

Again that uncertain fluster of hands. “She offered me more wine. I drank, felt sleepy. She took me somewhere. Then his voice pounded in my skull. If I tried to ignore him, it hurt. He”—a pause—“questioned me about Aric.”

“And you answered?”

Pairas flinched. “The Three help me, I think I did. It’s a blur. Like a nightmare, one where you can’t move or get away.”

A potion containing dream grass, perhaps?

“Priestess.” He gripped his thighs as he leaned. “I told them about the treaty, about Aric riding for Dal-Kanu. The man grew angry. I felt his knife at my throat. I could do nothing. Only wait for him to kill me. The woman stopped him.”

Aingear nodded thoughtfully. “If their purpose is secret—and why else should a Damadar Lord be in Tide’s End unannounced—then he was right to want to silence you.”

The boat rocked and yawed through headlands towards the shore. Tide sucked from sand. Jordan drew in the oars and jumped into shallow water to pull the craft in.

“I woke in a ditch outside the city,” Pairas said. “Maybe I was drunk. Imagined it all.”

Imagined a Damadar lord seeking information about Aric? That stank of plots and malice. “I think it was real enough. Now he’s safe in Tide’s End, you must tell Aric of this.”

“I’m reluctant to add to his troubles. What do they want with him?”

“Did you hear a name?”

His fingers strayed to his knife. “She called him Heath. He called her Judith.”

"Heath." Aingear clasped hands around the boatman's neck as he carried her ashore.

"A dangerous young man. A little too clever. He visited the Isles as a boy with his father and brother years ago. Judith. I know nothing of her. The elder girl is most frightening. Myranthe." She nodded. "Yes, Myranthe. She is steeped in their hateful beliefs."

"Sorcery?" Pairas circled his knife hilt with long fingers.

Aingear nodded. Dark, forbidden magic. Blood magic.

THE ISLAND THRUMMED with cicadas and beetles. Dragonflies whirred. Aingear slapped at a mosquito, squelching its moist body against her skin. A breeze stirred through the dark knot of trees before her, but the sea was quiet.

At her back, left together near the boat, neither Pairas nor Jordan spoke.

Aingear hoisted the lantern high, but the second moon already speckled the well-worn path to the caves. Late, then. Though the gods did not mark time like men and women.

Nor did their servants. And Aingear was a faithful servant. First a novice of just nine, then a journeywoman, then a priestess. A good life. A worthy life.

Men like Pairas recalled girlish dreams, long put aside, of a husband and children. But she did not regret her choices. Her life blazed with purpose.

Aingear passed a hand over her brow, her skin clammy. Then why, why, couldn't she shake off her nightmares of late? That last execution. That boy, just twenty. A child, deluded, led astray by others stupid enough to believe a dead king returned.

She had begged him to recant. He would not. A waste.

Despite his age, she could not show mercy. If this dangerous lie spread, if too many believed the dead Roaran Caelan was their true lord, the entire structure of rule collapsed.

They would refuse to pay taxes to the king, Hatton. Refuse to obey his laws, fight in his armies. The false king would strike, taking advantage of the absence of order and power.

She shook her head. All such nonsense. Roaran Caelan would no more rise from his nameless grave and save the Isles than the three moons plunge into the sea.

Scents mingled: dew on grass, salt and sea, spearmint crushed by her heels. Far away, dogs bayed at the turning tide. Only the gods knew how these beasts sensed shifting waters. As it should be. Power belonged to The Three.

Not dead kings.

INSIDE THE CAVE, that damp, dank chill of night and circling rock lashed. Nevertheless, she slipped off her cloak and knelt beside a pool. Her face, square and strong, stared back.

She was old enough to know a man like Pairas would look past her in a crowded room. Young enough to wish he wouldn't.

A sandalled foot scraped rock. Aingear lifted her head. *What was that?* Brine-scented air breathed with the thinnest thread of hyacinths. Then she heard a girl's sweet song quavering with strangeness from welling darkness, glimpsed a bobbing light.

A leather book clasped to her breast, Ethne tiptoed into the cavern.

Aingear drew back against the wall. With a vague suspicion this untrustworthy child was up to mischief, she held her breath.

Ethne broke off her song. She waved a torch about the chamber. Then with a satisfied nod, she lit a candle, placed it upon a rock beside the open book. Knelt to chant.

A binding spell. Aingear strained to hear. Or…

Her mouth tasted butyric with fear.

A summoning.

A chill eddied. Aingear thought shadows grouped, moulded

shapes, twitched, fell away.

Stop her. Stop this dangerous magic.

Except the intoxicating aroma of enchantment mesmerised her. She wanted to draw near, to see, to touch, to know the feeling of such power. If she was only bold enough to surrender to the allure of dark magic. If she was less afraid. Less dutiful.

Ethne's chant rose to a cry then fell away into the strangled silence. The girl drew a phial from her pocket, ripped out the cork, and dripped its contents onto the book.

Like a dreamer, Aingear watched. The heady magic held her. So tempting to embrace its potency, its possibilities. The control it offered.

The air thickened. Beyond the tiny pool of light, the darkness sat vast and empty, the rock walls close. Then from nothing, wind bellowed. Distant waves boiled over rocks as though a storm whipped in. Outside, gusts ground branches together like grating swords.

A shape formed, soundless, lifeless as an echo, a man's silhouette carved from shadows, a flicker on the periphery of her vision.

Someone, something, awakened. Dark and powerful and relentless. Aingear trembled with a chill not of the cave. Fascinated, horrified, she still could not move, only stare.

Ethne, too, stood transfixed. The wind died away. Beneath the candle flame's strum, impossibly loud, another sound echoed.

A drag of cloth against stone. A footstep.

Someone stood in the darkness.

"It's you," Ethne whispered. "Oh at last, at last. My lord, my king, reveal yourself again. Our enemies destroyed your magic. Save us. Save your beloved Isles."

The candle's flicker etched a single outline on the wall. A fragrance caressed Aingear with the warm scents of Isles summers. Her eyes clouded with memory. The cave dissipated.

She ran along the grainy shore, laughing, her bare feet covered with foam and seaweed left by the retreating tide. Her sister skipped at her side.

They both wore circlets of amaryllis in their unbound hair, the rims of their gowns wet, the sting of sand in their eyes. The wind carried sharp scents of spiced clove and pepperbush.

She reached for her sister, wanting to touch her hair. See her beloved face.

Glass smashed. The sound shattered the silence, shattered that memory of childhood.

Aingear was once more in the cave, aware Ethne was staring at her with guilty shock. Fragments from the broken phial littered the ground at the girl's feet. A dark liquid oozed.

Aingear snapped free of her stupor. This was dangerous magic. Even she felt its appeal, its seductive lure of power.

Stumbling to the makeshift altar, she bunted the candle and book aside. As they clattered to the floor, light again sieved the darkness. Shadows stilled. The air thinned.

Ethne clawed at her own gown. "No, no. You ruined everything."

That shadow. That fragrance. Summer. Childhood. Aingear groped at the wall.

"What was that? What did I see?"

"Then you saw him too?"

Aingear hesitated. She needed to know what happened here before she conceded anything. "I thought at first you tried to raise the dead. But that was a summoning spell. Who did you summon?"

The girl tilted her chin haughtily. "Do I answer to you?"

"I am high priestess. If not me, you arrogant child, then to whom?"

Ethne did not reply. Slumping to her knees, she scrabbled at the stained pieces of broken glass. "So close. So close."

"Give me those."

The girl sprang up, clutching the fragments to her chest.

Aingear tore a piece of glass from her, careless of how it cut her fingers. She sniffed. "Blood." With angry disbelief, she hurled the glass away. "Aric's blood, perhaps?"

No answer. Ethne's glance slid left and right.

"You wretched, wretched girl. Did you steal in while he slept? Thinking no one would notice one more scratch amid the other gashes left by the king's interrogators."

"I only took a little," the girl said, sullen. "Every sorceress knows how powerful Caelan blood is. The ichor of the gods."

"You had no right."

"You rode to the tower, saw the defiled sacrifice. We must restore Roaran's enchantments, Aingear. The gods showed me their chosen sacrifice. He's worthy, priestess."

That dreadful tower. "I searched my books to find Roaran's spell," Aingear said coldly. "Now I am here to ask the gods to choose a new sacrifice."

"I know who they desire, Aingear. *He* came to me in a dream. Told me how to prepare the boy. I offered the one he named to our gods when I tended to him in Dal-Kanu, though he does not know it. He has magic in his blood, the perfect sacrifice to The Three."

"You think the gods speak to you?" Aingear angrily stomped on broken glass. "You ignorant, conceited child. The gods will show *me* who they choose. I am high priestess. Leave. I have their work to do. I will settle with you about your reckless spell casting later."

Ethne left her.

THAT FRAGRANCE LINGERED. Aingear could not be rid of it. Nor her unease.

An unworldly, compelling presence had been in the cave. It bewitched her with memories of her childhood, of summer breezes dancing on waves. Her sister.

At last, my lord, my king. Reveal yourself.

My lord. My king. It was too clear. Ethne had tried to summon the dead Roaran Caelan to restore his broken enchantments.

Or… A shudder writhed down her backbone. No. No. Not that.

He came to me in a dream… My king, reveal yourself.

Aingear dragged her hands down her face. The girl's foolish words condemned her. That wasn't a spell to raise the dead. She summoned Roaran to this cave. Not thinking him dead, only hidden. Waiting to return.

She sagged, impossibly weary, her will frayed. How many must she kill? Cultists spread like sickness, challenging the gods and the rightful king, seeking answers from a dead seer. All a dangerous lie. Whatever, whoever she had glimpsed, it was not him.

Roaran slumbered in death. No one knew where or if he slept peacefully. Likely not. But he slept.

Aingear straightened her shoulders. The carnage in the tower stripped age-old defences protecting the Isles. First, seek answers from The Three. Then deal with Ethne.

The wind plunged to muttering. Waves gurgled around rocks. Aingear blanked her mind. She slowed her breaths until they rose and fell like water droplets into the pool.

"Saarn, Sartaen, Sauveroken," she whispered. "Hear your servant. I thank you for the life of my lord's son, Aric. Now I must ask for more. Name your new sacrifice. Reveal him. Tell me how I can serve you as those of the Isles have since the god-king Caelan first stood upon these shores."

Aingear peered into inky water. Her reflection dissolved into a forest. It was green and cool and damp, its scents of leafy earth, of raindrops shimmering on leaves.

Pink buds withered on branches. Autumn's pelt pooled in orange clumps at the base of trunks. The last, wilting blossoms spilled fragrance.

She swayed. Waves lapped a distant shore. But she fell away from the gurgling sea, away from the cave, crying out as she tumbled and tumbled. Until a forest surrounded her.

AINGEAR WEARS A STRANGER'S FACE. She rides through sun-speckled trees, flanked by men cloaked in black and grey. Her body aches from wounds an Isles prince inflicted, but her spirit rallies at the scent of battle.

A terrible blade slumbers at her side. Its hunger burns cold through the scabbard to her skin. No one else knows about its grim darkness—this is a secret between them.

When a man leans to whisper a story, she laughs, feeling that warm embrace of friendship. She belongs here, with this man, with the others.

In her companion's glinting helm, her green eyes framed by dark lashes stare back, unafraid.

She flicks strands of pale hair from her brow with a muscular arm. A sigil scars her skin. A half-moon. A sword. Other marks swirl up her arms towards her shoulders.

Then the sun slinks below the trees. The men, the horses disappear.

She runs through darkness, breathless, cold, alone.

Afraid.

Not of her pursuers, though she hears their taunts.

She is afraid because the forest no longer smells of damp, tumbled earth or fallen leaves.

It smells of blood. Of defeat.

AINGEAR BURST through iron-studded wooden doors. Respectful guards fell back.

"Where?" Her gaze flickered about the tower room. "Where?"

Aric lay on a pallet, a blanket screening his nakedness as the physician stitched his wounds. His father stood taut with anxiety at his younger son's bedside. A scowling Gendrick poked a stick in cold embers, detached. Ethne fidgeted at Aric's shoulder.

Aingear brushed past her king to Aric. The horse-faced physician rocked aside, his long jaw dropping. The odour of his lotions stung her throat.

Bandaged, bruised, broken, Aric's skin mottled purple, his sword arm in a sling. Candlelight contorted his gaunt face.

They had pulled him from his horse that morning, more dead than alive, his saddle slick with blood. "I didn't dare stop," his uncle had told the king. "Cathmor's men hunted us. But his wounds keep bleeding, may The Three help him."

Gods help him, indeed. If Tide's End fell, he'd hang—if Cathmor was generous. Burn in a traitor's fire if not.

Aingear looked away for a heartbeat to banish compassion. "Describe Khir's warrior."

"Well hello to you, too, priestess." Aric grinned wearily. "You clearly missed me."

She bunted air with her palm. "I have no time for polite words. The gods showed me something strange. Too strange. Tell me of this man."

"Kaell? Why?"

"Just answer. What does he look like?"

"Kaell is my equal in height and easily as broad."

That described half the warriors in Telor. Pairas. Aric's lover, Aiden Saltman.

Aingear hissed impatiently. "Obtuse prince. Describe him so I would know him."

Aric's gaze cut through her, questioning. "His hair is pale. A golden brown. Not washed-out straw like those brutes from Veniva. His eyes, green. Ask Ethne. She tended to him."

Tended. Oh, she knew too well how Ethne *tended* to Kaell.

Aingear cast the girl a hard look. Deluded child. History was clear: a Cahirean king murdered Roaran at Dal-Kanu. These rumours he lived did not start until many years after the seer's death. How could an intelligent woman like Ethne believe them?

Such treacherous lies. Cultists stirred discontent, even revolt.

A story recently reached Tide's End of merchants who ejected the king's tax collector from their town because they would only pay into the coffers of Roaran Caelan upon his return. In the eastern Isles, peasants armed with pitchforks burned their liege lord's house, declaring they knew no masters but the seer king.

His name had become a rally cry for malcontents. What if his followers sought to overthrow Hatton, to prepare the way for their dead master to return to power?

Yet for a moment, unlikely pity softened her outrage. Must she condemn Ethne to a cultist's death? The sorceress was young, like that boy Aingear had sacrificed. Foolish. Seduced by legends and lies.

An ancient voice stirred like a cold caress down her spine. Aingear stiffened her resolve.

Ethne meddled in magic she did not understand. Her meddling could cost Kaell his life, cost the Isles gods their prize.

"You struck him down. But what other bond ties you to this Kaell? What bond could tie him to the Isles? It is to do with you, I know it. Tell me."

Glances shifted. Feet scuffled. Hands fluttered. Gendrick tossed his stick into the ash.

The king tapped fingers against his belt. "The gods are good." He beat out the words. Gods are good, gods are good. A scream echoed silently in Aingear's head.

"Thanks to our gods, this boy returned Aric to us with little harm."

What did he call harm? His daughter—dead. The peace with Dal-Kanu—broken. Come spring, Cathmor's soldiers would pound Tide's End's proud walls.

"Do you mean he rescued Aric?" Aingear spread her hands. "That makes no sense."

Nor did it make sense for the Isles gods to show Kaell in her vision. A bonded warrior served Khir. He knew nothing of The

Three. She misunderstood. It must be another.

She said, "Kaell has scars?"

Aric laughed. "What warrior hasn't?"

"A bad warrior," Gendrick said without turning. "A dead warrior."

"Swirls, symbols on his chest, shoulders, and arms." Ethne avoided Aingear's eyes. "A half-crescent moon on his arm. Other marks carved by dagger or sword. Khir's wounds. I am told there is a ceremony—"

Aingear's knees buckled. Fragments of her vision snapped. A half-crescent moon. A forest. The scent of blood. Aric's words confirmed who she had glimpsed in her vision.

But it was too late. All too late. Kaell was lost to them.

Aric struggled to lift himself on the pillows. "Priestess, are you ill?"

"Old mother, what is it?" Ethne grasped her arm.

Aingear braced the bed. "You wretched girl. What have you done?"

At the vitriol in her tone, Ethne took a step back.

"Priestess?" Aric frowned. "What's going on?"

"This warrior from Vraymorg rides into an ambush. His gods have abandoned him—because of what this foolish girl did."

"Me?" Ethne spluttered in disbelief. "I saved him."

"You saved him with blood magic. Magic that broke his bond to Khir. There is only one reason why the gods showed me Kaell's fate. And that is impossible. Unthinkable."

Aric shook his head. "Priestess, I still don't understand. Why did the gods show you Kaell?"

"I asked them to show me who they chose as a sacrifice—to restore Roaran's protective spells. They showed me him. Him. A warrior bonded to other gods. That's why I say it's impossible. But even if it were not, this meddling sorceress has decided his fate."

Aingear drew herself tall. She stabbed a finger at Ethne. "Guards, arrest her. She is a cultist, a traitor to her true king. She must die."

ARIC

Pairas slouched at the foot of Aric's bed, long legs crossed at the ankles, his gaze brooding and distant.

If another man demanded punishment for falling prey to a woman's wiles, Aric might tease him about her eyes like deep, shadowed pools, her hair of silken midnight.

But Pairas? No.

His captain too quickly drew blame upon his shoulders. Aric knew the cause: a raving, drunken father who berated his young son daily as stupid and useless.

Pairas had fled to Tide's End as a thin child wearing rags, eyes hollowed by misery, unable to take the beatings any longer. He had found some sense of self as a soldier, but Aric recognised the fragile spirit beneath that rigid, patterned shield of duty.

"The Quisnaf trained Judith Damadar as a seductress. She's a weapon, not a woman," he said. "Of course you liked her."

Pairas shifted irritably. "I didn't say I liked her. Just when we talked, something stirred—"

Aric wriggled his brows. "Stirred."

His captain forced a half-hearted grin and lumbered to his feet. "What do the Damadars want with you, Aric? Your cursed blood? I heard a few drops brew up nicely in a potion."

Aric shrugged. He had other concerns. Cathmor, for one, intent on spilling *every* drop of his blood. All that morning, the king's messenger had argued with his father and uncle behind closed doors. Threatening, cajoling, bargaining.

"Why should it be my blood for brewing? Maybe Judith Damadar heard I'm charming. She hopes to, ah, stir me, the way she stirred you."

"Ha, ha. Throw on a funny hat, and you can entertain us all as a jester."

Grief lumped in Aric's belly. Azenor had teased him about his jests before the ambush.

Ambush. He'd led his sister to her death. He, the commander of Tide's End, tournament champion of Telor, could not save her or his men.

Now he couldn't save Kaell.

When ghouls seized him and Azenor, he was helpless, his skill as a bladesman worthless. Imprisoned by the king, helpless again. He was free only because of a stranger's kind heart and courage. A stranger about to ride into an ambush.

"Stirring or not," Pairas muttered. "Judith comes with an appendage—her brother. He's the one asking questions about you."

"The appendage is a fire dancer. Not beaten in the arena since he was sixteen."

One summer he and Heath had become unlikely friends while their elders hammered out a marriage contract between Gendrick and Heath's eldest sister, Deborah. It came to nothing.

Deborah died—suspiciously.

But what Aric remembered most of that summer was Heath's sarcastic wit. He liked him. He hoped fate didn't demand he kill Heath Damadar… one day.

"A what?"

"Fire dancer. A fire dance is a ritualistic fight in an abyss of flames. The defeated warrior's death is an offering to those cruel Icelands gods."

Pairas looked astonished. “How do you know this?”

Aric grinned. “How do we learn anything in Tide’s End? The rumour cesspool of the world. Isn’t that what they call this city in Dal-Kanu? You hear everything here: the Venivans plot about their princes, the Wardorians boast of war and plunder. And Icemen whisper in awe about Heath Damadar, beloved of the gods.”

“The gods do not love him near as much as he loves himself.” Pairas rocked to his feet. “I know what you’re thinking, Aric. But it’s too late. That boy from Vraymorg is already dead. You’d never reach Thom to warn him. You can’t hold the reins, let alone a sword.”

Aric squeezed his eyes shut. He imagined the scene the high priestess described: the knot of men, their desperate shouts, the clanging steel, the iron taste of blood, and pungent fear as wave after wave of ghouls fell upon them like beasts.

He pictured the ravens circling, foxes slinking from the trees to sniff at the stench of death. Sweat wet his armpits. It was all a terrible echo of Dal-Gorma.

“Kaell is alone,” Aingear had told him when he begged to know the reason for her questions. “Badly wounded, tracked by his enemies. They will have him.”

Aric shifted his sling. Before he lifted a sword again, Kaell would be dead. Helplessness, as heavy as armour after a battle, bowed his shoulders.

“I owe Kaell my life.”

“He’s a warrior bonded to Khir,” Pairas said. “He’ll die young. You know this. You’re the one who reads old stories in your creepy tower.”

“It’s called a library, Pairas.”

“Whatever. It still creeps. So you tell me, Aric. How long do bonded warriors live?”

As long as the gods willed. And who was he to defy gods that weren’t his? Gods—according to the high priestess—who had now abandoned Kaell.

THE SADDLE CRASHED to the ground. Aric fell after it. He struggled to his hands and knees to crawl. Blood from ripped wounds dripped on dirty straw stinking of horseflesh and manure.

He slapped a palm into the ground, furious at his weakness.

The Three help him. He must at least save Kaell, *must*. His fault, all of it.

"Do you know what you've done?" he shouted at Ethne in his dreams. "He rides into an ambush; he dies because his gods turned from him. Your magic did that. The magic you used to save me. I would rather die than carry this guilt."

He glimpsed Kaell, arms bound. But when Aric stretched a hand to help, the dream always slipped away.

Dust motes danced in sunlight through the stable door. The early morning light dazed. He clambered to his knees, his fingers clamped to his sticky belly. The world tilted, blurred into nonsensical images, snatches of memory. Aric slumped into emptiness.

When his wits returned, his cheek lay in straw. A face faded in and out. "I've found him." Hands lifted and carried him. Darkness rushed him, tossed and tumbled him like a stormy sea, and he fell into it with a sigh.

"MY SON IS MAD. His wounds, the torture, made him so."

Through a fog of sleep, Aric recognised his father's voice. Reluctantly, he stirred. Sunlight warmed his face. Damp cloth cooled his brow. The scent of sea and old parchment swirled, tantalisingly familiar.

Where was he? Not the stables. Nor his bedchamber, though he lay on a feather mattress. Stone walls circled. Leather-bound books cluttered shelves, and a tangy breeze through a low window rippled papers scattered on a table.

The Sea Tower. Why was he here?

His father leaned from a bedside stool. "How do you feel?"

Aric thought about that. "I don't know. A little strange."

"You lost more blood. The physician tended to you day and night. I thank The Three you live." His father's lined face clouded with pain. "I could not lose another child—could not."

Aric looked away, unable to bear this man's grief. *Do you blame me? Do you hate me? I didn't save her. Couldn't.*

Sorrow and guilt warred in his gut. *No, do not think of Azenor.*

He coughed. "How long—"

"You slept two days."

"Why am I in the Sea Tower? Not my chamber?"

"I ordered a bed moved here. This room has a heavy door and lock."

"You've locked me in? How dare you."

His father shot to his feet. "I dare because you're a reckless fool. You were in the stables. Muttering in your delirium about riding to warn that boy."

Aric rose to his elbows. "Is there any word? Of Kaell?"

"Nothing."

"Father, let me find him. Warn him."

Hatton did not reply, only went to the door to issue a command. When a servant returned with a tray, he sat in silence as Aric ate. More than once his gaze fell upon his son then darted away.

Aric put down his spoon. "What? What won't you say?"

Shoulders hunched, his father still didn't speak. The castle bristled with sounds, voices, thuds, footfall. Like a menacing undertone, the broiling ocean surged against the tower walls.

Aric sighed, understanding. "The king demands you surrender me. You should do it."

"You are my son."

"I am also guilty."

"No." Hatton rose, went to the window, and flung the shutters wider. Wind flickered his greying hair about his face. He looked weary. Pity tugged at Aric.

I couldn't save her, Father. I'm sorry. Gods, I'd willingly give my life for hers.

"Father—"

"No." Hatton gazed at the waves or perhaps a ship entering the bay. The sea lanes about Tide's End thickened with vessels at this time of year. "I won't offer you up to appease this vicious man's anger. If Cathmor wants war, then so be it."

"Father."

This time Hatton turned.

Aric snatched a heavy breath. He tried again. "Let me go. I must warn him. Kaell. He risked punishment or even execution to free me. Now he rides towards certain death."

His father's expression softened. "There is nothing you can do. I sent a messenger, but the river is up at Dal-Gorma."

"I must try. I failed to save my men, my sister. Let me at least try to save him."

"Enough." Hatton tapped his fingers on the wall. "That boy's fate lies with his gods."

"Kaell rides into an ambush because those gods turned from him," Aric said. "Because of Ethne. She only healed Kaell with blood magic in the hope Cathmor wouldn't execute me if Kaell survived. This is a matter of honour. If you stop me, you shame me."

"Honour is an empty word, Aric. You're ill. You won't get to the mountains in time to warn him. You'd risk your life for nothing." Still his fingers tapped. The beat jarred in Aric's temples. Tap. Tap. Tap. *Stop it,* he wanted to shout. *Just stop it.*

"I can't just let him die."

His father turned, advanced. He gripped Aric's arm. "Swear you won't leave Tide's End. Vow you won't go after this boy who may already be dead."

"I cannot."

Long seconds passed in silence. Hatton drew his hand away. "Then you will remain here, a guard at your door, until you see sense."

Aric's shoulders stiffened in disbelief. "So I am a prisoner. You can't do that."

The king's gaze held no sympathy. "I can, and I will."

"I was ready to die in Dal-Kanu," Aric said coldly. "I wronged not only Kaell but the men who rode with me. Cass—" His voice shattered.

Azenor. Dead, because he did not save her. Where was her accusing ghost? Where were the ghosts of those he didn't protect? He deserved their curses.

"I led my men into an ambush. I was ready to pay for that, to put my head on the block for Cathmor's executioner. Let me go. Helping this man will ease my guilt."

"No. You'll stay here until you see sense or—" His father shook his head.

"Or?"

Shoulders bowed, Hatton walked to the door. He paused.

For a moment Aric thought his father would turn and explain what he meant.

He did not. He walked out.

HEATH

"We are but dutiful flies in fate's knotted web." Heath flicked his hand dramatically to an unseen audience. The gods, perhaps? Theatrical nonsense but only nonsense rattled about in his wine-soaked head.

Beside him on the castle walk, Judith hunched in her cloak. A miserable wind lashed banners bright with the Lord of Vraymorg's insignia. Armed riders knitted through iron gates towards the frost-wet road to the lake.

Black clouds wreathed an ashen sky, dampening the dawn's birdsong. Beneath the prick of rain, the air smelt of damp and cold.

His sister twisted her hair into a knot, a sure sign of irritation.

"Who's the spider in your metaphorical web, Heath?" she said. "Kaell? Because he executed your oh-so-careful plan? How funny. Kaell snatches Aric before you snatch Aric."

"A spider indeed." Heath sighed to the heavens. The gods understood, surely, even if Judith did not. Life proved—bizarre. It entangled into confusion then unravelled into disarray. Ah, how poetic his drunken nonsense.

"Your tangled webs and your tangled words belong in a cesspool. You're still drunk from last night. More wine than blood in your veins and this comes out of your mouth. Webs. Spiders. I've had enough of it."

Heath hiccupped. "I am drunk. What else is there to do?"

"I should push you off this wall, but you're so full of wine you'd only float," Judith muttered. "Once again, Aric Caelan is beyond our grasp. For we are here in Dal-Kanu," she gestured. "And Aric is safely in Tide's End."

"Safely. An interesting word—"

Judith flicked hair from her brow with a frown. "You think Cathmor will tear down the walls of Tide's End just to take Aric Caelan and hang him?"

"Come summer, Cathmor will tear down every wall between here and the sea to get at Aric. Oh, he wants Kaell in chains, too, but that's a pleasure he'll delay until that young hunter slays a few more ghouls. The greater good of the realm and all that."

Again Heath elegantly fluttered a breezy hand.

"Stop waving your hands about. You'll knock yourself out. So the king believes Kaell freed Aric?"

Heath glanced down at riders milling in the ward. Kaell sat tall in the saddle as if pretending his wounds did not trouble him. "I saw him do it, Judith. I hid in the shadows near that tower. I had a plan. Cursed boy had a plan, too."

"Why not just take Aric from Kaell?"

"That spider had a bigger spider with him." Who started this spider nonsense? Oh, that's right. He did, with his blathering about webs. Served him right, then.

"I got this close to them in the ward." He held out his palms. "I considered knocking Kaell out and grabbing Aric. But the fool boy turned around. I needed two of you, Judith. One Judith to distract the king. One to distract the spiders. Clear the way for little old me."

"I hate you when you're sarcastic."

Heath smiled coldly. "I hate me when I lose." Probably why he drank so much. "Kaell and that man Arn moved quickly. Their plan echoed mine though I intended to be quieter and sneakier. Kaell proves very interesting, don't you think? Why risk Cathmor's wrath to save a man who tried to kill him?"

Judith fell silent. At length, she said, "He went to the crypt again before joining his men."

"Kaell? Maybe bonded warriors talk to the dead."

"Maybe you should go talk to the dead. When you're drunk at least."

"I'm worried they might answer back."

She pressed her palms into the stone balustrade, her gaze determinedly on the men in the ward as if to ignore his nonsense. "You told Cathmor we'd send soldiers to help take Tide's End."

He shrugged. "I made that up on the spot to appease him."

"But what if we do? What if we side with the king and snatch Aric when Tide's End falls?"

Heath gripped the wall. What was that expression? Out of the mouths of babes—and sisters. If Cathmor marched on Tide's End, every great lord would take sides. The king's side, of course. The side of justice and all that.

Ah, Heath. I hate me when I'm sarcastic too.

He grasped Judith's hand. "We have no time to spare."

"Where are you taking me?"

"Home. Before winter cuts off the Icelands."

Judith halted on the stairs. "We can't go home. Myranthe said—"

"I know what Myranthe said. She doesn't scare me."

"She scares everyone. She scares me."

"I'm too drunk for Myranthe to scare me. Anyway, thanks to you I have a plan."

"You always have a plan," she grumbled, dragging her feet as she followed. "She'll still turn you into a toad."

He flashed a lopsided smile. "I'd make a charming toad, don't you think? Princesses will line up to kiss me."

KAELL

Guards in the towers muttered about the "goat wind." It blew in from the Mountains at dawn, its gusts driving cold rain and offering an excuse to mock the riders grouped inside the gate.

"We don't want your foul wind here, goats," soldiers jeered from the wall. A sentry leaning from the battlements crudely gestured.

"Want me to do that to you?" Smiler groped for his sword.

Kaell shook his head as he limped to his horse. The youngest Mountains warrior easily rose to provocation.

"Tired of screwing goats?" a guard called. "A pox on—" A soldier clouted his ears and pointed at Kaell. The sentries backed off. When Kaell looked up, none met his eyes.

"No discipline in Dal-Kanu," Arn said.

Kaell shrugged and adjusted his bridle with stiff fingers. He wore moulded leather over mail, a shirt beneath, but still the wind, whatever its origin, blistered with autumn's damp, miserable bitterness.

Riders huddled in grey and black capes cursed the gods for a likely dismal journey. Olier twisted him a grin, others nodded or greeted him. But some looked away.

Unease curdled in his gut. Did his loss to Aric diminish him in their eyes? Did they doubt him? Did his lord also doubt him? Was that why he rushed to Kaell's bedside?

Kaell slapped on gloves, resolute. This hunt was a chance to prove to Vraymorg that even without visions he could serve his gods. He must not disappoint his lord again.

At an odd creep at his neck, Kaell glanced up at the wall. Movement blurred. Streaming brown hair, a woman's whirling skirts. A man laughed. Boots clattered on stairs.

A hand pecked at his sleeve. Kaell turned. The king's brother stood at his shoulder. A thin smile slitted grape-red lips beneath his beard.

"Cael-Carren?"

"I bring the king's wishes for success. Good speed. Good hunting." Cael-Carren nodded curtly. He turned and strode off. Disappeared as though never really there.

Kaell stood for a spell. Then laughed. A kinder farewell than he deserved. Generous, too, for Cathmor to send archers.

They clumped apart, rubbing gloved hands, hats pulled low, expressions sour, their billowing dark-blue capes blooming among the Mountains men's grey weeds.

Kaell always thought dark blue a curious choice for king's men. Once only Serravan knights wore that colour, knights who long ago fought for Ryol Caelan when Cathmor's ancestor Devarsi seized his throne.

"My weapons masters taught me the Serravan way." Aric's words snapped in his head.

Irritated, Kaell thrust the Isles man away. Bad enough Aric forced his way into his dreams. The familiar nightmare had struck near dawn with an assassin's fury—the door, the raven-haired girl. And Aric, grinning as he hewed with steel.

Curse him. Would he, too, haunt Kaell?

My weapons masters taught me the Serravan way.

Which meant what? Kaell's books hinted at secret rites

Serravan warriors undertook beyond the Enarae, the veil-shadowing otherworld. Yet Aric's style of swordplay held few surprises. Only the Isles man's intentions deceived.

He swung into the saddle. Stifled a groan. Khir take Aric for this wound. Battle fever would mask the pain. When it washed away, he'd hurt.

Still, only one ghoul nest to destroy. A hunt to regain his companions' trust, to prove his worth to his lord. Then home to the Mountains and whatever nastiness the priests intended to "fix" him.

Again, all because of Aric. Kaell really must thank him sometime.

Arn edged his horse close. "I rebuked young Smiler about his outburst."

"The boy reminds me of a younger me."

"Boy? Look who's talking? Old-man Kaell. You flare up all right. But you were never that stupid." Arn watched the portcullis lift. "Where were you?"

"The tombs."

Arn glowered. "Let it go, Kaell. Let her go. She's been dead three years now. Can't imagine how you limped down to the crypt with that leg. How's the wound?"

"It aches." Everything ached, even his head—thanks to that cursed dream stealing sleep.

"Surely the king could wait until you were stronger."

"It's as well we're away. Cathmor's temper smoulders over Aric's escape. He's no fool. He knows it was us but can't prove it."

"Give him time," Arn said. "Wonder what you'll look like without a head?"

HOOVES CLATTERED ON COBBLES. Dawn fell soft as silk upon alleys, temples, and homes worn with age. The stench from the king's head house pawed, but beneath Dal-Kanu breathed with fragrant spices from its markets and storehouses. *Exotic*, Kaell thought. *Exciting.*

The slumbering city slowly woke inside its grimy walls.

Grumbling traders, carts piled high, reluctantly parted for the riders. A cowled priest stopped to gape. A wiry drunk stumbled from horses. A girl carrying a basket of apples blew Kaell a kiss and earned a distant smile.

"Poor lass doesn't know she's competing with a dead girl," Arn muttered as the walls fell behind and the road wound through cropped, soil-scented fields towards the lake. A rising wind banked grey clouds.

"Hmm?" Kaell rubbed an itchy shoulder beneath his shirt, wondering if he should send outriders ahead. No danger yet, but perhaps in the Downs.

"Remember the king's feast welcoming us to Dal-Kanu? Beautiful women smiled at you, watched you, hoped you'd seduce them."

"I don't remember." Kaell had fallen into talk with a Falls warrior about an odd counterweight siege weapon the King of Wardour used against a traitor lord.

Arn heaved an exaggerated sigh. "Very sad, my young friend. How about Judith Damadar? Word is she's a Quisnaf-trained seductress. Mind you." He scratched his bristling chin, thoughtful. "They say the king's betrothed Azenor is almost as striking."

"The king's betrothed is dead," Kaell growled. Guilt battered him. With Aric safe, he hoped it might lift. But still it palled, gloomy, heavy like a snow-draped winter.

"Prickly," Arn muttered. "Didn't sleep then?"

They rode in silence until the lake rippled inky at their backs.

Fields fell to forest. Leaves dripped with rain; trees shivered, bent, soughed, swept green-jacketed branches low. Banners snapped. Cold, damp scents of autumn swirled. To Kaell these soft lands wafted of life. Unlike the Mountains where autumn smelt dead. Empty.

"No woman is as striking as the queen who visited Vraymorg when I was a child," he offered as amends for his bluntness.

"Oh?"

Did Arn stiffen? Strange.

"Rozenn of Cahir. I was about nine. She and her soldiers found me on the road. Or I found them. I can't quite remember."

"The Queen of Cahir was at the castle for Cathmor's wedding. You didn't see her? She is exquisite. But as dangerous as a snake. You'd think *he* had more sense. Though it shows he's not always so cold."

Kaell turned to stare. "He?"

"Ah, something you don't know." Arn's grin was more a leer. "Maybe I won't tell you unless you promise no singing for the next two days."

"Or I sing loudly and out of tune to torture you into speaking."

"Ah, a brute hides behind that young face."

"A singing brute. Queen Rozenn?"

Arn clicked his tongue against his teeth. "I suppose it's hardly gossip soldiers or servants would tell a child."

"Gossip about what?"

"About that visit from the Queen of Cahir and where exactly she spent the night."

"No, don't tell me." Kaell thrust a gloved hand over his ear. He spurred his horse forward. Rozenn was as perfect as the girl he dreamed of. A lovely vision, untouchable.

Arn bellowed laughter. His captain still laughed when Kaell fell back. "Tell me."

"Promise you won't turn it into a rhyme?"

Kaell touched hand to breast. "Promise."

"She bedded our noble lord. Or he bedded her. Not for the last time, either. Rumour is they meet sometimes in the forest. A stranger delivers a single rose—Vraymorg disappears."

"What?"

"Vraymorg. Our lord and master is flesh and blood after all."

Kaell wriggled, uncomfortable at such talk about his lord behind his back.

Vraymorg was a force in the Mountains, hard, resolute but not unkind. He raised Kaell to survive, and if that meant a firm hand, then so what? Kaell had no right to expect more.

But he did want more. More of his lord's attention, praise, his lord's time. Just more.

Love?

If only that fear beneath his lord's anger at Dal-Kanu meant he cared. Maybe Vraymorg couldn't love him because Kaell disappointed him. Because he feared he raised a damaged, flawed boy.

He must show his lord he wasn't.

"What did you make of our young Ice lord?" Arn asked.

"Heath Damadar?" Kaell welcomed distracting talk. "I wish I'd seen him. Everyone says they rarely leave the Icelands. The Damadars, that is."

"A good thing that. On top of their wealth and power, they're enchanters."

Kaell laughed. "You make them sound frightening."

"The eldest girl is. Myranthe. Some say her magic rivals Roaran Caelan's, though it comes from a darker source."

Kaell shivered. He glanced over his shoulder.

Arn laughed. "She's not here, Kaell. Myranthe doesn't leave her den."

"So you say. But what do you know? Did you see him, Arn? Heath Damadar?"

His captain chewed his lip. "I saw him in the hall when they arrested Aric. Didn't speak to him. Not for the likes of me to rub shoulders with wealthy, young Ice lords. But I swear a chill clung to that castle."

"That's poetic." Kaell grinned. "Thought you hated poetry. But don't discard your sword yet for a life of song, Arn. Poets are unappreciated."

"I appreciate you—when you're quiet. As I began to say, Heath's not only a fire dancer but an enforcer, a warrior who serves his father then his brother with his blade."

"An odd word, that. Enforcer."

Arn clapped Kaell's shoulder. "Make up a poem about that, boy. Go on. I dare you to find a word that rhymes with enforcer."

Kaell thought for a moment then shook his head. "No, I'm stumped."

"First time for everything. From now on, all poems must have the word enforcer in them. Ha, that'll shut you up."

THEY PITCHED TENTS among the broken stones of Martenhold. Wind gnawed and whistled through crumbled, moss-stained towers. The starless sky blanketed with blackness.

Legend said the first Lord Marten haunted the ancient castle shell, but Kaell slept deeply, undisturbed by ghosts, until rain pattered at dawn.

The rain drizzled all that day and the next as sloping hills crested to mountains. The trails narrowed, forests thinned, and tall weeds bobbed and bowed in a stiffened wind. Making camp that night in a hollow, an archer wondered at buzzing flies and found a corpse.

"Not long dead." Olier poked the man's body with a stick, cursing at the gashed neck.

Kaell ordered stakes surround the perimeter that night and set extra sentries.

The rain departed the next day, but as they wound into the mountains, a biting wind brawled with trees and grass and men—a goat wind, Olier declared, chuckling.

At dusk, they forded the Great Digger at Dal-Cross. The village rimmed the gorge with flickering torchlight. It was stone walled, gated, ringed by orchards and farms.

Kaell reined in his horse to stare across the ravine. Fading light silhouetted Vraymorg's distant and forbidding towers against stark, hulked mountains.

Loneliness cut though him like the wind. The fortress was the only home he knew.

"I miss it too." Arn appeared at his elbow. "Though if I were you, I'd be reluctant to return given Vraymorg intends to summon Khir's priests again."

Kaell hunched his stiff shoulders. More mysterious rites. More knives, pain. Unfair. Not his fault the witch cast whatever spells over him.

And again, all thanks to Aric.

He recalled an old Mountains' expression: if a man or woman sorely wounded you in this life, the gods bound you to them in the next.

What would Aric make of that? Fortunate, perhaps, their paths would not cross again.

AT DAYBREAK, the windswept mountain passes surrendered to a forested plateau. Grassland and cloudless sky curved to the horizon, the sun impotent against a dry, chill squall that ruffled cloaks, lifted gooseflesh on bare skin.

Wilted saplings clawed the banks of an ice-blue crater lake, the scent of its dank weed pricking his nostrils. An empty, remote land. When a migrating bird screeched, Kaell jumped.

"Gods," he said, when Arn laughed. "I'm as nervous as a cat in a yard full of dogs."

"Turn that into a rhyme if you can, poet boy."

"The dog barked, and the fool cried: I'm as nervous as that cat I spied. Hmm. Not so good."

"The ban on singing remains, though," Arn said.

A rider ahead shouted. Kaell shadowed his eyes with his hand.

A man rode hard at them. At Olier's challenge, he slowed.

Kaell urged his horse forward. "Name yourself and your business."

The blunt-faced, brown-haired stranger glared from beneath bushy eyebrows. A knife poked from his muddy breeches below a long-sleeved, woollen tunic.

"I seek Khir's bonded warrior." The rider clipped Telorian words like a Cahirean.

"I asked who you are."

The man passed brown eyes over him scornfully. "I am Rendell of Thom. I seek the Battle God's bonded warrior."

"You found him."

"Do you mock me? I seek a *man*. A warrior. You're a boy."

"Friend." Arn joined Kaell, his tone disarming. "Hunters are always young because—" He broke off.

Rendell scowled, as if still suspecting a senseless joke.

"You're from Thom?" Kaell said. "The king sent us after a plea from two villagers."

"Jocelyn and Lynden." Rendell tore fingers through his untidy, mopped hair. "Not all of us favour seeking help. We always sort our own problems. But then more died."

"Cursed ghouls," Arn muttered.

"Eleven villagers missing, taken in the night." Rendell frowned at Arn. "Here, do I know you?"

"Not unless you've travelled beyond these hills, friend. Did you find bodies?"

"None. But I'll say no more. The elders will speak of our troubles."

"Lead the way to Thom, Rendell," Kaell said.

He and Arn fell in beside the villager.

"What's the lake called?" Arn asked.

"The lake."

"Poetic," Arn said. "One for you, Kaell."

The road veered through grass, its green and brown pelt broken by slanted, weathered rocks and pebbled riverbeds. Wind tormented land and riders alike. When Kaell pulled his cloak tight, Rendell sneered and muttered.

"Friendly, isn't he?" Olier rode up. "What did he call you?"

Kaell shrugged. "A weak flatlander or something. Take no notice."

Olier turned in the saddle to shake a fist at the villager. "Look here, you. Most of us are from Vraymorg. Vray-morg. See those peaks." He pointed.

Rendell snorted his contempt.

"How far to Thom?" Kaell asked the villager.

"Not far."

"I was right," Arn said. "This one has the rich language of a poet."

THEY SPLASHED through mountain streams and waded muddy marshlands. As the sun dipped, wilderness softened. Sheep bleated in fenced meadows. Farmers drove teams of oxen. Women bending in furrowed fields lifted their heads to stare dull-eyed at the riders.

Thom knotted beside a deep green river gurgling over mossy rocks. Kaell glimpsed a mill upstream, and a square circled by houses, their walls stone from who knew where but surely not this empty downlands.

"Could be from an abandoned castle," Arn said. "You know the stories about ancient ruins in the Waste Mountains. Lost cities of stone."

"We're not in the Waste Mountains."

"Close enough."

A stone bridge straddled the river to the cobbled square. Villagers waited, loosely bunched. A white-haired man leaning upon a stick stood at the fore.

"Well met," he said as Kaell and Arn dismounted. His smile welcomed, a contrast to his companions' suspicious glances.

"We're grateful for your help." He addressed Arn. "And honoured to have the battle god's warrior with us."

Arn gestured at Kaell. "He's Khir's weapon. And a poet. Fancies himself as a singer too."

"Shut up, Arn."

A shadow crossed the old man's face. "But you're so very—"

"Young?" Arn finished for him. "He is all of twenty, but his heart is big. His voice is sweet—sometimes—and his friends are handsome and clever."

"I'm Kaell."

"Kaell." The man studied him with dark-brown eyes. "My name is Eelidaran. Aemeon here," he gestured to a beak-nosed man with lank brown hair, "and I are Thom's elders."

"It is a village to be proud of," Kaell said.

"We are blessed," Eelidaran said. "Until now. But before we speak of our troubles, let me show you our hall. It will shelter you all after your long journey."

"We won't trouble you. We can camp beyond the village."

"No, we won't hear of it," Aemeon slapped Kaell's shoulder. "The women cooked all day. The least we can do is show you hospitality."

Arn cast Kaell a glance then shrugged. "And our horses?"

Aemeon puffed out his chest. "The stables hold fifty beasts."

UNLIKE MOST OF THOM, the hall was built of wood. It was long, narrow, and set upon stumps with a ladder propped against a door. Smoke rose from the flat roof.

"Big hall," Arn mouthed at Kaell, drawing a grin. Another sign of Thom's blessings. The village was surprisingly wealthy given the Mountains' infertile soils and sparse crops compared to the rich, wet plains and pastures near Dal-Kanu.

Kaell left Arn ordering men about and followed Eelidaran into the hall. A stove's heat struck him at once. Most of its smoke escaped through an iron pipe in the roof.

"You'll be glad of the warmth tonight when frosts set in," Eelidaran said. "In winter, many villagers sleep here."

"I can well imagine." He fidgeted. "But this hall. It has just the one entrance?"

At his obvious unease, Eelidaran smiled. "A warrior's first thought is always defence." He hobbled to a panelled floor to lift a hatch.

"We built the hall as a refuge against Varee raiders. With one entrance it's easy to defend, but another way out is wise." He kicked the panel shut.

Kaell nodded. All the same, he'd double the sentries. A wooden hall easily blazed.

Trust very few, Vraymorg taught him, *even those behaving like friends*. Pity he forgot that when Aric challenged him.

"Cold enough to freeze your balls off." Olier squeezed inside, straightened, and stamped his feet. At the sight of the stove, his grin lifted. Other Vraymorg warriors followed him.

Kaell found Arn in the barn, scolding men unloading pack horses.

"I tended to your horse." He whipped up a hand to silence a protest. "I don't want to hear any nonsense about how you can look after your own horse."

"You treat me like a child."

"I treat you like a warrior who shouldn't be in the saddle at all. No, don't say a word. Your wounds trouble you. You're pale at the end of each day. No better when you wake." His dark eyes dwelled hard. "It's that cursed dream, isn't it. I heard you yelling near dawn. And no wonder. Night's Kiss. No one survives that."

"I'm all right."

"You're not. But when we return to Vraymorg and the priests

mutter their mumbo jumbo, you'll be fine. We'll clear out this nest of blood thieves quickly and be on our way."

THE WIND DIED AT DUSK, but cold misted like a damp blanket.

Kaell gladly sank beside Olier on a bench inside the smoky hall. A sullen villager tended the stove. Others set platters of food before their guests: mostly fish but also roasted mutton, cheese, and honey cakes. Unsmiling women offered ale.

"I sent food to the sentries," Olier said.

Kaell nodded.

"Arn put young Jarlen on duty again. That's two nights of four. Arn's got it in for him."

"Jarlen's insolent." Undisciplined. But one of Olier's dice-playing companions.

"He's spirited," Olier grumbled. "What did you learn from Eelidaran? I tell you, Kaell, I don't trust him. Any of them."

Kaell threw him a warning look. The two elders approached, accompanied by a boy.

"Ah, Kaell." Eelidaran rested his stick against his knee as he sat. "Is all to your satisfaction?"

"Indeed. Thank you for your hospitality."

"We are in your debt. Is now a good time to tell what we know?"

"A moment." Kaell gestured to Arn drinking with other warriors near the stove.

His captain wiped his mouth with the back of his hand, rose, and pulled up a stool.

"This is Brok. He has a story to tell." Eelidaran rested his hand on the boy's arm.

Brok trembled. He was about fifteen, with brown curls that tumbled wilfully across his eyes. Kaell wanted to muss his hair, reassure him with a smile.

"Don't be afraid," he said. "Just tell me what you saw."

Brok blinked. "I—"

"Just tell your story," Eelidaran said firmly.

The boy fixed his gaze on Kaell. "My lord, sir."

"A lord now," Arn muttered. "Won't hear the end of that, either."

"It's just Kaell."

"Sir," Brok said. "I was in the far, far fields, watching the sheep. I saw them."

"Ghouls?"

Brok nodded furiously. "Eight of them. It was dusk. I knew I was out too late, that ghouls"—he bit his lip—"took Jonathan, and then Niall vanished, and all—all the rest."

"Where did they go, lad?" Arn said.

"Into the caves, sir."

Kaell raised an eyebrow at Eelidaran.

"There are caves a short ride from Thom," he said. "Just beyond the pine forest."

"How many nights ago was this?" Olier asked Brok.

"Three nights."

"And you saw only eight. No more?"

"I saw eight," Brok said. "Or it might have been seven."

"And no one else has seen more? It's only a handful?"

Eelidaran and Aemeon both shook their heads.

Kaell turned to Eelidaran. "Can you draw a map to these caves?"

"Gladly. It's an easy distance from Thom. I'd send a guide, but the harvest is late and everyone tends the fields. What else can I tell you?"

"You've helped a lot. But I have one question."

"Yes?"

Kaell smiled. "Would there be in these parts a young woman with dark hair and a mark on her breast like a scar from a knife wound?"

Eelidaran tilted his brows.

"He asks everyone that," Olier stared unhappily into his empty cup.

"Because he's a poet," Arn told Olier.

"Is that what he is? I wondered."

Eelidaran considered Kaell solemnly. "I know of no one with such a mark. Why?"

Olier grunted in disgust. "Some girl he dreams about. Pay no attention. We don't." He waved his cup at a woman carrying a jug.

"IT SEEMS STRAIGHTFORWARD," said Arn, when Eelidaran and Aemeon left with the boy.

Olier scratched his chin. "Don't know. It's not right."

"You don't believe the boy?" Kaell asked.

"He seems a simple lad. No, it's the rest. The way they look at us."

"The women in the fields, the villagers," Arn said. "They don't like strangers."

"It's more than that. That man Aemeon stared oddly at you, Kaell, as though he pities you. And how did they know we drew near?"

"That's easy enough," Kaell said. "From the bridge you can see the track twisting through the mountains for miles and miles. I stood there earlier."

"Something's not right," Olier insisted. "I tell you, I won't sleep much tonight."

THE STOVE'S FIRE GLOWED. Opaque light chinked beneath the door. For a moment Kaell lay listening to Olier's grumbling snores. Remembering his captain's words, he laughed to himself.

He peeled off a blanket, gathered his cloak, and crept outside. A sentry touched hand to brow.

"All quiet?"

The guardsman was a Dal-Kanu archer, Ricker or some name similar. The second sentry, Jarlen, blew on frozen fingers on the bridge.

"Like a tomb. Bitter cold, though."

"A man will replace you at the second moon."

Leaving Richer stamping his feet, Kaell crossed the square to the river. The first moon threaded silver streaks across gleaming water. Stars dusted the sky. An owl hooted. A scampering paw stirred dead leaves.

Tightly cloaked, spine bent against the cold, Kaell stood staring at this strange beauty.

At a footstep, he groped at his sword.

"You're about late," Eelidaran said.

Kaell's fingers fell away. "Olier's snoring is loud enough to disturb the dead, and my leg aches—a recent wound."

Eelidaran leaned on his stick to peer across the light-streaked river to ragged peaks.

"It's spectacular," Kaell breathed.

"It is beautiful country. We have a good life here. A man must protect that."

Kaell sensed an undercurrent of meaning. Should he try to uncover it? Likely it had nothing to do with him. "Do you often walk alone at night?"

Eelidaran shrugged. "The mountains say much in the hush of night. You'll understand for you are a man of Vraymorg." He looked across the valley. "I hear the castle is formidable."

"Formidable is a good word. But as a child I always felt safe there."

Eelidaran turned to look at him. "Yours is a strange life, I think. Forgive me, but I must say, you are surprisingly young."

"I'm twenty. It's old enough." Older than some hunters lived.

He mentally shrugged. His lord never sweetened the truth about his life. Except Kaell never really thought he could die. Not until Aric poisoned him.

"Only twenty." Eelidaran's eyebrows furrowed. "But with such a reputation. You've killed how many ghouls?"

An odd question. Uncomfortable, Kaell huddled in his cloak. "Hundreds, I suppose."

"Very modest. You've hunted ghouls for five or six years? It must be close to 1000, surely. That makes you quite a killer. We should all fear you, I think, Kaell of Vraymorg."

"That's a grand title I have no right to." Eelidaran's gently mocking tone niggled. Olier might be right. Something felt amiss in Thom.

"Then we should fear Kaell 'no name'? Not so terrifying."

"You have nothing to fear from me." Stung, Kaell answered truthfully. "Every bonded warrior vows never to take up the sword against his own kind. It's so I can never fight for kings or lords, turn the tide of battles."

Eelidaran threw him a curious look. "I did not know."

They stood in stillness. Eelidaran cast a final glance at the bubbling river. "Well, goodnight then." He covered a yawn with his palm. "I hope you can rest before daylight."

Kaell stripped off his sword belt and knelt. Head bowed, he listened for his gods in the quiet mystery of a Mountains night. Had they really abandoned him? What if Khir now judged him unworthy?

He laughed mirthlessly. He? Doubting his skill? Had he failed? Had he ever led his men to defeat? *Answer that, Kaell. Never.*

And yet a stranger with a silken Isles tongue defeated him. His gods tested him with silence. And his lord…

Foolish tears wet his lashes.

His lord watched him with shadowed eyes. Afraid.

The gentle noises of darkness shifted. Trickling water. A bird's caw. Rustling grass. The wind murmuring through leaves. Then a sound he couldn't place.

Kaell spun.

Arn's blade glimmered in moonlight. His captain touched a finger to his lips. "Heard something." He stalked towards the trees, returning a moment later. "My imagination. Are you alone? Where's your sword?"

"Close." Kaell dragged the scabbard towards him.

"Not close enough. You didn't hear me behind you. What if I meant you harm?"

"There's no one here." Just whispering trees and silent gods. And doubt.

Arn stared. A muscle twitched in his cheek. "It's late. You need to sleep."

"That cursed dream awaits."

Arn dropped to his haunches. "You might dream of the girl. The one who kisses you."

"Last night I dreamt only of the door." Kaell shuddered. "Whatever my fate is, it draws closer, Arn. The door draws closer."

"It's just a dream, Kaell. A dream."

Kaell hunched weary shoulders. "I know. But it's always the same dream."

"It may never happen. Or it might happen years from now." Arn frowned. "There's no shame in fear. If you think this journey takes us towards that door, we should turn back."

Kaell dragged his hands over the soft bristle on his jaw. "My lord taught me to face fear head on. I'm a bonded warrior. Even if I'm afraid, it can't paralyse me."

"And your visions? Have they returned?"

"No."

"Then you can't see what happens tomorrow. What we'll ride into?"

Kaell glanced up sharply. "No. Why? Are you worried?"

Arn patted his shoulder. "I'm always worried, boy."

DAWN BROKE COLD, a pallet of grey and rose. Riders drew cloaks tight, their gloved hands numbly fumbling at reins.

Eelidaran and a handful of grim-faced villagers farewelled them. "Hunt well," the elder said. "Return to us unharmed and with good news."

The sun brightened without heat as the riders crested hills. At Kaell's back, thin, black smoke puffed from Thom's hall. Trees clustered ahead in a verdant, dark-trunked forest.

"A villager told me Cahireans used to raid these parts." Arn squinted. "Maybe your vision of loveliness, Rozenn, stopped it."

"She's not *my* vision."

"My, you're in a sour mood. Don't take it out on me. Not my fault you refused to sleep until near dawn."

Kaell rubbed his gritty eyes. "I kept thinking about something before I fell asleep. Aric's reply when I asked about a girl with a scar. Remember his words?"

"Yes, as it happens. He muttered, 'do you think that's funny?' Something like that."

"Senseless words unless—"

"Unless he knows someone with that mark. Kaell, about that girl—"

"The girl I dream of?"

Arn hesitated.

"What about her?"

Arn studied his face for a moment, then sighed. "Don't try too hard to find her."

"Why not?"

"You think only of her kiss, how sweet it is. But your visions are warnings. This girl might mean you harm. Think about that."

"And sometimes they're just a glimpse of what will happen, who I'll meet. Like that girl. It's some kiss, Arn. A wondrous kiss. Worth the risk." Kaell laughed. "You know, Aric was right about one thing, my friend. You do fuss."

No retort. Arn stared ahead, hands white on the reins.

Kaell's scalp tingled with unease. Around him were familiar sounds: men talking, whinnying horses, the jingle of harnesses. Everything about Arn, too, was familiar. Everything except his indrawn cheeks, his clouded eyes.

"I was wrong to stop you, Kaell," Arn said softly. "When you had doubts. When you wanted to run away to Tide's End or the Damadar twin cities."

Kaell forced a laugh. "I wasn't really going to run. I wasn't serious."

"I'm serious," Arn said. "Do you ever wonder, Kaell, what might be? That there could be another, different life—"

Astonished, Kaell arched a brow. "For me?"

"You could turn away from it all. Find a girl—"

"Or a queen, like Rozenn." Kaell grinned, trying to lighten the tension.

"Find a girl, settle somewhere. Or find a ship in Tide's End, sail to Veniva or beyond the Ice Sea. Fight for some fat, greedy lord you don't like for a lot of gold. An entire world awaits. Freedom."

"This is strange talk, Arn." Kaell scratched an itch beneath his shirt. He shook his head.

"What other life? Why? Freedom, you say? I don't feel trapped. Even on the Downs when I had doubts, that was just mindless fear. How can I turn from what's expected of me? The gods chose me, Arn. My duty is to them, to my lord, to the men we ride with. To Telor."

"Says who? Vraymorg?"

"Why do you say it like that?"

"No reason," Arn said. "Forget it."

KAELL STUDIED Eelidaran's map with Arn. "This is the forest." He stabbed a finger at the cloth. "Here. And the caves. We'll wait for the outriders to return before going on."

"As you say. Best to be careful."

Arn moved off to spread the word: a short break, then weapons ready, be on your guard.

Iron jangled as men dismounted beside a glazed stream rolling through a muddy, fern-swept gully. Twisted, light-barked trees swept low branches, their leaves bronzed and curled.

The wind's soft voice carried a feathery scent of mud and the sharp prick of rain. A single sodden grey cloud shadowed land then surrendered to dull sunlight.

Kaell put the map in his saddlebag and trod to the stream. As he knelt to splash icy water on his face, men nibbling dried meat or cleaning swords watched him. Some curious. Others wary.

Remembering the shadowed glances at Dal-Kanu, he wanted to shout: *You know me. Yes, my hair, my eyes aren't like yours. I might not marry or have children like you. I'm born to fight and die, probably soon. But I'm not so different. I belong here.*

Arn was wrong. He could live no other life.

"Cold enough to shrivel a goat's balls." Olier offered chunked bread. "The outriders are back."

"And?" Kaell bit into the bread.

A shrug. "All quiet in that forest. Empty. Dark though and dusk falls soon."

"We must be quick. Make use of the last daylight."

Olier chewed a lip. "We're close to the Waste Mountains. Too many ghouls there."

"We won't go into the mountains."

"No. But we could find more than eight ghouls in those caves."

"I've thought of that."

"At the Hall of Rollo, we faced thirty ghouls."

"We're a match for thirty ghouls." Kaell drew his knees to his chest to check cords fastening knives to his shins, then tightened the strap holding a blade to his upper arm.

Olier grimaced. "Three knives. One, I understand, but three? I'd leak like a broken bucket from the stab wounds."

"You adjust." Kaell forced a laugh. A shadow nagged in a recess of his mind. Eelidaran's manner last night? Arn's strange words?

Olier watched him. "You've seen nothing?"

"Nothing. Dreams yes, but not visions. Do the men know I'm, well, blind?"

"They know." Olier's frown deepened. "It was that witch, wasn't it? That sorceress from the Isles. It's unnatural magic they use in the Isles. That's what I've heard."

AUTUMN DAYLIGHT SLANTED low as they reached the forest. Towering trees packed close. A chill crept up from the earth. Unsettling dewy perfumes of approaching night scratched at Kaell's throat. Time ran out fast.

He signalled caution and led the line of riders beneath canopied leaves and vines. Gloom cloaked the wood. The sunlight that did fall only speckled shadows. Men twitched. Uneasy hands strayed to sword hilts.

No bird sang. Nothing chirred, nothing rustled, except a low branch Kaell brushed aside. Olier clutched a neck amulet. Kaell did not blame him. The woods shouted with silence.

"This is the right path?" Arn brought his horse up.

"The outriders say it's the only path," Kaell said.

Soon embracing branches shut out even dappling, fading sun. Sharp-pronged bushes swished as horses crushed past. Tree limbs rattled against helms and swords. Carpeting pine needles concealed the thud of hoofs. No one spoke.

Daylight sped its retreat as the trees fell away into a lush, grassy clearing. Kaell gestured to Arn and drew his blade. Arn signalled along the column.

"I don't like this," he said as men slid swords from scabbards.

Kaell shivered. "It feels wrong. And we've lost the light. Give the word to turn about."

Leaves rustled. Within shadows, a shape moved.

Hairs shot up along Kaell's arms. He yelled, "Ambush!" just as whooping ghouls surged from the trunks. Men wheeled horses to meet them.

For a heartbeat time stilled, as though men and ghouls froze in an eddy of eerie, breathless suspense. Then steel clashed in a mighty shriek: swords, axes, flesh tangled in a thunderous chaos of clanging, whirring metal, of howls and curses.

"Stand firm," Kaell's shout competed with ringing blades and screeches. "Archers to the side. Find cover then find targets."

Arrows thrummed. Ghouls fell. But more stormed out to fall upon the men. Kaell struck down two with one sweep of steel, straining to see in the gathering darkness. More ghouls than he could count. Too many.

A knowing shudder whipped his back. He would die today.

With a bellow of rage, Kaell rode into the tide of ghouls, his hungry sword streaming blood as he cleaved limbs and heads. The blade hummed a terrible, lustful song, a familiar song. A death dance gripped him—his dance—and he savagely swept ghouls from his path.

Mashed bodies heaped in Kaell's wake. His sword, his hair, his face darkened with blood. Sweat ran hot; his heart clamoured. Battle fever braced his sagging muscles, stiffened his resolve.

His men outnumbered. *Curse them. Curse them!*

"I'm here, cowards," he cried. "Kill me if you can."

Hands groped his legs. He kicked, swept his blade. Ghouls plunged back. One leapt in, jabbing. Kaell parried. Stabbed. His foe jerked and died.

Olier crashed from his horse. A ghoul rushed the fallen man, sword raised.

Kaell rode in hard. He slashed. The blade sheared bone and flesh. Blood choked chill air. Olier scrambled up, touched hand to brow, and leapt into a tumult of convulsing figures, shuddering blows, wailing iron, and screams.

Everywhere swords hunted, harried, struck. Men and ghouls howled in pain. Amid bloody disarray, horses whinnied.

Kaell tore into seething bodies and slashing, hacking, cutting blades. His sword mashed limbs, pulped guts. His horse's hooves crushed bones. A dark melody beat in his skull. Thought distilled to one intent. Kill.

Death coated his tongue, its sludge at the back of his throat as he pulverised flesh. Ghouls convulsed, screamed, and died in pools of blood and earth sodden with gore.

A horse bolted into the forest, a body slumped against its neck. Arrows twanged. Some pierced flesh. Others rattled to the ground. The king's man Ricker substituted bow for sword to hack at three ghouls. Kaell rode to help. His blade carved, crunched bone. A head spun.

As spouting blood blinded him, instinct screamed a warning. Unseeing, Kaell parried low against thrust steel. He blocked a blade. Swung. Killed.

Swiping his eyes, he shouted his defiance. "Attack me, cowards!"

An arrow whistled. Air swished his scalp. A voice cried, "Fool. Aim lower."

Pain jagged through his shoulder, toppled him from the saddle. Kaell tried to rise. A sword hilt smashed into his head. The blow spun him into blackness.

HE CAME TO dazed and nauseous, his cheek in blood, his shoulder a fireball. Touching fingers to the source, he found an arrow's fletching and pulled. This time the agony ripped a scream up his dry throat.

Teeth clenched, Kaell thrashed in pain. Shock numbed his mind. He couldn't think properly. Couldn't understand where he was.

Firelight chinked through branches, their groaning limbs naked against a dark satin sky. Tiny, white alyssum bobbed near his head, weaving their honey into stinging air.

Noises rippled. Fragmented, uncertain. Meaningless. Was that the wind scurrying dead leaves into buttressed shadows? Was that a brook's murmur? Maybe. Did he hear voices?

Nothing seemed real. But it didn't feel like a dream, either.

A man sobbed. Kaell knew he heard that. It cut through him with horror, exploded the block in his tormented mind. In grotesque flashes, memory slammed into him.

The darkening forest. Trap. Ghouls. Too many of them. Dying men. *His* men. Where were they? Dead?

On elbows and knees, he dragged his broken body through mud, through the sickeningly sweet alyssum towards the flickering light.

Between trunks, a fire's distorting glow fell on a ring of figures, on strewn steel, on bodies dumped in a pile. He would not look at faces.

Someone laughed. A man begged for mercy. Kaell jolted. Oh gods, some of his friends, his companions lived. He had to help them, draw the ghouls away from the wounded at least.

Through dizzying, knife-hot pain, Kaell forced himself to his knees, then to his feet. "Cowards," he screamed into the night. "Vile beasts. Face me!"

Blurred shapes turned, sneering. No one challenged him.

"Face me," he cried, brushing branches aside as he stumbled towards the clearing.

About the fire, ghouls feasted on wounded men. Some moaned, others briefly struggled. A dark stream washed into the earth. Wings beat overhead. Crows circled, cawing.

Frozen in horror, Kaell could only stare at this sick nightmare, at ghouls discarding dead prey, laughing as they grabbed others to feed upon.

Then fury raged through him, his sight dim with it. He had no thoughts of running, surviving. Only of how to kill. He would destroy them, reap every ghoul.

Tearing a sword from a corpse, he staggered forward, screaming, "You foul beasts. Leave them alone. Face me. It's me you want."

Anger became puppeteer to his arms waving the blade, his mind shut down to all but that fury. That need to kill. Bloodily.

An arrow whirred, puncturing flesh above his knee. Kaell screamed but did not stop. His lips stretched back from his teeth. Destroy them in a harvest of death.

Figures surrounded him, silhouettes against the fire. He whipped the sword about in a half circle, then stabbed, hearing a satisfying howl.

Shadows rushed along the ground, rising up, taking form. A blow from behind knocked him to his knees. A boot flew at his head. Kaell plunged back, drifting towards darkness, haunted by the fading cries of dying men.

HE SURFACED INTO BLINKING TORCHLIGHT. Rope bound his arms to his side, his shoulders cramped. Dispersed starbursts of pain blurred together: his thigh, his back, his skull, his throat as he gasped for air. The gods only knew where else he hurt.

Get free. The thought hammered. *Get free. Then get revenge.*

Kaell squirmed, arched his back, limbs contorted as he fumbled with his bound hands for his blades. All gone but one. He wriggled it loose from his forearm, took it in shaky fingers to hack and saw at the cords, gashing his wrists again and again in his haste.

The ropes fell away. But into a terrible silence. No more voices begged for mercy.

Too late. He was too late. Kaell's sobs wracked his broken body like a sickness. He crawled. Not knowing where, only far from the bloody clearing.

Beneath the trees, alyssum crushed against his blood-caked tunic, he retched, his body purging what his mind could not.

His men, his friends. Dead. He buried his head in his hands, moaning. Only a handful of ghouls, the villagers said. Yet scores hid in the forest, waiting.

A trap, surely. But why?

Faded blossoms trembled on trees. A boot scrunched dead leaves. Close. Voices drifted and gathered like wind: "Find him. Spread out. Find him."

Panicked, Kaell stumbled up and lurched through menacing trunks, through shadows. Starlight gleamed the edges of banking clouds, the air sharp as winter in his lungs.

His pursuers thrashed the underbrush, taunting in singsong voices. "Kaaaaelll. Where are you? You can't hide from us, Kaeeelll."

Kaell stumbled over a root. Fell. Pain ripped through his injured shoulder. He choked off a cry, found his feet, staggered on. *Keep moving. Just one more step.*

Rasped breath burned his throat. Sweat drenched his bloody tunic, clammy on his skin.

Thought condensed to survival. *Do not stop.* But his strength drained fast, and his wounds bled an easy trail.

Crooked trees with knife-sharp twigs rent his skin. New gashes dripped unchecked. He fought off slapping, needled boughs only to slip to his knees in soggy ground.

Kaell didn't want to rise, wanted only to surrender to exhaustion, to despair.

Why bother running? His dream unfolded. Surely it began like this, his desperate flight, ghouls hunting him. No matter what he did, where he ran, fate led him to that ruined castle where torch flames slapped cool air in the passage leading to the door.

A man might escape death once—he had survived Aric's poison—but twice? No, they would have him. Soon. When he could no longer crawl. At least here, now, he died with his men. With Olier. Arn.

Arn… What would he say if he knew Kaell cowered here? What would his lord say?

Shame flushed through him. His lord would want him to fight, to seek vengeance for his fallen comrades. Not huddle in self-pity.

Exhausted by shock and pain, Kaell braced the trunk to rise. His knees nearly buckled, his harried mind hooked on another wretched thought. His enemy overpowered him, took him. Why didn't they kill him?

Now his breath stalled. Wings beat against a black-domed sky. Falling blackness, blackness ready to suffocate him with terror.

Only one answer. Alive, they could drag him back to their god. A trophy, a prisoner to torture. Not just over days but months. No, the ghouls must not capture him again. If he could not get away, he must drive his own knife into his heart.

Kaell staggered a few steps. A light winked through trees. His heart hit ribs. A village. Cottages with window boxes spilling with flowers circled a grassy clearing. Goats bleated behind wooden fences.

He lurched towards raised voices, laughter, scents of ale and roasting meat. Armed men drank around a crackling fire. One leaned against a wooden barrel beneath an ancient, gnarled tree.

"Help me."

The men fell silent and stared. A woman with long, auburn hair stepped from a cottage. She turned a flat gaze on him.

"Help me."

A thick-waisted man with a slashed mouth and bristled brown hair lumbered to his feet. Dew wet the rim of a cloak draping his sturdy shoulders. "Help you?" He turned to the others. "He wants us to help him."

They all laughed. Some rose and surrounded Kaell. He recoiled, not understanding.

The brown-haired man threw a fist. Surprised, Kaell blocked the blow with his forearm. He groped for his knife. But other hands grabbed him from behind, held him.

"Help you?" The man sneered. "We're in these woods tonight to make sure none of you get away."

He punched. Kaell fell back against the others, blood metallic on his lips. Still laughing, they let him go. Dazed, disorientated, he slumped to his knees.

The man with brown hair grasped his chin. "I'll help you," he jeered. "Pass out." His fist came at Kaell again.

ARIC

Aric leaned his elbows on the window edge. A westward wind gusted, hot for autumn. He hardly felt it. Nor did his stare take in the sea frothing and breaking over rocks beneath.

Fists knotted, he bristled with frustration. Come spring, the false king intended to sunder their gates with his beasts of siege engines. The Isles must be ready. But how, when his father locked up his best warrior?

He leaned to brush fingers over the tower's rough stone, its chipped blocks warm from the sun. So many other hands must have touched these walls.

Maybe Ryol Caelan stood at this very window as his cousin Devarsi invested the castle with soldiers and towering trebuchets. Had Ryol felt as restless as he did? Had he yearned to do something, anything, rather than wait for defeat?

A key rattled in the lock. Aric turned, expecting his father or uncle to appear to berate him again for his wilfulness. Or a servant, eyes averted as they left a tray of food and wine while an insolent guard smirked from the passage.

Pairas stepped inside, grim-faced. "You're free to leave this room."

Alarm kicked in Aric's gut. "Why?"

Pairas said nothing. He did not look at him.

"*Why?*"

"That boy, Kaell—" Pairas's voice trailed off.

"Tell me."

"We've received word by raven from some place called Thom. About a massacre."

Aric recoiled. "They're all dead? And—" He dragged in a breath. "And Kaell?"

Pairas hesitated for barely a second. "Dead, Aric. Just as Aingear saw. I'm sorry."

But Aric caught his pause. "What are you not telling me?"

His friend would not meet his eyes. "Nothing. They're all dead."

KAELL

Fragrances of tallow, dried herbs and honeysuckle drifted as gently as a lazy, warm breeze.

Still half asleep, Kaell smiled. The scents belonged to Mountains summers, to long, carefree days when he stole away after his lessons to pick blueberries with Alyssa.

He did not want to surface from this sweet torpor, but someone shook him.

A woman bent over him. “I must check your wounds.”

“I’m wounded?” Kaell lifted his head. Nausea speared his belly. He groaned and dropped back on a pillow until the sickness passed.

Why was he wounded? *Remember.* But his thoughts shredded into a black, empty mire.

“Quiet, blossom.” Dark-red hair wisped the woman’s brow, the rest weaved into a long plait tickling his arm. Capable hands prodded his naked body beneath a prickling blanket.

Where were his clothes? Where was *he?*

Straw rustled on the cot beneath his back. An ember-red fire spat in a hearth. Tallow from candles in holders adorned a stained table. Beeswax and the faintest hint of lavender drenched the air’s smoky warmth.

Dull, yellowed light streaked through shutters upon sachets, bottles, and earthenware jars. They crammed untidily onto shelves upon a hut's walls. Dried herbs and flowers bunched from rafters.

"Who are you?" Kaell croaked. "What happened to me?"

"All is well." The woman did not smile. "After many days, the crisis came last night, and your fever broke. I removed the arrow heads while you slept, stopped the bleeding."

"Bleeding." Kaell fought a moment of disorientated panic. His dulled wits strained at shadows draping his memory. "Yet nothing hurts."

The woman rested her hand at the nape of his neck to hold a cup to his lips. "Salve on the wounds. And poppy juice to mask the pain."

And bring sleep. He sipped, wanting to surrender to the languid wave sinking his limbs… except for a niggle of unease, an inner voice warning him to stay awake.

"Where are my clothes?"

"Shy are we? I cut them off to clean and bandage your thigh. Your shoulder, too, is gouged. An arrow scraped bone in your ankle. There's an old scar there."

An old scar. That seemed important. Part of who he was. Kaell sank down. "Who are you?" How did he get here? Why couldn't he remember?

"Don't talk, blossom. Sleep."

His eyelids drooped. "My name's—not blossom." That sounded ungracious, so he added, "Thank you for helping me."

Sleep rushed him. He thought he heard: "I do not need your thanks, blossom. *He* shall reward me." But the words might be part of a dream. It might all be a dream.

NIGHT FELL AND DEEPENED. Fragmented images, faces, played behind his eyelids.

He wandered in a forest perfumed of rain and drizzling mist, searching. A man sobbed. Kaell followed the sound. But it faded until he stood alone and confused among dark trunks.

"My lord, Raggamirron. It's still too soon. He's still too ill to move."

Golden hair. Dark eyes. Cool hands on his skin. A whisper.

"It's been three days. He'll heal fast now. We'll return at sunset."

Kaell woke in hard light. A new fire burned in the hearth. Shadows yawed, the air cold. Shivering, he reached for the blanket. His hand caught. *What?* He tugged. Rope looped his wrists to the cot.

"Did you bind me? Why?"

No answer. No sign of the woman.

Panicked, Kaell thrashed about, twisted his hands. The cords bit but held firm.

"Are you there? Cut me free."

The woman appeared. She touched fingertips to his brow. "Warm. I'll check your wounds then bring more poppy juice."

"Why won't you release me? I'll not hurt you."

She stripped back the blanket and peeled blood-soaked cloths from his wounds. "They're right. You *do* heal quickly." Her voice shrilled in surprise.

"Answer me!" Kaell jerked at the ropes, arched his back, squirmed. Snatches of his dream returned to him. *Return at sunset. Sunset.*

What happened at sunset? From the harsh light the day already aged.

Nameless fear tore through him. Again he writhed, panting until he collapsed with exhaustion.

"Still, still," the woman said. "It's no good, blossom. You only tire yourself."

She covered his wounds and pulled up the blanket. "I'll fetch you something to eat."

"I don't care about food. Tell me why you trussed me like a beast?"

She dropped her hands to her waist. "Very well. Since you won't leave it alone. It's because they don't want trouble. When they return to take you."

Take him? Who? Where was he? That veil on his mind shrouded something important. He must remember. Must.

Dal-Kanu. With a jolt he recalled the city. The king. Aric. A journey. Thom.

Thom.

As if a hand squeezed his heart, memory ripped up his breast. His breath disappeared. Arn. Olier. Kaell wanted to scream, weep. Run. Fight. Hide.

Die.

Oh gods, his friends, warriors he'd known since childhood, all dead. It wasn't right they had died and he hadn't. A beast's sounds, not words, caught in his throat.

"Witless." The woman tapped her temple. "I suppose it's better for you that way."

She moved away, humming.

"Let me be dead too," Kaell whispered. "Khir, please. If you hear me, I can't stand this ache. I don't want to survive if I'm alone."

Alone. With ghouls about to come for him. He groaned in despair.

The woman returned with a cup. Kaell listlessly shook his head.

"It's water. Not poppy juice."

His throat as dry as sand, Kaell drank.

"That wasn't so bad, was it?" The woman turned away.

"They will torture and kill me," Kaell blurted.

She stopped. Turned back. Regarded him with eyes as hard and lifeless as unpolished diamonds. Empty of compassion. "Why should I care, blossom?"

"I'm Kaell, not some flower. I heard what they said: they return at sunset. You can't deliver me to them."

"I'm losing patience with your nonsense. One more word and I'll gag you."

Kaell fell silent. Light dulled towards dusk. Beneath a soft wind, crickets chirred.

"How can you do this? I'm human, like you. Why help ghouls?"

The woman took up knitting needles near the fire. "Spare me your tiresome cries for pity. Everyone knows Khir's warrior is not quite human."

She knew who he was. Ice fingers trailed across Kaell's scalp.

"Why bother to treat my wounds? Better to let me die. They'll just kill me, anyway."

The woman dropped her knitting, rose, found a cloth.

"I will be silent," Kaell muttered.

"See you are, blossom. Still, too." She glared, then shrugged and sat. Her needles clicked time away. Time he didn't have. Kaell glanced at the windows. Dusk gathered like storm clouds. He could not just lie there and wait for whatever happened at dusk.

Desperately, violently, he hurled himself back and forward.

The woman flew at him, her face twisted with fury. "Stop this nonsense."

Kaell thrashed. The cot creaked and shook.

"You wicked, wicked child. I'll force a sleeping draught down your throat." With clunked footsteps she trod off, returning with a bottle. She grasped his chin.

Kaell twisted his head away.

A fist thudded against the door. Two ghouls entered. The last light fled as though they marched darkness into the room.

Kaell stared in shock. One was the ghoul from the tournament. Lastenarron.

"You," he seethed, wrenching at his bonds. "You killed those men to spite me. You'll pay."

Lastenarron blew Kaell a kiss. "Threats now. Such a fierce child. I missed you."

The other ghoul addressed the woman. "He is well enough to travel?"

She nodded. "His wounds healed quickly, as you said. Be wary, my lord."

"Wary is Raggamirron's second name." Lastenarron barked laughter. "His first is duty. His others—honour and courage. My friend is very dull. I wonder why we are friends at all."

Raggamirron stood over Kaell. He was blond, tall, and as elegantly lovely as every ghoul, his face as splendid as a bird of prey's. A fur-lined cloak brushed boots of tanned hide. An embroidered leather doublet tapered to a sword belted around slender hips.

Yet despite the ghoul's graceful form, Kaell sensed bull strength, a contained menace.

"This is the warrior you fought, Lastenarron?"

Lastenarron swaggered closer. "Pretty isn't he?" He thrust his knife to Kaell's throat, forcing his head back with the tip. "A pretty beast."

"Beast?" Kaell curved a brow, determined to show no fear. "She says I'm a blossom."

The woman tapped her head. "He hit his head. Something not right there."

Lastenarron sighed. "I've slaughtered two bonded warriors. Children, like you. Why does your god send boys against us?"

"I'm no boy. I'm a blossom. Ask her."

"Mad," the woman said.

"Or pretending to be. How sweet." Lastenarron leaned to sniff. "He'll taste sweet too."

"Cut him free," Raggamirron said. "Wrap him in something—you and I both shall suffer if he freezes to death—and bind him."

Lastenarron tickled his blade across Kaell's cheek. "Maybe our lord will give him to me. When he's done with him." With a leer, he dug a knee into Kaell's hip and slashed at cords.

Lord? Done with him? Kaell thrashed hard. Once bound and their prisoner, he was lost.

Lastenarron struck him a numbing blow. "Settle down, sweetness."

He rose off Kaell and sauntered off.

"Woman," Raggamirron said. "I can't take him through the mountains naked."

She brought a tunic and pants. "Will these do? His are bloody rags."

"Dress." Raggamirron shoved the garments at Kaell.

Kaell struggled into tight clothing. He huddled on the cot, shielding his shivering body with his arms. Dread bowed his shoulders. Only pain and humiliation lay ahead. Shame.

Vraymorg would soon learn of the ambush. He'd think Kaell recklessly led his men to their slaughter. His lord would shake his head, his lips grim with disappointment.

Kaell blinked the terrible image away. If only he had a blade to drive into his heart. End this struggle, end this unendurable grief and guilt.

Yet despite his hopelessness, the prospect of torture and a slow death endured alone, part of him bucked at such cowardly surrender.

Would his lord, if held captive, give up? No. Even from that dark pit where all seemed lost, Vraymorg would shout his defiance, scornfully tell his captors to do their worst.

Kaell could not let his lord down, even in thought. He'd die well, be worthy of the man who raised him.

Lastenarron dangled coiled rope. "Wrists together, little beast."

"I'm a blossom," Kaell laughed. And laughed. It was better than weeping.

"Wrists together, little flower."

Kaell sprang at him. He landed a blow hard enough to knock Lastenarron off his feet. But pain snapped like steel teeth about his wounded ankle. Kaell moaned and toppled.

Lastenarron rose. "Naughty child." He hauled Kaell up, an arm to his windpipe as Raggamirron bound his hands.

Kaell winced as cord bit. "This won't stop me. You'll have to kill me."

"Sweet boy." Lastenarron kissed his brow. "So fierce. But you said you were a flower."

Raggamirron tied a cloak about Kaell's trembling shoulders. "Walk."

He took a step. Fire seared his ankle. His leg buckled.

With a patient sigh, Raggamirron circled an arm about his waist and half dragged, half pulled him outside.

Icy air stung Kaell's face and neck. Gooseflesh blistered his arms as vicious as the glares from ghouls turning to stare. Ranks of them. Some stoop-shouldered with weariness. Others bloody. Their lips curled in snarling hatred.

Raggamirron barked orders. A ghoul brought forward a horse dragging a wooden frame.

Outraged, Kaell blenched. "You expect me to submit, to let you lug me about like a beast."

"Be grateful you're injured. Otherwise I'd loop rope about your neck and make you run." Raggamirron shoved.

Kaell sprawled on frost-hard ground. He glared up. "I won't make this easy for you."

Ghouls pounced. Cursing, kicking, flailing, he fought them as they hurled him onto the frame and bound him to its slabs.

"He's stronger than he looks," one laughed, slapping his head.

"Sweet isn't he." Lastenarron strode from the darkness. "He's a blossom."

"He's a killer."

Kaell traced the new voice. For a moment, shock numbed him. Wind nipped his skin through cloth, coldly ruffled his hair. The coarse cloak's musk caught in his throat.

Beneath the forest's pungent, earthy fragrances, beneath the wind, beneath the high-pitched bats in trees, the hum of insects, Kaell stiffened with anger.

Eelidaran.

"You sent us to our deaths!" He lurched against ropes, desperate to get at the man.

The Thom elder shrugged dispassionately. "We offered you and your men to our god."

What god? Didn't these villagers serve Khir?

"I swear I'll make you answer for this."

"You'll be dead or worse." Sneering, Eelidaran tilted his head to study Kaell. "Not so proud now, are we, Kaell of Vraymorg. I cannot pity you."

He turned away.

The ghouls set off. Kaell stared after Eelidaran until the lights of the village faded. "Khir, hear my oath," he whispered to the night. "I will deliver vengeance for my men."

Horses plodded through gloved darkness. The ghouls carried torches, pale, insignificant, flickering beacons in a sea of murky emptiness. Every so often a shadow hulked, a towering tree or mountain, the landscape alien and hostile.

Kaell tried to peer into the darkness, listened, smelt, seeking anything that revealed where he was.

"Where are you taking me?" he shouted. Armed ghouls trudged about him, cloaked against the cold. None answered.

The moonless night and his captors' menacing silence swallowed Kaell's hope. All he had was vengeance, a knot of it stiffening his backbone and shoulders, a whisper in his head, *do not give up*, a spark lit by his need to avenge his friends.

Until even that whisper, that spark died. His body sagged beneath the burden of despair and loneliness, and the dreadful knowledge he failed his lord.

The frame bumped and scraped over stones. Eventually, against the slow clip-clop of the horses, worn out by anger and fear, Kaell slept.

HE WOKE SHIVERING, his toes numb. If only Khir had let him freeze. But he'd displeased his gods. Why else would they abandon him?

Would his lord, if he were here, abandon him also? Would he accuse with sharp words and quivering lips? Better to die than see his shame reflected in Vraymorg's eyes.

At last they stopped. A spine of massed rock jagged against pink-rimmed blackness. Walls of stone folded like resting wings. A gorge? A steep-rutted gully?

"We will not reach the castle tonight." Raggamirron.

"*He* will be angry."

"Daylight overtakes us. The caves are nearby."

The horses clopped forward, but soon Raggamirron called a halt. Ghouls dismounted, removed packs, and unbridled horses.

One freed Kaell, threw him over his shoulder, and bore him, struggling, wriggling, towards a cave in a soaring rock wall. Dumped on hard ground, Kaell tensed his muscles. If he could break free, approaching daylight might hide him.

A shadow fell upon him. Lastenarron shook his head sadly. "I'll take my little flower. I believe he intends mischief."

He dragged Kaell by the hair into the cave's gaping darkness where shapes convulsed in flurried activity. Torches flared. Ghouls cast Kaell spiteful or curious glances as they huddled in corners to sleep.

Kaell squirmed. Lastenarron's grip tightened. "You might be a bonded warrior, but even you can't escape hundreds of us. How far do you think you'll get?"

Another ghoul approached and bowed to Lastenarron. "Raggamirron says the prisoner needs water. Like a horse."

Lastenarron grinned. "Like a dog." He threw Kaell down. "Well then, give him water."

The ghoul trembled as he pressed a cup into Kaell's bound hands. Odd how his fear comforted. His enemies still considered him dangerous even if his self-belief wavered.

"He's just a boy." The newcomer barked a surprised laugh. "Look, Lastenarron."

"All bonded warriors are young." Lastenarron covered a disinterested yawn with his palm. "The gods of men demand it. But even wounded, this one is lethal."

"Maverran says our lord will torture him for months. That's why he demanded—upon pain of death—we bring him back alive?"

Kaell stiffened. Death he could face. That would end his gnawing, helpless rage, his sorrow. But painful, humiliating torture? He was no fool. The moment they captured him, it became a real peril. But to hear it said raked up new horror.

Lastenarron laughed. "You've scared my little flower."

Raggamirron appeared, needling his temples with ringed fingers.

"He's stronger," Lastenarron warned in a low voice. "Ropes might not hold him. Best to break an ankle. We can't lose our lord's prize now."

"Our lord wants his prize in one piece. Bind him to me."

No. Kaell choked on an outraged cry. He crawled away.

Lastenarron grasped his hair. "Well, sweet boy, do as our lord's favourite says."

Kaell uselessly struggled.

With an impatient growl, Raggamirron grabbed his shoulders and sank with him to their knees. Lastenarron lashed them together, Kaell's back to his captor's chest, his head on the ghoul's breast.

Raggamirron slept at once. Crushed against his enemy's body, the ghoul's breath warm in his hair, Kaell shrank away as far as the ropes allowed. He ached with misery, his mind in turmoil. Indignant anger roiled. This was insufferable. Why didn't Khir let him die in battle?

The day crawled towards dusk. He squirmed, groaned, silently wept. Until at last, worn out by his wild, black imaginings, Kaell plunged into an exhausted sleep.

Water trickled on stone. A girl rose on tiptoes to kiss his lips.

"Where are you?" he whispered. "Don't go. Please don't leave me."

But ghouls groped him in the dark cave. They pulled him away from the girl and her sweet kiss, cut him free of Raggamirron, wrenched him up.

Kaell's teeth chattered. Hunger cramped his belly. He tested his weight on his injured leg. A nip of pain but bearable.

Raggamirron commanded bustling activity. He stopped a scurrying ghoul. "Chall. Take the captive outside so he can piss. Then find him water."

"Why bother?" the ghoul said. "Let him go thirsty."

"Do as I say."

"Is there anything to eat?" Kaell asked.

"There's you." Chall bared his teeth.

Raggamirron growled. "Don't be a fool."

"Aww, it's a joke. So serious, Raggamirron. I know what our lord said. He's his. But Lastenarron boasts if you take only a drop, nothing tastes as sweet as a warrior of Khir's."

Not true. Kaell worked at loosening his bonds. Nothing tasted as sweet as Cahirean wine after hunting ghouls. He savoured the thought. It reminded him of who he was.

Raggamirron stilled, his face hard with anger. "Try it. He's bound. Taste him."

Chall blinked. Then he looked to the ground, stammering, "I also heard a bonded warrior's blood kills."

"You heard right, fool. Lastenarron talks big about the two bonded warriors he's killed, but most of what he says is nonsense."

Chall grabbed Kaell's arm, spun him and shoved him outside. "Quick now."

Kaell limped into a violet, blossom-scented twilight. A whisper ran through soughing trees, black cutouts against the sky. A few steps to that forest and freedom.

"Well, do what you have to," Chall said disinterestedly.

Kaell fumbled with his pants. "I'm sorry. I can't stand."

A sneer. "Do you want me to hold it or something?" He stepped in.

Kaell drove his palm up into the ghoul's chin. Chall plunged back. Kaell leapt on top of him, pounding his face again and again until the flesh pulped.

Breathing hard, Kaell scrambled up and groped into darkness swirling between trunks, seeking something sharp to free his hands. Wet grass plastered his ankles. Paws scuttled from his path.

A ghoul grasped his shoulder. Yelping, Kaell twisted free. They snatched at him. He flailed. Broke clear. Blindly stumbled away. Ghouls closed in to trap him with their bodies, pinned his arms to his sides. "No, no," he yelled in helpless rage.

His captors brutally lugged him back to the cave. Hurled down so hard his cheek ripped on a stone, Kaell curled to protect his gut from their kicks. Everywhere ghouls flitted like yawing shades, their voices a swill of angry murmurs.

Raggamirron stood over him. "Young fool, I like your spirit. But save your strength."

"Why don't you kill me?" Kaell hissed. "I'm your enemy."

Raggamirron sighed. "I understand you better than you know. I, too, would seek death if I were you. But you lost your chance to die the moment we took you alive."

He pointed at towering rock. "Do you know where we are, child? We're in the foothills of the Waste Mountains. Once in those mountains, no one will ever come after you. No one will ever find you. You are alone. Put aside foolish hopes of rescue or escape."

No. Please no. Kaell dragged himself away on his elbows. Raggamirron let him crawl.

Footsteps crunched. Lastenarron pushed forward, his fists bunched.

"He killed Chall." The ghoul's eyes bulged with hatred. Before Raggamirron could stop him, he kicked Kaell hard in the ribs.

Groaning, Kaell drew his knees to his chest and tried to roll. A boot struck his head. Merciful blackness rushed him.

KAELL LAY ON HARD, cold floor. Grotesque shapes blurred with formless shadows. Jigging light hurt his eyes and voices chirred like an angry buzzing.

"Are you nearly done? We must finish before Raggamirron returns."

"Phhaa," a second voice spat. "That one wants too much. It will be done when it is done."

"Be quick. He's stirring. Should we hit him or something? What if he escapes?"

"Call out to the guards if you're afraid, you big baby. Besides, where would he go?"

A grunt then metal scraped stone. "There," the second voice pronounced, satisfied. "Help me lift him."

Kaell groaned as they hoisted him. He blinked. Two ghouls studied him.

"He's awake."

"More pity for him. Here, you hold him."

Thick arms enfolded his body. Kaell's legs seemed useless. Trembling with sickness, he squinted. An ocean of rounded pillars surrounded him, their stone spearing a cavernous hall from marbled floor to vaulted ceiling. Candles smoked from sconces on hewn walls and ebony statues of nightmarish, winged creatures watched with shining, dead eyes.

A sword draped an elaborately carved chair upon a dais. His sword?

"It's done. Bring him."

The ghoul dragged Kaell to a pillar. He slumped against his captor, too weak to protest as the ghoul snapped iron about his wrists. Tightened chains clinked, bit into his flesh.

The ghoul stepped back. "Better."

Chains strung Kaell between pillars, arms extended, his back and chest aflame. Despondent with defeat, sick with pain, he moaned.

"Aw, it hurts? Too bad." A ghoul checked the manacles. Hesitant fingers edged to Kaell's arm. "I wonder if his kind tastes as good as they say?"

Kaell shuddered, disgusted at the ghoul's caress.

His companion hissed, "Are you weak in the head? His blood kills. Leave him be."

The ghoul laughed, grasped Kaell's chin, and spat in his face. At the door, he called over his shoulder, "Time to make peace with your gods, boy. Worthless though they are."

Darkness settled. Kaell drifted in and out of consciousness, his hungry, broken body shackled too tightly to slump. Pain plunged him into blackness, only to wrench him back to the pillared room, to his chains. His failure.

Sometime in the long hours, a door creaked. Timid footsteps approached. A light struck his eyes, achingly bright, and he wrenched his head sideways.

"Sorry." The light dipped.

Kaell squinted. A girl stood before him. Dark hair swept sun-bronzed arms. She wore a simple, dark-blue linen gown, gathered at her slender waist and billowing to her calves.

"Who are you?" he croaked.

"I'm Caitlyn."

Kaell coughed a laugh. Caitlyn, the name of a Cahirean river goddess. Stupidly, he said, "Are you here to wash me away, Ceet-lan?"

The girl scoffed as though she thought him unhinged. Perhaps he was. Did it matter? He would be dead soon. *Dead, dead.* The word throbbed through his skull.

"It's Caitlyn, not Ceet-lan." She fumbled inside a bag for a wineskin. "What a stupid way of talking. You sing your words."

"That's because I'm a poet. That's what Arn says." Arn. Sorrow rushed up in him.

"Poet are you? I heard you were a warrior. Here. Raggamirron bid me bring you water with a little poppy juice in it."

She held the skin to his lips, standing so close he caught her scent, golden like honey, earthy like a drenched forest. Kaell sipped, able to take only a little at a time. She waited patiently until he finished then returned the skin to her bag.

"Why are you in this dreadful place?"

Caitlyn did not look up. "I serve the old ones."

"I don't understand. Aren't you afraid they'll kill you?"

The girl flashed scorn. "Don't be stupid."

"They're killers. They need blood to live."

"You know nothing of these mountains. Can a boy raised at Vraymorg really be that ignorant? Ghouls need blood but do not take all blood. Do you see? The pact between the ancient ones and my people is centuries old. It is honourable to serve them."

Kaell rocked his head dizzily. Their conversation felt unreal as though he fell into a dream. He blinked, wondering if Caitlyn would still be there.

She was.

"So I didn't dream you."

Again contempt. "How can you dream of someone you've never met before?" Her face softened. "But maybe you'll see me now in a sweet poppy sleep."

"Maybe I won't wake." Kaell smiled.

"You'll wake. When he wants you to wake, you'll wake."

"Who's he?"

"Why *him*, of course." She edged closer. "You'd best not fight. Listen. Do not fight him."

Kaell offered her a weary grin. "I think I have to." Fight, then die.

"Then don't look at him."

Kaell stared. Something in her manner had changed.

"Why not?"

"You're so ignorant. And they say, Raggamirron and the others, you're a bonded one and all." Caitlyn heaved an exaggerated sigh as though explaining to a difficult child. "To behold *him* is dangerous. His face. Remember that, hunter."

She slung her bag across her shoulder. "Anyhow, they'll blindfold you. You're precious to our lord. A prize. He'll keep you to himself, savour that moment when he sees your sweet face, just you and him."

She strode away. Light patched at the door then disappeared. Stillness settled about Kaell once more.

THE POPPY JUICE blissfully carried him from his aching body. Dreams winked in and out, murky fragments of dulled voices and shifting images. He wanted to stay in this safe, comforting half world, but light and noise forced him back to the hall.

Kaell jerked awake. Hands held his head. A musty cloth tightened over his eyes. He panicked, forgot to breathe. *Blindfolded,* his tormented mind reasoned. *That's all.*

He gulped in air, hearing feet shuffle, benches scraping stone and rumbling voices. The ghoul words reminded him of sullen captives forced to teach him their tongue. Kaell was a quick student. An official sent from Dal-Kanu to assess him once remarked to Vraymorg: "The child has a good ear."

The praise warmed until his lord's sharp retort: "Every bonded warrior has."

Voices fell away into an expectant hush.

Measured footsteps approached. Stopped. In the stillness, he heard breaths, soft as silk. Someone stood close, wordless, just watching.

Kaell knew fear well enough. But what hit him then scorched like fire, cut like ice, held like steel. A scream rose in tortured lungs, died in his throat.

He gagged. A voice snapped a command. Hands pulled back his head.

"Breathe, just breathe." Raggamirron, his tone surprisingly gentle. The ghoul held a cup to his lips. Kaell drank.

The footsteps moved away. A chair scraped. But that menacing, powerful gaze still locked on him. Hairs spiked along his arms. But for the chains, he would reel back or fall to his knees in terror.

"This is him? The one I seek?" The male voice was soft and melodious, but grim with mystery. A tingling crept beneath Kaell's skin. Not with fear this time, but with a reluctant, terrible longing.

A muttering rose in a nervous crescendo then drifted off.

"Do you deceive me? I see nothing but grimy flesh plastered on bones. Is it even human?"

Uneasy laughter cut short.

"Speak. Lastenarron. I see Khir's marks, but surely this wretched piece of filth is not the bonded one I sought?"

"This is the warrior I fought."

A weary sigh. "Another child, another offering from my brother Khir. How generous."

"This *child* killed hundreds of our kind." Another ghoul's tone dripped venom. "At the battle of Dal-Benden he spared no one. Remember the slaughter at the Hall of Rollo? Him. The signs of Khir scar his skin, witness to his vicious nature."

A low, angry murmur coiled about the hall.

"Who else will speak?" The voice was calm but carried.

"I will," a ghoul cried. Then another. "I was at the Hall of Rollo."

Shouts. Hisses. Noise. Kaell drifted. Whatever he had drunk swept him far from the voices, from the accusations. A sharp slap forced him back.

"Be gentle, Lastenarron." The speaker stood close, his words like warm fingers on naked skin. That strange tingling ripped up Kaell's back again.

"Who are you?" he whispered.

"I am he who gathered with my brothers and sisters at the dawn of this age. My people call me Lord of Blood, their god. I am Archanin. You will know me, obey me, and kneel to me, as your lord."

Kaell's heart skidded in his chest. No. Archanin was a myth.

"What answer do you make?"

He trembled. "Every accusation is true, no doubt. I am your enemy. Kill me."

An amused laugh echoed. "Your lord taught you a bonded warrior's destiny is to fight and die. That he serves his king, his lord. And then his gods grant him death. Peace."

"I am your enemy. You must kill me."

The hush prickled with expectation. Into that chasm, Archanin laughed. A gloating laugh that lifted hairs on Kaell's arms. "Kill you? Lastenarron, you served me in the desert before my brothers and sisters banished us. What do you say?"

"I want to hear his screams. Then I want him dead."

A furious tumult broke out. "Yes, kill him. Punish him, then kill him."

Kaell tried to slip away from their hatred, but pain trapped him in this nightmare. He hoped death neared. Surely it would be gentle, like the girl's kiss in his dreams.

"Silence." Archanin's voice cut through the uproar. "You forget my words when I learned of that cursed book. You forget that he is the key to my freedom, to our victory."

A sullen quiet settled on the hall. Alive, surely. Waiting. Watchful.

"How short-sighted you all are. You think only of your rage, of vengeance. I could so easily satisfy your thirst. I could butcher him right now with his sword. I have it here, the instrument of his lethal destiny. Or I could drain every drop of his wretched life."

"You cannot drain a bonded warrior," a ghoul yelled. "His blood poisons us."

Breath lost within, stiff with fear, Kaell strained to see through the cloth.

Quietly, Archanin said, “You forget who I am.”

“We forget nothing, my lord. We remember who our enemies are.”

“And you would give those enemies peace?”

“What would you give them? A kiss?” They all laughed then.

“A bitter kiss, yes.”

Another uneasy hush fell. Lengthened. Beneath it rolled darkness and blazing power as though this chamber could not contain Archanin’s presence, his will.

Cold sweat broke out at the back of Kaell’s neck. He trembled from head to toe.

“My lord, what do you mean?” Lastenarron said.

“Just this. I will not give this warrior the peace of death.”

Kaell sobbed a panicked breath. Sick, his spirit frayed, he wanted only to die.

“I know your anger.” Archanin’s voice rose above their muttering. “I understand your fear. He is a hunter, yes. But what if he hunted men? What if my brother’s weapon belonged to me? A bonded warrior who fights with us, not against us.”

“Impossible.”

“Who said that? Nothing is impossible for your god. His hair is pale. I am told he has green eyes. You know what that means.”

“He must die. Punish him, lord. Kill him.”

“Yes. Kill him.” Others fell upon the words as a chant.

“Fools!”

Kaell shuddered at the contained fury in Archanin’s tone. He imagined ghouls reeling back as fear hunted like a chill wind about the hall.

“Every bonded warrior desires death. I will not give it to him. Not to this one. No, I will make him what he hates most.”

Archanin paused. When not even a breath stirred air, he said, “One of us.”

No one spoke. Then a ghoul snickered. A second joined in. Then another. Until ugly, mocking laughter rang through the hall.

It rolled like a wave, then ebbed away. As if a storm approached, the air charged with excitement, a cruel, knife-thin expectation.

Stunned, Kaell struggled to understand. Then terror leapt at him like flames. “No, no, no!” Twisting, wrenching, he tore at the irons until blood streamed down his wrists and arms.

Air shifted heavy and grim. A scent swirled. It was tantalisingly gentle, only a thread of sand, heat, and wild roses. Another’s breath flowed in and out, slower than his inflamed heart, hammering the silence with dread.

Fingers touched his cheek. Kaell choked on a scream.

“Be still. Still.” The softly spoken words rang with power. Those fingers stroked his lank hair. Limp in his chains, Kaell whimpered and was at once ashamed.

His captor grasped his chin. Breath warmed his neck.

Kaell could not move a muscle. Then, like hot knives, pain erupted, convulsing through his body. And he knew nothing.

VAL ARQUES

Vraymorg woke with a cry, his heart stormy against his ribs. What was that sound? He peered about his bedchamber. A shutter thumped against the stone wall.

Tossing furs aside, he padded to the window, the floor boards cool beneath his soles. Grey dawn welled in hollows between distant peaks, its ghastly light pallid on frost-covered fields. A vicious, skirring wind whipped his hair.

His nakedness adorned in gooseflesh, he fastened the shutter and crawled into bed, a sting behind his eyelids.

How *she* would laugh if he wept. Bloodless, Devarsi had called him. A man too afraid to feel. Why think of a long-dead queen now? Because his curse had started with his oath to her?

Or because of the boy.

I knew the danger. Surely I did not let myself care?

Restless, a tug at his heart, he rose again, threw a blanket about his shoulders, and paced. A wall tapestry, the only colour in his drab chamber, caught his eye. Faded threads depicted a warrior on his knees, sword and helm spilled, an enemy's steel at his bowed neck.

Centuries ago when this castle belonged to the Serravan order of warriors, the tapestry had hung in the great hall. Vraymorg, then a naïve student, often stared at it, puzzled. At last he asked the weapons master why the Serravan displayed a symbol of defeat.

"To warn against pride," the man said. "Every bladesman knows defeat—sooner or later."

I was proud, Vraymorg thought, tracing the kneeling warrior's embroidered face with stiff fingers. *Proud of Kaell. Of his quick wits, his speed. The way the sword answered to him.*

Had he let himself care too much? Was he kind when he should have been strict?

Had his pride failed Kaell?

Reluctantly, grief a cold, hard spear in his breast, he thought back to the previous night. To drinking beside the fire with the king's messenger, Patric of the Falls.

"The villagers of Thom sent word to Caelmarsh, and he to the king, when your men didn't return," Patric had said. "They were afraid to enter the forest. But Caelmarsh's soldiers did. I went with them as the king's representative."

He stirred the fire with a tong. "Your men were dead. I'd spare you the grizzly details, my lord."

"No. Tell me what you saw."

The messenger released a drawn-out, bleak sigh. "Some died from sword thrusts or blows from axes. But the wounded—" His voice fell away.

Vraymorg leaned, hands clasped tightly on his thighs. "Tell me."

"It's not pretty, my lord. Ghouls fed upon them. We buried the bodies in the forest."

And Kaell? He could not ask. He could not. "All of them dead? And—"

Patric studied a green-stoned ring on his middle finger. The silence lengthened. Bawling wind rattled a branch against a window. Crisp autumn air smelt of snow.

And Kaell. What of Kaell?

The messenger looked at him. "We did not find his body, my lord."

"Are you certain? Was he—" Vraymorg closed his eyes. "Was Kaell disfigured, unrecognisable?"

Again a pause. In a quiet voice, Patric said, "The dead all had dark hair, my lord."

VRAYMORG DROPPED his shaking hand from the tapestry. Like a malignant beast, ashen morning crept across the great pass and into his chamber. Cold rattled his teeth.

He forced himself to confront Patric's words.

Then the ghouls took Kaell's body, or worse, took him, to torture or humiliate.

A wretched thought, too huge, too terrible to bear. If he were a wolf, he might howl out his grief. If he believed in gods, he'd fall to his knees and beg them to kill Kaell sooner than his captors intended.

Kaell gone. He could not take it in. Didn't want to accept it. Wouldn't. Would—*not.*

No. The soldiers didn't find Kaell's body. Maybe, maybe, he had escaped.

"The villagers say they warned Kaell one hundred ghouls or more waited in the forest," Patric's words repeated in his mind. "Outnumbered, he still insisted on attacking."

Pride. Vraymorg's gaze dwelled on the tapestry. A warning against pride.

A NIGHTMARE SNARED him the moment he slept. With a soundless cry of terror, he jerked awake. Bright sunlight pierced the shutters. It hurt his eyes.

Ewen stood over him, puffing as if he had sprinted up the stairs.

"You must see this."

Blunt words. No apology for disturbing him.

Trouble then.

Vraymorg stumbled from the bed. Chill air stabbed his ankles. Last night's fire had died to ash. He dressed quickly.

"Where?"

"At the gates."

He followed Ewen from the room and into the stairwell. Nothing to hear but their boots tapping stone. A hush shrouded the castle.

"The dead gather," Arn had told Kaell on a morning like this when the boy was younger. "The souls of those who froze in the night mask every noise."

Kaell had shivered. "What makes them go away?"

"Laughter," Arn said. "Or one of your rhyming songs, little one." He'd chuckled deep in his throat the way he always did.

Vraymorg almost paused to listen, as though Arn's laugh might echo about the stairwell.

Ewen grasped his elbow to steer him on. "Val. Quickly."

Soft snow carpeted dead grass in the ward. By noon it would churn to mush. That was autumn in the Silent Mountains. Ice, drizzle, the stink of mud, and bitter winds carrying the voices of the dead.

Figures huddled by the gates. Quiet, like the keep. They parted for him. A sentry dropped his eyes to his boots. A stable boy, too young to know better, stared boldly.

At the foot of the wall, snow partly covered a long bundle. Vraymorg dropped to his knees. With a shaking hand he untied cord.

Ewen fidgeted at his shoulder. "Is it his, then?"

Vraymorg pulled the sword clear. A woman gasped. A young voice sobbed.

He wound numb fingers around the hilt. The familiar blade's glint mocked. A burst of wind iced his neck. It blew hard then fell away like a trumpet blast heralding what? An end? A beginning?

Soon the wind would turn. Soon it would bring spring's riotous colour to the land. Then summer's frolicking, honeyed warmth. Followed by winter, bleak winter, again. Another year. Then another. Until Khir whispered about another boy.

Vraymorg would not care about that boy. Not again. Yet…

"When was it found? Who left it?"

A guardsman stepped forward. "Just before dawn, my lord. I was in the tower and saw a figure approach the gates. I challenged them. Then I loosed a few arrows."

He jerked his head towards the treeless ground rolling from the walls. "I called Garth. We went to look, retrieve my arrows. That's when we saw the bundle. We woke the captain, and he sought Ewen."

Vraymorg nodded. He beckoned his new watch captain to his side.

Philip rubbed smudged eyes, his face gaunt. A candle had burned in his rooms when Vraymorg retired to bed. With the king's demands for men and weapons, too few men defended the castle. The young captain's burdens sat heavily.

"They could still be close," Philip said. "Hiding, now the sun's up."

"I doubt it." This was a message, not a trap. "But take some of the new men to check the woods. They're raw so be careful." He could ill afford to lose more warriors, trained or otherwise.

They were yet to count the dead from Thom.

PHILIP BROUGHT news to the hall of a fruitless search. Back to the fire, Vraymorg thumbed the thread on Fortitude's hilt. Ewen lifted his head from the account books to listen.

"That boy has a good head about him," he muttered when Vraymorg sent Philip off to sleep. "But there's talk. Hard to miss the resemblance."

Vraymorg shrugged, unconcerned by gossip.

He stroked the sword's tapered steel, so smooth beneath his fingertips. Years ago, in this very room, he'd first put Fortitude in Kaell's hands. The boy could not suppress a beaming smile.

He didn't know his lord was handing him death.

Vraymorg's eyes smarted. No. No tears. *Shields up. Do not think about Kaell.*

Dully, he polished a spot on the glinting blade. How did Seithin blade smiths make this terrible weapon? How did they produce enough heat to fold the metal hundreds of times?

The sword's secrets did not frighten him. Too much in this castle groaned with the otherworld's chill whispers. Some folk, the more superstitious, might even call *him* a thing of darkness—if they knew the truth.

Ewen scratched a mark in a book. "This coming war will break us. Do you know how expensive rope is? Every rope maker in the Mountains works day and night, but we won't be able to supply all the king needs."

"Without rope the king's siege engines are useless. Arbalests, mangonels." Vraymorg laughed at a memory. "When I was a boy, Isles engineers preferred to use hair for siege engines. Perhaps Aric is right now cutting off women's braids to defend Tide's End."

Ewen snorted. "Cutting off men's braids, more likely. Can't tell the difference in the Isles." He bent over his books again. "This castle has more arrows than snowflakes."

"The kings of Telor have always stored weapons here." He stroked the sword's steel again. Sleek. Dangerous.

Ewen looked up and glared. "Put down that cursed blade. What did the paper say?"

What quick eyes he had. "Paper?"

Ewen wagged a finger. "I saw you hide it beneath your cloak. What was it? A ghoul threat? What?"

"How is Philip performing as captain, do you think?"

"So you don't want to tell me?"

Vraymorg sighed. He took rolled parchment from his sleeve and flattened it.

"Four words, that's all."

"Yes?"

"It says: 'For the next one.'"

Ewen stormed to his feet. His mouth formed words that didn't come.

"They'll pay." Vraymorg stared bleakly into the flames. Wood crackled then popped as though the fire jeered. Pay? Gods help him. How? The monsters taunted him. And he didn't even know where to search for them.

"Evil." Ewen shook his head. "Monstrous. That poor child—"

Grew up. Grew careless. "Is gone." With deliberate care he placed the sword down and clutched the table, his legs wobbly.

"Val." Ewen plucked at his sleeve. His face was tight with worry.

"I'm all right."

He wasn't. For all his shields, grief bowed his shoulders, weighed his spirit. It crept through his blood, exhaled in every breath; a malicious shadow beneath every thought.

"I think it's time for you to die," Ewen said.

"What?"

"You left it too long. There's been mutterings about how young you look. You should have pretended to die when the last king did."

"How could I?" Vraymorg spread his arms. "Kaell was only eight."

"Kaell's dead," Ewen said flatly. "Now might be the time to grow a thick beard, catch a chill, and die. I'll spread word about your bastard son. In a few months, you can reappear, minus the beard, and say you're Vraymorg's son. I'll back you up, just as my ancestors always backed you up."

"It isn't the right time. Come spring, the king will march on the Isles."

Philip entered and dipped his head. "My lord."

"I told you to sleep." Vraymorg's voice was gruffer than he intended.

"A guardsman brought this." Philip thrust a rose at him. "Someone left it at the gates."

A perfect bud, silky to touch, its petals an exquisite dark red, but with little scent. Just like the gift giver, perhaps? Beautiful to look at but everything else a lie.

Philip's questioning gaze bore into him.

"I must go." Vraymorg shoved Kaell's sword into his belt beside his own.

"Now?" Ewen cast a doubtful look at darkness gathering beyond the windows. "It's nearly nightfall."

Nightfall. At dawn. Whenever. Just so long as it was now. He wanted an end to the pain.

RIPPED BRANCHES from black-barked trees littered the path through the forest. Beneath his horse's churning hooves, leaves billowed, their red and gold tarnished beneath the grey palate of rain clouds.

The lashing wind at last lost its voice. Sullen air, thick with silence, left Vraymorg alone with his wretched thoughts.

He could not brush off his nightmare. It layered his skin like a cold sweat, insubstantial but stirring a queasy foreboding in his gut.

Because of the sword? Why send it back except to taunt him?

I want an end to it. All the heartache. I want to forget.

Vraymorg scratched his neck beneath his damp cloak. Water dripped from his eyelashes, from matted hair. The relentless drizzle chaffed his skin.

"Curse the rain that stings," a Telorian poet once wrote. "And the misery it brings."

Vraymorg had no time for poets. Yet sometimes they hit a

curious mark.

Unsettled, he fingered one of the two sword hilts at his hip. This forest scratched with memories—bad memories, the sort that tainted his dreams.

Once his past had nearly caught him here. And it all started with a game. Just a stupid game between him and Kaell.

A spring day. Yes, he remembered its scents. Dewy grass. That dry aroma of sage and doughy earth. Violets and bluebells sprayed across this very path, but crisp, windless air stung his cheeks, and shadows cast from lofty trunks overwhelmed pale sunlight.

He rode with his horse tightly reined, his glance flickering left and right. Somewhere in the trees, Kaell stole towards the waterfall Mountains folk called the Crystal Drop.

"Be as lithe as creeping darkness," Vraymorg instructed the boy before they set out. A phrase his tutors had taught him centuries ago. Be swift. Be silent. Be smart.

All just words. Useless words. Kaell might be swift but reckless as well. What happened at Thom proved that.

But that spring day he had clue Kaell could be so rash.

He remembered Kaell flashing a brash grin as he slipped into the undergrowth. He even remembered thrashing a gloved hand at bushes scratching his legs as he stared after the boy, wondering if he had been that cocky at fourteen.

Just as Kaell disappeared, Vraymorg heard a woman singing, her voice clear and sweet. A girl from a nearby village, perhaps, searching for early raspberries.

Vraymorg forgot her as he splashed across a stream and onto a path through low-swept boughs. Ahead, a figure stood silhouetted against the dark trunks.

He squinted. As the figure came into focus, Vraymorg recognised Kaell and laughed.

"I don't think you grasped the point of this, young fool. You're meant to be stealthy. Not just stand there on the path and wait for me to find you."

Kaell did not answer.

"Kaell?"

The boy turned, his smile remote. "Don't you hear it, my lord?"

Hear what? Only the woman's high-pitched song carried in the stillness.

"She's calling. I must go to her, my lord."

Her? Go? A prickling at Vraymorg's neck became a shudder. "Kaell! Come here."

Without looking at him, the boy stepped off the path into the trees.

"Stop!"

Vraymorg sprang from his horse and peered into a tangle of gloomy trunks, of snaked vines and red-berried bushes. No sign of the boy.

"Kaell!" Panic laced his shout. Uneasily he remembered Kaell's rapt look. What was happening here? Some spell? Yes, beneath the soft, lyric tone, the song held power.

Grasping the horse's bridle, he pursued into the unwelcoming forest. Creaking branches clawed his face. Roots spread as though to trip him. Whispers drifted. Rich, deep caramel scents of earth whorled with threads of mud, pine, and the sweat beading on his brow.

A crackle of dead leaves fractured the quiet. Vraymorg wrenched his sword free. A rough-skinned lizard considered him then scuttled off.

Other eyes watched from the undergrowth. A fox? A bird? The mare whinnied. Absently he stroked her nose.

The song broke off. Vraymorg hissed in a breath. No beacon to track Kaell. He forced down paralysing fear. Which way now? One black-barked tree looked like the next.

The thud in his chest belted ribs. *Breathe. Decide. Do nothing and achieve nothing.* More words from the past when he trained as a Serravan warrior. *Indecision is action's enemy.*

Vraymorg hurried straight on, marking trunks with his knife.

No birdsong, no wind. Sodden leaves piled as though undisturbed for months. Surely no one had come this way.

As he retraced his steps, the cut trees mocked him. *You won't find him. The Silent Mountains take the lost.*

Vraymorg veered right, slipping on sloped ground. The mare snorted as he jerked the bridle. He patted her flank and clambered down knotted roots into a gully dense with delicate ferns. Water trickled through the muddy bottom. In soft earth, a heel imprinted. A booted heel.

Vraymorg released his held breath. Thank The Three for Kaell's careless haste.

He led the mare back up to a clearing, only to trip over a stump. Cleanly cut as if felled by an axe. Further on, a second stunted trunk then a third marked a trail.

The mare pulled back, nostrils flared. When he tried to coax her forward, she bucked. The forest's stillness unsettled him, too: the black trunks, the eerie absence of birdsong, the changing shape of shadows.

Looping the horse's reins about a bush, Vraymorg put aside his prickling apprehension and followed the stumps into a shady grove. He stepped from the trees into drenching sunlight and drew up short, hand on hilt, the thinnest breeze stirring his hair, breath stalled.

Near a derelict woodsman's hut, Kaell knelt before a young woman, his sword sheathed, neck bent and bared, stretched, vulnerable.

The woman lifted her head and locked her eyes with Vraymorg's. For a second that stare snared him. Then he curled his fingers about his hilt and strode at her.

The woman smiled. She broke into song. The melody hit Vraymorg like a wall. He slammed to a stop. Her song flowed into him, a dusting over his skin, a sweet burning in his veins, a dizzying drum beat in his skull.

"Kaell. Step away. Fight this. Fight. Draw your sword."

The woman sang louder. She tilted Kaell's chin with a finger. A tiny gesture, but possessive. Taunting. *Come, take him. I dare you.*

Anger knotted in his belly and flowed into his limbs. Shoulders hunched, Vraymorg pressed through air viscous with dark music as though wading a battering storm.

A sword length from her, he levelled his blade. "Move away from the boy."

The woman quietened. Sunlight struck a silver brooch clasping a cloak over a fustian gown. Reddish-brown hair spilled beneath a ruby-encrusted band as she tilted her head to consider him. She was young and pretty with freckles sprinkled on a delicate nose. Soft but for her eyes. They were hard and unafraid.

"Why don't you hear me?" Her voice thrummed with power.

For the briefest moment that voice lulled him. He shook it off. "Witch. Let the boy go."

"So I shall. For I did not call him." She twitched a triumphant smile. "I called you."

Boiling emotions plugged his throat, briefly burying his voice within. Surprise. Alarm. Who was she? What did she mean "called him?" Why him? Because he was lord of these Mountains? Or because she knew he was… someone else?

"Let him go, witch."

"That word again. Witch." She rolled it about her mouth with disgust. "Your ignorance surprises me. Your strength does not. Though perhaps you wear a protective charm."

"Who are you?"

"Someone sent to trap you. You hid for centuries, Val Arques. But now you are both betrayed and exposed."

His body stiffened with panic. He knew only too well who hunted him, who'd hunted him for centuries. Could he bluff? Deny who he was? Or had they watched him a while?

Swallowing hard, he managed, "You're Quisnaf. You must be."

The woman pushed back her hair. A tattoo swirled from her shoulder to neck, its writhing reds and greens vibrant and alive.

The mark of the Quisnaf goddess Cyrah. He clicked his tongue against teeth, fighting panic. Keep control. For Kaell's sake.

"What now?"

She stroked Kaell's hair. "You drop your sword and fall to your knees. Or I hurt the boy."

"Let the boy go."

The woman laughed and tossed her head with a swing of auburn hair.

"Why? Because he's yours? No. Your hair is dark and his pale. Yet you came for him, so you value him."

One lunge and he could grab Kaell. Unless her magic held him off.

Get closer. Do, say, promise, whatever it takes to save the boy. That was all that mattered. Kaell. Keeping him safe. It was all that ever mattered.

As if guessing his thoughts, the woman uncurled a smug smile. She whipped out a knife and thrust it to Kaell's throat. The boy peered up at her with trusting eyes.

Vraymorg flung down his sword. "Don't hurt him."

"Go inside," she said. "Fetch the blue bottle on the table. Be quick, or I slit his throat."

Vraymorg stood his ground, his body tight with rage. How to escape her trap? Think.

The woman sighed. Slowly, precisely, she caressed Kaell's jaw with the blade.

"Stop." He threw up his empty hands. Sweat broke out on his back.

"The bottle."

With dragging footsteps, Vraymorg trudged to the thatched hut and kicked the door in so hard it dangled from hinges.

The gloomy room inside stank of mildew and trapped smoke from a fire blackening the hearth. Weeds sprouted between slanting, grubby floorboards. Cloudy webs clung like hoarfrost to a splintering, wooden pole supporting a sagged roof.

It contained only a mattress, table, and chair. And one blue bottle.

Vraymorg snatched it up and stomped outside. "I have it. Let him go."

"On your knees."

Reluctantly he dropped. "Let him go."

"Uncork the bottle. Drink."

Ah, he wondered how she hoped to control him. The bottle must hold a sleeping draught. Drink and he'd wake a prisoner on a ship sailing for Quisnaf.

The knife glinted. A thin, red line streaked Kaell's neck. Still the boy did nothing, only looked at her with dazed, unquestioning eyes.

Anger shut down reason. His every muscle compressed, ready to spring.

Vraymorg seized a breath. *Think, fool. Submit, or she'll hurt Kaell. Save Kaell.*

Do whatever it took. Offer himself up. Did it matter, did it really matter what happened to him? He was damaged already.

Vraymorg ripped the cork out. "Swear you won't hurt him."

She shrugged. "I have no interest in him. I want you."

He drank.

"All of it."

She watched with a thin smile as he drained the bottle and hurled it away. "You'll sleep now. Long enough for my warrior sisters to come for you. I sent my servant to fetch them the moment I glimpsed you in the forest. They're close."

Vraymorg swayed on his knees. "It's a long way to Quisnaf. Not so easy to take a man so far against his will. Especially as I'll fight you every step."

She mocked him with lifted brows. "My sisters are prepared." Her knife fell from Kaell's throat. At least Vraymorg thought it did. Trees moved around him. Shadows flickered.

The woman cupped Kaell's face. "Guard this man until he sleeps. Then drag him inside."

The boy shot to his feet, ripped his sword from its scabbard, and pointed it at Vraymorg.

"His sword." The woman jabbed a trembling hand. "I recognise that design on the hilt, the etching along the blade. This is an evil sword."

"What?" Kaell carried a centuries-old blade of Seithin steel. Why evil?

"From all they told me of you, Val Arques, I didn't pick you for a fool. You do not give such a vicious weapon to a child."

Words thickened in his throat. Too tired. "This boy is destined to carry that sword."

"You lie. Only a warrior of Khir's, or a seer, a true seer, should carry such a blade. Is he Roaran Caelan in disguise? Impossible. He must not touch that sword."

Vraymorg teetered, eyelids drooping. Sleep plucked with velvet hands. So easy to let it have him. "Why should I lie? Now free him, or risk the wrath of the god who marked him."

"Marked?" She fumbled beneath Kaell's sleeve. To Vraymorg's alarm, she laughed, her fear gone. "Khir's sigils. A bonded warrior. A prize my sisters shall gladly take too."

"No!" What had he done? Instead of frightening her about gods and their vengeance, he only betrayed Kaell's value.

She rubbed ringed hands. "All this while I waited in this foul hut for you to return to this forest. This makes up for my misery. The Quisnaf council will reward me well."

Vraymorg thrust out a palm. Blackness spun on the edge of his vision. His cheek cushioned on dew-scented grass. A storm of darkness swept in.

HE WOKE WITH A THROBBING SKULL, woodsmoke in his nostrils, and dread pulsing his heart.

Vraymorg straightened stiff legs. Iron welted his wrists at the back of a rotting post in the hut stinking of neglect. His captor, it seemed, took no chances.

"You're awake already." The Quisnaf woman huddled in a chair by the fire.

Smoke twisted into shapes that seemed to float above her then spiral into darkness. It stung his eyes. Air bitter with cold and prickling with damp defied the crackling flames.

The woman rose. "I thought my draught stronger."

"Where's Kaell?"

She gestured to a mattress. "He's sleeping. Now I know what he is, I'll be very careful with him. Such a prize."

Vraymorg sighed with relief. With stiff fingers he scrabbled at planks behind the post. If he could break off a splinter, he might spring the lock.

"I found your horse. A mare? How untypical."

"I have a healthy respect for females. Even Quisnaf women who chain me up."

"Very wise, given what's ahead of you. I set your mare free to run home. No doubt they'll look for you. They won't find you. Not before my sisters arrive at dawn."

Vraymorg scratched a moan from his dry throat. His temple throbbed.

The woman passed amber eyes over him leisurely. She smoothed her hair.

"You must be thirsty." She knelt and put a waterskin to his lips. He caught a wisp of lilac as she needlessly pressed against him. "Drink."

Vraymorg wrenched his head aside, too aware of her breast against his ribs.

"You don't trust me?" She swigged water then brushed his lips with her wet mouth. "I should put you to sleep again, but we've a long night ahead."

Groggy, thirsty, Vraymorg drank. Water trickled down his chin. When she pulled the skin away, he leaned his head against the post with a sigh, surprised at a slow heat moving through his body, a softening of the edges in his mind, a relaxation of tension.

"Better?" Fingers traced beads of moisture on his throat. "Mmm, your skin is cool."

Her hand lingered.

"Take your hand off me."

"What do you imagine our blood keepers intend? With your precious Caelan blood, they'll make good use of you." Slowly, slowly, she walked fingers to his breast and unlaced his shirt. Her caress glided beneath to bare flesh.

He growled. "Don't touch me."

"You're in no position to object, Val Arques. Iron on your wrists. My sisters on their way. How shall we fill the time? Hmm? Why not enjoy an hour of pleasure? You're very pretty, and it can be lonely in this silent forest night after night."

"Do—not—touch—me."

"You don't mean that." She fisted his hair, pulling his head close. He could not stop his lips parting as hers pressed, allowing her tongue to thrust and flicker in his mouth.

Her breath fluttered over his cheek. One hand stroked ridged muscles beneath his shirt; the other gripped his hip to hold him against her.

Vraymorg's senses blurred until he knew only the touch of fingers, the perfume of her hair, a crush of heavy breasts.

Shame flushed up his neck into his jaw. What was he doing? Thinking? No, not thinking. Groaning, Vraymorg pulled from her embrace. "What did you give me?"

"It's called Black Velvet." She ran her palm over his shoulder. "Don't fight it. It can be very pleasant. If you're worried about the boy, he won't wake for hours."

She touched a droplet of sweat on his collarbone. "Time enough for us to take our pleasure. It's a while since I've been with a man." Undeterred, she brushed soft lips over his again.

Vraymorg pressed his back into the post. "Get off me. I don't want this."

"A lie." Her hand fondled between his thighs. "Yes, a lie. Be nice, and I'll tell you who betrayed you, told us where to find you."

He bucked. Still her hand encouraged too-willing flesh. Bound, his body responding to whatever Black Velvet was, his best weapon was his tongue. "You show your true Quisnaf skin. You bed men only to prove them weak."

The woman rose off him gracefully. "Or because I'm bored. I've been in this hateful forest for a long time. Often, all by myself."

"How sad."

She tapped his cheek. "What a proud fool. Beg to touch me, and I might free one hand. A chance to manipulate me, convince me to release you? I won't. Though I might pretend to want to. But since you're so disagreeable, you can sit there in discomfort all night, longing for any kind of sensation."

Vraymorg scraped a nail at a board. Wood splintered into soft skin beneath. He winced.

The woman considered him for a long moment. Shrugging, she returned to her chair.

He clutched the splinter in his fingertips. His wrists burned and bled as he twisted. At last the splinter slid into the lock. Patiently he worked it back and forth.

"You have a look." The woman squinted. "What mischief are you up to?"

"I'm hungry."

She rose to tend the fire. "What were your words? How sad?"

The lock clicked. Vraymorg ripped his hands free and sprang up. The woman spun. She flung up her arms as though expecting him to hit her.

He didn't. He punched the post. Hard. The blow held every bit of his fear for Kaell, his despair at his powerlessness. The chains, captivity snapped back nightmares, buried deep where they only poisoned his dreams.

The woman dashed for her knives. Vraymorg blocked her.

She rocked to a halt. Her face was contorted with spite. When she tried to edge around, he snatched up Kaell's blade and put his bulk between her and the weapons. "I intend to walk out of here with Kaell. Do not try to stop me. You're no bladeswoman, and your magic doesn't work on me."

Her lips thinned with loathing. She said nothing.

He turned and lifted Kaell to carry him to safety, leaving her staring after him in that cold, quiet hut that reeked of damp and decay.

He didn't know her name. He didn't care.

VRAYMORG'S CHATTERING TEETH snapped him from the past, from uncomfortable memories of a nameless Quisnaf woman. His frozen fingers struggled to hold the reins. A wolf howled in the distance for the absent moon.

"By moonlight, she loves me," Vraymorg sang to the trees. "Her name lost to time. When tides turn, I howl at the moon: she'll never be mine."

Where did he hear that? From a minstrel singing at the Mountains castle for a meal and a silver coin? No, an Isles song. From his youth.

"When tides turn, I howl at the moon," he sang louder. "A curse is upon me, she'll never be—" He broke off. A glow in a window pierced the gloom.

Shoulders hunched, he urged the horse forward.

The manor house sat in a tangle of branches and trunks. Leaves clotted on a sloping roof. Pine-scented smoke puffed from a stone chimney.

A young man with fringed black hair and sun-brown skin took his horse. A stranger. The second man, though—oh, he remembered the insolent Tarvan Blackstone.

"Look who's here." Blackstone slouched near the door. "Our splendid, brave, excellent, and always handsome Lord of the Mountains."

"I hear your sister is the king's new torturer," Vraymorg said. "My, my. How you must wish you could rise to such lofty heights."

He stepped around the sneering Blackstone and bobbed his head at a third figure, a woman dressed in fur. She threw him a distracted nod.

As he ducked beneath the overhanging roof, Rozenn flung the door open.

"Welcome." She wore an enticing smile that could mean anything and a gown that hugged every delicious curve. Her beauty always struck him anew. But what lay beneath?

He remembered a bleak night, miserable with shadows. How the wind howled outside and a lonely man looked up from his books to find Rozenn at his door. How she let her cloak fall to the floor. How her bare skin glistened in spluttering candlelight.

Even then, as he took her in his arms, he sensed she wanted something from him.

Tonight you delivered me the throne.

A threat in that. But Gendrick Caelan claimed Rozenn's son as his, the fruits of the queen's visit to the Isles nine months before the birth.

"I wanted to unsettle you. To punish you for unsettling me," she had explained that first time they met in the forest. He went to reason with her about Kaell. That's what he told himself.

Whatever she kept from him, he had secrets too. Deeds stained with shame he locked within. Never to look at.

"Come inside," Rozenn whispered. "I missed you."

Vraymorg swept her hand to his lips. She wore a different ring. Wrought gold, set with pearl and jade.

He stilled, his lips caught on warm flesh. A deathly, ghastly moon at last poked through clouds. Its wan glitter fell on shadowy trees, gleamed on Rozenn's perfect skin.

A memory ripped through him like a knife cut. Kaell's story about the woman who had tried to smother him. The boy remembered her perfume. And glimpsed beneath his blindfold a ring on slender fingers. A ring of gold and pearl and jade.

Slowly Vraymorg lifted his eyes from her hand to her face. Moonlight beat upon bright hair, but the roof's treacherous shadow hid her expression.

"Ah," she said. "He did see my ring. Safer to discard it. But my father gave it to me."

"Kaell remembered your scent. Vanilla and rose. Why didn't I realise at once?"

"That is unfortunate," Rozenn said.

No denial. No protests. No look of remorse. Just three useless words.

Anger kindled in his veins, a need to punish her for trying to hurt Kaell.

Rozenn turned and walked inside. Vraymorg stalked after her. "I warned you," he said. "But you went after him again. Gods, Rozenn. He was so young."

A floorboard creaked. Candlelight struck metal. Vraymorg groped for his sword.

"Tarvan, no." Rozenn waved the man back. The bladesman glared at Vraymorg, his fingers restless on the hilt of his raised weapon. Hostility smouldered between them.

"He dares raise his voice at you. He dares threaten you, my Queen."

"It's all right."

Scowling, Tarvan lowered his sword, shoved it into its scabbard and stomped outside.

Vraymorg wheeled on Rozenn, his breath ragged. "We agreed you'd stand down. Kaell was my problem."

"Yet you did nothing." Her low voice carved every word with contempt. "Your arrogance astounds even me, your stubborn belief you're always right. That you can control everything."

"I don't kill children because of words in a stupid book. But you do. Just how cold are you? You even knew not to spill his blood. What stopped you smothering him?"

She dropped her gaze and muttered, "My son convinced me of my error."

"Just like the last error? When you sent your own cousin to a tournament to kill him?"

"And paid for it." Her slender shoulders shook. She looked younger, vulnerable. The anger blew out of him—as it always did.

"Rozenn—" Before her grief, Vraymorg stood helpless. Unspoken words piled up in him.

I'm sorry. I didn't mean to wound you. It's just I'm afraid. Not ready to accept Kaell is dead. No. I must feel nothing. Nothing.

"A mistake, Val. I couldn't just trust the gods. Not like you."

He touched a tear on her eyelash. "Don't cry. I've made mistakes, too."

A branch grated against the shutters. Sparks danced in the hearth as a charred log rolled.

Against the red ember fire, the candles seemed like a tiny oasis of light in the vast night. A silence sat beneath the wind's moan, beneath the rustling leaves, beneath that incessant, nagging tap, tap, tap against the window.

He rubbed his temples with taut fingers. "I don't want to fight."

"Nor do I. Not with you. Not tonight." Rozenn lifted her hand to his hair. Her touch was tender, but his scalp tingled beneath the heat of her fingers.

"I heard about Thom, about Kaell," she said. "That he's missing. I know how much you hurt, not knowing what's happened to him. Whether he's a prisoner—or—" She dug her teeth into her bottom lip. "Val, let me comfort you."

The branch tapped and tapped. A grinding in his skull. *Stop,* he thought. *Stop. Just stop.*

Vraymorg stumbled to the fire, his legs unsteady. He gripped the hearth's warm, uneven stones. The heat did not penetrate his body. Cold, everything cold. The emptiness within him, cold. His pushed-back grief, its hollow pit in his belly, cold.

"Nothing seems to matter," he said. "Not now."

Rozenn unclasped his cloak. Carefully she laid it over a chair. "I've a hot bath ready. I know what you want."

"I want you." A desperation lay beneath his blurted words. I want you to take away this ache, he could have said. With your lips, your caresses. I want to lose myself in desire, empty or not so empty, to dull every wretched thought with mindless pleasure.

He drew her against him, breathing in not only vanilla and rose, but woodsmoke and the lavender candles she burnt when they met. A wonderful ménage of fragrances so rich he could nearly taste them.

"How long do we have?" How long could he hide here?

"Only tonight. It's dangerous enough. If Cathmor knew we conspired, he'd behead you."

Conspired. A curious word for seeking comfort in her bed. Beyond the sensual release of their lovemaking, he often wondered if Rozenn, too, desired to escape duty for a few hours in this wood, with a man who'd tell no one.

She didn't love him. Yet on every journey to Dal-Kanu, she called to him, her rose a signal. *I'm waiting, Val. Come to our special place.* He wasn't sure how she slipped away, but no one apart from Ewen questioned his absences. They knew better.

"Only tonight?" Vraymorg kissed her hard. "Are you sure?"

"Your lips are cold. And your hands." She gestured to a wooden tub. "Be quick. The water won't stay hot."

"Curse the water. There's heat enough in this room as it is."

Rozenn laughed. She boldly watched him strip off boots, gloves, weapons belt, tunic, and pants. Steam reddened his cheeks and neck as he slid into the tub.

"I'm content to look at you." She brought him a cup of wine then propped her elbows on the tub's rim. Vraymorg sipped. He leaned back, rose-scented water lapping his throat.

"I see you have one of your women with you. I met her outside."

"Mmm, Alfreda." Rozenn drifted a hand through water. She glanced at his discarded sword. Kaell's lay beside it, wrapped in cloth. "She's discreet."

"Who's your new groomsman? The black-haired boy. He doesn't look Cahirean."

"We found him. A Telorian merchant's son. Varee outlaws attacked Reman and his father in the pass. The boy wandered for days, wounded, weak from blood loss." Her smile edged with mischief. "You must deal with these Varee wolf's heads, my lord. Up the bounty again on their war lord. The one you say is clever. What's his name?"

"Dannon Bloodtaker, they call him. Fortunate for this Reman you found him."

"Most fortunate. I tended his wounds."

"Oh, tended," he teased, not jealous but glad of the distracting banter. "Is that what you call it in Cahir?"

Rozenn slapped his arm and rocked to her feet. "Healed. He's loyal, grateful for my care. Useful, too. Filled your bath, cut wood for the fire."

"Does he, hmm, cut wood as well as I do?"

Rozenn offered that secret smile of hers. "I will not flatter your big head with a reply, my lord." She made a mock bow. "What shall we do tonight? Perhaps you'll share more stories of the Quisnaf and how they seek you?"

Vraymorg winced. "I should never have told you about that witch in the forest."

"It was raw in your mind when we met. You can be forgiven an indiscretion, Val."

"I want to forget that happened." It hardly mattered now. Nothing did.

Her throaty laugh always roused his desire. "As you wish—my lord."

"If only all Cahirean queens proved so obedient." He sighed dramatically.

"How dull obedient queens are. I don't suppose you'll say what the Quisnaf want of you? Whenever we come here now, I always expect a Quisnaf warrior to jump out at me."

"I don't suppose I will." He reached to smooth her hair streaked golden by candlelight. "Let's forget the Quisnaf. I know other stories."

"My favourites are about Roaran."

"Because he had magic. Like you."

She splashed water into his face. "Roaran had Quisnaf blood, desert magic. It's very different to Cahirean magic."

Different. His brother's child was that. Karolus had struggled to comfort his young son when strange visions troubled Roaran. What do you say to a child when you didn't quite understand what they are?

Like Kaell.

Kaell. Oh gods, Kaell. Where was he? What had happened to him? He had to be alive. But what if—No, no, no. *Do not even think it.*

Vraymorg slipped beneath the water. He held his breath, reluctant to surface from this muffled world. When at last he did, ice pinpricked his damp skin. Rising, he stepped out and dripped water to the fire. Rozenn held a cloth.

"I have his sword. Kaell's. I don't know why I brought it." He lifted his shoulders, then let them drop. "It's like I expect him to come for it, to find me. Or he's somehow closer when I feel its weight against my hip."

She blinked, astonished. "Wasn't the sword with him?"

Vraymorg did not trust himself to speak. The fire crackled. Rain pattered. A new wind swooped, high pitched and sibilant.

As a child, he had stood on the cliffs at Tide's End as the wind whipped across lathered waves with the scents of other lands and promised adventure. He let it pass through him, unafraid. What had happened to that boy who turned his face to the wind?

"How, Val?"

"The ghouls sent it back." Abruptly he crossed his arms. To hold in the pain. To hold himself upright. He was so dreadfully tired. Exhausted by the burden of gossamer-thin hope, the act of will it took to believe Kaell lived.

Rozenn removed the sword from its covering. As she might his skin, she stroked its gleaming metal. "It's a memory sword."

"I don't know what that is."

Rozenn glanced up sharply. "You're shaking. Are you cold?"

He turned to hide his expression. "Yes, cold."

"Val." She slid her hands about his waist. "You're thinking of Kaell. I'm sorry. What can I do? I didn't realise how much you love him."

"No." Vraymorg broke away. "I don't. I'm afraid for him, so afraid for this boy I raised. But not love. Never that. Love is a vicious master, Rozenn."

"Val—"

"I'm fond of him." Vraymorg nodded to himself. "Very fond. How couldn't I be?"

"Fond," she said.

The muscles in his back contracted hard. "Rozenn. Please. I can't think about him. Tell me about this sword. What is a memory sword?"

She watched him in silence. Then with an almost imperceptible shrug, she returned to the weapon. Closing her eyes, she said, "It hums."

Kaell said that. Vraymorg thought the boy too imaginative. Yet he, too, had sensed the blade's power fester for centuries.

"It's Seithin steel," he said distantly. "But why a memory sword?"

Few Seithin blades survived the desert city's immolation. Aric Caelan carried the infamous The Cup. A ridiculous name. Cup of sorrow? Cup of blood?

Perhaps Aric knew the meaning. He didn't really care. He couldn't care about much right now. At least beyond drinking and finding pleasure in her bed.

Rozenn traced etched symbols near the hilt. "I don't know this sword's story. Not really. I only know how the magic within might work."

"It has magic?"

She did not answer at once. Carefully, lovingly, she touched the iron. "I didn't expect you to have the sword, Val. That changes everything."

"I don't understand."

Reflected in the blade's glimmering steel, her face distorted with excitement. "This sword can do so much. It can even take away your pain."

"How?"

"You need only tell it stories."

Cold air stabbed at the base of his spine. Vraymorg wrapped cloth tight about his hips.

Is that what he wanted? To be done with pain? Why else shield his heart? Why else shape his world so he need not love or remember or feel too much? So he need not break.

"I am afraid."

"Of this blade? No. I know you too well, Val Arques. You fear the past."

VRAYMORG LAY ON cushions before the fire, naked beneath his cloak. Lavender-scented candles ringed with yellow light. His goblet spilled near his hand. Whatever Rozenn added to the wine tingled in his blood.

I should care, he thought. *But I can't.* With a curious detachment, he wondered if it even mattered if she drove a blade into his heart.

A temporary release, death. But a release. Better than sleep that brought only nightmares. Shut his eyes, and his worst fears played out: chains on Kaell's wrists, the boy's scream as a ghoul bent his head to his neck.

Vraymorg rocked his head to shake the images away. Just a dream. It didn't happen. It couldn't. But the ghouls had Kaell's blade. Did they hold Kaell too?

Rozenn knelt and brushed damp hair from his eyes, her touch tender.

"You put something in the wine," he muttered. "I can trust you, Rozenn, can't I?"

He laughed mirthlessly. "What am I saying? A Mountains lord knows you can't trust a Cahirean of royal blood. Yet I can't see how it benefits you to hurt me."

"Hush. The wine will calm you. We embark on a strange journey." She laid Kaell's sword against his bare breast, its cool steel oddly clammy.

"What do I do?" he whispered. "Can this blade really stop the nightmares?"

"The sword feeds upon stories." Rozenn smoothed his brow with a thumb. "Tell it about Kaell."

"Where do I start?"

"Your first memory of him. Where you found him. Start there."

Vraymorg fidgeted. "I can't talk about that."

"If you think I can't guess"—Rozenn shrugged—"it doesn't matter what memories you share as long as they're strong."

His head fell back. A heady mix of scents swirled: vanilla, woodsmoke, wine, lavender. "The strongest memory then."

That meant Paulin. And the girl.

NATE CAELMARSH RODE into the castle as imperious and ridiculous as a dressed-up toad.

As the Downs lord and his soldiers threaded through the gatehouse into the ward, Kaell bristled with excitement at Vraymorg's side on the guard walk.

At sixteen, he stood as tall as his lord. A belt slung around his hips accentuated his long legs. His cape billowed grey and black, Vraymorg's colours. A tunic of white silk draped black pants.

Vraymorg had instructed servants to lay out these garments. With polished boots and groomed hair, the boy looked more courtier than warrior, but Caelmarsh must understand Kaell's worth. A bonded warrior served gods, not lords or even kings.

"That's Caelmarsh's captain." Vraymorg stabbed the air. "Paulin the Pious men call him—behind his back. Say it to his face, and he'll poke a knife in your ribs."

"Why pious?"

"Studied to be a priest. The story goes he attacked a fellow student who bored him. Not Paulin's calling, the priesthood. He makes a better soldier as long as you watch your back. Next to him"—he pointed—"Caelmarsh. The greasy-haired mutt in the green doublet."

Kaell shot him a shocked look. "I guessed as much, my lord. But who's that girl?"

Vraymorg squinted through the afternoon glare at a young woman riding beside Caelmarsh. He remembered Annatise as a long-legged, awkward child with freckles. Now, even from the wall walk, he glimpsed the hint of sweet curves beneath her gown.

"His daughter, Annatise." It meant Brile flower—a delicate orange and pink autumn blossom that wilted in winter's frosts. Its bright petals hid poisonous sap. A warning in that?

"She's pretty." Kaell's voice sounded breathy.

"Keep away from that one, Kaell. Caelmarsh aims high there." The Downs Lord hoped Annatise might catch the king's eye. Poor child.

Kaell tossed his head like a riled stallion. "You mean I'm too lowly born for the lady."

"No one's high born enough for Nate Caelmarsh." The grand constable's sense of his own worth equalled only the king's ego. If they fell out, gods help this land.

He squeezed Kaell's shoulder. "No need to court trouble, Kaell. Plenty of pretty girls."

"Not in Vraymorg," the boy replied sullenly. "Not since Alyssa wed."

The cook's niece. So that wound still seeped. He hoped Annatise did not open another.

"A sensible girl, Alyssa." Sharp words, but true. Alyssa recognised childhood friendship for just that, marrying a young forester called Will.

Kaell glowered. "And we must all be sensible, mustn't we, my lord." He gave an exaggerated bow and turned to the stairs.

Vraymorg followed, grinning. The boy prickled these days, strained against his lord's authority. He considered Kaell's stiff back, his adolescent swagger. All very well, but he still expected obedience.

The last riders plodded into the ward between villagers and farmers seeking protection behind high walls ahead of a three-moon night.

Groomsmen rushed to help the Downs newcomers. Servants waited to be useful. Vraymorg counted the soldiers then greeted Caelmarsh.

"Caelmarsh. A safe journey, I trust. And, of course, you are welcome." As long as he didn't linger too long.

"Vraymorg." The man's cold, slate eyes settled like a shroud. Lank hair brushed stooped shoulders; his pinched face was at odds with flushed red lips.

The girl's full lips sat far better on her, complementing fawn-like brown eyes and milky skin. "My lady." He allowed an admiring glance.

Caelmarsh grunted. "My daughter, Annatise." He swept his arm towards the villagers. "Why is this rabble here?"

"The three-moon night," Vraymorg said. "It's safest behind these walls."

"Superstitious nonsense." He nodded towards a young, ruddy-cheeked man dismounting amid rattling steel. "The king's sword, Goffren of Burrow."

"I know that name."

Goffren grasped his arm. "Vraymorg. The last time we met you knocked me down, thrust a sword to my throat, and demanded I yield."

His chortle drew startled stares. Vraymorg recalled that same booming laugh in the king's great hall. Usually after a drunken Goffren picked a fight.

"Luck favoured me that day."

"The gods take luck. You dizzied me with fancy footwork. Didn't know where the next blow might land."

Kaell caught his eye, his brows edged up. Curious about the where and how of that fight.

Vraymorg turned to Caelmarsh. "Your men understand the danger tonight?"

"This nonsense about ghosts and don't venture beyond the walls?"

"Not nonsense, Caelmarsh. The Lost will rise. Many in the Mountains see them. But the sentries will burn fires all night to keep them away."

He gestured to a man and woman. "My steward and his wife will show you and the lady to your chambers. You'll wish to rest. Then perhaps—" The king's business. Best be done with it and send Caelmarsh on his way. He and his dangerous-looking daughter.

"Who's this peacock?" Goffren looked Kaell up and down. "With that pretty hair, he must be some fancy chamber boy. Is he yours, Vraymorg?"

A Downs soldier sniggered and nudged a companion.

Vraymorg rested a hand on Kaell's stiffened shoulder. *Chamber boy.* Slang for a younger man kept for carnal purposes. He should draw steel on the fool.

Goffren deliberately sought to rile either him or Kaell. Goffren liked to stir up trouble.

Vraymorg once heard him call the Lord of the Falls' sword Jason Roya a snivelling sooka who screwed goats. The two fought below the king's window, both so drunk they toppled every time they swung their swords.

A stern-faced Cathmor flung them in a cell—together. They threw drunken punches then. The jailer left them to it. The next morning, bruised and sore-headed, the fools slapped each other's backs, declaring a lifelong bond as they staggered off to drink the king's wine.

Something like that.

"Watch your tongue, Goffren." Paulin's empty, black stare fell on Kaell. "Vraymorg has a certain type. Women above his station."

Vraymorg slitted his eyes. What exactly did Paulin think he knew? He understood Goffren's game but Paulin's? It would be viciously subtle.

"You have a short memory, Goffren." Vraymorg kept his tone even. "Didn't this boy put you and many others in the dirt in that tourney in Dal-Decma?" He forbade Kaell to enter, but the boy went anyway.

Kaell slid him a grateful glance.

"You say this piece of fluff is Khir's warrior?" Goffren looked Kaell up and down. "You dressed the child in pants, but my lord—surely she's a girl." He flicked hair off Kaell's brow.

Shoulders hunched, his breaths thick, Kaell threw Vraymorg a pleading look. *Let me show him. Let me put him in the dirt again.*

"Leave the girl alone." Paulin's sly gaze fixed on Kaell. "Pick on someone not so tough, Goffren. Someone you can actually beat."

"Like a mouse," a soldier said.

"A wounded mouse," Paulin corrected, still watching Kaell. "Not children."

Kaell bristled, a fist curled against his empty scabbard.

"Don't know how he put me in the dirt. A trick? He's not so tough. But pretty. Yes." Goffren tilted Kaell's chin with a gloved hand. "I think I'll give the pretty girl a big kiss."

Kaell shoved him. The bladesman stumbled a step, sneering. "You even push like a girl."

"Stand away, Kaell." Vraymorg blocked him. He knew that look, the storm building beneath Kaell's flattened, green gaze.

Through clenched teeth, Kaell strained words. "But my lord—"

"Yes, stand away—darling," Goffren taunted.

Kaell roared and leapt at him. Goffren hit the ground, his breath lost in a whoosh. Kaell scrambled off him, his fist swinging as soon as the man reeled to his feet. The blow smacked Goffren's head back. He staggered.

Arn grabbed Kaell's shoulders. The boy thrashed. "Let me—let go!"

"Most entertaining." Caelmarsh smacked his red lips together. "So the boy has a temper."

"I'd strike Goffren too," Annatise said. "If the brute tried to kiss me."

Downs men laughed. Goffren slapped dirt from his pants. "I'd do the same to myself." He made a farce of slapping his face and falling down. A grinning soldier pulled him up.

Arn whispered to the boy then at his nod released him.

"Kaell. Attend me," Vraymorg said.

With an embarrassed glance at the girl, the young man wandered to his lord.

Annatise flicked hair over her shoulder. Her brazen gaze swept Kaell from head to foot.

Caelmarsh thrust his hands to his waist. "Annatise!"

The girl offered her father a wide-eyed look of innocence.

"Quite a performance," Caelmarsh said. "If your steward shows us our chambers, we'll wash the dust off." He squinted at Kaell. "Then I'll question him."

NEAR THE FIRE, the wine's heat in his veins, his body grew languid and heavy. The warmth, the room's perfumes, the tangle of Rozenn's fingers in his hair, all lulled.

Her touch was gentle as though he was infinitely precious. He might even think she cared. Maybe she did—in her way.

“Don’t stop,” she said.

Vraymorg shifted his head on the cushion. He realised then he did not wish to tell this story. It had a benign beginning, true: a memory of an autumn day, of a night when the Lost walked, of a sixteen-year-old boy on the verge of adulthood testing the boundaries of his lord’s authority.

It was what happened later…

“I think I must,” he said with a short, humourless laugh. “I don’t know why I began this tale. There is nothing good in it. Nothing good at all.”

Rozenn stroked his hair. “I’m not afraid to hear it, Val.”

No, but he was afraid to tell it.

“Just a little more,” she said. “There can be no harm in that. It’s just a story.”

No harm. Despite the room’s stifling warmth, he shivered. No harm in words, perhaps. But in intentions, in deeds? No harm in murder?

“Perhaps a little more,” he said. “But only a little.”

THE COURTYARD BUSTLED with rushing figures, rang with jingling harnesses and snorting horses. Ewen directed men to unload trunks. Arn and Paulin discussed billeting Downs soldiers. On the walls, men bundled cut wood, ready for the all-night fires.

Everything as Vraymorg commanded. Grooms, servants, soldiers—even the castle dogs did as he ordered. Only the boy disobeyed him.

He faced Kaell with a heavy sigh. “I warned you. They’re king’s men. Their orders are to provoke you, pry out weakness.”

“You heard his insult,” Kaell protested. “If I did nothing—” A pretty girl sitting on a horse might think him a coward. Oh yes, Vraymorg understood.

“I didn’t draw my sword.”

"Just as well."

"I thought about my knife," Kaell said. "I wanted to shut his foul mouth."

"Men like Goffren aren't worth the trouble, Kaell. There will always be fools who want to test themselves against you. To prove their courage to others, to themselves."

"Not this again. Blah, blah, blah."

"Men who hate you because of what you are, who think you believe you're better than them, that you live a privileged life while they strain and suffer."

Kaell's face clouded with impatience. "We've had this talk before. Just saying it all again doesn't make it simpler. Why can't I strike back?"

"You can defend yourself. But a bonded warrior must never kill men or women."

"It's not fair."

"Is it fair if the gods gift a man with strength and speed to defeat evil only for that warrior to use his gifts against others?"

Kaell shifted his weight. "I understand. My lord, I do. It's just—"

"The chamber boy insult?"

"Ah, that nonsense. These flatlanders throw stupid taunts about. I know I don't look like a girl but…" He paused. "Do I dress like a peacock?"

Vraymorg tilted an eyebrow. He found nothing amiss with Kaell's clasped cloak or silver bracelet snaking his upper arm.

His thoughts plunged back to Isles warriors who rode to battle with his father. He could not remember all their names. But faces, yes. The silver-tongued Grantam Northman, who could forget him? Or the Lightning Sword.

Until he understood men's winks meant something more lascivious, he supposed the warrior's nickname reflected his flashing blade. An Isles swordsman to the core. His boots always shone, he wore crisp, white, linen tunics and scented his skin with oils.

"No." Vraymorg fingered a silver chain. "You dress like an Isles man."

His fault. The boy imitated him. Not just how he dressed; sometimes Kaell unconsciously mimicked his gestures or posture.

"Is that good? I've never met anyone from the Isles."

"Others might mock them as strutting peacocks, but Isles folk take pride in their appearance, prize beauty and elegance in both men and women."

He shrugged. "Choose for yourself how you wish to look. Let no one tell you what you must do. Except me, of course." He grinned. "Now I need you to prepare. Caelmarsh wants to see you. This time, no matter who says what, hold your tongue—and your temper."

"DID HE?" Rozenn begged.

Vraymorg blinked away the past. The fire's glint etched her golden hair. He wanted to touch its flooding silk, its ethereal wisps. Too much trouble. Too hard to move, to care.

"Don't stop there. I hope the boy heeded your words and minded his temper."

He snorted. "Kaell? Heed my words? Does your son Alecc heed yours? Within minutes he was free with his fists again."

VRAYMORG FOUND Arn in the stables ordering Caelmarsh's soldiers about. Some tended to horses, others carried tents to the ward. No sign of Paulin—the one man he must keep close until he left. Which wouldn't be soon enough.

"Paulin?"

Arn looked about. "Here a moment ago. Feel that chill?"

"What about Kaell?"

"I sent him off. He yabbered nonsense about pretty girls and how she's too good for him but maybe he can talk to her anyhow. Went to the crypt." Arn nodded towards the walls.

Vraymorg trudged outside.

Kaell strode under the wall walk near the forge.

One of the blacksmith's sons leaned against the doorway, swiping sweat from a broad forehead below spiked brown hair. His cheeks flushed from the furnace and soot stained his leather apron. He took a long look at Kaell.

"Hey freak. Where did you get those fancy clothes?"

Kaell stopped. "You want trouble, Pen-John?"

Vraymorg started forward. *Laugh it off, boy. Pick your fights—but don't pick all of them.*

"Me? With you?" Pen-John jeered. "Don't waste my time seeking trouble with freaks. Who made that cloak then? Your mother? Wait. You don't know who she is. I do. Some blonde Venivan tart. Maybe I did her last time I was in Tide's End."

Kaell scoffed. "You couldn't get it up." He walked on.

Vraymorg halted with a sigh of relief. The boy had avoided a fight—this time.

Pen-John's brother appeared, wiping grimy hands on pants. "You don't want trouble with him. You might catch something nasty."

"Trouble?" Pen-John laughed. "He's all troubled out. Tried throwing his weight around with some Downs men. They put the freak in his place. Besides, he's dressed up in his best. Doesn't want to dirty his fancy cloak by tangling with the likes of me."

Kaell's shoulders rose. He stopped, turned.

Curse it. Vraymorg edged closer.

"Leave it, my lord." Arn appeared at his elbow. "The boy can sort it out."

"Two against one. Three, if the smith steps in."

"Happens all the time. Caught Kaell scrapping with them both a few days ago. The boy can look after himself."

"Ha," said Vraymorg, secretly pleased.

"You want at me, Pen-John?" Kaell shouted. "You sure? I busted your nose last time."

The man scoffed. "You got lucky with a swinging arm. But if we dance in the dirt, you'll mess up that nice cloak."

"So I will," Kaell said calmly. Removing his cloak, he folded it and placed it on grass.

"I should stop this," Vraymorg muttered.

Arn shook his head. "Kaell's not a child anymore."

"And get blood on that tunic?" Pen-John said. "Cost more than I earn in a year, I'd say."

"You're right. No need to spoil my garments over you." Kaell pulled the tunic over his head and put it on the cloak. He stood naked to the waist, sun beating on blond hair.

"Nice boots," Pen-John said. "Pity to get blood on them."

His brother grabbed his arm. "Are you witless? You know how this ends."

Vraymorg thought he knew how this ended too. He took a step.

"Let it play out," Arn said.

Pen-John shook off his brother's grasp. "Leave me be." He scowled at Kaell. "Best take off those pants because I'm going to make you bleed."

"I can beat you clothed or naked," Kaell said.

Pen-John spluttered with rage. "Brat bastard. Think you're so much better than us—"

"I certainly *look* better," Kaell said.

"You, you—" Pen-John hunched like an ogre, breathing hard. Then with a roar, he ran head down at Kaell. The boy stepped aside, grabbed his shoulders, and flung him down.

"One thing about Kaell." Arn smirked. "You show him a move, he practises it, and he's got it. Now that hold is handy when Olier is drunk and spoils for a fight."

"Pen-John's always spoiling for a fight, drunk or not."

Vraymorg fisted his hands at his side, every instinct shouting to step in. But Arn was right. Kaell was old enough to swing in his own battles—as the Isles saying went.

Kaell pinned Pen-John with a knee to his chest. The man bucked. "Get him off me, Vince. What do you wait for?"

"You. Get off my brother." Vince wrapped burly arms about Kaell's chest and hurled him sideways. The boy sprawled. Vince kicked at his head. Kaell rolled away safely. He scrambled up. Vince came at him, huffing, fists swinging.

Kaell ducked, grabbed the man's waist, and threw him into the dirt.

"A variation on the move." Arn nodded approval. "Good boy."

Pen-John circled behind. He grasped Kaell's arms and yanked them back. Kaell writhed as Vince rose, panting. "You don't play nice, brat." He pummelled the boy's belly.

"Leave it, my lord," Arn warned once more when Vraymorg tensed. "Let them sort it out."

"Ha," said Vraymorg again.

Kaell grunted as each blow landed. He bent over as far as the yoking grip allowed.

Pen-John grinned. "Hit him, Vince."

Vince gripped Kaell's hair, bunched his hand. "Can't mess up your cloak since it's all nicely folded, but I can mess up your face."

Kaell kicked his shin. Hard. The smith reeled back, howling. The boy twisted free, ducked beneath his second assailant's flailing arms and punched soft flesh below ribs. A breathless Pen-John skidded onto his knees.

Vraymorg choked off a cheer. A lord must keep the peace, not barrack for combatants.

Vince circled, cursing. Kaell jabbed a fist into his jaw. The smith's head jerked back, but he stood his ground, spitting blood. "You'll pay for that."

He swung. Kaell swayed clear, bellowed, and threw himself at the man. Both hit the dirt, Kaell on top. He lifted Vince's head, slugged him. The man lay still.

Vraymorg relaxed, willing him to stay down.

Pen-John wheezed on his knees. Between broken breaths, he snarled, "Freak. Think you're the little lord. All dressed up in fine clothes like someone born all high and mighty. But you're nothing but a bastard with no second name."

Kaell grasped Pen-John's hair. Sweat glistened off his bare chest. "The cloak, the boots. All of it. It's small compensation for dying young and bloody. Dying for the likes of you."

He hurled Pen-John down, cheek to dirt, gathered his cloak and tunic, and stalked off.

Vraymorg tasted bitterness on his tongue. "Is that really how he sees his life?"

Arn shrugged. "There's truth in what he says."

"IT'S THE WAY WITH WARRIORS." Rozenn broke into his memories. "They get the best food, the best chambers. Women. We tolerate warriors' excesses because they're certain to die."

Die. Such a short word. It contained too much but offered nothing. For it was an ugly word too. A suffocating, poisoning wound of a word.

It's small compensation for dying young and bloody. He could still hear how Kaell said that. Without fear. But with an undertone of resignation no sixteen-year-old should feel.

"Different rules, especially moral standards, apply to swordsmen," he said, thinking of his cousin Dace, long dead. A celebrated warrior who slew a tyrant in the ruins of Seithin. He hid his pain with potions and drink. Everyone pretended not to know.

"What happened next?" Rozenn said.

Vraymorg's throat lumped. "The next I knew from Kaell. He had a book he scribbled in." He shifted, uneasy, the room too hot. "I've said enough, Rozenn. I can't talk about this."

She kissed his brow. "You'll feel better sharing it. Tell me what Kaell wrote?"

He shut his eyes, remembering how he found Kaell's book beneath the boy's bed. It was later, much later, when Kaell's wounds had healed and he could walk again.

Part of him wished he had never read it.

"Straight after Kaell dumped Penn-John in the dirt, he went to the crypt," he said.

"Why the crypt?"

"I often found him there. It's quiet, and the priest, Gabrian Eastman, rarely speaks. What I tell you now I recall from his book, the story as he wrote it down."

KAELL

He felt safe in the sanctum. He knew every cobweb in every murky corner, every crack, every slanting shadow. He knew how shards of sunlight washed stone walls golden, how the moons bewildered darkness with silver beams.

In summer, the airless chamber hazed with heat. In deep winter, the afternoon sun struck the chamber's imposing statue of Khir, and the god's marble eyes glittered knowingly.

Khir often watched him. Sometimes a floorboard creaked in an empty room. Alone in the mountains, eyes followed him. Maybe a lizard in grass. Or a bird on a branch.

It never scared him. Real fear, the terror that woke him sweating, Kaell had known only once. That was the night the sanctum became a prison, when priests bound him and marked him as Khir's. Six priests, one from each domain of Telor, even the Icelands, though his tutors taught that the Damadars bent their stiff necks to a deity called Ghani-Jai.

"An old god, that one," Arn once told him. "Vengeful. Sent his death riders to punish kinslayers and oath breakers. No one escaped a death rider. Even kings and lords."

Kaell shivered, fascinated. "I read about death riders. You can't kill them with steel."

Arn knew the stories from his father. "More truth to these old tales than what's in those books Vraymorg makes you study." He tapped his nose. "The past will out, Kaell."

The past will out. Arn said that a lot. Along with "you're as prickly as a mountain pear," or, "drink and swing, boy."

At a step, he half turned. The priest, Gabrian Eastman, nodded and moved away. Kaell often wondered at the man's past. Two names meant Eastman was someone. Of noble birth.

Another footstep. Stealthy. Close. Kaell slipped his knife into his palm and sprang up.

"Stop! It's only me." Annatise Caelmarsh flung her hands to her face.

Kaell gaped. "Sorry. I thought—"

She smiled. A warm, wide smile, full of promise.

His skin oddly warm, legs unsteady, Kaell hastily returned his knife to his belt.

"I should know better than to creep up on a hunter. Are you praying to Khir?" She dropped beside him and peered about. "This chamber is smaller than it looks outside."

Kaell knelt again. His knee touched hers. Should he move it? That felt rude somehow.

"We have a crypt and a temple at Knight's Spike." Annatise shook her dark hair loose onto her back. It was not straight like Alyssa's but curled at the ends. Kaell thought it beautiful.

"The Spike was an important shrine to both Khir and Cyrah. Before King Roaran that is."

"Really?" She must hear his rattled heart.

Annatise nodded. "Roaran destroyed the temple. My ancestors rebuilt it when he died."

"I see." He didn't. Words did not translate. Not with her blouse laced tightly at her breast.

Annatise caught him staring. "You looked at me like that before."

"What?" His cheeks fired.

"It's all right. I looked at you too. Made father angry. I just suffered his ranting about keeping away from you. Said you were—it doesn't matter. What does he know, anyway?"

Her breasts moved as she gestured. Kaell watched with an uncomfortable fascination. "He'll be angry to find you here."

She flashed him a conspiring grin. "He thinks I'm resting."

"Why are you—did you follow me?"

"I saw you from my window. Are you upset I'm here?"

He gulped. "No."

"Good." She slid her hand across the floor to cover his. It was small and soft. Kaell wondered if her red lips would be as soft if he kissed her. A dangerous thought. Dangerous but thrilling at the same time. That racket picked up in his chest.

"You can meet me here later," Annatise said. "During the feast. There'll be a feast, won't there? Always is. Meet me here then. No one notices who's missing at a feast."

Kaell laughed nervously. "I can't. I promised my lord I won't make trouble."

Annatise snatched her hand away. "What do you care? You serve Khir. Everyone knows a bonded warrior does not bow, even to kings. You should do as you like."

"It's not like that. It's just"—he snatched a ragged breath—"you're to wed the king. Everyone says so. I shouldn't even be here alone with you. Your father would have me whipped if he knew."

"My father doesn't know a thing. He drags me around from one boring castle to another, one feast to another. He only cares that I smile and simper and look pretty."

"You are pretty," he blurted. "More than pretty."

She unfolded a pleased smile. "Do you want to kiss me?"

Kaell stilled, shocked. He did but knew he shouldn't. "If I kiss you, the king's intended, I'll end up in his head house. Besides, my lord said—"

"My lord said. My lord said. Do you always do what you're told?"

Kaell thought of the times he had run away. "Don't you?"

"Why should I?" She tossed her head again. Such glorious hair. Dark brown but glinting red in the afternoon sun. Not gleaming blue-black like Vraymorg's. His lord looked different to most Mountains men.

"If I did, I'd have no fun." Annatise's bottom lip jutted. "And I want to have fun. Before my father weds me to some old king."

"Cathmor? He's young, I think." Kaell couldn't remember.

"He's old. I've seen him. Twenty-five or something."

"You saw him? In Dal-Kanu?" Wide-eyed, he forgot her hair, even her breasts.

"Many times," she replied loftily. "Haven't you been to Dal-Kanu?"

"No," Kaell admitted.

"Have you been anywhere?"

"Dal-Decma, for a tournament. I disobeyed my lord," he said boldly. Though Dal-Decma, the Place of the Rivers, didn't sound as impressive as Dal-Kanu, the Place of Kings. "Did you see the blood lake?"

"You see it from every castle balcony." Still that imperious tone. "But it never flows blood anymore. Not like it once did when a king of Telor died. I bet you don't know why."

He smiled. "I bet I do." If not worldly, he was at least well read. "Centuries ago, King Rainer cast a spell to make it a lake like any other."

"A pity." Annatise rose, skirt lifting to reveal bare calves and ankles. "Imagine the thrill of those old ceremonies when the priests cut the new king's wrist so his Caelan blood turns the red lake to water again. So—will you meet me later?"

He hesitated. "We shouldn't." Then more firmly. "No. If we're found together, your father will drag me before the king and demand he punishes me for the insult. Whipping's one thing; execution is quite another."

"No one will catch us."

"My lord will know. He always does. I think he sees through walls." Kaell laughed self-consciously. "Then he'll have this disappointed look on his face. Such a look. Arn says it's enough to shame even a seasoned courtesan."

She slid her hands to her hips. "What would you know of courtesans? My lord this, my lord that. I can't disappoint my lord. Goffren was right—you're a child."

"Don't say that." Kaell jerked to his feet.

"A man would want to be alone with me. Maybe you don't like me."

"I like you," he protested.

Mischief glinted in her brown eyes. "Maybe you don't like women. Goffren says you like goats."

"That's stupid."

"He says all the women here are ugly and men prefer goats or sheep or something."

"That's even stupider." His anger at Goffren grew. He didn't hit the fool hard enough.

"If you're not brave enough." Annatise flicked hair behind her shoulder. "I'll bet Goffren will meet me."

"Goffren? You wouldn't." That sly beast didn't deserve a pretty girl like her. That decided him as she clearly knew it would.

"I'll meet you," Kaell said. "On the second moon."

VAL ARQUES

Sweat trickled down Vraymorg's jaw. The fire's heat, the scents of lavender and rose oppressed. The sword weighed on his ribs like a stone.

He could no longer talk about Kaell. It hurt to even think of him.

Rozenn traced a bead of moisture down his neck onto his breast. Her touch was careful as though she feared breaking his powerful warrior's body.

But it was his mind that was fragile. And he didn't even know it. He thought it protected, like his heart. He didn't realise that something broke in him until he unwrapped Kaell's sword in the snow and held it in his fingertips. Now all of him felt raw. Exposed.

"Val Arques Caelan. I remember the first time I heard your name," Rozenn said. "You weren't real. Just a name, a story from the past. A possibility." She sighed. "I am almost sorry—"

"Sorry?"

She looked away. "Nothing. A musing. About what might happen if neither of us were who we are. If our choices did not already define us. Go on with your story, Val."

"I can't." His mouth tasted stale. "I cannot tell it. I'm not sure why I spoke of this at all."

"You cannot stop now. You're so close, Val."

"Rozenn, please." He rocked his head on the pillow. "I can't."

"Make me understand what was so terrible. So far, you've only told me you had to suffer a visit from the vile Caelmarsh, and his petulant daughter manipulated Kaell into a secret assignation."

Vraymorg shivered. "I didn't realise the danger. They were king's men, you see. Surely Kaell was safe with king's men."

He thought back. "The next part of the story is mine. I suppose it began about the time Kaell and Annatise were in the crypt, arranging to meet later that night."

NATE CAELMARSH ADVANCED the instant Vraymorg entered the guest chamber. "It's intolerable," he snapped. "I sent for that wretched boy half an hour ago."

You sent for him? Whose castle was this? "Kaell should be at his books." He kept his tone even. "I'll have him found."

"His books?" Caelmarsh scoffed as Vraymorg sent a guardsman off. "That's how you prepare a warrior? The boy must train from dawn to dusk, don't you say, Paulin?"

His captain contemplated something beyond the window. "That's how it's done on the Downs where I trained as a bladesman."

Caelmarsh pounced. "Exactly. You're soft on him, Vraymorg."

"The Lord of the Mountains knows best, I'm sure," Paulin said.

Vraymorg threw him a hard smile. He longed to retort that while Paulin learned to swing a blade on the Downs, harsh Serravan masters, long dead, had taught *him* the language of swords.

"On most days, the master-at-arms drills Kaell until dusk, often with weights on arms and legs to build strength."

He detailed specifics of the boy's training with sword, spear, and bow. "He's proficient in each weapon but excels with the sword. I doubt anyone this side of Dal-Kanu can beat him." Certainly no one from the Downs.

Paulin laughed. "That leaves the other side of Dal-Kanu."

Vraymorg eyed him acidly. Kaell would undoubtedly thrash this braggart. "If you mean the Isles, I studied every text on Serravan methods. Kaell is a match—"

"For Aric Caelan even?" Paulin sneered.

"I've not seen the boy fight."

"If your pup is as good as Aric Caelan, then you stand to make a fortune." Caelmarsh sniffed. "The king puts up gold at every tournament for anyone, heralded or not, who can put the Isles whelp in the dirt. Break a bone or two, and Cathmor would knight them on the spot."

"Men say the Caelan brat's secret is his tactical knowledge," Paulin said. "Aric's fast, I'll give him that. But for one so young he outthinks opponents as much as outfights them."

Vraymorg nodded. "A good warrior is more than a machine. He needs instinct. Knowledge. I've taught Kaell not only swordplay but lessons learnt from past battles."

On more than one night he and Kaell had argued until dawn about the strategies of commanders and kings, dissecting sieges and skirmishes. Not Paulin's business. Nor the bruises, the nights Kaell could hardly crawl into bed, the wounds, the broken bones, the tears. The arguments.

"I recently instructed Kaell on using a cape as a shield. It's obscure, but a bladesman must be able to turn anything to advantage."

"You train him yourself, then?"

Vraymorg held Paulin's insolent gaze. "When I can. If duty draws me away, my captain drills Kaell. Arn Tranter. A Downs man. Perhaps you've crossed swords with him?"

"The man who pulled your bad-tempered boy off Goffren?" Paulin's lips twitched. "Why should I know him? I don't trade blows with peasants unless it's on the field of war."

Vraymorg showed his contempt. "Arn *Tranter*. He's as wellborn as you."

"Tranter? That's a name I've not heard in a long—" Paulin frowned. "Still, I don't trade blows with those beneath me."

What did that frown mean? "Instead, you set your acolytes on boys half your age."

Another sneer. "I doubt Goffren will thank you for calling him my acolyte. If this boy half my age can't take a verbal lashing, how can he lead men against ghouls?"

"He's led my men against ghouls, more than once. Successfully."

Caelmarsh whipped up a hand. "Enough. Isn't that our purpose here? The boy is now sixteen. The king must be confident this bonded warrior will not turn against his own kind. As well you know from an incident in the past, a rogue servant of Khir's is dangerous."

He yawned. "All this tedious talk of training. Paulin and Goffren can test the boy's skill tomorrow. Tonight, I test his temperament. If we find the wretched child, that is."

"Kaell," Vraymorg said. "His name is Kaell."

"*Kaell* is in the odd-looking building near the walls," Paulin said. "I saw him go in."

And said nothing? "I'll send a guardsman."

"No need." Paulin resembled a cat set to pounce. "A guardsman sent him this way."

Someone knocked at the door. Paulin edged up a brow. "And that will be him."

"My lord?" A guard peered in. "You sent for Kaell?"

Vraymorg beckoned to the figure behind. Kaell rushed in and dropped to one knee.

"Forgive me. I was in the crypt."

"With the dead?" Caelmarsh sounded puzzled. "Whatever for?"

Vraymorg pondered Kaell's guilty face. "It has a sanctum," he said.

"And what were you doing, boy?" Caelmarsh rapped fingers against his belt. "I ordered you here a while ago."

"Praying, grand constable."

"Praying?"

Paulin laughed loudly. "Is that what they call it here?"

Vraymorg considered Paulin uneasily. The man behaved like he *knew* something.

"Well get up," Caelmarsh said. "You wasted enough of my time. Stand straight." He rubbed Kaell's shirt. "Silk? My, my. Paulin is right. You look like some effeminate fool from the Isles. Get rid of that. The cloak too."

"My lord constable?"

"Grand constable," Caelmarsh corrected. "Take it off."

Kaell glanced at Vraymorg. He paused then nodded. Caelmarsh might be horse dung, but he was the king's chief law bringer.

"Don't look at Vraymorg." A vein throbbed in Caelmarsh's throat. "I act for the king, and you will obey me without hesitation."

Kaell untied his cloak and folded it over a chair.

"What are you, boy?" Paulin crossed the room in two strides. "A washerwoman?" He grabbed the silk shirt and ripped. "The grand constable told you to take it off."

Kaell's breath hissed out. "Get your—"

Vraymorg grasped Paulin. "You forget your place, captain. The *Lord* of the Downs may be the king's constable, but who are you?" Captain of the Cesspool, he guessed. "Lay a hand on Kaell again, and I'll instruct you on how we do things in my lands."

The strained silence held too long. Then Paulin laughed. He swept Vraymorg a mock bow. "As you say, my lord."

Caelmarsh clucked. "Yes, you forget your place, captain." The pair exchanged a look Vraymorg couldn't unravel.

The Downs lord rounded on Kaell. "I told you to undress."

Cheeks flushed, the young man untied laces and dragged his torn shirt over his head.

"The rest."

"Stop." Vraymorg thrust his bulk forward. "What do you think you're about?"

Caelmarsh did not bother to hide the fury glinting in his eyes. "Keep out of this, Vraymorg. The boy is bonded to the gods, the property of the king and the temple. Valuable property I must examine to make certain it is unflawed and properly kept."

Shoulders tensed with disgust, Vraymorg slapped the air with a palm. "He's not a slave on the block. Not a possession."

"The king declares he is." Caelmarsh's lips slitted to a sneer. "How dare you question your king. In fact, I'm fed up with your presence. I tolerated it until now, but if you cannot shut up then leave." He paused, then in a tone laced with contempt added, "My lord."

Vraymorg thrust his balled fists beneath his cloak. He ached with the strain of containing his anger. One word and it ignited. So he said nothing.

Beyond the windows, dusk weaved a dissonant array of grey and pink. The wind carried the scent of ash from the walls and the kitchen's clatter of pans and plates.

"I will shut up," he muttered, his anger tamed to a simmer.

"My lord?" Kaell still held his discarded shirt, his arm suspended in the air.

"You, boy." Caelmarsh jabbed a finger. "What did I tell you to do?"

Kaell slid another glance at Vraymorg.

"You insolent whelp. I told you not to look at him. Do as I say."

Kaell fumbled at breeches. He stepped out of them, teeth snapped down, expression hooded, the bared body hard with muscle.

The child slipped away, Vraymorg thought with an odd mix of pride and disquiet. Even his bruised cheeks angled with a new sharpness. He knew what lay beneath. Enough coldness, he hoped, to keep Kaell alive.

Caelmarsh clicked his tongue again. He circled, fingers squeezing flesh.

Paulin leaned against the wall, arms folded. His low-lidded gaze held something Vraymorg didn't like. Stories spread about Paulin's violent appetites, lies an enemy might invent. And Paulin had enemies enough. But that look—

"Nothing strips our defences quicker than stripping away our garments," Caelmarsh said. "It's the first lesson a good interrogator learns."

Interrogator? Vraymorg didn't like what was playing out here.

"What are these bruises?" Caelmarsh touched Kaell's cheek. "On his face, his ribs."

"The boy fought some peasant," Paulin said. "Only minutes after hitting Goffren."

Vraymorg glowered. Captain of the Cesspool and castle gossip, apparently.

"A bad-tempered boy, indeed." Caelmarsh's yellowed nails traced Khir's sigils. "These are frightening. The ceremony. He was how old?"

"Fourteen."

"And sixteen now? His Majesty read me your report about that last hunt, Vraymorg. Ten ghouls killed? How many fell to his sword? You let him carry the sword, did you?"

"I killed three," Kaell said.

Caelmarsh slapped his cheek. "Did I speak to you? No."

Kaell stiffened, rebellion flattening his green eyes.

Caelmarsh smiled sourly. "The façade—let's call it that—seems in order. That should please the king, at least. But his temper, Vraymorg. His arrogance. How he talks back. The boy needs discipline."

"You're soft on him," Paulin said, his tone oily. "I'll teach him properly."

Vraymorg's temper exploded. "This ends now. No more prodding and poking. A bonded warrior answers to the gods—and to me."

"He answers to the king, and that means me, the king's representative."

"You would rewrite the law, Caelmarsh?" He grabbed Kaell's cloak and draped it over the boy's shoulders. "Go to your room. The steward will bring you something to eat."

Kaell scooped up his tunic and pants. Vraymorg pushed him through the door.

"What? Banishing him to his room?" Paulin's silky sly voice raised Vraymorg's hackles. "Afraid if he joins us in the feasting hall we'll see more of his bad temper, his ill-discipline?"

Spittle hit the air as Caelmarsh hissed, "You don't say when this ends, Vraymorg. I do. The king needs to know what manner of man he'll entrust soldiers to."

"And the king approves of your methods?" Vraymorg let Caelmarsh hear the steel in his voice. "Granted, it's tradition to question and test a new bonded warrior, but your two trained dogs yapped too loudly this afternoon. Now you try a different humiliation."

Caelmarsh thrust a finger into Vraymorg's face. "My dogs, as you rudely call them, hardly barked, and your prize warrior showed his temper. Another push and what? He bites? Like an animal? A bonded warrior you can't control is dangerous."

"You said it, my lord. The boy needs discipline," Paulin said.

"Can you control this one, Vraymorg? If not, the king will give him to someone who can."

Like you? Vraymorg bit back a scornful laugh. *Or the king*? Now he understood their intent. That scheming Cathmor wanted Kaell. The gods didn't care who controlled Kaell just so long as he killed for them.

A bonded warrior was a powerful weapon in a king's hands. Cathmor just needed a reason to declare Vraymorg did not properly prepare the boy.

"There's no risk Kaell will turn on his own. The boy is entirely sane." And dutiful. Mostly. "I assure you, he's ready to fight."

Caelmarsh rudely stuck his face in Vraymorg's. "Ready to fight. But is he ready to be unleashed? I determine this. How dare you interfere."

Vraymorg held his tongue. Stupid to rise to anger. If he controlled his temper, Caelmarsh questioned Kaell, the boy fought and defeated Paulin or Goffren tomorrow, and this ended.

"As you say, grand constable. I understand my error. I had no right to interfere. Let me call Kaell back."

Caelmarsh looked mollified. "Well—"

Paulin began a slow handclap. "And they say Heath Damadar has a honeyed tongue, hmm, Vraymorg. I see yours is just as smooth."

My blade is smooth, too, Vraymorg thought. *Slides in and out in a heartbeat.* "If I gave offence—" *It isn't nearly enough.*

"Offence? No. But I begin to understand you." Another insolent bow. "My lord."

You'll understand me better if I show you my smooth sword. Vraymorg flung his hands onto his hips. "Is that a challenge in your words?"

Caelmarsh grunted. "Pay no attention, Vraymorg. Paulin is unpleasant when he's hungry." He sniffed. "The boy can wait until tomorrow. When do we eat? Drink. I heard you have enough Cahirean wine to bathe in."

"When they bathe at all," Paulin muttered.

"Mountains men bathe in blood, or nothing," Vraymorg said. "Blood from the Downs won't do, though. Too thin."

Paulin laughed. But his fingers slipped to his dagger. "Harder to spill than Mountains blood."

"Shall we test that?"

"Oh, enough," Caelmarsh interjected pleasantly. "Paulin. Vraymorg. Stop this nonsense."

"My lord, he—"

Caelmarsh held up a hand. "Enough. I did not make this journey through foul weather and equally foul country to watch you two gut each other. No, Vraymorg. Say nothing. Unless it is about Cahirean reds."

"We have enough wine to flood the Downs."

"Then bring on the wine."

Vraymorg gestured to the door. He didn't trust Caelmarsh's sudden good humour. The man let Paulin spit out his bile before. Why stop him now? "I ordered a barrel opened. A spicy red. We serve it warm in the Mountains."

"And does the boy like spicy reds?" Paulin said. "Served warm."

"Kaell rarely touches wine, so it hardly matters what he likes."

"Surely it matters a lot." Paulin offered Vraymorg a sickly sweet smile. "From what I saw today, this young bastard has a taste for things above his position."

THE RED-EMBER FIRE in the hall warmed his back. The Cahirean wine warmed his blood. Nothing soothed his unease.

This young bastard has a taste for things above his position.

What did Paulin mean? Vraymorg tasted his disquiet as though Paulin's bile slipped down his throat. *I should have gutted him. Right there. Grand constable or not.*

Wind banged a faraway shutter. Flames atop the walls jigged black silhouettes through window cracks. Vraymorg's flesh prickled. The Lost walked. No, not the Lost. Someone near oozed hatred as tangible as a knife prick. Who?

Moodily he stared about. Trestle tables and benches, tightly packed with men and women, filled the usually stark hall of hewed stone, smoke, and shadows. Servants tended a roaring fire in the hearth, but a draught forced its way through arrow loops and beneath doors.

From a lower table, Paulin caught his eye. He lifted his cup in a mocking salute.

Him?

A shutter crashed again. Vraymorg jerked.

Caelmarsh patted his arm with fingers like scalloped claws. “This wind rips through a man like a sword cut. And not yet winter. No wonder only wolf’s heads and fools live in these cursed hills.”

Down the table, Goffren puffed out his cheeks. “What does that make you, Vraymorg?” His burst of laugher broke into talk and drew stares.

“I am no doubt a fool.” A fool who warned Kaell to bite his tongue then almost drew steel over a foolish taunt. A fool who knew something played out but could not stop it.

A serving woman with sweat-drenched brown hair weaved past Goffren’s outstretched hands to slide a tray of steaming bread onto the table.

Goffren tried again to grab her. She dodged. Bellowing in disappointment, he turned to shake his spoon at a man across the table.

Drunk. Vraymorg held up his cup to a servant carrying a jug. *Let’s hope Goffren passes out before he starts a fight.*

“And for the lady.” He nodded towards Annatise seated between Caelmarsh and Arn.

“No more wine.” Her father nudged her cup away.

The girl pouted prettily. Her brown eyes drifted to rising moons beyond the windows.

Caelmarsh bent his head. “You’re far from a fool, Vraymorg. You keep your own counsel, avoid the intrigues of Dal-Kanu. But you still need friends.”

Not friends like you. “I am loyal to the king. Why would I need *other* friends?”

The man flashed stained teeth. Vraymorg did his best not to recoil from the stench of his mouth. “Who knows when we might need friends, Vraymorg?” He leaned closer. “The king is capricious. Young. I need not tell you that.”

“Maybe. But do not underestimate him. His is what singers call a harsh bloodline.”

Caelmarsh rasped a guttural sound. "You mean his father?" He threw off a laugh. "Cathmor is not his father. He wishes he were, but he'll never live up to the old king."

"Yet you're eager this young, capricious king weds your daughter?"

"The king must marry suitably. He needs, hmm, guidance."

And you need to drink less, say less, Vraymorg thought.

"There's talk." Caelmarsh dropped his voice. "That girl from the Isles. Azenor Caelan. Cathmor sent his uncle to look at her. We can't let it happen."

We? "I heard the Isles girl is wanton. Surely you have nothing to worry about there."

Servants brought the fish course. Vraymorg tried it, nodded, and bid him serve his guest.

"She's quite wild," Caelmarsh said. "Her father and brothers let her do as she wishes. Word is she's had a string of lovers. Even her brother's captain. No, once the king sees Annatise—" He turned his head. Frowned. "Annatise?"

A plate shattered on stone. A cursing Goffren surged up, kicked his chair away, and waved a knife. Vraymorg nodded to Arn.

"Son of a sooka. You'll regret those words." Goffren lunged. Those closest scattered, knocking benches over in their haste.

A man huddled, arms protecting his head against flailing fists. Goffren swung a kick, overbalanced, fell over his target with a stifled yell.

Arn grabbed his arms, tore the knife from him. Goffren yelped a protest.

"My daughter." Caelmarsh thumped his fist on the table. "Where is my daughter?"

Into the silence, Paulin lumbered to his feet. "I know where she is. I know who's with her." His gaze slid to Vraymorg.

And coldness fanged Vraymorg's scalp, knowing Paulin played the game's next move.

HINGES SCREAMED a protest as Paulin flung back the sanctum door.

Vraymorg shouldered through ahead of Caelmarsh. Light from his burning torch spilled on tangled arms and legs just before the boy and girl broke apart. Annatise wore only undergarments, her blouse and skirt discarded. Kaell was bare-chested, bare-buttocked.

Paulin laughed.

Vraymorg shoved the torch into a sconce, sickness balling in his belly.

"Annatise!"

The girl whipped a startled look at her father. She scrambled up, torchlight and moonlight gleaming on unruly hair.

"You shame me." Caelmarsh took one step and slapped her mouth.

Glaring, Annatise stood her ground. "Don't you dare strike me. Don't you—" She dropped her head in her hands to sob.

"Annatise." Kaell staggered to his feet, arms stretched to comfort her.

Vraymorg grasped his shoulder. "You young fool. I warned you. Get dressed."

"My lord." Hastily Kaell yanked up his pants. "It's not—nothing happened."

"You!" Caelmarsh rounded on him. "You!" He whipped the knife from his belt.

Vraymorg moved between them, arms raised. "Caelmarsh, stop. It's not what it seems."

"Get out of my way." The grand constable tried to dart around.

Vraymorg blocked him. "Calm down. This is wrong, I grant you. But they're children."

Caelmarsh's mouth twisted to a snarl. "Children?" He shook the knife at Kaell. "How dare this bastard touch my daughter! He'll pay for it. Get out of my way."

"Father, no." Annatise clasped her hands together in a plea. "Please."

In the doorway, Paulin rocked with laughter, his lips thin as a sword slash. The sound rippled gooseflesh down Vraymorg's arms.

"I said: move aside." Caelmarsh lunged at Kaell. Vraymorg grabbed his wrist.

The grand constable swung his other arm. The blow struck Vraymorg's shoulder but did not break his hold. He twisted harder. At last Caelmarsh yelped and dropped the knife. It clunked to the floor. Vraymorg kicked it away.

"Curse you," Caelmarsh muttered. "Curse you. Who do you think you are?"

Vraymorg released him and backed towards Kaell. The boy rocked from foot to foot, arms shielding his shivering, half-naked body. He looked young and too vulnerable.

"Nothing happened, my lord. We kissed. That's all."

"It's true." Annatise tugged her father's arm. "That's all. A few kisses."

Caelmarsh rubbed his wrist. "Cover yourself, girl." He thrust his cloak at her. Then his glower swung to Paulin. "You knew. You knew they were here."

The warrior shrugged brutish shoulders. "Hardly that."

"I said: 'where is my daughter.' You said you knew."

"I guessed." Another shrug. "Because of how he looked at her when we arrived. You saw that look too."

A silence, then Caelmarsh brushed off Annatise's hands. He jabbed a finger at Kaell. "I want him punished, Vraymorg. Do you hear me?"

"He will be punished."

"Hanged by the neck. He has humiliated me."

"Don't be stupid."

Caelmarsh breathed hard. "Whipped. My daughter is not some tavern slattern. She is wellborn and intended for the king. It's treason for this bastard to touch not only a lady but his future queen. I want him publicly whipped, then he'll answer to the king."

Kaell recoiled. "That's not fair." He turned to Vraymorg. "My lord, *nothing happened.*"

Vraymorg struck him with the back of his hand. The boy stumbled.

"I don't like that tone. No," he said, silencing a protest. "Say nothing. You disobeyed me." He grabbed Kaell's shoulder again and dragged him to the door.

The second moon pierced veiled clouds. The wind chipped and roared, its breath damp on his skin.

Arn waited outside, shoulders hunched against the cold. Vraymorg shoved Kaell at him. "Find him some clothes and lock him up."

Vraymorg snatched slow breaths, fighting for calm. He badly wanted to pound his fist against a wall, to shout. Caelmarsh would not let this go.

Kaell panted slightly, his shivers violent. Vraymorg placed his cloak over the boy's shoulders. "Lock him up," he said again.

Paulin emerged from the crypt. Again he laughed.

HIS LIMBS NUMBED. So cold. The fire's heat no longer touched him.

"What's happening to me, Rozenn? I can't feel my legs."

"Finish this. Then everything will be all right."

"I can't. Not this. I've said enough."

Rozenn threw a blanket over him. "There now," she said. "There now."

There now. That's what he said to Kaell that night. Knowing the words were meaningless but needing to say something. Anything.

"I think, I think, I want to forget the rest, Rozenn."

"Be brave, Val." She touched fingertips to his jaw. "I promise you, you'll know no pain when this is done."

No pain. He desperately wanted to believe her. With a deep sigh, he said, "Then—the next—this is what Kaell wrote in his book." That cursed book. If only he never read it.

KAELL

The door above Kaell's head creaked. He shaded slitted eyes as a lantern bobbed. A ladder dropped into the hole.

"Out."

Kaell didn't recognise the voice. Stubbornly he folded his arms over his chest.

"Out. Your lord wants you."

At last. Vraymorg wouldn't leave him in the dark.

Kaell climbed. A figure edged back to let him stand. "Who are—?"

The lantern flew like a fist. Pain lanced his temple. Groaning, Kaell collapsed to his hands and knees. The lantern swung again. He blacked out.

STONE PRESSED AGAINST HIS BACK, cold and hard. Rope welted his wrists. Hot breath pawed his face. He gagged at a pungent odour of sweat and unwashed flesh.

A man laughed. Slowly Kaell's blurred gaze cleared.

"Paulin?" His head spun. A dream. Let it be a dream.

"Paulin, what is this?"

"Caelmarsh will force Vraymorg to give you up." The man's rank breaths, sharp and almost pained, steamed Kaell's cheek. *No dream.* "The king wants you brought to Dal-Kanu. If Cathmor thinks you're too dangerous, he'll sell you. Maybe to the Quisnaf."

Kaell's skull thumped. Blood dripped from his forehead to stone. "I don't understand."

Paulin waved a knife. Kaell squirmed back on his elbows.

"Stay still," Paulin said. "I'm not going to hurt you. I'm going to do this." He slashed at his own breast. The blade cut through his tunic and into flesh. Blood spilled from a long cut.

"What are you doing? You're mad."

"I'm not doing anything. You did this." He dug his knee hard into Kaell's hip. "You were escaping. When I tried to stop you, you came at me with a knife. I sought to reason with you, but you were crazed, like a beast."

"I didn't—" A slap. A ringing in his ears.

"When Caelmarsh learns you attacked me, he'll insist Vraymorg surrenders you."

Kaell writhed. The knee hurt his hip.

"My lord would never surrender me to you."

"Caelmarsh is the king's grand constable. Vraymorg must obey. Besides, why should he care about you? You're a burden. A bastard with no name. No one."

Kaell arched his back. The brute pinned him.

"Settle down." Paulin smeared his blood on Kaell's tunic. "I'll give you a chance to run."

"I won't run," Kaell said. "I did nothing wrong."

"You attacked me. That's after you put your bastard's hands all over Caelmarsh's daughter. Your lord can't save you from what's ahead. Life as a slave."

"You snake. Why are you doing this?"

Paulin laughed. "I have reason enough. Reason you won't understand—boy." With one flick he cut Kaell's hands free and rose, looking down with a knife-edged smile. "Your life here is over. Unless you run. Why don't you run?"

Kaell struggled to his knees. Then to his feet. He ran.

VAL ARQUES

"His book." Cold sweat trickled down Vraymorg's brow. "When I read it later, I understood just how devious they were. That night, I didn't know the whole of it. A guard fetched me to say Paulin had barged into the storeroom where I put Kaell—to keep him safe."

He groaned. "Safe. He was never safe."

"What did you do?"

"On that awful night?" Vraymorg shuddered. "I went after Paulin."

HIS ARM BRUISED Paulin's windpipe. "You did something. That's why he bolted."

Paulin choked out sounds.

"Vraymorg." Caelmarsh tried to pull his arm away. "He can hardly answer if you strangle him. The boy's out of control. He attacked Paulin, and now he's fled to escape punishment."

"Kaell would not." Confident words. But doubt nagged. Kaell had run before.

With an angry hiss, he shoved Paulin at Arn and a guardsman

called Aalart Hillborn, barely old enough to shave. The two held the brute while Vraymorg paced and thought.

A three-moon night. The spectres of the Lost walked. Kaell knew not to venture beyond the castle walls. Unless terrified. But what terrified him? Ghouls didn't. The Lost? Maybe.

He kicked the hatch shut on the storeroom. With Aalart on guard, the boy should have been safe there. Yet Paulin still found him.

He whirled on Aalart. "Why did you leave?"

"Paulin ordered me gone. I knew something was up, so I sought you at once."

"Why obey?" Paulin might be a lord's captain, but Vraymorg trained his men better than that. Obedience to him first. Regardless of what lord—or king—threw their weight about.

Beneath Vraymorg's angry stare, Aalart did not flinch. "He said the grand constable told him to question the boy."

"My lord."

Vraymorg turned. His foot slid on a wet patch. Blood?

Ewen approached at a rush. "Kaell's not in the castle. The men are ready to search the grounds. We've torches."

"Get out your dogs." Paulin sneered. Menace oozed from him like sickness. "Or let me hunt him down. I'll take him to Dal-Kanu in irons."

"Dal-Kanu?" Vraymorg glared at Caelmarsh.

"What did you expect?" The grand constable flared up. "First, this brat humiliates me, now he stabs my sword. The king will deal with him. Kaell will be fortunate if he doesn't hang. And you, Vraymorg, will be fortunate to keep your head."

Ewen plucked at his sleeve. "Kaell knows the danger on a three-moon night. We locked down the castle, so he's inside the grounds."

"You're right. He's here." Somewhere.

Caelmarsh coughed to clear phlegm. "Release Paulin. He answers to the king, not you."

Vraymorg grunted angrily. "Unhand the snake, Arn. Just keep him out of my sight."

Cloak drawn tight, he stomped out and ran up the stairs to the ward.

Ewen followed, grumbling. "Slow down. Wait for me."

Vraymorg remembered his brother calling those same words as they raced up sand banks near Tide's End. The two boys slid down on shields "borrowed" from the armoury.

Once the bank collapsed on Vraymorg. He panicked, gasped for air that wasn't there, choked on sand. Karolus had pulled him out.

That same sick band of dread tightened at his throat now.

Men in the ward held torches. Fires leapt from braziers on the walls, the flames' bizarre wind dance etching stone. The air was dense with cold, with scents of smoke and pine.

A three-moon night when folk cowered beneath blankets, letting lust or love silence the cries of the dead. Kaell knew better than to wander on such a night.

Arn joined him in the chill-swept courtyard. Ewen doubled over, hands to knees, catching his breath. He cast a doubtful look at the moons rising together.

"He's only a boy. And mist rolls in."

"We'll find him." Vraymorg shoved down panic. Surely Kaell would not leave the castle when the Lost rose outside. "Have them search this ward then the bailey. And the crypt."

Ewen trod off.

"Arn, we'll take the orchard and the ruins."

Arn nodded, fisted a torch, and trudged towards the collapsed tower on an overgrown mound. Men tended fires on the outer wall above their heads. Vraymorg hailed them.

"We heard, my lord," one called back. "No sign of him."

Arn waved the torch about the crumbling ruin. Builders long ago removed most of its stone for the new keep. But some hewed blocks, green and slippery with moss, formed broken walls. Trees claimed the subsiding husk, their roots piercing ancient stone.

Vraymorg lifted a rusted metal cover to a cellar.

Arn dropped to his belly and waved the torch inside. "Empty, my lord."

Vraymorg slammed the cover closed. If not there… where?

A dull ache pounded to his core. His fault. He'd locked Kaell in that hole to keep him safe, not make him easy prey for Paulin and Caelmarsh to manipulate.

Arn lifted the light to the keep's ivy-strangled walls. "Broken branch."

His lord shrugged. Ghosts, lovers stealing kisses, and children playing at knights all haunted the old keep. Anyone could have snapped that bough.

Arn stepped over a root and rounded the shell. He swung the flame.

"Kaell!" Vraymorg cried. Caught in the light, the boy scrambled up the broken earth through a gaping breach in the stone.

"Kaell!"

Vraymorg clambered after him. A stiff branch stabbed his shoulder. Another slapped his face as he crawled, broken stone grazing palms.

He straightened. No sign of Kaell in the orchard. Where? *Where?*

A shout from the wall. "I see him, my lord. To your right."

Darkness closed as clouds blanked the moons.

"No, he's gone again." Then the guard cursed. Clamouring footsteps and alarmed, belligerent voices carried from the wall. "Someone's there. They're armed. Seize them."

Arn rushed up. "Paulin's on the walk."

Moonlight split clouds. Vraymorg glimpsed a figure running through trees. He looked up fast at the wall. Paulin held a bow, its string drawn back.

"No!" He sprinted at the wall. The arrow whirred. Vraymorg jerked to a halt, whirled to see Kaell spin backwards. Hit the ground.

"Arn, stop Paulin." Vraymorg weaved to Kaell, blocking Paulin's sight. Another arrow hissed above his head. Kaell yelped.

A racket broke out on the wall: shouts, a thudding scuffle, Paulin's protests.

Vraymorg dropped beside Kaell. The boy clutched his arm, breaths fast and hard.

"You told them to shoot me?"

"Paulin shot you. Why did you run when I called out?"

Kaell groaned with pain. "I saw lights. I panicked. Thought it was *him*."

"Paulin? Why run from *him*?" Vraymorg brushed an arrow's fletching with taut fingers. He pushed Kaell's hands away to examine the boy's bleeding ankle. It must hurt.

No answer.

"Tell me, Kaell."

The boy's voice sounded tiny. "Paulin said you had to surrender me to the king."

Vraymorg rocked back on his heels. "You believed it?"

In the moonlight, Kaell's eyes rounded like an owl's. A sob mewed in his throat. Vraymorg felt helpless. No cloak. No words.

Kaell whispered, "He stabbed himself, said he'd tell everyone I did it, that Caelmarsh would force you give me to the king. That Cathmor would sell me." Frightened tears welled.

Vraymorg heard only his own ragged breaths, in and out, in and out. Cold wind brushed his face. Kaell's blood coated his fingers.

"Do not cry, Kaell. Warriors do not cry. I taught you better than that."

"My lord." Arn stood at the front of men carrying torches.

"Where?"

No need to say who he meant. Aalart shoved Paulin forward. Caelmarsh's captain looked from their angry faces to Kaell and laughed out aloud.

"A tricky shot that second one. I did well to only wound him."

Vraymorg surged up, cold with rage. He scraped his sword free.

Arn grabbed his shoulders. “Think, my lord. Think.”

“He’ll answer for it,” Vraymorg seethed.

“So he will. He spilled a bonded warrior’s blood. His fate is set. The brute awakened magic and can’t escape it. That is far, far worse than to die quickly from a sword thrust.”

Slowly Vraymorg lowered the blade.

Arn released him and turned on Paulin. “You shot him. Are you mad? You must be. That or you serve the Blood Lord.”

Parents told their children stories of the fabled Blood Lord so they stayed inside after dark. Yet Arn spat his name with certainty, his face twisted with loathing.

Paulin sneered. “I stopped him fleeing just punishment. That’s all. How do you stop them here? Kiss them?” He laughed again. “Filthy goat screwers. All of you.”

“Take that back, or I’ll—” A guardsman started.

Paulin thrust his hands to a belted waist. “Or you’ll what? I’m the grand constable’s sword. I’m here to judge, not be judged. I did what you cowards were too gutless to do.”

He shouldered through simmering men. “You’ll find me with the grand constable. Telling him a sorry tale. The boy seduced Annatise and attacked me. A flawed bonded warrior. The king must take charge of him. If he can’t redeem Kaell, Cathmor will kill him or sell him.”

As he stomped away a mutter rose at his back.

“My lord,” Aalart said. “He can’t—”

“Let him go. But this isn’t finished.” Vraymorg scooped Kaell into his arms. The boy sobbed in pain.

“No crying, Kaell.” His curt tone covered his relief. Even if the boy’s wounds kept him in bed a week or two, he was safe. He nodded to Arn to take Kaell’s legs. Torch-waving men accompanied them back to the keep.

“The physician will have to cut that arrow in his ankle out,” Vraymorg told Arn.

Overhearing, Kaell groaned.

"Yes, it will hurt," Vraymorg said. "I'd take the pain for you if I could."

Anger flared through his body. He fought it, knowing it was unfair, knowing his anger hid something else. Guilt? That Kaell should think so little of himself must be his fault.

Then he gave up, blurted, "You believed him?" His breath steamed out in cold air. "You believe I'd surrender you to Paulin or the king? Because that monster said so?"

Kaell hung his head. "Paulin said you had to obey. I thought—"

"What? That you're a bale of hay? For others to barter, pass around like spoils of battle?"

"I don't know."

Vraymorg cast Arn a look. The captain concentrated on the ground.

"How can you think you have so little value? By all the Mountains gods, Kaell, this castle is your home."

The boy lifted his head. "Is it, my lord?"

"What do you mean?"

Arn lost his hold. Kaell hissed a breath as his foot scraped the ground.

"Sorry." The captain re-established his grip. Vraymorg considered him again. Would Arn take his words back to the barracks? No. He was fond of Kaell. He'd say nothing.

"Well, Kaell. I await your answer. What do you mean?" He was too heartsick to soften his sharp tone.

"I don't have a second name. You reminded me of that when the grand constable rode in. That means I'm no one."

"It's no shame to have only one name, Kaell. Few are born into the great houses of Telor. Do you think any less of Ewen because he has one name only? Or Alyssa? Olier?"

"No. But then—who am I? I'm not your son. Yet everything I have is yours. Even the sword. It's mine only until—" He bit his lip.

"Careful my lord," Arn said. "There's a step."

They reached the keep. The physician Robbie Teverall tut-tutted from the doorway. "Bring him out of the cold." He shook his balding head. "What is it this time, young man?"

Arn grunted. "Gods, you're heavy, Kaell. Next time a man shoots you, find another slave to carry you. I'll need Teverall to fix my broken back."

The boy grinned then winced again.

"Shot?" The physician's eyebrows drew down. "How?"

"Twice." Vraymorg backed up the stairs. Raised voices carried from above; Paulin and Caelmarsh were arguing. He and Arn laid Kaell on a cot in the physician's room and stepped away.

"Twice." Teverall stooped over his patient. "What next?"

Arn rubbed his arms. "Got to check on the sentries," he mumbled to Vraymorg. "Three-moon night and all." He smiled at Kaell. "I'll check on you tomorrow, young'un."

"No point," Teverall grumbled. "A long poppy-juice sleep for this one." He shook his head sadly. "Shot. In the middle of the night, mind you. You'd think the Lost had attacked."

Vraymorg stayed as Teverall cleaned and bandaged Kaell's shoulder. Bone-weary, he reeled with the strain of worry and fear, knowing this long, awful night was far from over.

Paulin. He did not intend to let the gods deal with the snake.

The physician bid him hold Kaell down as he dug the bolt out. The boy screamed and blacked out briefly. Vraymorg winced as though the knife was cutting *him.*

Teverall bound Kaell's ankle. Then he stirred more poppy juice into wine. Kaell's eyes hazed. Vraymorg pulled up a stool. "There now, Kaell. There now. Sleep."

"You didn't answer my question," the boy murmured.

"I didn't like your answer to mine." Why run? Because of words. Empty words? Because he really thought his lord would believe Paulin over him?

Vraymorg knew he should hold his tongue until morning. Kaell looked beaten. But frustration and fear nagged. "You believed that brute? You believed I'd give you up?"

Kaell wrenched his head away. "Paulin made it sound possible."

"Possible." His anger rekindled. "Let's have it then. Exactly how worthless do you think you are?"

Kaell swallowed. He cast a hesitant, almost hopeful look at his lord. "Paulin said I was like a slave. A burden. A bastard with one name. Not someone who belongs here."

Bleakly, Vraymorg stared at the floor. Words tumbled through his mind, things he might say but would not. *You're loved here. You belong here. Like a son—*

No, no. Say these words, and they became real. He could not bear that again. To feel. To love. There was nothing kind about love. Raising a child was fraught with not just struggle but fear. Beneath those moments of joy, even pride, there was always fear.

It was why a man's arms might tighten when he hugged his child. Why his throat might close up the first time a small hand clasped a sword hilt, why he might hold back tears at a bright, undaunted smile before his child rode out to fight that first battle.

Teverall pounced. "No more talk. Sleep. My lord, a word."

He drew Vraymorg aside. "Something odd here, my lord. Nur weed on his breath. It heightens panic. Nasty stuff. Might explain why he ran."

"You didn't answer," Kaell whispered in a dreamy voice. "What am I?"

Vraymorg hesitated, tempted to let the boy drift to sleep. He knew what Kaell wanted to hear, what he deserved. But he would not love him like a son. Care for him, yes. Prepare him.

But love meant loss. Kaell would die. Vraymorg would not.

With a sigh, he sat and stroked Kaell's hair. "This is your home, and you are my ward."

"Ward." Kaell's voice held an ethereal sweetness. "King Rollo had a ward. The orphaned Lord of the Plains. Long ago. The king treated him like a son."

"Like that, yes."

"So I'm like a lord." Kaell's lips curled into a smile, and he closed his eyes.

Then a man screamed.

"THERE NOW." Rozenn touched his hair. "Nearly done. The sword hungers for this story, Val. Soon you'll know neither fear nor pain."

She pulled her hand away. "My, how hot you are. You're burning up."

Burning up. But it was cold that night, the night of the Lost. The three-moon night when Paulin fell to his death. No. Tell it correctly. When Arn Tranter pushed Paulin to his death.

TEVERALL'S HEAD JERKED AROUND. "By Khir. What was that?"

Vraymorg rushed to the window. The three moons washed the castle with white light. Smouldering fires twitched shadows on towers. In a scape of metal, Arn leaned over the roof balustrade. "He fell, my lord. Paulin. I tried to grab him. But he fell."

Vraymorg looked down. The grand constable's captain sprawled in the snow.

TOO HOT. Sweat poured down his throat. Vraymorg tried to swipe it away. His hand did not obey him. The sword burned his flesh. He moaned. Rozenn lifted it from him. Sorrow rimmed her eyes like a dark halo, but triumph glimmered beneath.

Why? What had he surrendered? Just words. Just a story.

"Please," he gasped, his tongue thick. "Tell me about the sword."

"Shhh. It doesn't matter. It doesn't even matter I'm sorry. Not now."

What did matter? He tried to remember. But his head hurt. "Why sorry?"

Rozenn watched him. Expectantly. Waiting. "It gives me no pleasure to see you in pain, Val." She stroked his cheek. "Especially as you gave me a precious gift. But I must fulfil my part of the bargain."

Her words made no sense. All he knew was he hurt and somehow she'd tricked him.

"You poisoned me." He tried to roll. His body was as heavy as lead.

A shadow shifted at the back of the room. Someone else was here.

"Who's there?" His breath rasped.

Rozenn mopped his brow with a cloth. "Only Tarvan. Don't worry. He won't hurt you. No one will. They'll take good care of you. You're precious to them, Val."

They? Vraymorg licked cracked lips. "Who?"

Rozenn sighed. "I didn't expect it to be this hard. But I cannot turn back. Not when you're worth so much gold. Gold my son can use to buy an army, to take the Telorian throne. Restore Cahir to its former greatness."

He groaned. "You sold me to the Quisnaf. And before—that was you, too. You told them how to find me. Why this lie about the sword freeing me of sorrow? Why not just drug me?"

"That was the intent. Until you foolishly brought the sword. They didn't expect that. But they told me what to do just in case. With this blade, the Quisnaf can control you."

She trailed a hand down his breast. "They fear you, Val."

"Why do this?" Neither ever spoke of what bound them, but

affection surely did. "I could have loved you, Rozenn. If either of us had been honest—not afraid."

Rozenn made no reply, only rose to talk to her captain.

"What do we do with him?" Tarvan's voice rumbled.

"When he passes out, tie him up then leave him here. I sent word. The Quisnaf are coming for him. No need for us to wait. The king expects us in Dal-Kanu."

"We should kill him. What if he comes after you? He's dangerous."

"He won't ever come after me. You know why. Besides, once they take him, he'll never be free again. I'll speak to Alfreda about our preparations to leave." Light footsteps tramped to the door.

Someone stood over him. A guttering candle flared its last light upon Tarvan's face, his expression remote as though bewitched.

The man lifted his sword. "This is because of what you had of my queen."

Running steps. Rozenn screamed, "No!" But her captain drove steel into Vraymorg's chest.

COLDNESS NUMBED, its gentle cocoon protecting him from feeling, thinking, or remembering.

Into this comfortable void, sounds intruded. Branches soughed in a harassing wind. Grass rustled as if fingers sifted downy tips.

Vraymorg opened his eyes. A fox sat on his ankle, its eyes gleaming in the darkness. At his twitch, it slinked off. He sat up in a shallow grave, his naked limbs splattered with mud and wet leaves. Icy rain slivered down his goose-fleshed skin.

Like the rain falling around Paulin's body, washing blood into tiny rivulets in the dirt.

A MAN BENT over Kaell's bed, his face shadowed.

"Arn?"

Arn thrust something beneath his tunic and turned. "He wounded him. Caelmarsh's sword. A man who should protect this boy."

So Arn killed him?

Vraymorg wrapped his arms across his breast. Nearly dawn. He ached with weariness.

"Paulin was a pig. No one will mourn him."

Arn set his lips in a hard line. "No one."

In silence, they watched Kaell sleep.

"The physician said the ankle might not heal right," Arn said.

"It will heal just fine."

"And if he's crippled?"

"A good swordsman can compensate for a weak ankle."

"I hope you're right, my lord. Well, I should—I just came to make sure he's all right."

Arn left him. Vraymorg wondered at his lie. A warrior used his weaknesses as well as his strengths. But a bladesman couldn't afford physical defects.

"Vraymorg!" Caelmarsh burst into the room. "You killed him. The king will hear of this."

Vraymorg scoffed. "Killed him? Paulin fell."

The grand constable accused with a stabbing finger. "You killed him because he shot that hot-headed bastard of yours."

"I was with the physician." Vraymorg tired of accusations and games. He longed for his bed. "My captain, Arn Tranter, saw the drunken fool fall."

"Tranter. The man with the scar. He's your creature. He'll lie for you."

"The physician and I both heard the cry. No one pushed Paulin. He fell."

"More lies. You murdered him. I knew you were ruthless, Vraymorg. Cold. Like your father. You wouldn't hesitate to kill because of a grudge."

True. But Arn dealt with Paulin first. "I was with Kaell. Not at the top of the tower." He frowned. No reason for Paulin to be there. Or Arn.

Caelmarsh jabbed a finger again. "You can't fool me. And you won't fool the king. He'll have your head for this. He has a penchant for heads."

Vraymorg grimaced. The stories of Cathmor's gruesome "head house" appalled him.

"The king will learn what you did. I intend to tell him everything that happened here."

"Everything?"

"Everything."

"Then he'll have your head, too, Caelmarsh."

"What?"

"You're right; the king should know—everything. I'm sure you told him your daughter is innocent, unblemished. Just as Cathmor's queen must be." Vraymorg clucked his tongue to his teeth. "What will he say when he learns how we found them—Kaell and your daughter?"

A muscle in Caelmarsh's cheek twitched.

"A pity." He had the other man's measure now. Just reel him in, and the man would agree to whatever he proposed. "She is lovely. But the king will put her aside. He might decide you sought to mislead him, to trick—"

"Stop." Caelmarsh threw up a hand. "You can't tell him. Why, you even said they are just children. Nothing happened. Annatise swore it was a few kisses."

"I'm sure the king will accept that when he hears about it."

Caelmarsh's face bloomed rosebud pink. "He can't hear. Vraymorg, listen. He must marry Annatise. For the good of the realm. Imagine if he turned his gaze to that Isles girl? What happens then? Isles princes at Dal-Kanu, in the king's ear. Unthinkable."

Vraymorg stroked his chin, pretending to consider. "As you

say. But the king surely has a right to know—everything."

Caelmarsh fidgeted with those ugly hands. "You'll say nothing, do you hear?"

"My good grand constable. Are you asking me to lie to the king?"

"I'm asking you to be circumspect in what you say."

"And in return?"

The other man's knuckles paled. "Curse you, Vraymorg. Curse you. I shall tell the king Paulin fell. He drank too much and fell. The king need not hear everything."

"He does not," Vraymorg agreed, hiding a satisfied smile.

THE NIGHT FOREST flowed about him. Scampering paws, an owl's hoot, the sky a discord of black and grey curving into the horizon. The earth gritty and moist on his bare skin, the indistinct buds on a drooping autumn vine, their milky perfume lyric in the air.

Vraymorg wanted to hide in this darkness, in the past.

But Rozenn had poisoned him. Her captain had tried to kill him. They must answer for it. Then he'd grab Kaell's sword and run—fast—before Quisnaf warriors arrived to take him.

He rose and staggered towards chinked light. Clouds whipped overhead. Icy rain beat at his face. Blinded, he tripped on a loose stone, straightened, stumbled to a window. A doused fire smoked in an empty room.

A door stood ajar. Sounds of jangling harnesses, voices, rushed steps carried. On unsteady legs, he crept inside, teeth rattling like coins in a merchant's purse.

Kaell's sword lay beside pooled blood, its trail a crimson ribbon across the floor to the door. Like the blood in Kaell's bedchamber the night a ghoul assassin came for the boy.

Woken by Kaell's cries, Vraymorg rushed in to cut the ghoul's head off.

Kaell huddled on the bed, a stained knife clutched tight. "I saw a shape by the window," he whispered. "They must badly want me dead to risk coming here."

Vraymorg threw an arm about his trembling shoulders. "There now." It was what he said when he couldn't find the right words. "There now. You're safe."

Safe. He could not keep Kaell safe. Nor any of these young men the gods chose to fight and die young. The weight of it, of their deaths, fell on his shoulders, a wretched burden.

He pressed a palm to the stone wall. So cold, this room. Yet a short time ago that fire had blazed and Rozenn stroked his hair, whispering that soon he'd feel no pain.

Vraymorg lifted Kaell's sword. So how did this work? How did this blade and his story give others power over him?

A boot scuffed a floorboard. A man called to someone.

Vraymorg shoved the weapon up the chimney. He brushed telltale ash and soot from his arms, grabbed his own discarded sword and flung it beside his blood.

Tarvan Blackstone trod inside. He stilled in shock. "You. But you're dead. I killed you."

"Not quite."

"Then I'll make sure this time." Fisting his sword, the Cahirean captain rushed him.

Vraymorg let him come. At the last moment, he jerked sideways. Steel swished air as Tarvan cut at nothing.

The man yanked the sword back and spun. Vraymorg leapt in to grasp his wrist, forcing the tip down. He drove his knee into the man's gut. The Cahirean doubled over. His sword clattered on stone. Vraymorg slugged him in the jaw. The punch felt right. He didn't need to see Tarvan go down.

"It's true then. You can't die."

Rozenn watched from the doorway. Her cool smile told him nothing.

Vraymorg scooped up Tarvan's blade. "It's true."

"I heard whispers through the Enarae but didn't quite understand how your immortality worked. Whether you didn't age or whether no one could kill you. Tell me your story."

"I'm done with stories."

"Stories show us who we are. They show us who we can trust, who we cannot. There is no surer way to know another person than listening to their stories." Her gaze fell on his pooled blood. "I'm sorry Tarvan did that. Because I took you into my bed, he was jealous."

"Oh, I'm sure you inspire that a lot. Your Grace."

Rozenn tilted her head. "Is that how it will be between us? Politely formal. How sad."

She crouched beside Tarvan. "I'm grateful you didn't kill him. Easy for you to do that. A prince of the Isles. A bladesman trained by the legendary Serravan."

Vraymorg put the sword to her breast to force her up. "Tell me about Kaell's blade. The truth." He knew how he must look, his naked body splattered with mud and blood, his eyes terrible. Yet she did not look afraid, only thoughtful.

"No."

He pressed steel into her ribs. "You betrayed me. For gold."

"For *a lot* of gold. For an army."

"I almost pity you."

Rozenn smiled that secret smile he had foolishly thought was just for him. "Why? Because I'm as ruthless as you?"

"I might be ruthless, but I'm never intentionally cruel."

"Cruel?" She touched cool fingertips to his cheek. "Did you ever think you might belong in Quisnaf? That a man like you will always be sought, desired, held?"

When he said nothing, she sighed and drew back her hand. "I'm leaving with the sword. If you're quick, you'll evade the Quisnaf—this time. But they won't give up."

"You're not leaving. Tell me the truth about Kaell's sword."

Rozenn's clear blue eyes dwelled on his face. Though anger

squeezed his heart, her beauty still moved him. "Kaell's dead, Val."

"No." He shook his head. "No, he's not. He can't be."

She shrugged. "It's for the best. I warned you. The nineteenth bladesman. You did nothing."

"That foul book with its foolish prophecies? You cursed me, Rozenn. Try as I might, I could not stop looking for signs, wondering if it were true. Even if the book referred to Kaell, if that was his destiny, how could I kill him?"

"We all do what we must, Val. You of all people know that." She dropped her eyes to his wrists. "Though you didn't do enough, did you? Didn't turn to magic, dangerous blood magic to save yourself. What happened to you all those centuries ago is your fault."

Vraymorg drew down a laboured breath, pushing away her cruel words. "Tell me about the sword."

"If I tell you, will you let me live?"

"Yes." *No.* She had betrayed him, poisoned him, buried him.

"You lie. You intend to kill me."

"Yes," he said.

A smile curled the edges of her soft, soft mouth. "Kill the mother of your son?"

"Wh—what?" he stammered, throat tight, heart rioting.

A bird cawed from the roof, took flight with flapping wings. The rising wind hunted through the ill-fitting door, rattling dead leaves into corners. But beneath the sounds, an unbroken stillness brooded.

"I wondered about your son… until Gendrick Caelan claimed Alecc as his."

His sword drooped. A bewilderment of thoughts assaulted him. A son. Did he believe her? Maybe she was lying to save her life? But if it was true—that meant another child he would one day mourn. He could not open himself up to that pain.

Rozenn challenged his bemused stare. "You didn't think I might have reasons to let Gendrick think Alecc is his?"

A shadow rose at his back. Vraymorg whirled in time to see Tarvan, blood streaming from his gashed face. In time to see Tarvan's snarl as he threw a fist.

It crunched into his jaw. He sank to the floor and into blackness.

VRAYMORG RODE HARD from the forest towards the dawn. In the castle ward, he left his horse with a groom. He hurled Kaell's blade down in the hall. But his anger, his sorrow he carried to the boy's room. The door fell open at his touch.

"Is someone there?" He stepped inside.

A young woman sat in pale sunlight by the window, her dark head bowed, her hands clasped across the book in her lap.

"Alyssa?"

The woman staggered clumsily to her feet and stood holding her swollen belly. "My lord."

"You're with child?"

"I'm close to my time, lord. Will is taking me to his mother's house in the valley town. The road passes the castle. I wanted to greet my aunt, to see—"

She choked a sound. Then words rushed out. "Kaell. Oh, by all the old gods. Kaell. I didn't know. Our home is so remote. We don't hear from anyone for months."

Her dismay struck like a blow. He almost reeled.

"You loved him."

Alyssa managed a sad smile. "Always, my lord. But not as Kaell wanted. Never like that. Then I met Will."

Vraymorg looked at the book spilled on Kaell's bed.

"You knew he kept that?"

"Yes." Another sad smile. "I suppose you think I'm wrong to read it." Her voice cracked. She turned to hide her tears.

"No. I understand."

"I'd see him scribbling, but when I asked what he wrote he smiled in that way of his and said it was thoughts. Thoughts." She paused. "Perhaps that's why he was so right in his head." Her glance challenged. "He was, wasn't he? Steady in the head. For a bonded warrior. My nan as a child knew a hunter who muttered to himself and saw things not there."

Vraymorg remembered the young man, how his mind had fractured when ghouls slaughtered men he led, how he wandered about the castle like a ghost, dishevelled, barefoot. Lost. Until he hanged himself in the ruins near the orchard.

"But that wasn't Kaell," Alyssa said. "He was steady, too cheerful sometimes, given what happens to bonded ones. The only time he wasn't—" She bit her lip.

"He missed you, but he was glad William made you happy," Vraymorg said kindly.

"Was he?" Alyssa brushed fingers over the book. "I didn't mean to read this. But I wanted something of Kaell's."

She threw Vraymorg an embarrassed look. "My lord, may I sit? It's just the child—"

His grief made him thoughtless. "I'm sorry. Sit. Please."

Alyssa gathered her skirts and eased into the chair. Vraymorg turned away. The room seemed unchanged. A carelessly flung cape draped a chair. Books piled beside the bed. Kaell often read by candlelight. Sometimes he fell asleep in a chair, head thrown back, mouth open.

A prowling Vraymorg, unable to escape dreams, always shook Kaell awake, ordered him to bed, snuffed out the candle, and paused at the door, listening to his breaths.

"He thought I didn't know about this book," he said. "I found it soon after that Downs man fell from the wall."

"I remember that night. I cried for hours. I thought Kaell might die. My aunt told me bonded warriors are strong, but I didn't believe her." She swept a gaze about the chamber. "Only a few things. Yet I feel him here."

Vraymorg wished the room felt long abandoned, empty of ghosts and memories. When he looked back, Alyssa was quietly sobbing into her hands. "Alyssa—"

She pushed to her feet. "I can't be here, my lord. Forgive me. I should not have come."

HE DID NOT KNOW how long he sat in that room after she left. Too many thoughts slammed into his mind. A bewildering jumble of disbelief, of anger and sorrow.

Alecc, his son. A boy already ten and he had been oblivious. Just as he was about Philip. Ewen was right: there could be wonder and joy in fatherhood, even with its struggle. But there was something else dark beneath.

Loss. He had loved and lost. Loved again, lost again. Until he could not bear the first because it came only with the other.

"My lord?" Ewen stood in the doorway. "The sentries said you returned."

Vraymorg dragged fingers through his thick hair, reluctant to leave this room. The past lingered here. Any moment Kaell must walk in, fling his cloak and knife aside, and eagerly tell him about that day's swordplay.

But what if he didn't? What if this room stayed like this? Empty. Gathering dust. Gathering silence.

"Where did you go?" Ewen dropped his pretence of formality. "To see her? You can't go off like that. Not now the Quisnaf know your name and where you are."

Vraymorg hid a fond smile. Ewen often treated him like a wayward nephew.

"From your first grey hair, you've scolded me. I'm centuries older than you, young man."

"I scold because you're reckless, Val. You don't care what happens to you. Do you understand what the Quisnaf blood keepers want of you? Better to drive a sword into that cold heart of yours."

"As it happens, Quisnaf warriors are in the forest."

"No!"

"I eluded them." But Rozenn was right: they would never stop hunting him. Maybe her other words were also true; his fate was to be sought, possessed.

What if he returned to the forest, begged the Quisnaf to take him? Could the surrender of his body, even his will, bring an end to struggle?

Except he could not offer up his fear. They could not ache for Kaell, worry for Kaell. If only caring was an act of will. Then he could put it aside.

"Your wrists." Alarm etched Ewen's face. "Rope burns. Who bound you? It was her, wasn't it? I warned you. You can't trust Cahireans."

Vraymorg sighed. "The sweet Rozenn and her captain left me tied up for the Quisnaf. After said captain first stabbed then hit me. I must thank him sometime."

"And you escaped? Thank Khir."

"I hid Kaell's blade up the chimney. Useful for cutting ropes. Rozenn took mine, thinking it was Kaell's. A long story. What brought you up here in a rush? What's happened this time?"

"This time?" Ewen flung his arms up in exasperation. "We're at war, Val. The king has expectations of you."

"Kings, lords, Quisnaf warriors—you." Vraymorg shrugged. "Don't tell me Cathmor turned up." He laughed. "No, stupid. He might soil his cloak travelling in this weather."

"Cathmor. No." Ewen sounded displeased at his lord's levity. "But his messenger arrived this morning. I put him in the small hall. He's comfortable beside the fire."

Vraymorg rose. That world of kings, of sieges, battles, lords, and their feuds beckoned.

"What's he want? The messenger."

"The king demands more rope, more arrows. At once. Cathmor's also sent someone to make sure he gets them."

"He'll get them when he gets them." He sounded like a petulant child. No wonder Ewen corrected him. "Who's he sent?"

Ewen looked hard at him. "Caelmarsh."

KAELL

His ragged breath hit air as sharp as ice. His bare feet bled. The sword slapped his back. It bruised and cut his skin, but Kaell ran. He would not stop until his lord allowed it.

Then I'll lie in the snow and sleep.

"Then you'll die," Vraymorg said.

"Then let me die," Kaell whispered. He thought he heard a chuckle, glimpsed blond hair, breathed an exotic scent unlike the forest's pine, churned earth, and dew-wet grass.

"It's been four days." A voice drifted through his scrambled mind. "Time enough for his strength to return. No more sleeping draughts. Get rid of the dirt. Bring him to my chamber."

Hands lifted him. His heels skidded on stone. Blackness folded like wings then slowly opened. So cold. Everything cold.

"Kaell, listen." A woman. "I must be quick before they miss me."

"Who are you?" he croaked. "Am I in the forest? Where is my lord?"

"What's wrong with you? You're a prisoner." She sounded angry. Why? He ran, didn't he? As his lord commanded. "Pretend to submit. Do not fight. Once they lower their guard, you must find me. Please help me, Kaell. Help me."

Fight? Find her? He wanted only to sleep in the snow.

"If you sleep in the snow, you die," his lord said.

Tiptoed steps faded. In the stillness, Kaell drifted in a carefree ether. Dreams winked in and out until a throb in his skull pierced deep, dragging him back to wakefulness.

His cheek was pressed against cold tiles, his body thick as sludge. He moved an arm. No clink of chains. How long had he sprawled here—wherever here was? His last clear memory was the hall, Archanin's breath on his face, his teeth nipping his throat. Then nothing.

Kaell lifted his head. His sight fractured as though he twisted on a rope. Groaning, he sank down and shut his eyes. Languor swept over him as sweetly as a tendril of fragrance.

Cloth brushed his arm. A woman, her perfume creamy, smoothed matted hair from his forehead. Bare feet padded away over stone.

Kaell forced open his heavy eyelids. He was in a circular room, its stone walls unbroken by windows, with one wooden door. Steam shrouded flickering, scented candlelight.

A bathhouse? Like the one he and Arn had visited in Dal-Kanu. He liked Dal-Kanu. The king said it stank of mud, but Kaell thought its narrow streets smelt of spices.

He rose on one elbow. A blanket fell away. Beneath, he was naked, his skin slick, his bedraggled hair plastering his face.

"About time you fled one nightmare and woke to another."

Kaell traced the female voice through curling steam to a figure leaning against a huge wooden tub. From her pale hair, her luminous skin, a ghoul. Words from dreams niggled. "Don't fight. You're a prisoner."

Kaell clawed his neck for the wound. Archanin's prisoner. He tried to rise only to fall down. In vain, he groped for his sword. No sword. No clothes, even. No escape.

The ghoul moved through damp mist like a wraith. She

grabbed his arm. "Be still. The guards outside will gladly hurt you if you cause trouble."

She peered at his face. "You look wan. I suppose it has only been a matter of days since our lord drained most of your blood. Take a breath. You'll feel better after a bath."

Better? A jester, this one. His dizziness and weakness shocked him.

The door crashed into a wall. A girl carried buckets of steaming water inside.

Caitlyn. Another dam of memory burst. The hall. Jeering laughter. A voice. He fingered the neck wound again.

"Caitlyn. Be quick then on with your work."

The girl emptied water into the tub, shamelessly swept Kaell a leer, grinned, and left.

The ghoul glared. "You, bathe."

"Who are you?"

"You may call me Terissada. Now obey. Bathe, or the guards throw you in."

Kaell folded his arms over his breast.

"Stubborn fool." Her gown swished mosaic tiles as she padded to the door, returning with two armed ghouls. They seized his shoulders. Kaell bucked. A blow snapped his head back.

"Careful." Terissada protested with raised hands. "Don't harm him more than necessary."

Dazed, Kaell hardly struggled as they hurled him into the tub.

"We should bind him."

Terissada shook her head. "He'll settle."

The guards stepped back. Kaell considered them angrily as dizziness faded. No point resisting until he had the strength to fight.

He sank into heat-misted water, sighing with reluctant pleasure. Dirt and blood floated off. Pleasing scents of freesia and lavender soap swirled. His knotted muscles loosened.

"This water is black already." Wearing only a shift, Terissada splashed into the tub. "Why, you're as filthy as a pig rolling in mud. Here, let me scrub your back, little pig."

Kaell flinched. "I don't want my back scrubbed."

She grabbed his arm. "Turn your back. My lord bid me prepare you."

"For what?" His voice cracked.

"Shut up. Do as I ask." Terissada lathered soap.

"Or what?"

"Or the guards restrain you. They won't be as gentle as me. Your choice."

His choice was *do not submit.* But restraints? No.

With a frustrated sigh, Kaell folded his arms on the rim as she scrubbed. At each stroke, his tension surprisingly seeped away.

"Turn again."

Kaell rolled. She soaped his chest and belly. When she groped lower, he growled and caught her wrist.

Terissada slapped his hand away. A guard started forward. She waved him back. "You can go, both of you. He won't cause trouble."

Kaell forced down anger, a need to throw his fists about to prove her wrong. Do not react. Let her—them—think him broken. One careless moment and he'd escape.

Terissada washed blood from his stiff hair, sponged his shoulders, her fingertips lingering on bulked muscle. Her breast pressed his arm. He didn't bother shrinking away.

When she left him to soak, Kaell floated, eyes closed, the heated water lulling his fears. Thoughts tried to ambush him, but he held them off. Thoughts hurt. Better an empty mind.

"Out." Terissada splashed water in his face. She wore a different gown, damp where it clung to her lithe body.

Unsteadily, embarrassed by a faint stirring in his groin, Kaell climbed from the tub and squeezed water from dripping hair.

Terissada held a cloth. She did not give it him, only swept an admiring look up and down.

Kaell tolerated it. Even in the prudish Mountains, there was little shame in nudity. Though, unlike the decadent Isles, it was common only in bathhouses.

"I traced your scars." Her voice husked. "It should sicken me to touch you, given what you are. And yet"—she sighed—"I didn't expect to find you so pleasing. Like a desert warrior from the past."

Glaring, Kaell snatched the cloth from her. He wrapped it about his waist.

"So modest." Terissada laughed. "A blushing Telorian will find our ways wanton. Now for that stubble. He prefers it gone. Come here."

He? Archanin? Kaell trembled. No, he must not think.

She bid him sit on a low bench, fetched a knife, wet the edge, and put it to his throat. Their eyes locked. Above lapping water, a faint murmur of voices outside, Kaell's breaths hammered, too loud, too fast. Steam swirled with floral scents.

He seized her wrist and pressed the knife into his skin. Blood lined a thin cut.

"Do it," he said. "Cut your enemy's throat."

Terissada carefully removed his hand. "If you fear what's ahead, you're not so stupid."

Shame heated his skin. It was one thing to want to die, another to let his enemy think he sought death because of fear.

Stunned by his weakness, he sat docilely as she shaved him then rolled onto his belly at her command. Terissada spilled scented lotions onto her palms.

Despite her previous lewd look, her hands moved over his body with impersonal precision, kneading and soothing tight muscles. Kaell drifted towards sleep.

A pounding roused him. An armed ghoul pushed inside. "Our lord grows impatient."

"He will be prepared in a few moments. Wait there."

Prepared. Dread unwound like a spring within him. "Prepared for what? Am I food at a feast?" Humiliating to die like that.

But the prospect of another, shocking fate festered in the darkest recesses of his mind. Ghouls were licentious and immoral. What if they used him shamefully? What if preparing him meant readying him to service their lord in his bedchamber?

Kaell gripped the bench hard, fighting panic. As a child he once overheard his lord tell Arn that beauty carried its own curse. Now he thought he understood what that meant.

"The main course." A teasing smile touched her lips. "Ah, the look on your face." She laughed. "Calm yourself. You're precious to our lord."

"Your lord—Archanin? If he does not want to kill me—"

"He does not."

"But he must kill me," Kaell whispered, his heart breaking into an uneven thud. "He must." His gods promised a hard, righteous fight then death. That kick of danger cut his breath. Torture wasn't the worst that could happen to a captive.

Terissada flashed a disbelieving look. "Do you have ears, boy? You heard our lord's words in the hall as surely as I. He doesn't intend to kill you. Not with your blood."

Kaell bunched his fists. "I'm still human. I feel it. He failed. He can't turn me. He must kill me."

Terissada shook her head. "Silly child. Believe what you want."

She threw open a chest and tossed him pants and a tunic, its colour the deep blue-green of the lake at Dal-Kanu. Why think of that? Because he'd never see Dal-Kanu again. Or Vraymorg. Or anywhere, except here.

Wherever *here* was.

"Where am I?" Kaell pulled the tunic over his head, relieved to be clothed again.

Terissada did not answer. She pressed fingers to his jaw to turn his head.

"Yes, you'll please him. He likes beautiful things. That's the way with gods. Though he is fickle in his affection and desires."

Desires? Kaell jolted at the now too-real prospect Archanin had a carnal use for him. He shielded his body with his arms, holding in a shiver as his imagination took over.

Terissada flung back the door and called to the guards.

"Why is my hair like yours?" Kaell snatched at something ordinary to thrash down his rising alarm.

She raised an eyebrow, amused. "Who do you think we are, Kaell?"

He shrugged.

"Where do you think we came from?"

"I don't know."

Terissada shoved him at a guard. "And if I said you and I share a common bloodline?"

"You were human? I don't understand."

She sniffed. "Poor child. This lord of yours treats you like a beast. Expects you to fight and die and tells you nothing. You don't even know who you are?"

Kaell's mouth tasted like sand. His lord rebuffed every question about his parents or where he was from. "Who am I?"

But Terissada turned away.

GHOUL GUARDS FELL in around him, gripped his shoulders, forced him forward. They carried swords, their watchful gazes surly with mistrust.

Kaell let training and instinct kick in, assessing options to break free. Unarmed, alone, could he overpower them? Run? To where?

He hung his head. His capture dented his belief in his skill. What he wouldn't do for his lord's comforting presence. His strength.

The guards shadowed him along a passage, its stone worn beneath his bare feet.

But for their boots and his reluctant steps, a silence palled. From sconces on hewed walls torches flickered golden light. A cool wind snaked through high, slanted shadows.

They pushed him up a crumbling staircase to a columned balcony. Kaell drew up hard. He expelled an astonished breath.

Clouds in a midnight sky webbed above broken, blackened roof beams. A ruined hall sprawled below, a dusting of shadows and moonbeams, of gleaming marble and pillars tangled with thorns and ivy.

A guard barked in the ghoul tongue. He shoved. Kaell stumbled, steadied, looked up.

And saw the door from his nightmares.

His breath clipped then choked. Terror sped through him like wildfire. *No!* The scream unwound silently in his tight rib cage. *No. Not in there.*

He backed up into bodies, tried to turn. The ghouls blocked him, grabbed him, dragged him forward. Kaell flailed with his arms and jammed heels into stone, that soundless scream drowned in his lungs. Step by step, they pulled him to the door.

He knew every carving, knew how the dark wood might feel beneath his fingers. His mind unravelled into disbelief. Sick dread ripped like a lance across his gut.

A guard rapped. Kaell's horrified stare held on the door. It swung open. With a bestial cry, he reeled back. The ghouls tightened their hold.

"Why the delay?" Another female peered out. "Bring him in at once."

Desperately, Kaell jerked his elbow into a guard's face. The ghoul stumbled, grunting in pain. Kaell swung an arm. A second fell back. He broke free of clutching hands and ran.

Footsteps pounded behind. Close. Voices erupted to shouts. Closer.

Weak, dizzy with fear, Kaell had no clue where he was or how to elude them.

The floor floated. Shattered light blurred his vision. A wall that wasn't there a heartbeat before reared up. He bounced off it, moaned, scrambled upright. Staggered a step. Yawed. Lurched. Ran.

Breath burned his ribs. He hit a long corridor. A man stepped through a far door. Turned.

"Arn!" Kaell froze. "You're alive." No time to unravel how. "Arn, we have to get out of here."

Even as the words fell out, he knew no one was there. Loneliness and guilt tore this illusion from his tormented mind. Yet the ghost, or whatever it was, stared over his shoulder.

Kaell wheeled, arms flung up as a fist flew. The blow crunched into his jaw. Dazed, he fell. Ghouls caught him, snatched up his feet, his arms.

He shook off his haze and thrashed, screaming, "Arn! Help me!" He squirmed, kicked until they dropped his legs, scrabbled at a jagged edge of stone, and hung on.

His captors peeled his fingers away. They struck him again. The blow stunned him. He didn't realise at once they carried him back to the door.

Through the door.

Fear stopped his breath. Blind with panic, Kaell jerked his legs, tore a hand loose, and clawed uselessly at air.

A guard laughed. "Our lord likes them feisty." They dropped him on his feet, bound him to a rounded pillar with thick cord. All but the female ghoul withdrew. The door clanged shut.

A sob died in Kaell's throat. Not here. Not this room. No, he could not weep, must not.

"Be silent and still." She thrust hands to her waist. "Enough of your childish nonsense."

"Arn. I saw my friend, Arn. He's alive. What have you done to him?"

She sneered as she retreated with a drag of her gown over carpet. "Fool. Your companions are dead. All of them. You are alone, child."

Alone. Behind the door.

PANIC WHIPPED HIM into a frenzied bucking, twisting, and writhing. Kaell screamed at the walls, drummed his heels, yelled until he was hoarse and exhausted. At last he slumped, the ropes all that held him up, his uneasy gaze flickering about his prison.

An ornate prison. His toes curled into a thick rug. The stone beneath his palms marble. Candles in tall holders glowed upon intricately carved tables, high-backed, padded chairs, dark-wood chests, and patterned screens. Tapestries and woven carpets covered walls.

Small-leafed vines embraced fluted columns spilling upon a vaulted ceiling. He smelt clotted soil in ceramic pots, mixed with a creamy scent like peaches or figs.

More rugs of spun gold, purple, and green and pillows of every shape and size were splayed upon a divan near doors opened onto a balcony. A moon-washed sky, awash with blinking stars, cruelly whispered of freedom beyond this room, impossible freedom.

"Are you done with struggle, then?"

Kaell jerked in alarm. The silky, male voice drifted from the balcony. Someone leaned against the balustrade, arms folded as they watched him.

No, gods help him. He knew that voice from the hall. Archanin's voice.

Terror ignited new strength. Kaell strained against the ropes until blood trickled down his arms and cords welted his thighs and chest.

"So—not done."

"No, not done," he hissed. "Never done."

Archanin sighed. He stepped inside the door, stooping to light a candle. Its flame glinted on golden hair, his face hidden. "How sad. Do you believe in fate?"

Back hard against the pillar, every breath chipped with fear, Kaell managed a scornful laugh. What did it matter? Nothing mattered except how quickly this god killed him.

"No."

"Except your struggle is against just that, Kaell. Fate. The moment this lord you call Vraymorg walked through the Enarae and brought you back as a child of what? Three? four? Your path led to this room."

"What?" Kaell's heart skidded. The newly lit candle spilled incense laced with a dizzying, sickly sweet fragrance. He coughed. "The Enarae? I don't understand."

"The Enarae's perfume clings to you. It had to be, to explain who you are."

Kaell fisted a hand against the pillar. His core wanted to twist away, not just from Archanin and his words but the desperate, shameful need in him to know the truth. Dry mouthed, he whispered, "Who am I?"

"You don't know?" Archanin's laugh was mirthless. "You really don't know?"

Every muscle in Kaell's back clenched. The room closed in, the cloying incense, the marble hard against his thighs, the narrowing yellow glow of torches on walls.

"What would you give me to tell you, I wonder? Oh your lord kept this close, but I tasted your blood, and I know the truth. So we come back to it—fate."

Kaell recoiled as far as his bonds allowed. The candle's smoke suffocated; it was on his tongue, in his lungs, in his throat. Archanin's velvet voice, its rhythm, washed his rage into a listless docility. He should fight it, but he couldn't seem to care.

So we come back to it. Fate.

Didn't he always know he'd die young? But death in battle. Not this. Bound. Defeated. Alone. That most of all. Alone. Unshed tears burned his eyes. Ashamed, he forced them back.

"There is a Venivan rhyme about fate." Archanin's voice possessed an ethereal whimsy. "It starts like this: A warrior's death they say is set…"

"By lords and gods and fate… and yet." Kaell took up the second line. The words seemed apart from him, the verse recited by someone else, somewhere else.

"My blade answers to my song,

My life is mine, my will too strong."

"You surprise me," Archanin said with a gentle laugh. "Few know this poem."

"I like words." Kaell struggled to shake off his sluggishness, that cloud dulling his mind.

Archanin leaned a shoulder against the wall. "Words hold power. Songs. Poetry. They all weave magic of one sort or another. My favourite poems are Venivan."

"Like King Cerall's odes to his queen, Eleanor."

"His poems are little known—in these vicious times." Archanin released a wistful sigh. "You are different. No wonder fate brought you to me, Kaell. You belong here."

A spell's rhythm throbbed beneath the words. Unheard before.

Kaell scraped his nails into his palms to clear his apathy. "Stop it," he hissed. "Whatever you're doing. Stop it."

Archanin's laugh pealed as chillingly silver and dark as midnight. He pushed off the wall and came out of the shadows.

"I will not look at you." Kaell screwed his eyes shut. "I won't let you bewitch me."

"You will do exactly as I say, Kaell. You'll look at me, obey me, and even love me."

Footsteps. Cloth whispered over rugs. Archanin stood close. Kaell knew it. His own breath dragged, too loud. Cold sweat beaded on his brow.

"I am your true god. You must learn to obey. Look at me."

The command tore into him like an arrow. Unbidden, Kaell looked, a startled look that became a stare.

He wasn't sure what a god should be like. Perhaps like this, as untamed and dangerously beautiful as a lashing storm. Golden hair cascaded onto broad shoulders. Flowing red silk, woven with silver thread, draped lean muscles.

Yet for all his beauty, Archanin possessed a warrior's contained menace, a formidable, alarming power.

Kaell mouthed a protection prayer to Khir. It tasted ashen. Desperately he heaved against the ropes again until blood oozed along his arms from new cuts.

No one warned him of Archanin's grim strength. He could not be here, must not be here. More hot tears welled, tears of helplessness.

His captor watched his useless struggle with pitiless, heavy-lidded eyes of an inhuman shade of blue. Translucent, almost silver at the edges but dark about the pupil.

"Why thrash about again? Only struggle hurts, Kaell."

Kaell had to fight. Only pain lay ahead. He couldn't just accept that.

"I won't obey you, so just get on with it." He etched each word with scorn.

"With what exactly?" Archanin's tone rippled with amusement. "You think I intend to tear and slash at you in some dark, dank prison?"

Kaell lifted his chin. "I am not afraid."

"Liar. I smell your fear. It almost makes me want to torture you. Your screams might please me for a time, but I can't risk killing you. You're too valuable."

"Valuable?" An irrational hope stirred. "Do you mean to ransom me?"

Archanin chuckled. "Cruel to tease one so young and naive. Do you see that steel ring?" He gestured. "That's where I chained the last bonded warrior your gods let me take alive."

Dry mouthed, Kaell swallowed. He tried in vain not to look at the ring. "What did you do to him?"

"That one was of no use to me. I did not treat him as kindly as you."

"Kind?"

"You're uncomfortable. Weary, afraid, as I want you to be. But that's all. I allowed you time to heal after I took your blood. I do not even intend to break you, Kaell. At least, not through pain."

"I should be grateful?" Kaell jeered.

"Oh you'll be grateful. But let me be clear so you don't cling to futile hope. You won't leave here, Kaell. I meant what I said in the hall. It will take patience, but I will make you a thing men hunt."

"You can't," Kaell whispered. "Even the bite of a ghoul kills—"

He broke off with a shudder. Archanin drank his blood. He should be dead. "No. No." A madness leapt upon him. He slammed his head against the pillar. And again.

"I prefer you don't hurt yourself," Archanin said dispassionately. "Stop, or I'll tie you so you cannot even twitch. That's better. Now, shall we get to know each other?"

Back taut, his fists knuckling stone, Kaell said, "I want only to kill you."

Archanin's smile unnerved him. It was so confident, so unafraid. "Then you should try. So you learn you can never hurt me, Kaell. Only obey."

The ghoul god waved a hand. The ropes dropped. For a heartbeat Kaell froze. Then he sprang at his captor.

Archanin spat a word. His palm carved air. Pain flooded Kaell's body, battered him down to the rug. Moaning, he balled knees to chest.

"That won't do." Archanin frowned. "Why can I hurt you so easily?"

The pain disappeared fast. Shaken, Kaell pushed to his knees. What just happened?

"Your bond to my brother Khir should protect you from Seithin magic. Didn't the priests, didn't your lord, prepare you?"

Stung, Kaell lifted his head to glare. "My lord taught me enough."

Archanin's clear blue eyes dwelt for a long moment. A smile flitted across his face, a knowing smile. "You're very loyal. But loyal to a man who can never accept you, Kaell."

Kaell barely hid a flinch. "You're wrong."

"Am I? I think I touched a wound. I think you long for that man's love. Yet with your blood, men and women will always fear you. Never love you."

"You don't know me. Stop pretending you do."

"I know I can give you all you've yearned for, Kaell. Everything your lord withheld. Poor child. Raised by a cold, distant man, never the father you sought. But you need never feel alone or different again. Not here. Not with me."

"You're wrong," Kaell answered fast, refusing to let the words sink into him. "I don't feel alone or a freak. If he knew where to look, my lord would come for me."

"Is that what you think?" Archanin heaved an exaggerated sigh. "Beneath your defiance, I hear doubt. You don't know if you're loved or where you really belong. Forget that other life. It meant nothing. Your real life begins here, with me."

"No."

"So easy to break you," Archanin said. "Easier than the others. Every other bonded warrior could withstand Seithin magic. But not you." He stared over Kaell's head, frowning.

"Was the ceremony binding you to Khir flawed? Or did someone, unwittingly or deliberately, break the bond? Blood magic might do that." He sighed. "I must be gentle, it seems, or I may unintentionally kill you."

"Then kill me," Kaell shot back hotly. He could stand the pain. He must. "That's all you can do to me."

The ghoul god arched finely shaped dark brows. "Even *you* don't believe that."

ARCHANIN LEFT him curled on the floor, too weary to crawl. Head on hands, he collapsed into sleep.

"Kaell."

Reluctantly he stirred. From a tall-backed chair, Archanin

watched him, his expression masked behind otherworldly eyes.

Kaell struggled to his knees. Sleep weighted his body and wits, a thankfully dreamless but too-short sleep. Darkness still hulked beyond the balcony.

Archanin leaned towards him. "Why did you make me hurt you, Kaell?"

"Wh—what?" He shook his head to clear it.

"That isn't why I had you bathed and dressed and brought to my chambers. I don't want to hurt you. I want you to accept me as your lord, to love me."

"You're deluded," Kaell jeered. "I have a lord. A god."

"A god who abandoned you. A lord who cannot love you."

"You don't know me or my lord."

Archanin sighed. He sat back. "Did you ever wonder at your name?"

"I'm your prisoner, and you want to talk about my name?"

A smile curved Archanin's perfect lips. "Kaell is a common name among my people. Caolin in its female form. My queen's name. A beautiful, graceful creature. I miss her, though she died many centuries ago."

"Should I care?"

A shrug. "I tell you this because I want no secrets between us. You belong here, Kaell. With me. No one will judge you for the colour of your hair, condemn you as different. That's what you want, isn't it? Acceptance. Love."

"Don't do that," said Kaell.

"Do what?"

"Think you know me. Think you know what I want. You don't."

Archanin pressed a finger to his lips, thoughtful. "This lord, this man—Vraymorg."

"What about him?" Kaell's voice cracked with unease.

"He'll never be what you want. Never give you what you want."

"Shut up," Kaell said.

"He can't accept you, because he knows what you are. Knows—and never told you. Did you ever glimpse fear flicker behind his eyes when he glanced at you? Did he stiffen when you hugged him as a child?"

"No. You're wrong."

"This man will never love you, Kaell."

Kaell clamped his hands over his ears. He swayed on his knees. Thoughts strummed with a despairing rhythm.

Candlelight straightened then flared as Archanin stood over him. "Reflect upon my words, about why you think you owe this flawed man your loyalty."

He stooped to snap a metal cuff about Kaell's wrist, then fastened the chain to the floor ring. Kaell did not resist. No point to it.

"When I return, we'll test just how open you are to my magic."

Archanin left him with disturbed thoughts.

HE REMEMBERED WRITHING TORCHLIGHT, smoke stinging his eyes, the wind's icy breath pawing his moist skin. He remembered faceless, hooded priests lifting him onto a slab. A sheer slope of walls closed.

Wet rock, sweat, incense. These scents always threw him back to the terror of that night.

"My lord?" Kaell whispered.

Forbidden to speak, Vraymorg briefly squeezed his hand as the priests bound Kaell's wrists and ankles. Rough stone indented his thighs, his naked back.

When the priests picked up their knives, Kaell's breath stalled. He followed the knives with wide eyes, determined to show no fear. Make his lord proud.

"With your blood," a hooded figure demanded, "with your life, will you serve Khir, god of battles, ancient lord of men and of this land, protector?"

"Yes." Beneath his terror, Kaell's voice crumpled.

"Do you accept his protection?"

"Yes."

"And will you in return surrender your will to the ancient one?"

"Yes."

The priest cut him. Kaell did not scream. Not then, nor at the next cut, or the next. He no longer heard their chants, aware only of his pooling blood, sticky beneath him, of its slow drip to the floor.

Tears streamed like that blood. Silent tears of pain. He clenched his teeth until his jaw ached. It would end. Everything ended.

"You did well." His lord rubbed balm into his wounds. They were alone in the sanctum, the priests gone. "You pleased the gods."

Kaell accepted the praise with a weary nod. Eyes closed, he let Vraymorg's hands soothe, summoning strength for the rest of the ritual. He did not—would not—look at the shadows. But a presence, as intangible as a reflection in a polished shield, waited.

His lord left him.

Alone, feeble from blood loss, Kaell struggled to sit up. His body throbbed. Fevered sweat matted his hair. The smoke reeked of sickly incense. Rising on shaking legs, he took the sword stained with his blood and sank to his knees before the statue of Khir.

Near dawn, the vigil ending, he fell into an exhausted sleep. For the first time he dreamt of the girl. For the first time he dreamt of his death.

Kaell was fourteen and knew he would not reach twenty-four.

"TELL ME OF THE DREAM." Archanin brushed hair from his brow.

Kaell jolted. There was no rock-walled sanctum. No priests. No praise from his lord as he rubbed balm into his wounds. This was

Archanin's chamber with all its luxurious tapestries and carved tables, its rich fabrics and rich perfumes.

He lay on a rug, his head in Archanin's lap. With a yelp of disgust, Kaell scrambled up in a clatter of chains. How did he end up there? He had no memory of what came before.

Archanin smiled. "The spell lasted longer that time. But again that lovely haze cleared from your eyes. What did that? Memories of your lord, perhaps?"

He stretched. Yawned. "A curious man, this Vraymorg. He teaches you Venivan poetry and the song of swords but shares nothing of himself."

Kaell hunched. "You know nothing about him or me."

"I know you desire this man's love. I could give you what he cannot."

"You know nothing of love."

Silence. But only between them. Beneath it crept a rumbling of sounds: distant voices distorted to an echo by caging walls, a breath of wind through broken stone, a bird's caw, a pitiful beat of wings.

"I've loved, Kaell," Archanin said softly. "I've lost."

"What? Your freedom? Your kingdom. You think that is loss?"

"That, yes," Archanin's gaze passed over Kaell to the shadows behind. "And my queen." He leaned against a chair leg. Even relaxed, arms hugging drawn-up knees, he looked elegant and beautiful.

Kaell swallowed. "How?"

"How," the ghoul god echoed. His stare fell on nothing.

"Do you know why I'm trapped in this ruin? Because of a spell cast by a long-dead king. If I could summon Roaran Caelan from death to pay for his vicious deeds, I would. His curse killed my queen, killed hundreds of my people, imprisoned me."

Unlikely compassion stirred. Kaell did not know what to say.

Archanin pressed his lips into a sad smile. "When she died, I knew only despair. It consumed me. Like the words of the Venivan song, "The Sorrowful Night." You know it?"

"I know it."

Kaell remembered a Mountains night when mist lingered and warriors huddled around a fire. A creeping night when men heard a dark song in the wind and shivered for no reason.

He could see Olier, flame light hollowing his cheeks, hands clasped about his knees, his eyes hazy as he sang the words his Venivan grandmother taught him.

"Despair consumes me, hollows me with grief,
It robs me of every hope—a vicious, taunting thief,
Broken, my heart bleeds sorrow,
There's death at least, if no tomorrow."

Tears pricked his eyelids. Olier was dead. He would never hear him singing, or fighting with Arn again. Oh gods, Arn. So many Mountains men butchered in that foul forest.

Archanin nodded slowly. "Do not think I cannot understand you Kaell, that I cannot understand your yearning for love, whether it is love lost or love desperately sought."

Uncomfortable, Kaell shifted his weight. What was happening here? How could he pity this monster? His enemy. Snatching at coldness, he uttered in a voice sharp with contempt, "I do not want your love."

Archanin said nothing. But for a slight spasm in his jaw, he might not have heard.

Then he shrugged. "The hard way, then."

Kaell braced. Just as before, Archanin did not touch him, only drove his palm through air. His lips formed words. But this time the torrent of agony was unbearable. It swallowed Kaell until he no longer existed, only his body jerking, convulsing, shuddering, his mind shattered.

"Stop!" he screamed. "Stop! Please!"

As fast as it came, the pain disappeared.

"So fragile." Archanin shook his head. "Turn over."

Beaten, Kaell crawled onto his belly. He buried his face in a cushion.

Despair consumes me. The words echoed miserably in his skull as if written for him alone. Until now, he didn't really understand them.

Archanin rubbed his back. Kaell's shoulders shot up.

"Be still," the ghoul god soothed. "I liked the story about your lord rubbing balm in your wounds. You felt safe. You can feel safe again, Kaell. Then you'll tell me other stories."

"Don't touch me." Beneath the caress, his muscles twitched.

"Ah, still fight in you."

Kaell growled.

"Just that last flare of defiance, like a cornered dog." With long, deep strokes, Archanin's hands tamed and humiliated. "Have you ever done this to a snarling dog? Force him to his belly then stroke his back until he accepts your training?"

Candles hissed against cool air, their scent heavy in Kaell's throat, in his lungs. Whatever the smoke did to him, he couldn't rally the will to fight it.

His eyelids drooped. His weighted limbs pinned him to the floor, his thoughts tangled. If he snatched at one, tried to focus on who he was, pain flared in his temple. Easier to drift.

Archanin rolled him onto pillows. "Those defences came down faster this time. No more growl in you." He reached for his dagger.

Lethargic, the cloying incense in his nostrils, Kaell only watched.

"You're stronger. And the spell holds. I can bring you the first death."

Kaell sighed in relief. "You intend to kill me."

"For one breath, no more." Archanin gently touched his hair. "This time when I drain your blood, precious child, I'll let your heart stop then bring you back with my blood."

"Why?" Kaell wasn't sure he cared.

"To make you like me, this must happen three times. Then a fourth death, which you must seek willingly. After all, magic is magic, and we gods will not be denied its ceremony."

Archanin slashed Kaell's wrist. He gasped in pain. His captor pressed his mouth to the wound. Kaell's awareness seeped away into a dreamscape of blurring colours and ragged shapes.

VOICES SLOWLY DESCENDED into layers of sleep. Quarrelling voices.

Kaell registered sensations. Stone at his back. Its chill clawed through thin cloth into his bones. Cool air laced with citrus and wood moss brushed his clammy forehead. Metal clinked as he moved a foot. Rippling, lambent candle flames still spewed nauseating odours.

"Do not succumb to needless fear." Archanin.

"But the prophecy. Kill him." Raggamirron, his tone stiff.

"No."

"Already talk spreads. The boy has dark-blond hair. It is written a warrior with the blood of the desert and the blood of Caelan—"

"And my blood."

"It's written a warrior with these three bloodlines will kill you, my lord. If you give this boy your blood, he will have two of the three."

Kaell forced open heavy eyes. Archanin sprawled in a padded chair, his chin propped on a hand resting upon the armrest. Raggamirron knelt on cushions at his god's feet.

"The prophecy is nonsense," Archanin said. "Impossible. A deception, even. I've waited for this child for centuries, fearing the seer's words might be wrong. Now it begins."

"What begins? A thread unravelling to your death?"

Archanin's laugh shivered foreboding down Kaell's spine. "A thread that unravels to my freedom, to my return to power."

Raggamirron sighed. "If you will not turn from this path, break him. Completely, absolutely. Destroy his will. Mould him anew."

Break? No. Kaell jerked in alarm. Jangling chains jarred the quiet.

Both ghouls looked his way.

"I think someone wakes." Archanin drummed the chair arm with tight fingers.

"My lord, you know I love you. I do not say this lightly. Kill him."

"No."

"My lord—"

"Enough." Archanin beat a furious rhythm. "Roaran's magic at long last fades. When this boy kneels to me, I'll walk free from this prison. I'll scatter blood and death and take this land. Every ancient doorway to the Enarae will be mine. Even Tide's End."

Raggamirron shuddered. "Tide's End? But that was Roaran's stronghold. The last true heir to Caelan himself. No, keep away from Tide's End, my lord."

His god laughed. "Tide's End will fall. Lastenarron destroyed Roaran's warding. The seer king sacrificed some poor fool centuries ago in a dismal tower tomb. Can you imagine?"

"But Roaran Caelan—"

"What of him? The seer king is long dead, his flesh rotted."

"And if he's not?"

A silence fogged, heavy and cold. Archanin's drilling fingers thumped in Kaell's skull.

He did not know why he listened for birdsong. None. The absence of the world beyond speared him with hopelessness.

"You don't think I'd know?" Archanin's voice fell empty, stripped of everything. "You don't think I'd sense the man I hate beyond all others?"

"Yes," Raggamirron said. "You would know."

Another tense, prickling hush fell. Kaell recognised an argument as timeless as this ruined castle. And between these two a bond like the one he shared with Arn.

Arn. Sorrow swooped in his gut, loneliness with it.

"Your fear is needless," Archanin said. "Roaran is dead. His prophecy impossible. It speaks of a warrior born of two Caelan parents."

"True Caelan, they call it."

"No Caelan warrior could also have Seithin blood and my blood. Especially our young captive."

"If Cathmor had wed Azenor Caelan—"

Archanin scoffed. "Cathmor is no more Caelan than I. His blood is tainted. No, the Caelan line survived only in the Isles."

He swept a hand at Kaell. "Free him, then leave us. I will win him, Raggamirron. Tonight, he and I begin an intimate acquaintance."

Intimate? Unease lifted gooseflesh on Kaell's arms.

Raggamirron rose, bowed, and walked to him. His look dwelled as though seeking to unlock a mystery. Kaell returned the inspection with a glare.

The ghoul shook his head and bent to unlock the ankle manacle.

The door thudded shut after him.

ARCHANIN SAT BACK. His face fell into shadow, but Kaell sensed those jewelled eyes upon him.

He reeled to his feet, his chin tilted in a small, futile gesture of defiance. The candles spat out their scent, that viscous, suffocating perfume that softened his will.

"You're not bound. You could run." Archanin waved a hand at the door.

"Do you deliberately test me? I might yet."

"You might. Or you might come to me."

Kaell forced a sneer, his bold front all bluster. A storm of fear tossed within. He badly wanted to turn and flee. To where? Where was this ruin?

Archanin leaned, hands gripping his knees. "Come to me, Kaell." His voice thrummed like music, beautiful but fierce. The command forced a staggering step. Just one step.

With an anguished cry, Kaell clamped down on the assault in his head, an overpowering need to obey. He summoned memories of his lord, of Arn, anything to hold on to who he was.

"The other one struggled too," Archanin said. "Until he collapsed, sobbing."

Kaell gritted his teeth in a snarl. "I won't sob. And I *will* kill you."

"Do you hide a host of armed men outside this room?" A snigger of amusement. "No? You are alone, Kaell. No one is coming for you. Not your lord. No one. Beyond these walls, you're dead. The sooner you accept this new life, the better. Now, *obey me*."

The words hammered. Not just in his head, along his backbone. His feet moved against his will. Kaell stumbled to the ghoul god.

"So it's true. Something frayed your bond to Khir. I can command you."

Kaell dropped his eyes, ashamed. "With magic. That is no victory."

"Victory? You think this is a battle between us? No, Kaell, it is a lesson. Now—"

Archanin's gaze trailed up and down. His breaths quickened. "Terissada choses well, as always. That tunic highlights the green of your eyes. I want to look at you. Disrobe."

No. Kaell jammed his feet into stone.

"Let me look at you."

The words beat at him, pulsing fire through his torso and limbs. The room's scents choked. His thoughts blurred.

Angrily Kaell swept a candle to the floor. He shouted, knuckled fists against his breast, shuddered, wailed. Anything but obey.

"Only resistance hurts, Kaell. Do not fight."

"Do your worst. I refuse to obey you."

Archanin shook his head. "I don't wish to hurt you, Kaell. But you are so ridiculously stubborn." He waved his hand.

At once a maelstrom of agony, scorching, knifing, throbbing, exploded through Kaell's body. He slammed to his knees, screaming, "Stop it! Stop it!" With desperate fingers, he clawed his tunic off. If Archanin demanded he rip his skin away too, he'd do it.

The pain dissolved to a dull ache.

"Stand."

Trembling, Kaell straightened on numb legs. The remaining candles flickered like wing beats. Archanin's gaze lingered.

Kaell made a despairing sound. Oh gods, not that.

"I remember men and women with that hair, those eyes," Archanin said. "My queen's eyes." He sighed, reached for a carafe, and pressed a cup upon Kaell. "Drink and tell me who in this land of dark-eyed men and women has eyes like yours."

"What sort of question is that?" Kaell folded his arms across his naked breast. "No one."

"Exactly."

"Then." He hesitated. "Where am I from?"

"Shall we bargain for the truth? Drink, and I may tell you."

Kaell took the cup and sniffed. The dark liquid smelt of hot spices. "What is this poison?"

"Life. I poured it down your throat after I drained you. You brought it back up the first few times, but by the third night you took it. It's why you're alive. That—and your blood."

Kaell hesitated. Then he gulped it down, angry that Archanin manipulated him but desperate for answers. "I drank your poison, so tell me. Who am I?"

"I said I might tell you, not that I would. Kneel on these cushions. I want to see those green eyes change as you bend to my will."

Outrage fired his courage. "No. You will have nothing from me."

"I'll have whatever I want of you. Obey."

Again he waved his hand. Pain crushed Kaell's skull. It didn't build; it was just there. Screaming, Kaell clutched his head. "It hurts, but I won't play your twisted games. You'll have to kill me."

"Obey."

Kaell fell to all fours. His body pulsed with vicious sensation, killing thought, allowing nowhere to hide. He crawled, but like a beast the pain pursued him.

"Obey!" Archanin's voice compelled.

A lance needled his head, stabbing, stabbing, stabbing. Sobbing in despair, panting, Kaell threw himself on the cushions, frightened he could hurt that much.

The pain disappeared. Archanin drew his head against his knees. "I can be everything to you, Kaell. Everything he cannot. Friend. Father." He paused. "Lover."

As his captor stroked his hair, Kaell muttered a half-hearted protest. A hateful longing whispered, a desire to surrender his fear, to let this god comfort him, consume him.

"I will teach you more than obedience." Archanin kissed his mouth. "In my arms, you'll learn life is not about duty. It is about pleasure. The pursuits of the flesh, without shame."

Shame. He should feel ashamed he did not draw away. That he didn't fight. Instead, he only watched as Archanin fluttered a wet tongue along his arm.

Thought and time stalled. Sensation splintered into lips kissing damp skin, hands stroking his body, sharp breath, Archanin disrobing, his touch on Kaell's thigh, his fingers running through his hair, the candles' scent, the perfumed oil, thick in his throat.

All the while, Archanin whispered, the words soft and seductive.

"You belong with me, Kaell. That other life, that other world, it means nothing. Forget it. Forget this man, this lord, who withholds his love from you. Think only of me. Think only of my hands on your skin, of how pleasurable it feels."

Beneath Archanin's caresses, his kisses, Kaell's mouth softened, lips parting to permit his captor's tongue. The alluring words bewitched like a potion.

When his body roused, he could not hold it back. The shuddering release was better than the agony Archanin brought him before.

Except there was silence. An awful silence drenched with regret and shame. Stunned by his submission, Kaell lay very still, his nakedness moulded against the ghoul god's.

"You're everything I hoped," said Archanin, still holding him, still stroking his hair. "I am more impatient now to bring you to this new life. So tonight, the second death."

He grabbed his captive's wrist. When he bit, Kaell's every muscle, every tendon and vein inflamed. A relief of pain. Welcome pain that at last plunged him into blissful emptiness.

HE DRIFTED ON sleep's sweet edge, a place free of hurt and shame. Sounds tried to intrude, to push down into his slumber. He thought he heard footsteps, a breath of cloth over stone. It was too hard to open his eyes; his body was part of the floor, an unmovable weight. His mind dulled.

A fragrance danced, rose-petal soft. Kaell made a sound that wasn't a word, wasn't a moan.

"Drink." A woman's voice. A memory nagged. Steamy, soap-scented air, warm water unknotting muscles. "Do not fight," she had said. "Let them think you're beaten."

Whoever she was, she lifted his head slightly, put a cup to his lips, helped him drink. Kaell coughed, the sticky liquid like molasses on his tongue.

"Finish it."

He accepted a little more, hoping she might then leave him alone.

Instead, she traced his lips with warm fingers. Sighed. "I wish I could see you."

Slowly, gently, as if savouring the sensuous touch of skin, she trailed her hand across his breastbone to his shoulders. "I remember Pairas. How he looked after we made love—his hair tousled, those wondrously dark eyes sleepy. Your shoulders feel as muscled as his."

Whatever he drank dissolved the haze. Kaell grew aware of the pillow beneath his head, the stone about him. Her hands on his naked body.

Exhausted from blood loss, he summoned the last of his strength to croak, "Cover me, please." He could hardly lift his arm. "I can't move or even open my eyes."

A coarse, itchy blanket fell over his hips. Her fingertips shifted to his gashed wrist. "He did this? And to your neck?"

"Kill me," Kaell rasped. "Please. If you have any pity, kill me."

"It will be over soon."

"What—" Sharp pain ripped his gut. It arched his back, tore breath from his lungs.

"It hurts." Kaell gasped through clenched teeth. "What did you give me?"

"It hurts, but it will prevent him enslaving you with magic again. He must give you his blood, but you cannot become his. When it's done, Kaell, find me."

"Who are you?"

She did not answer. He heard tiptoed steps and a door close.

THE CHAMBER DRAINED OF SOUND. It was like a deep, secret pool enfolding Kaell in its somnolence. There was only him, his loneliness, and this new tormenting pain.

In disbelief, he curled his knees to his knotted belly. The woman had poisoned him. Why?

At another long shudder of agony, his body convulsed. "Make it stop," he howled to the empty room. "Please. Make it stop."

The pain broke into waves, spasms through his limbs that

peaked then fell away into blessed moments of nothing. Except in those moments, memory gnawed and gnawed. Whatever he drank freed his body from its languor but also cleared the haze from his mind.

With shattering, sickening shame, he remembered Archanin's seduction. What did he allow his captor? How did his body betray him? Why, why didn't he fight?

More pain rolled through his core like fiery thunder. This time Kaell didn't resent it. It punished his weakness. It punished him for letting himself disappear, for retreating into his mind instead of resisting Archanin's beguiling words and soft caresses.

He lurched to his feet. Shoved his torn tunic down over his head and stumbled to the door. Impatiently he scrabbled at the latch. Run. Escape.

"Kaell?" Archanin filled the doorway, a guardsman at his back.

Pain built again. Cold sweat tickled his neck. He threw a steadying hand against the wall.

"Look at me." The ghoul god grasped his jaw. "You're ill."

Kaell's legs buckled. Slumped against his captor, he managed a grim smile. "I'm dying. I feel it. So you lose."

Archanin stared, unblinking. Then he turned on the guardsman. "Who was here?"

"No one entered, my lord. I swear it."

"Find Raggamirron. At once."

The guard retreated. Archanin scooped Kaell up and carried him to the bed. "What did you take?" He leaned. "I smell something syrupy on your breath."

"I willingly drank poison. To escape you. So you can't use me to be free. That's what you want, isn't it? But I won't let you. You'll forever be trapped here in this cursed castle."

Raggamirron appeared at a run. He looked in bewilderment from his lord to Kaell.

"What happened here?"

"Someone poisoned him."

"No one entered, my lord."

Kaell laced a laugh with scorn. "I poisoned myself. To escape you."

"Silence." Archanin wound a fist through Kaell's hair, dragging him close. "The only sounds I want from that lovely mouth are moans of pleasure." His kiss bruised. Then he shoved Kaell down and licked his lips.

"That taste." He frowned, tonguing his lips again. Shock then horror darkened his inhumanly blue eyes. "Gudverinal. Impossible. No one knows how to use Gudverinal. Only a sorcerer with real power could understand."

Kaell balled, wheezing.

"What's wrong with him?" A stunned Raggamirron stared at Kaell. "Is it this Gudverinal? What does it do?"

"It dissolves magic. Now it's in his blood, I can't control him. But to a mortal, it's deadly." Archanin's frown tightened. "How? No one has this knowledge. Myranthe Damadar? Roaran Caelan, yes, but he's long dead."

"Is the boy—?" Raggamirron tongued his top lips. "Dying?"

Archanin tapped a fist against his chin. "Whoever did this, they're foolish to think they can trade magic with me. They will not rob me of what's mine. Bring me blood wine."

Raggamirron returned with a cup. Archanin took it, stooped, and pressed the rim to Kaell's closed lips. "If you want to live, drink."

Kaell whipped his head away. Archanin gripped his jaw, forcing his mouth open. Wine splashed Kaell's face and neck. Some he spat out. Some he could not help swallowing.

"Stop fighting. Gudverinal will kill you if you remain human. I must quickly complete your transformation. One last time, I'll stop your heart. Then my blood will save you."

Warm breath tickled his throat. Pain erupted. Kaell screamed. Blackness rushed in.

He resurfaced in Archanin's arms, still screaming, spun into emptiness until relentless torment roused him to groggy, wretched wakefulness.

Archanin forced Kaell's head down, his lips to the ghoul god's wrist. Kaell's mouth filled with blood. He swallowed, gagged on blood, metallic on his teeth, thick in his throat.

"Enough, enough." Archanin pushed him off. Kaell curled, a gnawing in his gut.

The ghoul god stroked his face. "I need your surrender, Kaell. That was the third death. Surrender your will, or you'll suffer unimaginable agonies."

Kaell pulled away. He rolled with a thud onto the floor and crawled on his elbows. Raggamirron scooped him up like a toddler and flung him back on the bed.

He thrashed a pillow with his fist. "I won't give in to you."

"You must bow to me, accept me as your lord and god. Until you do, until you beg for death, until I kill you a final time, the agony twisting through you will only grow until you do truly die."

"I don't care."

"I have no time for this nonsense. You will surrender. Or I'll butcher those of your men still alive."

A cold fear snaked across his scalp. "You lie," Kaell whispered. "They're all dead."

Archanin shook his head, his look hard and merciless.

"We always take prisoners. To feed upon later. I'll leave you to wrestle with your thoughts while I prepare for the ceremony. I doubt you're selfish enough to sacrifice others for the sake of stubborn pride."

KAELL HOWLED. He thumped the bed, screamed, retched to spew out Archanin's blood.

None of his men lived. He knew it. When he shut his eyes, the nightmare of that ambush played out in all its brutal horror—the scent of blood, his helpless rage as ghouls dragged wounded captives to the fire.

No, Archanin was lying. This foul god needed his surrender to turn him into a monster. Maybe he was a monster already. All because of his hair, his eyes that marked him as different.

No wonder his lord Vraymorg could not love him. Who could love him now after he'd let a ghoul god, his enemy, seduce him?

A blitz of pain ripped breath from his lungs. Kaell wished he could black out. But he could only beat the mattress, shouting out his misery.

Then at last, his strength drained, he collapsed and wept into a pillow.

ARCHANIN FOUND him huddled on the bed, shoulders heaving, his body jarred by huge sobs. The ghoul god sat and pulled him to his breast. He stroked his damp hair. "Hush, hush. Accept me as your god. Then this all stops."

"Please," Kaell sobbed. "It hurts."

"I can end the pain. Kneel. Offer your pledge."

"No."

Archanin sighed. "I didn't intend it to be like this. Such a momentous occasion demands an elaborate ceremony—the hall ablaze with candles, everyone gathered, awestruck, gasping as they witness your surrender. To see my release from this prison after so many centuries."

"You'll never be free. I'll never turn from my gods."

"How can you be this stubborn? Must you suffer? Must your men suffer and die?"

"They're dead already."

"Two live. One is called Olier, the other says he's known as Smiler. They'll die horribly unless you obey me. I'm so close, Kaell. So close. Give me what I want. It is written you will serve me."

Kaell lifted a tear-stained face and spat, "Never. Whatever it costs me, I'll defy you."

Archanin's fingers stilled in his hair. His roused breaths rent the curtained stillness.

Darkness gloved about Kaell as though awakened shadows crept forward untroubled by a flame's pitiful flicker. Better the shadows than this tormenting half-light. Better to see nothing. To feel nothing. Better to be dead.

"Defy?" Archanin said. Then louder: "Defy?" Coldly, with deliberate control, he backhanded Kaell across the mouth. "I will not be denied. Not this close to freedom. You will submit."

"No." Kaell forced the word through split lips.

"Wretched child." Archanin dragged him from the bed and dumped him on a rug. He strode to the door, shoved it back, and jabbed a finger at a guard.

"Bring in the girl."

Girl? Kaell dragged his bruised body to his knees.

Guards shoved a protesting Caitlyn inside. Kaell bucked. A ghoul pressed him down.

"What is this?" Dread ran cold through him. "Why is she here?"

Dispassionately, Archanin said, "Kill her."

"No, wait. She means nothing to me. I don't know her."

"Kill her. Then if he is still stubborn, bring in the prisoners from Thom."

"No," Kaell shouted, his resistance shattered. Another young woman could not die because of him. First Azenor, now this girl. Even if Archanin bluffed about his men, Caitlin was right here. Defenceless. Blameless.

Archanin's pitiless stare did not move from him. "Poor Caitlin. So unfair she must die because you are obstinate. I hear you like her. That you had a moment together in the hall. That she spoke kindly to you."

"Don't. Please. This is between you and me."

"I've no patience left. Accept me as your god. Or she dies and your men follow."

A door banged far way. Footsteps tapped stone. What if guards dragged Olier into this chamber? If by some small chance he and Smiler lived, Kaell must do anything to save them.

"Kill me," he pleaded. "Don't hurt her. Don't hurt them. I'm your enemy."

"Beg to serve me. Renounce your gods. Beg me to give you my blood."

Kaell trembled. "If I do, you won't hurt her or my men?"

"You have my word."

"Then—" The word was little more than a sliver of breath through his clenched teeth. "Then—"

"Then?"

All sound drained. Archanin tensed like a bowstring, expectant. A guard turned to stare. A candlewick flared in a draught then stiffened. Caitlyn's wide eyes held a plea.

Each of them waiting.

Instinct screamed *do not do this.* But if he saved this girl, if he saved even one of his men, then he had to put aside Khir, accept the shame and guilt.

"What do I do? What do I say?"

Every breath released. Caitlyn dropped her head into her hands and wept. A storm of emotions exploded across Archanin's face. Joy. Elation. Triumph.

He pressed a knife into Kaell's hands. "Spill your blood with this Seithin temple knife. This is dark magic, like the sort that bound you to Khir. I need a blood oath to once and forever break that bond."

Kaell held the knife in shaking fingers. Jewels the colour of claret glittered in its hilt. Its long, silver blade gleamed, but beneath its brightness burned an awakening power.

"Spill your blood."

Kaell cut his palm. As though caught in a spell, he stared at the slow, mesmerising drip of blood to the floor. That blood, the knife, this chamber seemed unreal; his mind was buckling in disbelief.

Archanin gripped his shoulder. "Say these words: I pledge my life, my body, my will to Archanin."

"I pledge my life, my body, my will to Archanin—"

"God of Seithin. I renounce all other gods, all other lords."

"God of Seithin." The words choked in his throat. He swallowed. "I renounce all other gods, all other lords."

Archanin's eyes blazed with smouldering fires. He knelt beside Kaell. "Ask me."

In a shaking voice, Kaell whispered, "Give me your blood. Take my life."

The god sighed. It was a drawn-out sound, ancient and terrible like a wordless cry in a void. In its wake a hush fell, so deep, so bare, Kaell could hear droplets of his own blood strike the floor.

The room quaked. The tremor threw him flat. Wind rattled branches. A high-pitched wail, a shrieking, grated his backbone with cold horror.

Kaell scrambled to his knees, hands clamped over his ears, his teeth gritted against the boiling, thundering chaos. Candlesticks crashed. Glass shattered. A toppled pot plant spilled vine and dirt. Somewhere close a dog howled.

Archanin snatched up the spilled knife and slashed his own wrist. He pulled Kaell into a fierce embrace, hand on the nape of his neck, thrusting his captive's mouth to the wound. "Drink."

Choking, gasping, Kaell swallowed blood. It tasted hot and strange, as though he drank down darkness—drowning, unable to scream, unable to struggle in its ugly fetters.

Archanin's arms closed about him, his tongue at his throat. When the ghoul god bit, Kaell's inflamed body convulsed.

As he wavered at the edge of a black chasm, Kaell glimpsed Archanin rising, face turned to the maelstrom, arms spread. "Your spell breaks, Roaran Caelan," he shouted into the darkness. "You've lost. I only wish you lived to see my triumph."

PAIN POSSESSED HIM. Kaell no longer knew where it ended and he began.

Through its ether, he thought he heard whispers, felt soothing hands on his skin or cool cloths on his brow. Sometimes he tasted blood on his tongue or numbing poppy juice.

Yet even in slumber, his dreams writhed with fragmented images and the cries of dead friends. He woke drenched in sweat, sobbing.

Kaell could not grasp how much time passed while he lay like a stone, aware of little beyond pain burning like venom. When he at last opened his eyes, his dulled mind struggled to take in where he was.

He curled on a straw pallet, his unwashed body sluggish, his skin feverishly slick.

Stone walls caged an inky stillness, empty at first of memory. Slowly it rose from a black pit of delirium. Kaell tossed. Moaned. He dug nails into his cheekbones to shield against it.

But Archanin's cry of triumph echoed in his mind. With it, those nauseating scents of beeswax and incense from that chamber where he knelt to deny his god and his lord.

What had he done?

Appalled, Kaell ran his hands down his breast over his hips and groin, onto his thighs. He touched his face. In appearance he seemed unchanged. But within? Did he really become a ghoul? Would he soon be no better than a slavering beast? Hideous. Disgusting.

A monster his lord must despise. Hunt.

Kaell scrambled back against the wall. This shell, this flesh, was no longer him. He wanted to rip free of it, to take his spirit away. Escape the terror swilling in his gut. A beast awoke inside, and he could not stop it.

His captors left him a candle and flint, but Kaell did not light it. He belonged in this shifting darkness, the stagnant air fetid, where ghosts tormented with accusing voices.

Shapes, faces, rose from shadows like slashed patchwork—a hazy, delusional nightmare playing out in his troubled mind. "Why have you come?" Kaell whimpered, shrinking away. His words echoed off walls.

"You abandoned us."

"I didn't want to," he sobbed. "I wanted to stay and die with you."

Gorged shades closed to take him, their moans like an aimless wind. Kaell covered his ears until he realised the gruesome sounds came from him.

Sleep offered no release. Broken memories twisted into ghastly dreams.

He dreamt he hunted in the forest with Arn. Their prey didn't matter, only being together, laughing. Then Arn screamed. Kaell whipped about to see Archanin snap his neck.

"Parry," Vraymorg instructed. "Parry quicker, Kaell, or you'll die in the snow with a sword in your side."

Kaell jolted awake, arms flailing, howling out his despair. Then he wept and wept.

"KAELL, CAN YOU HEAR ME?"

"My lord." A yearning sigh released. "You came."

But the fingertips on his brow weren't Vraymorg's. Raggamirron lifted a lantern to his face. "You look better than the last time I was here. When you're well enough, your lord and god is impatient to embrace you."

"I want only death's embrace." Kaell rolled onto his side. "Go away."

Raggamirron's short laugh echoed. "Always so stubborn. I left wine by the pallet. It's been two weeks. You need blood." Footsteps rang on stone. A door scraped.

Kaell sat up. Hunger coiled like a fanged snake. He resisted it.

And resisted. The wine's ferrous odour infused his pores. He imagined that first sip, the hot, smooth blood in his mouth, its thickness coating his tongue.

With an angry cry at his weakness, he snatched up the cup and drained it.

Strength blasted through him. Kaell managed to stand, to stagger a step. The floor tilted. He plunged to his knees. Helpless tears welled again. Why did he cry? Warriors didn't cry. They endured. They fought. They died.

The stone walls rippled like a dreamscape, hardly real. Nothing was real. Not even him. There was only blackness.

THE NEXT TIME Kaell lurched to his feet, he stayed upright. His body enlivened with a giddying power, his every sense heightened and intense.

When he traced the floor's flagstones, his subtle fingers identified every grainy crevice, every abrasive lump, the silt in corners, slime on walls.

He tasted distinct juices in his mouth, the pleasurable remnants of blood wine.

Every scent broke down to its essence: the damp, the mould, the cinders of distant fires. A rat's scuttle in the murk resounded like booted steps. Darkness no longer veiled the faint outlines of a door.

He marvelled briefly at his new abilities. Then terror beat up. This strength. His sharper senses. All because of how Archanin changed him. Kaell had to escape himself.

Staggering to the door, he thumped fists against its iron until his knuckles bled.

No one came. They had entombed him in stone. Alone.

Kaell slumped, his mind splintered in despair. Captivity and the shocking knowledge of what he had become were all too much to bear.

He began to rock, back and forth, back and forth, singing a nonsense song.

A KEY RATTLED. Raggamirron lifted his lantern.

"This can't go on. It's been a month. Are you ready to greet your god? You gave him a great gift, Kaell. He only wants to reward you."

"Go away."

The door shut.

That night—or day, Kaell could no longer tell—the old dream waited. He breathed in the scent of damp earth. Water trickled down stone glowing with moss. The girl with dark hair trailed fingers through his hair.

"I must find you." Kaell ached with need at her touch. "Tell me where to look?"

"A secret," she whispered as she rose on tiptoes to kiss him.

Cold snatched him from her and from the comfort of dreams. Miserable, he curled into a ball. Maybe she was dead like the others. Only he remained.

"WHAT DO YOU SAY NOW?" Raggamirron brought more wine. "Will you greet your lord with a kiss or a curse?"

"I'll never serve him. I'd rather die."

"You can rot, but he won't let you die. You're precious to him."

KAELL PUT HIS back to the wall. Even through dense stone, sounds and scents carried with impossible clarity: chirring insects at dusk, a bird's gilt melody, wings like a composition of drums.

Distant rain, silver as mist. Dew.

But his keener senses, the strength surging through his muscles shamed him. His altered body revealed his weakness. It meant one thing: He failed his lord.

Weak. Flawed. Different. Why should his lord love him? Vraymorg knew the truth. That he raised a flawed boy to become a flawed bonded warrior. That's what his lord feared when he rushed to Kaell's bedside in Dal-Kanu.

Kaell thumped his head against the wall until blood dripped onto his shoulder. He deserved this. This cell. Punishment.

IN HIS DREAMS THAT NIGHT, Kaell stood on the edge of a line of trees, unable to move or speak, unable to look away as the blurred shapes of men strained against tall, blond figures.

Tendrils of fog swirled, muting the shriek of metal against metal, dulling the screams. Until the shapes became huddled men and the grey cloud absorbed every sound except a pitiful weeping. There was only that weeping.

"I'll avenge you," he cried.

"How?" Their voices edged with scorn.

"Somehow," Kaell said. "Somehow."

LIGHT BLINDED HIM. Raggamirron grabbed his shoulder. "Two months of this. I've had enough. Put aside your stupid pride, and let him reward you. In return, you need only obey."

Kaell thought about the raven-haired girl from his dreams. Did she wait beyond death? If he roused Archanin's fury so the ghoul god killed him, he could join his dead comrades.

"I will obey," he said.

THEY TOOK HIM to that hall of drifting shadows and golden, leaping flames, of vaulted marble pillars cradling an arched roof. Smoke from braziers oozed sickly incense.

Ghouls crowded onto fur-covered benches or leaned against walls. At the sight of Kaell, voices faltered. They all watched him, their gazes expectant but cold with suspicion.

His escort dropped Kaell on his knees before Archanin. The ghoul god leaned from an ornate chair of gleaming bronze. "Kaell," he said. "You are welcome."

Kaell said nothing. He bit down on anger. Did Archanin trick him? Or did he save his friends?

"I am free, Kaell," Archanin said. "For the first time in centuries, I can leave this dread place. Because of you. I would reward you, a reward worthy of what you gave me."

Kaell lifted his head. His captors clamped his shoulders as though afraid he'd rile up.

"The only reward I desire is death. I disgust myself."

A shocked murmur snaked, trapped like a flitting moth by circling walls. Archanin rested back against cushions, his expression complacent. "I can be patient. You are young and yet to understand how precious my gift of life is."

Gift? This fallen god had made him a monster, a cursed thing of darkness that must die. He belonged nowhere. Not here, nor with men and women. Not with his lord. Archanin had robbed him of everything.

His despair exploded to fury. Breaking free of the guards, he sprang at Archanin like a rabid dog, snarling, fingers clawed as he gripped the ghoul god's throat.

Archanin grabbed his arms and hurled him off. Kaell skidded into a pillar. He bounced and sprawled, arms and legs splayed. Guards seized him. They dragged him up by the arms.

Archanin reared over him. He shook his head, his tone mild as he said, "Ungrateful child. I wish to honour you, to cherish you, to let you serve me as a warrior."

Blood from his torn lips clogged Kaell's mouth. He spat it out. Spat out words, too, his hatred with them. "I despise you. I will never serve you."

"Lock him up," Archanin said, still calm. "No, beat him." He smiled. "Beat him so I hear his screams everywhere in this castle. I shall enjoy that."

THEY STRIPPED and beat him again and again, ghouls with hard faces and harder fists, yelling at him to submit. He spat blood and shook his head. Each time they left him bleeding on the floor of that dark, empty cell.

Kaell could only roll onto his back, his mouth dry with suffering, waiting for that gentle embrace of blackness. His new body healed quickly, but it was hardly a blessing when his captors returned to bruise and punish his flesh once more.

The third day, or perhaps the fourth, Raggamirron appeared. He tossed Kaell a tunic and pants. "You are stubborn and wilful. But your god takes pity on you."

"What?" Kaell lifted his head off knees.

"You need blood. Come."

Kaell didn't move. "I'm done with your filthy blood."

"Defiance takes strength, Kaell. You'll weaken if you don't feed."

"Good."

Raggamirron smoothed the folds of his tunic with a palm. The darkness hid his expression, but sadness edged his sigh.

"You won't die, if that's what you think, child. Without blood your flesh will slowly decay, your bones rot, but there will be no release from this life."

The words struck Kaell with dread. If he couldn't starve to

death, how could he escape the burden of what he had become?

Shaken, Kaell reluctantly rose, dressed, and followed Raggamirron into a passage of age-blackened stone lit with candelabra burning high on racks.

A faint breeze stirred his dirty hair, but the air smelt of nothing as though the walls dampened not only sound but scent. A hush beat so loud he clenched his teeth.

They passed wooden doors. At the sight of sunlight chinked beneath, a sharp flare of hope shook him. Sunlight burned all but the oldest, most powerful ghouls. A few minutes of pain, intense perhaps, then an end. Oh gods, an end.

Raggamirron thrust a knife to his throat. "Will you run?"

"To where?" Kaell said.

"That's true." Raggamirron searched his face. "Where would you go?"

With another heavy sigh, he shoved the knife into his belt and grabbed Kaell's arm to drag him on. A woman lighting candles bowed.

"Who are they?" Kaell asked. "That woman, the girl Caitlyn. They're not ghouls."

"They are the Varee."

"What?" Kaell stopped to stare at him. "The Varee are thieves, slavers. Do you mean they serve him? Archanin."

"Yes."

Kaell trembled with anger. "Is Thom a Varee village? Did they entice us to these mountains so you could slaughter us?"

"The world beyond the gorge is complex, Kaell." Raggamirron took his arm again. "The Varee, including the villagers of Thom, are our lord's chosen. For centuries they've served him. In return, Archanin protects them."

"That ambush. I should be dead," Kaell muttered. "I should have died with my friends."

"Archanin demanded we take you alive."

"Why? Because of my blood? What's so special about it?"

Raggamirron did not answer.

"Who am I?" Kaell's shoulders hunched. His breast ached.

His lord had always evaded that question. As a boy Kaell shrugged it off, his interest at once moving on to the excitement each day held, the prospect of mastering a new parry or reading a story about a warrior or battle from Telor's past.

They reached a timber-beamed hall with high windows shuttered against daylight. It was dimly lit by sparse torches in cressets. Kaell absorbed its aromas of candle wax, smoke, drying herbs… and blood.

His body quickened with hunger, an appalling reminder of what he was. Groaning, he pressed his palms to his belly.

Raggamirron nodded slowly. "You'll learn to control that craving in time." He bid Kaell sit at a table. A bowing servant set a jug and cup down.

"Drink."

Kaell drained the cup. He slid a look behind. No guards. Just Raggamirron.

"Who am I, Raggamirron?"

The ghoul sat opposite. "It's for Archanin to tell you." He nodded at the jug. "More."

Kaell picked up the jug. His knee hit the table.

Reflected in polished metal, his eyes were no longer green but as black as buffed obsidian. As black as a ghoul's.

He spluttered a bitter laugh. No one need tell him who he was. He was a monster.

Raggamirron grasped his arm. His face creased in concern. "What? What is it?"

Kaell smashed the jug into Raggamirron's face. The ghoul crashed back. His wooden chair broke apart as it hit the ground.

Kaell leapt up and ran for the wooden doors. An astonished servant stared after him, his dropped bowl clattering on the floor. Raggamirron yelled for guards.

"You! What are you doing?" A man blocked him. Kaell shoved

him aside. He reached the doors, rattled the handle. Locked.

A clamour broke out. Running feet pounded. Raggamirron stumbled towards him, clutching his head. "Kaell, this is useless. Stop."

Kaell hurled his weight into the doors. The wood splintered. He scrambled through shards into daylight, his breath snapping out in relief.

Across an expanse of lawn, wind rippled a river's turquoise surface, its cool breath teasing fingers in his hair. After the heavy stillness of closed-in passages, the perfumes of grass, May bushes, and spidery, yellow wildflowers intoxicated.

Water lapped a boardwalk. Bobbing boats strained against anchors.

Spring. The season of budding blossoms, of shooting green leaves on boughs, of song and verdant life. The wrong season to die.

Kaell tilted his face to the sun. "Turn me to ash," he cried. "Let me die."

Hands grappled at him. Kaell threw them off. A fist struck his chin. Stunned, he reeled. A second blow knocked him flat, sun beating upon his face. It must burn him. Must.

Men, not ghouls, yanked him up and pounded his midriff. He doubled over, wheezing.

"Yield."

Kaell broke free, stumbled to his knees, tried to crawl. "Let me die. Just let me die."

Men pinned him. He thrashed in a frenzy that quickly emptied his body even of ghoul strength. Only then as he panted, exhausted, did they pull him up to bind his wrists.

His captors marched him inside and surrendered him to ghouls. As they forced him back to that hateful cell, Kaell glimpsed a figure watching.

"Arn," he whispered in disbelief. Why did this ghost torment him? He shouted, "Arn!"

Ghouls flung him into the cell. Kaell fell face down. Hands bound, he used an elbow to roll.

Raggamirron stood at the door, blood dripping from his temple. "That was futile." He tore the torch from its bracket and turned. "Think about that as you rot."

Kaell thumped his trussed fists on stone. "Daylight. Raggamirron, why aren't I dead?"

"You have his blood, fool. A god's blood."

Raggamirron doused the torch, leaving Kaell in darkness once more.

THE BEATINGS BEGAN AGAIN. The ghouls took to their task dispassionately, their punches to his face careful and well placed. But his body they pummelled. Relentlessly. Brutally.

Hands tied, Kaell could only curl to protect his midriff. That forced them to stretch him out, a canvas for fists as they painted his flesh a mottled purple and red.

Beneath the vicious rhythm of blows, his thoughts blurred. Then fell apart. Sometimes Kaell wasn't sure when the battering stopped. When it started again. The nightmare of pain only rolled on and on, and he could not escape it.

"That's enough," someone said from the doorway. On elbows and knees, Kaell peered up through sweat-drenched hair. A guard smirked. "You're summoned."

The other ghouls dropped him. The newcomer yanked him up and half carried, half dragged him to Archanin's rooms. At the door he freed Kaell's hands. "Go in."

Kaell lurched inside. From the carved wooden chests, the thick carpets, and the divans bright with silk and velvet cushions, the chamber seemed unchanged. Light from torches in sconces menaced moon-streaked shadows. An owl in trees hooted.

Archanin reclined in a tall-backed chair, a goblet in one hand.

He jabbed a finger at a ghoul at his feet, her arms and legs spread like a beached starfish.

"I should take your heart. You served me poorly, Tristana."

"Forgive me, lord." The prostrate Tristana sobbed. "I shall keep a closer watch."

"Do so. If she slips away again, I shall not be so lenient."

The weeping ghoul clambered up and scuttled through a curtain to a side door.

"Kaell." Archanin stretched his long legs. "From your blood dripping onto my rug, you remain stubborn. Don't you tire of pain?"

Kaell clamped a palm onto his thigh. Blood oozed between fingers. He swayed, weak and disoriented by blood loss and hunger. "I prefer pain to serving you, monster."

"That's very naughty." Archanin's tone was a parent's correcting a wayward child. "Why invite my anger? My patience is not infinite."

"I don't fear you. There's nothing left you can take from me."

Archanin smiled.

Pain threw Kaell to the floor. He screamed, his body ripping inside, his mind collapsing to a haze. Then it swept away. Fast. Flat on his back, Kaell stared up at rafters, weeping.

"Why make me punish you?" Archanin drained his cup. "You gave me a great gift, Kaell. I want to repay you. In return I demand only obedience."

Kaell had no breath to answer. He shut his eyes, frightened by what happened. He could not withstand even minutes of what Archanin put him through. Yet to die, he must force the ghoul god to hurt him more than that.

Panting, he struggled to his knees. "I won't give it." He braced. "Do your worst."

When pain did not pummel him, he cast his captor a puzzled look.

Archanin offered a careless shrug. "Your game is obvious. I'll admit to a grudging respect for your courage. Come and sit by my feet."

Kaell made no move.

"Must everything be a battle? Shall I call my guards just to drag you a step closer?"

"No." Seething with resentment, Kaell crawled through smeared blood to kneel before Archanin. The ghoul god cupped his chin. "Let me look at you."

"I am what you made me," Kaell said tonelessly. "A beast belonging nowhere."

"You belong *here,* Kaell. You always did. In time you'll understand that. Then you'll regret this foolish bid to seek daylight to die."

"I only regret the sun didn't kill me."

Archanin sighed. "This battle of wills is tiring. I made a mistake, Kaell. I was impatient for your obedience and love. Now I'll do what I should have all along. Keep you close until you appreciate me and my gift."

"There's that word again. Gift. This is no gift. I don't even understand how you changed me. Why am I different?" He paused, his heart skidding and skipping. Words crept out in a scratchy whisper. "Who am I? You promised to tell me."

"I will—in time. I won't lie to you, Kaell, not like your lord. How poorly he treated you. Punished you by withholding his love. Such a cold, distant man."

"You're wrong," Kaell muttered. "Everything my lord did prepared me to fight, to be a warrior."

"A warrior with no defences against magic. A warrior he abandoned to his fate. You should hate him, not me."

"He didn't abandon me. He thinks I'm dead. He must."

Archanin touched Kaell's bruised jaw with his fingertips. "Do you believe he'd come for you, Kaell, if he knew you were here? Do you really think this man would come?"

"Yes." Kaell lifted his chin. "Yes, he'll always come for me."

Archanin laughed. With the back of his hand he stroked Kaell's cheek.

"How fiercely you defend him. He begins to take shape for me, this man you love. By reputation he is a formidable swordsman. The Varee fear him."

"He's the best bladesman I've seen."

"Is he? Such awe in your voice. Perhaps when I take the castle of Vraymorg, I won't kill him until I've brought you together one last time. What will he see when he looks upon you, Kaell? The boy he raised? Or some perverted version of that boy he could never love."

Torchlight spilled around Archanin like pooled rays. It fell on golden hair, on a cruel, knowing smile.

Kaell turned away. Despair squeezed his heart. It was as though his ribs caved in, trapping breath.

Once his lord would have come. Before. Not now. Not if Vraymorg knew what Kaell now was. A sob forced its way up his throat where air could not.

The guard returned with a bowl of water and cloth.

Archanin gestured. "Clean him up, Dharam."

The ghoul washed and bound Kaell's wounds then soundlessly left.

Archanin gripped Kaell's chin again. "I still see rebellion in those darkened eyes. Soon you'll forget why you're angry. You'll forget that other life. Time means nothing now."

He leaned, his hand at the nape of Kaell's neck to draw his head close. His lips brushed Kaell's mouth. He edged his captive's tunic off his shoulder, his fingers caressing bare skin.

So easy to surrender. So easy to close his eyes and let these hands, these lips bring pleasure rather than hurt. To feel something, anything, other than this misery and loneliness.

Kaell pulled away. "I know what I let you do. I can't hide from it, but it won't happen again."

Archanin sat back. He considered Kaell not with anger but

regret. "You're so young." The ghoul god carefully unknotted his hands. "Until that childish outburst, I forgot that."

With a sigh, he pressed his head into the chair. His gaze softened as it dwelled upon the shadows.

Lamplight, candlelight highlighted the planes of a near-perfect face, on eyes unnaturally, shallowly blue. Yet gloom thickened in corners, the room closing in.

"I thought you might be the one." Archanin's voice was low and uneven. "You're lettered. More than a brute warrior. But you are a child. A child cannot know or understand me. You cannot be the companion I seek, that man or woman, a sophisticate to share all I am."

Repulsed, Kaell drew back. Not at the thought of a male companion. But his captor was a ghoul god, his enemy. How could Archanin imagine he would ever want to understand him?

Archanin stirred and clicked fingers. This time Dharam carried a long chain inside.

"This is where I chained the last one," the guard said as he stooped to shackle Kaell's ankle. "A bonded warrior no older than you." Dharam smirked, bowed, and left.

Kaell tugged half-heartedly at the chain. "What's the point? You said I'll never be what you want."

Archanin touched his cheek. "You freed me, Kaell. Your blood oath destroyed Roaran's magic binding me to this ruin. My gratitude is deep. I will take the time to win you. How valuable a warrior with your skills will prove when I conquer this land."

He rose. "So we must play out this game. Let me explain its simple rules. You remain here alone. Only I visit you. Soon you'll miss me, despair when I leave. Then you'll beg me to stay even for a few moments."

Kaell mustered a sneer. "I won't beg you for anything."

"I'll remind you of that, Kaell, when you plead with me not to abandon you to loneliness."

KAELL DREW HIS knees to his belly, head to breast. In silver-hued darkness, Dharam's words taunted. "This is where I chained the last one."

He flattened a palm against cold stone to reach through time to this unknown man.

Who were you? Did you curse the gods who allowed your capture? With no hope of rescue, did you, too, succumb to despair?

When at last Kaell slept, a voice called down to him through tiers of slumber. At first, he thought it was in his dream. But it was here in the room with him, a young man's voice echoing from the past, clear enough to wake him. "Bonded warrior. Listen."

Startled, he rose to his knees. "Who's there? What do you want?"

The room was empty. But a voice said, "We're the same, Kaell. Warriors bonded to Khir. Except I could not escape him. You can. Archanin's blood makes you strong. Strong enough to break these chains, stronger than even Archanin realises."

"Why can I hear you? I've never heard another bonded warrior before."

"You never died before."

A man wept. The pitiful sobs faded into the wind.

Kaell dragged a hand over his eyes, a dull ache in his temples. That didn't feel like a dream. More like a vision. *Both warriors of Khir*, the voice said. *Archanin's blood makes you strong.*

His body did throb with power. Enough to break free?

With no great hope, he grasped the link of chain closest to the ring and heaved. Metal snapped at his ankle, leaving only the iron band.

For a moment Kaell stared at the broken pieces in surprise. Then he laughed, still stunned, rolled to his feet, and lit a candle.

Beyond its tiny spill of light, darkness clouded. He hugged his breast, thinking hard. Unfettered, he might escape. But to where?

The answer leapt at him. He could trust only one man to end his nightmare. Vraymorg always did the right thing.

His lord would kill him.

Kaell pressed an ear to the door. Feet shuffled outside. Guards. He leaned his back against wood and peered about the chamber. Tristana had left another way.

Clutching the candle, Kaell brushed through a curtain hiding a door. He pushed. It swung open. He took a hesitant step inside.

"Who's there?" A high-pitched voice cried. "Is it you, monster?"

Astonished, Kaell waved the light. A young woman huddled on a bed, a fury of black hair tumbling about her drawn-up knees.

"Who is it?" she said. "Tell me."

"A friend." A thud bruised his chest. She seemed familiar. How?

The girl gasped. Then softly laughed. "I recognise your voice. Kaell."

"You know me?"

Her laugh flowed carefree this time. "You took an age. I told you to find me."

Kaell's breath snagged. Memories stormed back. A woman whispering to him in that bathhouse. A woman who put a cup to his lips.

"I—" He stammered, lost. "You poisoned me. Why? I don't understand."

"Of course you don't. You're male and obtuse. So just listen. I've been waiting for you. Together we must escape and find my lord."

Bewildered, Kaell sank onto the edge of the bed. "Who's your lord?"

"Come closer."

"What?"

"Close."

Kaell wriggled nearer. She groped for his tunic then slid a warm hand beneath. Such comfort in her touch. So unlike the indifferent precision of ghoul hands. Her scent, too, like honey.

His muscles contracted, his skin hot. His heart paced as loud as her rushing blood.

Her blood. The sound of it. Its aroma.

Dizziness struck him: a need to push her back, run his palms along her arms to her wrists, feel her weight against him as he put his lips, his teeth to her throat. Taste. Feed.

Kaell pulled back, disgusted at his sick desire.

"I didn't mean to make you uncomfortable," she said. "I wanted to trace Khir's marks, to make sure it is you." A pause. "I felt other wounds. Bruises."

Kaell hunched. "They beat me. I'm apparently stubborn."

"I'm sorry for it, Kaell. Sorry you're hurting. But it will all make sense soon."

He pressed his fingers into his eye sockets, mystified not just by her words but that certainty he knew her. By candlelight her features blurred to waves of glossily dark hair and oval eyes. Hollows of weariness accented their darkness as they stared past him, unseeing.

Unseeing—that's why she spoke of recognising only his voice. A memory niggled, but he could not grasp it. Bemused, he could only mutter, "Why should a stranger be sorry?"

"Because"—she drew down a torn breath—"because of what he says he does to you."

"No, don't."

"He boasts of it, to torment me. Tells me not even Khir's bonded warrior can help me, that you are also a prisoner, that you also submit—"

Ashamed, Kaell dropped his head.

"You're silent? Why? Is it true? You submit to him?"

"No."

"Then he lied. I knew he lied."

Kaell's tongue coated with bile. His ribs contracted hard. All of it, the shame, the anger at his helplessness, tangled within. Tighter, tighter. Squeezing until it imploded.

He began to sob, terrible sobs that racked his body like blows.

She rested her hand on his bent head. “I know. I really do, Kaell. About everything.”

“Who are you?”

She sat back into shadows. She said, “I didn’t tell you? I am sorry. My name is Azenor.”

Her name meant nothing at first. Then it sank into him.

“Azenor,” he repeated, his voice dulled with shock. “Aric’s sister, Azenor.”

“Yes,” she said with an odd laugh. “I suppose in the end that’s really all I am. Aric’s sister, Azenor.”

AZENOR

Raiders burned the Isles, so the swaggering dancers stole Aric.

That's how Azenor Caelan remembered *that* summer. A summer three years ago when she learned about duty and love, loss and deception, and how fate tangled them all up.

Yet it began like every other. Long, honey-scented days of simmering heat, of storms clawing a velvet sky with jagged light, of a glistening ocean boiling with sleek ships bringing death.

"The seas are not still," the old men muttered as fires flared along the line of watchtowers, warning Tide's End of the shimmer of white sails and black hulls on roiling waves.

The seas are not still. Which meant her brother must disappear into that world of swords and strategy, of blood and battles forbidden to her.

"The swaggering dancers took him," she announced to Isobel Cross as they leaned against the wall on the castle walk. Frothing waters smashed against rocks below, their glaring counterpoint of blue and green too bright to look at.

"You and your childish nonsense, Azenor," the older girl replied primly. "They're warriors, that's all. Aric's with them because he's Isles commander. He has responsibilities."

"Childish, am I?" Azenor scowled with distaste at Isobel's pinched mouth. A Cross mouth, indeed. *Ha, you're so funny, Azenor*, she thought.

Isobel's brother Sherrin—the warrior men called the Stone Knight—had those same lips. That insolent mouth sat well on him though. Isobel looked as though she choked on seawater.

"And you're what? Queen of Duty?" *Or the Cross Queen? Oh, give up now, Azenor. The joke is already lame.*

"And you're Queen of Disobedience." Isobel swatted a fly. "It's too hot. Let's find shade."

Azenor dug her elbows into the wall. The coarse stone burned her skin. "So we can braid our hair, pick daisies, and giggle as we share our girlish secrets?"

Isobel sniffed. "You don't have secrets. You're too indiscreet. Can't we go inside? I'm thirsty, and my gown's damp and prickly."

"No one asked you to follow me up here. I like the heat."

The lie trickled off her lips as easily as sweat trickled down her neck. Sun bit to her scalp, but she'd never admit her discomfort to Isobel.

The wind whipped up burning sand and snapped banners upon the towers. Hot scents swirled; salty sea mingled with jasmine. The air rang with the clang and shriek of steel as warriors traded blows in the ward.

She glimpsed Aric grinning beneath his helm as he sent off another challenger, no doubt with a bruised body and ego.

At a sharp stab of loneliness, Azenor swung her foot into the wall. If only she, too, were male. Then she might be down there with every other wellborn son of the Isles, with her eldest brother, Gendrick, seeking out Aric, testing her skill against the young champion.

But no. She was stuck here with Isobel, the Queen of Cross.

Beating off Isobel's fly, Azenor shoved her back against the parapet, irritably watching men wave pointy metal sticks. Sun struck hats of steel, heels flattened dying grass, boastful shouts celebrated thrusts that broke through an opponent's defence.

All to do with balance, footwork, timing, and tactics. Aric explained it often enough.

Azenor had sat on the walk a thousand times listening to her brother talk about the knight of this and the knight of that, of forgotten battles, of blades and grips, of circular or lateral parries and lunges. She knew how to recognise a good sword and a good swaggerer.

But now, with only the Queen of Cross for company, her belly twisted every time she watched him on the training field. She'd lost her brother, her playmate, to duty. Because Aric had grown up and she—she what? Didn't want to?

Why did everything have to change? Why couldn't it stay like it was when she and Aric were children? Always summer. Lazy hours of scorched sand between her toes, of swatting flies and nonsense and laughter, of exploring the caves below the castle together or at low tide swimming out to the rusted bones of an old wreck to find treasure.

"Oh, good stroke. Did you see that, Azenor?" Isobel brightened. "That's Nicholas Hengeman. He's a stone man. That's who we need to stop these raiders. Stone men. *Your* brother sent word to the Henge. *My* brother brings forty men."

"Sherrin is an excellent swordsman," Azenor said distantly, her gaze drawn to another dancer waving steel in the dust. With a long-limbed body moulded to muscle by years of fighting, with that ready laugh, Pairas always attracted appreciative glances.

"Aric once told me he's glad Sherrin rides with him and not against him. He only says the same of Pairas."

"Pairas." Isobel sniffed. "My brother is twice the bladesman. Why didn't Aric name him his captain? Pairas hasn't got two fish to his name and is as crude as a fishhook."

Azenor fisted a hand. "How can you say that? He's wellborn. Descended from Ryol Caelan's half-brother Morgan. His father fell on troubled times, that's all."

"His father fell on something all right—a wine bottle."

"And you fell on a stick. It's so far up your—" Azenor clamped her lips tight. Isobel would only tell the king, the treacherous little tale-teller. With a big salt-sour mouth.

She released a breath. Unfair. The king ordered Isobel to watch his rueful daughter. The girl had no choice but to spy and tattle.

DUSK FELL. The swaggerers freed her brother from their dance, only to whisk him off to plot in the sea tower. "The seas are not still," the older men muttered again, shaking their heads.

Azenor understood. Really, she did. But a restless yearning stirred at the sight of lamplight flickering behind the tower shutters, a beacon to this exclusively male rite.

"It does no good gaping at that room." Isobel appeared at her shoulder. Her shadow. "Aric's Commander of the Isles. He has more important things to worry about than you."

"Aric no longer has time for me. He belongs to them now." There, she'd admitted it, but she felt no better.

"He has responsibilities."

That word again. "Duty, duty, duty. I'm tired of duty."

"Boo, hoo. Grow up Azenor. Without duty we have nothing. Time you realised that and took your responsibilities seriously instead of demanding your brother's attention like a brat. Time you stopped drooling over that drunk's son Pairas, too. He's no good."

Drunk's son? Brat? All Azenor's simmering resentment spilled over. How dare her haughty Majesty of Muck judge her or Pairas? Who was she? Queen of the Sticks up the—

"Duty is boring," she flared. "Like you."

Isobel's plain face reddened. "And you're mean."

"At least I'm not stupid."

The girl's heavy-lidded eyes squinted to a glare. "You're the stupid one."

"I'm not stupid."

"Stupid and pathetic. Following your brother like a puppy. He has no time for children."

"I'm eighteen. Not a child."

"A child making puppy eyes at Pairas, the Isles' most notorious rake. Princess Puppy, that's you." Isobel tossed her long hair over her shoulder and sniffed.

Such a pompous tone. Azenor laughed. *Princess Puppy. Not half bad.*

"Oh, I'm funny now?"

Azenor giggled. "You sound like that old dragon who taught Aric and me languages. She 'tut-tutted' all the time and said I behaved like a bedraggled street urchin."

"If you mean Lady Carolyn Saltman, she's nearly as wellborn as you. Poor woman. You're worse than a street urchin. You rarely wear shoes, and your gown is too short."

"You can't run or ride in long gowns. Who needs them?"

Isobel brushed hands down her skirt. "A Princess of the Isles. A princess soon to wed."

"I'm in no hurry to wed."

Isobel's mouth twitched. "You mean no one told you—?" She broke off and dropped her eyes, but not before Azenor caught a gleam of venom.

"Told me what?"

ISOBEL REGALLY SWEPT off to bed leaving Azenor fidgeting at the window.

The night cloaked, heavy and hot, its stillness dense with orange blossom. Light streaked the sky, a guttering candle above an inky sea. Rain-scented air dusted her skin with moisture.

Still that lamp gleamed in the Sea Tower, its shutters flung wide.

Snatching a candle, Azenor tiptoed to the ward. Her bare feet made no sound on the stairs to the tower's top chamber. She watched unnoticed from the doorway as her brothers and their captains huddled over maps.

"The watchmen report ships sailing south," Aric said. Except it wasn't her brother. It was this other man who hid behind a steel helm as he danced. A frowning stranger.

"There's a pattern to their attacks." Pairas jabbed the map. "Dal-Ford then Dark Cliff. Lastly Dal-Henge. Each time the raiders hit further south, towards Tide's End. Between attacks they hide somewhere. Perhaps in a river up a snake valley."

"Will they attack Tide's End?" Azenor blurted. Impatient glances swung at her.

"You shouldn't be here, child." Aric still wore his frown face. Not her brother. The aloof, stern Isles commander.

"They'd be stupid to do so, Princess." Pairas bowed his head without lowering his eyes. His look was bold, his smile quiet and secret.

Azenor's belly fluttered, remembering the exquisite sensation of his lips on hers, of entangling her fingers in hair like black satin, before he slipped from her bed at dawn.

"What do you want?" Her eldest brother, Gendrick, scowled. A cross man. Perhaps Isobel's match? The King and Queen of Cross. "This is no place for you."

Azenor folded her arms. "Where is my place then, Gendrick? In the Stone Knight's bed?"

"Who's been—" He shrugged irritably. "Nothing is decided."

"According to gossip, I'm to wed the Stone Knight." Azenor cast a quick look at Pairas. Shoulders stooped, he turned to the window and gripped the sill.

"Stupid name." Gendrick's attention returned to the map. "This isn't the time, Azenor. Father will talk to you. Haven't you a gown to sew or something?"

She'd like to sew his lips together. With a haughty sniff, she wheeled and stomped down the stairs. In her haste, her foot slipped on worn stone. A hand grabbed her elbow.

"Careful, little one." Still Aric the soldier, not Aric, her brother. "Want me to escort you to your rooms?"

Azenor tossed her head. "Am I a child? Besides, you've got male things to do."

Her brother laughed. "It's what I'm trained for, Azenor. It's my duty."

That word again. The old Isles tongue had three words for duty. Telorian had one. A harsh, cold word.

"Yes, yes, yes. It's easy for you. Duty means playing with swords or sailing ships. You don't have to marry some simpering lord."

"Simpering? Hardly. Sherrin is courageous and sharp-witted."

"You knew!"

"Not the details. Who told you?"

"Isobel."

He ran fingers through thick hair. His frown face appeared. "She should know better."

"It will be all over Tide's End by now." Azenor clenched her hands. "Don't you think I should have some say?"

"I don't, no."

"No?" Anger balled in place of that flutter.

"It's a matter for Father and Gendrick as his heir. It'll be the same when I wed. Any bonds of marriage must keep our family strong. You know that."

Her anger smouldered. She expected Aric, at least, to take her side. "I won't marry some stupid knight I don't love. It's not fair."

"Nothing's fair, Azenor. It's a good match. Better than—" He shook his head.

Better than an Isles captain with a drunken father ruling a barren rock?

"Sherrin Cross admires you." Aric continued in his careful, frown-face tone. "Men call him the Stone Knight because the family owns the only quarry in the Isles, but Sherrin is passionate, forthright. You'll like him and"—he paused—"he'll forgive much."

"And you think he has much to forgive?"

"Don't you?"

Azenor thought about Pairas's lashes on his high-boned cheeks, his calloused hands on her skin. The enticing male taste of him.

"I won't give Pairas up," she said to shock him. "I love him." Well, desire, at least.

"Curse your foolishness, Azenor," Aric stormed. "I hoped I imagined that look between you and Pairas just now. What are you doing?"

Azenor laughed, wickedly enjoying his attention. "Nothing you don't do and often."

He tore a weary hand through his dark hair again as he seized a steadying breath. His temper ran hot like hers. But Aric could push it down in a way she never could.

"It's different. I know you're Caelan-born but even so."

"Don't 'even so' me. Gendrick says that. Then he strokes that pathetic little beard on his chin and looks stern. Say it often enough, and you'll forget how to smile."

A pulse beat in his temple. He didn't smile. "Even so, you can't take whoever you choose to bed. Azenor, listen. I trust Pairas with my life, but that man knows more women than there are grains of sand."

"I'll wed him or no one." Azenor enjoyed her game. His fault anyway she found time to play with Pairas. Aric was too busy swaggering with swords.

"You sound like a petulant child. Duty, Azenor. Both of us must keep the Isles safe. Me with the sword, with my wits. You with—"

"What's between my legs? I may as well be an alley girl."

"You share Pairas with them already. This has to stop, Azenor. I can easily send Pairas away."

"And I can easily go after him. Why must everyone tell me what to do? I'm not free. I'm a gilded prisoner."

"You mean you're in a gilded prison. Wrong. You need to be responsible."

"Well, I'm sick of it." She stamped a foot. "Everyone makes decisions about me, for me."

"Oh, poor you."

Azenor blinked in astonishment. Instead of his frown face, her brother wore a furious face. Or a sarcastic face? She disliked all of them. As for his belittling tone—

"Oh, go away, Aric." She spun and marched down the stairs. Her game had turned on her, soured like Isobel's mouth. "Go dance with your pointed stick."

"Dance? Stick? Are you witless? Azenor, come back here."

She ignored him. Her temper carried her down the stairs and into the ward.

"Poor you," she imitated. "You sound like a petulant child." A child? How dare he. What did he know? Frown face. Frown brain, more likely. "I'll show you childish, Aric."

Her hands fell as fists as she stomped on. "You haven't seen anything yet. If you think I'm childish now, just you wait."

She'd make him sorry. He'd frown if she was gone. He'd miss her, wish he'd been kinder, defended her, taken her side about Sherrin instead of dismissing her as a child so he could pore over stupid maps with Gendrick.

Witless man. He grew up and become stupid. How ridiculous the Isles commander would look if she rode off—on his horse. With his sword. Then he would regret that sarcastic face. That sarcastic tone. *Petulant child. Huh.*

She wet her lips, the prospect of mischief softening her anger. Time to show him what childish was.

Laughing softly, Azenor crept to her brother's room, dressed in Aric's clothes, strapped her hair back, thrust his best sword in a belt, and clasped his cloak at her throat.

She grinned at her mirrored reflection. Less a child and more an Isles prince, Frown Face? No one stopped Aric going or doing what he pleased.

In her rooms she pulled on boots then tramped to the stables to saddle Aric's horse. A sleepy groom stumbled in. "My lord?" Head down, Azenor waved a gloved hand to dismiss him. He shuffled off.

The disguise did not work as well at the gatehouse. "It's not yet dawn, my lady," a sentry said when she bid him raise the portcullis. "Does your brother know you're leaving?"

"Do I answer to Frown Face?" she snapped. "I want to collect flowers in the forest." For her gilded cage. "Let me through." Why did men have more freedom than her? It wasn't fair.

"Yes, my lady." He slid a nod to his companion. The second man drifted away.

"Call him back," Azenor said.

"Who?" the sentry said blandly.

"That man."

"Call of nature."

Call of duty, more like. Loyalty to Aric and all that nonsense. "Just hurry up."

When the portcullis lifted, Azenor walked the horse through the gatehouse.

Murmurs broke out at her back. No doubt dutiful guards arguing about fetching Aric.

Too late. If he wanted his beloved sister back, he'd have to come after her. Apologise. Yes, that. Only when he said sorry for his sarcastic words would she return.

She swung into the saddle and rode across the bridge into the town, a mass of stone and timber behind flanking walls, never still despite the early hour.

A yawning shop owner unlocked his door as she passed. In a fetid alley she glimpsed a man's straining back and a fair-haired woman, her skirts hitched high.

A friend of Pairas? Azenor giggled.

The sentry at the town gate stammered her brother's name and bowed. She put a copper coin in his palm as he pulled the gate aside. A reward for stupidity.

Beyond the walls the road knotted like a frayed cord through sloping hills etched against a sky curtained with sleek darkness. Dew sprinkled grass meadows.

Grazing cattle paid no heed as she rode past. Distant thunder squalled, its low rumble no match for birdsong or the patter of paws through tall grass.

As the third moon slid into the soft, nectar-scented dawn, she reached a crossroads.

Straight ahead lay the gentler route of merchants, priests, and officials to Goradin's Ford and Dal-Decma. But adventure beckoned on the other road, the one through dark-trunked woods drenched with swirling silences, swollen streams, and stone bridges over the Great Digger to the Mountains.

Azenor let the hood shadow her face and turned left.

SHE MET FEW travellers on this road. A weary soldier wearing Falls' insignia nodded, head bent against the stiffening wind. A farmer atop a cart loaded with baskets and barrels glanced at her sword and averted his eyes. No one ever looked too hard or too long at armed men.

As the track ground through a rock-walled valley, a long line of riders appeared amid clattering chain mail, jangling harnesses, and voices.

Azenor tugged the hood lower and studied badges on shoulders. The thorn tree and mermaid. Lord Fitzroy, the Shield Lord. She stiffened. He'd know her. But the grey-bearded border warden did not appear, and the riders threw her only a passing glance.

She laughed then at how easy deception proved, imagining Aric's fury when he discovered his missing sword and horse. A naughty, petulant child, eh, Frown Face? He'd be sorry. When Aric came after her, she'd refuse to come home. Until he begged.

In late afternoon, dark clouds burst in a cold, hissing torrent. Azenor left the road to take shelter, shoulders hunched against a fanged wind and driving rain.

Her temper as sodden as Aric's clothes, that giddy elation at punishing her brother seeped away. She was lost. And how exactly did she think Aric would find her?

"Seems *I'm* the stupid one," she confided to the horse. "Not Isobel."

The rain pattered as night dropped. A starless sky bowed overhead in utter blackness, the moon masked by billowing clouds. Azenor splashed through puddles, squelched through mud, fought bushes and rending branches, but could not find the road.

"Curse it. The stupid child is even more lost." She patted the horse absently. "Don't suppose you remember which way we came?"

With an exasperated sigh, she turned back, crossing a fast-flowing creek. That wasn't right. Panic churned in her gut. She beat it down, tied the horse to a sapling, and crawled beneath clotted leaves to keep warm. Her belly rumbled.

Tomorrow. She'd find the road, return to Tide's End. A brighter day, tomorrow. With this thought, despite hunger and itching wet clothes, she slept.

AZENOR WOKE in bleak light barely splintering a canopy of leafy, dark-timbered trees. She stretched, shivering. Damp garments clung to her skin. Water dripped from her hair down her neck. Her empty belly hurt.

Tears brimmed. Angrily she swiped her eyes. When Aric found her, he would not see her crying. Besides, this was an adventure.

With trudged steps, she led her horse into a clearing of wind-flattened grass.

A patchwork of grey and black clouds sped overhead, shadowing land. Wind skittled leaves into piles at the base of trunks. Water burbled close, a rush of sound that lifted her spirits. A river meant villages.

Unless—unless she'd wandered into a snake valley.

"I haven't seen any snakes," she reasoned with the horse to fight down alarm. "It can't be a snake valley. Though what do I know? I'm losing my wits as I'm talking to a horse."

Hood down, cape tight against the brawling wind, she followed a stream through mushed grass and mud to a wide river, its currents wrinkles in its meandering, green-grey surface.

Drooping trees lined the banks, thick with crisscrossed boughs and leaves glistening with raindrops. Yellow flowers flattened by last night's squall spilled between moss-green trunks and the reedy water.

The scent of mud was everywhere: on her clothes, in the air, rising from the turgid river. On its far side, woods pressed in a dark mass. The slate sky was mottled with clouds, the light a dismal ash.

Azenor didn't see the ship at once. Just an odd shape jutting from the bank. She drew up, staring. Strewn branches hid a deck.

A hand clamped her mouth. Cold metal pricked her throat as someone grabbed her from behind and pulled her against them.

"Make a sound, and you're dead." A man's voice. "Do you understand?"

Her heart too fast, Azenor swivelled her eyes towards a cowl hiding all but a man's bristled chin.

"Do you understand?"

She managed a curt nod. His hand fell away.

"Let's see who you are, little spy." The man tipped back her hood. "But you're a woman!"

"Really?" Her voice cracked. "If only someone told me before. It explains a lot."

Leaves rustled. The wind carried low voices. Close.

"Quickly. Come with me." The man pulled her back into long grass, a firm, strong body pressed against her. A woodsman perhaps? Who else skulked about in forests in cowls?

"I tell you, I heard something." Heavily accented Venivan words.

Her new companion pressed a ringed finger to his lips. Azenor jerked a nod, her eyes hooked on that ring. Sapphire set in a silver band. An expensive trinket for a woodsman.

Boots padded over wet leaves. The man gripped his knife.

The Venivan spluttered in surprise. "Why, it's a horse."

"Threw its rider?" Another man, also Venivan. "Might be an accident that someone's here."

"No one comes by accident into a snake valley. Find them."

A sword swished and slashed through bushes.

The stranger tensed, holding her close as they crouched in the grass. The uneven beat in his chest drummed. Or was that her heart? Azenor thrust her fist in her mouth as men circled, thrashing at undergrowth.

They moved away. Her companion yanked her up. Again he tapped a finger to lips and pointed to an embrace of trees across a meadow of bobbing orange wildflowers and mud.

Azenor followed. He seemed friendlier than the Venivans.

He reached the trees with a swordsman's lithe, sweet-footed speed. Aric had taught her to recognise those who danced with steel. That catlike balance marked this stranger, a man with a bladesman's shoulders, a cloak of fine wool, and a ring of silver and sapphire.

A man who did not belong in a snake valley.

They trod on in silence as forest thinned to a grassy hill, and Azenor's pent-up fear at last released in a torrent of questions. "Where are you taking me? Who are those men? They spoke Venivan. Did you hear? We must go back. My horse is there."

"There isn't time for talk. They'll be on our trail."

"Make time, or I go no further." The retort shot out hotter than she intended. Tough. Her belly rumbled, her clothes prickled with damp and she was lost. "Tell me who you are and where you're taking me?"

The stranger drew up so fast she nearly barrelled into him. He laughed softly. "Yes, let's sit down and chat. Who cares that those Venivans are likely slavers and we'll end up in irons in the Icelands caverns."

Irritated, fed up, Azenor shoved him. He reeled a step. Then the ground collapsed beneath him and with a blink of surprise, he tumbled backwards.

Guiltily she peered down. The stranger sprawled at the bottom of the hill, his hood flung back from black, glossy hair spilling in rain-misted waves onto a fine-boned face. He was older than she expected, at least thirty-five, but striking none the less.

"I didn't mean—"

He glared. "That's quite a temper you have, girl."

"That's quite a big sarcastic mouth you have."

"I'm told it's one of my best features." He shifted, groaning.

"I wouldn't move if I were you."

"Why? If I come back up there, do you intend to push me again?"

"A Jape snake is sizing you up. It's big enough to swallow you whole."

The man grinned. "Surely it will choke on my big sarcastic mouth."

"Well, since you have the situation in hand," Azenor declared, not really worried for him. The snake wasn't as huge as she pretended. "I'll leave you to it."

"Wait!"

She looked back, eyebrow raised.

"I dropped my knife up there. At least toss it down. Give me some chance."

Azenor found the blade. "Here." She hurled it high. The knife thudded in clumped grass about a body's length from him. A poor shot. Too close to the snake. It coiled, hissing.

Alarm ripped through her. She didn't really wish to see him hurt.

"Good throw."

"I aimed for your big sarcastic mouth."

"May the gods keep you far from crossbows." He lunged for the knife. The snake tensed like a spring. Azenor's hand flew to her mouth. Curse her temper; he was in real danger.

Then he and the snake blurred. She thought it struck at him, that he ripped the knife back and forth, too fast to see. An ugly head flew skywards. A whiplike body thrashed, its tail gashing his arm. Yelping, he sprang away, hands raised.

"Are you all right?"

He looked up. His face changed. He scrambled to his feet, shouting, "Behind you!"

Azenor turned. Glinting metal whirred. Sharp pain burst through her chest. Her knees hit the dirt. A rage of sounds erupted: a drawn-out scream, a terrible gurgling, a thud. A man collapsed beside her, eyes gaping on nothing. Blood trickled from a slack mouth.

She swept fingers across her breast. Blood? How? Dizzy, she swayed, her mind and body soft with shock.

The stranger thrust his wet knife into his belt and caught her, whispering, "Gods help me. She's dying. That's not right. It doesn't happen like that."

Azenor only half heard the words. Darkness embraced, as welcome as a lover.

Firm lips brushed hers. Her limbs flooded with warmth and strength. He'd kissed her. In fact, he was still kissing her. Spluttering with outrage, she demanded, "How dare you!"

"You're wounded. I'm kissing you better."

"Wounded?" That still made no sense. "How?"

"One of those cursed Venivans. Probably thought you were a

man and armed. Press here." He guided her hands to blood pooling on her chest. "Press hard. Three more are coming through the trees."

She trembled. "They'll kill us."

The stranger unfolded a grim smile. Completely without fear. Now Azenor had his measure. She may not know *who* he was, but she knew *what* he was. A swaggering dancer. Just as brazenly cocksure as Pairas or Aric.

"I need your sword," he said.

"Where's yours?"

"I left it in the cave."

"You live in a cave?"

He laughed, a warm sound that unexpectedly shivered through her like an erotic caress. Azenor considered the pleasingly strong, elegant lines of his face. Arrogance carved those lips, and a darkness clung to him.

"It's a very special cave," he said.

Of course. A swaggerer's cave. She laughed with him, then broke into a fit of coughing. "Take it," she gasped.

The man lifted Aric's blade. His eyes flared hard and cold like a gold ingot, his irises the deepest of blues, a shimmering of light and shadow caught beneath long lashes and arched brows.

"I hoped not to spill blood for one day. Though I didn't count on them."

Azenor squinted. Three men with short-cropped blond hair plunged from the trees, roaring. Two carried swords, the third an axe.

The stranger laughed, bitter this time.

"Only three against one. It hardly seems fair." With a yell, he ran to meet them, swinging.

In his hands, her brother's sword brutally carved flesh and bone. A blond man shrieked and toppled in spouting blood, his belly opened, an axe slipping from his flaccid fingers.

The other two jerked to a halt. Cautiously they ringed their target. He grinned. Azenor thought she heard him shout "for Ghani-Jai" as they came at him. Swords clashed in a spray of screeching metal, then blood. A Venivan reeled, clutching his shoulder. His companion hammered at the swordsman, but he sweetly matched every desperate stroke.

He knows the dance well. A master swaggerer, then.

Gaping, Azenor watched swords weave and cut, hew and thrust. The air rang with clamouring, battering steel, with sharp breath, with the odours of blood and sweat.

The wounded man staggered to his feet and circled.

"Behind you."

The black-haired warrior already whirled. Bone crunched. The wounded man dropped. He coughed a woman's name and died.

Enraged, the last Venivan unleashed a stream of vindictive curses. His heavy blows clapped like thunder. The stranger parried with blue-sparked metal.

The ground shook as they pummelled each other with whistling, shrieking, clanging blades. Deflections answered ferocious thrusts. The two lunged, swept, jabbed, retreated, circled.

Until her brother's sword sang a vicious song. A deceptive feint, a parry a heartbeat too late, a blade humming as it parted air then mutilated flesh. Blood pulsed in dark-red spurts.

The Venivan clutched at his groin, trying to clamp the flow. He collapsed to his knees.

The black-haired stranger stood over him. He lifted Aric's sword. As it cleaved bone, Azenor thought a shape rose at his back like a cape fanned by wind. Gooseflesh rose along her arms. She blinked yet saw nothing. Her imagination, surely.

The man rushed back to her, hair damp, his tunic, face, and neck splattered red. He shoved Aric's sword into his belt beside the knife.

"We must move. Others will look for them, for us too. Unpleasant sorts, these Venivans."

"They're the raiders my brother—" She dug teeth into her lips, uncertain it was wise to reveal who she might be. But he did not react. "My horse. I must go back."

"Too dangerous. Three against one is no matter. But they have horses on that cursed ship. If five or six or more ride us down, I don't know if I can keep you safe."

Azenor bristled. The arrogance of the man. Like Aric, like every swaggering dancer. "I didn't ask you to keep me safe. Just point me to the road, give me my sword, and I'll go."

"*Your* sword? Doubtful. Your brother's perhaps."

Azenor glared. "How do you know that?"

He whipped out the blade and held the hilt close to his face. "Chiselled iron, encrusted with niello. A shape inlaid in the metal, a broken crown. An Isles sword for certain."

"How clever. Finding an Isles sword in the Isles. I'm shocked."

His eyes held genuine amusement. Their unusual colour, an otherworldly glimmer, drew her shiver. But she didn't fear him. Not a conceited, swaggering dancer.

"I've more to tell you. Seithin steel, so a lord's sword. The broken crown dates it to Queen Devarsi's rule. I'd guess Ryol Caelan, the king who never was, owned this blade. Or one of his Serravan warriors. Though, given it's your brother's, I'm certain Ryol carried it."

"So you know about swords. But who is this brother you throw at me?"

The heavy, dark-blue gaze held hers.

"Ryol's descendant, Aric Caelan. The young Isles commander."

"Ha," she said.

"Which makes you either a thief—and a good one if you took this blade from Aric—or his sister, Azenor. And that is who you are. Even with knotted hair, the blood and mud all over you, anyone can tell you have Caelan blood."

His face softened. Boldly he spread his gaze, let it linger. Aware of clinging wet clothes, Azenor's cheeks heated.

That gaze flattered her. Unlike most of Caelan's descendants, her face was far from perfect. Her lips were too large, her teeth not quite straight, her hair always unruly.

What did it matter what he thought? Who was he anyway? A dancer, that's all. Tide's End was full of handsome, brazen warriors. Azenor had grown up around bladesmen, and she had their measure. They were all the same.

The man reached to steady her. "You're cold, and we must tend to that wound. Come. I'll have a fire started before you know it. Food, too."

"Come where? I don't know who you are."

"Enough time for questions later. You're exhausted, child."

"I'm not a child." Her legs collapsed. She cried out as pain again lanced her chest.

The man tucked Aric's blade in his belt and scooped her into his arms. Muscles shifted in his breast and shoulders. Hands about his neck, she breathed in an exotic but male scent.

"I've never been stabbed before. Wait until I show Aric this wound. He'll be jealous. He and Pairas always boast about their scars."

"Hush." He carried her through grass whipped by blistering wind, across bulging streams.

He stopped only once to slow his breath and peer at faraway peaks. "It rains hard in the mountains. It'll flood these lush Isles meadows soon enough. Such a soft land, the Isles; it's a soft land that produces hard men and women. But not as hard as they'll need to be."

Azenor murmured unintelligent sounds. The rhythm of his strides as he bore her into a green-leafed forest soothed her. She watched the treetops moving against the grey sky, eyelids heavy. And as fat, steamed drops of rain fell, she plunged into darkness.

AZENOR WANDERED through the hall at Tide's End. The same, yet...

Seizing a torch from an iron bracket she studied the wood-beamed roof, the high windows, and walls bright with murals. In the flickering flame, sea serpents twitched; a painted warrior, tall and broad, stared back, a bow and quiver of arrows slung over a shoulder.

Not the mural she knew on the walls. Why were they different in her dream?

Fear boiled up. She ran, crashing through wooden doors into the council chamber where the Isles lords met. No sign of the long table and her father's seat at its head. Bare stone walls, not whitewashed, surrounded her.

"Azenor? Child?"

Azenor whirled. Her dead mother sat beside the window, hands folded in her lap. An older man at her shoulder wore a black-work cloak. A lord's silver chain draped his neck.

"Mother?"

The woman smiled, but her knuckles whitened. "You shouldn't be here, child. Not yet."

Frightened, disoriented, Azenor quivered. What was happening to her? Was this a dream? She brushed a hand down a pillar, its marble smooth and tangible.

"Are you real? Please be real. Where are we?"

Her mother's gaze flew to the doorway. "No," she whispered. "Not you. Not this."

"Mother? I don't understand." Panicked, Azenor backed up. She turned. The man with the sapphire ring stood behind her, those blue-black eyes hard.

Her mother dropped her face into cradled hands. "Destiny shadows you, seer. But it's too cruel," she sobbed. "Must it be this way? Oh, Azenor. Aric. My children. How is your fate entwined with theirs? And that boy with desert eyes. Oh, too cruel. Too cruel."

"It can only be this way," the man said. "This foul god must fall."

Azenor reeled, frightened. *A dream,* she thought wildly. That was it. A fever dream.

The man pulled her to him.

Her mother shot to her feet. "No. Please, seer. Choose another path."

"The dead should stay silent," he said.

Hand on the nape of Azenor's neck, he bent his head and kissed her. Outraged at his daring, she beat fists against his chest. But an ache of longing, sweet and powerful, flamed.

His scent, the weight of his firm body against her, his sensual lips were all so heady. She wanted to touch his breast, to tangle fingers through wavy hair. Her hands fell away. She closed her eyes, breathed him in—and woke on a bed of fur.

Only a dream. Sadness shook her. How she wanted her mother to be real. And that unsettling kiss? Did she want that, too, to be real?

Azenor scrunched fur in her hand, bewildered, embarrassed by the heat beneath her skin.

The man, at least, was real. Wasn't he? He brought her here… wherever here was.

Blinking, she let shadows take shape. Flames writhed on cracked rock. Rain still drummed. Scents of wet earth and stone mingled with woodsmoke.

A cave. How did she get here? Uneasy, she shifted on the bed, thinking back.

Grey skies, flashing steel, a desperate face. Pain. Such pain. Yes, a Venivan raider had stabbed her. She groped at her breast, touched fingertips to a rough mound like a scar, hardly there at all. Except…

Azenor nearly shredded the fur. From the light, the rain, she had slept a very short time. Not long enough for a wound to heal. What was happening here?

Alarmed, she jerked upright and saw—him.

Her breath escaped as a gasp, her pulse chaotic. She

remembered that kiss, its mystery, its sweetness. Her face flushed. Curse her hot Caelan blood. Now she longed for another kiss.

Through her confusion, she realised the man sang, a beautiful, sorrowful melody that seeped into her mind as the sun might soak warmth into her limbs. Her fear fell away. There was only the caress of his voice, that mesmerising beat of rain, his song.

It carried her to the cliffs at Tide's End. A winter wind burned her cheeks and ears. The sea frosted and gurgled over rocks below. Helmed men moved about her. Their long-bladed swords flashed in pale sunlight.

The man was there, covered in iron. His hand rested on his hilt, that dark-blue gaze searching the horizon. "The seas are restless," he said grimly.

Azenor touched his arm. He did not feel it. Nor did he look at her, only at the white-crested waves.

The song broke off. The cliffs and sea disappeared. The cave's stone surrounded her once again. In dim light and wispy smoke, the stranger stripped off blood-soaked garments.

In front of her? Did he have no shame? Not afraid any more, only indignant, she snapped, "What do you think you're doing?"

He turned, revealing all. She shouldn't look. Why not? She was an Isles woman after all.

She swept her eyes over a warrior's body, from the breadth of muscular shoulders to narrow hips and long legs. A tattoo swirled across his breast. Another ringed an arm in an inked bracelet, its whorled tentacles writhing up his shoulder.

Isles men often tattooed their bodies with depictions of sea serpents, ships or anchors, even swords, but nothing like these patterned sigils.

"I thought you were sleeping," he said, his tone unapologetic. "I stripped to wash the blood off in the rain. You should do the same."

By The Three, did he wink? "I'll do no such thing."

"Then at least take off those damp clothes. You'll catch a fever."

She frowned. Her clothes could not be damp if she'd slept long enough for her wound to heal. "I will," Azenor replied carefully. "When you're not here."

He nodded, his smile subtly teasing. "I left a tunic on the bed."

Without him there, the cave felt empty and frightening. She almost called him back. Not just for the comfort of his presence but for another kiss, like the one in her dream.

She laughed at her own nonsense. First she had dreamed this stranger kissed her, now she wanted his arms around her, his lips on hers.

"I can't decide if your Caelan blood is a curse or a blessing," Ethne often said when Azenor took a new lover. "Life is more than conquest and pursuing pleasure."

"In the hedonistic Isles? Silly Ethne," she had teased.

The new tunic reached her knees. She smoothed cloth against her breast, feeling only a tiny bump on her chest. A chill iced her neck. Did she imagine the raider had stabbed her?

The man returned and moved to the fire with a bladesman's grace. Yet that body looked anything but soft. Corded muscles strained across his naked shoulders and back as he dried off with a cloth. This time Azenor averted her eyes.

"Isles women these days. So prudish," he said. "Once they bathed naked in the sea on summer's eves. Now if a man so much as shows his ankle, they blush and giggle."

Azenor took up his challenge. "I don't blush and giggle at the sight of male flesh." Openly, boldly, she stared.

He possessed that dark beauty bards and poets attributed to Isles men: his cheekbones angular, his body all shadowed muscle, powerful legs, and wide, strong shoulders. Raven hair fell in wild, wet curls about a haughty face. Firelight danced on his glistening skin, sun-brown and smooth beneath scars.

Yet the dark-blue hue of his long-lashed, mocking eyes did not belong to the Isles. Belonged nowhere in Telor.

"I don't even know your name." She sounded breathless. His

fault for standing unclothed before her.

"Is my name important? You learnt more in that leer right now than my name will tell you." His eyes whipped with mischief as he wrapped a cloth about his waist.

Now he was laughing at her. Curse him.

"If you won't tell me who you are, then tell me this. That Venivan stabbed me." She traced the scar. "The wound healed. How is that possible?"

"Hard to explain. It comes down to a kiss. Simpler to answer your first question."

"So I didn't dream that kiss. That's twice you've brazenly kissed me."

"I apologise for my bold behaviour, Azenor Caelan." He bowed, a lock of hair falling over one eye. "And I suppose if I can kiss you, I should offer my name. I'm Roaran."

Roaran? Indeed. Eagerly Azenor seized the chance to tease, to create something ordinary between them, like banter about a name.

"No wonder you didn't wish to tell me. You're ashamed your parents punished you so."

"What?"

"I knew a Roaran. The son of our steward. Children tormented him, accused him of pretentiousness. No one calls their sons Roaran."

"Why? Because it was the name of a king?"

"A dangerous king. People still whisper of him in awe. As for these stupid cultists—"

Roaran looked hard at her. "Are you certain they're stupid, Azenor?"

"My brother explained it. They're traitors to their king—whether you believe it's that boy king in Dal-Kanu or my father. If they accept a dead king as liege lord, what's stopping them rebelling or not paying taxes? Or refusing to take up arms when their real king goes to war."

"That boy king," Roaran said, "is twenty-seven. Besides"—he smiled—"no one ever teased me."

She could well believe that. Every part of him was muscled. And he was as tall as Aric. Not even Pairas was as tall or as powerful as Aric. "So—Roaran. Is that all you'll reveal?"

"Actually, I think I've revealed a lot."

"Except now you're wearing an evil cloth. Since you're shy, I'll tell you who you are, just as you reasoned my name from my brother's sword. To begin with, you know the song of swords well, so you're a warrior. And you look every bit an Isles man."

"Every bit?" He released that mischievous grin. An ache kicked hard in her chest. Her breath caught in surprise then slowly freed.

I want him. A dangerous, exciting thought. Not the first time she had seduced a stranger for no reason except she found him pleasing to look upon. Or because her Caelan blood heated. "I'd like another eyeful. Why is that cloth there?"

One last fling. When she returned to Tide's End, she would wed Sherrin. No more Pairas. No more enticing handsome guards to her bedchamber.

Roaran laughed. She already liked his laugh. It pleased like a summer breeze on her skin. "By The Three, girl, you're bold. No one could doubt you're an Isles lass."

"My brother says I'm shameless."

"Well, shameless one." Roaran slipped a shirt over his head and laced it carelessly. "Should we eat? There's fish. Hunger and fish in the river drew me out in the first place."

Azenor sniffed. Whatever he cooked smelt good. She settled beside him near the fire. "You've dressed. That's sad. If I were a Quisnaf warrior and you belonged to me, I'd keep you naked."

Roaran shoved a crudely cut wooden plate at her. "Eat, shameless girl."

They ate in a hush both companionable and tense. Azenor deliberately listened to the thudding rain, the crackling fire. All familiar. Ordinary.

Yet the air shimmered with tension as though a storm whipped in. What did she see at his back when he plunged his sword into the raider's chest? A shadow? Wings?

"Why is an Isles warrior in this snake valley?" she asked. "Do the king's sheriffs hunt you? Are you hiding out in your special cave? I take it *this* is your special cave?"

"It is."

"And?"

"And what?"

"What makes this cave special?"

Roaran did not answer at once, only traced a circle in the dirt with a twig. Azenor's neck prickled. She glanced behind. Nothing stirred in the gloom.

"Answer me this," Roaran said. "Do you want the truth or something else?"

I want to hear waves crashing against rocks below Tide's End, she thought. *I want to hear my brother arguing with Pairas. I want to sit and just look at you.*

"I want the truth," she said.

He hesitated. Carefully he put down his plate. "The truth then. The cave is a gateway."

"Gateway? What does that mean?"

Roaran sighed and stretched. Muscles rippled beneath his shirt. "A gateway." He pressed tongue to teeth. "To the Enarae."

Azenor poked a stick at the fire, her heart breaking into an uneven beat. She wasn't ready for what this truth might mean. No, in fact, she refused to think about it.

"Azenor, did you hear me?"

"Yes."

"Say something."

"You smell nice."

Roaran shot out a breath. "You know about the ancient gateways?"

"Am I uneducated? Of course I know about gateways. And I want you."

"What?"

"I want you."

"Gateways," Roaran repeated, a breathless edge to his voice. "Heavily protected with blood magic. There's one at Tide's End, one in Dal-Kanu. The most dangerous at Vraymorg. Caelan Godsson—your ancestor—built fortresses at these places to protect these gateways."

Azenor pressed a finger to his lips. "Stop talking."

He tilted a brow, smiled faintly. Yet a silence grew about her words.

She searched his face. Behind that smile, his blue eyes shadowed with disquiet. He held his body stiffly as though on the edge of surrendering secrets he wasn't ready to reveal.

Azenor pressed her mouth against his. His lips yielded. She loosened the laces of his tunic. Her caress slipped inside to bare skin. Beneath her fingertips, his heart slammed.

Roaran pulled away. "This is happening too quickly."

"If you're worried about children, don't be," she whispered in his ear. "I've silphium."

"It only grows in Quisnaf."

"My friend Ethne's a sorceress. She knows how to get every strange herb."

"Nevertheless, we have a ways to go, you and I."

"You speak in riddles. It makes my head spin when all I want is a hundred kisses like that last one."

"We need to talk about that." Roaran broke off, moaning as she dropped a hand to his thigh then to the thickening bulge beneath tunic and cloth. "Slow. Slow. The gods may frown on this."

"Why? Are you my cousin, abducted at birth and now returned?"

"No. But I'm—no matter." Roaran pulled her against him and fiercely kissed her mouth, his soft, wet tongue plundering and exploring. Fire shot through her. He tasted wild, of enchantment and mystery. Like in the dream.

Murmuring with pleasure through his kiss, she tangled her fingers in his curling, damp hair and flung a leg about his hip.

Their beating breaths drowned the fire's crackle. Beneath her strokes, his erection strained. "The gods be gone. Do with me what you will," he groaned.

"Oh, I will." One last exciting conquest before she wed Sherrin.

Laughing softly, Roaran lifted her and carried her to the bed. He laid her down and eased her shirt off.

Azenor reached up to draw his tunic over dark hair. She groped at the cloth then leaned back, drinking in the sight of him, every muscle, every hollow formed by elegant, perfectly sculptured bone. Naked, aroused, he was magnificent.

With a soft hiss of air through bared teeth, she pulled him down onto her, felt his shudder as damp skin slid against damp skin. A lustful heat flared, the strength of her desire shocking and exciting. Azenor did not want a tender, slow mating. She must have him now.

Her hand slid down his hard belly, rubbing, stoking his arousal. Roaran flung his head back. A long moan escaped his flushed lips.

Azenor caught his hair in a fist, drew his mouth to hers. Her tongue teased. Her hand's rhythm matched his harsh, quick breaths.

"Witch," Roaran whispered through her kisses. "Who taught you that?"

"Enough talking." Azenor circled legs about his waist, fingers gliding around him, hips tilted, guiding him until he plunged into her.

As he thrust, his shoulders flexed. The strength of his body, the warm, clean scent of him, the strain of muscles beneath her fingers blurred into simple joy. Roaran pushed deeper, holding her against him, his skin moist and hot.

Sensation after sensation flooded, fractured. His full weight on her, his tongue, his breath in her mouth.

For the briefest moment, a distant echo of alarm brushed down her bare back as though an ancient power cried out through her.

But the velvet touch of his hands, his lips, the feel of the slick length of him sheathed inside her, the delicious irritation of skin, overwhelmed. She closed her eyes, lost in their rhythm, hearing the soft sounds he made and surrendering with a cry of pleasure.

His body tightened then shuddered. He collapsed against her, straining for breath.

They lay entwined, limbs, hair, lips. Roaran was in no hurry to end their joining but stayed deep within her, watching her face with those curiously blue eyes.

What was he thinking about? The idle thought fast retreated. A delicious weariness in her limbs stole the need for words or questions.

When he finally broke apart from her, Azenor curled her knees to her belly. An otherworldly scent swirled as thick as smoke, faintly disturbing. Roaran folded her in an embrace.

"This was always to be," he whispered. "Even so, I thought I'd need patience to win you."

"I'm an Isles woman," Azenor said sleepily. "I take what I want."

ROARAN SLEPT, his breaths slow and even. Azenor rose, threw on her drying clothes, and thought about his words. Always to be? This was lust, nothing more. Just like her other conquests. Isles women did not hold back, did not deny their desires.

Her close brush with death also aroused her hunger for pleasure. Ethne explained once how those stalked by death—warriors after battle—sought life.

She took a last look at his pleasing face. Asleep, Roaran looked younger; his raven hair was dishevelled, his palm curled, dark lashes fanning a sun-bronzed cheek.

He stretched on his back, the ridges of old scars from the nicks and cuts of swords pale against his skin. No surprises there. She had traced Pairas's wounds often enough.

Yet one mark puzzled her. A raw, angry blemish. Just above his heart.

That uncomfortable chill tore into her again. She shook it off. A wound that healed poorly. Probably not as deep as it looked.

Azenor rounded the dying fire. Dawn broke outside, grey and silent, the raucous whistling and chittering of birds absent. She shivered, pulled Aric's cloak tight, stepped outside the cave… and found herself back inside.

What had just happened? She rubbed her eyes, spluttering a laugh. *Foolish girl. You're still half asleep.* Again she circled the fire—surely she did that before—and walked into the light. And once more was inside the cave.

Walls closed. Panic stripped her breath. Gasping, she fell to her knees.

Roaran dropped beside her. "Azenor, it's all right."

"I've lost my wits." She clutched at him.

"It's all right." He guided her to the bed and draped fur over her trembling shoulders.

"I tried to leave and could not. Why can't I leave?"

"It's a gateway, Azenor. I was about to explain but you"—his smile wavered—"distracted me."

Gateway. No. She didn't want to think about that.

"I have to leave." Azenor tried to rise on wobbling legs, her breath quickening again to panic. "I have to leave. I have to leave. I have to leave."

Roaran drew her to his breast. "I know you don't want to hear, but you must."

"No." She pulled away.

"Azenor, it's a gateway to the Enarae. I brought you here because—"

"No!" If only he'd shut up. The odour of smoke lingered. Rain pattered outside. That would make her journey home harder. *Aric is looking for me. He'll be worried.*

"Azenor."

"No, no, no. I know what the Enarae is." Fear coiled about her ribs. She surged to her feet, faced him, threw at him, "I'm dead. Is that what you want to tell me? I don't believe you. I can't be. I feel so alive."

"Azenor—"

She flung away from him, her eyes stinging. Disjointed thoughts rushed at her. It wasn't possible. She could not be dead. But that blow. The nauseating, shattering pain as the Venivan's knife drove through her breastbone.

Crouching at Roaran's feet, she grasped his hands and held them against her cheek. "Tell me, can the dead feel the way we felt just now?"

His sigh weighed with regret. "My first kiss strengthened you for a time. But you died in my arms. I carried you through this gateway then went after you into the lands of the dead. My second kiss brought you back."

The dream. Her mother, long dead. Weeping for her children. No. It made no sense.

"Your kiss brought me back? This is madness. Who or what can do that?"

Roaran did not speak.

"Answer me, curse you."

His dark-flecked blue gaze hardened. He dragged hands down his face. Beneath the pelt of stubble, his skin looked paler.

"What?" Azenor demanded.

Roaran pressed his palms together, his reluctance tangible. He said, "A death rider."

"No. You lie. They don't exist. Not anymore. Maybe never. They're just a story so people fear disobeying the gods. There's no such thing."

"What did you see, Azenor Caelan, when I killed those raiders?"

"I don't know. Something. Nothing. My eyes played tricks."

Roaran laughed mirthlessly. "You don't believe that."

Azenor rested her head on his lap. She was dizzy with the strangeness of it all, her thoughts detached. Words of a nursery rhyme from her childhood snapped into her mind. She whispered:

"*The death rider's blade cuts swift and deep.*
But his kiss wakes even the dead from sleep."

"It's just an old rhyme, just an old rhyme." She sobbed.

Roaran slid to the floor beside her. He held her, stroked her hair. "There's more to that old rhyme, Azenor." Softly, he recited:

"Kiss so sweet from one so cold,
But now your life is his to hold."

Azenor sought to focus only on his curious lilt—an Isles lilt—but the half-forgotten words, their meaning hammered and hammered. Dread then anger flushed heat through her veins.

"Curse you." She shoved him away. "What did you do to me? I asked for none of this. How dare you. My life belongs to you? Well, I won't have it. I won't."

Roaran sprang up, shoulders rigid, his jaw tightening. "I give it back to you, Azenor Caelan. I'll take your hand and lead you to the gates of Tide's End. If that's what you want."

"That's what I want." She gulped in a torn breath. "Yes. That's what I want." Wasn't it? She met his fierce gaze. He looked dangerously wild and dangerously beautiful.

Confined by stone, his presence was overpowering, overwhelming. Azenor turned her head aside, trying to hold on to that anger so she would not cry.

"What have you done to me?" Her voice splintered. "I have to leave. I have—" She laughed bitterly. Isobel would like this. "Responsibilities."

Roaran pulled her into his arms, his kiss this time firm and demanding. He tasted, smelt, felt wondrously exotic, mysterious, male. "Stay with me," he whispered when he drew back his head. "We'll have an eternity together. Duty will wait. I mean that, Azenor. If I take you with me into the Enarae, time will mean nothing. I'll bring you back to this very day."

Azenor clung to him. "You said this was always to be. Do you mean you saw what would happen? Did I say yes?"

"Not like this. Not so soon. But yes, I saw this."

"How? Only a seer glimpses the future." She was close enough to glimpse the tiny lines about his eyes. His face, partly shadowed, seemed only stark cheekbones and hollows.

I was wrong. Not a swaggerer at all. Much more.

"I think you know who I am." He held out his hand. Azenor took it.

HE TOOK HER to cities of golden stone that once thrived beside sapphire seas, to shores empty of all but cawing birds where the wind stung her eyes with grains of sand.

To the desert city of Seithin before it fell so she could walk barefoot on cool marble in the temples and trail her hand through fountains beneath shady jacaranda trees, their purple flowers bobbing in crystal water or carpeting cobbled stone.

To vast deserts of red earth, rich with pungent aromas, to sun-bleached lands beneath endless skies sprinkled with diamonds, to white-tipped mountains capped with pine trees.

And when she tired of wondrous places, of markets and palaces and taverns, Roaran Caelan brought her back to the cave.

There they lived simply, loved with a desperate fierceness that came of knowing time fast ran out, or sat together about the fire, dreaming and talking softly. Wondering what it might be like to be together always.

There was always so much to talk about. The past, her brothers and father, Pairas, of gossiping in the courtyard with Ethne, of the war with the false king. Of the cave city of Quisnaf where a sorceress trained him, a prisoner, to harness the Enarae.

Thoughts. Feelings. Everything shared. How a sunset moved

him. How the aroma of soap always reminded Azenor of her grandmother.

In summer, the cave was cool. Beyond its gaping mouth, butterflies danced in honeyed warmth. Jasmine sprawled in vines and bushes, its scents perfuming the night.

In winter it was damp and dark, but the thundering winds whipped past as they clung to each other, naked beneath the furs.

Regardless of the season, Roaran often ventured outside to hunt or forage for mushrooms and firewood. Every time he returned, she would run to him as if they had been long parted, and he would enfold her in his arms.

When did she love him? That first year together? Longer? She could not say. One day it was just there. Yet her awe at the seer part of him never changed.

Azenor remembered nights when she woke to find Roaran staring glassy-eyed at the fire, the aroma of dream grass in its smoke. And a breath warmed her neck as if something unseen brushed by into the dawn.

Only then did Roaran gasp and blink, freed from whatever spell held him. Shaking and weak, he could only crawl into their bed and fall into a soundless sleep.

One night, exhausted by a vision, he said, "How long has it been?"

"How long have we been together, here, in the Enarae? Years and years. Why?"

He did not answer at once. He sighed, then said, "Long enough so you trust me? Do you trust me, Azenor?"

She nuzzled closer. "How can you even ask? Of course I trust you."

"Enough so you won't doubt, even if it seems I do terrible things?"

"I trust you."

"Enough so even when we're apart your feelings for others won't sway you?"

She rose to one elbow to study his face. "What is this about?"

He closed his eyes. His grip on her shoulders tightened. It was as though he wanted to hold her close because she was about to slip away and he would forget her.

"And if I do something that hurts you? What then, Azenor?"

"You will never hurt me," she said, pushing an unruly lock of hair from his eyebrows. The dawn clouded to a sickly grey at their backs. When he opened his eyes, his expression was as bleak as that light. Haunted.

"It's time then," she said, aware of his sadness. "We're going back."

Roaran turned his head, his cheek denting the pillow. "It's been a decade. But when I take you beyond the Enarae, when we walk outside this cave, no time will have passed. It will be that day I found you in that snake valley."

She slapped his arm. "That's not how I remember it. I think I found you."

"You'll be the same. We've lived outside time, and neither of us has aged. They won't have had time to miss you. Do you understand?"

She drew away. "I don't want us to part. It must happen, I know. But I don't want it to."

"We'll be together again. I swear it. Have I ever lied to you?"

No. But there were things he hadn't said. About the past. A part of him lingered there with a queen who had died centuries ago. Foolish to be jealous of a dead woman, but there it was.

"You'll hear things," Roaran said. "Doubt me. Doubt what I've told you. Perhaps my intent will no longer make sense. Or you'll doubt yourself. Question if you can do this."

"I can," Azenor said, her voice cold. "I am an Isles princess. I understand duty."

Roaran shook his head. "No. I don't want you to trust me from duty. I want you to trust me from love."

"For me they are the same."

"A STORM BLOWS IN." Roaran's fingers choked the rein.

Azenor peered at a cloudless sky above Tide's End's stone walls. Its deep blue curved to cage a jewelled sea against the horizon, unbroken but for a flock of languid birds.

It promised heat, more flies, but no storm, unless a wind-whipped tempest of dust.

"A storm of blood? That brings Archanin down?"

The scales of chain mail jangled as she leaned back against his hard body, the curve of shoulder to breast beneath her head achingly familiar. "What are you thinking?"

Roaran stared at the castle, his face clouding. He did not speak.

"The past snares you again, my love," she said.

"I'm thinking about what's ahead, how it will stain and perhaps destroy us both."

"Liar. You're not here. You're there, in Tide's End."

Thinking of men and battles long forgotten. Or remembering hot Isles nights when he slept beside *her* and the sea breeze drifted over their bare skin.

"Enough," Roaran broke in angrily. "Azenor, enough. I drown in sorrow. And not because of the past. Because of you."

"They've seen us." Azenor pointed at the walls with a wavering finger. She shook, sick with grief. *I long for him already. How do I do this?* The answer: Do it quickly. Walk away from him and don't glance back.

She slipped from the horse. "Don't come closer. There will be questions as it is."

"They hardly had time to miss you, girl. Do you remember what you did a decade ago?"

Argue with some silly girl. What was her name? Isobel. Argue with Aric. Over nothing.

"I remember, yes. And I remember what I have to do. All of it."

Would her courage fail? A curse to know what must happen,

all of it—the ambush, the monster who would imprison her.

The boy.

Of him, Roaran said least. "Kaell's story is not yours," her lover whispered one night as they lay arms and legs entangled, drowsy with spent passion.

"How can you say that? I'm his doom."

Roaran stroked her hair. "The fate of one man, young I know, can't outweigh the fate of so many. I pity him too. But I waited centuries. I can't let pity stop me."

Too cruel, her mother whispered in that shadow land where painted serpents spat and shapes writhed in a castle that looked like her home but wasn't. *Too cruel.*

Shivering, Azenor shoved away the past. The portcullis rose in the gatehouse.

"They'll see you're armed. The watch captain will demand to know who you are and what you want. It's dangerous times, Roaran. If they don't like your answers, they'll lock you up as a spy, hurt you."

He bared white, even teeth. "I dare them to take me."

Azenor shook her head. "I swear you sometimes act barely twenty with this male posturing. Isn't age supposed to bring wisdom?"

"Who said that? Some minstrel still sucking at his mother's teats? It brings only regret."

Azenor walked away.

"Azenor."

Walk away and don't look back. Her brother's sword slapped her thigh.

"Azenor." She turned. Roaran dismounted. He stood holding the reins, uncertain.

"I'll come for you," he said. "The night a man I cannot yet tell you about puts aside his doubts and picks up a cursed Seithin sword named Fortitude."

STRETCHED ON HER BED, Azenor closed her eyes as servants fussed with damp cloths on her brow and her brother fussed with questions.

"He was armed with steel, Azenor."

"I don't know his name," she repeated for the third time. "I went into the forest to gather flowers, like I told the sentries. A storm came, and I got lost. This man found me. Brought me back to the castle. He didn't give a name, and I didn't ask."

Aric scoffed. "You didn't ask? Did a flower bite your tongue? What are you hiding? I know when you're keeping something from me."

"All right. You caught me out. I went to meet my lover. His name is Cathmor. He says he's a king or something. I didn't believe it. Men will say anything to have their way."

"Ha, ha. Where's my horse?"

"Aric." Reluctantly she opened her eyes. "Enough questions. I'm tired and dizzy from the heat. Why does it matter? The stranger is not a raider. They're Venivan."

"How do you know that?" Aric leaned from a stool, his tone sharp.

"Surely it's likely."

He rose in one graceful movement. She had forgotten how he moved. How he brooded. But other gestures felt so familiar she wanted to cradle his beloved face and kiss him.

Next she'd want to kiss Isobel. Then the palace dogs.

"Not the king," her brother muttered. "But a king's man? Spying on us. We'll know soon enough. I sent men to hunt him down."

Azenor dragged her fist to her mouth. *The Three give Roaran the sense to be far from here.*

If Aric's men caught him, they would drag him back to the castle, chain him in that hideous pit where they kept suspected spies. A place of no light or hope. The guards left prisoners hungry and thirsty until they dragged them out to question.

She trembled. No sword could kill a death rider, but Roaran could bleed. And hurt.

"This stranger did us no harm. You can't arrest someone because they carry a sword of Seithin steel. Why should he be a spy? You're too suspicious."

"I've good reason, Azenor. This land is about to erupt. The king's spies are everywhere."

"Tell me what is about to happen? You used to tell me everything."

"You used to listen. Now you fault everything I say."

"You say things I don't like." *Said things*. That was in the past. Her anger, all of it.

He grimaced. "Now we come to it. The reason you stole away—with my sword, by the way." He patted the hilt in his belt. "This is no toy."

"About the sword—I'm sorry."

Aric edged up a brow. "Did some changeling swap places with my sister in the forest? The Azenor Caelan I know never uses that word."

"Nevertheless, I am sorry. It's a valuable weapon. Once belonging to King Ryol. You can tell that from the broken crown cut into the metal."

"I'm impressed."

"But here's the mystery, Aric." Azenor could not resist showing off. "The Seithin no longer existed in Ryol's time. So how can a sword of Seithin steel carry his mark?"

"It was melted down from another weapon. Or the broken crown added later."

"I thought you'd know. You spend so many hours studying old writings."

Aric's dark gaze held hers. "Some things the past can't teach us."

"Like how to tell a woman she must marry for the sake of her family, her people?"

He laughed. "Yes, like that. About the Stone Knight, Azenor—"

She silenced him with a gesture. "Whatever I said the other night, it's forgotten." Certainly by her. How long ago it seemed.

"Sherrin Cross." That sounded right. "Brings two hundred swords. His lands border the Isles and the Mountains. Sometimes the Henge fights for Dal-Kanu, sometimes for the Isles. You want to bind Sherrin through wedlock to ensure the Henge fights for the Isles. So war is coming?"

"Gods." Aric stared at her. "I thought you ignored our tutors. Yes, we'll soon be at war."

"I'm listening."

Aric studied her for a long moment. "You seem different. Why is that?"

When she said nothing, he shrugged. "What I tell you does not leave this room. The king has made certain demands. Unreasonable demands. We will reject them. For our defiance, he will bring war to the Isles."

So Roaran had told her. So many nights they had sat together as candles guttered, talking of what he glimpsed in visions. Of a ghoul god about to break free of Roaran's prison, of how they might defeat that god.

It all began now. With the king marching on the Isles. With Aric defeating Cathmor near Dal-Gorma. After a hasty cease-fire, drawn-out negotiations followed where they bartered over land, gold—and her.

Then her brother, her beloved brother, would ride to Dal-Kanu to murder a boy.

So the threads weaved together.

"You'll defeat the king," she said.

Aric unfolded a broad but sceptical smile. "It may not come to anything." He smoothed her hair. "You do look tired. I'll ask Ethne to tend to you."

ALONE, AZENOR DREW her knees to her chest. Misery roiled. Roaran had told her it would pass, that everything passed. But he had centuries to learn that.

Azenor had not.

"Azenor?" Ethne nudged the door open with her foot. She carried a basket of cloths and bottles no doubt containing weird balms. Their scents struck Azenor from across the room, a ménage of pungent herbs and resinous earthy roots.

"Whatever you have there, it surely stinks. If this is some torture Aric dreamed up to make me confess I met my mysterious lover in the forest, tell him I surrender."

Ethne laughed. She put the basket on the table and sat on the bed. "Aric says you feel dizzy." She touched Azenor's arm then whipped her hand back with a yelp. "By The Three, Azenor. The Enarae is all over you. How? I thought magic sealed this castle's gateway."

Gateway? Of course. Roaran had said as much. At Tide's End, Dal-Kanu. Vraymorg.

"I don't know what you're talking about."

Ethne did not hear. "The high priestess," she muttered. "She'll know what to do. She'll know if the magic protecting the gateway fades."

"Nothing fades. You're talking rubbish. I got lost in the forest, spent a miserable night in the mud, and then a stranger brought me back." She shrugged. "That's all there is to tell."

Ethne forcefully shook her head. "I smell the Enarae, Azenor, feel its enchantment like a tingling along your arm. You forget what I am."

"You're wrong."

"Why do you lie to me? I thought we were friends."

"We are."

"I can keep a secret. You know that. Whatever you say, it stays between us."

Azenor covered her mouth with her cupped palms. The unsaid words burned. She ached for that comfort of shared confidences.

Even in these few hours since she had walked away from Roaran, her loneliness had grown too much to bear. If only she could talk about her lover, about the Enarae, about Roaran's prophecy and that awful burden of knowing what she must let happen.

"There's no secret," she said firmly. "I told you what happened."

Ethne's gaze hung on her face. Then she shrugged. "Have it your way."

"Ethne—"

The young sorceress did not look at her. She determinedly focused on rummaging among bottles and sachets in the basket.

"Oh gods, Ethne." Azenor's voice broke up. Her eyes pricked with tears. "I'm so miserable. It's all so awful."

The girl dropped the sachets. At once she was beside Azenor, her arms about her. "Hush, hush," she comforted. "It's all right. It will be all right."

"It isn't. It's so hard. Why is it this hard?"

Ethne squeezed her hand. "How long did the Enarae trap you? Let me fetch Aingear. She'll help."

"No. She can't know."

"But you walked through the Enarae. How? Because of your Caelan blood?"

Azenor sucked in a deep breath. "A death rider took me."

Ethne shot up, shuddering in horror. "That's impossible. A sorcerer killed every death rider centuries ago. The Damadars lost the knowledge of how to make them."

Azenor thought about Roaran's strong arms, his soft lips. Her heart surged with longing but also with pity. A Damadar sorceress long ago stole his body, woke him from death to serve her god. Roaran didn't ask for it. "A Damadar sorceress knew just enough to make one more."

"You're serious," Ethne stammered. "Except—if a death rider took you through the Enarae that means you died."

"I died."

A silence grew around them, laden with undercurrents. Ethne's shock and disbelief. That ghosting of strangeness. Tide's End, even with its scents of sea and salt and blossom, no longer felt like her home. How lonely and disconcerting to no longer belong here.

Ethne entwined her fingers then released them. "Was it his kiss? Is that part of the legend true? But that means he holds the measure of your years."

"I know what warning you will give me." Azenor's tone dulled with resignation.

"Do you, princess? Do you really?"

"My sight will fade. I have a few weeks, at best, until I see only shadows and shapes."

Glumly, Ethne nodded. "A death rider's touch binds you to him. Wander too far from his side, and your sight goes, or so legend says. That first, then—" She wet her lips. "But that isn't the warning I would give you." Ethne exhaled, a reluctant puff of breath as fragile as driftwood in a heaving sea. "He's dangerous, Azenor. A death rider is the god Ghani-Jai's weapon."

"I trust him."

"You trust a dead warrior? A creature restored to life through a blood rite so horrific the presiding priest or priestess risked death. A death rider sacrifices to his god with his blade. Kinslayers. Murderers. All face his justice. And Ghani-Jai is righteous and hungry."

"I trust him."

"Why?" Ethne grabbed her arm. "Why do you trust him?"

Azenor swallowed hard. "Please don't ask me anything more. It isn't fair to tell you. It would destroy you, put you in danger. Especially here."

"So you trust a death rider, but you don't trust me?" Ethne swept a candle holder from the table. "Why should I expect anything else? You're an Isles princess. In your eyes I'm so far below you I deserve only lies."

"That's not true. It's because we're friends I can't tell you."

"Whatever you say." Ethne turned her back. "My lady."

Azenor stormed to her feet, her hands fisted at her side. "You want to know why I trust him? You won't thank me for it, but I'll tell you if that's what you really want."

Ethne slowly faced her. "I'm not afraid."

"You should be. You will be."

"No."

"Very well." There was a hardness in her that was new, her words stiff and emotionless. "I trust him because of who he is. Because this death rider is Roaran Caelan."

Ethne took a step back.

"Are you satisfied?" Azenor said. "Are you glad I destroyed everything you believe in?"

"No." Ethne threw up her arms as if to fend off the words. "No."

"It's true. The seer king lives. Just as those cultists always believed."

"It can't be true." Ethne voice trembled.

Azenor seized her hands. "I've been with him for ten years. I journeyed with him beyond the Enarae. Touched him." She briefly closed her eyes against another stab of loss and longing. "I know him, Ethne. I do not lie. Roaran Caelan is alive."

The young sorceress struggled to speak. Her voice, when it at last came, rustled like an autumn leaf. "What have we done? All those innocents the high priestess executed. Oh gods. I must tell Aingear. She has to know."

"She can't. Certain things have to happen."

"It's to do with a prophecy then." Ethne groaned. "It has to be if the seer king really doesn't rest. I don't know what to think. Prophecies are vicious things, Azenor. Never what they seem."

"Will you tell Aric something for me?"

Eyes still dulled with shock, Ethne stared through her. "I could summon him. Roaran. Oh, how I should like to see him. Is he as extraordinary as the bards say?"

"Ethne, listen. I need you to tell Aric those raiders are Venivan. They're hiding in a snake valley a day's ride from here. Will you do that?"

The young sorceress blinked. "I'll tell Aric I had a dream. What else can I do, Azenor? How can I help you?" She nibbled her lip. "Help him. The seer."

At the unsettling fervour gleaming in Ethne's eyes, hairs lifted on Azenor's arms. Just his name, his legend drew unsought devotion. A good thing Roaran didn't want to take back his throne. At least—she paused. At least, he had never said he sought that.

"There's one thing," she said. "Will you come with me to Dal-Decma? To a tournament. There's someone I must see."

"Pairas intends to compete in Dal-Decma." Ethne raised a suggestive eyebrow. "The prize money is significant."

"And he is penniless, as usual." The two women exchanged indulgent smiles.

"Then Pairas draws you there?"

"No." That was done with. Azenor hardly remembered why he enticed her. That with few prospects he was forbidden to her? "It is someone else." Someone she must betray.

THE TWO MEN huddled by a fire beneath a cloudy sky. They cradled cups in gloved hands, unnoticed in their frieze tunics and black kersey cloaks amid the cheerful tournament crowd.

The younger had curling hair the dark-brown of cinnamon and wide, hazel eyes. Cold reddened boyish cheeks that contradicted his stubborn mouth and firm jaw. His older companion's wispy auburn hair thinned upon his brow but thickly pelted to broad shoulders.

At their furtive manner, their careful glances, Azenor nudged

Ethne seated beside her on a log. "What plots are those two about?"

The young sorceress sniffed in disgust. "Cahirean. Trying to pass as Mountains men."

Azenor pulled her cloak tight. Wind from distant snow-tipped mountains gnawed. She thought the Downs a soft land, warm and honey-scented, but autumn blistered cruelly.

"How can you tell? They might be from the Mountains."

"Trust your nose. These two bathed once in their lives." Ethne thrust crusted bread at her. "The next round of the contest of swords begins soon. We'll need a place near the field to see whoever you wish to see." She flicked up a brow.

"Be patient. I'll point him out. Just don't ask me why."

"More mystery. Like what you did all those years with Roaran. I'm bursting at the sides to know all about him. Maybe I should use a potion to make you tell me."

"I wouldn't want to destroy your illusions, Ethne."

Azenor chewed bread, watching the crowd in the makeshift field tavern. It thronged with Downs soldiers, merchants and their wives, peasants, thieves even, seeking food and drink between pursuing entertainment, riches, or advancement.

A tournament offered more than a test of skill and courage or a chance to win gold. Warriors might offer their services to wealthy nobles. Men bartered over lands, priests and priestesses sought grants for temples from the powerful Nate Caelmarsh.

From his name, she and Caelmarsh shared a common ancestor. But beyond that the Downs lord did not interest her. Sly, everyone said. Gendrick used the word ambitious and made it sound like a bad thing. Well, Caelmarsh had a daughter. And the king was yet to wed.

A torturous ache began behind her eyes, like her skin stretched too tightly across her brow. It was sharp and dizzying then gone. *No. Not yet. Just let me keep my sight a few days longer.*

Azenor dug her thumbs into her temples. Seeking distraction, she considered the markets that always sprang up at tournaments.

Craftsmen and traders sold finely crafted pewter and silver jewellery, charred meat, mandarins, apples, grapes, spices, and silk from stalls or carts.

Whatever you sought, you'd find here. Except flesh. Its sale, legal across the sea in Veniva and Wardour, was forbidden in every region of Telor but the Icelands, where the Damadars grew rich on the slave trade deep within their ice caverns.

Azenor had wandered the markets that morning. A trader sold her a wrought gold-handed dagger, declaring it worthy of a champion. She chuckled at his smooth lies. The thing was a bauble. Though she felt safer with it in her belt.

"He left men twice his age in the dust." The Cahireans still plotted. "We must be careful."

Ethne dragged a finger over her throat. "Someone's for it."

"What if they're talking about an Isles man? Pairas is here. And Sherrin Cross."

"More likely some Mountains wretch. There's always tension between Mountains folk and Cahireans. Their queen retains some ancient claim to the lands around the gorge. But she'll not raise a hand against a man like Vraymorg."

"Vraymorg. I know little about him." Roaran avoided her questions about the Lord of the Pass.

"Not much to know. Just another Mountains thug. Come on." Ethne pulled Azenor to her feet. "We'll pay for a seat. Near the fence, but not so close we're ducking swinging swords."

Wind whipped hair about their faces as they walked through sprawled pavilions circling a gated field. Voices rumbled behind canvas, mingling with groaning leather, the scrape of iron, and scattered laughter. Banners fluttered from poles.

Cold scents swirled, edged with damp and a feculent stink from a stray dog wandering unnoticed through the crowd.

For a bronze coin each, they bought seats in a wooden stand overlooking a platform in the field's centre. Robed officials watched the gate. Azenor knew from Isles tournaments they would judge the winner if neither combatant yielded nor wounded the other.

"Good enough?" Ethne raised an eyebrow.

Azenor could only nod, her mouth dry. She'd see him soon. Kaell. From what Roaran told her, when next they met, she would be nearly blind. *I must remember all I can. His face, eyes, expressions. How he moves.* She owed him that respect.

Laughter and the chime of clinked glass carried from a raised, covered stand, brightly decorated in swirling flags. Richly clad men and women found cushioned seats. Servants moved among them, filling goblets from silver carafes.

A cheer lifted as a man and a girl climbed stairs to the stand. He wore a damask cloak and lawn tunic. A circlet of silver banded a forehead below greying hair. Jewelled rings glittered from fingers. The girl held her head proudly, combs capturing dark-brown hair in a knot.

Ethne nudged Azenor. "Caelmarsh. Very unlordly. The daughter, Annatise, though, has all the grace her father lacks. Thanks to her Damadar mother. Did you hear? She's to wed Cathmor next month. It's decided."

She broke off at a roar from spectators. Heralds carried banners and swords onto the field. Behind them strode two men wearing helmets, their tunics emblazoned with the insignia and colours of their lords. Neither wore expensive body armour or mail.

The heralds proclaimed the warriors' names and achievements. It meant little to Azenor though the crowd cheered and whistled. Everyone sat or pressed forward.

No tournament event equalled the contest of swords. Men might win silver in the melee where a warrior could wield any weapon, but Telorians valued bladesmen above all else.

"Who are these two? I don't know their houses."

Ethne squinted as the warriors clambered onto the platform. "A silver dog and a tower. The House of May. Minor Downs family. I can't make out the other man's heraldry."

An official stood between the combatants, speaking rapidly. Both nodded. He raised his arm, dropped it, and backed away.

A tense hush fell. The fighters circled. At the first clash of steel, the crowd screamed as though woken from a trance. Their yelling nearly drowned the shriek of cutting blades as a fierce dance unfolded.

"Our silver dog is the favourite," Ethne said. "The crowd roars every time he lands a blow."

Azenor could not concentrate on the fight. Her gaze strayed into the crowd. *He's here. Somewhere. What might he look like?*

That ache started again behind the bridge of her nose. Her vision broke up, the tents, the pennants, the spectators dissolving in a murky blur of grey and black. Panicked she rubbed her eyes. *Not yet. Please, not yet.* The web fell from her eyes, the tournament field and its two combatants again clear.

A cry rose up from the crowd as Ethne's silver dog thrust deep to wound his opponent in the side. As the warrior slumped, the dog whipped off his helm and lifted his sword to a ruckus of applause. Attendants carried the injured man to a physician's tent.

More heralds and bladesmen took their places. Azenor sat through the next few fights with little interest. Her thoughts whirled, her palms damp, her pulse jittery. It wasn't just knowing Kaell was here, somewhere; she knew her vision must soon cloud. She could not imagine her life then.

Ethne watched every fight from the edge of her seat, gasping at blows or sighing if a quickly found favourite lost. Then she seized Azenor's hand.

"By The Three, did you hear that?"

Azenor had not. "What?"

"That herald named his fighter as Griffin Damadar."

"A Damadar? Here?"

A young man accepted a sword with an embellished enamel hilt from his herald. A distinctive shard of ice splashed a too-neat tunic.

“The Damadar pup, if I recall. Griffin has two older brothers, Velleran and Heath. Few expectations, then. He’s probably here for the gold.”

“Who’s he fighting?”

His opponent only now wandered leisurely onto the field, staging an entrance. With wavy black hair sweeping broad shoulders beneath a flowing, crimson cape, the swaggering newcomer cut a romantic figure.

When the herald shouted his name, another expectant muttering spread. An Isles man. Onlookers nodded knowingly. Likely a good bladesman, then. Both women giggled.

“My intended.” Azenor thrust a hand to her breast. “The Stone Knight himself.”

“Not who you came to see?”

“No.” But Azenor watched this bout, at least, with unwavering attention. When Sherrin Cross thrust steel to the young Ice lord’s throat, she nodded. A man who knew the language of swords. The delighted mob cheered when he tore off his helmet and gracefully bowed.

Three more bouts followed, quickly decided. Winners’ names filled a wooden board.

Then a ripple stirred through the crowd. Chatter faltered. Other warriors waiting at the gates to compete turned to gape.

A young man strode onto the field, his chin thrust forward as if daring anyone to judge him. A sword swung against his thigh, his hair escaping a capped helm like waves of honey.

The silence deepened. Then an undercurrent of whispers rose to a low murmur. For no reason that made sense, Azenor’s gaze tore to the stand and its finely dressed spectators.

Nate Caelmarsh sat up, fingers strangling his chair arm, his shoulders stiff with outrage.

“Made quick work of it in the first round,” a nearby spectator whispered to a companion. “Too quick. Crowd likes more drama.”

“Can’t be more than seventeen,” the other man muttered. “Not natural that. Saw his lord fight once, years ago. Never forgot it. Such a controlled display of skill."

Azenor rose as though her heart's momentum threw her forward. Ethne grasped her sleeve. "This one? Him? By all our gods, no. There's too much doom and mystery about these warriors of Khir, Azenor."

Quickly Azenor sat down. Her breath locked in her lungs; her gaze locked on the bladesman. He boldly wore Vraymorg's ensign on his tunic and held his fair head fearlessly high. Khir's warrior, blessed by the God of Battles. Trained to fight. Expected to die young.

Look at me, Kaell, Azenor willed. *Know I am sorry for it.*

Kaell turned his head then, though only to watch his opponent enter the field to a burst of shouting from a fast-swelling mob.

"The Bastard of Bearclaw," Ethne muttered. "Michael Bearclaw. A Downs man who wins often, so popular here. Aric once put him in the dirt but only after a fierce struggle."

A herald carried not only his master's sword but a banner displaying four claws and a solitary star, symbolising the warrior's bastardy. Little shame in that, but men rarely celebrated it as he did.

"Champion of the Downs," the herald proclaimed to a roar. "Champion of the Melee."

"Where was Pairas when this fool won the melee? Drunk probably," Ethne said. "Still, your young Mountains warrior can't win. The bastard is a head taller and thicker."

"I'll bet a gold coin the bastard only claws the dirt."

The young priestess laughed. "I'll take your money."

Both women leaned. The crowd also packed close, straining to see. Warriors, physicians, and servants emerged from tents, forcing their way to the field's edge.

Voices faded. Scattered laughter died. The emptiness filled with a slap of cloth in gusting wind and nervous excitement as tangible as tendrils of mist.

"Shouldn't allow it," a man muttered behind his hand to another. "Listen to the stories, these bonded warriors aren't human."

"Want to bet on it then?"

The first man shook his head. "Nah. Blondie's just a boy. Got lucky yesterday. The Claw will sort him out with a few well-placed blows."

The Claw did trade, if not land, a few blows with the young man. But then, too soon, he rolled in the dirt, and Kaell stood over him, sword tip at his breast.

"I think you cheated," Ethne complained as she pressed a coin into Azenor's palm, the sound of the Claw's "I yield," ringing in their ears.

"You knew what he was."

"I didn't know how well he fights."

Azenor grinned as Kaell raised his sword to hesitant applause. A muttering tore about the field. Onlookers uneasily shuffled their feet. *He frightens them*, she thought.

Kaell shoved his blade into his belt and turned for the gate.

"If we hurry, we can get close." Ethne grabbed Azenor's hand. "Come on. That's what you want, isn't it?"

Is it? Her belly churned with nerves.

She pulled her hood over her head and let Ethne drag her through knotted men and women. Wind drove a few splatters of rain, but sun also pierced scattering clouds. Peat scents swirled above the odour of mud.

"Azenor?" Pairas pushed off the fence. "And Ethne?" He peered about. "Priestess, are you witless bringing her here with no escort?"

Azenor thrust her fists to her hips. "No one brings me anywhere."

"We're on an adventure," Ethne said. "Thought we'd watch you fight."

Pairas's dark glance leapt hopefully towards Azenor. "You came to see me?"

She winced, hardly able to remember waking beside him, limbs and bedclothes tangled, in effect only days ago. Pairas did not reproach her for her sudden coldness, but there was an edge to his shrug and smile.

Perhaps she might have loved him; perhaps she might in time have loved Sherrin.

Except for Roaran. He consumed her. Everything else before—there could be nothing after—felt like childish infatuation. Tender perhaps, but shallow.

"Forgive me." Pairas offered her a flamboyant bow. "Isles princesses do not waste their time on men with few prospects. Unless they're bored. You came to watch Sherrin."

That stung. Clearly she had hurt him. Kaell reached the gate, saving her the need to reply.

Pairas turned. "Nicely fought. You're quick. I hope we meet in the final."

Azenor hung back. She let the hood shadow her face. She hadn't told Roaran she intended to seek Kaell out. Perhaps there was a reason she shouldn't.

The young man dragged gloved fingers through damp, darkly golden hair. His eyes, too, were singular, like the dappled green of a deep, rolling sea. He said something to Pairas, but Azenor couldn't understand his Mountains accent.

She exchanged a puzzled look with Ethne.

Pairas frowned. "What's that you say?"

"Kaell!"

A man forced his way through a grumbling crowd, a powerful, dark-haired man moving with a warrior's speed and balance. He reached the boy and grabbed his arm.

Pairas moved between the women and the newcomer, his hand falling to his blade hilt. "The Lord of Vraymorg," he muttered to Azenor. "Careful."

"By Khir." The man shook Kaell by the shoulders. "What do you think you're doing?"

Voices and laughter hushed. Men and women turned to stare. Spectators at the fence and in stands craned necks, distracted from swordplay.

Azenor, too, gaped, fascinated. With those eyes of polished ebony, that burnished hair, surely Vraymorg must be an Isles man. But a shadow clung to him, an unworldly, invisible shimmer like a chord of sorrowful melody in still air.

She felt an urge to step back, as if drawing too near this man would rip her into a maelstrom, a violent world with rules and expectations far beyond the Isles.

"My lord," Kaell stammered. "I wanted to know—"

"If you could kill? Gods help you, Kaell, if you did."

"No, not kill." The boy irritably shoved off his lord's grasp. "I need to test myself. To see if I'm ready."

"You're ready when I say so."

"You say I'm never ready. It's always when I'm older."

The Mountains Lord knuckled a fist. "You don't answer me back, Kaell."

"My lord," Pairas interjected boldly. "This young man fought well. Both yesterday and today. Fairly, too. He's more than ready to be unleashed in battle."

Vraymorg threw him a look that would make most men quiver.

"Who are you? Some pretty bauble from the Isles? Butt out."

Pairas blinked, his jaw tightening in a way Azenor recognised. *No, no, no. Do not erupt. This Mountains lord is too dangerous to rouse. I feel it.*

Pairas this time fought down his anger. Curtly, he said, "I thought you should know."

"Well, now I do. It changes nothing. The boy disobeyed me. Not that it is your business."

"My business is warfare," Pairas said. "As captain at Tide's End, I know swordsmen. If you won't let him fight, I'll take him. We can use him in the Isles."

Azenor sucked in a breath at his daring. This man, Vraymorg, was Lord of the Mountains. The force of his will, his power, blazed off him; just his stare was enough to cut a man down. But Pairas stood his ground.

"Do you still yabber at me?" Vraymorg's hand slipped to his sword. "Back away. Captain or not, you know nothing about what a bonded warrior is. Not that it is your concern, but Kaell has no right to be here. He once again disobeyed me. Deliberately."

Vraymorg shot him a final, threatening glare then shoved Kaell. "We're leaving."

The young man bristled, his embarrassed gaze sweeping from Pairas to Azenor and Ethne to the mob gathering to watch the fun.

"I want to fight," he said. "I can win this tournament, my lord."

"Enough." Vraymorg stopped him with a gesture. "Give me your sword. A bonded one does not waste his skills playing at tournaments."

"He serves the gods. Yes, yes, yes." With an angry mutter, Kaell surrendered his blade.

Vraymorg thrust it into his belt beside his own and stalked off. Kaell scuffed dirt with a boot. Head down, he followed.

"Now that one," said Pairas, as they disappeared into a sea of surging bodies and clashing colours. "Knows the meaning of obedience."

"Let's see where they go." Ethne shot Azenor a mischievous grin.

Pairas glowered. "Let's not, priestess. That man Vraymorg is dangerous. The boy as well. No need to seek trouble."

"I think we should."

"Should?"

Ethne adopted her serious priestess expression. Azenor coughed to cover a giggle.

"I feel something, Pairas. They might need your help."

Pairas nibbled his bottom lip. "Do you mean some witch-sense thing?"

"Crude but accurate. That sums you up, actually."

Azenor sighed. These two always argued. Ethne thought the Isles captain a libertine. Pairas once called the sorceress a meddling schemer.

"They went this way," she said.

Pairas led them through rows of silken and canvas pavilions. From one, a man shrieked, and a calm voice urged, "Hold him."

The tournament's sounds seeped away to a distant rumble, though every so often voices rose to a clashing roar and hewing metal clanged. The earth drummed as onlookers stomped their feet to salute a lusty blow.

Vraymorg strode towards a man waiting with horses beyond the pavilions, Kaell close behind. A figure slid from lengthening shadows to go after them.

Azenor grabbed Pairas's arm. "Someone's following them."

"That's one of those Cahireans," Ethne said. "From the tavern."

Steel scraped leather. The servant with the horses shouted a warning as an armed man moved in fast with a swinging blade. Vraymorg whipped out his sword and whirled. He shoved Kaell behind him. Braced.

The man thrust. Iron rang in a mighty crash as the Mountains lord deflected the blow.

Weak sunlight flashed on metal. A second assailant sprang at Kaell. Unarmed, Kaell dodged a lethal cut. Pairas cursed and broke into a run.

Like trying to watch different combatants in the melee, Azenor struggled to follow what happened. The two Cahireans, Vraymorg, Kaell, Pairas all blurred into a flurry of straining figures, a storm of streaking metal, of shouts, curses, and ringing steel.

The first bladesman hacked hard at Vraymorg. The second forced Kaell back, step by step. Trapped in hemming pavilions, Kaell flung up his arms as his assailant lifted his weapon.

Pairas shouted a challenge. He leapt in, slashing. The man spun and ripped up a parry that ground blades together in a cloud of blue sparks. A dagger glinted in his other hand. He stabbed. Blood burst on Pairas's tunic. Azenor cried out in dismay as the Isles warrior reeled.

The Cahirean turned on Kaell. He cut high. The boy dropped beneath steel a whisker from his scalp, rolled to his feet, and crouched. The man chopped at him. Kaell weaved aside. The sword followed. Dirt puffed as he dived.

Grinning, his attacker stomped after him. Kaell scrambled back on his hands. Vraymorg shouted, "Kaell!" Just one word but Azenor heard his desperate, gut-wrenching fear.

Her mouth stale with panic, she could hardly separate what happened next.

Pairas staggered up, yelling. The Cahirean wheeled from Kaell. Pairas thrust at his midriff, little strength in the stroke. The man easily swept the blade aside. "Prancing Isles peacock," he taunted. "I'll kill you then him."

Kaell launched at him. The Cahirean crashed into trampled grass. He elbowed the boy off and clawed at his spilt weapon.

Pairas stumbled in. His sword rose. He drove it shuddering into the man's ribs. The Cahirean jerked like a puppet. Blood and entrails sprayed. The air thickened with the nauseating odour of death.

Kaell safe, Azenor's panicked glance flew to Vraymorg in time to see him cut down the first bladesman. The force of his terrible stroke spun the Cahirean about and then into a bloody, twitching heap.

Azenor opened a clenched palm. Her held breath released. *Thank the Three.*

But now a shadow thickened off canvas. A third man rushed at Kaell, steel in his hand. Kaell edged back, blank surprise on his face as if the gods had failed him.

With a heartbreaking cry of fear and rage, Vraymorg sprang at the man. His thundering blow ripped the sword from his opponent's grip. The man hurled his palms up to shield his head. The Mountains lord ruptured his chest with iron.

Pairas, his tunic crimson at his hip, limped to Vraymorg. The Mountains lord's shoulders heaved. His breaths racked out in jarring gasps.

"A pity." Pairas nudged a body. "You can't question them about why they came at you."

"They didn't come for me," Vraymorg answered grimly, already looking away to Kaell. "You, boy. Are you hurt?"

Kaell dusted his tunic. Sullenly, he muttered, "You shouldn't have taken my sword. I couldn't defend myself."

"No." Vraymorg said. "I shouldn't have taken your sword." A faint smile shaped his lips. For a heartbeat, beneath that darkness, he looked barely older than Kaell.

Azenor blinked. Impossible. A trick of fading light. Or her fading vision.

Ethne crouched beside a dead man. "They're Cahirean," she told Vraymorg. "We saw them plotting in the field tavern earlier."

"Cahirean." Kaell frowned. "My lord, why?"

Vraymorg sheathed his sword and dragged bloody fingers through his matted, dark hair. To Pairas, he said gruffly, "You're wounded."

The Isles captain shrugged. "A scratch."

"I suppose you have my gratitude. But this is still not your business."

For a thank you, hardly gracious. Azenor burst out laughing. Such arrogance.

Vraymorg's scowl swung to her.

Even though she knew he couldn't see her face, Azenor dropped her head. An ache ribboned in her brow. Her eyesight blurred, the dizziness this time stirring up her gut. She pressed her fingertips into the bridge of her nose, breathing through pain until it ebbed away.

The servant rushed up with two soldiers.

"My lord, I fetched help." His glance fell on the broken, bloodied bodies. The stench of iron was overpowering. "Which you don't need. Who are they? Are they—?"

"What goes on here?" A soldier wearing a captain's shoulder clasp pressed forward. "Who are these men? Who killed them?"

"They attacked us, captain," Kaell said. "We defended ourselves."

The captain wheeled with a glare. "I didn't address you, boy." He faced Vraymorg. "Is that true, my lord?"

"It's true."

"We all saw it," Pairas said. "They attacked without provocation, weapons drawn."

"And who exactly are you?"

Kaell stalked away from the raised voices towards the horses. Azenor made certain her hood covered her face and followed.

"Why do Cahireans want you dead?" she said.

Kaell turned in surprise. Wind stirred hair the colour of darkly woven gold. "There's some who have good reason. But Cahireans? I don't understand."

"Kaell." Vraymorg advanced. "We're leaving."

"Yes, my lord." Kaell dragged mutinous feet towards his lord. Unexpectedly he glanced back at her with a charming grin then strode on.

As Azenor stared, he blurred. Then a fog covered him. *No, no, no.* She blinked to clear her vision, rubbed her eyes, but the shroud this time came down completely. Shapes floated in a soup of grey. A violent shiver lifted gooseflesh on her arms.

Not yet, she thought. *I'm not ready.*

Her knees hit hard ground. Like blood from a wound, panic drained her will and strength. She heard rushing footsteps, felt Ethne touch her shoulder.

Azenor's stunned disbelief froze out the world. She knelt in the dirt, hardly aware of their questions, only staring at shadows. Etched figures moved about her. Voices assaulted her like a distant buzzing.

Then she beat the ground with her fists, shrieking out her fear and frustration, thrashing against their hands as they tried to grab her. Until finally Pairas held her to his breast, and she sobbed and sobbed.

KAELL

Azenor. Her name stung with memory. Sun upon his face. Aric's taunts as they hewed and thrust with steel in that dusty yard at Dal-Kanu. Writhing in agony in a hot, darkened room, his broken body aflame. Wretched. Alone.

"Your brother—"

Azenor clutched at his arm. "No. Then he is dead. I feared it when I knew you lived."

"Aric is in the Isles. Alive."

To his surprise, Azenor flared up. "You lie. Aric is no coward. The ghouls told him to poison you to save me. My brother would never leave me to this fate."

"No, listen," Kaell broke in. "He struck me down to save you, believed he killed me."

Candlelight lit a faraway flame within her dark eyes. "Then *he* told me the truth. I began to doubt, to think he lied when he said no lasting harm befell Aric."

"Who is this *he*?"

"A sweet, powerful lord." Her voice hushed with reverence. "He'll tell you everything when I take you to him. Quickly, now. We must flee before Archanin misses you."

"Did he hurt you?" Kaell blurted. "Archanin?"

Azenor let out a soft sigh. “A bit,” she whispered. “Disobedience displeases him.”

And she, a prisoner with as little hope as he, disobeyed? When he submitted? Shame roiled, rancid in his mouth.

“No more talking.” Azenor grasped his hand. “We need to escape. What’s your plan?”

A plan? When he was broken by guilt, no longer human, barely holding onto his reason. A plan? Put one foot after the other?

“There’s a river.” Kaell remembered sun in his eyes, boats bobbing at anchor. “The fortress of Vraymorg can’t be far away. Maybe a week’s walk. If we get to my lord, he’ll know what to do.”

“What do you mean?” she said sharply.

Kaell sighed. “You know what I am. My lord will do what’s right.”

“Do you mean kill you?” Her voice lifted a notch. “Is that what you mean?”

“Yes. That’s what I mean.”

“No. He won’t.” Azenor dug strong fingers into his arm. “Take me to the Isles. You’ll be safe there.”

So fierce. Strong-willed. Kaell gave a short laugh. “Are all Isles women like you?”

“I don’t know,” Azenor said impatiently. “Are all bonded warriors like you? Do they all speak oddly? I can hardly understand you.”

Kaell grinned. Despite all that befell him, the emptying misery, he enjoyed her biting retorts. Perhaps the gods willed he lived just to save her.

“There might be a way to escape.” Her courage gave him the strength to at least say the words, to find something among the shattered parts of his mind and will.

Azenor swiped at a frustrated tear. “How can you doubt it? It’s foretold we’ll reach the Isles.”

More strange words. But no time to ponder them. Kaell took her hand. “Come.”

Azenor did not hesitate nor waste precious moments asking questions. Kaell liked that about her. Along with her courage—and sharp tongue.

He led her back to the chamber where Archanin had shackled him. The chains' glint mocked as though awaiting his return to them.

Run, the ghost from his dreams whispered.

Guards still shuffled in the passage. Kaell crept to the balcony and leaned out, brushing stone with his fingers. Rough, though no obvious footholds. He returned to Azenor.

"We'll climb down. I can carry you on my back."

"Or I could stick a knife in my ribs. Are you witless? We'll fall." Her mouth twisted.

The door smashed inwards. Two guards stomped in.

At the sight of Kaell and Azenor, they drew swords. "What do you two think you're doing?" one sneered. "Going to fly off the balcony? Fall to your knees and put your hands together at your back."

"Make me," Kaell said. The words felt good. Defiance felt good.

He pushed Azenor down against the wall to keep her clear of swinging weapons. Crouched, braced as the nearest guard lunged low to wound him.

Kaell seized the blade between his palms. Pain ripped like fire, but he ignored it, yanking hard. The guard staggered, the sword yanked from his grip. Steel tore up Kaell's hand.

The second cut at Kaell's legs. He jumped then dived for the first ghoul's spilled blade, fisting it in time to smash metal aside.

The guard pressed his attack, hewing with his blade like an axe. Still on the floor, Kaell barely blocked, his palms stinging, the hilt slippery with blood. With a cry of anger, the ghoul tried to impale his thigh. Kaell rolled aside then sprang up. Extended the sword.

The first guard lurched to his feet. He slashed with a knife. Kaell jumped back. The thin blade uselessly swished through the air. The second ghoul fell upon Kaell with battering, heaving, clamouring blows. Kaell dodged and weaved, tried to find traction on the hilt.

They chased him about the room. Brutal swipes knocked candle holders to the floor, gashed tapestries, and smashed vases.

Kaell sidestepped a thrust. Steel impaled a pillow. The ghoul took a heartbeat too long to withdraw his sword. Kaell pounced, slicing. The guard screamed and reeled, a star of crimson exploding across his breast.

Kaell wrapped a strip of cloth from his tunic about the sword hilt as the other ghoul moved in with his companion's dropped weapon. He bellowed in fury, crashed iron down. Kaell caught the blow high on his blade. It shuddered through his shoulders.

The guard unleashed a ferocious assault, a whir of cuts and slashes. Now better able to control his weapon, Kaell met thrust for thrust, metal singing.

He yawed to avoid a crouching Azenor, her arms shielding her head. The guard came after him. Kaell steered the fight away, yelling as he jabbed and cut, his blade a grating, screeching blur. A furious strength fired his muscles, an awareness of his new power and stamina.

Kaell laughed. A cold, vicious laugh that didn't belong to him. "You can't kill me," he jeered. "I'm stronger now. I have your lord's blood."

The ghoul blinked in alarm. With another grim laugh, Kaell bunched a fist and swung. His blow snapped the guard's head into the wall. At once, Kaell swung high. His opponent's rushed parry drew their blades together.

This time Kaell did not withdraw but pushed with all his might, grinding his sword past raised steel into the ghoul's throat. Blood splattered his face. The guard's shriek choked off as Kaell rammed the blade deeper, impaling the ghoul against a wall.

For a moment he stayed like that, his weight against the body, his breaths sharp. Blood streamed from his aching palms down his arms. Ghoul blood, wet and hot on his cheeks, clotted his hair. His shoulders and back screamed a protest.

A black joy raced through Kaell's veins. Killing ghouls brought back some sense of who he once was. It was his purpose, his duty. What his lord had raised him to do.

He yanked out the sword. The dead ghoul slumped. Kaell felt no pity, only that detached coldness of battle fever. "We must go. Quickly." He reached down to Azenor.

The girl shrank away. "You laughed." Her voice quavered with horror. "You laughed as you slaughtered them."

Kaell's hand froze on her arm. "I did what I had to."

She made no reply, only clasped her knees.

A bolt of bitter anger choked his breath. How dare she judge? He killed to save her.

Impatiently he shoved the ghoul's sword into his belt and grabbed her hand. "Do you want to escape? This is your plan, remember."

She hesitated. Nodded. Trembling, she let him pull her up.

Kaell led her into a passage outside, his teeth snapped shut. Her fear and revulsion stung. *I know I'm a monster*, he wanted to shout. *But soon I'll be dead. You'll be safe then. Everyone will be safe.*

"You keep groaning. You're hurt?"

"What do you care?" he said. "I'm a monster. I deserve this."

"Kaell—"

"No. Don't—just don't talk."

Through shutters, daylight wisped as frail and tantalising as fragrance. Kaell listened for sounds of alarm. Only stillness rattled breathless air. Torches smoked, their flames forming pools of ivory that discoloured the gloom.

They stole down a stairwell then through empty halls of gleaming marble, of creeping ivy and shadows, to a door. It creaked open into an overgrown garden of bushes and puffy grass fading into entangled trees with roots like a tower's buttresses.

Faint birdsong twitted. Mist swirled, its damp fingers brushing skin. At Kaell's back, the castle loomed as stark as bones against a colourless sky. A husk, broken and twisted. Unreal. Vines entwined crumbling walls. A forbidding hush welled behind its stone.

"What is that?" Azenor wrinkled her nose.

Scents exploded. The deep richness of soil and rotting leaves. Rushing water. Then something rank and nasty. A cesspool? "Nothing." Kaell didn't want to know.

He led her into the trees. An uncomfortable prickling crept beneath his skin. Bewildered, he stopped. "Do you feel that?"

"A little. It's a magical barrier. Broken now. Thanks to you."

"What?"

Azenor grinned smugly. "You really know so little. And you, a bonded one."

Kaell was silent.

Azenor entwined her fingers with his. "I'm sorry. I didn't mean to be cruel. But I thought you understood. Your blood oath to Archanin, the oath of a warrior who served his brother, Khir, destroyed that barrier."

"You know about that." His voice cracked.

"Kaell, everything happened as it should. That magic was fading anyway. Even without you, Archanin would walk free sooner rather than later."

He had no words. Heaviness shrouded his heart. Disgust. Dread. Soon it wouldn't matter what he'd done. What he was. Soon he'd be dead.

"Aric says barriers like this exist across the Isles," Azenor said. "To keep ghouls out."

"Who created them?"

"A powerful seer. Guess."

An easy answer, but he shivered. "Your ancestor. Roaran." As though whipped up by the name, a fragment of wind fingered his neck. "We'd best move. Before they miss us."

"Mooove," Azenor echoed. "Why do you speak so strangely?"

"It's not strange to me. Or anyone else in the Mountains." He took her hand again. Lapping water sounded close. The stench of decay thickened.

"Mooove," Azenor teased. "Mooove."

"I don't see why that's so funny."

"Fooney. Fooney—" She broke off with a cry, her hand torn from his.

Earth collapsed beneath him. Kaell tumbled, his body thumping and rolling down a slope. His skidding heels sprayed up soil and dust until with a bump and a groan, he hit uneven ground. The dislodged sword hilt bruised his hip. Pebbles bounced in raining dirt.

"Azenor?"

The girl sprawled, coughing. Kaell swiped grime from his eyes. A pit's walls rose around them. His arm painfully pressed against bones. Shuddering, he shot to his feet.

"Kaell." Azenor groped about. "Kaell, where are you? What is this place?"

"We fell into a ditch." He scrambled to her. Azenor picked up a skull. She poked a finger through an eye socket, yelped, and flung it away.

Kaell folded his arms about her. "Hush, you're safe."

"Was that—" She clung to him. "Oh, by The Three. We're in a grave."

"Don't think about it. We're close to the river. I'll carry you."

Dazed, she made no protest as Kaell lifted her into his arms and bore her through the pit. Bones cut his bare feet, his eyes averted in case he recognised less decayed flesh. He helped her clamber to the top, straightened, and brushed bloody palms down his pants.

Just beyond the woodland, the river gurgled, spilling scents of wet soil and waterlilies.

A man laughed. "Bone dust. How pretty."

Three men emerged from the trees. Two carried swords, the third a bow. "Thought we'd have to haul you out," one sniggered.

Kaell looked at the men. He looked at the trees just a few steps away.

He swung Azenor over his shoulder and ran.

The men cursed and chased them. Trunks fell away to a muddy bank. Dawn's symphony of pinks played a soft melody across a river's mirrored surface. Birds nesting in reeds exploded into the sky, their flapping wings rending the quiet as a knife might rip canvas.

Kaell bundled Azenor into a flat-bottomed boat, jumped in, and snatched up an oar. He shoved the craft from the bank as the men pulled up, breathless and angry.

"Stop!" one shouted. "We'll shoot."

Kaell leaned on the oar. The boat yawed. An arrow thumped into wood at his feet. Azenor screamed. Another plucked at his arm. Blood dripped, but he kept at the oar.

"Fool. Correct your aim. Our lord will want them alive."

Hissing arrows shot up in a black cloud. They plunged wide. The boat hit the current. More arrows twanged, skidding harmlessly over the river's surface.

The archer lowered his bow. His companions shadowed the craft on foot along the shore.

Kaell dragged in the oar. The boat slid on dark, rippling water. Above the inky canopy of clustered trees, daylight bloomed. Branches scrabbled at banks. The pungent odour of mud and clotted reeds assaulted, drowning the river's cool freshness.

He helped Azenor sit, cursing at the sight of her cut feet. His bled too, but his mind detached from the pain, detached from all but one thing: Get to his lord. Die.

"You don't have shoes," he said.

"The Lord of Gore, Archanin, thought I might escape. Fooney, hey. Are we safe?"

"They'll come after us. But we have a start."

She huddled, her shoulder pressed to his as though his nearness no longer repulsed but comforted. Kaell forgot his anger. He knew he must seem monstrous. Even he feared that yawning chasm of darkness within.

He dipped the oar into fast-streaming water to keep them in

the current. Banks flashed past. A mountain bulked ahead, a silhouette blotting the rose-fluxed horizon.

They were somewhere in the Waste Mountains. Mountains he knew little about. Not safe but free. *Run,* the ghost said. *Yes,* Kaell whispered.

A WATERFALL'S THUNDER drowned out every other sound as dusk's crimson fugue splintered the horizon. In the churning river, the boat bucked and spun. Jutting rocks menaced. Reluctantly Kaell steered from the dangerous slipstream to the bank.

Unease gnawed at him, banishing exhaustion. At midday, he glimpsed a boat far behind. Though he did not see it again, he guessed their pursuers were closing in.

He jumped out to pull the craft through reeds. The forest thinned long ago to a treeless wetland, crowded with scraggly saltbushes, their bare branches rattling in a rising wind.

Azenor woke with a start. "Where am I?"

"In the boat. I hear a waterfall ahead. We must walk from here."

She stretched cramped limbs. Fascinated, he watched her, tracing Aric in the chiselled cheekbones, the lush mouth, dark lashes and brows. The same clay, a different mould.

"That's my first deep sleep since the ghoul ambush." She accepted his hand to scramble onto the muddy shore.

Kaell hid the boat in sickly bushes and smoothed mud with a leaf to hide their tracks. Probably useless. Any ghoul could track their scent. His own heightened senses proved that. Touch. Smell. Hearing… Azenor's blood pulsing. Its scent.

That terrible, shameful hunger uncoiled. Kaell shoved it down. *Do not think of blood. Think only of getting to his lord. To end this.*

"Where are we?" Azenor groped for his tunic.

"I don't know exactly. Somewhere in the Waste Mountains."

"Ugggh." She shuddered. "Waste Mountains? What's *in* them?"

"Ghouls."

She screwed up her face. "Oh, fooney."

"Well, you asked. Slavers. The Varee. I'm told they're Archanin's chosen people."

"Snakes? We've snake valleys in the Isles. Deserted except for venom hunters."

"Snakes, no doubt. I've heard stories, nonsense probably, about ancient crumbling cities in these mountains. Fields blackened by lightning. Many dangers."

"But nothing a bonded one fears." Azenor laughed. "A bonded warrior is just another swaggerer, isn't he? Like my brother. Swaggerers fear nothing."

"What's a swaggerer?"

"An arrogant, strutting dancer. Dances with swords."

"Ha. Did you hit your head in the boat?"

"Very fooney. If I hit yours, I bet it rattles."

"Come." Kaell took her hand, grinning. "I'll carry you. Your feet are bare."

"I'm not helpless, Kaell."

He swung her up. Azenor beat his chest. "What are you doing? Put me down."

"Stop fretting," he said. "My ghoul blood makes me strong."

"Fretting? You sound like Aric." She released a drawn-out sigh. "Oh, very well. Carry me away then, swaggerer. To the Isles, please."

"To this mysterious 'he'? Is he a swaggerer too?"

"A swaggering dancer of the first order."

"Swaggerers have orders?"

"For sure. And all sorts of rules."

"Ha. Only now do I fully understand my dire predicament. I'm lost in dangerous mountains with a girl with a sharp tongue. No plan, no help on the way. But all's well because I'm a swaggerer."

His grin faded. No, a monster.

PURPLE DUSK LINGERED as Kaell carried Azenor to a rocky mound. A rug of stunted bushes discoloured a plain sweeping to a darkling knob of distant pine forest.

An alien landscape. Far different to the valleys and wooded slopes of the Silent Mountains. Even the ugly, ruptured gorge seemed welcoming next to this dismal place, surely long abandoned by men and women.

"I'm truly lost," he said.

"What can you see?" Azenor wriggled to the ground.

"Saltbushes. From the little I know of these mountains we go south. But where's south?"

"Isles seafarers steer by the sun and stars. Aric says to sail south look for The Wolf."

"Huh?"

Azenor flung an arm up. "Exactly who hit their head? Look for a group of stars like a wolf's head and sail, or walk, towards it."

"Does it have a long snout?"

"How would I know? I haven't seen it lately, thick head."

"What sort of insult is thick head?" Kaell could not hold back another grin. "Actually, there's a rhyme in that. *Hit his head, and now his thoughts are thick and slow and out of sorts.*"

Azenor laughed. "Like I said. It rattles where your brain should be."

Kaell laced Azenor's warm fingers through his own. Her teasing lightened the darkness burdening his thoughts.

"Then south to the snout." He lifted her into his arms.

"Or north to nowhere? I trust you. You're Khir's Bonded Warrior."

"Khir surely turned from me," he muttered. "No warrior lets his enemies capture him alive." A yearning kindled. It wasn't Khir's approval he wanted, but his lord's.

"It's easy to die, Kaell," Azenor said. "Harder to survive."

Kaell plodded on in silence, careful not to stumble and drop her. Weariness blurred his footsteps. An eternity since he slept. An eternity since he fed. He dragged his tongue over his lips, too aware of her heart tolling against his chest, her pulsing blood.

So hungry. Hungry.

No. He dug his nails into his bloody palm. He must not lose control and hurt her.

DAWN TRAILED OPAL tails through a black satin sky. The Wolf faded above mountains glazed in mist. Thunder clapped. Light streaked between sky-flung walls of stone, like a lance smashing into a ribbed ravine. Then darkness curtained again.

Beneath the trill of birdsong, the ripple of breeze, another sound, taffeta-soft, intruded. A furtive sound. Kaell whipped about, seeking to strip the blackness with his eyes. Mist swirled in hoar light. A bush trembled. The wind? A scuttling. Paws?

"There! I see them." Through blindingly turbid, grey cloud, shapes lurched.

"Kaell." Azenor stiffened in his arms as he broke into a run. "Is it them? Is it?"

Steps pounded at his heels. A shape leapt at him. Kaell crashed down. The jolt tore Azenor from his arms. At once a ghoul fell on him, pinned him, a knee to his chest.

"I've got him. Here."

Kaell drove his thumb into the ghoul's eye. Howling, his attacker clutched at his face. Kaell hurled him off and rolled to his feet.

"It's me," he said, reaching to pull Azenor up. She sobbed in relief. He took her hand and fled into the ravine. Towering sheets of stark rock closed about them.

Kaell tripped often on uneven ground. Their pursuers fell also, their curses muffled, their steps eerily echoing in scattering fog.

"They're close," one said. "Work your way back. We'll find them."

Kaell led Azenor away from the voice. Dawn's fragile light at last broke up the darkness. Pebbles dislodged by his foot scuttled into emptiness. His breath cut. He flung out an arm to hold Azenor back. But for his ghoul senses he would not have seen it.

"What is it?"

They tottered on the edge of a cliff. Far below a flat wasteland of scarred black earth curved between mountains.

"That's a lightning plain." Lastenarron emerged from the mist with a handful of armed ghouls. At Kaell's startled look he laughed. "What? You don't know? Watch, fool."

With a metallic, scorched odour, thunder crackled. Jagged light punched at earth. An explosion of noise. Azenor clutched at Kaell's arm.

"Nowhere to go, little flower. You can't cross that plain. Surrender, and I won't hurt you"—Lastenarron grinned as he gestured to two ghouls with loaded bows—"too badly."

"I'm feeling particularly stubborn." Kaell tore out his sword. His palm ached.

"That's your most attractive quality. Drop the weapon, blossom. Or I'll put a bolt in you and carry you back, moaning and sobbing, to our lord."

How to escape? Even with the comfort of a sword, Kaell was less than he was. His humiliating capture broke his spirit, his confidence.

The archers edged closer. Azenor huddled against him. Her heart sang of fear, its pounding even now stirring that sickening hunger.

"Put the sword down, Kaell," Lastenarron said. "No doubt you think with our lord's blood you're special, strong enough to fight your way out of this. But it ends only one way, with or without violence. I hope it's with."

Kaell frowned. "What do you mean special? You have his blood, too."

"Only Raggamirron does. And you. What makes you so deserving?" Lastenarron hitched up a lip in disgust. "Not going to surrender? Good. It's violence then." At his signal, ghouls advanced but warily. "Don't hurt the girl." Lastenarron yawned. "Our lord is fond of her. But hurt Kaell all you like. Just leave him alive and in one piece. Makes it easier to drag him back rather than carry all the bits."

Azenor needled Kaell's arm with her fingers. "What do we do?"

"It took three arrows to bring you down when we hunted you near Thom," Lastenarron said. "I'll put three in you now, and we'll see how stubborn you feel, little flower."

Thom. His men slaughtered. Fury salted Kaell's mouth. A red mist fogged his eyes. *Make them pay.* That single thought flashed. *Make Lastenarron pay and pay.*

Rage, pain, burst out of him in a roar. With no plan, just the sword, Kaell ran at them.

For a heartbeat stunned ghouls gaped. Then Lastenarron shouted. An arrow's wind parted Kaell's hair. Another whistling shaft skimmed his wrist. His sword spun away.

He yelped, but the pain, the spurt of blood didn't stop him. He crashed into the archer. They hit the ground in a puff of dust. Kaell rolled to his feet. Kicked. The ghoul skidded across earth.

Such strength in his every blow now. Elated at his power, he flung a startled ghoul through air like a spear.

Arrows twanged. Kaell dived. More sank around him. Lastenarron drew back his bowstring. Kaell launched at him. The ghoul fell back. Kaell groped for a stone and smashed it into his face.

Scrambling up, he rushed to Azenor. Dazed, she huddled in a chaos of arrows and shouts, of surging bodies. He swung her over his shoulder and ran. Arrows zipped over his head. The ground rattled and throbbed as lightning flashed, the charged air hot and strange.

Another arrow seared into a gnarled bush beside them. Kaell glanced over his shoulder.

Lastenarron staggered up. Blood streamed from his gashed head. "You can't hide, Kaell," he shouted. "There's nowhere to hide. Not for you."

THEY PUT THE SALTBUSHES, the river, the ghouls behind them. After a few days, Kaell dared hope they had lost their pursuers in the shadowed valleys.

By the time they reached the Silent Mountain's darkling forests, terpenic with pine, he realised spring was upon this land, that he'd been a prisoner for three months. It was hard to make sense of that.

"I must have been in that dreadful place longer still," Azenor said. That was all she'd tell him about her time as a captive. But as they walked, they spoke of many things. Tide's End. Aric. Winters in the Mountains, the fortress of Vraymorg. Its lord.

"My lord will do the right thing," Kaell confided one night around a fire.

Azenor took a moment to work that out. Then she made an exasperated sound. "You expect him to kill you? You do, don't you?"

"You wouldn't understand."

She groped for his hand. "You don't have to die, Kaell. Take me to Tide's End. You'll be safe there, too."

"It's my duty to return to Vraymorg. To get you safely to the fortress."

A week into their journey, he told her about the tournament in the Downs where Caelmarsh sent soldiers to abduct him, and a woman had tried to smother him.

"You fell in a hole?" Azenor burst out laughing. "I'm sorry. It's not funny, I know."

"Maybe it's a bit funny," Kaell said. "In hindsight."

"Why would Caelmarsh risk the displeasure of the king and the gods—not to mention your lord—for the sake of throwing you in some dark cell?"

"He says I killed his daughter." Kaell didn't look at her. Easier to speak about this that way. "Or as good as."

"But Annatise Caelmarsh fell in the river or something."

"On her wedding night," Kaell said. "The king discovered she was with child and threw her out of not only his bed but of the castle."

"Oh."

"It wasn't my child. Caelmarsh thinks it was. But it wasn't."

"Oh," Azenor said again.

ANOTHER WEEK PASSED. Kaell hoped they might be safe. But in the dense forest beyond the ravine, drums pursued, their toneless beat creaking up his backbone.

"Is it about us?" Azenor whispered. "A message to someone?"

"I don't know."

He remembered standing as a child upon the walls of Vraymorg, listening to the rolling drums as sentries clutched at amulets and muttered to Khir.

"The Varee," Vraymorg once told him.

"We must hunt them, my lord," Kaell had declared with all the fierce clarity of a child of ten.

Vraymorg had laughed and clapped his shoulder. "That's my business, Kaell. Yours is to kill ghouls—when you're older, of course."

Kaell was older now but more afraid. When Kaell was a child, his lord seemed so powerful, so big nothing could harm a boy under his protection.

"Can we rest?" Azenor said. "I'm exhausted."

Kaell set her down and peered about.

The forest tangled with black trunks sunk deep in shed leaves, vines, and spindly bushes. Spikelets of pea-shaped citrina on shrubs spilled the last of their winter perfume. But elsewhere leaves budded on boughs. Wildflowers pushed up in grass. A stream murmured.

Twilight rimmed the black sky with a cacophony of red streaks. Two moons blinked through branches. A third clung to the horizon. Pale, full. Ready to ascend.

Kaell's blood iced. A three-moon night.

He jumped up. "We're in danger."

"No," Azenor wailed. "They can't have found us."

Panic spun Kaell's thoughts. Fire. That held off the Lost. Yes, start a fire.

The red dusk drained as though a whirlpool sucked its colours into a black pit. The last moon assaulted the night. Awakened shadows twitched. Trees soughed with murmurs.

"What was that?" Azenor's voice shrilled. "Kaell, something's there."

Kaell pulled her to him, his arms a shield. Three moons towered in shards of silver brilliance. Branches creaked. A shape wisped, lifelessly pale. Figures staggered from the trees, wraithlike, arms outstretched.

He knew what they were. But he only ever glimpsed them from the safety of Vraymorg's high walls. Now terror stripped his breath. Even if he had a sword, steel did not kill the Lost.

"Don't move or speak."

Azenor trembled. "I don't understand. What's there?"

A wraith turned. Arms outstretched, fingers curled as claws, it lumbered towards them. It was the shape of a man, but ragged cloth hung from a body little more than ghastly flesh covering bone. A sickly sweet odour cloyed. A crackling scraped from its throat.

Kaell put his lips to Azenor's ear. "Do not move."

The wraith's breath chilled his face. Moonlight fell on pallid skin, on gleaming teeth. Its flailing limb swatted Azenor. She slumped in his arms.

Quietly, shaking, Kaell lowered her to the ground. He stood

over her, his body the only protection he could offer.

More misshapen figures lurched their way. Flat gazes frosted. The first wraith groped at Kaell's face. He gagged at the waxy stench.

"Let me in." Its voice rustled, its touch icy.

He dared not move. Dared not breathe. The wraith pawed his lips. "I want to be free," it hissed, forcing his mouth open. "Let me in. Let me go home."

Swooping coldness burnt his throat. Kaell gasped, spluttered. He could not run. His scream caught against his ribs.

"Get away, unclean thing." A man poked a flaming torch at the wraith. Howling, it fell back.

As though released from a spell, Kaell dropped to the ground beside Azenor, coughing. His breath frosted. The air smelt of ash, burning pitch. Bobbing torches carved flames through silver-flecked darkness. Wraiths screeched.

"Quickly, come with us." A man beckoned.

Still shaken, Kaell staggered up. He slung Azenor over his shoulder and followed the stranger. The man's companions fell in behind, jabbing at the Lost with flaming pitch.

More wraiths emerged from the trees, their cries an awful pleading. "Let us in. Free us."

"This way," the stranger said. "It's not far."

He led Kaell through forest etched with opaque light, along overgrown trails where sharp branches cut and bruised skin. The crisp air beneath the trees hardly breathed, spidery, stark bushes still, but a breeze trilled through the top canopy of leaves.

Pines drowned the sickly stink as the Lost pursued, their shuffling feet crackling leaves, their hissing a sibilant curse. Paws pattered from their path. The chirr of insects faded only to pick up once they passed.

The strangers shouted and thrust flames at wraiths. One caught alight. It thrashed soundlessly as the fire took hold, collapsing to a blackened, smoking hulk.

A mountain's bulk loomed. A light glimmered. Kaell followed his guide onto a sloping path strewn with sharp stones. He stumbled. Azenor groaned but did not stir.

Across a gaping cave mouth a fire pit glowed. Two men stoking embers looked up sharply at their approach.

"It's us," the man said. He beckoned to Kaell. "Inside. You'll be safe."

Kaell carried Azenor into an enormous cavern. Men crouched around cook fires turned to stare. Flames in another pit threw shapes on a far wall. It was a sheer pane of stone, intricately carved. The façade of an ancient crumbling ruin. An arch in its centre framed a passage burrowing into the mountain.

Kaell wanted to sweep his palm over the majestic carvings. He turned to his guide. "What is this place?"

"A gateway to a long-forgotten city, abandoned for centuries."

"How did you come to be here? Who are you? Who are all these men?"

"You ask a lot of questions."

"Sorry." Carefully he laid Azenor down. "I am grateful you came along."

"Came along?" The man smiled. A satisfied smile, so guileless Kaell's scalp crept.

"No, no. We were out searching for you. Just as the drums bid us do."

The meaning sank into him. Kaell took a step back. Air parted in a soft whoosh. Pain shot through his neck. "What—?" His clutching fingers closed around a feathered dart.

"Stay calm," the man said. "It will only hurt for a moment."

Kaell's knees buckled. He hit the floor hard. The drums picked up. Their thump vibrated through the ground beneath his cheek, beating down the seconds until blackness closed in.

KAELL WOKE in a small chamber carved into stone, an ache behind his brows, his wrists bound by prickling weed to the arms of a solid chair. He twisted his hands, only to yelp as the weed burned his skin.

"Witch weed." Their guide leaned a shoulder against a wall. Lamplight fell on shaggy, brown hair. Beneath unflattering, thick brows, his gaze was expressionless. "Poison to ghouls. So sit quietly."

Kaell strained against the bonds. The vine tightened and burned. Again he winced.

"I only tried to help," the man said. "But go ahead, be stupid. Find out for yourself."

"Khir take your help. Cut me loose." Kaell yanked at the bonds again—more pain.

"More you struggle. More it hurts."

Cursing, Kaell tugged until blood streamed down his arms. With an angry huff, he stilled. "Where's the girl I was with?"

"Safe enough."

"Who are you?"

"Names are dangerous. You don't need to know mine."

"What do you intend to do with us?"

"Hear those drums?" The man looked towards a grilled door. "It's a message. About you and that girl. That's how we knew to look for you. Now listen hard."

A second beat, the tone lower, resounded very near.

His captor watched him. "That's our answer. Know what it says?"

Kaell's belly dived. He knew. The drums called Lastenarron.

"Says we have you. Safe and tight. Says: Come and collect."

"In return for what?"

"Archanin's good will."

"You're Varee." His shoulders sagged. "His people."

The man looked pleased. "You're not so ignorant after all. Yes, we serve Archanin. He is our lord, our god. Soon lord and god of all this land."

Kaell rocked his head. "I'll never serve him."

"Then you'll suffer some." With a disinterested shrug, the stranger grabbed the lamp and turned for the door.

"Wait. The girl. Don't surrender her to Archanin. Her father will pay if you ransom her."

The man paused to lift the lamp. Frowned. "You look ill."

He disappeared through the door, returning with a young woman. Smiling, she knelt before Kaell and cut her wrist over a cup.

His spine slammed into the chair. "What's she doing?"

"Feed," the man said. "We're to care for you. Our lord expects it."

She put the cup to his lips. Pulse inflamed, giddy at the scent of her blood, Kaell whipped his head aside. He could taste that blood, ferrous on his tongue, hot and smooth.

How repulsive, how disgusting, this need. Each time he drank he wore away the links to his humanity. Until the tether snapped, and he became a debased thing. A beast.

"I will not drink. Why does she do this? Did you threaten her?"

His captor waved the woman away. With a disappointed pout, she rose and backed out.

"We all open our veins for them," the man said. "Our masters take only what we can afford to give. Once a year Archanin demands a tribute. For the chosen, an ecstatic death."

Kaell recoiled in horror. "You just let him kill you?"

"We serve him."

"You should fight." Kaell tugged at the vine. Its knots seared his torn skin.

The man carried the lamp to the door. "You know nothing of us. But you will learn."

KAELL YELLED AT THE WALLS. He thumped his heels on stone. Thrashed until fire ringed his wrists. He had to get to his lord. Get Azenor to safety. Instead, he was helpless, a prisoner tormented by thoughts of what that poor woman's blood might taste like.

Just how sick was he? Only a monster thought like that.

Monster, monster, monster. The drums pulsed. No, not drums. He sat up. Screams. Shouting. Iron scraping iron. Clashing swords.

Unable to understand what was happening, he tore at the vine and violently rocked the chair until it toppled. His head struck the floor.

The door creaked. Footsteps approached.

"Who's there?"

A candle bobbed, its tallow overlaid by the odours of sweat and oil. Someone righted the chair. A man with a gleaming dome of a skull and sorrowful brown eyes studied him.

"You found him?"

The bald man nodded.

A second stranger sauntered through flickering light. One of Azenor's "swaggering dancers." With that complacent, arrogant smile, his gloved hand thrust onto his hip, his prowling strides, he had to be.

Where his companion was stocky with a brutishly powerful body, this man was tall, leanly muscled, and fluidly elegant. Short-cut black hair bristled at the nape of his neck, but a thick fringe swept long and curling onto a haughty face.

With an elaborate flourish, the swaggering dancer drove his sword into its scabbard. His polished boots squeaked as he knelt to touch the sigils on Kaell's neck and shoulder.

Kaell bristled. "Take your hands off me."

The man rose smoothly. "This is the one our lord seeks. Thank The Three we're in time."

The Three? "You're Isles men." Kaell released a relieved breath. "Azenor Caelan. She's here somewhere. Help her."

The stranger rattled a laugh. "Long while since I considered myself an Isles man, hey Joss."

"Nicky, those drums." The bald man swiped a moist brow. "We must be quick."

"Cut him free. Bring him."

"He's tied with witch vine for good reason."

"Keep the vine. But no chair. Unless you mean to carry him like that, chair and all?"

Joss dropped his head. "No, Nicky."

No Nicky. Kaell mouthed the words.

"Quickly."

"Yes, Nicky."

Yes, Nicky, Kaell silently jeered. *No, Nicky. Go screw a goat, Nicky.* He kicked the chair with his heel. "Curse it. Free me so I can find Azenor."

"But what will Joss do with all the lovely witch weed he collected?"

Kaell shrugged. "Hang himself?"

"And they say no one in these cursed hills has a sense of humour." With a white-toothed grin, Nicky looped vine around Kaell's neck and pulled it tight. "Pretty. Just your colour."

"Don't you mean the colour of your blood? The blood I'm about to spill."

"I like you," Nicky said. "You're funny." He scrunched the end of the vine in a fist and turned to his companion. "Release him, Joss. Now he's leashed, our young warrior won't struggle—too hard."

"Yes, Nicky. Whatever you say, Nicky," Kaell taunted the bald man. "Do you tug your forelock, too, when you curtsey?"

Scowling, Joss hacked through the bonds. Kaell surged up and knocked him aside.

Nicky yanked. The vine sliced into Kaell's throat. Choking, gasping, he clutched at the ligature. The Isles man threw a punch. The blow knocked him flat. Nicky kicked his belly.

"Naughty." He kicked Kaell again. "Let's be clear from the start, boy." He stooped to tie Kaell's wrists at his back with vine. "Joke away all you like. But disobey, and you suffer."

Trussed like a beast, helpless, Kaell could only glare.

Joss swayed to his feet. "Could have killed me, Nicky."

"You live a charmed life, friend." He hurled Kaell up and shoved.

He stumbled. It tore the vine from his captor's hands. Hardly able to believe his luck, Kaell broke away into a whitewashed passage. At his back, Nicky laughed.

Thick, stale air blanketed. Torches smoked in brackets. Kaell's bound hands threw off his balance as he staggered along the walls.

Nicky's laugh pursued. The tap, tap, of his steps echoed, unhurried, as though he knew Kaell had nowhere to go.

In his haste, Kaell smacked into a wall. He shook off dizziness and twisted his hands in a frenzy. When the vine came off, blood oozed from deep ruts in his wrists. The pain didn't matter. *Azenor. Find Azenor. Get away.*

"Where are you going, Kaell?" Nicky taunted. "There's no place to run."

Kaell lurched towards a fire's glow. He passed beneath an arch, part of the stone façade.

Silver-hued night beckoned at the mouth of the main cavern. But between him and escape, men prowled. Torchlight glistened on their swords, on dark stains on rock, on broken bodies and smashed weapons strewn about.

One looked his way. He called to his companions. Kaell retreated fast. From the passage Nicky's laugh floated. Kaell spun back. The men closed in, blocked him, snatched at him.

Unarmed, desperate, Kaell lashed out with ghoul strength. He kicked, punched, swung his arms. His attackers reeled. Kaell belted a shin, drawing a howl. He threw a fist, heard a crunch as a collarbone shattered.

Bodies fell on him, too many of them, forcing him down cheek to stone. Pinned by knees and elbows, he could not stop them tying his hands again with that cursed witch weed.

Nicky emerged through the arch. He leaned a shoulder to the wall, watching with a serene smile as men hurled Kaell up. "Well that was stupid, don't you think?"

No, Nicky.

"We're not here to hurt you, fool. *He* demanded we bring you to him."

"Archanin." Drained, weary to the bone, Kaell's head drooped. All he had left he threw into fighting. They could do what they wanted with him. Beat him. Humiliate him. Kill him.

"Who comes in empty night?" He mouthed an old Mountains saying. "No, not death. It is I, despair."

"Not Archanin." Nicky pushed off the wall. He grasped Kaell's jaw, his face close. Tiny lines pinched a vibrant mouth. A mass of wrinkles framed dark eyes. Not so young, then. And slender for a bladesman though his arms corded with muscle. "A lord of hope, not darkness."

Kaell cast a sneering look about. "You killed so many for your lord of hope?"

"They're Varee. Murderers and slavers. What do you care?" Nicky spun Kaell towards the moonlit entrance. "Let's move. Bring torches. Those wretched wraiths will be about."

"Azenor," Kaell said. "She's here. If you're from the Isles, please help her."

"Once an Isles man, always an Isles man, is that what you think?" Nicky turned to Joss. "Find the girl."

Joss protested. "Nicky, she'll slow us down."

"You-know-who said bring them both. Besides, threaten her, and this one behaves."

Men brought Azenor into the cavern. She struggled in their hold. "Kaell. Where's Kaell?"

"Azenor, I'm here. It's all right."

"She's safe for now." Nicky patted Kaell's cheek. "So be a good boy."

"Good?" Someone laughed. "He's a wicked little blossom."

Bile shot into Kaell's throat. He knew that voice, that laugh.

Lastenarron strolled in, blade levelled, more ghouls at his back. Iron clattered as men ripped swords free.

"Give me a sword," Kaell said. A familiar, sweet ache kicked, beating down exhaustion.

Nicky glared at Lastenarron. "Back off—thing!"

"Not until I get my flower. I'm very grateful you rounded him and the girl up for me. So grateful I might let you live—if you hand them over now."

"He's lying," Kaell said. "Give me a sword."

"No chance."

Stubborn fool. "I'm your only hope. Give me a blade."

"What part of being my prisoner don't you understand?"

Stubborn, dead fool. "What part of dying don't you understand?"

The ghouls fanned out. Men packed closer, swords levelled. A pulse bloomed in Nicky's temple. He swept his eyes over the number against them. With a grunt, he cut Kaell free.

The ghouls charged, their yells bloodcurdling. Men ran to meet them.

Kaell grabbed a discarded blade as the whirlpool caught him up, a chaos of howling, hacking, clattering metal, of groans and screams. Firelight blazed off hewing steel.

He slashed and smote, bellowing in fury as he tore apart ghouls. At each stroke, not just battle fever but a terrible song of death rose in his throat. They would not take him. He would cut down every ghoul until none stood in his way.

Nicky dismembered a ghoul with one stroke then whirled to fend off a swinging blade. Blood fountained as his riposte skewered a rib cage. A dancer, indeed.

Men dropped Azenor and leapt into the vicious fray. She cowered, arms protecting her head as swords wrought bloody destruction around her.

Kaell fought towards her, scything ghouls as he might

wildflowers. That furious strength, that dread power burned through him. Archanin's blood enhanced his skill and training. It pumped like rage, firing his sword arm, his muscles, and his will.

He decapitated two ghouls with a swish. Nicky paused for a heartbeat to stare. Then the Isles bladesman disappeared into a savage, bloody confusion of flesh and metal.

More ghouls sprang at Kaell. He swatted them back then stalked after them, impaling their bodies into the ground before they could rise. Blood, gore exploded, the dirt a slick mire. Everywhere men and ghouls cursed and panted. Steel clanged and whirred.

A ghoul cut at Kaell's legs. He jumped, thrust with iron. Hot liquid spurted. He swiped his eyes.

"Disarm him, lackwit." Lastenarron. Somewhere in the tumult.

A man spun into him then spun down, thrashing in pain. Kaell cleaved his attacker in two then ripped another apart with a one-two slash.

Heat from the fire pit walled at his back, its spitting flames gleaming on pooled blood and painting the walls with grotesque shapes. Sweat poured off his face. Clanking blades tolled in air silted with that stink of death.

A voice lanced the din. "Kaell, I'll kill her, Kaell."

Lastenarron held Azenor against him, a knife to her throat.

"Hold." Nicky gestured. Combatants broke apart. Thundering steel quietened. Ghouls retreated towards Lastenarron. Weary, panting men lowered weapons.

Lastenarron smirked at Kaell. "Put the sword down, little flower."

Nicky grabbed his arm, the fire's reflection sparking in his dark eyes. "Don't do it."

Kaell threw off his hand. He faced Lastenarron. "Only if she and these men go free."

"Done." Lastenarron slid back his lips in a half smile. "What do I care about these fools?"

"Don't do it." Nicky's stare held Kaell's. "You can't trust him."

"Decide, bonded warrior." Lastenarron pricked Azenor's throat to draw blood. Cursing, she tried to force his arm down.

"Stop." Kaell dropped his sword onto his foot. Ghouls grabbed him.

"No!" Nicky yelled. "They'll kill you. You fool—" The words choked off. A dark stain burst on his chest. Mouth slack, he collapsed in a heap.

As if she sensed Lastenarron's distraction, Azenor bit his hand. He cried out and dropped her.

Kaell kicked his sword high, flung off ghouls, and smashed into Lastenarron. The ghoul thumped into a wall. Two more attacked just as Kaell caught the somersaulting blade.

He cut them down, grabbed Azenor, and pulled her towards the entrance. The last moon dipped into a sky woven with pink and ivory.

Lastenarron staggered after him. "Daylight won't save you. I'll always find you."

Kaell lifted Azenor into his aching arms. That strength fighting unleashed leached away. A flat numbness took its place. He had nothing left. "Who comes in empty night," he whispered again. "No, not death."

"Kaell." Azenor trembled against him. "I don't know what's happening."

"It's all right. You're with me. You're safe."

Safe. He had to find something within, something beneath his exhaustion so he could defend her and get to his lord. Because Lastenarron would not give up. Kaell knew it.

BY LATE MORNING, they crossed the great gorge into the black-barked woodlands near the fortress.

Soon, the stark, square keep at Vraymorg winked through trees in cloud-dappled sunlight. Ancient towers flanking sheer walls spawned shadows over circling ditches and the gorge.

Sadness squeezed Kaell's ribs. When last he approached these gates, he was bone-tired, fingers cramped from gripping the reins, his tunic stained from a seeping wound. But returning in triumph, one of a brotherhood.

Now he came upon the gates disgraced, an outcast, with footsteps as heavy as his heart.

He dragged the hood over tousled, dirty hair. One last duty to do.

"We're close," he said. "I see Vraymorg's towers."

Azenor fisted her hands. Her voice, though, dealt the blows. "So now you can die? Well, go ahead. Just don't expect me to stay and watch."

"I won't ask you to do that, Azenor. Just as you can't ask me to live like this."

He passed a hand over gritty eyes, his tone bleak and resigned. "You know what I am. If I'm dead, I can't hurt you or anyone. In that dreadful castle when you flinched away, your instinct was right. What's inside me is monstrous."

"Why do you punish me with that again?" Her tone cut like a midwinter wind. "I no longer fear what's inside you, Kaell. Nor should you. It makes you strong."

She didn't see the danger. Or refused to recognise it.

"I hear your blood," he said quietly. "Smell it. All the time, Azenor. It awakens a terrible hunger. Like desire. Sometimes all I can think about is my lips on your throat, how your blood will taste."

He shuddered. Through sheer will he resisted. But will, even reason, would not always be enough. "So tell me, Azenor Caelan. Should I fear this darkness? Should you?"

Her bottom lip trembled. Abruptly she turned away.

Kaell sagged. Why didn't she understand his torment? He wanted an end to his misery, an end to the struggle of holding back his sick hunger for blood.

His lord would do the right thing. The only thing he could. Kill him.

But this close to the castle, to dutiful death, Kaell's feet mired in reluctance.

Once through those gates he must confront his lord. Tell him what he was. Look into his face, wanting only compassion, forgiveness, knowing that was impossible. Knowing if his lord looked upon him with disgust, he'd shrivel inside.

Azenor stood as he left her, her shoulders tight. Kaell sighed. "Azenor—"

She whipped up a palm, a barrier. Her eyes were wet.

Thinking she feared for him, he muttered, "My lord will know what to do. It will be all right."

The girl swiped at tears. "I'm not crying for you. I'm crying because. Just because." She shook her head.

THE ROAD SLASHED the forest then meandered through fields of sun-bleached grass and wind-rippled sweetbox. Kaell looked for outriders but saw none. He frowned.

Near the walls and still no challenge, Kaell's unease grew. Crouching, he sought signs of a battle. No churned earth or flattened grass. No broken arrowheads.

Azenor sensed his restlessness. "What is it?"

"I don't know. Maybe nothing."

She held his arm, taking this last chance to throw stale words. He knew them so well he could mouth them with her. "Don't do this, Kaell. At Tide's End we'll both be safe."

"Safe," he muttered. "Ha. Will I be safe from myself?"

The fortress gates gaped, the portcullis roped high. Only two guardsmen defended the gatehouse. One levelled his sword. "State your business."

"Surely you know me, Salwyn?"

Nothing. Then a tremulous, "Kaell? It is you?" The grey-bearded soldier drew taller. "But we thought—it's been months. They said you were dead."

If only. "Where is everyone?"

Salwyn swept a puzzled frown to Azenor. "The king is marching on the Isles. Many of the fighting men have already joined him. The rest leave soon with Vraymorg."

"Where will I find my lord?"

"In the great hall."

Kaell felt the guardsman follow them with his eyes as they crossed the near-empty ward.

Leather groaned as a stableboy tended to two sweat-lathered horses. From the forge, a man he once wrestled into the dirt flung down tools and wiped grubby hands on a soot-stained apron. Only a handful of soldiers commanded the walls.

The ward usually bustled with noise and movement, with shouts, laughter, the clip-clop of hooves, hammering iron, yapping dogs. A tumult of life overpowering the slow tolling bell in the well house. But now its ominous echo resonated through the earth.

A stranger barred their way at the steps to the hall, barked, "You cannot enter."

Weary, impatient, and sorrow sick, Kaell didn't argue. He flung the guard into the ward. The man lay groaning.

Hand in Azenor's, Kaell shouldered inside. At the sight of the hall, his heart splintered.

So unchanged, from the guards lining hewed walls, to the roaring fire, to the odours of beeswax and ash, to the castle's bored lord seated high, chin resting on his palm.

A stoop-shouldered man addressing Vraymorg turned to stare. *Him? Here?* Caelmarsh, soon to witness his humiliation. Kaell nearly laughed, a mad cackle for the cruel gods.

The wooden doors clanged shut at their backs. Guards rushed to surround them, swords drawn. Kaell squeezed Azenor's shaking hand. "Everything's fine. My lord will protect you."

He dropped his hood.

Silence. It sank down into the hall like a prowling beast. It sank down into him.

Faces turned inch by inch to him, every movement sluggish as though time stalled then only slowly released. Weighted hands lifted to cover gaping mouths.

Kaell's breaths beat in his skull, a laboured inhalation, a forced release. An endless, dismal thrumming. He was aware of Azenor's fingers gripping his, that her lips formed words he didn't hear.

Then the spell lifted. Sound and movement exploded. Gasps, mutters, disbelieving stares, shuffled feet. But beneath, that tremolo of silence sang unbroken.

"Kaell." Azenor's voice shrilled as guards grabbed her. "What's happening?"

Throat pinched, limbs like jelly, he could not answer. A pain burst in his heart. For at last, Kaell must lift his eyes to that chair. To his lord.

Vraymorg surged to his feet. He stood stunned. For a heartbeat. For another beat. A third. Then, like an arrow loosed, he strode at Kaell with furious vigour.

"Vraymorg," Caelmarsh said. "Beware. His eyes are black."

His lord shuddered to a halt before Kaell. "No." A single word, torn out. "No. Your eyes. Kaell, it can't mean—it can't—"

Kaell hung his head. Shame blocked his throat. He swallowed hard. "Ghouls took my blood, my lord."

Shock stirred through the long hall, a whisper, a sigh that hit stone walls and fragmented into a cacophony of venomous murmurs. The sounds knifed Kaell's back.

He met his lord's eyes. They thrust like blunted daggers, seeking to pierce his defences. Filled not just with anger. That he could bear. But misery? That he could not.

"They took your blood." Vraymorg carved words with disbelief. "And you live? How?"

Because the gods play with me, he might answer. *Because I failed you.* He said nothing.

"Who is this?" Vraymorg whirled on Azenor. "Is she cursed also?"

"No, no, my lord," Kaell said quickly. "This is Azenor of the Isles. Archanin's prisoner but free now. I beg you; return her safely to her father and brothers."

Muttering fell away into that boiling silence. Every breath held. Only the fire's crackle and a rush of wind beyond the walls silted the hush.

Vraymorg tapped fingers on his belt. "You are Azenor Caelan?"

"I am. Tell these oafs to release me."

"My lady." Vraymorg paused halfway into a bow as though noting her unseeing stare. "You are unharmed?"

"I am unharmed, my lord." She traced his voice. "Kaell freed me."

"Kaell freed you?"

"Must I say it twice? Kaell freed me."

Caelmarsh bristled at Vraymorg's side. "Look at him. He is a ghoul. Strike him down."

"I see what he is."

"He is a ghoul. Kill him."

"Curb your bloodthirsty impatience. I will do my duty." Vraymorg gestured to a servant.

"Take the lady to suitable chambers. Look after her." He closed his hand about the hilt of a hip sword. "As for Kaell. Disarm him. Bind him—chain not rope."

"My lord." A guardsman nervously levelled his sword. "Where shall we put him? In the tower?"

"Take him below. Bring me the key."

HIS PRISON WAS a den of slippery stone below the hall. Cold and damp seeped through his clothes. Iron circled his wrists. The stench from a forgotten slop bucket tasted acidic at the back of his parched throat.

Kaell's shoulders ached. His belly growled with hunger. But he could wait. His lord would come. He had to come.

Darkness absorbed a line of torchlight beneath the door. Back to the wall, legs stretched, Kaell fell into a shallow sleep where Archanin stroked his cheek. He fled in horror back to wakefulness and the chilled cell.

Where was Vraymorg? Had he forgotten him? Left him to rot in this black hole, alone?

A tear strained. Ashamed, he wanted to brush it aside but could not. It ran down his cheek to his lips. Kaell gagged. Even his tears now tasted foul.

A key turned. Air fanned as iron creaked. A brand flared in a sconce, splattering light on a man in the doorway.

Shrouded in stillness, torchlight rimming his dark hair, he might be but a shadow except for a restless patter of fingers on steel and forced breaths that shattered the emptiness.

Kaell almost sobbed with longing. If only this man knelt beside him, brushed hair from his brow and whispered it was all right, that he need no longer face this alone.

Yet beneath that yearning, that splinter-thin hope, there was a voice, so soft and malicious, so relentless. He was everything his lord hated. There could be no comfort. Kaell turned his head aside, ashamed, wanting to hide from his lord's gaze.

"The guards shackled you tight, I see." Vraymorg's tone was as bleak as his dull-eyed stare, his grimly set mouth. "They fear you no doubt. Are you uncomfortable?"

"Not so much."

"Do you need—have you fed?"

"I'm all right, my lord."

The quiet lengthened. A clandestine murmur of wind crept from the passage. A rat skittered in the gloom. His lord's fingers rapped, unnaturally loud.

"I would lock you in the tower, but—"

"No. I hate the tower. This is as good a place as any—for a monster." Kaell forced a laugh. No matter the breaking in his breast, he must be strong. His lord hated weakness.

Vraymorg crouched. With hesitant fingers he traced the scars on Kaell's neck.

A sob tried to push into Kaell's throat. But a weight trapped it within, a weight upon his ribs.

Those hands that touched the evidence of his shame once soothed his fears the night the priests had cut him. Those same hands had gripped a shoulder to encourage him when he fell or held him when he coughed with winter fevers.

He trusted those hands to take up his sword and end this.

A drumming began in his head. At first Kaell wondered if it ground through the earth. Then he knew it was only his breaths, too loud.

Vraymorg dropped his hand. Slowly he rose, his body locked with an awful tension. He drew Kaell's blade, its gleam sinister in torchlight.

Light beat upon his dark hair, dark eyes. His shallow breaths rasped. His fingertips stole along the blade as they might along a lover's body. The rest of him seemed very still.

Then Vraymorg hurled the sword against the wall. The clank smashed the silence. The man began to yell, to shout out anger and frustration he could no longer contain.

A storm raged, fierce but brief. When it passed, Vraymorg braced a palm against stone, drained, panting. Lost.

Kaell watched in astonishment, uncomfortable at his lord's unleashed despair. He did not understand it. In that moment, he wondered if he really knew this man at all.

Do not flinch from what you must do. I am a monster. I want you to end this.

His lord said, "You'll die at first light tomorrow." He dragged long fingers through his curling hair. He looked impossibly young, his face strained, all pretence at indifference gone.

Kaell wanted to comfort him, tell him this was what he wanted. That death would end the nightmares, the guilt.

"Kaell," his lord muttered. "Kaell. Was I kind when I should have been crueller? Did I fail you? Did I not prepare you? What can I do?"

"Your duty, my lord."

A skirring wind hunted the passage. Dense air prickled with damp. Vraymorg's haunted gaze dwelled. "Why?" he said. "Kaell, why did you return?"

When he made no answer, Vraymorg snatched up the torch and turned for the door.

"My lord." Chains jangled as Kaell pushed forward. "Don't leave me in darkness. Not tonight." He seized a breath. "Please stay. Just a while. I must tell you all—about what happened in Thom and everything I know about Archanin. Things you need to know."

"Is this why you returned?"

"I wanted Azenor safe. And"—he jerked his chin up, keeping back sadness—"I knew you'd know what to do. That you'd help me."

A bitter laugh burst from his lord. "Help you? I must execute you with that cursed sword."

"You taught me never to fear death," Kaell said.

His lord said nothing.

"I remember your words," Kaell said. "'There were far worse fates than death,' you said. 'And things beyond.'"

Vraymorg stared where there was nothing to see. "And there are," he said.

VAL ARQUES

Vraymorg's sword slapped his thigh as he strode away from that foul hole. He let it hit him, just as he let his anger and grief wash through him, not resisting it, not thinking on it. His body ached for combat against anyone who could hold a sword or throw a punch.

No time. The Isles girl waited. With accusations? Questions? And his duty was what?

Duty. It offered order when misery thought to strip his reason.

He burst through the doors into the lesser hall.

Azenor sat at a long table near the fire. The gown the servants had found for her tightly clung to her slim-waisted, full-bosomed figure. Her brushed hair fell in curls about bare shoulders. A generous mouth carved an impatient grimace as she traced his footsteps.

Surprised at what the dirt had hidden, Vraymorg could not help but stare. She wasn't beautiful, at least not in the elegant way Rozenn was. Her wide mouth was too obstinate, the ridges of her Isles cheekbones too stark.

But there was something wild and fascinating about her. Beneath level brows, her eyes were like storm clouds, the candlelight gleaming upon their dark brilliance, her untamed hair black and lush.

He was about to tear his gaze away when fine hairs lifted on his arms. The Enarae. It clung to this woman. He could smell it.

"Forgive my delay." He found his voice. "Caelmarsh will join us shortly. As the king's grand constable he has questions. I cannot put him off."

"You were with Kaell."

"Yes." Vraymorg waved the servants away and slid into a chair opposite her.

"I know what he wants, the stupid oaf. He wants you to kill him." Her voice rose as relentless and brittle as worn iron. "You won't. I know you won't. Not if you love him. And I think you love him."

Vraymorg drew a startled breath. Confronting words from a stranger. Few challenged him so forcefully. And usually only when they wielded steel.

He poured wine, refusing to think about her words, placing a glass by her hand.

"Wine, my lady?"

"Save him." Azenor groped for the glass. "If you love him, find a way."

Vraymorg gulped a mouthful. His gut swooped with sick despair at the memory of Kaell's sword on the floor in that damp prison. Too few hours until dawn.

"Kaell must die."

"Why? He hasn't killed. Not like a ghoul, at least. He's strong enough not to." Her eyes fixed on his face but looked beyond. Disconcerting.

Vraymorg pushed away her words, would not let them dwell in his mind. Could not. "You speak directly, my lady, so I will do the same."

Duty. Focus on duty. "I cannot return you to your father. He and the king, my liege lord, are at war. I am sorry, but Caelmarsh will question you and then deliver you to Cathmor."

"You're not sorry," she said. "You're like my brothers, my

father. All of them *dutiful.* Just as Kaell thinks his duty is to die. Why? If he hasn't killed, then why?"

He pressed his palms into the table. "I can't talk about this. About Kaell."

"Tell me why he must die?"

Vraymorg briefly closed his eyes. "Why won't you let this rest, girl? You know why. He is tainted, an abomination. A bonded warrior with ghoul blood. Unthinkable."

"It isn't his fault. He should not pay with his life."

"And if I let him live? What will he become? Not now, but in a year, a lifetime, a century? Sooner or later, he'll succumb to his appetites just as Archanin intends."

Her fingers tightened about the wineglass. "You don't know that. You don't. By what right do you judge him? Who are these vicious Mountains gods who say he must die?"

"Who are you to decide what's best for Kaell?"

Had she paced by his bed when Kaell burned with fever? Had she comforted him with stories when he woke screaming? Had she, knowing the hard task ahead, disciplined the boy when instinct shouted to ruffle his hair, smile, and shield him in his arms?

And yet, he could not forget how Kaell gazed fondly at her in the hall. Or her anger and fear when he surrendered. Something bound them.

"To spare him is cruel—to Kaell. He does not wish to become a monster."

"So you'd kill a boy you raised like a son?" Her voice whipped with contempt. *If she were a man, I'd look to my sword,* he thought. "A boy you love. You love him. I know it."

A rising wind moaned through a tower. Bells in the well house jangled softly.

Again he lowered his lids to shut out the room, her words. Except they would not retreat, only sat between them. An accusation.

He said, "I cannot love him."

A cold, sharp ache tore at his breast, his belly hollow, his shoulders so rigid they hurt. The tolling bells like splinters in his temples. Her hand frozen on the wineglass. Her lips pressed into a disbelieving sneer.

In a low voice, she said, "You sit there and say that? Just like that?"

He did not reply. What answer could he give?

"He loves you like a father. I hear it every time he says your name. My lord this, my lord that. He's about to die, miserable because he thinks he failed you. And all you can do is sit there and say you can't love him. Can't? *Can't!*"

"You don't understand."

"He's not a monster. The only monster in this castle is you!"

The chair scraped as he surged to his feet. "You go too far, girl. How dare you judge me!"

"You don't go far enough." Her anger sparked like lightning, a match for his. Yet he sensed something within it. Something she couldn't face. As if it was easier to lash out at him, a stranger, than accept an uncomfortable feeling.

Guilt?

"Why can't you love him? Tell me that, *my lord*. Make me understand what is so wrong with you that you can't love him?"

"You—don't—know," he said. "It hurts. Gods, how it hurts to love. I can't let myself. Not again. Never again."

"If you're so afraid to love, it's you who may as well be dead."

He sat down hard. Her words thrust like sharpened steel. Dully, he said, "You would not understand. How could you? You're a child. A pampered Isles princess." He rolled his wine cup in his hand. "You're not strong enough to hear uncomfortable truths."

Azenor thrust out her chin. "I have courage and strength enough for any truth."

Did she? If not for this undercurrent, this sense she, too, hid from something she couldn't accept, he might have believed her.

Vraymorg drank quickly. Part of him wanted to storm out, to

snatch up a sword, find one of his captains, and sweat out his doubts. The other part needed to unload his burden, share a part of himself, to breathe with a lightness of spirit, if only for an hour.

"Who are you, Azenor Caelan?" A woman of his blood. Who walked beyond the Enarae. Could such a woman understand his pain?

"I am a woman who is not afraid to feel."

But he was. Afraid. "Then you have not known real pain. The sort that grinds your heart to dust. If I let myself feel deeply again, Azenor Caelan, it shall destroy me. And what of Kaell then? If I let myself love then how can I do my duty to him?"

"Duty," she muttered.

"Yes, duty. Soon I must go to that prison and kill him. He trusts me to do that, this child I raised. No one else will do that for him."

"You speak as though death is the only answer."

"Life can be much crueller than death. I know this because—" He exhaled slowly. "Because Kaell isn't the first bonded warrior I've trained nor the first I've seen die."

"You mock me with lies because I can't see you. Your voice is a young man's. You move like a young man. How many warriors could you have trained?"

Vraymorg struck the table with his fist. She jumped.

"You said you had courage enough for the truth!" He let the silence linger, let it build around them.

"I do," she whispered.

"Then you will hear it all. But you will not tell Kaell what I've said."

Azenor passed a tongue over her lips. "Take me to him. Let me stay with him until dawn. That is when you will do it, isn't it?"

His voice caught. "Yes, dawn." A sigh. A snatched breath. "I will take you to him. If you say nothing of what we speak of now."

"I give you my word."

Such a fragile quality to her. Like an orchid's wondrous bloom that faded overnight. He guessed what had befallen her as

Archanin's captive. No king, no lord would want her now.

"Then I'll tell you a story, Azenor Caelan. I'll tell you who I am. If you can bear to hear it."

The fire crackled. The wind outside smote bitter and cold, its harsh song for him alone. He half heard footsteps, a murmur of voices as though far away. Strangeness eddied. It sat about them. Nothing existed beyond it. Only them.

"Tell me," she said.

Vraymorg gulped more wine. He longed to give voice to his darkness but feared memory's perilous, bitter sting. "Then make what you will of this. I am cursed to train every bonded one. And watch every one of them die."

Cinders whipped up like crimson stardust as a charred log clunked in the hearth. A curl of smoke rose off torches. A lambent flame hissed.

"I think I misheard you." Her voice shook. Torchlight caught a flicker of fear in her eyes.

"You heard."

"It can't be true," she said.

Vraymorg grasped her wrist. "I smell the Enarae on you. You've walked close to the otherworld, yet you doubt what I say?"

She paled, her eyes wide. "Go on."

Vraymorg released her. He sat back.

"Centuries ago, Queen Devarsi let a banished god and his people into this realm to help her steal the throne from your ancestor, Ryol. He turned on her, and she begged the ancient gods for help. Khir promised a bladesman of exceptional strength and skill to smite ghouls. The first bonded warrior. I raised him and taught him to fight. Survive." His voice cracked. "I loved that boy. I saw him die. I loved the next. I saw him die as well. Each time, grief settled within me, layers upon layers of sorrow. Love means pain. I can't love anymore."

And yet—Kaell. Oh gods, he tried to feel nothing. No. No. No. He *would* feel nothing. Through force of will alone. "Kaell was four, perhaps younger, when I took him—as Khir commanded—from his mother's arms. I did not question Khir's choice, only did my duty."

"Do you mean—" She closed a trembling hand about the glass stem. "Are you telling me you're centuries old?"

"Centuries old," he laughed bitterly. "A wise description. If you said I'd lived for centuries, I might dispute your words. I don't think I've been alive for years. Every time one of these young men died, I died with them. Or a part of me did—the best part. Sometimes I feel like a ghost, hardly able to care what happens to me anymore."

But for a breath of air cool in her hair, she did not move.

His mouth was stale. He had no idea what she might say. Or if he even wanted her to speak. The need to flee boiled up in him again, to shove every memory down. Forget.

The air thickened with smoke, with the aroma of their wine.

Azenor groped across the table for his hand then his arm. She lifted her fingertips to his face. As she slowly traced his brow, his cheekbones, his lips, he sat mesmerised.

A curious intimacy webbed them. His breath, her warmth, the tenderness of her touch.

"I don't think I would have the courage to go on," she said. "To be so alone."

The words sank into him. Roughly he pulled away. "I don't want your pity, Azenor Caelan. I told you the truth only to show you why I must shield my heart."

"And yet," she said softly. "Despite every shield you throw up, you love him."

You love him. His breath stripped away so fast it hurt. Vraymorg dragged taut fingers down his face.

"You love him. You love Kaell."

"Stop saying that." Vraymorg rose unsteadily. He gripped the chair back.

"Take me to him," she said. "Let me give him the comfort you won't."

He seized his cup and drained the wine. "Will you first answer me something?"

"If I can."

"Kaell told me Archanin took his blood. Is there more to know?"

Azenor again fell silent for so long he thought she would refuse to speak. Then she nodded. "There is more to know."

"He tortured him."

She hesitated. "Yes."

The back of his neck dampened with unease. "What happened to him?"

Azenor scraped a wounded noise in her throat. A shadow masked her brooding eyes. Gods, she was full of secrets. Strong but fragile. Fascinating.

"Tell me," he said, his voice hoarse with need. "Tell me only what you can bear to say."

Azenor clasped her hands tightly on the table. He knew her look from men on the battlefield seeking vengeance. However Archanin hurt her, she was using it to sharpen her anger.

"I shall tell you. Once said I will not say it again, not to my father, not to my brothers. So Kaell does not have to say it." A pause. A sigh. "They chained Kaell in their hall. Archanin drank from him. A spectacle." She spat the words in disgust. "He told me how Kaell screamed, how he tasted. So smug. Pleased with his captive. Pleased he submitted."

"What do you mean submitted?"

"Archanin is apparently unnaturally lovely. Blind, or nearly so, I could deny him all except what he took. But Kaell." Another pause. She inhaled slowly as if to keep control. "He had no choice—"

Vraymorg's glass shattered in his grip.

Azenor started. "What was that?"

"I do not believe you." His gut twisted. "Not with a ghoul god. Kaell wouldn't—"

He broke off. Why should she lie? He dropped his eyes to his scarred wrists. He, most of all, knew how powerless a captive was.

Azenor grasped his arm. "Do not judge him. Kaell was alone. Helpless. With no prospect of rescue or death. And this fallen god, this hateful god, is not only seductive but commands strong magic."

Like that sorcerer who had held Vraymorg so many centuries ago. How quickly his thoughts scurried to the past, finding no protection, only barbed memories buried so deep they surfaced only in nightmares. Time healed nothing.

"I beg you. If you will not spare him, then let me be with him until dawn, until he dies."

He took her to Kaell.

VRAYMORG SLUMPED IN his chair in the darkening hall. Embers glowed in the hearth. Wind hunted through towers. But beneath all sat his heart, thumping, hurting. He drank quickly to banish thought. Whatever else he did this night, he must not think.

Where was Caelmarsh? The brute made a good drinking companion.

With an unsteady hand, he emptied his glass. Cahirean wine. It filled his vaults. Enough to bathe in, as he once told that snake Paulin. Thanks to Rozenn. Payment. For use of his body.

Despite the ill she did him, a ripple of desire heated his blood. So beautiful, Rozenn. But so cold compared to the Isles girl he left kneeling beside Kaell. A girl who fell against Vraymorg, weeping. A girl with deft fingers that groped for keys.

"Take Kaell and run," he could have said. But he was the king's man, his duty clear. Execute Kaell. Deliver Azenor as a hostage to Cathmor.

Yet he didn't take the keys from her. Keys or no keys, they could hardly walk through the gates. Fate set their paths.

I could keep her here. The thought surprised him. *Make an offer for her. A spoil of war.*

A cry of terror rose from the wall. Vraymorg rushed to the windows. Men roiled between the towers, gestures wild, a bustle of steel and alarm.

Shapes dropped from the walls into the ward with a telltale flicker of torchlight on iron.

Not warriors of this castle.

Cold, hard fear speared him. How did strangers breach the walls? At dusk, the castle was locked down, its enormous gates shut, sentries upon the walk.

He scooped up his sword and ran from the hall, almost colliding with Philip on the steps. "How many?" Vraymorg said. "Who?"

The young soldier panted. "Two hundred or more. My lord, they're—"

"How did they get into the castle?" Vraymorg already moved past him.

"They appeared from nowhere. But my lord—"

Vraymorg turned.

"My lord," his captain rasped. "They're ghouls."

Shock numbed him. Too briefly. Then anger emptied his lungs.

Kaell. All a trick, his surrender, his pleas for death. The traitor had led ghouls here, told them how to take the castle. Fury nearly drove him back to the cell. One swing of that blade—

"Get everyone into the tower. I'll win you time."

Philip hastened away. Vraymorg raged down the stairs into the ward.

Beneath a fat, low moon, torchlight distorted shapes hewing and hacking with steel. Archers upon the walls loosed fire arrows at ghouls surging through the gaping metal gates. Broken timber from a brattice burned where it crashed.

The castle's keeper took it all in as he sprang and decapitated a ghoul with a swing and a yell. Even as his blade swept a head from shoulders, he fell upon another. This one screeched and reeled away, the blow only wounding.

No time to finish him. More ghouls attacked, slashing with axes and swords. Mercilessly, efficiently, he cut them down as he might lop off braids of hair. Blood spouted like dark, eerie fountains against moonlight.

Hopeless. There were too many invaders against just thirty defenders. Even with the ally of daylight in a few hours, none of his men would be alive then.

"To the old tower!" Vraymorg shoved a man towards the steps. "Get inside."

Despair fuelled his hatred and strength. Roaring, he slashed, thrust, his sword greedy for non-human blood. But still they came through the gates with trampling feet and hunting metal. More for him to slaughter.

Bodies heaped, both wounded and dead. Vraymorg's sword ripped and cleaved and scattered death, his shout of defiance rallying his outnumbered men. Blood and mashed innards splattered through his hair, stained his clothes. All impulse shut down to one thing: kill.

More ghouls circled. Then more still. Roaring, he leapt at them. Wild, useless thoughts flickered. Was Kaell safe? Philip? They were his last thoughts for a long while.

HIS CAPTORS CARRIED him into the hall amid a clamour of booted feet and raised voices. Dropped him on stone.

"You hit him hard, Raggamirron."

"He is an excellent bladesman. It was only luck we took him alive."

Vraymorg struggled to care. Every part of him throbbed. An exhausted stupor clung not just to his body but his mind as though it could not take any more.

"This man is surely too young to be the lord of this dread castle."

"This must be him. He fought with rare skill. I almost paused to watch."

"They all look young, I suppose."

The voices dimmed. Vraymorg drifted into blackness, thinly veiled, with sounds and shadows muffled through the ether. He surfaced with a groan. His head pounded.

Ghouls hurled him into a chair and bound his wrists to its arms. Forcing open heavy lids, he blinked into irritating torchlight in the room where he'd last sat—and argued, curse her daring—with Azenor. The pieces of his glass, the carafe, their trenchers still lay on the table.

A ghoul leaned over him. "He lives. I clearly didn't hit him hard enough." The ghoul moved aside, leaving Vraymorg staring at a creature so striking his breath fled.

Torchlight tinted golden hair, polished the unearthly blue of almond-shaped eyes. Booted, with a cape draping heavy shoulders, he wore an emerald tunic, its silk embroidered with silver thread, a knife and sword at a belted waist.

Anger burned away his exhaustion. Vraymorg knew who stood before him. Only Archanin could possess this repellent beauty and power.

"You unnatural beast," he shouted, tearing at his bonds. "I know what you did to Kaell. You'll suffer for it. I swear it."

Archanin levelled ice pale eyes. "Where is Kaell?"

Chained to a wall below this room. Easy to find. Vraymorg glared. "How should I know?"

"You're a better liar than the boy. But not good enough. You had Kaell in irons. I found your prison though he is gone. Tell me where you hid him. Azenor too." The ghoul swept a hand at the table. "She sat there and not long ago. I know the perfume of her skin well."

Vraymorg hissed, "How did you take this castle?"

"Far too easily." Archanin fluttered a hand. "The king stripped most of your warriors from you so he can assault the Isles. So foolish. He leaves this vital castle vulnerable to settle some petty dispute with his cousin."

"What do you know about it, snake?"

"Such an insolent tone for a man completely at my mercy. You should be afraid of what I intend to do to you."

Vraymorg shrugged.

Archanin leaned over his captive. "Curious. I sense resentment, anger, but not fear."

Vraymorg glared but said nothing.

"Yes," Archanin said softly. "You are the man who trained Kaell. Who else but a man without fear? A man, my faithful Raggamirron declares a swordsman without equal."

"You like the sound of your own voice, I see."

"I like to be obeyed. I like my questions answered. I begin to have questions about you."

He released a soft breath in his captive's face. An otherworldly scent swirled. Musky, dense as amber. It prickled Vraymorg's nostrils, his thoughts thick, his body sluggish.

Growling, he threw off the spell. "Keep out of my head."

Archanin stepped back. "Interesting. I sense you have no magic, yet you repel my spells. Tell me where Kaell is, and while my warriors fetch him, we'll talk about who you might be."

"If you're so sure he's here, find him." Vraymorg wrenched at the bonds. "This castle is yours. Open every door. Walk every passage."

"My warriors searched every crevice except the tower where your men cower with the women."

"And they call us craven dogs," a ghoul sniggered. His lord gestured for silence. Again he menaced with a lean. "I followed Kaell here. I will have him back."

"To kill him? If he came here, I would do that for you."

That drew a harsh, unpleasant laugh. "Kaell is very willing to die. You taught him well. In that, if nothing else. However"—Archanin stroked a lip—"I do not want him dead."

"Then what will you do with him?"

"I'll chain him in darkness until he breaks. And he will. Break and bow." The ghoul god sang the words. "Break and bow. Isn't that what the prophecy says? That the nineteenth bonded warrior will break, bow, and serve me in this coming war."

The prophecy. Vraymorg's heart tightened like tuned strings. "You're speaking nonsense."

"Surely your priests read the signs? The seer's enchantments fade." Archanin straightened with a sigh. "I sense torturing you for answers will take too long. So what to do with you?"

"Lord's blood," the other ghoul jeered. "Too thin to drink."

"A lord." Archanin rested a hand on the chair back. "A lord who looks too young to command this vile den of stone, a lord who stinks of the Enarae."

"If I knew to expect guests I'd have bathed in scented water. Roses perhaps?"

Archanin smiled, genuinely amused. "I recognise your black humour in Kaell. It hides much." He tore out a knife and slashed away ropes on Vraymorg's left wrist. With a gloved finger he traced the white scars. "What sort of despair makes a young lord do that?"

Vraymorg laughed coldly.

The blue gaze steadied on his face. "You're really not afraid of me, are you?"

"Not especially. You'll kill me. So what?"

"So what." Archanin tapped the chair arm. "It's not feigned, either, this lack of fear. It makes you singular." He paused. "What might frighten you, I wonder?"

Thoughtful, he removed his glove, circled the chair, and trailed a hand over his captive's shoulders.

Beneath his touch Vraymorg's skin crept. He forced himself to sit still.

"You're tense. Interesting."

"Your hand is cold."

The ghoul god strained a lock of hair through fingers. "So dark and thick. You cut it too short, like a brute warrior's. It should fall softly about your face, caress your neck, flow about these fine, muscular shoulders. If you were mine—"

Vraymorg jerked so hard the chair rocked.

Archanin laughed. "Now you're afraid. I think the chink in your armour shows, my lord." He grasped Vraymorg's scarred wrist and drew it to his lips, tonguing damp skin.

Vraymorg fought for indifference. His jaw tightened in disgust.

"Even more afraid. And now?" Yanking his head back, Archanin kissed his lips.

Rigid, he did not resist.

Archanin pulled away. "As lifeless as marble. I admire your control, but I'll force a reaction from you. We have a little time while my warriors search the grounds." He kissed Vraymorg harder, his tongue forcing its way through clenched lips.

A ghoul burst in, breathless. Archanin turned. "Well, do you have him?"

"Raggamirron tracked Kaell to a passage beneath the walls," the ghoul panted. "He also bid me tell you three warriors collapsed, sick."

Archanin drummed fingers on the chair back. "Time to abandon this dread fortress with walls reeking of enchantment."

Vraymorg knew the castle had hidden defences. Roaran's magic was why ghouls had never dared breach the fortress before.

Archanin spoke rapidly to the messenger in the ghoul tongue then bent over his prisoner again. "This passage. Kaell knows of it?"

"Kaell is as familiar with this castle as I am."

Archanin touched fingertips to Vraymorg's cheek. "You guard your words as carefully as you guard your emotions. How I would like to break you down, lay bare—shall we say—every hidden desire."

Another ghoul entered. "My lord." He bowed. "We cannot smash into that warded tower. More warriors complain of dizziness."

"That cursed Roaran Caelan and his nasty, sorcerous ways." Archanin pulled on a glove. "Put the word about: We leave at once." Pausing, gloved hand on his sword hilt, he considered his captive. "You flinched before. You knew Kaell was the nineteenth bonded warrior. But you arrogantly believed you could save him. You should have killed him."

Vraymorg wet his lips, remembering the awful words in Rozenn's book. "I could say the same for you."

"Nonsense prophecies about three bloodlines together? That a warrior with my blood, Seithin blood, and true Caelan blood, will kill me?"

"One can only hope."

Archanin peeled back a lip. "You don't believe your own words. You want me to fear Kaell and kill him. You seek to provoke me to kill you."

"My lord." The other ghoul shifted his weight. "Raggamirron says—"

His lord stopped him with a gesture. He did not shift his blue eyes from Vraymorg.

"I would like to take you with us and explore what we began to uncover. But it is self-indulgent to drag prisoners around simply because they fascinate me."

He drew his knife. Sighed. "Ah well. You must take your secrets to the grave. A pity. I might enjoy breaking a man with no fear. Forgive the lack of artistry, my lord, but time defeats me."

He stabbed Vraymorg in the heart.

KAELL

The tunnel's chill pawed bare skin, its air stale and thick. The low roof and narrow walls trapped odours of damp earth and moss. Water trickled down slimy stone, green glowing when Kaell's pitiful torch flamed past, barely licking the darkness.

Azenor held his arm, but neither spoke. Kaell's steps fell into a dazed staccato. His body tight, his throat constricted, he struggled to grasp how his fate had turned. He had been ready to die. Time, immeasurable in the blackness of that cell, led only to an end.

Until she came. Until his lord brought her to that prison. Until she unlocked his shackles, cruelly insisting he lived a little longer and returned her to the Isles.

"You shouldn't have freed me," he blurted at last. "I could have broken the chains. I chose not to. I accepted my fate, Azenor. Once I knew you were safe, I was ready to die."

She scoffed. "Safe? Your precious lord intended to give me to Cathmor."

"My lord would not do that." Kaell tapped his sword hilt with stiff fingers. "He'll protect you, Azenor. He knows his duty."

"His duty? Oh yes, his duty to bend and scrape to his vicious king. To kill you."

"Yes, his duty to kill me," Kaell snapped. "Why don't you

understand?" He seized a frustrated breath. "All right. I'll get you to the Isles. But then I'll return to my lord. I know my duty too."

Azenor drew up so abruptly he nearly fell against her. "What is it?" Kaell swung the torch.

"Duty." She bunted air with a palm. "I'm so sick of that word. I hear it constantly from Aric. Now for days and days it's all I hear from you. You'll live and die for duty. Is there nothing more, Kaell?"

"How can there be?" His mouth tasted acrid. "You know what I am. I don't get a fairy-tale ending, Azenor. No bonded warrior does. My lord will do what's right."

"You thick-headed fool." She slapped her thigh. "Why don't you see it? I don't want him to do what's right. I don't want—" Her voice fell away into a vacuum.

He shone the torch. Revealed in its bleak light Azenor seemed altered. Shoulders rigid, her brows drew down as if her outburst, her feelings surprised and frightened her. She clamped a palm over her mouth, holding in words.

"What do you mean?"

"Nothing. It's just"—she took a breath—"I don't want you to die."

She cared. Kaell smothered a giddy roar of lightness. She spoke as his friend, that was all. Why torment his heart with dreams of tenderness?

Azenor stood so close he glimpsed moisture beading her brow. She lifted a hand, hesitant. Then she touched his cheek. A spell fell upon him. Kaell could not move. Her fingertips stole to his lips. As she leaned to kiss him, her breath smelt of wine.

The dream.

Dank water streamed down jutting rocks. The scent of her hair and skin, the taste and touch of lips banished the mud and rotting moss. The weight of his body pressed down through feet rooted in stone, his mind emptied of everything but her.

She pulled away, a palm on his breast.

Kaell had no words. The stillness in his mind imploded into a confused chaos he could not unravel. He badly wanted to run his fingers through Azenor's hair. To kiss her again, let their hips and thighs melt together. She had haunted his dreams. Why?

If only there were hours, days, years where he and Azenor could break down that mystery of friendship, the vulnerability of it, its unspoken bonds of joy and pain and belonging.

With time, friendship could become something more. *Couldn't it?*

But time was like the sea, dark and silent and cold as it ebbed away. For a man no longer human, there were no days or years. No love. Only duty. His clear duty: Take her to the Isles then return to his lord.

Almost timidly Kaell placed her hand on his arm to lead her forward. They spoke little. When their shoulders rubbed, she flinched.

"Sorry," he mumbled.

"For what? One kiss and you're afraid to touch me?"

"Because I'm an oaf."

"Because you're a man, more like. Though the two naturally go together."

"Oafs, too, may learn to swagger," Kaell broke into song to break the tension. "To dance with swords or even daggers."

Azenor tugged at her hair. "I'm stuck in a mud tunnel with a failed poet. Is this death?"

"Sadly, no." He trudged on, too aware of her fingers entwined with his, this small touch as intimate as if their bodies pressed skin to skin. "How *did* you free me?"

"I stole the key to your chains when I fell against your lord—accidentally, of course."

At her smirk, Kaell grinned. The powerful Lord of the Pass deceived.

His smile died. What would Vraymorg think when he found them gone? That Kaell had cowardly fled death? Nausea churned in his belly. His duty to Azenor done, he would return. Explain. He could not bear it if his lord thought less of him then he must already.

WAN LIGHT BLINKED AHEAD. The last moon sank below a flushed horizon as the tunnel opened into a wild spray of trees and dew-wet bushes, their deep green foliage haloed by dawn. Birds chirruped. The rustling breeze carried a cool, sharp blast of mint mingled with soft gardenia.

"Where are we?" Azenor said.

"We're on the other side of the lake below the castle. Near the drowned forest."

"Drowned forest?"

"That's what they call it. The story goes that in the days of King Caelan, Venivan raiders landed in the Isles and marched to this place, plundering villages along the way. Caelan intercepted them. His men outnumbered, he spoke terrible words of magic, commanding the lake to flood its banks. A torrent of water cascaded upon the forest, drowning every raider."

"The gormel slayer is my ancestor, yet I don't know this awful tale." Azenor shivered.

Kaell instinctively reached for his cloak. No cloak. He had only Fortitude, left by his lord in that cell. Its dark whisper comforted. Did it hold a warning? His dreams did. And he dreamt often of Azenor. But what could be wrong about a wondrous kiss?

THEY WALKED UNTIL the sun peaked above the roof of leaves then slept beside a bubbling stream. Dusk's chill woke them. The forest was filled with shadows and soft rustles as they trudged on.

Moonlight fell fitfully, but Kaell's gaze easily pierced the rising darkness.

By dawn, they reached a lake, drooping trees mirrored in its rippling surface. On its quiet banks both plunged into sleep. A dream snatched at Kaell. He woke in a cold sweat, yelling.

"It's him, isn't it?" Azenor's face was drawn. "Archanin."

"He calls to me."

She trembled. "I also dreamt of him."

The land curved and climbed into knotted woods, thick and lush with vines and towering trunks sunk deep in cinnamon-scented soil. They walked in silence; her steps were fearless, confident he'd catch her if she stumbled. Comfortable now, like comrades in battle.

Azenor rarely complained, no matter how hard he pushed her. "I am the perfect companion to a changeling almost-ghoul," she said. "It means little to me whether it is day or night."

Despite their danger, his edginess, he laughed.

She groped for his hand and drew it to her lips. "I like your laugh. It's a good sound."

Kaell ached at her nearness. "How can you bear to touch me? Can't you see what I am?"

"Lackwit. I see nothing."

"Well, I deserve that."

"But I feel your courage and gentleness."

"Gentle! I'm a hunter, Azenor. I slaughtered my first ghoul at twelve. I only know how to fight."

A memory stirred of the Thom elder who had called him a killer. Let down his defences, and he'd become just that. Kaell shuddered. He must never give in to his bloodlust.

"My brother Aric is a warrior," Azenor said. "Some men in Dal-Kanu, the false king among them, call him a killer. I don't love him any less for it."

"Your brother Aric is a splendid swordsman." A craftsman with a blade. Smooth-tongued, true, but Aric's deception offered a lesson. One he learnt too late.

"Tell me of your fight," Azenor begged. "Tell me again everything Aric said, everything that happened. Oh, how I miss him. How did he return to the Isles?"

Kaell told her of potions that weren't drunk and daring rescues from towers. His cheeks flushed when he recounted finding Aric "not alone."

Azenor only laughed. "Another sweet dance, as Pairas might say. And how did Aric trick you into fighting?"

"Your brother's tongue is honeyed—"

"A swaggerer's tongue, in fact."

"But I badly wanted to test my skill against the Isles champion. I recognised the game he played, with the blade, at least." Kaell described their fight blow-by-blow.

Astonished, she said, "How can you remember in such detail?"

"My lord taught me to analyse every attack, every parry. It stood me well." Until Aric. Though that taught him something too. Not about beats or lunges, but about trust.

ANOTHER DAWN BROKE as they followed an overgrown trail through trees buttressed as close as warriors' shields in battle. Vines gnarled.

Ferns sprayed in muddy gullies; bluebells carpeted every tiny clearing. Pungent, earthy scents mingled with creamy moss and the fresh tang of rain.

A twig snapped. Kaell clamped a hand over Azenor's mouth as he dragged her behind a fallen log, its rotting wood home to bright blue orchids.

Two shapes moved through dark trunks. From their blond hair, their tall, elegant bodies, there was no mistaking what they were—ghouls.

Kaell gripped his sword hilt, fighting down panic. He could kill two. But if others followed, how could he keep Azenor safe?

The ghouls edged closer, their menace, their intent in how their heads shifted left and right. Searching. For them? With a shiver, Kaell waited. And waited.

A hush prowled. Kaell didn't trust it. Cautiously he lifted his head. No one. The woods empty. Rising, he reached for Azenor to lead her further into the trees.

"Kaell," she said at last. "Can't we rest?"

"Soon. We're near Dal-Gorma. I think."

"Dal-Gorma?" Her face brightened. "Then we've reached the Isles."

They scrambled up a wooded copse, then along a bleak, hushed valley before the land rose again. A road at the top wound through huddled trees, leaves sprinkled by raindrops. Kaell intended only to cross it. It offered too many dangers—not just ghouls but thieves and soldiers.

The rumble of fast-ridden horses cut the stillness, the sound lifting hairs on his arms.

In a storm of splayed mud, with thundering hooves striking loose stones, riders rounded the bend, their pace urgent. Kaell snatched a look as he pulled Azenor into the grass. Nine or ten men on horseback, bunched in twos or threes, their swords in shoulder holsters.

Breath held, he willed the riders to roar past. To his dismay a man shouted "halt." With a creak of leather, his companions reined in. The same man said, "I saw someone."

"You're still drunk from last night, imagining things."

"I'm no more hungover than usual. You in the grass, show yourself. I see you."

"Stay down," Kaell whispered to Azenor. Blade drawn, he rose. Barely a few paces from him, horsemen blocked the road, the forest at their backs. They whipped out swords. A horse whinnied. "I mean you no trouble," Kaell said. "Just ride on."

A man at the front spat at the ground. Darkly handsome, he sat tall in the saddle despite the mail beneath his dark-blue surcoat. "We'll ride on once you're dead, ghoul. Kill him."

"No!" Azenor stumbled out. "No, don't kill him. You can't."

Kaell's heart plunged. "Azenor, what are you doing?"

"Saving your life, lackwit."

"Azenor?" The dark-haired lead rider frowned in surprise.

"Pairas. Thank The Three."

"My lady, Azenor. How? We heard you were dead."

"Lackwit. Do I look dead? I'm alive and spitting, thanks to this warrior. So don't you dare hurt him. Do you hear?"

Pairas took off his helm. At his nod, a man dismounted, sword drawn. "Azenor, he's a—"

She stamped a foot. "You know nothing, thickhead."

Another thickhead? His kin under the skin, perhaps? Kaell remembered this man now, how he had insolently argued with his lord at a tournament.

"He rescued me. Wherever you're heading, turn around and take us to my father."

"My lady, Aric ordered us to Dal-Gorma. The false king is on the move."

"The false king will wait."

The captain exchanged glances with the thick-bodied man moving in to menace Kaell with steel. "As you say, my lady. Aiden, take half the men and escort them to Tide's End. I'll ride with you to the crossroads then press on with the others to Dal-Gorma."

Azenor stretched out her hand. "Kaell?"

He moved to her side. "I'm here."

"These are Aric's men. They'll take care of us."

Kaell caught Pairas's scowl. He knew the sort of care the captain intended. Tensing muscles, he slid a look at the trees. Azenor was safe. Time to run.

At a sound behind, he half turned. Pain burst in his skull. The blow knocked him to his knees. Fast moving, blurred figures surrounded him.

Azenor whipped her head around. “What’s happening?”

“My lady, he has a ghoul’s black eyes.” Pairas dismounted. “We must bind him.”

“You don’t understand. I don’t want him—” She broke off. Dazed, Kaell braced a hand against the ground as he tried to focus. Azenor was frowning. “Oh gods,” she whispered, her voice fractured in surprise. “I really don’t want him hurt. Pairas, don’t—hurt—him.”

“My lady, I must take precautions.” At his gesture, his companions lashed Kaell’s wrists. Azenor cursed Pairas colourfully. The man grinned.

Bound, dizzy, Kaell struggled in their grips. A frustrated anger boiled up. He had to return to his lord. “You have no right to hold me,” he growled. “Release me.”

“There’s something familiar about you.” Pairas grasped his chin. He stiffened then leaned towards Aiden. “I know him. And she called him Kaell. But that’s impossible.”

“Why impossible?”

A pause. Then Pairas said, “That’s the name of that dead warrior from Vraymorg.”

At Aiden’s bewildered splutter, Pairas dragged taut fingers through his hair. “This is a mess. I’ll let our king sort it out. But for now, I must protect my men.”

He drew his sword. Kaell tried to scramble back. The soldiers tightened their grips.

“No,” he said. “No.”

Pairas turned the weapon. The jab from the hilt only hurt for a moment. Then he fell away into nothing.

HEATH

From the edge of the forest, the king's monster trebuchet fired its unconventional load against Dal-Gorma's wooden walls. Archers' volleys blotted the sky like a flock of birds in flight.

Heath listened to the familiar creak of pulleys and ropes, the quiver in the air, and thunder through earth. How long until they could take a battering ram to the gates? Then the mayhem started. The fun bit—as he always told Judith.

With idle interest, he watched men load the trebuchet. The Beast, they called it. It took a dozen oxen to drag the terrible thing to Dal-Gorma. All to fire stinking missiles of excrement.

Heath vaguely remembered a story of a Wardorian castle subjected to this same bizarre assault. Perhaps Cathmor copied that siege commander to show his contempt for the Isles.

The ground rumbled, the air vibrated as The Beast unloaded. Excrement splattered over the walls. Soldiers cheered. Handkerchiefs tied over their noses and mouths, the engineers shovelled more cargo from carts into the bucket.

How did they get the right, hmm, thickness, so it was hard enough to hurl yet liquid enough to slop in Dal-Gorma? He laughed softly. Hardly the question he expected to ponder on the field of war.

Still smiling, Heath moved away from the rank carts. In the hollow of rolling hills, Dal-Gorma sprawled before him. The Place of the Brook. Named for the river coursing at its back, a glistening, blue streak. Buds burst upon trees lining its banks. Spring was upon the Isles early with all its blossoms and scents of heat and honey—at least away from The Beast.

Even on this hillside where the king camped, a warm breeze bowed daffodils and leaf-laden boughs. Insects chittered in dew-wet grass beneath a sky so blue it looked nearly purple. The perfect weather for war.

He sighed, almost content. Today, perhaps tomorrow, this Isles town would fall. Heath knew it. Every one of the king's soldiers knew it. Even Dal-Gorma's sentries in watchtowers along the timber stockade knew it as they assessed the force set to descend upon them.

He shaded his eyes with a hand. Surprising Dal-Gorma had not already descended into chaos. Someone must still be in charge, commanding bowmen to fire if the enemy got too close. Directing townsfolk to repair breaches with rocks.

Though, once they stood knee-deep in excrement—he chose the polite word—they must surrender. No fiery immolation, no thrilling and dangerously unpredictable battle.

No, the battle would begin when they fell upon Tide's End, the real prize, like hungry dogs. Then what might Cathmor do with Dal-Gorma, a town full of—well, filth?

Heath turned away. The king had summoned him a good half an hour ago. Not like him to avoid confrontation, but Cathmor had questions he didn't want to answer.

With ponderous steps, he trod to the king's pavilion at the peak on the hill, well away from The Beast. Guards admitted him at once.

He found Cathmor with his uncle. Cael-Carren thrust a cup of wine upon him. "Where were you? We're toasting the fall of Dal-Gorma."

"Cahirean?" Heath sniffed. "How do such savages produce these fine wines?"

"I'm told it is the soil and climate," Cathmor said. "No merit of the Cahireans."

Heath took a sip. Just a sip. He needed a clear head and a clever tongue. "Is there any merit in a Cahirean? Didn't King Dace say: 'Do not trust a Cahirean, even dead'?"

"Wasn't it Roaran"—the king unfolded a smile so deliciously sinister Heath was vaguely jealous—"who said: 'Do not trust a man of the Ice for it runs in his blood'?"

Heath raised his cup in a salute. "I'll take that as a compliment, Your Grace. Roaran was an admirable king. A man unafraid to use sorcery to achieve his ends."

"I admire Roaran also, but for different reasons. The last king to rule all of Telor."

"That will soon change," Heath said. "My father believes so."

Cathmor considered him over the rim of his cup. "So he sends me five thousand warriors to make sure? I am grateful. My father could never achieve this. They talk about him with such awe, about how powerful he was, and yet he could not take the Isles."

"As you say."

"I long to know"—Cathmor's tone disarmed—"what your father wants in return."

Heath chose a guileless smile. "I like your directness. I am not some fancy courtier who goes around and around."

"You sell yourself short."

Really? Everyone accused him of pride. Heath sipped wine. "Delicious. Perhaps I should go to Cahir one day. Or perhaps not. Such wine might make a man forget his duty."

"Not you. You prattle like a fool, but you don't deceive me. What does your father want?"

"He believes alliances are best secured through marriage. I have sisters. You are unwed. Or if that is distasteful, then you have all manner of cousins." Heath shrugged. "I am unwed."

"You know I'm betrothed to the Isles girl?"

"Who is surely dead. If not, a betrothal to a traitor's daughter means nothing."

"As you say. But this simple business could go before my council."

Heath paused. "There's another matter."

"Ah, now we come to it."

"A trifle really."

"Will I like this trifle?"

Not at all. "When Tide's End falls—and it will fall."

"I thank you for your confidence," Cathmor said. "So far I like your words. Continue. When Tide's End falls—"

"There is the question of prisoners. One in particular." He seized a quick breath. Plunged in. "Aric Caelan. I want him."

Cael-Carren nearly choked on his wine. "You jest, Damadar."

Cathmor shook his head. "If his brother dies, Aric is his father's heir. No. If by a stroke of luck we take my cousin alive, I'll execute him."

A silence stiffened with tension. Both men watched him, their faces hard. Heath chose his words carefully. "What if I assured you, Your Grace, that my sister Myranthe will most certainly kill Aric Caelan for you? He will not produce any troublesome heirs."

Cathmor recoiled. "This stinks of sorcery," he muttered, making no attempt to hide his contempt. "For what purpose do you want Aric?"

"Nothing unnatural, Your Grace."

"For what purpose?" the king hammered.

"I cannot tell you."

"Then I will not you give Aric."

Heath tongued his top lip. *Find the right words, sooth their fears.* Whatever it took. "We won't use Aric to claim the Isles. We just want his body. My sister Myranthe—" Heath sighed. No way to avoid the truth. "Intends to restore death riders."

Cael-Carren again spluttered wine. "Blood magic. I know your family's reputation, Damadar. There are those in Telor who will have nothing to do with you. Others think we should storm the Icelands and rid this land of your kind."

"My kind?" Heath echoed indignantly. "I am flesh and blood like you. My family never turned its back on Telor's past, that's all. Magic infuses this land, its history."

"Not your sort of magic," Cael-Carren said.

"Really? Your ancestor, Rainer, weaved words into spells. And what of Roaran? So admired, this son of a Quisnaf sorceress. Did he deny his talents? No, he went to Quisnaf to learn to control them."

"The Quisnaf took Roaran prisoner," Cathmor corrected tartly. "They wanted to use him because of those very abilities. Roaran was afraid of what he could do."

"The Ice lords are not afraid," Heath said. "We want only to serve Ghani-Jai." He dragged in slow breaths, snatching at calm. He did not intend to lose his temper.

"A foul god," Cael-Carren said. "Bloodthirsty."

"In return for Aric." Heath ignored the insulting words. "My father will keep his army in the field. No matter how long it takes to overwhelm Tide's End."

"Which may be months. No one has taken Tide's End by force," Cathmor said. "And we can't invest it unless we hold the sea. Which we don't."

"My captains assure me it will fall quickly. You have beasts of siege engines. No walls can withstand a day-in, day-out pounding. Let me say again, just to allay your concerns. We want only Aric's body. There will be no Caelan descendants to challenge you for the throne."

Cael-Carren spun to his king. "You cannot consider this, nephew. Not this, of all things. Death riders!"

With deliberate care, Cathmor put his goblet on the table. "Let me think on it. After all, I cannot pretend to care if your sister murders Aric."

Heath knew his smile did not reach his eyes. “Then I will be content with that, Your Grace.” Content? Not at all. If Cathmor didn’t give him Aric, he had another plan the king would choke on. It involved all he excelled at. Betrayal. Manipulation. Bloodshed.

Good times.

AINGEAR

Shoulders hunched, her steps brisk, Aingear paced the hall. Dust danced in fading sunlight dappling two columns of fluted pillars. They stretched from brass doors to the king's throne on a platform. Their shadows licked at the mosaicked floor, but a warm tang lingered in the air, the tide's hum a drowsy monotone.

She tapped her foot. Where was Gendrick? He promised to take her below—to him.

Aingear passed a hand over her eyes. Kaell was here. Right below her. Unconscious when guards carried him into the keep but alive. Within her reach.

As if unseen eyes watched her, her scalp prickled. She turned fast.

No one. The chamber empty except for a painted Rainer Caelan staring from a mural.

Though centuries of glaring sunlight had muted its vibrant colours, the fresco with its tale of carnage dominated the hall, its two central figures bigger than her and brilliantly, eerily real.

Such a strange scene for a palace wall in Tide's End. A scene from distant Quisnaf, of Rainer battling the demon god Aziarr, a wounded Roaran at his side.

In contrast to the morbid tale, the Telorian warriors wore sky-blue tunics, their cloaks scarlet. Their niello-encrusted sword hilts gleamed. The blood soaking Roaran's tunic looked wet. Their faces seemed impossibly lifelike as if the artist had imprisoned them in the work.

Aingear often imagined Rainer's eyes following her. They were dark, those eyes. Very dark and very serene, even though he was about to die. His smooth, shoulder-length hair was black, his face unlined. He had been barely twenty-two when he killed Aziarr.

As a girl, Aingear had been a little in love with him. She'd steal into the hall to trace his lips and sigh at the heroism of this young god-king who glimpsed his death in visions yet deliberately chose a path to that fate.

The words of a tutor, his beard the grey of an angry sea, stole back. "The enigma that is Rainer. Tell me why, novice?"

"Because he weaved words into magic," a solemn Aingear had said. A spell maker needing no potions or aids. Only the power of his rhymes. A rare gift.

As she grew older, though, the warrior at Rainer's side also drew her gaze.

Such a compelling man, Roaran, with the strong, straight lines of his face and cheekbones that would not appear so stark except in contrast to that full, decadent mouth.

His raven hair was curled, boyish for a man already a Serravan captain; his eyes were depicted as dark as his cousin Rainer's. But according to legend, they were blue, a strange blue, like a turgid sea stripped of light by storm clouds.

Despite his beauty, she could not look upon Roaran without anger. These foolish cultists. Such dangerous nonsense. For all the stories about this man, about his magic, Roaran was dead. Dead.

With a deliberate release of breath, Aingear opened her clenched hands and let them dangle at her side. Even more deliberately, she tried to turn from the mural and the past. But after the desecration in the secret tower tomb, the scenes of that fated battle in distant Quisnaf seemed a portent of evil, of nightmares still to come.

Beneath the tide's murmur, a drift of voices, low and indistinct, carried down the hall. Gendrick. At last. Aingear lifted her gown and hurried through the stone monoliths.

In an alcove below a glass window, two figures talked softly, their heads close like conspirators. With the same shade of ebony hair, a symmetry to their gestures, even a stranger might pick them as brother and sister.

Aric as always looked every bit a prince, his black hair striking against the blue of his linen shirt. Azenor, though, had not changed the ripped, dirty gown she had worn when soldiers returned her to the castle a matter of hours ago.

"That's impossible." Aric drove his hand through air. "He lied to you."

Azenor tugged at his sleeve. "I know how it sounds. I do. But I'm telling you the truth. His position in the Mountains is a disguise. He's an Isles man who can't be killed."

Can't be killed? Aingear pressed a palm to a pillar, startled. She edged nearer.

Azenor turned her head. "Aric, someone's there."

Cloth rustled, then rapid steps moved towards her. "Oh, it's you, priestess." Aric's fingers fell away from his sword hilt.

"I did not mean to disturb you." She looked for Azenor. The girl had disappeared. Given she saw only blurred shapes and colours, she moved fast. "The lady Azenor?"

"Gone to berate Father again for locking Kaell up like a brigand or murderer."

Aingear snatched at his arm. "About that boy, Kaell—"

"Below." Aric smoothed his hair, the gesture weary. "Gendrick thinks he's dangerous."

"Priestess?" Gendrick stomped into the hall. "I ask you to reconsider. The prisons are no place for any woman."

Aingear pulled her cloak tight. "I need to see the boy."

"The beast, you mean." Gendrick's laugh held a sneer. "This way."

She turned to follow. For a moment her gaze lingered on the mural. Rainer's painted eyes still bore into hers, warning her to turn back. *Too late,* she thought. *Too late.*

AINGEAR GROPED DOWN narrow steps cut from rock to the prison beneath the hall. Behind slimy walls, the sea rumbled. Fetid air stank of damp and brine and hopelessness. Darkness quickly swallowed Gendrick's torchlight.

"This is a foul place," Aric muttered. "Better the axe or the sword than this."

Gendrick jeered. "Worried you'll wet your dainty feet? No one asked you to come."

"Where you go, brother, et cetera, et cetera."

Gendrick halted. Half turning, he lifted the torch to Aric's face.

"My path is truly set, Aric," he said, an odd undercurrent in his voice. "No one can follow. Especially you."

"I have no clue what you're on about."

"Of course you don't." Gendrick swung the torch ahead. His boots clipped stone, their echo melting into the fading murmur of waves and wind.

The steps ended in a low-roofed passage. Water dripped down walls and pooled on a rough-hewn floor. Rust flaked off iron doors. Gendrick stopped before a door and turned a key. Metal clanked as if someone within moved.

"Azenor." A voice floated from the blackness. "Is that you? You shouldn't have come."

Gendrick shoved his torch into a bracket inside the cramped, windowless cell. A single prisoner shackled to the grime-crusted walls threw up an arm to shield his eyes.

"She didn't," Gendrick said. "She's sobbing in Father's

chambers as he stares helplessly at her, wondering why his beloved daughter pleads for a monster."

"Why are you here?" Thick chains jangled as the prisoner shifted. Kaell appeared leaner than in Aingear's visions, harder too, with a grim wariness. Though not as tall as Aric, he could not stand in this forsaken hole without bending.

"Well?" Beneath her scrutiny he bristled. "What do you see? What do you want?" He passed his eyes over her robes. "Priestess."

"I want to know if you can bend your knee to our gods," Aingear said. "If you do, then I can rid you of this monster's blood."

"What?" Aric turned to frown. "Why didn't you tell me before?"

"It's dangerous, uncertain magic. It may not work. Not unless he's willing."

Kaell leaned a shoulder against the cell wall. "Who are you?"

"I am Aingear, High Priestess of The Three. My gods have shown me a way to save you."

"Save?" His laugh was bitter. "Nothing but death can save me."

Aingear couldn't look away. She thought him dead in an ambush, lost to her. Now he was within reach, tantalisingly familiar with that pale hair and Khir's sigils scarring muscular arms. Except he also looked unreal as someone from a dream often did, as though he belonged only to her visions and could never be flesh and blood.

"If I cannot save you. I will end your misery."

Kaell pushed off the wall. "Will you swear to it?"

"No." Aric burst forward. "I won't let you kill him. Azenor and I owe him our lives. And to repay him, we chained him up like an animal."

Gendrick laughed, an unpleasant, caustic echo on stone.

Aric spun, hands fisted at his thighs. "What is wrong with you?"

"What do you think is wrong with me? You, dear brother. It's bad enough Azenor is pathetically pleading for this abomination.

Seems she acquired a taste for his sort."

"Take that back. Or I'll ram those words down your throat."

Gendrick thrust his hands to his hips. "Why do you think her captors didn't kill her? Why does she look at him as she does? She debased herself with a thing that's not human anymore. Just a monster who'll succumb to his sordid, unnatural instincts if he hasn't already."

"You always did have a foul mind, Gendrick."

"I dreamt of her," Kaell said. Torchlight lit eyes hazed with memory. "Azenor. Even before we met."

Dreamt of her. Aingear clutched at the wall, her neck moist with sweat. So simple, yet so unexpected. Something bound him and Azenor. Use it, and she could also bind Kaell to the Isles gods.

"Priestess, are you unwell?" Aric took her arm to steady her.

Aingear brushed off his hand. She faced Kaell. "Is Gendrick right? Are you and Azenor—" She licked dry lips. "Are you lovers?"

Kaell edged back as if escaping her words. "No," he said, his voice quiet.

"I've had enough of this." Gendrick drew his blade. "I'll take off his head. Right now. Then we'll be safe."

Safe? Aingear laughed, an empty rattle without merriment. With Roaran's magic destroyed? With the usurper king about to march on Tide's End. Safe? Not yet.

"I have need of him," she said. "The gods chose him. Now I understand why."

ARIC

Shadows blurred in the tower room's eight corners. Moonlight bled into pale candlelight spilling upon shelves of books. A breeze scented of salt and sea sifted Aric's hair as he bent over dispatches. The thud of hammers echoed.

He knuckled the table's age-worn wood. Unease churned in his gut. His plan had to work. It simply had to. All the same, it was a risk letting Dal-Gorma fall without a fight.

But why sacrifice men defending a town not walled by stone? No, let Cathmor have it. Then let him march to Tide's End, sit in his tent and drink wine, grow tired of the flies and the dysentery, and leave. To find trouble waiting.

Aric smoothed a map with his palm. Cathmor's siege engines trundled from Dal-Gorma. His men harried the transport, taking out a few guards at night then melting away.

Spark panic, he had ordered. Don't stay to fight. Still, he had lost men. Cathmor had lost more. But he had more to begin with. Thanks to the Damadar Ice lord, Rolland.

With a weary sigh, Aric rose, stretched, and wandered to the window.

There were two figures on the sea path below. Aingear and a man.

Aric pressed his palms into the sill, his neck prickling with unease. It wasn't just because of the high priestess's stiff-backed stance, her arms crossed in a barrier.

That man. There was something uncanny about him. Seithin steel gleamed at his hip, ice-blue. Moonlight lit curious insignia—a bird, a circlet, a blindfolded figure—stitched into his leather doublet beneath a cloak billowing off powerfully built shoulders.

A sea bird meant the god Saarn. So an Isles man. The circlet. A king or prince.

Aric's scalp crept. Who dared wear such a doublet? Who exactly stood below?

Beating wings broke above the incoming tide's rumble. A raven flapped into a crevice. Aric stared through it. He knew that insignia from somewhere.

He spun, grabbed a book from the shelves, sat, and flicked pages.

Perfumed night deepened. His candle guttered. He put a taper to a new one.

A blinded man. Where had he seen it? A crest, a shield. In the king's hall? A mural.

His breath stalled. Yes, a mural. But not in Dal-Kanu.

Aric snatched up a candle. His heels tapped stone in the stairwell, an eerie midnight echo. Even the hammers beating metal in the forge, the wooden arms of mangonels creaking on the breakwaters hushed.

At the entrance to the hall, he hesitated. Already he wrestled with Azenor's uncomfortable story. Did he want to learn another dangerous truth? No. Not at all. But his duty was to understand, to decide if what he uncovered threatened the Isles.

Resolved, he pushed through doors and lifted the candle to the wall.

King Rainer mocked him from the mural. Aric looked not at Rainer, but at the man kneeling at his side, sword spilled, his hand clasping a seeping wound. A man whose tunic bore an insignia not yet this king's, but one an artist years after Roaran's death had painted with hindsight.

A bird. A circlet. A blindfolded man wielding a sword.

Aric reeled a step. *Impossible.*

Shadows ran about him. The wind hunted and howled. Beneath the walls, waves rolled like thunderheads. Aric hardly heard them. His thoughts whirled in disbelief.

At a footstep, he spun.

His brother waved a torch. "You look like you expected a ghost."

Not a ghost. The dead. "You startled me."

Gendrick poked the torch at the mural. "I never liked this. When I'm lord, I'll have it painted over. There are other heroes besides Rainer and Roaran. The Ice Rider, for one."

"They pale beside Roaran." Aric struggled to control his rising disquiet. "A capable, strong king who united Telor against formidable enemies. A mystic."

That was it. The blindfolded man. A seer's sign. No other Telorian king used this insignia. Except this was nonsense. Roaran was long dead. Not stalking the sea path.

Gendrick snorted. "Whatever you say, Aric. You always liked old stories."

Aric slid his brother a look. "Why are you about?"

"A messenger just rode in. Dal-Gorma fell to the king a few hours ago."

"As expected. Pairas? Is he returned?"

Gendrick hesitated.

"Gendrick?"

His brother sighed. "The messenger says he fell wounded. No sign of him."

Aric braced a hand against the wall, his legs unsteady. "No," he muttered. "No. Pairas knows what he's about. He's an excellent bladesman. He's on his way here."

"Just like the king," Gendrick said. "Before you head to your bed, best hear everything the messenger has to say."

"Oh?"

"The king's advance force has already reached the forest." Gendrick grinned wearily. "Let the games begin. Cathmor can't invest us because we hold the sea. But sometime tomorrow we'll be officially besieged."

HEATH

The flap rippled in a thin wind. A swirling of sea fog escaped into Heath's tent along with the aroma of smoke from cook fires and the ocean's brine.

Salt and sweat. The distinctive perfume of the Isles. It clung to his garments even at dawn when he'd wandered to the edge of the king's camp to stare up at Tide's End, majestic above the marble wasteland of grey sea and drifting storm clouds.

It coated his skin as he sat in his tent now, unable to concentrate on words in a book, wondering how long before the king's engines breached this bastion of the Isles.

Only a handful of days ago, Dal-Gorma had fallen. Now the dull, dull business of besieging proper castles began. What he wouldn't give for diverting nonsense. Perhaps he could pick a fight, insult some pimply lord?

A hand appeared through the flap. The king's field captain Bora pushed uninvited through canvas ahead of the king's interrogator. Bellicent Blackstone flung a bound, hooded man down.

"The king wants you to question him." Bora studied his knife hilt, disinterested. "He says you have a taste for this sort of thing."

Heath considered Bora with displeasure. A furtive rat with squinting, dead eyes and a mail-clad, thick body that might be strong but was far from elegant.

"I have a taste for many bloody things." Cutting up rats, for one. "Who is this? Someone close to Aric? Highborn?" He clicked his tongue. "Very careless, falling into our hands."

"This man fell wounded at Dal-Gorma. Townsfolk hid him in a cellar."

At a shout outside, Bora glanced at the tent opening. Laughter broke out, then a clang of iron and more yelling. Ringing steel was common in a besiegers' encampment as men sought to pass the time.

Bora shrugged. Yawned. "Someone betrayed him for a fistful of silver."

"Greedy, these Isles traitors," said Heath.

"The king thinks a less brutal approach might work better with this prisoner. If there's anything left when you're done, give him to Blackstone."

"My lord, give me the traitor now." Blackstone edged forward, just as cloud shadowed the tent. Dramatic, except the laden air and scent of rain heralded more cursed thunderheads. Summer in the Isles. Sweat sticky on his thighs, the air too hot to breathe. Endless storms.

"I like your enthusiasm for your work," Heath said. Not much else about Blackstone pleased him. "But a subtler hand first. Let's see what we have, shall we?"

Bora whipped the hood off. The prisoner pushed to his knees, blinked.

Heath's fingers curled around his hilt. This was a surprise. Not unwelcome. Intriguing.

He laughed aloud, tempted to ruffle the captive's hair. Hard to tell this man's pain-gaunt, bruised face had once been handsome. A dirty cloth crudely bandaged his thigh; his body was as ripped as his bloody tunic.

"I know him, my lord," Blackstone said in that oily voice of hers. "His father is the lord of Mar-marin. The rock in the sea. A drunkard and a fool."

Heath tilted an eyebrow. "The father or the son? Never mind. I know him too. Pairas Morgan." He shot the bleeding man an amused look. "Aric's captain."

Pairas slowly lifted his head. His eyes stretched with alarm, then anger. "You." He tried to lunge at Heath, but Bora pressed him to his knees.

Heath only laughed again with genuine pleasure. Unfinished business this. The gods surely loved him. Why else gift a man with wit and skill? Tolerable looks. Then return to him the one man he had foolishly spared. Yes, his gods favoured him.

Judith always warned fate slapped the prideful down. Maybe. But not today.

Pairas swiped his split lips with a bloody sleeve. He glared at Heath. "The king wants you to question me? Just the low task I'd expect for an Ice lord."

"Such a busy boy. Acquiring useless nonsense."

"I should have recognised that brooch at once. Or at least recognised the arrogance."

"Where's the insult in that? Try again, captain. Use smaller words so I understand."

Pairas sneered. "Why waste my breath? Your sort is impervious to words."

Heath crouched. When he touched the man's jaw, Pairas flinched.

"I'm sorry to see you in pain, Pairas. May I call you that? I feel close to you. It's very intimate drugging a man and dragging him into your bedchamber to question him." He shot his companions a quick look, realising he'd revealed too much.

"Fists?" Heath turned Pairas's head. "The physician can make you all pretty again, Isles man."

"If I answer your questions, you'll tend my wounds?" Pairas spat at the ground. "I'm loyal to my king. Do you think I care what you do to me? I'll bleed out before I help you."

"Pairas, really. I won't let you bleed out. But bleed, yes."

Heath rose. Pity someone else had to make Pairas bleed. Judith's little spell was spoiling all his fun. "I wish you told me you enjoyed punishment. That could add a layer of perversion to our friendship."

Snarling, Pairas tried to spring at him again. Bora thrust him down.

Heath sighed. "I admire loyalty, captain. Really, I do. I am infinitely loyal to my family. But answer me this: Why did Aric send you to hold Dal-Gorma? Why are you a prisoner when your fearless commander hides behind strong walls? I call that misplaced loyalty."

Pairas mumbled, "We didn't intend to hold Dal-Gorma."

"So Aric ordered you to delay us then slip away? You didn't manage the slip away bit so well, Pairas. Nor the delay bit. We smashed the town in two days."

Pairas looked at the ground, his face tight with anger.

"I think Aric let us overrun Dal-Gorma while he took a hard look at our numbers. What now? Will he cower in Tide's End until we give up the siege? Or march against us?"

Pairas lifted his head. His stare stabbed with hatred. "You'll learn nothing from me."

"My good captain," Heath said. "There's no Judith with her soft heart to save you today. You see this woman here? Her name is Bellicent Blackstone."

Pairas shrank back onto his heels.

"You're famous, Blackstone. He's heard of you."

"I know what she did to Aric. She's a monster," Pairas said.

"So the misguided might say. What do you say, Blackstone?"

"I am an artist, my lord. I enjoy a challenge."

"And the captain will present you with one?"

"If only, my lord. This one looks half broken already." Blackstone passed low-lidded eyes over the captive, assessing. "Still, we'll find some amusing games to play."

"You play," said Heath. "I'll watch."

HEATH PRESENTED AT the king's pavilion, his skin soap-scented, hair damp, boots cleaned of Pairas's blood. He wore clothes well. If men misjudged him as a pampered nobleman, they quickly learnt their mistake when he effortlessly—oh, and elegantly, he hoped—ran them through with steel.

In fact, the deception suited him well. A man might hide all manner of ambitious plots behind a guileless smile and a crisp, clean tunic.

He found the king and Cael-Carren bent over maps. Cathmor edged up a brow.

"He's said nothing useful yet, Your Grace. I left him with Blackstone."

The king nodded. "He'll break. They always do. Surprising Aric so readily surrendered Dal-Gorma. He sent only a small force to hold the town."

"Aric Caelan is practical," Heath said. "Dal-Gorma could not be defended. Besides, he knows Tide's End is the only prize. Take Tide's End, and you take the Isles."

Cathmor's shrewd eyes flickered. "According to gossip, you know Aric."

Heath lifted and dropped his fire dancer's shoulders.

"As a boy, I journeyed with my brother Velleran to the Isles. Our elders talked, leaving Aric and I together. We had a common interest in swordplay. And fishing."

"Do you know enough of my cousin to outguess him?"

"I knew him only a few days. Aric wielded a sword well, even then. An excellent fisherman." Heath extended his arms to show the size of the catch. "Though surely we grapple not only with Aric's intelligence but his father and elder brother's."

Cael-Carren jeered. "Have you ice in your ears? Aric Caelan commands the Isles."

"Gendrick is his father's heir," Cathmor instructed. "The role of Isles commander falls to the best soldier and tactician. A Serravan tradition."

Heath scratched an artfully stubbled chin as he puzzled over this. "Curious. Does this strange system work, I wonder? If I tried to order Velleran about, he'd slit my throat."

"I doubt that." Cathmor unfolded a smile entirely without warmth. "You are a fire dancer. A violent man. I'm surprised you didn't stay to torment our captive yourself."

"I watched for a bit, just to maintain my brutish reputation and all that. Truthfully, Your Grace, I prefer those I torment to be able to defend themselves with steel. Still, I'll lash Pairas with my tongue if Blackstone fails."

Cathmor scolded with a wagging finger. "Such lack of faith. Bellicent is thorough."

"And if the captain survives? He's of good birth. You'll ransom him to his father?" For Judith's sake, Heath hoped so. She seemed irrationally fond of this man.

"Or just hang him," Cael-Carren muttered.

Cathmor grimaced. "Hang a nobleman? The law forbids it. Though"—he tapped a finger against tight lips—"it says nothing about hurling him over Tide's End's walls from a trebuchet."

"You're serious?" Heath looked from one to the other. Neither smiled. "You're serious," he repeated. First excrement, now Isles captains. War seemed much simpler in the Icelands.

"Your Grace?" A soldier appeared at the tent entrance.

Cathmor whirled. "What news?"

"Vraymorg just rode into camp. With your Grand Constable. You wished to be told."

Vraymorg. A prickle of anticipation ran along Heath's backbone. He remembered leaning his elbows on a castle balustrade as a silence fell at this man's name. How the Queen of Cahir had said only, "He is very beautiful."

"Yes, yes." Cathmor flicked an impatient hand. "Have Vraymorg attend me at once."

Cael-Carren touched his sleeve. "You'll offend Caelmarsh if you don't receive him first."

The king flashed that cold smile. "Vraymorg sent word ahead he possesses dangerous and secret information. I want to hear it at once."

"Dangerous and secret?" Heath arched his brows. "About what?"

Cathmor shrugged. "I have no idea, Damadar. But let's hear what Vraymorg says then call Caelmarsh in so he can spray accusations. Sometimes he hits a curious mark."

A SHARP TONGUE, a sharper temper, and sharper yet with a blade.

That was Vraymorg's reputation.

A hard man who held the Mountains against ghouls, against the Cahireans with their schemes to invade, against Varee slavers who robbed merchants travelling through the great gorge of their furs, their jewels, their silk, and their sons and daughters.

Heath didn't expect this striking creature who thrust inside with an unconscious swagger. A man too ornamental and too young to be the king's sword in those cursed Mountains. He certainly looked out of place in a muddy camp of tents. With that haughty, defiant mouth, those impressive shoulders, that sweep of attractive stubble darkening his jaw, he belonged on a Quisnaf woman's arm. Prized, pampered, protected.

Yet his youth, his beauty, his unaffected assurance, did not explain why Cathmor tensed, why resentment boiled behind the king's cool eyes as Vraymorg elegantly fell to one knee.

"You seem much recovered." Cathmor did not permit the newcomer to rise. "Given they found you in a pool of blood after the ghoul attack."

"My strength is returning, Your Grace."

Cathmor knuckled the table. "Report to my physician later so he can treat your wounds. Now, how many men did you bring?"

"Only five hundred more, Your Grace. Many untrained. With this attack on top of those lost near Thom and most of the garrison already with Your Majesty's forces—" He shrugged.

"*Fortunate* most of your men already joined my host," Cathmor said, his tone sharp. "Or they'd lie dead, too, slaughtered by those ghouls who overran the fortress."

"As you say, Your Grace."

The king at last, curtly, waved him up.

Vraymorg straightened, grimacing as he fought down pain through what Heath guessed was a sheer act of will. What would it take to break a man like this? What might such a man be worth in the slavers' caverns? Unbroken, of course.

His fire dancer's gaze took in the long legs and broad shoulders, the play of tight muscle beneath the newcomer's tunic. A slaver, though, might nibble his lip at that seductive mouth, that perfect moulding of bone and flesh into a shockingly lovely face.

"How did these cursed fiends breach the castle, Vraymorg?"

"Sorcery, Your Grace. This is what I must tell you—"

"Sorcery?" Cael-Carren echoed, startled.

Heath inwardly scoffed. Why did that surprise the old fool? Magic rippled through Telor's history, infused with the legends of its more infamous kings.

"Is this your secret news?" Cathmor tapped fingers on his belt. "Out with it. I have a siege to plan. Unless Aric Caelan loses his nerve and surrenders."

Heath chuckled.

Cathmor whipped about. "You assured me moments ago you knew only of Aric's skill with a fishing line. Now you laugh at the idea he'll surrender?"

"Who's he?" Vraymorg's hard gaze fell on Heath.

The king impatiently swept his arm. "Surely you noticed the ice warriors in camp, Vraymorg? This is Heath Damadar."

"Damadar?" The man spat the word like poison.

Heath offered an insolent smile. "That sounds vaguely threatening, my lord." His hand slipped to his empty scabbard. He liked Vraymorg already; the man bristled with tight-held menace. A little prod and he might explode.

"My lords, really," Cathmor cut in. "Take your posturing outside. Vraymorg, speak. Why did ghouls attack and how?"

The Mountains lord tore off a glove with one sharp tug. Its slap, slap, slap against his thigh tolled in Heath's skull. The man's breath laboured. In a voice stripped of everything, he said, "The ghouls were hunting Kaell."

A shiver rolled down Heath's spine. Kaell. Khir's bonded warrior. A dead warrior.

"Impossible." Cathmor bunted air with a fist. "The boy is dead. Along with his men. And some of mine, curse his recklessness. Why attack hundreds of ghouls with only thirty warriors?"

"Not dead." Vraymorg's voice shattered. "But by the gods, he should be."

The air in the tent surely thickened. The silence bristled uncomfortably, broken only by a creak of wood as Cathmor pressed his hands into the table.

"Not—dead?" He spaced the words. "How? Then where is he?"

"My guess is the Isles. Kaell wanted Azenor Caelan safe."

"By Kutron. By Khir. She is alive?" Cael-Carren said.

Cathmor stiffened. "Azenor Caelan found?" His voice simmered with fury. "And you didn't send word at once?"

"That news, surely, is too dangerous for a messenger," Vraymorg said quietly.

"Where is she?" Cathmor hammered. "Do you have her?"

Vraymorg dropped his head as though unable to face the question.

Heath could not drag his eyes from him. This man possessed an intense, contained physicality. From the moment he pushed into the tent every one of them had watched only him.

He must meet Vraymorg with steel in a fire dance. This man would not yield, surely. No, not at all. He would fight for his life with every strained breath. How thrilling to take that life from him.

"Do—you—have—her?" Cathmor said.

Slowly the man lifted his head. "No. By now, I hope she is safe in the Isles."

"Be very careful," the king said. "Your words border on treason. Surely you didn't let her go? Need I remind you, we're at war with her father?"

"No."

"Then what? Quickly now, Vraymorg. You test my patience."

Vraymorg forced another breath. "I told the girl I must send her to you. I imprisoned Kaell, intending to execute him the next dawn."

Heath stilled in surprise. Execute? For leading his men into an ambush? Was Vraymorg that harsh? That unforgiving? He knew nothing of Kaell or what sat between him and this Mountains lord. But there must be more to this.

Cathmor gripped the edge of the table, his stare fixed on Vraymorg.

"Ghouls attacked, led by their god, this so-called Lord of Blood," Vraymorg said. "He came for Kaell. Perhaps the girl, too. Kaell and Azenor escaped. To the Isles, I assume."

"Who," asked Heath, "is this blood lord?"

"A myth," muttered Cael-Carren. Yet fear flitted behind his blink.

"Archanin is a fallen god," Vraymorg said, his voice flat. Detached. "He stabbed me, left me for dead. He did not care that he had taken the castle. He only wanted Kaell."

Bewildered, Heath spread his arms. "Go back. Why execute the boy? Because he failed? Because he recklessly attacked so many ghouls?"

Vraymorg ripped his fingers through sweat-glistened hair. "Kaell was not reckless. The villagers of Thom deliberately sent him and his men into an ambush."

"Then it makes even less sense to execute him. Or did he lie about the villagers?"

"Kaell does not lie."

"Then why?"

"Indeed." The king's baleful gaze dwelled on the dark-haired lord. "Why?"

For a long moment Vraymorg said nothing. Then he clawed his cheeks.

"Kaell's eyes." His voice crept out as a disbelieving whisper. "No longer green but black. This ghoul god took his blood. And yet Kaell lives. Gods, help him, he lives."

All sound drained from the tent. In its place, a shocked hush scourged. Caught in its web, Heath struggled to understand. He knew little of ghouls, but surely their bite killed.

At last, his voice low, Cathmor said, "Khir's bonded warrior is turned. He is turned. He has Azenor, and he is with my enemies in the Isles."

ARIC

Aric leaned his elbows on sun-warmed battlements. Across a muddy field of white-tipped grass and daffodils, tents rimmed the forest. Figures bustled about the encampment, too far off to interest Isles archers. An occasional stone crashed well short of Tide's End as the king's engineers tested their mangonels.

From planted poles, from pavilions, pennons and flags fluttered, the standards of three hundred Telorian houses seeking to tear down his walls. Great lords and some not so great.

The Lord of the Plains' hoe and horse banner rippled beside the black axe and plough of the Downs. At least with Nate Caelmarsh against him, he need not watch his back.

At the sight of one wind-streamed, blue banner, Aric dug his nails into a chipped merlon. Why should Rolland Damadar take up arms against the distant Isles?

Aric remembered that summer when he and Rolland's son Heath had traded sword strokes in the ward and wild stories as they dangled their legs off rocks and fished for coral trout.

I liked him. His sarcastic wit. His audacious charm. I hope I don't cross swords with him. Kill him.

Aiden Saltman stomped onto the wall walk. "It appears most of

Telor wants to take us down." He brushed dust from his tunic. "The Icelands among them."

The Icelands. The Falls, the Plains, the Downs.

The Mountains.

Strangeness traced Aric's backbone. Azenor's story could not be true. But if it were? What did that make Vraymorg? No, it was too incredible. He didn't want to believe it.

"Not to mention the Henge," Aiden said. "If I meet Sherrin Cross in battle, I'll bring you his head."

"Better to take him alive, put him in chains, and force the Henge to submit. Are the scouts back? Any prisoners in the king's camp? Pairas?"

His new captain shook his head.

Dead then. Aric pushed sadness away. He'd mourn others soon. Too many.

"I'm sorry." Aiden covered Aric's hand with his own. "What can I do? Will I come to you, tonight? I would comfort you any way I can. You know that."

"I know. You always do."

"My lord." A sentry shouted from a corner tower. "Messenger, my lord."

A rider crossed the grassland between the king's camp and Tide's End, his pace unhurried, an orange ribbon streaming from his horse's bridle.

The game's first move: listening to Cathmor's tedious, predictable threats.

Aric flattened his palms on stone as he studied the messenger. Sunlight glistened on the man's glossy ebony hair and on a gold clasp fastening a grey and black cloak.

A man of worth. From the bulky shoulders, a warrior.

"Aric Caelan." The stranger called up. "Open your gates."

Aric showed himself. "To whom?"

"The king's messenger."

"You can deliver your nonsense from there."

A hush fell. Soldiers on the wall paused, listening.

"My words are for the castle lord only."

Aric frowned. He expected a demand to surrender the castle or the king's forces overwhelmed them. Or unacceptable terms he must refuse. New rules to the game? Ah well, he could adapt.

"Open the gates."

He took the steps to the ward, Aiden at his heels. The stranger dismounted and passed his horse to a groom. Stubble shadowed the man's jaw. A generous mouth curved as though to smile, but his dark eyes held an unfriendly shimmer.

"Search him carefully, Aiden," Aric said.

The messenger's deceptively soft lips parted in a sneer. "You think I'm an assassin?" He raised arms heavy with muscle so Aiden could pat him down. The captain shook his head.

"Who are you, and what do you want?"

The stranger's unyielding stare fell hard on Aric. A king's man might well assess him, but he caught an odd note of censure, even anger, in that look.

"I bring the king's words," the messenger said. "Then mine."

Who did think he was? Aric usually laughed at arrogance, but this man's confidence had a dangerous edge.

"As to who I am? I suppose there has been no reason for us to meet." A pause. Again that flicker of distaste as this man considered him. "I am Vraymorg."

Vraymorg. Just a name but it filled the silence.

Aric clasped his hands together so he did not fidget. A turmoil exploded in his mind.

The Mountains lord. Kaell's lord. A man who must hate him. Now he understood that judging look. But was Vraymorg here to exact revenge, or did he just bring a message?

"My father is in the hall," Aric said with rigid courtesy. "If you'd come with me—my lord."

VAL ARQUES

He followed Aric to the great hall, his steps brisk and regimented. As if that act of control could banish his disquiet.

Familiar sounds, scents—half forgotten—tugged at him with bittersweet memory. Lavender, brine, and seaweed, a wind perfumed of summer, cawing, languid birds, the tide's rumble—all plucked from his childhood.

Vraymorg had been born here, on a grey, heavy day: my winter son, his mother had called him.

In these wards he had wielded his first sword. If he paused, surely he'd hear an echo of his mother's cry when he fell and cut his head and feel his father's calloused hand help him rise. In this hall he had wed a girl betrothed to him since birth. Her face forgotten.

Too long ago. Someone else's life.

At their intrusion, two men rose from behind a table. A clerk gathered up papers and scurried off. Aric shut the doors behind him. "Father. The king's messenger."

The older man glanced at Vraymorg. "Whoever you are, state your business then go. Thanks to your king, we have work to do."

"Very well." Vraymorg quietened his tapping fingers.

Unsettling to be in this hall again. "The king's words—then my own."

Aric leaned to whisper. The Isles lord's face creased in surprise. "I've heard of you, Vraymorg," he said. "Until now, you kept apart from the distractions of Telorian politics."

"The Silent Mountains are too dangerous for distractions. Ghouls, the Varee, Cahirean raiders even, all leave little time to worry about matters beyond my lands."

"Why then involve yourself in this business?"

"It was forced upon me."

The younger man poked his chin up with contempt. "You would have us believe you are not our enemy?"

"Who are you?" Vraymorg matched the insolent tone.

Hatton waved a hand. "My son and heir, Gendrick. Say your words, Vraymorg, so we may send this loathsome invader our defiance."

"Then I shall say the king's words, the words you expect and will answer as expected. The king says: Your city is invested. Surrender, or Cathmor takes it by force."

"Not quite invested," Aric said. "The sea is ours. So what terms? Unconditional?"

"There are terms." Cathmor preferred to win the Isles without a fight. "Surrender Tide's End, and the king promises fair treatment to all within. No building will burn. His soldiers will hurt no one who does not resist."

"My cousin wants Tide's End intact." Aric nodded. "What else?"

Vraymorg pressed his tongue to teeth. The rest was less palatable. "The self-proclaimed 'king' of the Isles, his brother, his son Gendrick, and daughter Azenor will surrender to the king's captains. An escort will take them to Mazen-da castle. No harm will come to them."

"And my son, Aric?"

"Aric will remain here."

"It is reasonable." Aric turned to his father. "You, Azenor, and Gendrick will be safe."

"We will reject my nephew's terms." Hatton whipped up a hand to silence Aric's objection. He faced Vraymorg. "What do you say, Vraymorg? You've been direct so far. What will my nephew do with Aric?"

"Cathmor is a proud man. Your son struck down a warrior under his protection. He escaped the king's custody and now holds this castle against him. Cathmor will force Aric to kneel before your men. Before you. Then"—he wet his lips—"the king will execute him."

A silence fell. Their expressions revealed nothing. "There is more," Vraymorg said. "Another is within these walls. The king desires you also give him up."

"And who is that?"

"His name is Kaell."

"Kaell." Hatton wandered to the windows. His sons watched him uneasily as he rested his hands on a sill. "And *your* message?" he said at length.

"It is about Kaell."

"Of course. He is yours." Aric brightened.

Yours. Vraymorg brushed off a stab of loss. "I raised him, if that's what you mean. So I ask you: Surrender him to me." Let him determine the boy's fate. If Kaell fell into the king's cruel hands, he'd die slowly.

"He is not here," Hatton said.

"That's what you came for?" Gendrick twisted a snide smile. "This fool of a king is about to rip Telor apart, and you want that ghoul brat?"

Vraymorg turned with a withering glare. "No, boy. My message is this: Do not foolishly shelter Kaell. Deliver him up. Or he'll bring trouble down upon your heads."

"What do you mean?" Hatton said sharply.

"Ghouls followed Kaell to Vraymorg. Attacked the fortress. Do not think you are safe. Surrender him. He belongs, as your son says, to me."

Hatton tapped his fingers on the window edge. Fast, fast, slow. "He is not here."

"I followed his trail. He is here."

"He is no longer within the walls of Tide's End."

"Then I will have to be content with that," Vraymorg said.

ARIC

Aric escorted Vraymorg to the gates, his mind awhirl with questions. Azenor's story about this man, hastily shared in the long hall, could not be true.

He considered the Mountains lord's stiff back. Anyone immortal would seem different. With an aura of the otherworld cloaking him, perhaps.

Not that Vraymorg wasn't extraordinary. He was. Disturbingly so.

Physically imposing, he possessed not only a bladesman's grace but an intangible quality of excellence, a curious detachment Aric mistakenly first dismissed as arrogance. It was as though this man stepped back from the world even as he moved through it.

What did it hide? Deep-held pain, surely. Aric could not help but see the scars on the Mountains lord's wrists and wonder at them.

"Not that way, Vraymorg." He blocked the stairwell. "This way."

"I have no time for games. It is quicker to reach the gates through the inner ward."

Aric almost stumbled, a drumming in his skull. No Mountains lord had ever visited Tide's End as far as he knew. He scrunched a fistful of his tunic. "You know this castle?"

Vraymorg's pause was so indistinct Aric nearly missed it.

"How could I?" the man said. "But I know castle design, and we should go this way."

"Nevertheless." Aric gestured away from the stairs. Intriguing or not, this lord remained the king's man. The less he glimpsed of Tide's End's defences the better.

Vraymorg shrugged. "It hardly matters if I count your soldiers or mangonels. This castle will not withstand the assault. Not this time. You must know that."

"Tide's End has never fallen," Aric countered. "You must know that."

"I don't seek to destroy your morale, boy. Warfare has changed since Devarsi's time. The king's engines will breach your walls."

"You're only trying to help, is that it?"

"Not at all. I simply have no reason to lie. However, I will deliver the king your message of scorn, and then we will see." He turned.

"Wait." Aric grasped the man's arm.

Vraymorg looked down at his hand. "Take care not to provoke me. You tried to kill him. Kaell. For that, I bear you a grudge. I begged Cathmor to surrender you to me so I could drop you in a deep hole in the Mountains and teach you about despair."

Aric's grip fell away. "You are entitled to your hatred, Vraymorg. Come after me when this war is done. I'll answer your accusations with steel. For now, tell the king—" He bit his lip. Dare he defy his father? "Tell the king we will consider his terms."

"Consider."

"Yes, consider."

Vraymorg lifted his eyes to Aric's face. "Make no mistake, Aric Caelan. Cathmor will humiliate you, torture you, then kill you. I cannot pretend to be sorry."

"His other terms are fair. My aunt, Cathmor's mother, is custodian at Mazen-da Castle. My father, brother, and sister will be securely kept but comfortable."

Vraymorg turned away. "Very well. Lord Hatton is considering His Grace's terms."

King Hatton. Aric let it rest. "About Kaell."

Vraymorg whipped back, the small gesture telling. The man was desperate to find him.

"I'll say you asked after him."

Nodding slowly, Vraymorg said, "I guessed your father did not speak the entire truth."

"My sister told me a story," Aric blurted. "About you."

"I am not your business."

"Azenor says you're Isles-born, of Caelan blood."

Vraymorg drew very still. He looked right at Aric. Wariness glittered in long-lashed eyes indeed dark enough to belong to an Isles man.

"She says you do not die. That you trained every bonded warrior from the first."

"Your sister speaks nonsense."

"Does she? That stubble ages you, but beneath this deception, you're no older than Kaell."

The other man rested gloved hands on the stone balustrade, staring at nothing.

Dust swirled. Beating sun scorched Aric's scalp. The glinting sea frothed over reefs. Carts rumbled in the ward. Clanging steel, thudding axes, squeaking leather, and shouts of men on the wall ground together into a harsh melody.

Nothing louder, though, than his heart and its uneven, pounding rhythm. He forced a breath and waited for a stranger to explain away what he said, to laugh or mock him.

Instead, Vraymorg sighed. "You and I, Aric Caelan," he said quietly. "We won't meet again this side of death."

"You believe if not my cousin, then the gods will punish me?" Aric laughed mirthlessly. "Which gods, Vraymorg? Your gods?"

"Khir's curse is upon a man who sheds a bonded warrior's blood."

Yes, a shadow stalked him. Nothing mystical. Just guilt. About Kaell. About Aric's dead warriors. A bladesman trusted steel, not supernatural nonsense. He had to. "And is that the truth that explains you? Are you also a cursed man?"

"Cursed." Vraymorg's shoulders stooped as though laden with an unspoken misery. "Is that why I shared the burden of who I am with a spirited, young woman that night? I told your sister things, bitter things, someone so young should not hear. Because I thought she, an Isles princess of my blood, might understand."

"Who are you?" Aric whispered.

"Do you mean my name?" For the first time the other man smiled. He looked younger then, even younger, and Aric shivered.

"I shall tell you," Vraymorg said. "And you shall search for me in your books in the long, tedious weeks ahead while the king waits without and you wait within. But the king will prevail. I am sorry for it. For I was born a son of the Isles in this very castle."

"It's not possible—" Aric broke off, trembling.

Again the man's dark eyes settled on him. "As you say. And yet..."

"How?"

"A sorcerer sought something from me. I tried to escape him." Vraymorg absently touched a wrist bracelet. "He imprisoned me, condemned me to an eternity of darkness. Until Devarsi heard me weeping and freed me."

"A cursed queen," Aric muttered.

"Cursed or not, I loved her, vowed to serve those of her blood, like Cathmor. Even though their gods aren't mine. Even when they war against the city of my birth, against those I would rather cut off my arm than fight."

"Then do not." Aric struggled to make sense of this. "You're an Isles man. Fight with us. Take our side."

Vraymorg curled a gloved hand. Slowly. As if drawing every bit of inconvenient emotion into that clench to control it. "We are both on a path, Aric Caelan," he said. "We met here, briefly, because I sought word of Kaell. I told you the truth because you will die soon. If by chance you do not and you tell my secret, I will deny it. No one will believe you."

"They might."

"I've had centuries to learn how to hide. The Lords of Vraymorg always die soon after their monarchs. They leave behind with a faithful servant letters and sworn documents naming a bastard as their successor—me. I change my appearance a little, my servant remarks about how I look like my father." He shrugged. "In time, I present myself at court to the new king as my father's son. No one has suspected anything. No one will."

"We share blood. My father, my brother, Azenor, we're your kin. Yet you do not take our part." Anger burst through him. "You disgust me."

"I owe no debt to those of my blood." Vraymorg's voice was cold.

Aric stared. None of it could be true. "Who are you?" he said again.

HEATH

The camp echoed with thudding axes. Bora demanded wood for battering rams, and wood he would have. Once the engines pierced the walls, he intended to ram the gates.

"They'll expect us to pour through the breach," the king's captain explained to the war council that morning. "Not come through the gates."

"The problem is," Heath told his captain, Dillon, afterwards, "we can't get anywhere near the gates without losing a lot of men. Aric's archers will pick us off."

"It might work if it's a double bluff," Dillon said. "Both the charge at the gates and the breach feints. Attack from the sea side."

"Very good." Heath tilted a brow. "With those wits, we're clearly kin, cousin. I'm still better looking of course."

Leaving Dillon at the king's pavilion, he stomped around bogs and rain puddles, weaving through carts and cook fires to his tent on a flat hill. Hearing singing, he grinned as he pushed through the flaps. "Judith."

His sister soaped an arm extended from a wooden tub. She broke off her song. "Heath dear, be more than decorative for once, and tell that girl I need more hot water."

Like an obedient puppy, Heath found the servant then

wandered back to watch Bora's men fell trees. One must find entertainment where one could. A dull business, sieges.

He returned to find Judith dressed and towelling her hair.

"I hope you didn't mean to keep my presence secret, Heath," she said. "Men scuttled off to tell the king when we rode in."

Heath swept up her hand to kiss her fingers. "You're hardly the only woman in camp so Cathmor won't wonder if I'm up to mischief."

"Camp followers," she sniffed.

"And a bejewelled mistress or two. The Lord of the Plains brought his wife and daughter. He thought a siege might amuse them. Or maybe he hopes to find a husband for the girl. What a fat fool. Gods help him if there's actual fighting."

Judith snatched up a comb to attack her hair. With wet locks sticking to her cheeks, she looked young and vulnerable. A useful disguise. Judith wasn't that even in the womb.

"Your message said you have a task for me?"

"I do. A fish to catch."

"Am I to look ravishing at dinner with the king and his lords tonight? For this fish?"

"Perceptive girl. Yes, no doubt the king will insist we dine with him."

"And?" Judith tugged at a knot. "Am I to hook the king?"

"Not Cathmor. You reeled him in months ago. No, this fish will be slippery. I have no idea what bait to use. Does he prefer women or goats? Perhaps he abstains from all that is fleshly and embraces his blade at night for comfort. Who can tell?"

Judith raised an eyebrow. "Does this abstaining, blade-embracing fish have a name?"

"He does." He ducked as she hurled the comb.

"Tease. Is this to do with Aric? It seems hopeless. You and I are here, on a small hill overlooking a field of mud and tents."

"We are *without*," Heath said. "As those involved in sieges say."

"And Aric Caelan is behind Tide's End's walls, looking down at us and our mud."

"He is *within.*"

Judith laughed. "Be serious. I'm assuming your fish is 'without' and not 'within'. A pity I can't play with Aric. He's almost as pretty as his captain, the one you nearly cut up."

"Don't forget I didn't cut up the pretty captain, just to please you." No need to tell her Pairas's fate now. Judith did not need pretty distractions. "No, even if without, you can't play with Aric. Myranthe wants to torment that fish."

She feigned a pout. "You spoil my fun."

"This fish will be fun—and to your taste."

"Promises, promises. Well, go on with your fish nonsense."

"Our fish is a young lord. One I never encountered until two days ago when he came into the king's tent, weary, wounded, and rather grimy from a long ride."

"That's to my taste? Grimy and weary? No doubt stinking of sweat."

Heath grinned, enjoying their game. "He brought important news for the king, so one can forgive him for looking dishevelled. He'll scrub up nicely, you'll see."

"Was this important news about Khir's bonded warrior? Don't look shocked. It's all over camp about Kaell. That means this lord who brought the tale is Vraymorg."

"Ah, so sharp you'll cut yourself one day."

"I've heard that said of you. No one seems to understand that beneath the charm you're really very tedious." Judith frowned. "Why do you want me to get close to Vraymorg?"

"Because I don't understand him, because he's very prickly, and the king resents him."

"Prickly. Hmm. If you're interested, he must be a swordsman."

"He moves like a swordsman. But there's so much more, Judith. This is a powerful man, an intense man. Quite fascinating. He almost frightens me."

That snagged her attention. "Frightens? That makes him singular."

Heath laughed. “Oh little sister, I am easily frightened. I’m terrified of muddying my boots on this hill. So troublesome. When I asked that servant of yours to bring hot water, I trembled at her glare. Not to mention when the king flies into a rage, I want to cry.”

“There, there,” she comforted, laughing.

But she was right. Vraymorg was singular. Heath wanted to know why.

Before he killed him.

KAELL

Wind lifted his hair, its tangy breath pleasantly warm. White-tipped waves foamed over reef and rocks, brushing sand with damp fingers.

Kaell stripped off his pants. Naked, he let the tide lap his toes. Until Archanin took him prisoner in that vile ruin, he had never felt ashamed of his hard body. Now it no longer seemed a part of him. Its flesh, bone, and skin a shell for his impure blood.

Gripped by a strange calm, he waded out. His breaths matched the waves' rhythm, their hum a song in his head. Hip-deep, he dropped beneath the water.

The shrieking of sea birds and the wind's roar fell away. Time moved softly. Deeper and deeper he sank. Why not just let his breath go and drift into death? No more shame. No fear, no doubts.

Sun broke through clouds, filtering down through the rippling sea. Kaell squinted, an uncomfortable ache behind his eye sockets heralding a vision.

It came from nowhere; the sea was gone in a heartbeat. His back pressed against chafing wood. Iron bruised his ankles and wrists. Limp pennons and standards drooped from tent poles. Mist swirled, damp on his skin. A man stood before him. His lord, his face gaunt with pain. He held a sword. The blade swung. At Kaell.

Kaell's breath rushed out. Flailing, a weight on his chest, he kicked until he surfaced above cresting waves. Desperately he gulped in air, unable to stop the vision rolling on.

Oars splashed waves. Wind streamed Azenor's hair, her hands clasped about her knees as a boat yawed. "Kaell," she said. Just "Kaell," and laughed.

They sank onto the sand, shoulders touching, watching the boat pull away towards a red-hued horizon.

"Where does it go?"

"Beyond the Enarae," she said. "Through the veil."

"Why are you here?"

Azenor stroked his face, her fingers clammy. "Don't you know? What do your dreams tell you? You should listen to their warning."

She disappeared. Despite the late afternoon sun, gooseflesh pimpled Kaell's arms. His shadow clouded the waves. The vision made no sense. But it was a bad portent.

HE FOUND AINGEAR crouched by a stream in a forest-ringed grove above the cliffs. A stiffening breeze creaked through soughing trees, its summer breath nectar. Alyssum and bluebells patterned a rippling white and blue rug. Butterflies danced in balmy air that defied the approaching dusk.

"Did you immerse your head beneath the waves?" she said. "It is part of the ritual."

Kaell nodded and looked about him. "What is this place?"

"The island is a temple to The Three."

"A temple?"

"Listen."

Bees droned. Down a rolling hillside, waves foamed on rocks. Yet as twilight lengthened shadows, the wind groaned an eerie song and the stream whispered over pebbles.

Kaell shivered. This island and its strange gods repelled him.

She considered him in silence for a moment.

"Tell me of your life. I hear the Mountains fortress is a forbidding place."

"I felt safe there. Because of my lord." Kaell smiled. "I remember the first time he gave me a real sword, steel, not wood. My lord dismissed the weapons master and said, 'Show me what you know. And I'll show you why it's not enough.'"

How he had glowed with pleasure to have Vraymorg's attention focused only on him.

"A harsh man."

"A truthful man," Kaell said. "No one ever matched him with the blade." His belly twisted—a sharp, painful lurch of loss and loneliness. His lord had always shielded him. He was the one certainty in his life. Whatever the trouble, he knew what to do.

But Vraymorg wasn't here. Kaell was alone in a land with gods he didn't understand, in a body with appetites he wasn't certain he could control.

He closed his eyes, remembering how his lord had hurled the sword in that cell as though he could not contain his despair. Did he care? Could he?

The priestess rose. "Let me show you something."

She led him up a fat, earthy-scented hill in the island's centre, its slopes tangled with small-leafed bushes. Feathery grass brushed his legs. Across twilight-dark waves, islands bobbed like beaten husks on a horizon ablaze with swirling orange and pink.

The high priestess pushed through bushes towards a black stone. It was low and long with iron bands hammer struck into its wind-beaten, flat surface.

Kaell paused beside a nearby oval-shaped rock. Though worn, its edges crumbling, it was free of weeds, with words carved into its seaward face.

"What does it say?"

Solemnly, Aingear replied, “It says, ‘Karmarna. The king’s sword. The man’s friend.’ *He* came back and buried the body. That stone is a grave marker.”

“He?”

“Roaran Caelan nearly lost his life here long ago.”

“When he was king? Why was he here?”

“To pay homage to The Three as the Lord of the Isles must do each midsummer. One year, Adorean soldiers ambushed Roaran and his escort. Trapped, outnumbered, his king’s sword, Karmarna of the Icelands, sacrificed his life to delay the Adoreans so Roaran could escape.” She brushed a palm over the black stone. “His sacrifice makes this a place of power.”

The unknown laid a bewildering hand on Kaell. Dry-mouthed, he shifted his eyes to the dark stains beneath Aingear’s hand. “What are the iron bands for?”

But the priestess already turned away. He trudged after her back to the stream.

She sent him to gather more wood. When he returned, she jiggled a pan in the fire.

Kaell dumped an armful of branches. The aroma of frying fish roused a nagging hunger for both food and blood. He had built inner walls to cage that blood lust. But should they crumble and he killed, he was lost. A pariah.

“You promised your gods could save me. Is it true? Even if they’re not my gods?”

“Yes. Because I now know how to bind you to them.” She hugged her knees. “It is easier, though, if you could put aside your gods—”

“No.”

“They failed you, Kaell. Did Khir hear your pleas when Archanin held you prisoner?”

“You don’t know what you ask.” Kaell slumped beside her. “In battle, Khir grants me strength and Kutron the wind’s speed. I belong to these jealous Mountains gods.”

He would not tell her of the wretched oath he had reluctantly sworn to Archanin. Would not.

Coiling smoke hid her expression. "Then it will be harder for us both," she said.

"Why? What must happen? When?"

"Soon."

Irritated, he hurled a stick into the fire. It caught alight and quickly charred. Like a warrior's life. A fast burn, bright. Then gone.

"Priestess, I want to trust you. But what do you intend to do?"

The silence lengthened. Kaell's frustration ripped to anger. He stormed to his feet. "You promised to heal me. When? Why do we bathe, cook fish, do nothing?"

Aingear only said, "Soon."

IN DREAMS THAT NIGHT the old Mountains gods, ghost pale, called to him. *Come,* they whispered, their emerald eyes glittering. *Follow us.* And he followed them, laughing, into a thick forest.

Deep in the bowing trees, wet grass on his toes, Kaell looked for them. He was alone.

"My lord," he cried, forgetting the gods, wanting only Vraymorg's comforting presence. "Where are you? I trusted you to save me."

A ragged breeze rustled leaves. A bird swooped, its caw the only answer.

Kaell woke sweating. Aingear touched fingertips to his cheek. "Hush, hush. A dream."

"I couldn't find my lord." Kaell blinked away tears. "I couldn't find the gods."

"Leave those gods be." She offered him a cup. "Drink. I prepared wine mixed with blood. It will keep you strong. You must be strong."

Thirsty, hungry, his thoughts scrambled by nightmares, Kaell drained the cup then curled, listening to the wind trailing through grass like gloved hands. The salt scents of a roiling ocean mingled with the aroma of fennel.

The sea's chill, whipped by gusts that frothed waves, seemed too alive, unlike the sterile cold of the Mountains. As a child, Kaell had slept in a fur-lined bed, a fire in his chamber, but in deepest winter nothing kept him warm.

He remembered wandering barefoot into his lord's solar one bitter night after a dream had torn him from sleep. Vraymorg was drinking alone by the fire. "Go back to sleep, Kaell," he said.

"If I sleep, the nightmare returns."

Vraymorg had stared into the flames. "I, too, flee from dreams tonight."

"What's in your dreams?"

"The past," his lord said quietly. He blinked, smiled, bid Kaell sit beside him, and told him stories until dawn of warriors of Telor, long dead. Of Dace Caelan, who defeated a tyrant in the desert city of Seithin, of Rainer who disobeyed the gods and sired a daughter who stole the throne from her cousin.

A wide-eyed Kaell listened to the tale of a jealous sorcerer who destroyed Seithin because the desert city's beautiful, green-eyed queen loved a Telorian king called Rollo. He liked best the stories of Caelan, the son of a god and a Cahirean princess.

"They called Caelan the gormel slayer," his lord said. "He must have been a vengeful, driven man for he did not stop until he had killed every gormel."

"What is a gormel? Is it like a ghoul?"

"Gormels served the demon lord Aziarr." Vraymorg shifted burning wood with a poker. "When Caelan died, the people feared Aziarr's wrath. But another hero came. Then another. Until Rainer at last slew Aziarr in far-away Quisnaf."

And Kaell, falling towards sleep as wind howled across the sea and across an island temple, wondered why his lord had never told him stories about Roaran.

HE WOKE BESIDE a cold fire pit. Alone. A dull ache beat behind his eyes the way it did when the physician allowed him poppy juice for battle wounds.

Yawning, hungry, Kaell rose and stretched.

How long had he slept? Already twilight's sounds thrummed: an owl's hoot, the rustle of paws through grass, a chirr of insects. The sun quickly vanished towards a rusted horizon.

Through swaying branches, a light blinked from the hill and its forbidding black stone.

A beacon—to him.

As though disembodied by Aingear's draught, his feet carried him towards the light.

The priestess called that hilltop a place of power because a man died to save his king there. For honour? Duty? Maybe love.

Kaell would die for his lord in a heartbeat, without question. This warrior, Karmarna. He must have loved Roaran Caelan with that same fierce devotion Kaell felt for the man who had raised him. How strange to think some Ice lord loved a Caelan king like that.

The night wisped with scents and sounds: churned earth, mud, orange blossom, a rustle of wind through dead leaves. Early moonlight bathed the grove a silver-grey. But that wasn't the light that drew him. That light flamed. It flickered through dripping branches, dimming stars.

An otherworldly web folded about him as Kaell moved like a ghost towards the flames. Two rows of blazing torches lit a path to the stone. And beside the stone, hair streaming like silken midnight, her skin pale perfection in the silvery light, stood Azenor.

Kaell's heart lurched then sang, as he stumbled through dew-wet grass.

The dream. That kiss in the tunnel as water trickled.

Azenor turned her head. Her beauty was unearthly. “Kaell?”

“I’m here.”

With shaking fingers she released a clasp. Her cloak fluttered down. Her nakedness stole his breath, whipped up heat in his blood and loins. Not like the dream at all.

He struggled from his pants, heart unsteady against caging ribs, aching for her urgently.

“Kaell,” Azenor held out her arms.

AZENOR

His sighs were like a song's low notes. Did he dream? Sweet, sweet dreams of torches burning low. Of soft touches, murmurs. Of desire.

Azenor slid a lock of Kaell's hair between her fingers, imagining its pale colour. She traced his face: the curved jaw and angled cheekbones, the shape of a brow. Lips.

She remembered his kiss, the vulnerability, the wonder in it, how his tongue teased, how he drew her down, whispering she must tell him if he hurt her.

"You will never hurt me," she said, stroking, circling, rubbing until she found the rhythm that most excited him. His groans, his hands hot on her skin, flamed a frantic need to fall into his embrace, into that moment, and banish everything else. Duty and guilt done with. Except when she licked his neck, his sweat and the sea's salt was the taste of her betrayal. Betrayal shouldn't taste so good.

Kaell stirred in sleep. Huddled against him, Azenor touched his scarred breast. How those muscles had strained beneath her hands such a short time ago. How he had moaned with pleasure as she shifted, gripping his hips to take him deeper.

When his thrusts came faster, when he cried out, a beat

resounded through the earth, primal, exciting, then an ethereal sigh as though the gods watched with pleasure.

She had become their instrument. Like Roaran.

Bile curdled in her throat. *You ask too much, Roaran,* she whispered to the darkness. *I thought I could do your will. Except you didn't say I'd care.*

Kaell woke with a soft release of breath. Murmuring her name, his mouth sought hers, lips parting. His kiss was uncomplicated. Hers was not. It was despairing, lost. She pressed against him, wanting to force the world away with all-consuming desire.

"You have a scar," he murmured. "Right above your heart. Just like in my dream."

"Yes. Like your dream."

"It's time," Aingear touched Azenor's shoulder. "You know what to do."

Kaell tensed. "Time?"

"Dress quickly. Then I'll explain." *About betrayal.*

"If this were a fairy tale." He laughed. "I'd wake to find the magical maiden gone."

If only this were a fairy tale.

Kaell moved a distance away, humming. The high priestess thrust a robe into her arms. As she threw it over her head, Azenor begged, "Tell me how he looks."

"You must forget him," Aingear said sharply. "You know what happens now."

She knew. Oh, how she knew. "Please. Before I—before it happens."

"Child, such words can only make you blush."

Blush? After months as Archanin's prisoner? Sob more likely. Or even laugh, a twisted sound that would shock the high priestess.

With a heavy sigh, Aingear relented. "He moves with an easy grace."

"He has many scars. I felt them."

"A warrior's scars and his god's frightening signs."

All warriors bore scars. She'd traced Roaran's often enough, though his deepest wounds inflamed within. He thought he hid them. But in his sleep he begged another woman for forgiveness.

Aingear closed Azenor's fingers around a knife. "The gods will help you," she said.

Steel in her hand. Cold. Only now did this seem real. She never imagined the churning in her gut, the hot, dizzy nausea throbbing up. The guilt. Was it too late to stop this? She could hurl away the knife. Tell Roaran to find another way.

What if she did? But what if that meant the future unfolded as Roaran warned? A bleak, terrible future where ghouls ruled Tide's End, their god's temple rising up taller than the walls. Where dull-eyed men, women, girls, boys trembled on their knees before their blood-thirsty masters.

The Three help her. Strengthen her resolve. She could not let that happen. No matter who she hurt.

At the sound of Kaell's steps, Azenor nearly shouted, "run." But a princess of the Isles knew about duty, more than any swaggering warrior with a sword.

Kaell drew her into his arms. She was starkly aware of him, of every breath, of the press of their thighs, of skin, of lips. Of the life in him.

The knife almost slid from her quivering fingers. One life to save her people. Just one. She dared not pause or think, for if she did, she could not do this. Even for Roaran. Even for the Isles.

Kaell held her so close Azenor had to pull back a little. With a swift breath in, she tore the knife down his belly. A shallow gash.

Kaell gasped, slumped against her. Hoarse with shock, he muttered, "Azenor?"

"Take him," the high priestess commanded.

The stillness exploded with a flurry of voices and movement. Booted steps. Kaell's protests. Azenor imagined rough hands hurling him up, holding his shoulders.

"Azenor. I don't understand. I thought—"

"That I cared?" She banished compassion, caged her heart as any dutiful swaggering dancer might. His blood wet her palms. Wipe it off, and that was an end to it.

"I did my duty. The high priestess prepared you; she bid you wash in sacred waters. You drank the sacred wine. Our joining binds you to an Isles princess and through me to our gods."

Kaell must have struggled then for she heard scuffling and a thud.

"Bring him," Aingear said.

"You're so cold," Kaell whispered. "I don't understand."

"You had warning enough, Kaell." Her bitterness surprised her—as if she blamed him for trusting her. "Your dreams. A warning, you said. Yet you never wondered about that kiss."

ARIC

Aric traced words in a book, its embossed pages yellowed by age. Sweat ran down his neck. A beeswax candle spluttered, its flame upright in steamy air faintly perfumed of jasmine and frangipani.

"A son born today to the Duke of Avanti," he read. "I shall name him Val Arques."

He leaned back. A few lines in the long-dead duke's diary, its vellum thinned and the writing faded. So little when he had so many questions.

A tap at the door broke into his thoughts. At his call of "come," a squire rushed inside, breathing hard.

Aric surged to his feet. "What's happened?"

The young man held out rolled-up parchment. "A man said to give you this," he stammered. "A lord. Yes, a lord. Or a prince."

"What lord?"

The squire dragged his tongue over his lips. "He did not give a name. He said only to tell you these exact words at this very hour, not a moment before or a moment later. To say you must stop the high priestess. You must repay your debt."

VAL ARQUES

The woman stole away from the feast. Vraymorg knew she wanted him to follow.

He drained his cup, wondering at her game.

When Judith Damadar and her brother had joined the king at his table, voices hushed, only picking up when servants brought more wine.

As an hour passed, then another, glances again and again fell upon her. But Judith had locked her eyes with his. Every tilt of that lovely head, every beguiling smile, every glimpse of ample breasts, became an offer, that last look before she slipped outside a promise.

Vraymorg gestured to a servant to refill his cup. He could drink and forget her. Or play her game. *Why not?* Only his empty bed, a drawn-out night and suffocating dawn lay ahead.

He sipped. Why not? Because her brother was a sharp-witted Ice lord.

Vraymorg put down the cup and rose.

Heath leaned towards the king, hand to lips as though sharing dangerous secrets. From Cathmor's smirk, probably a bawdy story.

Two men at a lower table discussed the spoils when Tide's End fell.

Vraymorg remembered Aric's stillness when he had delivered the king's demands. The Isles commander wasn't afraid. Nor was he about to give in. What was that expression? They counted coins not minted. Only stupid men thought of gain before winning the battle.

A drunken Nate Caelmarsh waved a knife at a man called Sherrin Cross, his voice strident. He'd likely use that knife or his fists, before the night grew much older.

Safer outside with a scheming daughter of the Icelands.

He pushed aside the tent flaps, passing bland guards.

The encampment blazed with cook fires, hundreds of them. Aric could count them from his battlements and know how many men stood against him. But the young Isles commander would not yield. Not him.

Across welling darkness, torches flamed on Tide's End's ancient walls and towers. Which light came from the room where Aric hunched over a table, searching his books for a man called Val Arques?

A man who no longer existed.

A man who had died aged nineteen, sobbing in a sunlit tower room.

Heat closed in on him: its thick taste in his mouth, its damp touch on his arms, and sultry air, aromatic with wormwood. The tide throbbed beneath murmuring voices, laughter, and footfall. A trebuchet's counterweight bucket gently creaked.

The scents, the sounds took him back to childhood, to nights lying beneath the window in his room at Tide's End, barely a feather of wind whispering across moist skin as he dreamed of honour and glory and other such nonsense. The stiff heat, the tide's hum, lightning splitting a velvet sky, these Isles fragrances of blossoms, salt, and pungent mud after rain brought back the past like nothing else. He wasn't sure he wanted it back.

At the sight of the woman waiting at the top of a rise, he hesitated. Judith turned and smiled. Pulse unsteady, he joined her. Her perfume was so gentle he caught only an intriguing hint. The air stirred with a heady mix of heat, desire, and anticipation.

"I hoped it would be you," she said.

"If I hadn't come, what would you have done?"

"But you did."

Vraymorg laughed. Men always behaved as she expected. Yet what would she have when her waist thickened and her glorious hair thinned? Her wits? Perhaps they mirrored her brother's.

"I know who you are," he said. "Every man in that pavilion tonight sought your name. Did your brother tell you to seduce me? What does he want of me, Judith Damadar?"

Judith did not bother with denials. "My brother finds you enigmatic." She giggled, a surprisingly innocent sound. "He even told me he is a little afraid of you."

Vraymorg pressed his tongue into the roof of his mouth. Heath blazed with the arrogance of a man confident of not only his status but his intelligence and skill. A man like that feared very few. No, something else played out here.

"I am also a little afraid of you." Judith touched his arm. "I like that feeling. Forget my brother and his games. Ask instead what I want of you."

Her eyes were hot, unlike the cool hand she boldly slid beneath his tunic. Her fingers roamed without haste over bare skin. His breath caught. The whisper of fingertips, the scent of her hair, the perfume of lust and need, awoke a ménage of sensations. Vraymorg had heard the stories about who had trained her, knew the delights a night with this woman promised.

He remembered then another night when the wind whispered through torn stonework and a woman came to his room. How he took her in his arms because she was beautiful and he was just as lonely as he was tonight.

"Is this what you want of me?" He drew Judith into an embrace and kissed her savagely.

"Come to our tent." Her voice thickened. "My brother won't return for hours."

Judith did not look back as she walked away.

Beyond the camp a light flared in the middle of the sea. Then more lights bobbed. Did something unfold on the Isle of the Gods?

Shrugging, he put it out of his mind and followed her.

ARIC

Aric crawled through bushes at the edge of the moon-frosted knoll. As he dropped to his belly, flames from a pit spat at warm air. A spark flew into grass. He swatted it, ears strained for his men moving into place around him.

Beneath a curlew's mournful song, a chant rose and fell, distorted by the wind into an eerie moan. Figures emerged from the trees, their hooded silhouettes grotesque against the writhing flames. They carried burning torches to a large, flat stone.

Aric knew this place, that stone. As a child he had traced the words in the grave marker, thinking about Roaran Caelan. About sacrifice.

Sacrifice. The word beat uneasily in his head. None of what he'd just seen made sense.

Azenor had stabbed Kaell. Then Aingear ordered robed figures to drag him off. And who was this stranger who sent a squire to tell him to stop this? A lord, the frightened boy said.

The figures thrust the torches into soft earth, their voices a low monotone. Others dragged a struggling Kaell towards the stone. He broke free only to stumble a step and slip to his hands and knees. His captors fell on him.

Throw them off, Aric willed. *Run.*

Yanked to his feet, held, Kaell uselessly writhed. One struck him a heavy blow that snapped his head back. He hung limply in their grasps as they stripped him naked and hoisted him onto the stone. Pinned his arms and legs until they shackled him.

The figures parted for Aingear. Aric's gut churned. He guessed what she intended but didn't know why. Interfere, and he defied the temple. But do nothing, and Kaell died.

Gesturing to his men to fan left and right, Aric crawled closer. Two moons, high and full, washed the knoll in light, soft as though filtered through mesh.

Their glitter struck steel as Aingear lifted a knife. The robed figures ringed the stone.

"An Isles princess bound him to our gods. She struck the first blow." Aingear's ceremonial voice carried across the hillside. "Each of us, each priest and priestess of The Three, must take up this blade to complete the spell."

The blade came down. Kaell jerked. Aingear stroked his hair, murmuring. A priest at her side took the knife and stabbed. This time Kaell cried out.

The last of Aric's men moved into place. He leapt up, sword drawn, bellowing, "Stop!"

Aingear whirled. "You." Her stirred-up gaze swung from Aric to the Isles soldiers surging from the trees. "How dare you! This is the will of The Three. Leave."

Her companions closed protectively about Kaell.

Aric walked purposely towards the stone. He didn't want a fight. Not with her. But now he drew steel he could not turn back. "Release him."

The high priestess stamped her foot in fury. "Have you lost your wits? With this sacrifice, we can again protect the Isles from Archanin and those who drink life."

"You intend to restore Roaran's blood spell."

"Yes." Surprise in her tone. She had underestimated him and had forgotten Aric had studied history along with swordplay. He knew every ancient text in Tide's End.

"Pairas told me about the defiled burial tower. This is not the answer, priestess. Do you even know how Roaran cast this spell? Are any of you as powerful as him?"

Beneath hoods, resentful faces glowered. Kaell shifted. Hands pressed him down.

"I have the words of Roaran's spell," Aingear said. "The Three showed me this boy in visions. They demand him as the sacrifice. Roaran's spell to keep ghouls from the Isles is blood magic, and the gods require a life."

Aric took a step towards Kaell. Robed figures blocked him. He pushed them aside. When others rushed him, his men shoved them back.

"My lord," one of his companions began uncertainly. "What if it *is* the will of our gods?"

Then Aric brought a storm of outrage and condemnation down upon his head.

Memories knocked together in his mind. An interrogator's moist palms on his buttocks. Leather slicing air, the starburst of agony across his shoulders. The odours of the king's prison, dust, blood, air rank enough to cut with a knife. His despair.

But most of all, he remembered a young man on top of a tower throwing back his hood and grinning as he bid him climb down to safety.

Aric shouldered through. Kaell groaned, his eyes shuttered with pain. Pooling blood from shallow wounds trickled from the stone to the ground.

Not allowing himself time to think, Aric crashed steel down on the chains.

For a heartbeat time stalled. The priests and priestesses drew in disbelieving breaths, the sound like swooping wings.

Then chaos erupted. Enraged, the high priestess clawed at him. Aric held her off. Her followers surged at the stone. His men kept them back.

"The king will hear of this." Aingear's voice rose to screech. "Take him then, you foolish prince. But I'll have him back. Your father is no ghoul lover like you."

"It's murder. Just like your so-called executions of cultists." The only just death was steel against steel where a man stood a chance to change his fate.

"Murder? Of a half-ghoul?" The high priestess laughed aloud. It whipped with coldness. "Fool, fool. You do our enemies' work."

Aric closed his mind to her taunts. "Can you walk?" he asked Kaell.

Kaell moaned and clutched his belly as he sat up. Blood streamed through his fingers. "Don't know."

"The two moons are full again tomorrow. And the night after," Aingear hurled at his back as Aric helped Kaell hobble. "All you did is delay this ceremony by a day."

All he did was make an enemy. Of her and of his gods.

AZENOR

She could not even retch. It would not be that easy. Nor could she run, flee the tears held close inside. Poisoning tears she had no right to.

Azenor could only collapse on the sand near her brother's boats, her drawn-up knees a wall against guilt. That sickening scene repeated again and again in her mind: the knife, how it tore into his skin, his blood slick on her hands. Kaell's weight on her. The hurt in his voice.

Cold, he had called her. A single word that shouldn't wound as it did.

"You must take it where it leads." Roaran's voice hammered, a dreadful echo in her mind. "Even to death."

One death to save the Isles, to save Telor. Just as Roaran promised. And she believed in Roaran. Who could not? He was extraordinary, the seer king returned. The only man able to stop Archanin.

Then why did her gut roil? Why did her breast ache?

"Azenor."

Him? Here? At last. Oh, at last. Blood pounded in her head as Roaran took her shoulders. She had long imagined this moment: how he reassured her with soft words, soft touches, told her everything was all right.

Except it wasn't. Her guilt soured it all.

Azenor beat her fists against his breast. "I disgust myself." Miserable tears strained at her eyes even as his death rider's touch restored her sight.

Slowly his face sharpened. She blinked, staring in wonder at shattering waves, at stars dimmed by the moons. "Oh." Azenor touched her eyes. "I forgot what it's like to see."

"I'm sorry it had to be like that, Azenor," Roaran said. "But everything's all right now."

She clutched at him. "Please tell me I don't have to be apart from you. Not again."

"You don't have to be apart from me," he said.

Was there an undercurrent in his voice? Or was it her? Her doubt.

She curled her hand. The hand that had held the knife. The hand she had furiously wiped on her gown, unable to forget how the blade had cut Kaell. No resistance. Just flesh tearing. Then blood. Sticky, warm blood.

"I did everything we planned," she said. "But it's too much, Roaran. I hurt him."

He drew her close, his body so familiar she melted into him. How she had ached for this man. But her lies tainted the comfort she thought she'd find in the press of his arms, his nearness.

"You bound the boy to us. Your part is done."

Azenor clung to him, dazzled by longing, by that half-forgotten, beautiful face. An artful symmetry of brow, cheek, and chin. Eyes no poet had ever properly described. A colour not like the sea or sky but that blue-black of twilight.

"Take me with you beyond the Enarae again. Just as you promised. You never lie."

"I said I'd come," Roaran smoothed her hair with his palm. "To take you back with a kiss."

"A kiss." Azenor remembered the words she had thrown at

Kaell to wound him, to cover her guilt.

You had warning enough. Yet you never wondered about that kiss.

At last her tears poured out. For Kaell. For herself. "You warned me not to care." Azenor pulled her hands free. "Do you think I could know him, lie with him, and feel nothing?"

"For duty? Why not?" His voice had a harsh edge. A stranger's voice. "I can. I have."

Sounds beat about her, through her. Wings. Caws. The sea's murmur. The startled clamour of her heart. Surely she misunderstood. "What?"

"Drink this." Her lover pressed an ampoule to her lips.

"What do you mean, Roaran?" Her voice shrilled. "I thought, I thought—"

"That I love you?"

His tone chilled. Yet his arms tightened about her as though holding something precious. "Love. What is that? I no longer know. Now quickly, for we have a ways to go, you and I."

"We have a ways to go. That's what you said the first day I met you."

"When you seduced me?" Roaran laughed. How warm that laugh had once seemed. Now, stripped of that warmth, it prickled her neck with alarm.

"I thought I'd have to work harder, Azenor Caelan: be charming, fascinating, play a part I've not had to play for a long time. But you made it easy—that bit at least."

"Roaran, you're frightening me."

"I do care, Azenor. Enough to spare you what happens next. We have a ways to go, but you can't be the one who goes with me. It can only be him—Kaell."

The words hung between them. Senseless words. She could not take them in. But slowly, slowly the truth beneath seeped into her.

Azenor began to laugh, the sound bitter even to her ears. How did this happen? The man she had spent a decade with beyond the

Enarae, her lover, had betrayed her. She thought she knew him, every breath, every expression. Every intention.

For Roaran she had become someone who could deceive Kaell. How horribly poetic that the man who had asked that of her was the one to deceive her.

Even then, she clutched at a faint hope she had misunderstood. Roaran patiently planned his moves over centuries, every piece put in place, but it achieved nothing, surely, to betray her.

"You sound so distant, my love. I don't understand—" She stopped. Stared at him. "You want me to hate you? Why? Because you hate yourself for what you must do?"

"Drink, Azenor."

She tried to pull away. Roaran pressed the ampoule to her mouth.

"I promise," he whispered. "Like a fairy tale I'll awaken this body with a kiss."

ARIC

His father sagged in his chair. "This cannot be true." He glared at Kaell, chained and on his knees before him in the long hall. "That my son should defy the temple to free this, this—"

Monster.

The word unsaid. But Kaell dropped his head. An angry mutter stirred through the crowd.

Every servant who could sneak away crammed between pillars, shoulder to shoulder with soldiers, officials, perfumed courtiers, even ladies of the court in cambric gowns that swished as they fidgeted in the heat. Aric knew most by name, but no one met his eyes.

He stood near Kaell at the front of the throng, a space about him as though defiance was contagious. Perhaps it was. Kaell had defied the king to free him; now he defied his gods.

"And Azenor?" Gendrick dug his fingers into the back of his father's chair. "Why won't she wake? Is it as the priestess says? A curse born of her bond to this changeling?"

At the shocked cries, the dismayed murmurs, Aingear thumped a stick into tiles.

"The princess will recover once I complete the ceremony."

Aric forced open his clenched hands. He'd found Azenor just hours ago lying on the pebbled shore near his boats, barely a breath in her. Neither the physician nor the high priestess could wake her. This spell, whatever it was, had nothing to do with Kaell.

"My sister's illness is your fault." Gendrick jabbed a finger at Aingear. "You bound her to a ghoul. Before the gods. Kill him, and that bond ends. No nonsense about sacrifices."

More murmurs coiled then fast fell away, expectant.

In the hush, Hatton rapped his fingers on the chair arm, the *tap, tap, tap* like axe blows.

"The king is at our gates," he said. "Roaran's magic is broken. And yet my son, the commander of the Isles, concerns himself not with defending this castle but rescuing ghouls."

A low hiss ballooned. Aric took a step back, surprised at the glares from men and women he'd known since childhood, from soldiers he commanded. Even the painted figure of Rainer Caelan dismissed him from the wall with steely eyed contempt.

No one understood. With an army besieging them, with the high priestess warning of ghouls and monsters, talk of honour and repaying debts sounded hollow and intangible.

Aingear thumped her stick again. "Your Grace, let me speak."

Righteous, always so righteous. Her blinkered certainty was surely dangerous. When Aric became Isles commander, his father bid him remember one thing: only a fool never doubted. Doubt meant examining decisions from all angles, seeking consequences.

Hatton again tapped his fingers. A bad sign. He gave a curt nod.

"Your Grace," Aingear said. "Our gods showed me Kaell in visions. They chose him. Even led him, a Mountains warrior, to me. I explained the ceremony to you. Let me finish what I began."

Gendrick swiped at air. "He does not serve our gods. What use is he to you?"

"What he believes is irrelevant." Aingear adopted the ringing tone she used for ceremonies. And executions. "I bound him to an Isles princess and thus to our gods."

A sharp rap pierced an outburst of discordant voices. Not Aingear's stick this time. A sword hilt against the door at the far end of the hall.

At the sight of Aiden, Aric turned cold. He strode to meet his new captain. The crowd reluctantly parted, their sullen glares torches on his back. "What news?"

The man glanced at those within earshot. "My prince, I have a message for His Grace."

"Go forward." Cathmor's beast of a siege engine must be here. Ready to test the strength of their walls. And their wills.

Aiden fell to one knee before the king.

"Captain," Hatton said. "You are a welcome diversion. Speak."

Aiden swallowed hard. "Your Majesty. I do not how to say this. It is unexpected. Impossible, even. However, here it is: We have taken the Fern Castle on the border."

The king clutched his knees. "A Mountains castle? How? Every Isles warrior is here."

"It seems." Aiden tore out a breath. "We have new allies."

A chorused gasp exploded. Men and women exchanged startled looks.

Aric did not know what in Aiden's words alarmed his brother, but Gendrick blenched, his face ashen, a muscle twitching below his eye.

Hatton frowned. "I still don't understand."

"Your Grace, I know only this," Aiden said. "The castle fell to an invader who declares it his gift to us. His warriors slaughtered all within the walls except one squire. He bid the squire bring a message, a specific message for Prince Gendrick."

"For me?" Gendrick flicked his tongue over his lips. "From whom?"

Aiden's glance flickered to Aric. In a voice thick with reluctance, he said, "The message is signed"—another pause, another uneasy glance—"Archanin."

In the wake of that single name, the hall seemed different.

Smaller, airless. Perilous. The sunlight splintering between fluted columns too bright.

Voices stripped away. Their absence exposed every other sound: the doleful beats of a smith's hammer, the ebbing tide's rasped whisper, the groaning rigging of ships at anchor in the bay below the windows.

Aric braced a palm against a pillar. As Isles commander, he should grab the message, decide what it meant. Except he could neither move nor speak, only stare at a bead of sweat on Gendrick's temple, at his curled hands gripping their father's chair.

Slowly Hatton rose. "Clear the hall. This is at an end." He looked to Gendrick, his voice not quite steady as he said, "We'll deal with this in private."

KAELL

A silence ripped through the emptied hall, broken only by the sound of Hatton's footsteps as he paced. They all watched him. Kaell, Aric, Gendrick. The priestess, knuckles white on her staff.

Kaell's shackled wrists dangled by his thighs. He was so weary, every limb heavy, his body battered and torn. Yet of all his knife wounds, only one hurt. The first cut.

The shiver of Azenor's hands on his skin, the taste of her lips lingered. For one heady moment he had foolishly let himself believe he could be like any other young man. He thought—no. No point dwelling on it. She deceived him. That was all.

Hatton broke off his pacing. Without his echoing steps, the hall sat quiet and vast. Too big to contain the clamouring sea or the wind slapping against pennants atop the towers. Too small, though, to contain this tension.

"What have you done?" Corded muscles strained in the Isles lord's neck. "Gendrick, what have you done?"

His son said nothing. Ankles crossed, he leaned a shoulder to a pillar.

"Answer me. Why does this Archanin send you a message?"

Gendrick's insolent gaze passed slowly over them all. Then he shrugged, smiled, and said, "Because Archanin is my ally, Father."

He spoke as he might repeat gossip about castle dalliances. Complacently. Dispassionately. But in the wake of those words, shock sank down, all of them shaken.

"No," said Aric, his voice strange.

Kaell struggled to understand. An Isles prince in league with Archanin? Impossible. Gendrick didn't realise how dangerous the ghoul god was.

"You fool." Hatton's bewildered expression fell away to fury. "Ally? Did you invite this creature to attack the Fern Castle? You put us in danger." He struck his son across the face.

Gendrick staggered. Straightening, he touched his jaw, still smiling.

"You invited ghouls here?" Aric shook his head in dismay. "Why?"

His brother rounded on him. "To save the Isles. Because you can't. You couldn't even save our sister."

Aric opened his mouth to speak then abruptly turned away.

Just like Kaell couldn't save his men at Thom. In his nightmares he heard their screams, watched, frozen and lost, as ghouls fed like beasts upon the wounded.

"The false king will bring down our walls." Gendrick fisted his hands. "You must see that, Father. With every lord against us, this castle is lost. Unless we accept Archanin's help."

"Gendrick." Aric grabbed his shoulder. "Tide's End will hold. Even if Cathmor breaches the walls, we'll defend the breach. And he doesn't know where I've sent our ships."

His brother shoved off his hand. "Ships." He sneered. "You place the future of the Isles on a reckless plan that can never work. I've found us a way to win, Aric. Win. To defeat this upstart from Dal-Kanu and unite Telor under a true Caelan king. Our father."

"You cannot trust Archanin," Kaell said.

"Do not speak." Gendrick stabbed a finger in his face. "Say another word, and I'll gag you. I don't even know why you're here and not below."

Hatton slumped into a chair. He gestured to Aric. "Read the message."

Aric straightened rolled parchment. "It says: 'By my hand, I, Archanin, who stood with the ancient ones before the dawn of time, send greetings to my ally, Gendrick Caelan.'"

Hatton stared beyond the window. He drummed his fingers on the chair arm.

"Archanin writes: 'As a demonstration of my intent to deliver up your enemies, I hold the Fern Castle. In return, I seek only what is mine, what I intimately claimed. This warrior you call—'" Aric hesitated. He kept his eyes on the parchment. He didn't look at Kaell.

"Say it," Gendrick said.

"He wants Kaell," Aric said.

Kaell dropped his head, numb.

Aingear whirled on Hatton. "Kaell belongs to our gods. I must have him back to complete the ceremony, restore Roaran's spells."

Gendrick laughed in her face. "You foolish woman. We have no need for spells. Archanin is no threat. He'll help us smash the false king."

"And in return?" Aric asked quietly.

"He wants the Mountains. That's all." Gendrick shrugged. "It's harsh, treacherous land anyway. Let him have it. The rest of Telor will be ours."

"You can't trust Archanin," Kaell said again. Gendrick took two steps and hit him. Kaell reeled. He tongued salty blood on his lips.

The Isles lord shook his head. "What have you done, Gendrick? What have you done?"

"What I've done? Won, Father. Won this war. With Archanin's help we'll take back Telor, bring this land firmly under the reign of a true Caelan king."

"This is nonsense." Aric threw his arms wide. "This god has deceived you."

"Our ally just delivered us a border castle at the false king's back. And all he wants in return is Kaell. So what? He's no longer human. Who cares what Archanin does with him?"

"I must complete the ceremony," Aingear protested. "If Aric had not interfered, we would be safe already. I demand he answers for his defiance before a temple court."

"Aric is yet to answer for the deaths of his men," Gendrick said. "He led them into an ambush. No one else. Him. But nothing touches him, it seems."

With restless fingers, Hatton beat out a furious rhythm. "I do not know what to make of this. My son in league with a fallen god. My priestess insisting we restore centuries-old magic. I cannot decide this matter tonight. I will summon the council of lords tomorrow."

He gestured at Kaell. "Lock him up until the council decides how we proceed. If they accept Gendrick's arguments, then we surrender him to Archanin. If they accept, Aingear must complete the ceremony, then she shall have him."

A crazed laugh died on Kaell's lips. Either a priestess butchered him on a slab, or Archanin took him. His legs folded.

Aric caught him. "I need to question him. Kaell has information about Cathmor's ally, Vraymorg. About how many men and weapons he likely brought from the Mountains."

"You have until dawn," Hatton said. "Then I want him in irons below."

"And Aric?" Gendrick said. "The high priestess brings a serious charge against him."

Hatton dragged fingers through his grey hair. His face was haggard and old. "Aric commands this castle in a time of war. This charge must wait until Tide's End falls or stands. If my son survives, then he will surrender to the temple."

Aric bunched his hands. "Once this war is done, I will submit." He swept an arm at Kaell. "Have the guards lock him up until I can question him."

THE CELL DOOR SLAMMED SHUT. Kaell slid his back down the wall, dizzy with shock. Death he no longer feared. But this? To be Archanin's prisoner or Aingear's sacrifice.

Despite the shackles on his wrists, he must escape. Overpower Aric, then the guards. Get to the Fern Castle and kill Archanin. Or die. Yes, probably die but at least with some dignity, knowing he had tried to avenge his men. Tried to make his lord proud.

Kaell closed his eyes, longing for the touch of Vraymorg's hand on his shoulder. Again he heard steel clattering on stone as Vraymorg hurled his sword in that prison as if unable to bear the turmoil of emotion within. Or afraid of it.

Afraid. He turned the word over in his mind. As a child he thought his lord feared nothing. But what if he did?

He pictured the cell below the fortress, remembering the look on Vraymorg's face.

Like a shout, understanding clamoured. His lord feared one thing. Love.

Kaell turned that over in his mind. Wasn't he just as afraid? He fixed only upon what he yearned for. Affection. Tenderness. Praise. He had never told his lord he loved him.

A sob rattled in his throat. It was too late. He was alone, about to die on a stone altar or become Archanin's prisoner.

Even if he escaped, his path did not lead to Vraymorg, to a chance to tell him he understood. That he loved him, even if his lord couldn't say the words.

Fetters sang a discordant song as Kaell fell to his knees, wretched. Perhaps in this bare cell, when every certainty broke inside him, the habit of prayer could fire his courage.

Sultry air nipped at his neck. Cold, though, rose from the stone floor into his bones. Through thick walls, the sea rumbled. Kaell muttered words that tasted ashen in his mouth.

A torch flared. Aric filled the doorway. "Do your gods answer you?" he said. "The last time I prayed to mine, they stayed silent, and I rode to Dal-Kanu to kill a stranger."

"So it's the gods' fault you tried to kill me?"

"They had a hand in it. Though they didn't force you to fight me."

"So it's my fault?" Azenor blamed Kaell, too—when she thrust a knife in him. A shadow woman, with secrets behind her kisses. An ache ripped his breast. *No, don't think of her.*

"The blame lies with me," Aric said. "Everything that happened that day and everything that's happened since. And just like that dreadful day in Dal-Kanu, I can hardly understand you, Kaell. You Mountains folk sing your words."

"Then let's limit our talk to the language of swords. I'm game if you are."

Aric leaned a shoulder against the wall. "Has anyone said you're prickly?"

Arn called him that. Kaell's irritation faded. "Like a Mountains pear."

"I like that. A pear."

"It's from a children's song. Cahirean. *Pears look sweet when Mountains bred, but prick their skin and end up dead.* It doesn't sound as silly when it's sung."

"Prickly." Aric studied him with eyes too like his sister's. *Azenor, why?* "A warrior who spins words and believes in his gods."

"Why is that peculiar? Unless you don't believe in anything."

Aric shrugged. "My ancestor Roaran didn't. He turned from the gods as false. He's on my mind tonight. Sometimes I think I'll turn a corner and find him walking these corridors."

"You believe in ghosts but not gods." Kaell found Aric just as bewildering as that day in Dal-Kanu when the Isles prince had baited him.

"All of us, fascinated by a dead king." Something flitted behind his eyes. Fear? "What would you say if I told you I thought I saw—" He broke off. Wet his lips. "Never mind."

Thought he saw a ghost? Roaran's ghost? Kaell's scalp crept with unease.

He remembered the dead bonded warrior he had heard when Archanin held him prisoner, a voice calling down into his dreams. Yes, there were ghosts.

"What *do* you believe in, Aric Caelan?"

Aric flashed a cocky smile, whatever doubt banished.

"Myself. My wit. The strength of my sword arm. All gifts of the gods. Here." He draped a cloak over Kaell's shoulders. "Come with me."

Kaell did not rise. "I like this cell. It's warmer than my last."

"I'm glad our prisons are superior. Still, I must insist, prickly pear though you are."

Kaell lifted his fettered arms. "Do I have a choice?"

THEIR BOOTS ECHOED loudly on stone as Kaell trudged after Aric up a tower stairwell spiralling into darkness. Only torches smoking in sconces challenged shadows. The castle slumbered, waiting for dawn.

Aric ushered Kaell into the top room. "Now." He lit a candle on a table. "We must talk."

Kaell peered about the circular chamber. Fading moonlight filtered through shutters. The sea heaved against the walls, its voice the perfect music for a chaotic room filled to every corner with stacked scrolls and leather-bound books.

He picked his way through scattered parchments. "This is a strange torture chamber. How do you expect to make me spill my secrets about my lord?"

Aric looked baffled. Then he chuckled. "These books are dangerous, Kaell. One fell off a shelf onto my head only two nights ago. I could threaten to choke you with dust if I must. But really, I don't have the heart for torture."

"What do you have the heart for?" His sister had the heart for lies, even murder.

"Winning. Here." Aric spread a map over books open on the table. A word on a page caught Kaell's eye.

"Val Arques. Who's Val Arques?"

Aric's hands froze on the map. "You don't know?"

"Should I know?"

Aric frowned. "Azenor said nothing? About what your lord told her?"

"No. What is this about?" So Azenor kept secrets all along? His lord's secrets? Kaell fumed. Only minutes ago he thought he understood Vraymorg.

"It's not my story, Kaell. You must ask him. Vraymorg."

Kaell considered Aric's guilty face. He knew more. Anger pricked up and down his arms. "You are a shadow man. Your sister tried to kill me, and you try to deceive me."

A shadow certainly crossed Aric's face. Pain too. "I saw," he muttered. "She stabbed you."

"Why?" Kaell threw up his arms. "Do you know?"

"Kaell." Aric dug his teeth into his bottom lip. "I can't think about it. About her, about what she did and why she won't wake. Any of it. Not yet. I must think only of defeating Cathmor and then this ghoul god my brother foolishly trusts."

Grim-faced, he stabbed the map. "The king has three camps. Here, here, and here. Guard posts here and here. Still, I'll get us through the king's lines. Here."

Get through? Bemused, Kaell could only stare.

Aric looked up. He grinned. "I read men well, Kaell. Know when they're lying, when they're desperate. That's why I win in swordplay. I smell a feint, sense when an attack is true. You don't just watch a man's eyes; you watch his feet and shoulders, the way he tenses."

Kaell nodded. "I do the same."

"I know why you sought your gods: for fortitude to face Archanin. What was the plan? Hit me and run? No need. I intend to free you and help you kill Archanin."

"My fight with Archanin does not concern you."

"Doesn't concern me?" Aric caught his arm. "This monster

seized a Mountains castle on the edge of the Isles, less than a day's ride away. My brother is a fool to plot with him."

"Not your fight. Mine. You need to worry about the king smashing your walls."

Aric broke away to pace. "It is not only your fight, Kaell. I know what he did to Azenor."

A shudder of shameful memory whipped him. Warm flesh. Archanin's kiss. Desire, guilt. Did part of her break as it did him? How else could she have betrayed him?

"Why should you risk your life? Just let me go. My life is over anyhow."

"It's not that simple. My brother has guards watching me so I don't just free you."

"Then this is pointless," Kaell shouted, surrendering to his anger. "You may as well march me back to that nice, warm cell."

"Kept tight until either Gendrick or Aingear marches you somewhere not so nice? No, I thought we'd leave." Aric pointed to the window. "That way. I learnt all about sliding down ropes from some fool who broke me free from the king's interrogators."

Kaell gaped. Then his anger fled with a burst of laughter. "After seeing how the king's mistress interrogated you, I wasn't sure you wanted to be free. Vicious it was."

"She was certainly skilled. And your timing was awful." He grinned. "Time to move."

"Aric, you can't come with me. Archanin wants to punish me. That gives me a chance to get close and kill him. You, he'll just butcher."

"When he and my brother are allies?" Aric shook his head. "I knew Gendrick sought power, but how can he believe he can use and trust a fallen god?"

"He can't," Kaell said. "Archanin is dangerous."

"Talking of dangerous. If by some chance I survive and you don't," Aric said with morbid cheerfulness as he freed Kaell. "Is there a message for your lord? He's with the king."

"He is?" Kaell arched a brow. "What am I saying? Of course he is." His gaze slid to the window. His lord. So close. That hurt more. Because beyond these windows was too far.

"You plan to ride into the king's camp to deliver my message?"

"Tempting." Aric's eyes shone with mischief. "What might Cathmor do if I did?"

"Put your neck in a noose."

"And your lord? If I should drop in to see him?"

"Give you to the king so he can put your neck in a noose."

Aric sighed. "I thought he had come to like me. Vraymorg that is. When we met yesterday. When he came to Tide's End."

Lost, Kaell stammered, "He? Here?"

"He brought the king's demands. Conditional surrender. All reasonable enough—even my cousin's plan to hang me. I'd hang me, too, if I were Cathmor. Spectacle is very welcome after besieging a castle. Otherwise it's boring sitting about watching someone's walls."

"You prattle on with a lot of nonsense," Kaell said.

"Does it provoke you?" Aric unlocked a chest. He drew out Fortitude and passed the blade to Kaell. "Vraymorg warned me not to provoke him; he said he bore me a grudge for poisoning you."

"Did he?" Kaell's voice lifted with gladness.

"He asked about you. I suspect that's why he really came: to find out about you."

Warmth fluttered in Kaell's belly. "And he is without? With the king?"

"He is the king's man," Aric said in a strange voice. "And, it seems, always will be."

ARIC

Waves breaking with thunder and clamour beneath the cliffs shrouded their footsteps to a boat on pebbly sand below the castle. An alert sentry shouted a challenge.

Aric showed his face. "All is well. Remain vigilant." The man saluted and melted into the darkness.

He and Kaell each took an oar. The craft glided around a headland into a narrow cove. Ragged clouds hunted a sinking moon. The remnants of night curtained, a veil of grey shadows and soft scents. Brine. The perfume of Murraya.

"My spies get in and out this way." Aric hauled the boat in. "Under the king's nose."

He groped up a rocky cliff path, starlight his only guide. The darkness tinted charcoal, rimmed by prowling dawn, its awakening a reminder of his father's order to surrender Kaell.

Guilt niggled at him. But not regret.

The king's interrogator had taught him a lesson in agony and degradation that would have ended with his humiliating execution. Kaell had risked his life in Dal-Kanu to save him. The man who had tried to kill him. Aric shook his head, still puzzled by that kindness.

"We go through caves up there. Isles lords kept these passages secret for centuries."

"Then how far to the Fern Castle?"

"On horse? A few hours. We'll be there by noon. Just when the ghouls are sleeping."

"Aric, no. You must turn back. The king is readying his men to attack Tide's End."

"They're still assembling his beast of a trebuchet. The battle, when it comes, will well and truly wait for me. Besides," Aric hesitated.

"Besides?"

Aric debated how much to say. Kaell could hardly betray him to the king. "I don't intend to sit and wait for Cathmor to haul missiles at our walls."

"The reckless plan your brother dismissed? Something to do with ships? I counted only five off Tide's End. The Isles fleet is triple that. Where have you sent them?"

Aric considered him. "It's as well you're not fighting for Cathmor. Work it out."

"I once read of a traitor lord who besieged King Rollo at Tide's End. Rollo left half his men guarding the walls and sailed with the rest to Cahir. They marched through the night and attacked the traitor's camp from behind. Cathmor should know this. It's a famous victory."

"And I thought I came up with the idea." Aric's foot slipped on shale as he clambered higher. "I didn't know about this Rollo and his ships so I doubt Cathmor will."

"So that's it?"

In grey light Aric glimpsed Kaell's eager face. Stories of battles and old heroes interested him also, could distract him, too, even in the worst moments. Under other circumstances—if he hadn't tried to kill Kaell—could they have been friends?

"Through Cahir. An interesting idea. But no. Even if I surprised the king, his army still outnumbers my men." Thanks to the Damadars. To think he once liked Heath. "My plan is a little more ambitious." Aric could not hold back a smirk. "What would you say if I told you the Isles fleet sailed east, not west? Towards the Falls."

"Khir be good." Kaell stopped to stare. "You mean to attack Dal-Kanu!"

"I mean to *take* Dal-Kanu. Yes, I know. Alecc of Adorean long ago sailed his ships up a river to the Falls, took the city, but then lost it within a day to King Rainer."

Rainer Caelan was a sorcerer. He expected Alecc's attack. Cathmor wouldn't.

The cave's entrance was barely a crack in the cliff. Aric fumbled for a torch and waved it about. The narrow space quickly widened to a cavern. "This way."

"It's too dark to see." Kaell groped along a wall. His boots crunched sand.

"What good are you then?" Aric said. "Next time I'll bring a proper ghoul."

"Sorry—my lord." Kaell touched his brow.

Torchlight revealed his grin. Aric smiled back. Gods help him, he did like Kaell.

A stone turned underfoot ahead. Kaell stilled. "What was that?"

Aric listened hard. Beyond the caves the retreating sea sucked and lapped at rocks. A gull shrieked, its winds fanning air. The wind surrendered to dawn's thick silence.

"Maybe nothing."

"Wait. I hear—" Kaell's words cut off with a grunt.

Aric swung the torch. His companion grappled with a dark-clad figure, their bodies locked in struggle. With an impatient cry, Kaell hurled his attacker off and tore out his sword.

Shadows ran about. Aric snatched for his hilt as a shape rushed him, hit him hard. He plunged down. The torch spilled. Steel pricked his throat.

"Light," a man called. "I need light."

Hewing blades clangored as Kaell exchanged blows with some unknown assailant. Booted steps hastened closer. Torches bobbed.

"Aric Caelan, by all the gods." Vraymorg stood above him, his sword to Aric's neck.

"Get off me." Aric tried to rise. The Mountains lord poked his throat with the tip. "Still."

Aric tensed, ready to seize his chance to knock the blade aside. Beyond the spill of light, figures writhed. Metal shrieked. Men cursed. One howled in pain.

"Whoever you are," Vraymorg shouted. "Put up your sword. I have your prince."

"My lord?" Kaell's voice was sharp with surprise. "Is that you?"

Vraymorg's head swung. His sword did not. "No. No. Not you too." His breath caught then dragged out. "Drop your sword, Kaell."

"Kaell, no!" Aric tried to shove the tip aside.

Vraymorg pressed a boot into his ribs to stop him rising. "Kaell will always do as I say, Aric Caelan."

Torchlight flickered shadows across the man's face. Vraymorg drew back his sword, his sigh heavy with regret. "I am sorry to find you here. You're not what I expected."

"No. Don't!" The hilt flew down. Aric's skull flamed. Then he slid into blackness.

HEATH

"Patience," Cathmor instructed Heath. "Brings its own rewards. It even delivers one's enemies to you." He heaved a satisfied sigh. "Bring them in."

Heath turned expectantly to the tent flaps, glad of the diversion.

The king proved tight-lipped about which particular enemies patience "delivered" but besieging castles proved a tiresome, bloodless business. A warrior sought relief by downing sour wine or downing some fool with a face he didn't like.

Or expressions he didn't like. If only he could swipe off Cathmor's smug look. One juicy blow. But as he complained often to Judith, you can't always have what you want.

The flaps opened. A guard dumped a man on his knees.

Heath gaped stupidly. Aric should be behind Tide's End's walls. Kept safe for him. Not bound and bleeding in Cathmor's tent.

"The gods sometimes spoil us." Cathmor laughed. That grated too. One little blow. All right. Maybe a slap. Just to wipe the smile from this vicious king's face.

Bora hurled a second prisoner inside. Rope circled his hands, but guards and the Telorian lords summoned to the tent edged back. Who was he? Venivan perhaps, given fair hair tumbled about a pleasingly boned face. Venivans, though, rarely had black eyes.

Cathmor circled his captives, humming. He flashed Heath a look of triumph—what does he want? Applause?—then demanded of Bora, "How? Where?"

"In the caves, Your Grace. We expected only to net a messenger."

"Ah, but this catch is sweeter." Cathmor rounded on the man who followed the second captive inside. "Vraymorg, you were right. They did use those caves."

"A fortunate guess, Your Majesty."

"Traitor! You swore to keep that secret." Aric sprang at the Mountains Lord. Guards grabbed him and threw him down.

Traitor? Curious. Aric was hardly a man who hurled careless words.

The king twitched a brow. "Whatever does he mean, Vraymorg?"

"I have no idea, Your Grace." Vraymorg held his warrior's body stiffly, hands clasped behind his back, his eyes as wary as a cornered beast's.

Heath knew that look, a bleak fury dulled by fear. Of what? Or for whom?

Cathmor turned on Aric. "Why 'traitor'? Oh, good gods. Someone find a bandage. My cousin is bleeding all over my expensive rug."

"He is that and more." Aric's voice whipped with scorn as he clambered to his knees. His gashed head dripped blood. "He knows why."

"Vraymorg?" The king raised another eyebrow.

The man only lifted massive shoulders. His anger slumbered like a sheathed blade, masked to those staring at Aric. Only Heath intently watched Vraymorg. That fierce longing twisted through him. He needed to fight this man. No. He needed to kill him.

"Deceptive words, Your Grace. Meant to distract us."

"Yes, but distract us from what?" Cathmor stroked his chin. "Just one more mystery my interrogators will uncover."

Aric jerked beneath the guards' hold. Heath had heard Blackstone tortured him in Dal-Kanu. Well, what did Aric expect? Defiance sowed pain unless a man proved careful or particularly clever.

Heath was both.

"I see from your wounds Vraymorg got rough—will someone do as I command and stop my cousin bleeding everywhere?—but he doesn't have the imagination for torture. My questioner, though, invents many unpleasant joys." Cathmor touched Aric's hair. "Blackstone. Remember her? She's terribly fond of you."

"And you're fond of your own voice." The fair-haired captive sneered.

Vraymorg slapped him. "You dare address the king? Be silent, or I'll gag you again."

The man grinned carelessly then broke into song. *"No words from me for kings, Your Grace. That falls to lords who know their place."*

Vraymorg said, "Shut up."

The young captive sought to mask fear behind a deceptively playful tone. Heath liked to think he'd do the same—if the king ever threw him in irons.

Cathmor patted the man's fair head. "I was coming to you."

"About time. I'm bored. Though your neglect allowed me to think up more rhymes."

"They're not very good rhymes," Aric said.

"You're a harsh critic, Aric."

Vraymorg hit the prisoner again.

Cathmor threw up a palm. "Now, now, Vraymorg. Don't discourage that creative tongue." He smiled sweetly at the prisoner. "Find me a rhyme about how the gods love me. They bring me not only my pretty cousin but you also. I shall praise them for a week."

Heath knew the pretty cousin but the other? The king valued his capture, so a nobleman? Yet every lord, besides those of the

Isles, was here and known.

He puzzled over it. A comely face but a bladesman's shoulders, long legs, and calloused hands, his accent that singsong Mountains nonsense. So less a lord, more a warrior.

"Praise the gods all you like," the man said. "Just so long as I don't have to hear it."

"I'd rather listen to your rhymes, poor though they may be," Aric said.

"That's very kind. Do you like Venivan poetry, Aric?"

Cathmor's smile widened. "I always liked your spirit. You'll need it when you die. What do you say, Vraymorg?"

The Mountains lord's voice seemed lost, his eyes hollowed by pain. He stammered, "He is your prisoner, Your Grace."

"He is that. Hold him. Let me look at him."

Soldiers pulled the prisoner upright.

The king fisted a lock of blond hair. "An abomination. A shame about your green eyes. Caelmarsh swore he'd cut them out and wear them on a neck chain. Where is he? He'll be sorry to miss the sight of you on your knees, about to die. But before you do, answer me this. How did you free Aric?"

Free Aric. Links clicked in Heath's mind. Kaell. Khir's warrior. The warrior raised by the very man who had just delivered him to the king.

Kaell laughed. "No art to it, Your Grace. I pretended to drink the physician's draught then escaped through the window—well, you know yourself, I like to climb—and set Aric free."

Cathmor let him go with a shove. "By yourself? Surely not."

"Did you write a poem about it?" Aric asked.

"I couldn't find anything to rhyme with Aric."

Vraymorg struck Kaell so hard he reeled. Grinning guards yanked him up.

"I'm sure you'll find something to rhyme with Kaell," the king said cheerfully. "And something to rhyme with dead."

Heath should have realised who this was at once. In his defence, he'd glimpsed Kaell only from a distance and then again as a figure in the darkened ward.

The king smirked. "How about, *hail, Kaell, how he did wail.* As for Aric, he can wail, gnash his teeth, or recite poetry for my interrogator. Once he's told all he knows about Tide's End and its defences, when he reveals where he sent half the Isles fleet—"

Aric shot Vraymorg a murderous look.

"Once he reveals everything I need to know and perhaps what I don't, then he'll stand, if he can, crawl, if he can't, below the walls and call upon his father to surrender."

"I won't do that." Aric's tone was mutinous.

"You'll do exactly as I say. My chief questioner boasts she can break any man. I intend to hold her to that. And then—" Cathmor's smile was hard. "And then," he repeated. "Once your warriors see you kneel to me. I'll hang you."

Gods forbid. Time for his smooth tongue to be—well—smooth. That, or face the storm his sister Myranthe would call down upon his head if Aric died here and not at her elegant hands.

Heath cleared his throat. "Your Grace, the gods willed Aric Caelan should fall into your hands so you may punish his defiance. But he is your cousin. These same gods frown at kinslayers. Imprison him. He'll make a useful hostage."

Cathmor nodded as though considering. "A pretty speech. What do you say, Vraymorg?"

"Damadar is right. Send Aric as a hostage to Dal-Kanu. For the rest of his life if you choose, Your Grace. But it is unlawful to hang a man of his birth."

"My council already sentenced Aric in his absence to hang."

"You are the king. You are above councils," Heath said.

"So I am. You both best remember it. And as the king, I say Aric dies."

A smattering of voices rumbled then fell away. Only Aric's breaths, uneven and loud, disturbed the stillness. Until another sound broke out, a ringing, then a toneless beat.

Cathmor dramatically raised a hand to his ear. "Do you hear?"

No one spoke.

"My builders. Oh no scaffold for you yet, cousin," he said as Aric fought to rise. "Not until Blackstone is done with you. No, this is a platform. High, so even your father on the walls of Tide's End sees the flames. It might draw the cowering traitor out."

"Flames?" Vraymorg repeated sharply.

"It's how you kill ghouls. Kaell will burn."

"No, you can't!" Roused at last, Vraymorg blazed with alarm. Heath instinctively backed up. That yearning tore through him. How to get this man to the Icelands?

"Can't?" Cathmor hissed. "Can't?"

Vraymorg stilled. Jaw locked, his lips clamped as if he struggled to contain his rage. "Your Grace, I grant your right to kill him. But the flames? Show mercy. Kaell could not prevent the ghoul god taking his blood. It is not his fault."

"Bring in the ghoul," Cathmor said, deceptively calm. "The other one."

Guards bustled away. Hammers thudded. Despite a warm breeze nipping through gaps in canvas, Heath shivered. A ghoul in camp? The king kept his pieces in this game close.

He stole a look at his companions. Cathmor gleeful. Vraymorg grim-faced. Aric stiff with scorn but unbowed. Kaell adrift, a sleepwalker, his dark eyes peering at nothing.

The guards returned with a tall, typically blond ghoul. Wind through the flap lifted strands of long hair as he shuffled in leg irons. Bands circled his wrists, but his clothes were clean, his body untouched by torture. They dropped him on his knees before the king.

"Who is this?" Vraymorg demanded. Menace rippled off him in waves, prickling Heath's skin with a longing akin to desire.

If he faced this formidable creature with steel, fire beneath his feet, surely fear would writhe down his spine. Surely the contest must enliven every sense, every appetite in a way he'd not felt for years. And victory, when it inevitably came, could taste no sweeter.

That fight must happen. With Judith's help, he'd abduct this man.

Cathmor tilted the ghoul's chin with a gloved finger. The captive smiled up at him.

"Who is this?" the king echoed. "Perhaps Kaell will tell us?"

The blond warrior muttered, "His name is Lastenarron."

"You admit you know him? And he serves this ghoul lord called Archanin?"

Kaell hesitated. Then nodded.

An ugly murmur stirred. Cathmor gestured for quiet. "My outriders captured Lastenarron in the woods. A spy for this creature calling himself a god who sacked the Fern Castle. Lastenarron has told us many interesting things."

The ghoul shrugged. "It is my nature to serve, Your Grace."

"Tell everyone what you know about Kaell."

"Do you mean"—Lastenarron paused dramatically—"about how he pledged himself to Archanin?"

Men gasped, muttered. Heath grimaced with distaste. The ghoul was enjoying himself too much. He might be a liar. He was certainly a disgusting pawn.

"How Kaell knelt, swore to serve—"

"It's not like that!" Kaell shouted, pushing to his feet. Guards shoved him down.

"How he willingly drank my master's blood to become one of us."

Kaell dropped his head. Condemning stares fell on him. The air in the tent thinned, changed. Faces, too, twisted with revulsion.

Vraymorg dropped a hand on Kaell's shoulder and squeezed, unsurprised by the words.

"Not his fault, Vraymorg?" Cathmor stabbed a finger, his eyes bright with the need to dominate. "A warrior dedicated to our gods bent his knee to this ghoul god. I have every right to not only kill him but burn him."

Then Heath understood. This wasn't about Kaell at all. It was about the Mountains Lord. Cathmor feared and envied him. He wanted to hurt him, put him in his place.

What was behind his resentment? Jealousy? Vraymorg was certainly impressive.

"Behead him," Vraymorg said dully. "That way is sure and tested. The other—cruel."

"You think me cruel, my lord," Cathmor said. "What will you make of this?"

He called Bora to him, snapping fingers at Kaell.

"Shackle him to a stake. Let the builders erect the platform around him. The sun may kill him, but if not, he can think upon what will come. What do you say to that, my lord?"

Vraymorg did not speak. The man drowned. Gods, that rage, the disbelief, the raw pain must be unendurable. Even without knowing Kaell, Heath's gut hollowed.

"But I have even more entertainment planned." Cathmor's smile flitted, blade thin. "Burn the other ghoul first. Let everyone see it." His gaze fell on Kaell. "Let him see it."

"No." Lastenarron sprang up. "I helped you. You said if I helped you would not kill me."

Cathmor shrugged. "Promises to a ghoul mean nothing. Take him and burn him."

Guards dragged the struggling, protesting Lastenarron off. Heath heard his shouts and curses for a long while then a sharp crack like a blow.

The king was right. Why honour a promise to a ghoul? But then why his disquiet, this stale taste on his tongue? He already knew what sort of man Cathmor was.

Cathmor turned to his prisoner. "Why so quiet, Kaell? Surely you can find something that rhymes with fire? Liar, sire perhaps? No, let me." He paused. "How about: *The king condemned him to a death so slow, to show his subjects what defiance sows.* Not bad?"

Head bent, his lord gripping his shoulder, Kaell stared through them all. No longer there.

Aric answered for him. "You are worthy of your ancestors, Cathmor," he sneered. "A true son of Penmar the Cursed and Mallon the Malicious."

"I have not finished, cousin," Cathmor said, his humour restored. "I was about to tell my loyal Vraymorg that when Kaell burns—" He settled his cold eyes on the dark-haired lord. "He'll put the torch to the wood himself. A test of that loyalty he proclaims."

The king slid those eyes to Aric. "What do you say to that? No." He shook his head. "Say nothing. Save it for Blackstone."

THE CAMP LIMPED to life in the clear, crisp morning. Dogs barked. Smoke from cook fires spiralled against an ivory haze of heat. Hammers clapped a doleful tone, the sound grinding up Heath's backbone. Sweat dampened the back of his neck.

How he longed for the Icelands and its familiar cold. Its familiar games and rules. He was no stranger to violence, hardly averse to it, but what unfolded here was vindictive and cruel.

Warriors wearing Mountains badges slouched outside a tent. At his approach, they fell silent. He passed on. Urgent whispers picked up. Heath heard "Kaell" and "the king."

Ice men roasted rabbit, their gossip about bonded warriors, ghouls, and Isles witches.

Shaking his head at such nonsense, Heath glimpsed Judith in a crowd jostling about carpenters building a platform. Necks extended, stones or rotting fruit in their fists, the throng pushed towards a figure chained to a stake. Guards forced them back.

Even in a fire hall, the bloodthirsty mob fed off each other's baser instincts, never falling back, repulsed, only pressing forward to watch a man plunge to his fiery death.

"Come to see the changeling ghoul, pretty?" A woman with

breasts spilling from a russet gown grinned at his sister. Heath shoved through sweating bodies towards Judith.

"That's 'my lady' to you." A soldier slid Judith an admiring look.

The woman shoved her hands to her hips and laughed. "It's 'my lady' to you, too, lackwit." But she dipped her head at Judith. "Beg pardon, my lady."

Judith noticed Heath. She dropped into an elaborate curtsey. "Am I a lady, Heath?" Her laugh bubbled. "That sounds terribly dull. I'd rather be not *quite* a lady."

"My dear, you could be *quite* anything and never dull."

"Damadar," an insolent voice interrupted. "I suppose you're well used to seeing someone burn. But surely you should spare your sister such a grizzly sight."

Nate Caelmarsh appeared. Heath fought the compulsion to edge back.

"Judith, sweetness." Heath frowned with mock concern. "Do you feel faint? Shall I fetch smelling salts or some strong, handsome young man to carry you off when you swoon?"

"The spectacle disgusts me," Judith said. "Surely it's usual to keep a condemned prisoner locked away from prying eyes and bring them out only to die? This is cruel."

Caelmarsh's lips twitched. He found this amusing? Revolting creature.

"It's so he sees what's coming," the lord said. "He'll have time to plead with his gods."

Judith squinted into the sun. "His gods serve him poorly to lead him here. But tell me, my lord. If he's a ghoul, why isn't he dead? Doesn't the light burn them?"

"This one has powerful blood, my lady."

"Powerful blood?" Judith scoffed with a short laugh.

"They say the ghoul god drank him dry then filled him with his own blood."

They also said magic bound Kaell to an Isles princess. Heath even overheard nonsense that a Seithin witch whelped Kaell. All ridiculous. A siege camp washed with silly lies.

"I saw a man burn once," Caelmarsh said. "Never heard anyone scream so much."

"Really?" He'd like to hear Caelmarsh scream in a fire pit, skewered on a sword tip. Actually, *his* sword tip.

"Screamed more than any man I've given to my questioners."

Judith summoned a haughty glare. "I hope Kaell does not give you the satisfaction—my lord." She grabbed her brother's arm and led him away.

DILLON WAITED OUTSIDE THEIR PAVILION, his round-cheeked face strained with weariness.

"We've landed in a murky muddle, friend," Heath said, as soon as Judith disappeared inside. "Cathmor has Aric—that boy Kaell too—and is unlikely to give them up. All thanks to Vraymorg. How did you take them?"

"Vraymorg guessed Aric used old caves to get messages in and out. We expected to arrest his spies. Instead, the Isles commander turned up, Kaell with him."

"Damned bad fortune," Heath muttered. "I understand Vraymorg surrendering Aric to the king—a valuable prisoner—but Kaell? He raised the boy, gods help him."

A dutiful man.

"The boy surrendered at his lord's command. Stupid. He gave us no end of trouble." Dillon laughed grimly. "If he hadn't put up his sword, I may not be standing here right now."

"You live a charmed life. Did Vraymorg say anything to him?"

"Vraymorg was too furious for words. Kaell, though, begged his lord to set him and Aric free, muttering about ghouls and the Fern Castle. Vraymorg gagged him."

The man couldn't bear to hear Kaell's pleas after all. So dutiful, but not an indifferent man.

The boy was his weakness. How could he use that? Heath always played a long game, put his pieces in place early. Judith, for example. But he was yet to see how to snare this lord.

Dillon fixed a hard look upon him. “Talk is the king plans to burn the boy.”

“It’s true. I wonder if Vraymorg would have been so dutiful had he known Kaell’s fate?”

“Vraymorg may act now. Would you be able to watch a child you raised die like that?”

“If I had to, yes.” Heath slapped Dillon’s back. “You would, too, if the gods demanded it. What is it flatlanders say of we Icelands folk? That ice is in our veins.”

“Then ice is in the Lord of Vraymorg’s veins, too.”

Heath could not fault that observation.

VAL ARQUES

Vraymorg jolted awake. The nightmare vanished like a wind sighing across the sea, its elusive, shadowy remnants sweat dampening his skin and a drumming in his chest.

He reached for Judith before remembering their farewell the night before, how she had waited at his tent wearing travelling cloak and boots, how he said only, "You're leaving."

"My brother thinks it's safer." She stretched on her toes to kiss his cheek. The stab of loss as he drew her to him, too aware of the perfume of her hair, her skin, surprised him.

Judith pulled away to see his face. "About the boy—"

"No, don't." He waved a hand through air. "Don't."

"You could defy the king. You could save him. Save Kaell."

"My duty is to the king. What else is there but duty?"

"There's love," she said softly.

"My duty is to the king," he repeated, his gaze falling away.

She put a hand on his arm. She looked into his eyes. She said, "Is it?"

In the quiet of dawn, alone in his tent, her words lingered. Uncomfortable. Confronting.

Vraymorg rose, pulled on pants and tunic, and draped a cloak over his shoulders. Every movement mechanical, his mind shut down.

He knew where he must go. He knew why he did not want to.

If he walked outside this tent now, he risked destroying his carefully structured world, the one where neither the past nor love could ambush him. The one where he was only Vraymorg, guardian of Khir's warriors, the king's man. That was all.

Was it all? What else was he? A son—once. A child longing for praise from his splendid father. Longing for attention. Like Kaell.

He closed his eyes. He could see his father, how he moved, the brisk strides Val never kept up with.

He could see Teynan Caelan thrust his calloused hands into gloves to snatch up his sword, every action, every gesture sharp with intent and a contained impatience.

He remembered the crisp linen of his father's shirts rubbing his cheek, the scent of leather and soap and warmth when Tey drew him into an embrace.

A lord. A man responsible for keeping the Isles safe. Keeping his sons safe.

Would this man hide behind his lordly mask if his young son needed him?

Gods, how he wished his father was here now, that he could ask him how to become someone other than the Lord of the Mountains, be who Kaell needed him to be.

Except—except if he let down his shield, what splintered him within would not be the world's envy or hatred or even judgement. It would be love, the joy and agony of it.

Love. Val could taste the word, smell it, and it was brackish. A brackish stream of doubt.

It shouldn't be like that. It should be simple.

I am a coward. How easy to risk my body as a warrior but never my heart. My position, my title, the rigid forms of duty, all a coward's barrier against the world.

What did Judith say? *There's love.* And he always knew he was loved.

Another image from the past came into his mind of his father stooped over a table, his curling, dark hair falling across his face, an iron-pommelled sword in his belt.

Despite lines of worry tightening his mouth and the warriors urgently gathered, he made time to lift his head at the sight of his son and smile. Then he called Val to him, threw an arm about his shoulder, held him close as men discussed war, tapping their fingers on maps.

Teynan Caelan feared nothing. He certainly didn't fear love.

With a sigh, Vraymorg pushed through tent flaps into the labyrinth of canvas and silk. Ivory light glazed lifting fog. Mist prowled over the sea to steam off dewy grass, wet on his bare feet. His body fell into a familiar stride, but his mind broke up into chaos.

Smouldering cook fires bloated crisp air with woodsmoke and charcoal. The silence fell soft, expectant, waiting to embrace the dull thud of hammers.

His backbone crept with unease. Too quiet. As if the ghoul's death cast a pall upon the camp.

Last night Vraymorg had stood at the king's side as commanded, gagging on the stench from the fire. He didn't see Lastenarron. It was Kaell he imagined against that stake.

When Vraymorg staggered, Cathmor reached to steady him. The king's lips thinned, but he said nothing.

Snared by memory, Vraymorg didn't realise he had paused.

Blankly he stared about. Above the tents, the stark wooden bones of the king's dreadful trebuchets etched the dawn. At night he lay on his pallet and listened to their eerie creak in the wind. But there was no wind now. There was nothing.

He strode on, his legs leaden. How could he be the man his father was? He dropped his eyes to his wrists. It took strength he didn't possess.

At the platform, a sentry thrust a spear in his path.

"Let me pass."

"My lord, the king says—"

"Let me pass." Vraymorg let the guard hear the iron in his voice, glimpse the threat in his expression. The man stood aside.

Slumped in fetters, back to the stake, Kaell slept. A bruise purpled his cheek, his tunic ripped away from his body. Gently Vraymorg touched his shoulder. Kaell blinked awake.

"You came," he said.

Words choked within. *I should have protected you. How do I save you? What do I say?*

Easier to surrender to anger. "Who hit you? The bruises, the gashes."

"Does it matter? Or does it matter because it wasn't you?"

The blows in Cathmor's tent. "I taught you to hold your tongue, boy. You're lucky the king didn't take it out."

Kaell's bitter laugh slipped into the mist. "He'd never do that. He wants to hear me scream. Lastenarron didn't scream. I knew he wouldn't. Not him."

In the half-light, Vraymorg glimpsed in Kaell's drawn face the child he had long ago taken from a sobbing woman in a city soon to burn, a child who beat small fists against a stranger's chest. A child he had failed. This was his fault. All of it, his fault.

"How can I—" His voice broke up.

Kaell did not look at him. "You can't save me, my lord."

"Kaell—" The back of his eyelids burned.

"Leave it be, my lord," the boy said quietly. "This will be over soon. It's better like this. You know what I am."

"I know *who* you are. Who you still are."

Kaell violently shook his head. "No. You don't understand. Even now, I hear your blood, my lord. Khir help me, I smell it. Every day it gets worse, this hunger. How long can I hold it back? How long until I become a monster? A week? A month? Am I even that strong?"

"Don't say that. You're not a monster. You're not like them."

"I'm becoming exactly like them. If I were free now, my lord, I might fall on you like a rabid beast. Part of me badly wants to sink my teeth into the soft tendons of your neck. You can't imagine this overpowering need to kill."

Vraymorg remembered that kick of fear and dread in his gut when Kaell had told him in the Mountains what he was. He knew he had to take up the sword and save him. Death was kind. Kinder than letting the child he raised become a monster.

"Let it end, my lord," Kaell said. "Or one day you'll have to hunt me down like any other ghoul. Let me die knowing at least I didn't become what Archanin wants. A killer."

The dawn fell away. Sunlight strained at mist. A gull wheeled.

Vraymorg dragged his hands over his eyes. His body ached from holding in pain, holding in rage.

Kaell said, "Is Aric alive?"

"For now. Cathmor intends to force him to call upon his father to surrender."

"He won't do that. He's stubborn."

Vraymorg released a breath. "About the girl—" The camp ran rife with gossip about evil ceremonies and secret rites.

Kaell wrenched his head aside. "She stabbed me," he said, his voice fractured. "So their high priestess could perform some foul ceremony."

"What?" Vraymorg tore fingers through sleep-knotted hair.

"She let me think she cared when she really wanted me dead."

"I don't understand. Azenor stabbed you?"

"No," Kaell muttered. "I can't talk of her. Not her. Not ever." He slid his lord a nervous look. The yearning in it cut at Vraymorg with guilt and pain.

"You told her something. A secret you kept from me. About you."

Vraymorg looked away. The camp stirred with muted voices and clattering cooking pots. Dampened by mist, the sounds were unreal, an echo of the real world. Somewhere.

The tension in him hurt. He longed to take up a sword, shrink his thoughts to that mechanical beat of kill, survive. The beat of battle. Tomorrow it began. That monstrous trebuchet The Beast would pound the walls of the city of his birth. After…

"Kaell." The disused words were there. So close. Words his father would never be afraid to say. *You never disappointed me. You're loved, like a son. That's what you are to me.*

"Kaell—"

Footsteps tapped the stairs. Vraymorg whirled. Guards grabbed his arms. Outraged, he thrashed in their grip. "What is this? Release me."

"My lord, the king bids you step away," Bora said.

"How dare you put your hands on me. Release me."

"Bring him." Bora snapped his fingers.

"Kaell," Vraymorg cried, as they bore him off. "They'll have to hear my words, but I have to tell you—Oh gods help me, it's too late. It's always too late."

THEY FORCED HIM back to his tent. The guards let him go, watching him with carefully impassive expressions.

"The king demands your word you won't again approach the prisoner," Bora said. "If you don't give it, I'm to clap you in irons. Do you give your word, my lord?"

Vraymorg fisted his hands at his side. A helpless fury boiled his blood. Time ran away from him. He needed to comfort Kaell, tell him words he should already have said, if not for his selfish, stupid fear. Even now he feared these words. Simple words that would strip him down to someone raw and vulnerable. *Coward,* he thought again. *Coward, coward, coward.*

"I have no time for this. I must speak to Kaell."

"Then." Bora's expression hardened. "You choose irons."

"Wait." Vraymorg whipped up a hand as men moved in. He panted in anger. "I give my word."

Bora searched his face. Then he nodded, gestured to his companions, and stomped away.

VRAYMORG SLUMPED beneath the bath water, escaping into the silence of this other world. But his despair pursued him, strangling the quiet with thumping breath in his skull.

Reluctantly he lifted his head. Sounds breached the tent's canvas. Laughter. Voices. A blade scraping stone. A fire's crackle. The distant, dull thud of hammers.

So ordinary. How could it be so ordinary? Tomorrow Kaell died.

A silhouette fell on canvas. "Who's there?" Water surged against the tub as he rose.

Shadows twitched. Boots padded across rugs. Someone waited beyond the wreath of candlelight.

"Ewen?"

"Don't move, Vraymorg. I only came to talk."

The voice had a hard edge but still he knew it, even before the man stepped forward, a crossbow in his hands.

Stunned, Vraymorg forced words through his tight throat. "You're dead."

Dead. The air soured. The silence that rose up—it, too, tasted bitter. He could not move. Water dripped from the fine, dark hairs on his chest, trickled down his thighs.

Arn Tranter lifted his eyes to his. Eyes dulled with anguish. Haunted eyes.

Arn here. Alive. Impossible unless he fled, abandoning Kaell to his enemies. This man dared come here now? With Kaell about to die he dared show sorrow?

This man had no right to feel anything but guilt and shame.

Vraymorg's disbelief contorted to fury. He leapt from the tub and surged at Arn. "Coward! You ran. You let ghouls take him, torture him."

Arn's finger twitched. A bolt tore into Vraymorg's thigh. He buckled, choked back a scream. Fell. Arn nocked another quarrel. "Please be still, my lord."

Panting, Vraymorg struggled to sit up. He clasped fingers to the bloody wound. Instinct shouted, yank the shaft out. But if he did that, he'd only bleed more, might pass out.

Arn tossed him a cloth. "Stop the bleeding."

Vraymorg pressed, trembling from shock. He must not surrender to it. Not until he knew what this man had done and what he wanted.

"Val?" Ewen stuck his head through the flaps. "I heard—" He gaped at Arn.

Arn swung the crossbow. "Back off, Ewen."

"What is this? How is he—?"

"Go," Vraymorg wheezed through clenched teeth.

"You're hurt."

"This is a command. Go. Say nothing."

Once Ewen disappeared, Vraymorg briefly squeezed his eyes shut, lightheaded. *Hold on.*

Arn circled. "Why make me shoot you? You always were stubborn."

"What I am hardly matters. What do you want?"

"I was sent to deliver a message," Arn said.

"What?"

"Do you think I want to be here? I had no choice. You need to understand what to do."

Vraymorg struggled to take the words in. His mind still snagged on how Arn was alive. "Did you run? Did you see them take Kaell? Did you know what they'd do to him?"

"I saw. I knew."

Anger blunted Vraymorg's pain. "You did nothing. You betrayed him." Unable to go on, he spat at Arn. It was vulgar, but his disgust was too big to contain.

Arn wiped his cheek. He said, "What can you, a Lord of Telor, know about betrayal?"

Vraymorg began to laugh.

Memory threw him back to a cave in hills above Dal-Kanu in the aftermath of battle, to hot blood spouting over his arms as he cut a guard's throat then whipped about to gut a second man with his sword.

So easy for a Serravan-trained warrior to kill. It shouldn't be that easy. Not really. Not for those stakes. For a kingdom.

He stalked into the darkness to find the boy. Hands bound, helpless, Ryol Caelan watched him approach with a quickening in his eyes. Not fear. Not—fear.

"You let him live?" His queen's slap stung his cheek. "My rival for the throne? You betrayed me, Val. You, who profess to love me."

Betrayal. It was that simple. Not so much what you did. But what you didn't do. Don't kill an unarmed boy in a cave. Don't find the courage to say words to comfort a child you raised. A young man who badly needed those words.

"How can you know?" Arn's voice banished the past, forced him back to that tent where he lay bleeding. "You serve your king. No doubts. But what if someone stripped away all you believed? Every certainty. Leaving only duty."

"Duty is cold," Vraymorg muttered as much to himself as the man with the crossbow.

The thick hush rubbed like shrouding sackcloth. Arn's eyes held that haunted look again. "Yes," he said softly. "But love is colder."

"I thought you loved Kaell. You even killed Paulin because the snake hurt him."

Arn's knuckles paled on the bow. "Paulin told me to meet him on the tower roof. I went to kill him. But not for Kaell. I pushed Paulin off that roof to shut him up."

"What?"

"I trained as a soldier with Paulin on the Downs. One night, both of us drunk, I foolishly said I was from Robba, a Varee village.

When Paulin saw me again in the Mountains, he realised a Varee man could only be there to watch Kaell."

"I don't understand."

"Don't you, my lord?" Arn's voice held the hint of a sneer. "So powerful, the king's man, with such a reputation, yet you know nothing of the world beyond the gorge or the Varee."

"I know they're slavers, thieves, killers."

"So *you* might say. Archanin calls us his chosen people. We offer our love, service. Blood even. In return, Archanin protects the Varee. There is complete order."

Horror lashed him. The Varee served Archanin? Let this be a nightmare. Then he could wake and find Arn gone. Not holding a crossbow on him and spitting out a vile confession.

"So you're not just a coward." Vraymorg let the other man hear his contempt. "You're Archanin's spy. Sent to the Mountains to watch Kaell. To tell your master what?"

"Whether he was the bonded warrior Archanin sought."

The Nineteenth Bonded Warrior will lead a path for evil.

Even after all that had happened, he would not kill Kaell because of these words. Prophecies proved two-edged. As if seers laughed at anyone who believed their mysterious mumbo jumbo.

"You don't want to talk. You came here to appease your guilt. You disgust me."

"No." Arn's look fell on him hard. "That is not my intent. My guilt is my own, and I must live with it. There can be no atonement, no forgiveness. Not for me."

"Then what do you want?"

"My lord has a message for you. The man I defied Archanin to serve."

"Who," Vraymorg said. "Who is this lord?"

A whipped-up wind rippled canvas. Beneath it, a whisper stirred as if the otherworld murmured: *The truth will change everything. Everything you believe, the way you see the world. Do not listen to this truth.*

Arn released breath in a soft sigh. Sounds from the camp flattened, distorted, then fell away to nothing.

"I have served two lords," Arn said, his face altered by awe. "One a lord of darkness. The other a lord like tarnished silver, a beautiful prince with a heart I fear is just as dark in parts. For his sake, I put aside Archanin, the god of my people."

"Who?" Vraymorg whispered. "Who?"

"He'll come for Kaell. He must. Please tell me you have the boy's sword."

Vraymorg glanced at the blade he took off Kaell in the caves. "That cursed thing. Why is everyone so interested in it? Even Rozenn bid me tell that sword stories of the boy."

"This is why I'm here. I am not here to justify my actions to a man who could not understand. My lord sent me to tell you we can use what she did. Your stories about Kaell. We can use that sword."

"Use it? To do what?"

The man's gaze held something Vraymorg didn't like. Pity.

Arn said, "Save Kaell."

Two words. How slowly their meaning leached into him. Vraymorg drove a palm through coiling smoke to push away hope. False hope hurt more than no hope.

He watched a candle flame jig at the command of every draught. He watched insects no bigger than black spots whir about it. He thought about his father, a man unafraid of battle and unafraid to do what was so much harder—feel.

At last he looked at Arn. He said, "What must I do?"

VRAYMORG POKED the torch at dry rushes. They caught at once.

As the flames danced, he felt nothing. His gaze whipped across the mob pressed as near as they dared. He even felt nothing for them. Not revulsion. Not hatred. They were just there, morbid spectators to another's pain, their excited whispers dying away.

The present scene in front of him unbearable, his numbed mind groped ahead. When this ended, when Tide's End fell—and it must fall—the gods would name the next bonded warrior. Another child...

His breath contorted to a sob. No, no. Blank his thoughts. Do not think of Kaell.

"My lord, step away." A guardsman confronted him.

Vraymorg blinked like a sleepwalker. "In a moment." Heat scorched his skin. He was aware of it as he might register a distant sound.

The guard shook his head and drew back towards Cathmor, sprawled in comfort with his noblemen beneath a rolled-up tent. The king leaned to Caelmarsh, patted his arm, and laughed.

Laughed.

The fire spat. Wood cracked. Flames reached the edge of the scaffold. At Kaell's cry of alarm, grief at last pierced Vraymorg's torpor. He looked up. "Kaell. I'm sorry."

Through billowing smoke, the boy shrugged. "For what? You taught me to be what the gods asked. When I let Archanin take me captive, I let you and the gods down."

"Vraymorg," the king called. "You're too close."

"My lord." Kaell coughed. "He's right. It's dangerous."

The fire leapt higher. A plank on the edge of the platform caught alight. How long, he wondered. How long? Smoke veiled Kaell, as though he was already lost to him. Gone.

I should have killed him that night the ghouls attacked. He deserved that, this child I raised. He trusted me to do the right thing. Now he'll die in the flames.

Flames. The past sprang at him.

Braziers upon the walls at Vraymorg, the smoke twisting into the dusk. Against an endless sky, violet and beautiful, three moons rose.

Kaell tore about the ward, a child of six waving his wooden

sword at the nesting plovers, shouting, "Silly pluckers, shut up, shut up, you silly pluckers."

Vraymorg was about to correct him, call out "plovers, Kaell," only to laugh. Pluckers suited the birds just as well. From now on that's what they would be.

He smiled at the memory: the boy, the sword, the indignant birds with their distinctive cries. The small child taking them on, unafraid.

Vraymorg shivered. How terrified that child who fearlessly ran about the ward must be now. Alone, back to that stake, watching the flames advance.

He could leap onto that platform and drag that child to safety. Except that meant breaking his vow to a dying queen hundreds of years ago. A vow to serve her ancestors. Like Cathmor. And he had done it. Whatever the cost.

"Gods—which ever gods," he whispered, "why do you ask this of me? I've done my duty, I've served the king."

He served the descendant of his queen, the woman who saved him from unending darkness. Yet a trembling tore through him, a stab of unwanted memories.

Devarsi ordering him to murder a boy. Devarsi with Archanin, heads close, conspirators.

No. No. Devarsi saved him.

Bile washed into his mouth. Devarsi had laughed as the Isles burned. Laughed, just like Cathmor laughed. Devarsi ordering her soldiers to execute every captured warrior.

"Vraymorg, I order you to step back," the king said.

His knees hit dirt. He beat the ground to force back memories. They hammered and hammered. Tears slid down his cheeks, salty on his lips.

His debt, whatever debt, was long paid. His duty was not to unworthy queens. Nor kings who asked this of him. It was to this boy he loved.

Loved. Oh gods, that was it. Such a simple word.

It was that look on his father's face when Val fell on the training field, that mix of pride and pain. It was his father's calloused hand helping him rise, his arms holding him close as though to immure him from the world.

He wanted that for Kaell. To hold him like his father held him. Protect him from kings, from ghouls and gods. From every hurt.

"I've done as you asked," he called to the king. "Release me from my bond."

"What are you talking about?" Cathmor was on his feet. "The only bond you owe me is that of a lord to his king."

"The other bond."

"There is no other bond."

Vraymorg trembled. Cathmor did not acknowledge the vow. Then surely, surely, that released him. He staggered up, drew Kaell's sword, and limped to the platform.

"What's he doing?" The king's voice rose in shock. "Someone stop him."

The heat from the wooden steps scorched through his boots to his soles. Flames writhed. Vraymorg laughed, unafraid of their physical threat.

Fire could burn him, hurt him, but not kill him. Its pain nothing compared to the terror of letting go, of admitting he loved this child he raised.

A Telorian king, his cousin, once braved fire beyond the Enarae to prove his worth as a Serravan warrior. He needed to prove so much more—his worth as a man. As a father.

What had Arn said? Love is colder than duty? For the coward, maybe. For a man, love must never be that. It must be warm, bright, unafraid, and vulnerable.

With one slash, he freed Kaell. The young man fell against him, coughing.

"My lord, what you doing?"

Vraymorg hugged him hard. "Forgive me."

"For what, my lord?"

It hurt to breathe. It hurt the way it did every time he sat by Kaell's bed while the boy tossed in pain or fever, never admitting to himself why he was there.

"I always knew what you wanted to hear," he said. "But I was afraid. Because if I cared and something hurt you, I'd shatter. Now I understand I must shatter. And shatter again. If that's what it takes."

Kaell said nothing, only stared.

Vraymorg clasped the young man's face between his palms. Only two things he could do for Kaell.

The first… He drew in a long breath.

"Once, on a terrible night when the Lost walked, you asked what you were to me. I could not admit it to myself. Not then. But I'll say it now." He paused, fighting a flicker of panic. "You never disappointed me, Kaell. I love you as I might love my son."

A tear wet Kaell's eyelashes. He did not swipe it away.

The second.

"You can save him," Arn's voice echoed, his words terrible and wonderful. "The priestess bound them together. Kaell and Azenor. Your stories bound Kaell to that sword. My lord planned this. Every step. It will take only a little blood."

Vraymorg pressed his lips to Kaell's brow. "They'll stop me if I try to get you away. Arrest us both. So I have to believe what the traitor told me. If there's a chance this magic works, I must take it."

He shuddered at the enormity of what he was about to do. Destroy a girl's life, perhaps. Tarnish his name, his spirit. "I'm told Azenor will never wake. It will be a mercy."

"My lord, I don't understand."

Vraymorg lifted the sword. Flames lashed his back with heat. "I can do this for you, at least. I can save you."

He could not hesitate. He took just one dizzying breath and stabbed.

Kaell collapsed to his knees, his lord's arms still about him. "It hurts," Kaell whispered. "I didn't think it would hurt like this. But it won't kill me. Please, if you love me, you know what you must do."

Vraymorg could no longer speak. He could only swing. Seithin steel. A single stroke.

Flames beat like red wings. Smoke stung his eyes. Shapes ran to and fro, a chaos of outrage and confusion that meant nothing.

Vraymorg flung the blade away. He reeled off the platform and knelt, coughing, spluttering, his body aching. Knees drawn up, he let himself remember a small child who had followed him about with endless questions, a boy who snuggled against him to listen to stories by the fire.

He remembered how Kaell, no older than four, wrapped his arms about his leg when he left to fight.

He remembered Kaell bursting into the hall the first time the boy killed a ghoul; the story came tumbling out, his gestures wild as he recounted the thrust and cut of the fight. How the words fell away before Vraymorg's silence and he looked to his lord, waiting. Waiting for praise. A nod, a smile. Anything. Then, as Vraymorg touched his hair and said, "You've done well," how his face blazed with elation.

Not knowing Vraymorg didn't care about the dead ghoul, only that Kaell was alive, unhurt. Not knowing to raise a child meant pain, even in the joy of it, beneath the shared moments of achievement or happiness. Because there was always fear.

THE FIRE SLAPPED AIR, its whip a heartbeat. Perhaps there were voices, commotion. He didn't care about the world beyond that space of ground where he sat, arms clasped about his knees, rocking. Minutes surely passed. He didn't care about that, either.

Guards seized his arms, a violent intrusion into his grief.

Cathmor stood over him. "By what right did you defy me to

give him a quick death?" he said. "This time your insolence will cost your life."

Vraymorg shrugged. "I am not as fond of this life as you may think."

"You fool." At the king's side, Cael-Carren shook his head. "I always knew your arrogance would be the death of you. Beg my nephew's forgiveness. Ask for mercy. Admit to a moment of weakness because of your grief over the boy. Tell your king you're sorry."

"I'm not sorry. Your nephew is cruel and repellent. Not worthy to be a king."

Hands drawn down to fists, Cathmor bellowed, "Find my executioner!"

Guards bound Vraymorg's wrists at his back and found a log to use as a block. Another spectacle for the swelling mob. Their murmurs rippled at his back; their callous, bloodthirsty anticipation was as tangible as the fire's heat.

"Nothing to say?" Cathmor said. "Nothing? Come, my lord, you disappoint me. Such an arrogant tongue, and it falls silent when you are about to die."

"I will say this, then." He raised his voice. "I am Vraymorg, Lord of the Pass. With me, men of the Mountains. To me!"

"Shut him up!" the king screamed.

"This king is false. He does not deserve our loyalty. To me!"

A fist knocked him flat. Hands dragged him forward, forced his head down. A sword screeched from a scabbard.

A man cried, "I stand with my lord, with Vraymorg."

"I, too, stand with Vraymorg," a second yelled. Then another and another, until voices rolled into each other in a riot of shouts, an eruption of shrieking blades and thudding feet.

In vain, Cathmor shouted for silence. Yet above the din, one voice carried.

"I am Damadar. I stand with Vraymorg. To me, men of the Ice."

Guards reeled back. Heath freed Vraymorg's hands, pulled him up and shoved a sword at him.

"Isn't this fun?" The young Ice lord grinned. "Mayhem, betrayal, the prospect of battle and—even better—we're outnumbered. Can you fight? I need every warrior who can stand."

Vraymorg grasped the unfamiliar sword, stunned at this bewildering turn. Amid the turmoil of his spinning thoughts, his weariness and sorrow, he wondered why he'd disliked this man.

"I can fight." That was all he could do.

Letting rage possess him, Vraymorg plunged into the chaos of shrieking, clanking metal, ready to deliver death with a coldness mirroring the intent in his heart.

A grim resolve to bring down a king.

If you love Kaell and Val (or even Heath!) ...

If you enjoyed this book, please consider leaving a review on Amazon or Goodreads or both! Reviews help other readers discover the Shadow Sword series.

Thank you!

And watch out for the second book in the series, *The Last Seer King,* coming out in May, 2019.

Feel free to drop me a line on Facebook (author SJ Hartland) or at my website www.sjhartland.com. There's nothing better than talking characters!

Warm regards, Susan.

ACKNOWLEDGMENTS

I'm fortunate to have so many fabulous friends, mentors, and family who helped bring the Shadow Sword series to life.

My amazing, wonderful mentor Dr Kathryn Heyman—where would I be without you? Kathryn not only believed in the series but taught me everything a journalist doesn't know about writing. Turns out that's a lot! Thank you, Kathryn, for too many things to list.

Many thanks to my Saturday night family, Sasha and Eleanora, who patiently listened to talk about characters and publishing. (*Hamilton* one day… maybe.)

Thank you to my Sunday "furniture night" family, Cat, Steve, and Hoges. "Dace the Virgin Knight" isn't in this series (and guys, hate to tell you but he's not a virgin!). Maybe one day Dace will appear…

Thanks to Annie and Dad, David and Annette and Kate who only ever encouraged me.

A thank you to my friend Meghan who ended up becoming a beta-reader before I knew what that was… and read the first three manuscripts, or 1800 pages! Thank you, Jo and Eva, for reading blurb after blurb.

Thank you to Sarah G. from Red Adept (that poem about enforcers is very cool) and to Hayley and Dallas from the University of Southern Queensland for helpful suggestions on writing and publishing.

ABOUT THE AUTHOR

S. J. Hartland is an emerging author of epic fantasy who calls the Darling Downs, Queensland, home.

She is an Australian journalist, former AAP finance editor and fencer who watches too much TV, spent too many holidays wandering around obscure castles, and is obsessed with anything medieval.

The 19th Bladesman is her first published novel. The second in the Shadow Sword series, *The Last Seer King,* will be released in mid-2019 and the third, *The Sword Brotherhood,* early in 2020.

Find out more about the series and the characters at www.sjhartland.com

Made in the USA
Coppell, TX
15 June 2020

27731150R10365